LIGHTNING FALLS

More from the Weeping Cedars Universe

Books
Shards of Amber
Welcome to Weeping Cedars

Podcasts
Weeping Cedars
Samite
Wrought of Amber

LIGHTNING FALLS

J.W.G. Wise

2025 Ikandaset Books Trade Paperback Edition

Published by Ikandaset Books.

Library of Congress Cataloging-in-Publication Data is available on file.
Cover design and artwork by J.W.G. Wise
Print ISBN:
978-0-9601305-1-1

WeepingCedars.com
3rd On-Demand Print Run

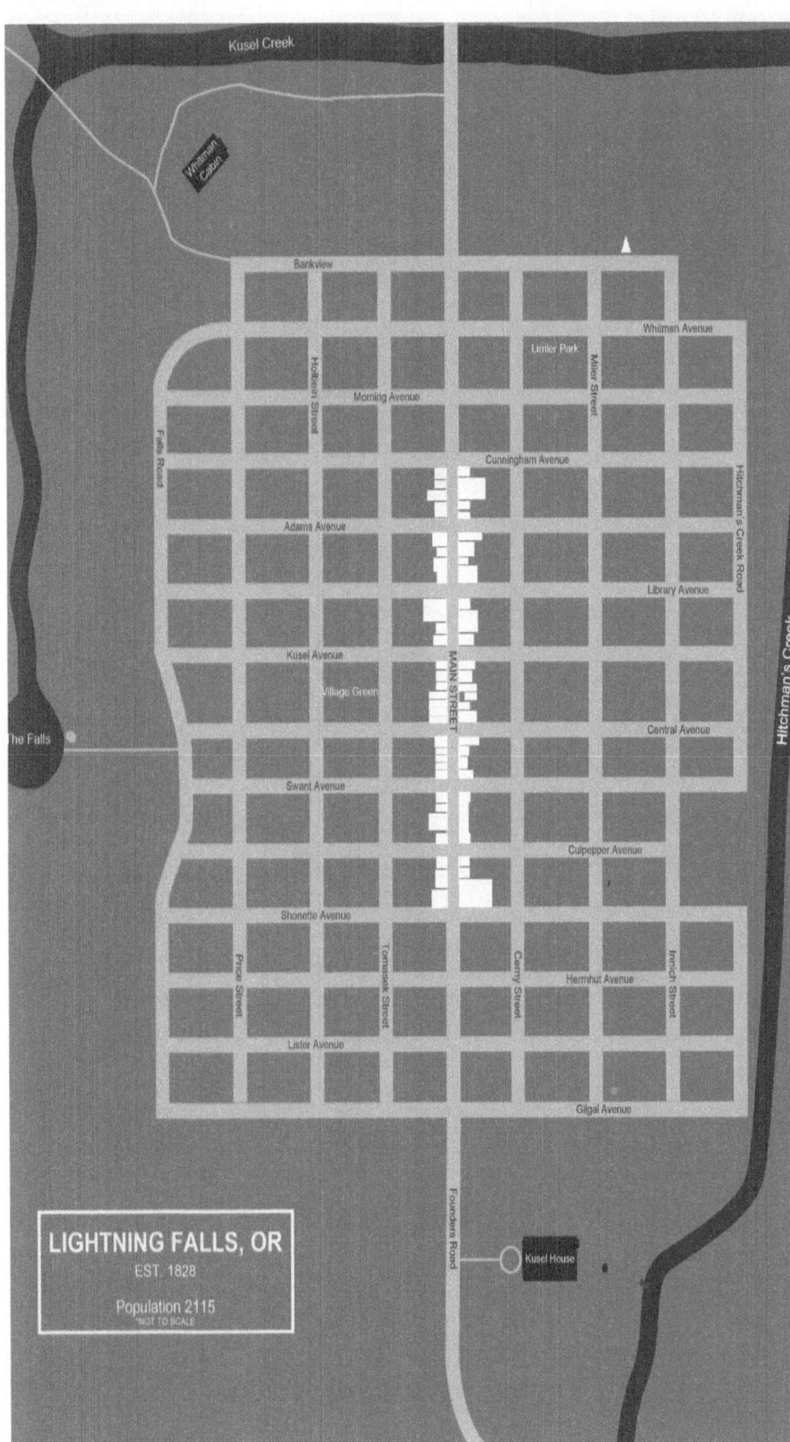

Kusel Creek
Whitman Cabin
Bankview
Whitman Avenue
Limler Park
Miller Street
Holtein Street
Morning Avenue
Falls Road
Cunningham Avenue
Hitchman's Creek Road
Adams Avenue
Library Avenue
Kusel Avenue
MAIN STREET
Village Green
Central Avenue
Hitchman's Creek
The Falls
Swant Avenue
Culpepper Avenue
Shonette Avenue
Price Street
Tornusek Street
Cenny Street
Hermhut Avenue
Innich Street
Lister Avenue
Gilgal Avenue
Founders Road
Kusel House
LIGHTNING FALLS, OR
EST. 1828
Population 2115
*NOT TO SCALE

LIGHTNING FALLS MAIN STREET

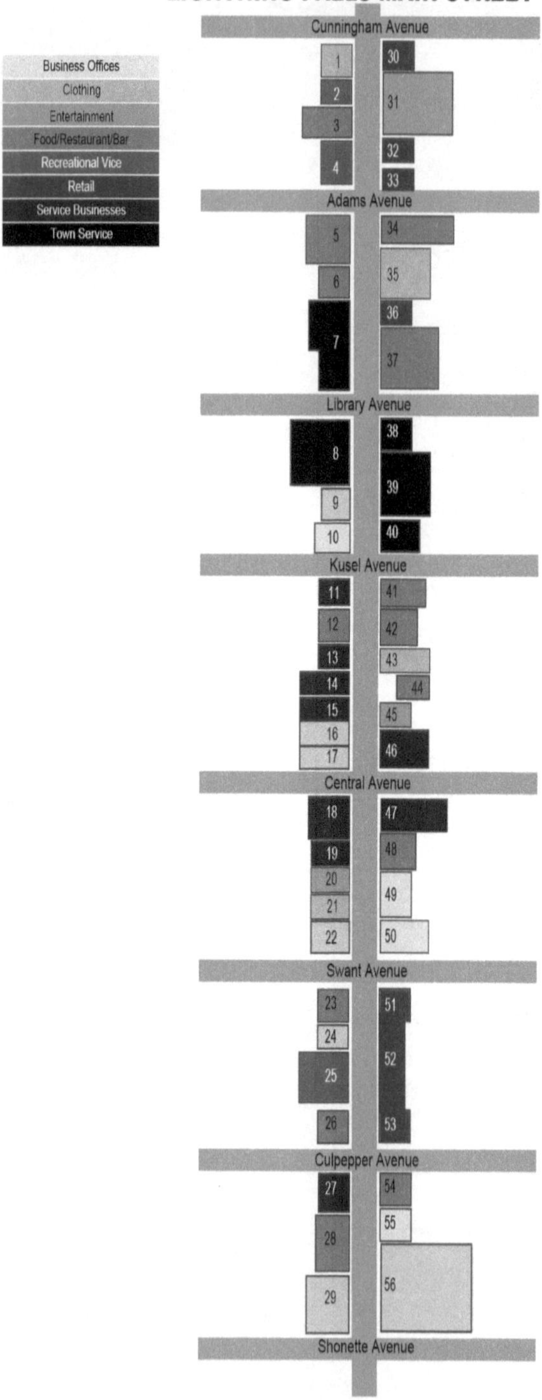

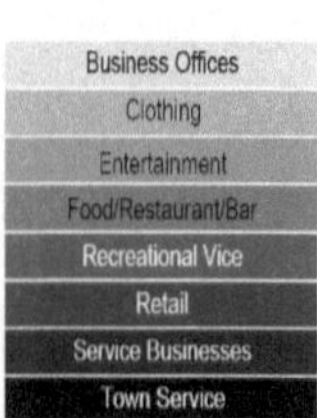

1 - Tied Died Dreams
2 - Flying Purple
3 - Mastino's Pizzaria
4 - Lightning Falls Tobacconist and Vape Shop
5 - The Timber
6 - North Garden Chinese Food
7 - Lightning Falls Fire Department
8 - Library
9 -
10 - Offices
11 - Fix-It Phone Repair
12 - Cinder's Remorse
13 - T. Havorford DDS
14 - Up Done Hair
15 - High Tops Barber
16 - Street Light Apartments
17 - Heart's Breath B&B
18 - Quickgo Gas
19 - Lichter Physical Therapy
20 - Lightning Falls Art Gallery
21 - Ermine's Consignment
22 - Congregation Study House
23 - The Mouse Trap Restaurant
24 -
25 - Something Wicked Liquors
26 - Rim Shot Bar
27 - Wallowa County Bank
28 - Montaña Esmerelda
29 - Private Residence
30 - Roundtree Antiques
31 - The Mist Theater
32 - Comin' Around Again
33 - Baker's Books
34 - Barry's Coffee
35 - Fashion Backward Vintage Clothing / Realistic Threads
36 - Steve's Cards and Games
37 - Second Wave Diner
38 - Post Office
39 - Town Hall
40 - Police Station
41 - Huckleberry Heaven Jams and Jellies
42 - Lost Boys Bakery
43 - Lightning Falls Outdoor Outfitter
44 - Aunt Erma's Candy & Creamery
45 - Lightning Falls Museum
46 - Pillar's Drugs
47 - Red's Grocery Store
48 - Sharko's Sandwiches
49 - Offices
50 - Sharework Working Spaces
51 - Autoparts Store
52 - Tek's Hardware
53 - Liedar Plumbing Supply
54 - Stollie's Corner Store
55 - Rebecca Nielman, Esq.
56 - Shonette Apartments

To my wife.

There is only love forever.

Introduction

LIGHTNING FALLS **IS A** strange book. It is the first novel in what has come to be known as the Weeping Cedars Universe, which currently consists of a series of podcasts and short stories, all of which, to some degree, intersect with this tale. The central story so far is the audio drama podcast *Weeping Cedars* (something like an old radio-drama, but conveniently located wherever you download podcasts). *Weeping Cedars* is a slow-burn horror story told by residents of the eponymous town in Northern Hamilton County, New York. It alternates between a documentary made by employees of the local historical society and episodes from a local late night radio show, called News at Night. It aired for three seasons between 2019 and 2021. Since then, I've written and produced two spin-offs: *Samite* and *Wrought of Amber*. The first book I released in this "universe" was earlier this year called *Shards of Amber*, which contains almost twenty short stories that flesh out the story of *Wrought of Amber*.

Though all these podcasts and short stories intersect with this novel, I have tried to make sure that you can enter Weeping Cedars through any door. You don't have to listen to those shows or read those stories first. They can sit tantalizingly behind Lightning Falls waiting for you if the world intrigues you enough to dig deeper. However, those who have listened to and read the rest of the stories may anticipate and understand elements of the novel that others won't until they have explored other parts of the world.

So, the first warning, in brief: This novel is part of a bigger story, but you can also get to that story later.

The second warning: This story trusts you to be smart, be curious, and maybe have a notebook sometimes. It also trusts you to put it all down if it's not for you. This is a dense tale, a lot happens, and not all of it will be explained. You'll get many of the pieces, but you won't get everything. So, there's some work to do, and I trust you.

The third: I know this is not for everyone. There are plenty of people who hate the original show for its slow pace, seeming endless stream of names, events, and historical details, and inclusion of certain types of characters. This book will likely endure some of the same critiques. But I promise, there are no ideal people here and no shining examples of any lifestyle. Everyone is broken.

Everyone, sometimes, is the villain.

J.W.G. Wise, 2025

Part 1 - Homecoming

"Any mind may shelter, but the broken may be worn most perfectly."

-Zuzanna Cerny, *The Book of Corrections*

"Of the four cressetmen that once beckoned the citizens of Fesoro to the great library, two remain in service to its chief. Ekt—he who beckons to secrets—and Eshe—the one who beckons to war. Of the other two, little is known, but that Ket—who beckons to study—serves another. None has preserved his original purpose, except perhaps Eshe whose nature, I am told, was always bloody."

- Mikuláš Vaclavek, *The First Book of Seeings*

Prologue
Camping Days

Friday, October 8, 2004 - Night

ROBERT BERGER FROWNED AT his eight-year-old daughter as she stood on the muddy bank of Kusel Creek in khaki shorts and a dirty, white camp T-shirt. The water burbled, night birds trilled, and insects chittered as she copied his posture and crouched to submerge her fingers into cold water under the dim glow of a hanging lantern. Ignoring his frown, she peered at him hopefully.

"It's good," she said.

"I think it's just too fast, Jenny," Robert said from a few paces upstream. "The rain swelled it, and I think it's just going to sweep us down way too fast."

"No, come on," Jenny said, swishing her hands around. "Dad, it would be so cool. We'll be like explorers."

Robert shook his head. "No, I don't think so. At this speed, we won't even be able to see if there're branches in the way. It's a bad idea."

"We could put a lantern in the front and one in the back. Come on, you promised we would."

"That was before it rained so much, honey," he said. "Maybe it'll be down by tomorrow night, and we can do it then."

"But we won't be out here tomorrow night, Camping Days will be over," Jenny pleaded, desperation creeping into her voice.

She was right—tomorrow was the parade and the festival in the park. There would be sun, music, and food, and he knew they would be too exhausted by nightfall to bring their boat back out. He could see her point that this was probably their last chance to take a night canoe trip for Camping Days. Of course, he thought, they could always come down next weekend.

"If we put a lantern in the front and one in the back, it will be like we have spotlights all around us!" She stood and ran over to their campsite, which consisted of a shabby, but sturdy, little shack of plywood with an old curtain nailed to the inside of the door.

She ducked inside and emerged a moment later with another battery-powered lantern.

"How's it going to stay on?" Robert asked.

"Um… I guess I'll hold it." He saw the frustration in her face and wondered if she had imagined the lights hanging before and behind them, as if they had some fancy gondola instead of their simple, little two-person canoe.

"So, I have to do all the paddling myself?" He laughed. She turned and gave him a withering look. "Can you keep the light up in front of you the whole time?"

Jenny held the lantern aloft like she was a figure from a bygone time, casting her light out, searching for ships dashed against a treacherous shore. The orange glow cast shadows deep into her eyes and under her nose, aging her and exaggerating the earnest plea on her face.

"You're not going to be able to hold it up like that, but can you keep it steady on your knees the whole time? Or on the bow in front of you?"

Jenny climbed inside of the canoe and put the lantern on the bow, kneeling down behind it. Robert smiled.

"All right. Let's take a look upstream at the bend. If that looks rough, we'll bring our canoe up there, and then we can take it back down here. If it looks okay, we can grab one from the rack at the pool and take that. But we aren't going to go much past here, okay?"

"But why?" Jenny asked, not looking at all like she was getting what she wanted.

"Because, if we go much farther, then I'm going to have to try to carry the canoe back all by myself."

"Not if we go all the way down to the second shed," Jenny said.

"Is the second shed lit up?" Robert asked. He stood and wiped his hands on his own khaki shorts.

"Maybe," she said with a shrug. But they both knew it wasn't. He raised his eyebrows, and she relented by dropping her shoulders and lowering her lantern.

"All right, come on then," Robert said, waving her on. She hurried after him as he trudged along beside the ponderosa pines. They walked for ten minutes in silence as Robert listened to the water grow louder the closer they got to the bend.

Kusel Creek ran north from the pool under the falls until it bent east, where it merged with Evans Creek. Normally, the meeting was gentle—little more than a ripple across the surface as the two waters became one. But that night there were rapids rolling white in the light of high-held lamps, loud with rushing, rumbling pour-overs and holes.

"Okay, so we'll start about twenty feet down that way," Robert said, pointing back the way they had come.

"What? No, we can do that easily!" Jenny said.

"If we had a raft, sure. But with a canoe in the dark? Not a chance."

"You don't think you can do it?" she challenged.

"Like I said, in a raft it would be okay. And alone in a kayak? I could definitely do it. Or, maybe with someone else paddling the canoe. But I've got to do it all by myself, so no. We'll bring ours down and put it in down there."

"But we could—" she started, pointing up the creek toward the waterfall whose characteristic low rumble had grown to a roar.

"No," he said, cutting her off, "we're going to do it my way, or we'll wait till tomorrow night. Or maybe next weekend."

Once more accepting defeat, she flopped her arms down dramatically. "Fine," Jenny exhaled before starting back toward their camp.

Robert watched her go, thinking to himself, *If this is how she is at eight, what the hell am I in for when she turns thirteen?*

He started after her, but froze at the sight of a dark, shadowy figure emerging from the trees. For a moment Robert's heart raced with dread, and his imagination filled with pictures of uncanny specters. But when he raised his lantern, he laughed.

"Freddy! Hey, how's it going?"

"Oh, just dandy," Frederico said, pulling a face. "The tribe is slowly torturing me to death. How about you?"

Robert listened for a moment and heard at least three of Frederico's five boys arguing about something.

"I feel for you," Robert said. "Thinking of drowning yourself?"

Frederico raised his eyebrows as if the idea were intriguing. "Sadly, no, just taking a minute's break to drain the lizard. What about you? Jenny driving you out of your mind yet?"

"Only a little. She's convinced me to do a little night canoeing."

"Yeah, I hear that. Izzy's already bossing me around and got her brothers doing her bidding. Carlos tried eating a banana with the peel on because she told him that's where all the vitamins were."

"They'll end up killing us," Robert said, rocking on his heels.

"If we're lucky," Frederico said.

"Dad!" Jenny's voice wafted down the creek toward them.

"Speak of the devil," Robert said. "Good luck with the mob."

"Be careful out there," Frederico said. "Sounds like it's moving."

Robert said he would, nodded, and then picked up his pace to catch up with his daughter.

Ten minutes later, as Robert pushed the canoe out into the creek, he felt the current's tug immediately and wondered if he had made a mistake.

"Make sure that light is steady," he said, plunging one of the paddles into the water and paddling backward twice on one side, and then twice on the other, trying to slow them down. "This was probably a bad idea," he said, dropping the oar back in on his right and pressing it hard against the hull to rudder them toward the center of the creek. "The water's going a lot faster than I thought, Jen."

"No, it's fine, look," she said, pointing ahead to the darkness, "it gets slower up there."

Robert squinted into the darkness and saw no sign that what she said was true. He wasn't even sure a person could see such a thing in the daytime, let alone the dark.

"I don't think so," he said.

"Then we'll get back to camp in like a minute, right?" Jenny said. At least that made some sense, and Robert thought that he could already see the lantern on the tree branch not too far away. He took a deep breath and resigned himself to a harrowing—if brief—journey.

Their trip down Kusel Creek took three minutes. For the first two, Jenny held the light up and called out branches when they got too close. Twice they had to duck, and once one of the branches scraped Robert's temple. He was already deeply regretting the experience when he saw the man standing on the north bank across from their camp. Dread and confusion returned. The man appeared to be wearing a heavy rain slicker with a hood, and he was holding his own, curious lantern high in an outstretched hand. It appeared to be a metal cage surrounded by a pale green nimbus that hardly touched the world around him, suggesting only the outlined sketches of ground, trees, and water's surface.

Even so, the light was enough to show something moving in the creek, a deeper, more perfect shade of black than the water around it. It snaked out from before the man and darted toward them. For a moment, Robert wondered if he was dreaming or hallucinating. Maybe he was suffering some kind of stroke or aneurysm. When the dark form broke the surface next to their canoe, showing rows of tiny, diamond-shaped black scales that reflected the light of Jenny's lantern, he thought he might be going crazy. But when it dove back under the surface and slammed into their keel, rocking them dangerously, he knew that whatever he was seeing was real enough to be afraid of.

"Shit, Jenny, you okay?"

"Dad, what was that? Was that a snake?"

She had seen it too. Part of Robert's brain was relieved; the other part slid into deeper terror.

"I'm not sure. I need to get us to the bank. Hold on, okay? If you need to put the light down, you just put it in the bottom of the boat and hold on. Stay low!"

He ruddered the canoe again, this time angling toward the south bank. The boat rocked harder, almost tipping them over. The creature—whatever it was—crashed into his paddle and almost stripped it from his hands.

"Shit, shit," he said. He looked around frantically and got a better look at the man standing on the bank. He had been wrong; the man wasn't wearing a slicker. Instead, a heavy cloak bunched around his shoulders and cowled up over his head, hiding most of his face. Only his mouth—dry, cracked, and cruel—was visible. Pale, it smiled in the dim emerald light and from its mouth wriggled a mass of what Robert thought looked like worms.

Worms were spilling out and over the man's chin.

It was then that Robert Berger, known to his friends as Bobby, believed that he was going to die. His brain kicked into overload, and the world slowed down.

This is what you see when you die. The ordered, sane world falls away, and madness breaks in. I thought I'd see an angel, but instead it's this. Oh God, please help Jenny! Please help my daughter!

The boat knocked again, and this time Robert's paddle was wrenched from his hands.

"Hold on, baby!" he shouted, gripping the sides of the canoe. "Help! Help! Someone help us!" he screamed into the night, hoping to rouse the others who slumbered in their little wooden shelters along Kusel Creek.

In response, voices rose from the darkness, calling back.

"Who is it?" one person yelled.

"Where are you?" That voice sounded like Frederico.

"The creek!" he shouted. "Help us!"

Robert opened his mouth again to scream, to say that Jenny was with him. He meant to tell them to save her, but his words died as he was thrown overboard. For a second, in the darkness, he thought that this was it. This was death. They would both drown. He flailed in a creek that would have normally been too shallow to cover them, and found his footing on the rocky bed. He planted his feet and pushed against the bottom. His head broke the surface, and he thought the world had disappeared. He was in total darkness.

"Dad!" Jennifer screamed. Her voice echoed oddly and Robert realized that they both had come up under the overturned canoe.

"Baby," Robert said, pulling himself along toward her, and ducking under one of the seats after bumping his head on it. "Baby, we've got to get out of here. Take a deep breath and hold it. We're going to swim for the side. Stay close to me … Actually, hold on to me. I'll swim. Okay? Just hold on. But if you need to, you push away to save yourself."

"No, no, no," she said even as she grabbed at him. She was crying, clutching, her fingers digging deep into his shoulders. He could feel her trembling with shock and fear.

"You do it. We'll make it together. But if I can't—you go, you don't wait for me. You do not wait for me! Now, ready?"

Robert felt something brush past his leg.

No. Ignore it. You get her to safety. You get her to safety. If it's the end, you at least do that.

"Deep breath!"

They took their breaths together and went down into darkness with Jenny clutching him tightly.

When they broke the surface again, the man was standing on the bank, the wavering green light before him. For a moment, Robert wondered how that could be. The creek must have pulled them down twenty feet already. How had the man moved so quickly?

Jenny pulled him, and he turned. On the south bank, a man was hurrying toward them.

Thank God, Robert thought.

"Help us!" he managed to choke out as water forced its way into his mouth. The man, tall and stocky, was wearing a real rain slicker and hat, and was holding his arms out to catch their attention.

"Jenny, swim to him!" Robert sputtered. He felt her pulled away from him and heard the splash of her body being sucked under the water. Robert forgot the two men on the creek's banks and dove down, as shouting voices broke through the pines, and people rushed to the creek with their own bright lights—searching for the man who had called for help.

Down into the darkness he went, praying that she had taken a breath before she went under.

The Quiet Rumble

Volume 10, Issue 64, Sunday, July 27, 2025

The Passing of a Friend

By Keith Lowry, Ed. In Chief.

THERE AREN'T ANY WORDS for what I'm feeling today. I'm sure many of you are going through something similar. But I suppose, since I run this little paper (if you can call it that now that it's almost entirely digital), it's my job to use words. Right now, they feel like paltry, cheap things, but they are all I have. So, I'm sorry Jack, but I'm going to try to sum up what I think about you in a few short paragraphs. Just know, if they get email newsletters in heaven, these meager syllables are only the outward sign of a much vaster inner reality.

I loved Jack McCallum. He'd want me to say, "Not in a gay way," but I suppose that's only somewhat true. I don't want to startle my wife, or my four children, by saying so, but there are times when you look at a person and think how beautiful they are, and you can't help but feel a deep attraction to them. Did I ever want to snuzzle up to that big-bearded man and play tonsil hockey with him? No, I can't say that I did. But I did, on more than one occasion, wish we could just be affectionate with each other beyond the man-hug. I did want to kiss that man on the cheek, or on the forehead, or, before God and his angels, on the lips, like friends used to before we got so damned scared of men touching lest they lose control and fondle each other's swimsuit areas.

I thought Jack was a beautiful man, and I wish I could have shown him that more.

Of course, we knew, each to the other, that there was love. But we weren't equipped to express it beyond a late-night beer-soaked, "I love you, man." But even those were rare. Instead, we were left with the nod, the handshake, and the man-hug. Of course, we had the rest of the language as well: house repairs; unsolicited advice about things we knew nothing about; and the steady silent sentinel solace of the man next to you on the night when your wife is in the hospital, or your kid isn't answering their phone. I think I speak this language pretty well, but Jacky was fluent in it. He might as well have had a PhD in the stuff. It's a flimsy thing to say, but Jacky cared, and people knew it. I knew it.

It's a hard thing when a man like that dies. Especially when he dies 'not old.' I won't say young. Jacky was pushing sixty, and his smoking, drinking, and occasional mushroom consumption hadn't left him looking any younger than his age. But he wasn't old enough yet to look back on his life and say, "I've done it. I managed to get to the end, and now, God who fashioned me from the earth, I am ready to meet you, if not proud, then at least a little unashamed of the man I was."

I think most men hope to get there. To that place. To be able to meet God, not exactly on their own terms, but at least with a little plot of ground under them, where they can stand and say, "I tried." And it's more than sad that Jacky won't get to stand on his little plot, his beard long and gray, his eyes dim with age, and say to the Maker, "Judge me. I know most of it won't be good, but I think maybe I've made something out of it all."

He won't get that chance because it was taken from him yesterday when someone broke into his house and murdered him. They didn't surprise him on the couch; they didn't come in to rob him and knock over a vase and wake him up. Instead, they crept up on him while his wife was out of the house, doing her job. They snuck up while he slept, put a knife into his neck, and jerked it free, killing him almost instantly.

My friend went to bed two nights ago, hoping to wake up to do some fishing before he stopped by the diner to say 'hi' to his wife and her colleagues, and then on to work at the repair shop. Instead of getting to do those normal, wonderful, glorious things that life is made of, he was wakened with only seconds to process the impossible fact that his life was over. I wonder if he recognized that or if the shock was too terrible. Did he have a chance for one last prayer? To ask for his wife, Cassandra? One last moment to say to God that he was sorry? Or to ask for help? Or mercy? Or—what I think is the deepest prayer of every human—that God should, in fact, be God. That there should be a good face behind this horrid world where people do these kinds of things.

I don't know if he had a chance to pray that prayer. So, here, as one last expression of love, one last bit of that old service language that we used so often, I'm going to pray it for him and, I suppose, for all of us who sojourn in this world, not knowing what will happen to us.

Oh God, may You be who we hope You are. May You not be a dream, a nightmare, or a let-down. May You be God, beyond our fears and our best expectations, beyond our evils, our prejudices, and our tiny, contorted pictures of You.

May You Be.

And, if You can see your way clear to taking Jacky into your house, we who knew him and loved him would be much obliged.

He deserved better. Please help him get it.

1
Object Permanence

Friday, August 01, 2025 - Morning

MOTTLED CRIMSON DAWN FORCED its way through Jenny's eyelids. She couldn't remember if she had ever thought about which way her childhood bedroom windows faced. Heavy black curtains had covered the windows the last time she slept here. More than a decade later, dawn slanted unhindered into her curtainless, box-crowded room that was half storage area and half museum.

Jenny tightened her eyes against the intruding light and the memory of her bygone, embarrassing self-expression. The teenage girl with the long, black hair, pale skin, monotone wardrobe, and macabre-cum-holier-than-thou attitude felt like a cringe-inducing stranger to the twenty-nine-year-old woman sporting a Spider-Man T-shirt.

She couldn't remember the last time she thought about her teenage years. She found that they slipped away like the details of a dream as she tried to recall them. Maybe too much had happened for her to remember who she had been. Though the dresser, comforter, and alarm clock radio were all familiar, she felt no closeness to the girl who had spent her nights here. She marveled at how someone could be a completely different person in so short a time. Groggily, she wondered how many more people she would end up being.

A flash of memory appeared and faded—waking up during high school, her mind fixed on prayer, her heart bent on condemnation. She shook her head at her younger self. That girl had known nothing about the world, neither its sin nor its beauty. She had been a blithering idiot in cheap black lipstick.

Still, Jenny thought, *at least she had curtains.*

Jenny groaned as she tasted the inside of her mouth and found it revolting.

Right, she thought, *there's a pool of vomit on the side of Route 3, between here and Enterprise.*

She kicked her covers and almost laughed at the pink pajama pants that rode high, like capris on her calves. She had grabbed them from a shelf, and tossed them into a cart, paying them almost no attention. Appraising them, she thought that at least she and her younger self would agree that they looked ridiculous.

Jenny sat up, rubbed her face, and pulled her forearms across her breasts, rubbing her suddenly hard and sore nipples. The morning air was cold. Proper cold. She sniffed, wrinkled her nose at herself, yawned, and thought about trying to go back to sleep. Instead, she stood, turned her head away from the eastern window's blinding light, and crossed her arms over the thin T-shirt that had followed the pajama pants into the cart. She shuffled over and gazed south from the nearest window to find Lightning Falls stretching out for more than a dozen blocks.

Houses, parceled out in groups of six or eight, rolled like hills before her. To her right, the taller buildings of Main Street obscured the west side of town. She knew that if she opened her window and leaned out, she could see the lines of ponderosa pines that boxed Lightning Falls on all sides, and above them to the west, the falls that rumbled down from Wayne Butte. She remembered doing just that when the mornings were warm in the summer, stretching out and taking in almost the whole of the small town from her aerie at the north end. If she stood on tip-toe and pushed herself dangerously far out, she could make out the top of the house at the far end of town, hidden in its own pocket of trees.

Jenny wanted to do that now: to suck in the cool, clean air, smell the pine, a wood fire, and probably someone's cooking breakfast. She wanted to hear the morning birds calling, and the low, distant rumble of the falls. But the morning air was too cold to dangle out the window and wish the world a good morning. Instead, she turned and shambled her way to the bathroom.

Jenny pursed her lips. It wasn't as bad as she'd feared. A spider had spun an impressive web in the shower, and the toilet water had mostly evaporated. But other than that, it was pretty much how she had left it. She flushed once to make sure that another spider wasn't hanging out in the bowl and then sat. There was no soap on the sink, and the water ran cloudy for ten seconds before clearing up. So, she let it run, rinsed her hands, wiped them on her pink pj's for lack of a hand towel, and then leaned on the sink to look at herself in the mirror.

She needed a haircut. Her black curls had gotten a little too wild over the last year. She hadn't trusted Sunrise's institutional staff to cut her hair, and she had already worn it long, so the year's neglect wasn't as obvious as it had been for some of the other women she had known at the facility. She pulled the dark curls back. Her cheeks were rounder than she liked, but the sedentary life of Sunrise hadn't done too much damage. A few weeks of running and eating less bread pudding after every meal would get her back to a place where she felt comfortable in her own body again.

Comfortable and profitable, she thought to herself. *That is, if you want to go back to making money like that.*

Her gray eyes squinted at her. Of course, she wanted to. How else was she supposed to keep herself in too-small pajamas and superhero T-shirts? How else would she pay rent to the woman who had disowned her more than a decade ago? She'd have to get back to her life. For that, though, she'd need to do more than just get into shape. She'd have to get her phone reactivated, and, well, a bundle of other things. There was plenty of time to drop a few pounds to avoid comments from her audience telling her she had gotten fat—which she hadn't—or that they liked her new look—which she didn't.

Jenny sucked at her teeth and was once more reminded of her need to brush. She opened her new toothbrush and paste and got to work. She thought about the jumble of things she needed to do to get her life back on track and realized she needed a checklist. And for a checklist, she needed a notebook. There, motivational goal number one: Get a notebook.

She put her hand on the light switch and turned toward the shower.

"This isn't going to work, you know?" she said, addressing the web, hoping the fellow who spun it was listening. "Maybe you can move down to Patty's shower. I'll give you the day to think about it."

She switched the light off, left her room, and walked down the short hallway to the stairs. On the second floor, she washed her hands properly in the bathroom sink before descending to the first floor.

Patty was in the kitchen, cooking bacon in a cast-iron skillet.

Jenny sniffed and nodded. "Morning."

"Morning, Jennifer," Patty said, poking at the bacon with a fork. "How did you sleep?"

"Fine, I guess. What time did we get in last night?"

"About one. Did you throw up again?"

Jenny shook her head. "Nope. I think it was just car sickness."

"Well, you take it easy today, I think it was all a big shock to your system," Patty said. She was the picture of a 1970's middle-aged homemaker: flowered calf-length dress, apron, glasses, and brown-dyed hair cut Mia Farrow Vidal Sassoon short.

"Yeah, you can say that again," Jenny said, opening the refrigerator.

"What do you want? I can make you herbal tea, or there's orange juice—"

"Coffee," Jenny said.

"Oh, I don't have coffee, I'm sorry."

Jenny took a deep breath. "Okay, how about just some regular tea then? English breakfast? Irish breakfast? Something with—"

"I have some herbal teas," Patty repeated, pointing her fork to a shelf in the corner of the yellow and white wallpapered kitchen.

"Decaf?"

Patty nodded.

"Decaf tea in the morning? What's the point?"

"I like it," Patty said. "And you know that I don't use any kind of drug now, I—"

"Right," Jenny said, putting her hand up to ward off the explanation.

"Speaking of, do you still eat meat?" Patty asked.

"Yes," Jenny said, walking over to the shelf, ignoring her automatic dirty joke detector's alarm, which was bleating fuzzily and half-heartedly in the back of her head.

"And bacon? I've heard—"

"Yes, bacon too. I fucking love bacon. Who doesn't love bacon?"

Patty frowned, and Jenny could tell that she was restraining herself. "Jewish people. And Muslims too. And I think some of the Hindus…"

"I'm not Jewish, or Muslim, or Hindu, Patty," Jenny said, picking up the tea box and closing her eyes. "Plus, like, I had a friend who was Jewish, she made the best bacon. Is there a coffee shop in town?"

"Yes, Barry's is still open."

"Huh. Well, that's not the worst news I've heard," Jenny said, putting the tea back. "You mind if I use your shower while you do that? There's a spider in mine and I'd rather not wrassle with him right now."

"I thought you'd be a fan," Patty said, smiling the old smile that Jenny knew was only for herself. Jenny's bad joke detector was apparently working more enthusiastically than her dirty joke apparatus because it blared with Klaxon clarity.

Stubbornly, Jenny stared at her for ten seconds, refusing to give in. Patty flipped bacon, seemingly oblivious to the look. Finally, Jenny asked, "Why would I be a fan of a spider in my shower?"

Patty turned and pointed her spatula at Jenny's shirt, her self-amused smile deepening. Jenny looked down to find Spidey swinging across her breasts. She let out a half-hearted chuckle. "I only like the ones with muscles in skin-tight spandex."

Patty raised her eyebrows with a look that was half-reproach and half-agreement as she walked over to the sink and turned it on full force.

Suddenly, Jenny was drowning. Water filled her mouth and nose, and the world was dark and surging around her. Jenny gripped the refrigerator door handle to steady herself. Water sloshed, she thrashed, and the world went black as her lungs burned with monstrous fire.

Then she was in the kitchen again.

"What's the matter?" Patty asked, tapping the faucet back down to a reasonable flow.

"Sorry, nothing, bad memory," she said, feeling the floor right itself under her as a strange and jarring feeling of wellness slammed back into place. "So, um, can I use it? Your shower?"

"Of course, there are towels in the hallway and … Well, I mean, everything's still the same as it was. Do you remember?"

"Um, yeah, I think so," Jenny said. She turned and started out of the kitchen, back toward the stairs.

"Oh, how do you want your eggs?" Patty called after her.

Jenny stopped, leaned back into the kitchen doorway, and said, "However you're doing yours is fine."

"Do you want me to wait until you're out to make them?" Patty called.

"No, just cover them, I won't be long."

She took the stairs two at a time, hoping Patty would take her urgency as eagerness for breakfast. When she reached her room on the third floor, she dropped onto the bed, put her hands over her face, and cried. Five minutes later, in Patty's shower, cluttered with shampoos, conditioners, scrubs, and moisturizing foams, she scrubbed furiously and shaved too quickly, nicking her ankles and knees three times as the need to feel clean competed with her terrible need to get out and away from the pouring water.

2
Connection

Friday, August 01, 2025 - Morning

JENNY PULLED THE CHAIN, turned the deadbolt, and unlocked the knob.

"Expecting invaders?" she asked as Patty stood behind her, wiping her hands on a dishtowel.

"No, but a man was murdered only a few nights ago," Patty said.

"Really?"

"Yes, in his home, while was sleeping. It's really terrible."

"Jeez," Jenny said. "In a town this size. I didn't think anyone got murdered in a place like this."

"You've been gone too long then," Patty said. "People die in small towns as much as anywhere else."

"I mean, I know people die. I just didn't think murder was a big reason."

"Well," Patty said, "it's not a big reason. I guess we've had half a dozen murders since I was born. Most of them are just arguments or someone so drunk that he had enough of one thing or another. But we haven't had something like this since I was a teenager."

Jenny thought about that for a moment and nodded. "You want me to pick up another lock?" she asked, patting the door.

"No, I'm perfectly happy with the locks I have, thank you."

"You want anything from Barry's?"

"No, I have plenty here. Besides, I need to get to work at the store. I won't be here when you get back. There's plenty of food, and there's a little extra cash in my nightstand drawer if you need anything before I get back this afternoon."

Jenny thanked Patty and walked out the front door. The house was red brick and had a cement stoop with iron rails that needed sanding and a new coat of paint. The path from the stoop to the sidewalk was also brick and shot straight between two small, well-trimmed hedges that flanked the steps. The lawn was overdue for a mow, and a stump that Jenny remembered as a perilously towering maple now jutted just above the uneven grass line.

Jenny turned right onto Bankview, toward Main Street. To her right, tall houses dominated the northern edge of town, standing two or three stories tall, their yards dappled with trees not native to land where only ponderosa grew. To her left, single-story houses reigned. Here and there, a two-story wooden house would fill a corner lot, but overwhelmingly the people of Lightning Falls lived in ranch-style homes. The lawns were generally solid green, except where they were marred by a rare patch of brown. The sidewalks were wide and neat and the streets almost empty of cars, as every house sported a spacious driveway.

The world appeared as a double exposure to Jenny—two pictures laid atop each other. The first showed her a familiar town where houses appeared as they should, and each block followed the other in appropriate succession. Trees grew where they were supposed to, streets bore their proper names, and fences marked off the right backyards.

The second image was of an alien world. Though the houses seemed to be where they belonged, none jogged her memory. None summoned faces, voices, or moments from her past. She knew that some must have been important to her. She had an idea that she had been to a pool party at one of the corner houses on Miler Street, but neither of the two pale blue buildings seemed right. Nor could she remember whose party it was or anything that had happened there. It sat in her mind as an emotionless fact, like the boiling point of water or the length of a mile.

Jenny felt like she was walking through a town she had only seen in pictures or on a virtual tour. She had flashcards with notes that told her that somewhere on this block she had watched a movie at a sleepover and that another house had given out great Halloween candy. But the flashcards might have been for a town in a foreign land she had never visited.

She passed Limler Park where she had had her first kiss on the merry-go-round in seventh grade. She knew that. But how had it felt? Who had it even been with? She didn't know. That was even odder than her disconnection from the houses. There had been only ten kids in her grade—six girls and four boys. Or was it the other way around? No, that was right, six girls, four boys. Four boys and she couldn't remember anything about them or if any of them had been her first kiss.

Jenny's heart pounded. She felt unsteady on her feet and almost retreated to Patty's. But when she reached Main Street, the double exposure faded a little. The alienness diminished. She felt emotion-infused memories seeping back into her mind. There was the theater, there she could see the diner, and there—poking out above the sidewalk—was the sign for Baker's Books.

A pickup drove past her and the man behind the wheel raised his hand in a polite wave as he drove north, into the pine forest that lay just beyond Bankview. She drew a hand from her pocket too late and tried to remember if she had been the kind of person who waved at people.

If I'm going to live here again, I should probably become one.

She passed an antique store and the Mist, the two-screen movie theater. It was advertising *The Maltese Falcon* and *The Big Sleep* for the following Saturday, along with a film called *Beyond a Second Chance* that Jenny wasn't familiar with. She stopped and peered into Comin' Around Again Records, where she had her first job, and Baker's Books where she had her second. She almost went into Delia's but decided she didn't have it in her to face her old boss and friend. Not yet. She needed a few days of recuperation before she was up for a big 'how have you been' conversation with someone she both cared about and hadn't spoken to in over a decade.

She crossed Adams and stopped in front of Barry's Cafe. The place had a rustic flair as if Elisha Kusel himself had carved it from the native pines back in the 1870's. The sign looked as if it might have loomed over shops immemorial, suffering sanding and repainting a hundred times, leaving behind scraps of paint from each bygone business. Its current coat was a field of light green broken by the shop's name painted in red and gold cursive, punctuated by a mug of unlikely proportion and perspective. Large windows cut across the front of the building, displaying a counter running along the right side of the shop and six two-person tables running along the left.

Jenny breathed deeply the familiar and exciting scent of roasting coffee. It was nice that Patty had found religion, as Jenny was confident that the woman would be dead by now if she hadn't, but she couldn't get behind any belief system that outlawed caffeine. Beyond the Congregation Church in town, Jenny knew that the Mormons weren't fans of the wonder drug either, but she wasn't sure if there was anyone else on Earth so misled as to forbid the most coveted of stimulants.

She peered through the glass into the warmly lit interior. It was almost exactly as she remembered. Barry had gotten new chairs, and an updated pride flag poked up from a coffee cup on the pastry case, but Barry's looked right in a way that nothing else had since Patty drove her back into town last night. She wanted to cry again.

The bell above the door rang, startling Jenny, as a woman holding two paper coffee cups pushed her way through. Jenny grabbed the handle and pulled it open for her.

"Thanks," the woman said, giving Jenny a short nod before doing a double take. "Holy shit, Jenny?" The woman moved as if to hug her and then glanced at her two full cups. She was shorter than Jenny, and her hair was just as dark as Jenny's, but straight, and came to her chin. She had wide, squinting eyes accentuated by her eyeliner and full burgundy lips. Jenny didn't recognize her at all.

"Um, hi," Jenny said. "Sorry, I …"

"It's me, Isabella!" the woman said. She put her cups down on the windowsill and pulled Jenny into a hug. "Oh, my goodness! You're back?"

"Um, yeah, I got in last night," Jenny said, tentatively hugging Isabella back. "Patty, I mean, my mom, drove me up from California last night."

Isabella stared wide-eyed and talked so fast that she kept interrupting herself. "Oh my gosh, yes! I see Patty all the time at—She didn't say anything about you coming—We have to hang—Shit, my boss is waiting for these—Are you back for good or just passing through? If you're heading out soon, I'll tell him they were out of coffee. You look great, by the way!"

"No, no, I'm here for good now … At least for a while anyway. Maybe we can grab lunch or dinner?"

"Yes! What's your number? I'll text you," Isabella said, pulling her phone from the back pocket of her jeans.

"I … I, um, don't have phone service right now. That's on my list of things to do. Can you call Patty's house?" Jenny said.

"Of course. I have her number. Okay, we'll talk. You look amazing. Did I already say that? Well, you do."

"Thanks, you're lying, but thanks. You do too, those jeans!" Jenny said. Isabella laughed and hugged Jenny again. This time she kissed Jenny on her cheek. Then, like a grandma, she rubbed at the spot with her thumb.

"Okay, I've got to run. It was amazing seeing you!" Isabella grabbed her cups and walked away. Jenny watched her go and appreciated that Isabella's tight jeans looked even better from her new vantage point. Isabella turned, caught her staring, winked, smiled, and lifted a cup in farewell.

Slow down, ma'am, Jenny thought. *Have your coffee before you start lusting after the locals.*

A wave of memories, which were, unlike her ghost images of Lightning Falls, brimming with emotional weight rolled through her, dragging with them shame, anxiety, and nausea. She put her hand on the window and tried to breathe through the sudden onslaught.

Breathe, the past can't hurt you anymore, she thought, mimicking her doctor's words.

Even so, as she took long, controlled breaths and told herself how powerless the past was, Aurora's green eyes peered up at her and blinked in wild, confused terror.

3
Steam

Friday, August 01, 2025 - Morning

STEAM TWINED UPWARD AS Jenny pushed the foam of her latte back with a disposable wooden spoon. She emptied two sweetener packets into the open space, stirred, sipped, added a third packet, and stirred again. Satisfied, she put the lid on, grateful that Barry hadn't recognized her. He had been busy with two high schoolers who ordered complicated drinks and a food order he had to hustle to fulfill. She thought it was better for both of them. Barry didn't have the time, and she wasn't sure she needed a morning full of prolonged conversations about where she'd been since she lit out for Portland ten years ago.

She pushed through the front door and almost crashed into a man carrying a stack of packages.

"Sorry," she said, holding the door open for him. He nodded his thanks, scooted in past her, dropped the three parcels on the counter, and rushed back out. He waved to Jenny as he jogged past her into his waiting van.

At least some things are as busy here as they are in the rest of the world.

That thought was countered as she glanced up Adams Avenue to see a lonely pickup pull out of a driveway onto the empty street. With the van gone, and the truck disappearing around a corner, the streets were devoid of drivers. It boggled her how little traffic there was here.

Well, at least the delivery drivers are still in a constant panic.

She walked three blocks down to Pillar's Drugs and opened a door that had been new when Carter was president. Jenny and an old woman behind the counter exchanged brief greetings before Jenny made her way back into the flickering fluorescent light under a yellowed drop ceiling. She found the shelves that passed for a stationary section and grabbed a notebook and a pack of cheap pens. Next to the notebooks were folders, tape, string, wrapping paper, and then a small collection of knock-off toys that would appeal to only the extremely young or old—people who didn't care about brands and what was currently popular. Jenny half-remembered a red and yellow water gun she had gotten from Pillar's one summer.

She wandered the store, idly appraising the inventory, letting the band-aids, pain-relievers, magazines, and marital aids suggest themselves to her. She found a strange pleasure in once more donning the role of consumer, all the while reminding herself that she had to be frugal, at least for the moment. She tossed tampons, deodorant, some placeholder makeup, and toothpaste into a hand-basket with her notebook and cheap pens.

When she brought her items to the counter, the woman stared at her for a long moment, as if trying to decide if she recognized her. Then, without saying anything, she rang Jenny up. Change stuffed into her front pocket, Jenny strolled back up Main, unsure of where to go next. She didn't want to go right back to Patty's. The freedom to walk around wherever she liked was too sweet to lock herself back in the house on such a fine, sunny morning. So, she decided to wander a bit.

She suddenly had a ravenous desire for an almond croissant from the Lost Boys Bakery. A friend of hers had worked there … But, no. That was gone too. She remembered the croissants, though, and could almost taste them.

Next week, she thought. *Lose some weight first, and then a reward croissant.* She remembered someone telling her that that kind of thinking wasn't the best way to go about things, but she'd always found that it had worked for her. Do the challenging thing first, reward yourself for the effort. She didn't think it would be hard for her in Lightning Falls. She had no car, so she'd have to walk everywhere, and she thought she remembered that the trails around town were impressive and challenging.

She considered ducking into the Lightning Falls Outdoor Outfitter, but frugality reared its head again. *I'm going to go buck-wild when I start getting money coming back in*, she thought. In the meantime, she needed something other than jeans and the one skirt she had in her bag. The mornings were cold, but the day was already warming up.

As she passed the Second Wave Diner, she saw Barry up the block, dragging a little, round table from the ally next to his coffee shop. Jenny trotted up and put her bag and coffee down before helping him carry it to its place.

"This saved for anyone?" she asked.

"Nope, first come, first served," he said. He was whip-thin and just shy of six feet tall. His skin was deeply tanned, and his light brown hair was sparse. He wore a soul patch, narrow sideburns, and a faded "Pet Sounds" T-shirt. His cadence and tone reminded her of men she had met in southern California, with their wind-swept hair and tanned faces. She wished he would end his sentence with 'man' or 'dude' to make them complete. But maybe a few decades east of the Cascades had stripped him of such verbal festoons. She moved her belongings to the table and helped him pull a second out. Then they brought four heavy, black-metal chairs out.

"Are you afraid someone's going to take them at night?" she asked as she hefted her second chair.

"Nah, they're so heavy they wouldn't get far. But the town has an ordinance, so I've gotta keep 'em close to the building during the day and off the sidewalk at night."

'—*man*,' she thought.

"Ah, gotcha. Well, I appreciate it. I thought I was going to have to sit in the park," Jenny said.

"Well, the parks around here are nice. But I got ya covered." He glanced down at her coffee cup. "Can I get you anything else?"

'—*dudette?*' Jenny had to suppress a laugh at her interior monologue. "No, I'm good. Thank you, Barry."

"Sure thing." He opened the door and stopped. "Sorry, lots of psychotropic drugs in the '60s, so the old noggin doesn't work like it should. But … have we met?"

"You were eight in '69," she said, smiling broadly. "And yeah, a long time ago. I'm Jenny Berger."

She watched his eyes squint, then widen as his mouth worked like a fish for a moment. He stepped back out of the coffee shop and spread his arms. "No way, holy shit, man! Come here!"

Jenny laughed out loud and stood. They wrapped each other in a bear hug, and Jenny suddenly found that she was crying.

"That's okay," he said, rubbing her back. Jenny's tears weren't the full-fledged flood of feeling that she knew was waiting somewhere inside. Instead, she felt like she was letting a head of steam out, easing the pressure a little.

"Sorry," she said, pulling back and wiping her eyes with her fingertips. "Sorry."

"No need, sister," he said. "That's the world, you know?"

She did know, she thought. She knew a hell of a lot more than the last time she had seen him. She wanted to cry again but instead sniffed and forced a smile.

"How have you been?" she asked, stepping back to grab her drink. She needed something to do with her hands or she'd try to hug him again.

"Oh, you know. The world keeps changing and staying the same. I just keep on truckin'. But what about you? I heard … well, I guess I heard you were dead."

Jenny nodded. "That was the rumor," she said. "Like Mark Twain."

"I know how that goes," he said.

She wasn't sure what that meant, but she remembered him repeating it a hundred times to people. She wondered if he meant it or if it was just something he said to ease over uncomfortable situations or to make a joke.

"Hey, look, I've gotta get back to the grind, so to speak, but are you around?"

"I'm back for good," she said.

"You got a job?"

"Sort of," she said. "But not like anything to fill the time. Why? You need a new barista?" she said, holding up her drink.

"Not right now, besides, you're way too old to work for me. I only hire the young, foxy ones," he said, laughing. She glanced into the coffee shop. Barry's white-haired mother was serving someone a slice of quiche.

"You're right," she said. "I missed my chance."

"No, but there might be a job you could do while you're getting on your feet—if that's something you'd be interested in."

"Really?"

"Yeah, pay is kind of okay, but the hours are shit. But there are perks. You'd love it. Let me talk to some people and see if it's still a thing. If you want."

She thought for a second and then shrugged. "Why not?" Jenny said.

Barry smiled, put his hands on her shoulders, and looked her over from head to toe. Men had stared at her since she was thirteen, but there was nothing lustful or objectifying in Barry's gaze. Instead, Jenny felt like he was really seeing her.

"Jenny Berger, back from the dead. Hallelujah!" he said, throwing his head back. Then he hugged her again quickly and went in.

Barry. She remembered Barry. She had never worked for him, but this place had been a refuge. She could remember open-mic nights and even recalled standing up and reading some of her excruciatingly obvious religious poetry. Jesus on the cross for our sins. Jesus in the tomb.

Why must He suffer when we are to blame?
Why do we crucify Him and praise His Name?

She shook her head and cringed, feeling second-hand first-hand embarrassment for her younger self. Jenny sat at one of the tables she had helped Barry move and opened her notebook and the pack of pens. She wrote the date in the top-right corner of the first page in blue ink. Then she drew a short line and wrote next to it, "Get notebook." She immediately put an "x" over the line and smiled. This she followed with:

___ Reactivate Phone
___ Access Accounts
___ Transfer Money
___ Get New Clothes
___ Decide What the Fuck To Do.

She looked at the list. She thought that maybe, just maybe, she'd get the first three done today. Then, feeling like she'd get a freebie, she added one more line.

___ Have Lunch with Isabella.

Right. Okay. She thought. *Not a bad list for your first twenty-four hours out of the nut house.*

4
Exchange

Friday, August 01, 2025 - Noon

JENNY HELD THE TIMBER*'S* front door to let an older couple out of the restaurant. A gust of wind blew down Main, tugging the curls of her hair and rippling flags along the increasingly busy street. The morning's quiet had grown into not quite a bustle as locals went about their business and tourists wandered, shopped, and set off for the hiking trails around town.

Jenny checked her phone and found that her service hadn't been reconnected yet. Her phone plan's website had told her that she'd be reconnected soon, but she felt strange anxiety for it to happen immediately. She wasn't sure why, as there was enough free Wi-Fi around town for her to stay in touch with ... Well, just Isabella, she supposed. Isabella and several dozen men waiting for her to reappear.

Jenny mused that her meandering path back to technology had involved Isabella calling her on Patty's beige, corded phone and Jenny writing Isabella's username on a Post-it note. Then, thankfully free of the archaism of the phone, they had decided on the Timber as a good first meal. There were several new eateries on Main Street that Isabella had suggested, but Jenny didn't want to do the work of sitting in a new place and racking her brain about what it had been in the past. The memory section of her brain felt overworked, swollen, and sore.

Jenny slid along the heavy door once the couple had thanked her and ducked into the restaurant. Compared to the bright day, the Timber was dark, and Jenny's eyes took a moment to adjust. When they did, she saw walls covered with photographs, posters, saws, axes, and other, unfamiliar tools Jenny assumed were once used to cut down trees. A newspaper declaring unrestricted cutting during the Second World War hung behind the hostess who wore a black T-shirt with a plunging neckline above the word 'Timber!' in a font composed of old logs stuck together.

The redheaded hostess couldn't have been more than twenty and Jenny didn't recognize her.

Who knows, maybe I babysat for her?

"How many?" the hostess asked her as she reached for a stack of paper menus.

"Two. She's not here yet."

"Do you want me to seat you, or—" The hostess glanced over Jenny's shoulder. Jenny turned and saw Isabella backlit by bright sunlight.

"Hey, Julie," Isabella said. "We're together. Can we get a corner booth?"

Julie rose on her tiptoes and peered out over the wall behind her. "Sure, I think it just needs to be bussed. Give me a minute."

Julie pulled two menus from the stack and carried them with her.

Isabella spread her arms tentatively, a small gift bag in one hand. They hugged briefly and Jenny stepped back, pushing her hair behind an ear.

"I'm glad you could get together so fast. What do you do?" Jenny asked.

"I work for Mike Koletz, do you remember him? Big guy, big black mustache, looks like he's going to tie you to a train track or make you a pizza?"

Jenny laughed and nodded. "Yeah, sure," Jenny lied. Or did she remember him? *I'd probably know him if I saw him*, she thought.

"Yeah, he looks exactly the same, not a gray hair on his head. I think he probably dyes it. Anyway, I do kind of everything for him."

"Really, what does he do?"

"Yeah, he runs a few businesses, owns some properties. We do a lot of rental listings too. Really smart guy when it comes to seeing opportunities, but he has no idea if he's already eaten lunch, or if he has plans, or, well, anything. So that's what I do, I keep him on track," Isabella said.

"So, he needs a mother," Jenny said.

"He needs a wife or a girlfriend," Isabella said, winking.

"Oh my god, you don't also...?" Jenny made a subtle lewd motion with her hand down by her thigh.

Isabella laughed so loudly that people from the bar looked up from their lunches and stared. The shorter woman put a hand on Jenny's shoulder and shook her head.

"No," she said after people returned to their food, "no, but I do have a story about that. But that's probably better if we're not in public and I've had a couple of shots. But no, Mike's not my type."

Julie reappeared at the side of the host's booth and gestured for them to follow her. Jenny thought how pretty the young woman was and wondered how long she'd stay in town. She had a look in her eyes that said, 'Just wait, small-town person, I'll be heading out to make it big soon, and then I'll forget all about you.'

Jenny knew that look well; she had practiced it in the mirror when she was fifteen.

After they sat, they stared at the menu for a few minutes. Jenny asked what Isabella was getting, and after the waitress came to take their orders, they sat sipping pints of beer, waiting for their food. Jenny racked her brain for something to talk to the woman about.

Finally, Isabella put her hands up, as if remembering something "Oh, so this is for you," Isabella said, sliding the small gift bag across the table. It had a wad of white tissue paper stuffed inside.

Jenny felt a wave of panic. "I–I'm sorry I didn't get you anything, I—"

"Shut up," Isabella said, "this is a welcome home gift. It's nothing."

Jenny reached into the bag and pulled out a small journal.

"I thought, since you're home now, you might want to literally start a new chapter. It's totally lame, I know, but—"

"No, it's cool," Jenny said. "I used to journal when I was like thirteen, I haven't really done it since then. This is sweet, thank you."

"You're welcome! Okay, so, tell me everything. What happened to you? Where have you been? Why do people think you're dead or in prison?"

"Well … shit, it's a long story. I won't bore you with the whole thing right now, but—"

"No, bore me, I want to know absolutely everything."

"Right. Well, I guess to answer your last question, I was dead, for like a minute. And I wasn't in prison, I was in a hospital."

"Wait, what does that mean? How were you dead for a minute?"

"I drowned. But I came back, like, super-fast. No permanent damage."

"Oh shit," Isabella said and reached across the table to take Jenny's hand. "Oh my God, that must have been terrifying."

"Yeah, it was," Jenny said, frowning down at her beer. "It really was. Anyway, after that I had to, you know, get my shit together in a big way. That took a while."

"God—" Isabella said again. "I can't even imagine. If that had … I mean, with your—You know … God."

"Yeah," Jenny said, not sure what to say next.

"Are you okay?" Isabella asked, squeezing her hand.

"No, not really," Jenny said, closing her eyes. "The last decade has been … a lot. Like, a lot, a lot. I just … Anyway, you know that I ran away when I was nineteen—"

"Wait, I'm sorry before we do that … I need to know. You actually died?"

"Yeah, for like a minute, I guess. Or, I mean, I don't know if that's really being dead. But my heart stopped, I stopped breathing." Jenny said, not sure what Isabella's point was.

"I'm sorry if this is a fucked-up thing to ask, but ... like, was there a light or something? Did you see anything?" Isabella pulled back, clenching her hands into fists in front of her.

Jenny forced a half-hearted chuckle. "Yes, and yes."

"Holy shit, really?" Isabella asked.

Jenny nodded. "Yeah. I didn't like, see my grandmother, or anything like that. But I saw something, and there was definitely a light."

Isabella took her pint and leaned back in her seat. She stared into the restaurant, shook her head, and sipped. "Okay, I'm going to put the whole 'I saw something' thing aside for now, but I'm definitely coming back to that later."

"That's fair," Jenny said. "But you'll be disappointed, I have no idea what I saw. It was just light. And ... I don't know, like someone was there."

"Who? God?"

Jenny shrugged.

Isabella pushed her pursed lips to the side and gave a long 'mmm,' before leaning forward again. "Okay, so you drowned, someone gave you CPR, you're back, you went to a hospital, how long does it take to recover from something like that? How long did you have to be in the hospital?"

Jenny cleared her throat. "Well, I didn't go to the hospital for the drowning thing, I ... Yeah, it wasn't like that. I checked myself into a mental health facility a few weeks later. That's where I've been—until yesterday, actually."

Isabella drew out another long sound, this time an 'ohhhh' while she nodded, as if everything made perfect sense. When she let the sound die, she stared at Jenny for a long moment. Jenny wasn't sure if Isabella was trying to decide if she was lying or crazy. She didn't like how it felt for Isabella to study her, and a sudden rush of fear bloomed. How many times would she have to have this exact conversation with people who used to know her? How many times would she have to sit under that gaze while people judged her?

"Okay," Isabella said. "Okay. Yeah. So, you just got out? What are you doing back here? No offense, not like you need a reason to come home."

Jenny shrugged again. "Nowhere else to go. All my people are gone, the ones I was living with the last decade."

"They're gone? What does that mean?"

Jenny shook her head. "They're just gone."

Jenny scanned the walls for something to focus on other than Isabella's intense stare. She found a framed black and white picture of a group of Asian men in mining gear standing beside a river.

"Okay. Bad memories, I get it. So, you ran away when you were nineteen. Why? I know shit was bad at your house, but, you know, there were people around here who would have helped," Isabella said. "You didn't have to stay there. My dad would have let you stay with us. You know, like, he was friends with your dad. And, I mean ... Actually, is it even running away when you're an adult?"

"Yeah, I don't know. I don't know why I didn't ask anyone here for help. But I definitely ran away. It wasn't some kind of planned thing where I just moved. I threw a bunch of stuff in a bag and hitch-hiked my way out. The day before I ran, I heard this girl talking ... shit it was in *here*. I was having lunch with my m—with Patty, and this girl was sitting over there." Jenny half stood up and turned in her seat, putting her knee on the old, dark, wood booth bench. She pointed to a table closer to the entrance. "This girl was sitting over there talking about living in Portland, and how there was just this big community of young people there, and how you could get by without much since there were so many people ... I don't know, it just felt like fate." She turned back around and sat. "So, the next day I hitched a ride to Enterprise and took a bus."

Isabella shook her head. "Wow ... hitchhiking? Did you have to," she raised her eyebrows and made the same hand motion Jenny had earlier.

Jenny nodded and Isabella's eyes grew even wider. "Yeah, a few times actually. Not like, full on, but some, y'know, stuff."

"Weren't you like, big Bible girl back then?"

"Yeah, but what's a handy when you're getting away from literal Hell?"

"Shit," Isabella said, shaking her head. "Damn, I'm sorry that happened."

Jenny shrugged. "Believe me, a lot more than that happened. And, honestly, there was something pretty pure about it."

Isabella nearly spit out her beer, her face a contortion of horror and amusement. "Pure? What the fuck are you talking about?"

"Just, you know, two people agreeing on the terms of how they'll help each other out. You give me a ride, I … you know."

Isabella shook her head. "Yeah, sorry, I couldn't."

"Yeah," Jenny said, looking back down at her beer wondering why she'd told Isabella. Jenny thought back to the last decade of her life and the conversations she'd had with people. Nearly every encounter had been an experience of acceptance and shared stories. Even in Sunrise, the other girls—when they weren't losing their shit—hadn't been judgmental. Jenny realized she had to reset her expectations. This wasn't Portland, Chico, or Sunrise. For all she knew, Isabella was one of a hundred different stripes of easily offended.

Suddenly, she remembered telling Aurora about her hitchhiking as they sat in her apartment, smoking. She remembered Aurora's hair falling out of the red kerchief tied over her head, and her laughing her ass off and wanting to know all about it. She had wanted details, and she couldn't stop laughing, but there had never been judgment in Aurora's eyes, not even at the end.

"Sorry," Isabella said, reaching back across the table as if reading Jenny's mind. "Sorry, I don't mean to judge you. You did what you had to do to survive. It's a fucked-up world."

Jenny nodded, agreeing with the last part of the sentiment.

Jenny steered the conversation away from sensitive topics as best she could for the rest of lunch. She asked questions about the town and let Isabella ramble on about her job, her boss, and a seemingly endless list of people Jenny didn't know. She was grateful when, after they'd paid the check, Isabella apologized for having to return to work. Politely, Jenny offered to walk her back and, to Jenny's disappointment, Isabella accepted.

They hugged again when they parted in front of Isabella's office—a small two-story brick building that housed several other small businesses including a dentist, an insurance agent, and a travel agent. Jenny shook her head at the last one, wondering how they could still be in business. Didn't everyone just use websites now?

Wondering if she was out of touch with small-town life, Jenny decided to walk up and down Main Street. It was warm, and she was glad she had changed from her jeans and jacket to one of the only other pieces of clothing she had stuffed into her bag when she had left Chico—a jean skirt. Jenny mused that she might decide to buy clothes of some other material sometime soon. With that in mind, she stopped in front of a retro clothing store called Fashion Backward and gazed through the window at dresses, tops, skirts, and shoes. She found a T-shirt that made her stomach flop with pleasant, nostalgic longing. She pulled the door open, and $15 later stepped out in a white tee with faded orange rings around the sleeves and neck that read 'Lake Sequoia.' Jenny thought it screamed 'Help me, I'm a busty camp counselor from Camp Crystal Lake,' and she loved it.

She paused, looking at her reflection in the store's front window. It felt strange thinking about her style again. She hadn't given it any consideration for the last year. And, she realized, the strangeness was accentuated in the town where her final three years had been spent assembling a wardrobe of pure black.

Hope you appreciated that one, Jesus, she thought. *I know it helped everyone to have me in mourning for how fucked the world is.*

She clasped her fingers behind her and walked further south, coming to the end of Main Street's businesses. She paused again in front of the old dark-brick Shonette Hotel, which had apparently been converted into apartments and workspaces. A keypad lay by the heavy glass and metal front door, which sported a large piece of paper with printed text taped on the inside.

At least they found a use for it, she thought. But she also found herself skeptical of how much Lightning Falls needed work-share spaces and apartments. How many people wanted to live out here? How many people could even find the town? She wondered if the building would be empty again in three years.

Jenny thought about walking down to the town square where she knew, but could not picture, town events were often held. She decided that scouting Main Street was enough for her first day back, she didn't need to branch off just yet.

She headed back north, feeling suddenly tired. She passed a Mexican restaurant called Montana Esmerelda, the bank, a bar, a liquor store, and another restaurant. This one was called The Mouse Trap. A large-eared mouse nibbled at cheese on the sign, and Jenny wondered how wise it was to associate your eatery with mice. She turned and stopped as an old woman came out of the next building, a stack of books cradled in the crook of her arm. She closed a bright red door behind her with the tinkle of an old shop bell. The woman descended three steps to the sidewalk, gave Jenny a neighborly wave, and then hurried up Main Street as if she were off to give a lecture from her books. Jenny approached the brick building's plate-glass window to read the gold lettering stenciled there.

'Congregational Study Room,' it said. Jenny cupped her hands close to the glass and saw a plain room with a little counter and several bookshelves full of books. The only other things in the room were a sturdy table with old wooden chairs, and a little, spindly-legged table to her right with a candle set on top. Jenny wondered if it was the kind of place Patty would go with her friends for a rousing study session.

She tried not to laugh. She hoped that such places comforted people, but she couldn't imagine spending her time in the hard-backed seats when the library had a much bigger selection and lovely, comfy chairs to curl up in. Hands once more behind her back, she gave the study room a not-entirely-dismissive shrug and continued past a consignment store, another apartment building, and a barber.

She stopped again to consider a statue flanked by neatly manicured bushes in front of the library. It depicted a thick, mutton-chopped man wearing a nineteenth-century suit and high-collared shirt, holding both a hammer and a book. He had his foot up on what looked like a facsimile of Proclamation Rock. The names and places jumbled in her head, whispering that she knew them from another life. She read the inscription under his feet.

Jasper Lundy
1872-1950
The head of one of the most important early families in Lightning Falls, Jasper Lundy led the reorganization project from 1908-1912. He served as Mayor from 1912-1924 and again from 1932-1940. Lundy's influence on local politics, commerce, and historical preservation has left an indelible mark on our town.

A thin, feeble fear twinged in her gut, confusing her. There was nothing about the man and his business suit, book, bald head, glasses, or benevolent look that Jenny thought was frightening. Nothing except that when she moved—and the shadows shifted on his face—he reminded her of someone. The thin fear spread until she stepped to the left and the effect was gone. For a moment he had looked like … but now, Jasper Lundy looked nothing like Joseph. Both had broad faces, but nothing about their features suggested the other. Still, from below, with the shadows falling exactly right …

Jenny turned and continued briskly up Main.

The fire station followed the town library and was succeeded by the local Chinese food place and the Timber. When she finally passed Mastino's, Patty's favorite pizza place, the tightness in her stomach had loosened. She slowed to savor the familiar scent of mozzarella, tomatoes, and spiced Italian meats. To the restaurant's right stood something new: a weed shop called Flying Purple. Jenny felt like she was sixty-five years old. She hated the smell of marijuana and hoped that Lightning Falls wasn't living under a perpetual cloud of its funk.

Well, I haven't smelled any yet. That's a good sign.

With that tentative observation, Jenny crossed the street to return home.

5
Where the World May See Them

Friday, August 01, 2025 - Afternoon

Cinnamon and the clanking of pots and pans greeted Jenny as she came through Patty's front door. *I thought you'd be at work a little longer,* Jenny thought, suddenly annoyed. She realized she had no idea how long Patty's shifts at the hardware store were, but something about what Patty had said that morning had suggested that Jenny would have a little more alone time. She considered going up to her room or back to Patty's computer to continue working on getting affairs in order, but figured that if she was going to do that, she should at least tell the owner of the house she was home. So, begrudgingly, Jenny walked up the short hallway to the kitchen and leaned against the doorframe.

Patty was scrubbing a metal cookie sheet in her basin sink and wearing big blue headphones and an apron that said, 'Congregation Bakeoff 2020.' She was singing a hymn that Jenny was unfamiliar with.

"Up high, where the world may see them,
High, where the light can free them,
High, where the sun doth eh-ver shine!"

She raised her voice in a trilling, affected vibrato, her sponge waving back and forth, suds dripping down her rubber glove. Jenny stifled her laughter and walked into the kitchen slowly, waving her arms. Patty must have seen Jenny in the cookie tray's reflection because she waved without looking as she worked at a particularly tough bit of burned dough. Finally, when the bits had come free, she slapped the faucet handle, dropped her sponge, and pulled her headphones down. Jenny could hear a choir tinnily singing about lifting something high.

"Where were you?" Patty asked, smiling.

"I had lunch with Isabella Delgado," Jenny said.

Patty's face lit up. "Oh? How was it?"

"It was ... awkward. But good, I guess. Good to reconnect with her." Jenny figured those were the words Patty would want to hear.

"Well, I'm sure there will be plenty of awkward-but-good coming down the line."

Jenny nodded, crossed her arms, and stared down at her feet.

"Were you able to access your money online?" Patty asked.

"Yeah, but it's going to take a few days to transfer. But my one credit card still works, so my phone will be up soon," Jenny said.

"Well, that's good that you'll be all connected back to the internet superhighway."

Jenny couldn't stop the smirk from tugging at one side of her lips. "Hey, by the way, do you mind if I borrow the car in the next day or two? I want to drive out to Walmart or something. I've been wearing the same five pairs of underwear for the last year."

Patty gave her a horrified look. "Well, I know that the drugstore has some—"

"Those are for emergencies, and I'd like to take my pants off in front of someone again before I'm ninety."

Patty shook her head. "I'm not sure if I feel good about lending you the car to go off and buy sexy underwear."

"One, not wanting a plastic pack of granny panties from the drug store isn't the same as wanting to go out and buy G-strings. Two, I'm twenty-nine, I think you can stop taking responsibility for what I buy."

Patty frowned. "Is that a new T-shirt? Did you go to, what is it, 'Sequoia Lake?'"

"Yes and no. And, sort of no and no," Jenny said, pulling the shirt out and looking down at the cracked words. "I picked it up from that retro place on Main Street. And no, before you ask, I'm not going to buy my underwear used."

Patty snorted a laugh and shook her head. "Did you buy it so people would ask if you vacationed at Sequoia Lake or wherever? Sorry to burst your bubble, but with the size of that T-shirt, no one's going to be paying any attention to what it says."

Jenny frowned and glanced down at her chest again. "Jeez, sorry grandma passed her boobs down to me. Not my fault."

"You could wear something a little looser," Patty said, untying her apron.

Jenny sighed and shrugged. "I don't remember you wearing loose shirts back in the day," Jenny said. "Or any shirts sometimes. Pretty sure there's still a picture in the back room of that dive—"

"There isn't, not anymore," Patty said. "John took that down when I asked him to. A lot has changed since you left, Jennifer."

"Yeah, I've been meaning to ask, when did you and Eric break up?" Jenny heard her tone become more combative and regretted it. She hated how she could be calm and diplomatic with everyone else in the world except for this woman.

Well, maybe not everyone.

"The same time I was asking John to take that picture down. The same time I stopped letting everyone know about my personal business. Six years ago. That was when I found my way."

Jenny nodded. Six years felt like a lifetime. Where had she been six years ago? In the Chico house, in love with Aurora, getting to know Matina, and trying to figure out what her life should be. She hadn't met Nolan yet, or Joseph. Almost nothing real had happened yet. Nothing but Aurora.

"Well, I guess I'm still looking for my way. And just in case you're wondering, I'm not really interested in learning more about your Lord and Savior. Me and Jesus have had an understanding for a while now."

Patty gave her a bemused look bordering on pity. "Oh really? What sort of understanding is that?"

"We help each other out when we can," Jenny said. "He's a busy guy, and I've got my own shit going on. But if we cross each other's paths, we'll give the other one a hand."

"Oh really?" Patty said, putting one yellow rubber gloved hand on her hip. "And how often does he cross your path?" She was almost laughing now.

Jenny smiled sadly. "More often than I'd like," she said. "You forget I knew him a hell of a lot earlier than you. He's in everyone, right? The least? He just doesn't seem to run across me that much."

She shrugged and left Patty staring at her with her mouth open and the suds sliding down her glove into the sink.

6
Buffs

Friday, August 01, 2025 - Afternoon

At three in the afternoon, under a gabled ceiling, Jenny lay atop her covers, running her bare feet across the comforter's fabric. The cloth bunched between her toes while she pulled at her new T-shirt and let it fall back to her stomach, wafting air against her pale skin. The room had grown stuffy despite the open windows.

Anxiety throbbed as she replayed her lunch with Isabella, the look of the statue on Main Street, and the near-miss of an almost argument with Patty. She felt she had already begun on the wrong foot and should scrap the idea of starting over in Lightning Falls. The thought occurred to her that she should pack her meager belongings and try somewhere else.

Sure, but where?

She glanced at her phone and sat up. She had service. The anxiety in her ebbed and flowed. The fact that Patty's Wi-Fi didn't reach the third floor was no longer an excuse for her not to check her site. She had justified not logging on in a public place, or downstairs where Patty might walk in. But now, as satellite data connected her with her different apps and services, she couldn't find a reason to put it off any longer. Of course, doing everything on her phone wasn't ideal, but this was a first step. She could transfer her money from the site, buy a laptop, figure out where she was financially …

Jenny opened the JustBuffs app to find that her message count was just over 3,000 and that her account balance rested at a similar number. She pursed her lips and pulled at her shirt again.

Okay, that could be worse. It could be a hell of a lot better, but it could be worse.

She went to her payouts page and started the money transfer immediately. She considered taking the hit to get the cash in a day, but she opted against that. She had an emergency credit card she could use until the money came in. There was no need to give the people who ran the site any more of her earnings.

Then she turned to the messages. The number was daunting, but she knew that most would be from a relatively small number of people. She was about to start replying when she had an idea. Jumping up, she hurried into the bathroom and appraised herself. She had done her makeup for lunch with Isabella and thought she still looked passable. It was certainly good enough for her almost entirely male audience.

She went back to the bed and wished she had a phone stand. That would have to go on a list right away. Jenny turned on the camera's burst fire option, held it out, and took several pictures of herself. Then she took her new T-shirt off, checked to confirm her bra wasn't unpresentable, and snapped a few more shots, trying to mimic the same pose as in the first set. Then she leaned back and reviewed the images. She thought most were terrible, but two from the first set and one from the second didn't make her cringe horribly. So, she did a little editing on her phone until she was happy with the light, color, and crop, and then posted them as a group to her JustBuffs page with the caption, *Guess who's back?*

She posted the first two images publicly. She blurred the third, more revealing image so only her paying supporters could see it. Then she started in on the messages. She had been right that most had come from a small, highly devoted group. That group was still over fifty people large, some of whom had been checking on her weekly for a year. One had sent her fifty messages, another a hundred, and another over three hundred. She didn't know how to feel about those people. She didn't understand their concern for someone they had never interacted with outside of a paid website.

Still, the kind messages were welcome compared to those that demanded that she return so they could get their money's worth, or the ones that said they had read about her in the news and called her terrible names. Others were limited to 'Where are you?' or some variation of complimenting her chest, which Jenny found oddly amusing in a non sequitur way. Did they think they'd coax her back to the website by telling her she had a great body? To the first and second groups and those who asked where she was, she sent a cookie-cutter message that thanked them for their support and concern and told them she was back and doing well. She politely thanked those who told her how fantastic her body was and told them they would see more soon. Those who called her terrible names she blocked.

She closed the app and considered her plain, beige bra. She needed new clothes. Jenny thought about how Patty would feel about housing a woman who bought underwear, not for people to see in person, but for hundreds or thousands of people to see on the internet. She imagined that that conversation wouldn't go well.

All I have to do is keep it secret long enough to be able to get myself settled. Then she can feel however she wants when I'm living in my nice, cozy house on the other side of town. Or, she thought, remembering her lunch with Isabella, *in another town far away.*

She pulled up her calculator app and decided she needed to make at least \$8,000 a month from her page to move anywhere but Lightning Falls or somewhere like it. Rent was ridiculous, and buying a place would be impossible unless she was making more than that. And since her page had generated only three grand in a year, she had a lot of rebuilding to do.

She wondered how long it would be feasible to live with Patty. She needed a plan that would let her leave if Patty ever found out or if things became too contentious. Her mind wandered to the other ramifications of her site being discovered by anyone in town. She guessed she'd probably get a few local husbands signing up, and as long as they were cool about it, she'd be grateful for the support. But then there was the possibility of people she knew signing up without her knowing. Jenny wasn't sure how she felt about Barry surfing her pictures late at night while randy. On the one hand, she didn't mind the idea much, but on the other, she would rather know than wonder. And the reality was, unless she outright asked, or someone volunteered the information, it would always be a nagging question.

She slid down over the covers and longed for her life in a larger, more anonymous place. Chico had been good, and Los Angeles had been better. No one knew her in either town, but in LA she could hide among the crowds. Even her work hadn't been exceptional in LA; no one had cared if she took her clothes off for money.

She sat bolt upright again and thought about her work in Los Angeles. Her time there had lasted only six months, but she had made a significant amount of content that still lived on some of the more popular adult sites, and it wasn't the quiet, mostly R-rated material she had made on her own. The idea of someone finding her JustBuffs page and searching for her other, more explicit content suddenly seemed inevitable. It would be one thing for Patty to find out that Jenny was selling pictures and videos of her naked body, it would be another if she found out that there were videos of Jenny engaging in adult activities with other people all over the internet.

Suddenly her anxiety roared, and she felt like she had to do something about it all immediately. She considered just deleting her page entirely. That wouldn't stop people from discovering her other videos, but she thought it would at least hide the trailhead under some brush. She could at least not put a sign up for everyone to follow. That felt too drastic, and it would wipe out any hope of a livable income in the near future. Of course, just being on the site and having her pictures and videos there wasn't the main issue. Just being on the site and having her pictures and videos there wasn't the main issue. If Patty thought she was a harlot for letting people see her nipples, then so be it, but the follow-up—people going from her page to the highly produced X-rated content she had made with dozens of people—scared her in a place as small as Lightning Falls. She didn't own the videos so she couldn't take them down, but she could at least take the sign down.

She opened the app on her phone and clicked on the settings button. Under her display name, she highlighted her stage name and typed 'Jenny' in its place. When she saved the change, it felt like an inadvertent rebirth—something she should mark. Remembering Isabella's gift, she pulled the little leather-bound journal from the gift bag and one of the pens she had bought earlier in the day. She cracked the journal open and giggled as she printed her name on the inside cover above the words 'For my eyes only!' Then, on the first lined page, she wrote the date in the upper left-hand corner, and on the first line she printed, 'Goodbye Venena.'

7
Sleep

Friday, August 01, 2025 - Evening

She was thirteen and trying out for track. Her shorts cut into her legs, and her oversized shirt billowed about her as she sprinted on the red-rubbery racetrack. On the sidelines, two coaches—a woman and a man—blew whistles and shouted at her to keep going. She lapped once, twice, three times, and the silver whistles never stopped. Finally, she broke away, her cleats hitting first gravel, then dirt, then grass. The whistles followed her across the soccer field and through the gate in the old chain-link fence along the back of the school's property. They followed her into the street and down the bank toward the creek. The high-pitched trills followed and morphed, first becoming long, screeching wires drawn across rusted metal, then the departing riffs of a half-remembered guitar solo.

She stood on the bank of the creek, panting and trying to remember the name of the song. As she stood, hands on knees, the water rippled. Her father's face peered up at her with swollen white eyes and a mouth full of worms.

"Your way leads through the water," a man's voice said in her ear as something black and glistening slithered between her feet.

Jenny jolted awake and clapped a hand over her mouth as fear and sorrow tried to force their way out as a groan. She didn't want to wake Veronica. Neither one of them would get back to sleep for hours.

Veronica isn't here. You aren't in Sunrise. You're alone.

The thought was ragged comfort. She would never have to worry about waking Veronica up again, never have to hear her cry herself to sleep for hours.

"Oh, fuck," she croaked into the moonlit room as the rock and roll song reached its conclusion. Jenny rubbed her eyes and realized that she had slept the rest of the day away. Her stomach rumbled as she pulled her hair back into a bun and wrapped a hair tie around it before swinging her legs over the side of the bed. *Guess I missed dinner*, she thought. As she stood to undress, visions of a late-night kitchen raid filled her mind, but she dispelled them. Only disappointment could be found in Patty's spare and wholesome pantry. Freed from skirt and bra, Jenny shambled to the bathroom.

Ten minutes later—her face clean and damp, her mouth minty— she slapped the light and flopped onto the bed. She was too awake to fall back to sleep. She reached over to turn the radio down and realized with confusion, that she had never turned it on.

She sat up and looked at the old black rectangle that sat on the nightstand. The time, 11:07 showed in blocky, red LED lights. Another song ended and a young woman's voice replaced it.

"Hey everyone, that was "Watermelon" by John and Jane Q. Public. I literally could listen to that over and over again. How about you all out there in night-land? Do you have songs that you could listen to on repeat? Oh, I know, maybe we can figure out what Lightning Falls' favorite song is!"

Jenny frowned. Did Lightning Falls have a radio station? Wasn't it too small—

Then it all came flooding back.

The radios.

The towers.

The Sleep Talkers.

"I think we could maybe have a bracket, and we could just play the same songs over and over and no one in the world would get insanely annoyed with us. What do you think—" A phone ringing cut the radio woman off. "Oh, phone call time. Hello, you're on the tower with Sydney!"

A young boy's voice said, "Hey, Sydney!"

"Hey, Bryce, how are you? Um … it's kind of late, isn't it? I figured you called Maddy tonight since I didn't hear from you."

"No, I got to stay up. Can you do it now?"

"Yeah, why not? And since it's so late maybe we'll be putting some older people to bed too. So, what kind of story do you want? Knights, spaceships, or tractors?"

"Spaceships," Bryce said.

"All right. Do you still need to get ready for bed?"

"Mhm."

"Okay, get yourself ready, brush your teeth, and I'll start the story in ten minutes, all right?"

"Thanks, Sydney!"

"Say 'hi' to your parents for me," the woman said. "Okay everybody, that means that in ten minutes we're going to do a bedtime story. So, if you don't want to hear about spaceships, tune in to Maddy or Charles."

Jenny's mind wandered. She had forgotten all about the three radio stations in Lightning Falls. The woman, Sydney, filled the ten minutes by talking about the weather and the next day's summer market on Main

Street. Patty had also said something about it before she had left that morning. Jenny wasn't sure if she had agreed to go, but she figured it might be good to get a taste of small-town life.

Jenny slid down under her covers as Sydney's voice soothed Jenny's mind. When the woman began to read the children's book, Jenny drifted. In her imagination, her father tuned the radio to the AM band. He asked her who she wanted to listen to. "Cassandra," she said. He turned the dial and sat next to Jenny, stroking her hair as the woman's rich, deep voice lulled her into dreams.

She sank into the void where dreams grow, and the world shifted. Her father led her through a crowd of adults to two men by the bank of a creek. She recognized one, tall, stocky, and sun-tanned. The other was tall and thin and facing away from her. He was looking across the creek at two women—too blurry for her to recognize—who were staring at Jenny. Everyone made her feel uneasy as if none of them should be there.

"Put one on," her father said. Jenny tried to respond, to ask him what he meant. But when she opened her mouth water gushed out.

Jenny woke, but not enough to remember waking. She would forget reaching out and turning the radio off, leaving only the night sounds of insects, a hawk, and the distant rumbling of the falls.

Within, a new voice whispered as she fell one more into the void of dreams, "Hello? Are you there?"

8
Summer Market

Saturday, August 2, 2025 - Morning

PATTY WOKE JENNY EARLY with a knock on her door, and Jenny resisted the urge to tell her to go away. An hour and a half later, full of bacon, eggs, and coffee longing, Jenny followed Patty downtown. A police car was parked across Main, blocking traffic south of Cunningham. A police officer, young, tall, and red-haired, leaned against the side of the car with his arms crossed, smiling and talking to a pretty blonde woman who was probably twenty years his senior. Jenny immediately clocked her stance, smile, and intense gaze.

"Well, she's hungry," Jenny said.

"What's that?" Patty asked as they approached Cunningham.

"Nothing," Jenny said.

"You're still hungry after the eggs and toast?"

"No," Jenny said, uncertain if she should sigh or laugh. "I just need Barry and his magical beans."

Beyond the police car, Main Street's transformation stretched for three blocks. Stalls stood on either side of the thoroughfare, facing each other around a growing crowd of milling people in jeans, boots, and assorted flannel and puffy vests. Stands for fresh produce, honey, soaps, candles, and crafts shouldered close to each other in cramped files. A woman with gray, braided hair sat in a folding chair next to a booth of impressive paintings of landscapes, Native Americans on horseback, and one of Elvis. Another booth sold T-shirts with political slogans, most of which were indecipherable to Jenny. They passed two older women who were leaning over rows of hand-made mugs.

"Good morning, Anna," Patty said, touching one of the women on the shoulder. Anna turned and smiled from behind round glasses. Once out of earshot, Patty leaned over and whispered to Jenny, "Lesbians," as if it were 1955. Jenny shook her head and stopped at a booth where a mustachioed man was selling clothes. The sign above the booth said, 'Fashion Backwards.'

"Oh, I was just in your shop yesterday," Jenny said. "I didn't see any of these."

"They're all overstock," the man said. "Stuff we keep in boxes in the back. What did you get yesterday?"

They chatted about vintage clothing for a few minutes, and he showed her a brown T-shirt with a roaring bear on the front. She loved it and paid him $6.

"Oh my god," a young woman with orange hair said, passing Jenny with another young woman in tow. The second woman—hair black, wavy, and long—reminded Jenny of herself as a teenager, though she put both into their mid-twenties. The girl with black hair flashed Jenny a look of recognition before her friend pulled her close in front of the Fashion Backwards table. They put their arms around each other and Jenny couldn't help herself. She rejoined Patty, leaned close to her ear, and whispered, "Lesbians."

It was Patty's turn to shake her head, but not in reproach. Jenny smirked and glanced back at the pair, this time catching the orange-haired woman's eye. Something fluttered in Jenny's stomach.

Oh no, Jenny thought. *Girl, you've got to calm down, seriously.* Another part of her mind suggested that the best way to do that was to get laid. With that idea came another lancing jab of guilt and shame. She looked away from the pair, ran her hand over her stomach, and tried to force the image of Nolan's blue eyes from her mind, and the feeling of his hands from her skin.

Aurora, Nolan, Matina.

Veronica and her crying. Grace and her vacant stare.

Joseph.

With the sense of shame came the feeling that someone was watching her. She turned to search the crowd for anyone looking at her, anyone who might be making the hairs on her arms stand at attention. But the only person looking directly at her was a young, freckle-faced teenage boy wearing a Lightning Falls Nighthawks jersey. He looked away when she met his eye. He had seemed curious, probably at the sight of an unfamiliar woman in tight jeans. She figured that it was nothing more sinister than garden-variety lust. Nothing that would make her feel as if Joseph were standing right behind her.

"You said you needed new underwear," Patty said, pulling on Jenny's arm.

"What?"

Patty didn't repeat herself, she just pointed. They stood in front of the historical society's booth, which had six mannequins flanking a folding table attended by a thin old woman with a bent back. One of the figures had overalls and a white collarless button-up shirt under it. Another had an elaborate dress with a wide skirt. The one that caught Jenny's eye was a short black dress with gold accents and beaded fringe on the bottom. Jenny reached out toward the cloth.

"Please don't touch," the woman said in a wavering voice.

"Oh, sorry," Jenny said.

"That's real. They're all real."

"Oh, wow, they're so well preserved."

Patty tugged on Jenny's arm. Jenny turned and finally saw the mannequin that was at the heart of Patty's joke. It wore a set of women's underwear that Jenny guessed was from before telephones were invented. It covered the figure from shoulder to knee.

"Ah," Jenny said. "Very funny."

"I thought so," Patty said with a grin.

They passed in front of Baker's Books. A stall was set up with a young man in a baseball cap setting out boxes of books with the help of a fit woman with short brown hair.

"Do you think Delia's here?"

"She usually is, but I think she's having one of her parties tonight. She'll be here for the next one though. You need something to read?"

"What? No, that's okay, I still have my library card," Jenny said, feeling a powerful combination of disappointment and relief. She wasn't sure why her feelings about seeing Delia were so fraught. She had worked for the woman for two years. Those years had been tumultuous, but the bookstore had been a refuge. She remembered it as a quiet place where she could do homework, read, or even sleep. She owed Delia a lot and they hadn't spoken in over a decade.

"Oh, look," Patty said, "they have soup!"

Twenty minutes later, Jenny sat sans soup in front of Barry's, sipping her latte while Patty talked to a tall, handsome man with flyers in his hand. Behind her two other men were conversing. They stood out from the rest of the crowd for Jenny. The first was shorter and had dark skin. Lightning Falls, Jenny mused, was the whitest town she'd ever been to. Other than her friend Delia, she only knew a couple of other black people in town, though now she couldn't remember who they were or how she knew them. For all she knew, she might be old friends with the stocky Van Dyke sporting man who stood under the Town Hall booth's banner.

The other man was conspicuous for his age. He was tall, slender, and wore a broad white beard. He must have been eighty, or perhaps even ninety. Jenny didn't recognize him either, but there was something about the man that tugged at her mind as if he reminded her of something she was supposed to do or something she had forgotten to do.

The feeling passed as Patty left her conversation and walked over.

"Well, are you feeling more energetic?" Patty asked.

"I'm getting there."

"Good. You'll be happy to know that I'm setting you up on a date then."

"I will? When will that be?" Jenny asked.

Patty made a face and shook her head. "You will once you meet him. Phil is a nice young man. And I think he's exactly what you need."

Jenny opened her mouth, felt herself about to say the word 'Mom' in an exasperated teenage voice, and decided that the better thing to do was to sip her latte a bit more. She had just been thinking about her need to get laid. Her thoughts had leaned more toward the sapphic side, but the idea of a tall mountain man welcoming her back to town wasn't without its charms.

"If you say so," Jenny said.

Patty frowned approvingly, doing her best Robert Dinero impersonation, and sat next to Jenny. "I think you'll like him very much. You probably remember him; his sister Leddy was one of your best friends."

Jenny knew Patty expected her to respond with a long 'ohhhh' of recognition, but no recognition came. She didn't remember anyone named Leddy. So, instead of an 'oh' she gave Patty an 'ah.' Short, sweet, and cut off by her latte.

Entry 2

Sunday, August 3, 2025

I guess I should write something other than a poignant, pithy one-line entry. So, okay, here goes. Yesterday Patty set me up with a guy she knows. Today I got his number, and we started texting. Well, sweet diary, his name is Phil and he's tall and dreamy. And every time I think about him, I want to puke my guts up. Why? Is his face a mess of scars? Is the word on the street that his dick is the size of a gherkin? No, it's because I see Nolan whenever I think about hanging out with this guy. It's like he's just standing there, looking at me with a blank face.

So yeah, tell me diary, what should I do? Do I go out with the tall lumberjack-looking guy and try to keep the fucking knife fight in my stomach from tearing me apart, or do I give myself some more time to grieve? How long does it take to get over your murdered boyfriend?

Volume 10, Issue 66, Monday, August 4, 2025

Time Travel

By Keith Lowry, Ed. In Chief.

A WEEK CAN BE an infinite amount of time. I first learned this fact when my brother, Mikey, went to Vietnam. The next time was when I came back from that same foreign land and had to readjust to being a normal person again. Time moves quickly when the world is on fire and slows to winter molasses when it suddenly quiets, and Death isn't gobbling people left and right.

This past week was a lesson in how true that is. I seem to have spent a million hours sitting with my friend's widow.

Widow.

It's a monstrous word because it corresponds to a monstrous reality. I'm tired, though I feel like I've slept for a hundred hours in the last seven days. I've been helping her make Jack's last arrangements. Like many couples around our age, they didn't have everything sorted. And, like many people who go through such things, I'm promising myself that I'll make all my own arrangements when this is done, but I probably won't.

The loss of someone like Jack is a pain that goes on for as long as the people who love him. Of course, I won't keep subjecting everyone to that pain, bringing it back up every issue or even every month. But, right now, I'm too close to it, and our little town is too quiet for me to write about much else today.

For me, Lightning Falls is a place where people happen. It's not a place of buildings, businesses, or landmarks except that they mean something to the people who are born, live, and die here. Main Street isn't the businesses, but the movies seen at the Mist, the meals eaten at Second Wave, and the Saturday morning conversations at High Tops. It's picnics by the falls and the hikes up to the High Path with the people who matter to you. Their spirits infuse the place with meaning and identity, so that Proclamation Rock isn't just the rock where people propose to each other, but the place where I proposed to my wife and Jack proposed to Cassandra. Stollie's Corner Store isn't just our local version of what they'd call a bodega in New York, but the place my nephews used to buy baseball cards and *Garbage Pail Kids* packs.

The people who give those places their identities are like time machines. When I'd walk into High Tops on a Saturday morning and see Jack there, ready to get that big beard of his trimmed, I had access to all the Saturdays before that going back to when we were kids getting our crew cuts. Together, we could travel through the years and find those places again, because the spirits that lived with us in those moments were with us. But, when Jack died, the past became something new and strange: the past.

I lost my father twenty years ago, and I remember having this experience but not knowing how to express it. My memories of my father, wonderful as they are, are not the same as those of one of my closest lifelong friends. But even then, I saw, at least a little, that the past had taken on a more solid, immovable character. And this week I've watched the past become ever more rigid and ever more inaccessible.

I wonder if the week has moved so slowly because I've lost something more than I realized with Jack. This town was our world together, and until someone took his life a little more than a week ago, I hadn't realized how easy it was to time-travel here. But now, on the other side of Jack's life, I've become stuck. I'm here in the future, and he's in the past, and we can't go back together to those wonderful days of racing down the street on our bikes, standing at each other's weddings, or sharing a quiet beer fishing at the creek. Those days are locked away, and I am H.G. Wells' time traveler, stuck in a future I never predicted.

9
Occupation

Tuesday, August 5, 2025 - Noon

THE TIMBER STOOD ON the southwest corner of Adams and Main. Three stories tall, the restaurant occupied the brick remains of the old Lightning Falls Lumber building. The business had never operated in town, as lumber contracts fell through after construction finished in the 1890s. The building stood vacant for five years before the township claimed it for the Town Hall for nine years. Then, during the period of reconciliation in the first decade of the twentieth century, the building was used as housing for those whose homes were being constructed.

Afterward, the first and second floors were used for storage. Patience Lustin, an artist whose work was considered far too abstract and disturbing for general consumption, occupied the third floor. In the 1920s, Gabriel Lundy—the mayor's brother—purchased the building and converted it into apartments. He used the rent to construct a hotel at the corner of Shonette and Main.

In the 1940s, the building was slowly transformed into offices and storage space. Then, in 1953, the first and second floors housed Millet's Department Store, before it moved to its more permanent location further down Main Street in 1965.

This began the building's tenure as an eatery. Split into two restaurants, the building featured a steak house on one side and served Italian food on the other. Since the '60s, the building had housed a Japanese restaurant, a second steak house, a Mexican restaurant, and a short-lived, seafood-focused eatery.

In 2010, after the last remaining restaurant closed, Carl Victorine purchased the building, took over its current leases, and renovated the first floor to create his vision of a rustic bar and restaurant—the Timber. He hoped it would celebrate the past, present, and future of Lightning Falls in a location rich with local lore and character.

Jenny sat in the Timber's foyer, reading the restaurant's history from the back of one of the menus. None of it rang any bells for her except the name 'Lundy,' which she was pretty sure was familiar only because of the statue on Main Street.

She frowned at the laminated history, feeling like it had either lied to her about the building being rich in local lore or just ignored that lore entirely. There was a sentence about the artist, but that was it. No scandalous murders, no torrid love affairs, no run-away servant girls, or secret brothels operating out of apartments. As far as Jenny could tell—one artist excepted—the building was entirely devoid of local lore.

The heavy wooden door of the Timber opened, and Jenny glanced up, expecting to see Isabella. Instead, sunlight backlit two figures, one tall and one short. When they entered, the dark figures resolved into a man and a woman who were—was it polite to say 'ancient?' If not, Jenny wasn't sure what adjective would be appropriate. She thought the old man looked familiar, and for a moment thought she might be remembering something from her time in town. But then it struck her that she had seen him at the market a few days earlier and her momentary excitement faded.

The woman was perhaps twenty years younger than him, which she thought put her in her seventies. Jenny guessed that she was seeing the strange pairing of an old person with their ancient—that was the only word she could think of—parent. A flash-forward nightmare suggested itself to her imagination, and Jenny pictured herself at seventy with a nonagenarian Patty toddling beside her.

"Good morning, you two! Your table is ready," Julie, the soon-to-leave-town-and-become-an-actress hostess said, grabbing menus and walking over to the man. He was tall, close to six and a half feet, and towered over both shorter women. Jenny watched as he released his daughter's hand and put his arm around the much younger woman's shoulder.

"Lead us on, Julie," the man said in a tired, rasping voice. "But not too quickly, I want you to tell me how you've been. I've been so busy with things that I haven't had time to talk to you."

She put her arm around his back and guided him slowly past the hostess booth. The elderly woman gazed at Jenny for a long moment with pale blue eyes. Jenny couldn't quite make out the expression in them. Was it curiosity? Pity? Concern? She couldn't tell. Feeling uncomfortable, Jenny uncrossed and recrossed her legs, glancing at the woman furtively. The woman continued to stare. Jenny was trying to build up the courage to ask her if she could help the woman when her phone buzzed.

Jenny glanced up from her phone. The old woman had finally moved on and was following the hostess. She wondered if the woman didn't approve of her clothing, or maybe she recognized her as Patty Berger's kid. Jenny could understand why that might upset someone.

Maybe she just used to know you, Jenny thought. *Maybe you were just incredibly rude.*

Before Jenny could consider the consequences of that thought, the front door opened and Isabella came bustling through.

"Sorry, Mike wouldn't let me go," she said, walking over to Jenny and holding her arms out. Jenny stood and gave her a reserved hug. Isabella, on the other hand, pulled her close and squeezed her. "How have you been? Are you all settled now?"

"Sure, I've got everything up and running, for the most part. I have internet guys coming to Patty's house tomorrow to upgrade her service. It's like the '90s in there. I'm surprised she doesn't still use dial-up."

Isabella laughed. "Well, that's good. Have you figured out what you're going to do for work?"

Jenny crossed her arms under her chest and shook her head. "No, not yet. I haven't really been looking. I had a few, um, projects going before I—"

"Two?" Julie asked from behind her.

Jenny turned and smiled. "Yeah, two."

"This way," Julie said, waving them on with menus. She sat them in the same corner booth as she had a few days earlier. Jenny had a clear view of the rest of the dining area and the tall old man who was looking studiously at his menu.

"So, you were saying about your work," Isabella said.

"Oh, right, anyway, I had some money put away, and I still have a little coming in from some work I did before, so I'm not in a rush. But if I have to pay rent or anything like that, I'll need to get something going soon."

Isabella nodded. "Well, I'd tell you to work with me, but Mike is so cheap he makes me do everything instead of hiring a second person. You've never shown rental properties to prospective tenants before, have you?"

"No," Jenny said.

"God, it's boring. Have you ever bartended before?"

"No, does being a barista count?"

Isabella shrugged. "Maybe? You'd have to ask Carl, who owns this place. I know he's always looking for hot women to bartend. I think he wishes this was one of those places where everyone has to wear a miniskirt and shows their tits."

Jenny cocked an eyebrow. "So, you mean like me."

Isabella laughed. "I mean, you look amazing, so if you got it—" She stopped. Jenny wondered if she was remembering their last conversation in the Timber. "But as far as being a barista goes—I don't know if Barry is looking for people right now."

The waitress appeared, took their drink orders, and left.

"Yeah, I don't think being a barista would pay enough for me to get my own place."

"Probably not," Isabella said. She smiled as if she were about to make a joke but stopped herself. Once more Jenny felt like the woman was remembering their conversation and censoring herself. Perhaps Isabella was the kind of person who liked to joke about sex work and was finding herself confounded by sitting across from someone who had done it.

Oh, if you only knew, sweet girl, Jenny thought.

"I feel like I don't recognize anyone," Jenny said, hoping to change the subject. "Like, who is she? She can't be more than five years older than me, but I don't recognize her."

Isabella regarded the short-haired, olive-skinned girl in the booth across from them and shook her head. "No idea, probably a tourist. See how she's dressed like she just came out of the outdoor store?" She scanned the room on one side and then leaned across her seat to look at the bar. "Okay, what about him?" Isabella said, pointing to someone behind the bar. Jenny scooted over and peered at the bartender. He was a bald man with a thick white mustache.

"Is that Carl?" Jenny asked.

"Yeah!" Isabella said. "See, you remember!"

"No, I just guessed because I read the sign at the front, and you said that Carl owns the place and wants to hire hot girls. I figured that guy isn't Carl's type."

Isabella smirked. "Okay, Sherlock, how about her?"

"In the blue?"

"No, in the red blazer."

Jenny shook her head at the woman hovering somewhere around seventy with obviously dyed-red hair.

"That's Mayor Hillard, she's been mayor since we were kids." Isabella propped herself up and craned her neck, not trying to be subtle. "Oh," she said and pointed across to one of the other booths. Waving, she called, "Chase, stand up!" A young man with red hair and a short-sleeved checked shirt stood up and waved back. "What about him?" Isabella asked.

"Well, I know his name is Chase," Jenny said, laughing. She scooted over to the end of her seat. "He's a cop, isn't he?"

"Chase, come here," Isabella said, waving him over. He obliged. "Do you remember Jenny Berger?"

Chase tilted his head to the side like a dog. A light scattering of freckles ran across the middle of his thin, deceptively youthful face. Jenny guessed he didn't have an ounce of fat on his body. "Um … yeah, I think so. You were the goth girl, right?"

Jenny nodded. "Yeah, that was me."

"Do you remember Chase?" Isabella asked.

Jenny shook her head slowly. "Kind of? I mean, you look a little familiar. I did see a woman flirting with you on Saturday."

Chase laughed and blushed. "I can't remember anyone flirting with me on Saturday. But, yeah, I was two grades below you, with Isabella," he said. "You wouldn't have any reason to remember me."

"Except that we all played kickball together during the summer, and you used to go with us down to the creek," Isabella said.

"Wait, how old are you?" Jenny asked.

"Twenty-seven," Chase said. "I know, I look young."

"Huh, yeah, I figured you were like, twenty-two."

"Well, I'll be grateful for that one day, right?" He joked. "But yeah, you don't remember me."

It wasn't a question. Jenny got the sense that Officer Chase didn't expect anyone to remember him. She smiled apologetically. "Yeah, I'm sorry. But don't take it personally. Isabella is making a scene because I can't remember much."

Chase laughed. "Well, that's not surprising. I don't think there's much to remember about Lightning Falls. But if you ever need a tour, I'd be happy to—"

"Officer! Are you hitting on our newly returned resident?" Isabella said.

"No, I—Well, you did call me over," he said, grinning widely. Suddenly Jenny understood why the older woman had been paying the young man so much attention. He was disarming in his innocence, but there was something else there, a hint that he wasn't just a golly-gee-shucks small-town deputy who couldn't unclasp a brassiere to save his life.

"If I need a big strong man to escort me around town, I'll let you know," Jenny said.

"If she needs someone to do that, I'll see to it," Isabella said, putting her hand on Jenny's.

"Ah," Chase said. "Well, good to know that you've got someone to help you if you need it. Anyway, I should get back to my lunch. It's nice to see you again."

Jenny returned the sentiment and Chase returned to his seat.

"He's cute, in a Ron Weasley kind of way," Jenny said, playing with the straw of her newly delivered drink.

"Sure, if you're into that kind of thing," Isabella said, frowning.

"What kind of thing?" Jenny said.

"Penis," Isabella whispered. She studied Jenny's face and pulled her hand back. "Which, you're not, right? Or have I totally misread you? You were definitely checking out my ass when we first met."

Jenny squinted at Isabella. "Yes, I was checking your ass out, and yes, I also like"—here she whispered to mimic Isabella—"penis. I'm bi."

Isabella looked up sharply. "Oh," Isabella said. Jenny thought she heard the same hint of judgment in the woman's voice that Isabella had given her the last time they had lunch.

"Is that not okay with you?" Jenny said, unsure why she was asking.

"No, no, it's fine," Isabella said. "Just, like, which way do you tend? Are you the chick who dates guys but dabbles with chicks on the side, or like, the 'I love women, and unfortunately I also need a dude sometimes' kind of girlie?"

"Um, neither," Jenny said. "I … I'm more about the person. I'm attracted to people, not their gender, I guess? I don't know. I've only been in one relationship with a woman, well two—"

"Two relationships?" Isabella asked, sounding hopeful.

"No, two women, one relationship. There was a guy involved too."

"What?"

"It was complicated."

"Yeah, sounds way too complicated for me," Isabella said. There was the judgment again.

"Well, I'm not looking for that again," Jenny said. "I wasn't looking for it back then, either. And honestly, I'm not really looking for anything right now. Though, Patty has set me up with this guy from town already."

"Oh, who?"

"A guy she works with at the hardware store, Phil."

"Oh, Phil's a nice guy, I guess. His sister is hot. But wait, you know her. Damn, you're infecting me with your memory bullshit. I keep thinking like you're new here."

Memory bullshit, Jenny thought, but let it go.

"Yeah, Patty said I know her too. Sorry, it's all just a little fucking weird."

"Yeah," Isabella said. After an awkwardly silent moment, she pushed herself up in her seat and scanned the room again. She patted the table and pointed, trying to be subtle. Jenny followed Isabella's gesture and found the tall old man who had come in earlier.

"What about him?"

Jenny frowned and shook her head. "Nope."

"Really?" Isabella said,

"Yeah, really. Who is he?"

"Mr. Grossman. He's like, the oldest guy in town. Everyone knows him since … I don't know … since a long time ago."

Jenny stared at the man and tried to summon any memory involving him. "What does he do?"

"He practically runs the town," Isabella said, laughing.

"I thought you said the other woman was the mayor," Jenny said.

"She is, but he's like, I don't know, the unofficial mayor. He knows everyone, and he gets stuff done. He's rich too. Like, the school needed new computers for the teachers a few years back and he made sure it happened, even though the township didn't have the money in the budget. He gets the library the latest books that all the middle schoolers want to read. And I'm pretty sure he's singlehandedly responsible for the renovations that they're going to do at the library."

"Mr. Grossman?"

"Yeah, I'm shocked you don't remember him. I mean, I get forgetting Chase, but Mr. Grossman? Weird. Did you get some kind of brain damage when you were in California?"

Jenny once more swallowed her response to the insensitive question. "I guess I don't know," Jenny said. "Maybe."

"Oh," Isabella said, lowering her voice to a conspiratorial whisper,

"Maybe you blocked it all out, you know? Your stepdad wasn't exactly the nicest guy, if I remember."

"No, he wasn't, but I don't think he was so bad that I would block out my entire life."

"He didn't like … you know?" Isabella made a lewd gesture with her hands in the direction of Jenny's chest.

Jenny laughed and shook her head. "No, but I would have let him if he wanted to."

"What?" Isabella ducked her head and further lowered her whisper.

"I would have. Not because he was hot or whatever, but because it would have been a fuck-you to Patty. And, I don't know, I liked the attention."

"I thought you were little Miss Gothic Jesus back then."

"I was, it doesn't mean I wasn't a vengeful little bitch though," Jenny said. "I was also pretty horny."

"And he never tried to, you know …?"

Jenny shook her head. "Never. Not even when they were breaking up and I kind of threw myself at him. Hell, I was eighteen by then. But no, as shitty as he was, I think he actually thought about me like I was his daughter."

Isabella frowned approvingly. "Does your—does Patty have anyone now?"

Jenny shook her head. "No, I think she's off men. She does have dinner planned for Friday with one of her friends. I think they're going to try to save me," Jenny said. "So, I guess maybe the man in her life is Jesus. Not like, real Jesus, but like whatever her church's version of him is."

Isabella frowned. "You know, like, Patty and I go to the same church."

Jenny smiled apologetically. "Sorry, no offense."

Tuesday, August 5, 2025

Dearest Diary, I have a secret. I am naked. Right now, as I'm writing this, I have literally no clothes on. Scandalous, right? I am, admittedly, in my own bedroom alone, though I still don't have any curtains, so maybe a passing bird will get a free look. Need to put that on my checklist (curtains, not bird). Now, you might ask, why am I naked? Did a bear devour my clothes? Did a walrus run off with them? Did a llama decide he wanted to live as a woman for a day? No, friend, I was working. I put on my makeup and took off my vestments for a series of scandalous photos for which men on the internet will give me money.

Now, this wasn't a fancy photo shoot, and the editing I did on the pictures was basic since I don't have my new laptop yet. BUT! But—butt... I said butt. See what I did there, dearest Diary? I said butt and my butt is out. My jokes are nothing if not relevant and timely.

Anyway, pictures, faux earnestness, and capitalism aside, I also had lunch with Isabella today. I think she doesn't like me, and that's probably good. I'm not sure I dig her vibe. She seems, pardon my French, like an uptight bitch. But then, maybe I'm just not giving her a chance. No one else wants to be my friend, so what can I do?

Oh, and I found my junior-year yearbook an hour ago. My makeup! Also, go Nighthawks!

10
Offer

Wednesday, August 6, 2025 - Morning

BARRY'S WAS MOSTLY EMPTY, except for a man alone with his laptop and a pair of gray-haired women talking in the back. Barry was leaning over the counter, engrossed in a badly beaten-up paperback.

"What's happening, Barry?" Jenny said as the bell above the door jingled.

"Hey, just the lady I was hoping to see!" Barry bent the corner of his page and put the book on the glass-topped counter.

"Really?" Jenny asked.

"Yeah, I talked to my friend about that thing," Barry said. In response, Jenny frowned. "The job that I said might be opening up. It is, and I put in a good word for you."

"Oh, that! Right, I honestly totally forgot about that," Jenny said.

"Oh. Well, you still wanna hear about it? Or'd you get something else?"

"No," Jenny said, resting her elbows beside Barry's book. Beneath the glass, dozens of stickers covered the old wood countertop. She half-remembered that they were for small, relatively local bands. There were so many that they overlapped, and Jenny wondered how old the oldest of them was. Were the members still alive? Were any of them famous? "I mean, no, I didn't get anything new. Yeah, tell me about it."

"There's a Sleep Talker position opening up," he said, pushing a glass down onto a rinser. "It's a weekday one, not a weekend. So, four nights, Monday through Thursday."

Jenny stared at him, trying to make sense of Barry's words for several seconds. Then her eyes went wide. "Wait, what? Really?"

"Yeah, Cassandra—who's been doing it for like forty years—is quitting. Her husband Jack died recently. Fucking horrible. She's moving away and they need someone to take her place."

"I, wow … Huh, I guess I have to think about it. I didn't expect that."

"Yeah, people don't really think about the Talkers changing much, but it's been happening a lot recently. This is our fifth change in the last five years. Only one old-timer left. But don't tell Charles I called him an old-timer, he'll come after me."

"Really?" Jenny said.

"No, not really, but he still kind of intimidates me. He's really smart."

"No, I mean—wouldn't there be a waiting list or something?"

"Not anymore. In fact, the last two were open for more than six months before they got filled. It's getting harder."

"Huh! I guess, I mean I really would have to think about it," Jenny said, shifting her weight from one leg to the other and then back again. She pursed her lips and studied the band names.

The Second Order, Jawbone's Cove, Faithless Friends, Whispering Cave, Carrows and Barrows.

Someone had slipped a ripped piece of a flyer for what looked like an anniversary at the local grange with the words 'Jacky and the Mans' written in the corner.

"I figured you would. Just so you know, it comes with housing, nothing fancy, but you'd get one of the apartments at the Kusel place."

"The house south of town?" Jenny asked.

"Um, yeah," he said, looking at her like she was crazy.

"Sorry, of course," she said, trying to cover her confusion up. "Yeah, that sounds great, I'd just—"

"Have to think about it," Barry said. He smiled and put the glass on a rack. "Yeah, I got that. Let me know if you have any questions though, I can put you in touch with Link at town hall, he's in charge of the assignments. Latte?"

Jenny nodded and stared at the counter as Barry made her drink.

Yellow Pie, Nodding Hyll, The Rhimes, Mighty 44.

She took her latte, backpack, and thoughts out to the metal tables on the sidewalk. She sat and pulled out a dinged and creased novel she had just checked out of the library: Glen Moat's latest, *Tomorrow's Queen.* Only four months old, Jenny was surprised to find no waiting list for the horror novel. Apparently, it had already made its way around town. Jenny had put off reading it at Sunrise; the idea of increasing her anxiety in a mental hospital seemed like a bad idea. She had also wanted to save some things to look forward to when she got out. Now she put the hardback on the metal table and stared at its cover. A bright house glowed with light on a hill above a dark forest.

She ran her fingers over the smooth, protective plastic cover and hoped it was another story in which his characters wandered into a dark alternate world. That idea never got old for Jenny. She felt like she needed Moat to take her childhood stories of Wonderland and Narnia and paint them in dark eldritch green and inky black.

She held the book to her nose, breathed deeply, and peered north up Main Street over its binding. Past the edge of town, the road turned east to cut back toward Route 3. Kusel Creek ran just before the bend, and on the near side stood the old Whitman log cabin. She could picture it with the historical information sign in front, its low-walled garden in the back, and the narrow antenna pole sticking up from the roof. She wondered why she could picture the building so clearly, but almost nothing about the people she had experienced it with, or the things that happened there.

She contemplated the radio antenna and the one that jutted up from the old fire-watch tower near the High Path, but she couldn't picture one on the old Kusel House. In fact, she couldn't picture the house except for a faint impression of its lawn and gravel driveway.

She wondered what it would be like to be a Sleep Talker. She'd been listening to Sydney over the weekend and last night she had heard the deep voice of another person whose name she couldn't remember. They had both lulled her to sleep while they spoke in hushed tones that crackled through her old clock radio.

Could I do that? I'm not even mildly qualified.

But Barry hadn't asked her about qualifications. He had said that the town was desperate to fill the position. She'd have her own apartment. That, in and of itself, was enough to make her seriously consider the possibility.

Jenny tried to picture staying up all night and sleeping during the day and thought that it must be a lonely life. She knew plenty of people worked the night shift, but not in Lightning Falls. There was no factory here to draw people out three times a day, no warehouses that needed nighttime security, no cabs that waited in queues to take anyone to the airport at 2 AM. The diner was open twenty-four hours, and she thought one of the corner stores and the gas station also were, but she guessed that was pretty much it.

She wondered if the Sleep Talkers were their own little group, living a life opposite the one that everyone else took part in. Could she live like that, with only a few other people in town on her schedule? It would be a small world. A small and lonely world.

But then, she thought, *that's what I have already.*

But was that what she wanted? To choose to be lonely? To keep her world small?

Yes, you stupid bitch, remember what happened the last time you let people in?

Water churned, eyes strained, and bubbles burst the surface of the roiling water. Jenny wrapped her arms around her stomach and closed her eyes, trying to force the image out of her head. It would be better if she kept her circle small. Maybe it would be better if she was alone entirely.

No, I can't manage that. I want to, I really want to, but I know myself. I will glom on to anyone who wants me, I'm a fucking leech.

So, maybe the thing to do was to build her world so that the number of people she could latch onto was small. Plus, if Patty—no, not *if, when*—when Patty found out how Jenny earned her spending money, she'd be out on the street anyway. It would be better to have her own place.

It would be the smart thing to do. But can I?

She decided to shelve the idea until later. If she lost the position through procrastination, then maybe that was a good thing. If it remained open until she decided, then maybe that was a sign. She laughed at the idea. She knew anything could be interpreted in any way someone liked, and remembered Aurora trying to divine meanings from all kinds of entirely mundane things. She pushed the memory aside and reopened the Glen Moat novel, trying to focus. After a long, slow, deep breath, she read:

In the waning hours of the Wandering City's blessed age, seven figures stood atop Fesoro's towers and welcomed the pulsing tide of shadow. They had all had a hand in summoning it, and they longed to grasp as much of its might as possible. All seven were alike in stature and countenance: tall, regal, grim, and dire. Among them stood queens, warriors, and those who thirsted first for knowledge. Each drank deeply of the dark emptiness that descended upon the Wandering City, their figures and visages changed by its unmaking emanations. Those who sought power found it, though they did not inherit power unalloyed. For what came to them was like a new self-knowledge, and with this new mind, a new being. With a new mode of being many curses came, including the curse of names, which forever subjected them to those who named them. Thus, in my world, the seven are known as Eridach the Swordmaster, Tosaich the Keeper of Books, Logol the Maker of Empty Things, Mistharis the Radiant Queen, Palamar the Oath Keeper, Shetziz the Eater of Tombs, and Chkeliach the Singer. But in other strange worlds, they bear other names. Some I have learned through my years in the city after its descent into madness and the unchanging curse greater than that of names.

— From the Writings of Eliach, son of Nagis the Midwife.

Texting

Thursday, August 7, 2025

> **_Treeman_**
> Sorry, work got busy

> **_Jenny_**
> No worries

> **_Treeman_**
> Do you want to grab a drink tonight?

> **_Jenny_**
> Can I keep putting it off without you getting pissed?

> **_Treeman_**
> Okay

> **_Jenny_**
> are you pissed?

> **_Jenny_**
> I also have this dinner with Patty and her friend tomorrow night. I'm just in a bad headspace for meeting hot guys.

> **_Treeman_**
> No, I get it. It's a lot.

> **_Treeman_**
> I see what you did there.

Treeman
It's cool though, Leddy wants to do something together and I was just going to use you as my excuse

Treeman
Joke

Jenny
Haha

Jenny
Seriously though I will figure my shit out soon and then I'll give you the privilege of buying me a drink.

Treeman
As long as I have dibs on first in line. There are going to be a lot of guys in town who want to buy you a drink.

Jenny
Are you saying I'm pretty?

Treeman
Small town.

Treeman
Joke

Treeman
Yes, you're pretty

Jenny
Haha.

11
Appeal

Friday, August 8, 2025 - Evening

RAIN TAPPED AGAINST JENNY'S bedroom window as she stepped over empty boxes to get to the bathroom. Her phone buzzed as she considered her new V-neck sweater in the mirror. She thought it was just tight enough that she'd want to wear it to something other than an old-lady dinner and not so tight Patty would give her shit for it. On the other hand, her jeans looked painted on, and Patty would have to deal with that. Both pairs she had ordered ended up a little snugger than she had anticipated, and she was tired of wearing the same pair for the last week. She regretted leaving some of her clothes behind, but she also hadn't wanted to run around in her institutional outfits any longer.

Jenny left the bathroom, kicked one of the empty boxes, and picked up her phone from where it lay next to her new laptop. Phil wished her a good dinner and offered her refuge at the Timber if it went badly. Jenny considered what to text back, not wanting to string him along or give him false hope. She had no idea if she was ready to meet a guy on a date. She decided to respond, 'Thanks, I'll definitely keep that in mind.' Then she slid her phone into her snug back pocket, considered the mess in her room, and left it for later.

Jenny found Patty in the kitchen making chicken Caesar salads with her friend from church. Marlene was older than Patty by about ten years, her face was round, her hair mostly gray, and she had a pleasant, matronly softness. She wore a fluffy turtleneck sweater and a long, floral skirt. Marlene seemed genuinely pleased to see Jenny. She told her she looked well and hugged her. The hug lasted a little longer than Jenny would have liked. Marlene leaned back and held Jenny at arm's length, looking her over as Barry had a week earlier.

"Doesn't she look wonderful?" Marlene asked Patty.

Patty turned from chopping chicken to give Jenny a once over. "That's a nice sweater," Patty said, though Jenny could feel her disapproving stare at her jeans.

"Thanks," Jenny said, the immediate desire to fight with the woman rising within her. Maybe she would need to take Phil up on his offer after dinner. Thankfully, the topic changed quickly, and Jenny was set to work chopping lettuce and opening bags of croutons to dump into a restaurant-sized metal bowl.

"No one has any allergies or anything, do they?" Jenny asked before adding the little bits of baked toast.

"What do you mean?" Patty asked.

"Like gluten or anything?" Jenny said.

Patty frowned at her.

"No," Marlene said. "No allergies here. Patty, you don't have any either."

"What is gluten?" Patty asked.

"It's a protein—" Marlene began.

"It's a bread thing," Jenny said.

"Lord, people are allergic to bread now?" Patty said.

"Where have you been?" Jenny asked.

"It's a protein—" Marlene began again before shaking her head and giving Jenny a wink. "We're all fine. Do you have anything that causes you stomach issues, dear?" Marlene rubbed her stomach as she said this, making a sympathetic face. "My niece has terrible IBS."

"Now what on earth is that?" Patty said.

"Nope," Jenny said. "Also, can I have my dressing on the side?"

"Absolutely not," Patty said. "One big communal bowl, just like they used to do."

"In the olden days where the tribe ate their Caesar salad out of the communal metal bowl?" Jenny said.

"That's right," Patty said, sticking out her tongue. "Calories don't exist when you're with friends."

No wonder I put on a few pounds then, Jenny thought. Immediately she felt guilty, picturing Veronica, who had comforted Jenny as much as Jenny had comforted her, and Grace who, though silent, had been kind. She didn't know if they were friends, or if she would ever see either of them again, but the callous thought still stung her conscience.

Despite the promise of ancient communal practices, they did not eat from one giant bowl. Instead, Patty doled out tongs full of salad into appropriately-sized wooden bowls before laying well-grilled sliced chicken on top. Once they were seated, Jenny changed the subject again and they chatted blandly about new shops in town, which Jenny had visited, and which she should try. They moved on to the clean-up of the village green where the fair would be held in October at the end of Camping Days. From there, they slipped into talking about the town in general, which allowed Jenny to start feeling comfortable. Her desire to fight with Patty ebbed away as they chatted about road repairs and the forecast for continued rain. That led to town drainage which brought them to the subject of the mayor. Marlene brought up a quiet little scandal about the mayor and a younger man. That younger man's cousin, it turned out, was Marlene's niece's friend's ex-boyfriend. Marlene told Jenny that he was 'a player' and not to be believed. Of course, they forgot to tell her his name before moving on to another quaint scandal in which the owner of the Mist had been giving a married woman free tickets for the past five years.

"Were they sleeping together?" Jenny asked, spearing the last of her salad with her fork.

"Oh, nothing like that," Marlene said. "But you know he wants to."

"Five years of free movie tickets and he hasn't sealed the deal? Feels like he should move on."

"Oh, you know how men are," Patty said. "Either they can't keep it in their pants or they can't get it out."

Marlene laughed as if this was the funniest thing she'd ever heard, and Jenny frowned trying to decide if she thought Patty was right.

"Oh, they just need to find the right woman to help them find their middle ground," Marlene said. "My Richie was like that, shy as a mouse before I showed him a thing or two." Patty opened her mouth to signal her scandal. "*After* we were married," Marlene finished. "Even so, I changed that man's world forever."

"Oh really?" Jenny said.

"We don't need to go into all that," Patty said.

"Really?" Jenny said, knowing that she should shut up. She also knew that what she was about to say was a lie. "But of all of us you've had the most—"

"Please!" Patty said, putting her fork down so hard onto the edge of her bowl that Jenny was afraid she'd crack it.

"Sorry," Jenny said.

"I'm not that person anymore, Jennifer. I haven't been for years."

"You're right, I'm sorry," Jenny said.

"I forgive you," Patty said.

"See?" Marlene said. "That's a sign that you've both grown so much. You make a mistake, you say you're sorry, and you move on."

Jenny nodded, suddenly wanting to leave the room.

Marlene seemed to read her mind. "Why don't we make some tea and have some pie on the back porch?"

Everyone agreed, and ten minutes later they sat in wicker chairs with rain pattering beyond screened-in windows.

"That's the kind of thing you learn at church," Patty said.

"What is?" Jenny asked, pausing with a forkful of peach pie hovering before her lips.

"Forgiveness," Patty said.

"Oh, Jennifer, you should come. I think you'd appreciate the community," Marlene said.

Jenny nodded slowly. "I'm not sure that it's the place for me," she said. She knew she should have just said 'thanks for the invitation, I'll think about it,' but the rejection just came out.

"Why not?" Marlene leaned over and patted Jenny's forearm. "You're newly back in town, it would be good to have a safe place to center yourself every week. That's how I see it. I don't go in for all the dogma, I just love the feeling of being close to people and, you know, the big man upstairs."

Jenny frowned as something tickled in the back of her mind. There was something about this—then it clicked. She understood what was happening. Patty didn't trust herself to get Jenny to go to church, so she recruited Marlene. Kind, motherly Marlene with her wide smile and warm voice. Patty knew Jenny would tell her where to stick her religion, but would she blow up at a friendly stranger? Would a new person trigger the same emotional knee-jerk rejection? No. No, Patty was clever, Jenny realized. It wasn't enough that her daughter was home, she had to figure out how to convert her. Jenny's conflicted mood started to resolve itself.

"I've had enough of"—she almost said 'cults,' but bit her tongue—"organized religion. At least for a while," she added, trying to soften the blow of her rejection. "I think I need to figure things out on my own for now."

Marlene nodded slowly, giving Jenny her best understanding smile. "I know what you mean. I do. I was there. I walked in your shoes." *Not likely*, Jenny thought. "And I know that it seems like a good idea to take your own judgment on these matters. But truly, you'll be happier and wiser in the company of others who have gone farther down the path than you have."

Jenny took a deep breath and forced her smile to remain. "I can see that. But for now, I really do just want to find my own way, at least for a bit."

"Oh, why do you trust yourself so much?" Patty snapped. Jenny and Marlene stared at her. Patty chuckled the way she did when she tried to pass her anger off as a joke. Jenny knew that this was a pivotal moment. If she responded in anger, Patty would be offended, as if Jenny had no right to be angry at the barb. If she didn't, Patty would keep pushing, keep poking, until Jenny responded.

Jenny tried a middle path, and calmly asked, "What do you mean?"

"I mean that … Well, we all make mistakes. And after we make a certain number of them, we should learn to take the advice of others with more experience."

"What kind of mistakes are you referring to?" Jenny asked. She knew the woman was right. She had made mistakes—quite a few of them. Some of them, she knew, would ride on her shoulders, and weigh her down with shame and self-hatred until she died.

"Well, let's not bring up specifics," Patty said, "but I think you might do well to listen to Marlene. She has helped me a lot."

"I'm really happy for you," Jenny said, trying to mean it. "And I'm glad you helped Patty, Marlene. Maybe I'm still too foolish to ask for help, but the last time I did that, things went really bad for me. So, for now, I'm just going to—"

"Just stop!" Patty said. "The last time you listened to someone else, two people died! Don't you think I know that? Don't you think I read about it? Don't you think I know—we all know—that you died? And that's the judgment you want to trust? Marlene cares about you and wants you to be better! So do I!"

"Marlene cares about me?" Jenny scoffed. She turned to the woman with chin-length, gray hair who was nodding with a look of concern etched into her face. But her kindness now seemed condescending to Jenny. "Sorry, Marlene, but I'm not interested! I don't know how you wrangled my mother into your cult. Maybe she hit rock bottom sleeping with every available man in town, and a few that weren't, if I remember correctly."

"Stop it!" Patty said.

"Or maybe you just had a quota. But however you weaseled your way in and made her your follower or whatever, you're not going to do that to me. I've seen this game played a hell of a lot better than you play it. And I've heard enough of that bullshit for one lifetime. And yes"—she turned to Patty and stood up, holding her plate—"people died. People I loved. And you throwing that in my face so that I can join a total stranger in your congregational temple or meetinghouse or whatever the hell you call it, is just sick. So, stop it. Stop trying to get me to become you."

The two older women stared at Jenny, their mouths open.

"Jennifer, I—" Marlene started, but Jenny wheeled on her.

She felt herself pulled back through time and space to a place where she wasn't alone. For a moment, Jenny felt like she didn't just stand for herself, but for Aurora, Matina, Nolan, and Joseph. Here was Venena whom Joseph had loved, not Jenny. Here was the passion and fire she had found and left behind.

"Seriously, lady. Who the fuck are you? Fuck all the way off!"

"Jennifer!" Patty yelled, standing up. "What is wrong with you?"

"No, what's wrong with you? How could you bring a stranger—"

"She's not a stranger, Jennifer," Patty said, her face a mask of confusion and anger.

"Stop calling me that! Stop acting like I'm one of your fucking church people. I've been there, I've done that, and it's bullshit! She might be your sponsor, or your faith mother, or whatever the hell you call it, but she's a stranger to me!"

"What are you talking about? Marlene was your teacher! Your-your middle school history teacher. How do you not remember her?"

Jenny froze. "What?" she said, her mouth suddenly dry.

"I taught you Social Studies from fifth to eighth grade," Marlene said, her face a mask of pain and confusion. "You always said I was your favorite teacher. I … I was at your high school graduation."

Marlene's words faded under the thunder of the pulse in Jenny's ears. The two women appeared as scared as Jenny felt. With a shaking hand, Marlene put her plate down on the wicker table next to her. She moved as if to speak, but Jenny shook her head. She didn't recognize her. And when she tried to remember anything about her classes in middle school, there was nothing.

"I …" she started, shaking her head. "I'm sorry."

Jenny turned and rushed into the house.

12
Regret

Saturday, August 9, 2025 – After Midnight

JENNY STUDIED THE TALL man lying under the sheet and hated herself. Nothing about his form—his well-shaped shoulders, flat but not chiseled stomach, and adequately attractive, but not stunning face—coaxed the feeling from her. It was only the fact, the sheer brute reality of being in his bed that conjured her self-loathing.

She took a long, steady breath and found remnants of his cologne, which was also perfectly nice, though it hadn't made her head swim with desire. Her head—it didn't hurt yet, but it would soon. She sat up and looked around for her clothes. Her jeans, she remembered, were in the living room. Her sweater should be near them. Her bra and underwear, however … Those she found on the floor with the help of her phone's flashlight. She gathered them as silently as she could before slipping out of the bedroom.

Thankfully, Phil lived alone, and she didn't have to risk a roommate coming out of his bedroom to find her hurriedly dressing in the dark. She felt hunted, like Phil was following her, and if she didn't hurry, he'd catch her. It was the same feeling she had in dreams sometimes. She had felt it with Aurora if she was cleaning and didn't want her to catch Jenny in the act. Jenny wanted Aurora to look in the bathroom and say, 'Wow, this is really clean!' not find her cleaning it. Now, she didn't want Phil to catch her escaping. Did she want him to wake up and think, 'Wow, she's so gone?' Jenny wasn't sure, but she was so caught up in contemplating her flight that she jumped, screamed, and fell onto the couch with one leg in her jeans when Phil spoke behind her.

"Sneaking out, really? Was it that bad? Oh God, are you okay?"

In her humiliation, Jenny noted that he had put his boxers on. He strode across the room as Jenny lay ass in the air, wishing she could somehow melt into the couch.

"No," Jenny said. "Kill me."

"I probably won't do that," Phil said, rolling her over and helping her work her foot through the bottom of her pantleg.

"I'm sorry, but I've got to go," Jenny said.

"Yeah, I was getting that," Phil said, sitting next to her. He was a little over six feet tall and had a short, brown beard that made him look more rugged than he was. His tight jeans and plaid shirt had done a lot of work for him. Physically, Phil was average in almost every way, which

Jenny thought would have been completely fine if Nolan didn't keep stepping into her mind with his blond hair, blue eyes, perfect body, and porn star's physical gifts. Everything about him had been beyond what Jenny had ever looked for or wanted. She had never wanted men like Nolan. She still didn't. She didn't want men like anything.

She wanted Nolan.

"It's not you, you didn't do anything wrong," Jenny said, standing and zipping her jeans. "I just need to get up early tomorrow and if I'm not home, Patty will wonder where I am."

"New job?" Phil asked.

"No, I—" Jenny pushed her head through her sweater. "Look, I just have to get up early. Let's not make this something it isn't, okay? I'm sorry I came over and used you, okay?"

"I'm not sad that you used me, I'm sad I don't get to take you to breakfast," Phil said.

"We can do breakfast another time," Jenny said, almost certain that she was lying.

"Right," Phil said, walking over to the front door of his apartment. "Well, if you want to keep talking, feel free to text me. I won't bother you though."

Jenny stared at him while she slipped her shoes on. "I will text you," she said. *Liar,* she thought.

"Great. Do you want me to walk you home? I can get dressed."

"No, I think I'll be okay. Not a lot of night predators in Lightning Falls."

Phil made a strained face before nodding. "All right. At least text me to let me know you got home okay. If you don't, I'll call Patty in a half hour."

"Okay!" Jenny said, standing. "I'll let you know. *Do not* call Patty."

"No text and her phone will be ringing. We'll have the cops out."

Jenny closed her eyes and sighed. "Okay. I'll text you when I get home." *And that will probably be the last time.*

He opened the door for her and stood behind it. He didn't try to kiss her or ask for a hug. He just let her go. She hurried down the carpeted hall, down the stairs to the first floor of the old, converted house. A moment later she was out onto Main Street and walking north.

Ten minutes later, she was quietly sneaking back into Patty's front door.

> **_Jenny_**
> Home. Sorry again

> **_Treeman_**
> No worries. Text me later if you want

> **_Jenny_**
> I will

Entry 4

Tuesday, August 12, 2025

Well, shit, diary. I have to say the last few days have me pretty messed up. I've been hiding from Patty like a spy, and I'm pretty good at it. I wake up late (something I'm already good at, thank you, new curtains!) and wait for her to leave for work or church. Then, after I shower and do my makeup, I take some pictures and try to earn that cash. That's been going okay, I have a few new followers, but nothing earth-shattering.

Why am I hiding from Patty, Diary? Well, you know that conversation where your mom finds out something is wrong and then asks a thousand questions you don't have answers to, or maybe you do but you don't want to tell her? Yeah, I'm trying to avoid that one. Not remembering my childhood other than a few little gems, like dad dying and walking in on Patty giving a random stranger head on the couch, is probably like a red flag for her. And, you know, I don't want to talk to her about it.

I've been hiding from everyone else too. I go to the library and Barry's. I got locked in last night (to the library, not Barry's). Don't worry, Diary, I got out. But I sometimes wonder if I could haunt the place like a library version of the Phantom. I think I'd be pretty good at that too. I need a long sheet I can clutch at my chest and drag behind me. I also need one of those old metal candle holders with the ring on the side, so I can hold it up in front of me and walk around the shelves. (I probably need a bag or something for the books too, since I'll be clutching the sheet and won't have any hands free.)

I was actually picturing that exact thing today. I almost fell asleep on the third floor, where no one goes, and I dreamed I turned a corner, and the library changed into this huge place with shelves that went up and down forever in darkness. And there were these hanging walkways and billions of books. Yeah, it freaked me the hell out. I don't remember what happened after that, but thinking about it makes me feel wonky.

Um, what else? Oh, still haven't texted Phil back. So, I'm a piece of shit. I have plans with Isabella later this week because even if she makes me feel like shit, she's my only friend right now. And … yeah, that's kind of it. I guess I haven't really been talking to you either Diary, but there are so many videos to watch online and men who will pay me $10 to tell them that they are too big or too small, where is a girl to find the time?

13
Baker's Books

Wednesday, August 13, 2025 — Early Afternoon

JENNY WAS SURPRISED TO find the parking spaces at the north end of Main Street full of trucks and SUVs. A local police car, flashing its lights, sped past her, disappearing into the woods north of town. Jenny frowned. She hadn't seen police lights since she came home and wondered if there was an accident. Hoping everyone involved was okay, she continued down Main until she reached Baker's Books. Her skin tingled with anticipation, and she wanted to turn around and go back home or hide in the library for another eight hours. But this was something she needed to do.

A familiar, tinkling bell greeted her as she pushed her way in. A cluttered path led straight up the middle of the shop to the front desk. Overflowing boxes nestled against old wooden bookcases, sporting piles of battered paperbacks, jacketless hardbacks, and a smattering of pocket-book-sized literary magazines. Both new and old copies of the least popular titles crammed the shelves. Delia Baker's philosophy, which Jenny saw that she still cleaved to, was to keep people out of the main aisle unless they were in line.

Jenny breathed deeply the scents of old paper and strawberry and remembered stalking into the shop, anguished because of a fight with Patty. Here, she remembered. She knew every corner, every plant, every framed picture jammed into the few places where the walls showed through the forest of bookshelves. She knew this world and, by extension, herself. The contrast to her experience on Main Street moments earlier was jarring, but pleasant.

The only element of the store unfamiliar to her was the young man behind the counter. He appeared to be in his early twenties, had shaggy, sandy hair, and was a little chubby. His freckled, open-mouthed face seemed to be in mild wonderment. Maybe, Jenny mused, the look was for her.

"Hi," she said as she walked up to the counter.

"Hi, welcome to Baker's Books," he said, swallowing. "How can I help you?"

"Um," Jenny said, smiling. "I'm—I mean, I actually used to work here. I'm Jenny," she said, holding out her hand. He glanced at it before shaking it damply.

"I'm Dylan," he said. He let her go and silently stared.

She smiled. "Uh, is Delia here? Miss Baker?"

He nodded. "Yeah, she's in the back, you want me to get her?"

"Please," Jenny said.

"Okay, it'll be a minute, I think, she's kind of buried under some boxes."

Jenny laughed, remembering. She could picture Delia piling boxes precariously around her, trying to sort through the copies of John Grisham, Tom Clancy, Jodi Picoult, and Stephen King, searching for something original in the mix of donations.

'My father used to complain about how Asimov, Bradbury, and Heinlein filled the boxes,' she would say. 'Now I would kill for a robot, or carnival, or problematic immortal.' Invariably, a box would slip and bruise her arm or leg. Then she'd be holding the piles back from burying her.

The memory was sweet, like fresh water after sour milk. Was that why she had been avoiding this place? Had she been afraid of remembering? With so much lost, she was overwhelmed by what remained among the books.

No, she thought. *I was afraid I wouldn't remember. I couldn't bear to lose this place too. This place where I was actually happy after Dad.*

"Jenny?" Delia's voice, deep and kind, came from behind her and Jenny immediately covered her face with her hands and started to cry. "Dylan, go into the back now and work on sorting things."

A moment later, Delia's arms were around her, and they were crying together. "I didn't think I'd see you again, honey," Delia said. Jenny tried to talk but couldn't. They stood like that for minutes, silent but for sounds of sorrow and joy. When they were still, Delia pulled back. "Let's take a walk. Here, let me get some tissues first."

Jenny nodded. Delia disappeared for a moment and then reappeared with her purse. She left the store in Dylan's care, and they headed east on Adams, walking and dabbing their eyes with tissues.

"Wow," Jenny said, trying to laugh. "I'm sorry. I didn't expect to come in and just start sobbing."

"I did," Delia said, smiling. "I figured we'd both start crying, and I was right. But I thought you'd come in a little sooner."

"I don't know why I didn't," Jenny said. Delia nodded.

Jenny risked another bout of tears by glancing at her old friend. Delia hadn't changed much. She still kept her hair closely cropped, still wore jeans to work, and still went sleeveless in the warm weather. She was ten years older now—so almost forty, Jenny realized—but she hardly looked it. Jenny hoped she would look so good a decade in the future.

"So, what have you heard?" Jenny asked.

Delia laughed. "Which parts? The part where you're in a relationship with a woman from Portland, or the one where you joined a cult, or the one where you got into porn, or the one where you killed some people and ended up in a mental institution? Or the one where you died?"

Jenny stopped and stared at Delia. "What the fuck?" Jenny said. Her throat was dry.

Delia shrugged. "I know, people said all kinds of shit while you were gone."

Jenny took a deep breath and started walking again.

"So, what really happened to you once you left? I know you ended up in Portland, but after that—"

"After that, most of what you heard was true. Though, I'm not currently dating anyone—" Jenny caught herself. She almost started crying again. "And I think that ... well, I didn't actually kill anyone myself."

That was the hardest to say because she didn't believe it.

It was Delia's turn to stop. She frowned, considering Jenny for a long moment. Then that frown eased and became a tentative smile. Jenny could see it on her face: was this woman teasing her?

Jenny shook her head. Delia's smile disappeared.

"You're serious."

Jenny nodded.

"A cult?" Delia stage-whispered.

"I'm glad that's the one you started with," Jenny said. "Yeah, though, I know this sounds about as stereotypical as a person can get, but it didn't feel like a cult. It was just people. Me and the woman I was dating—"

"Okay, I have to admit, that one surprises me too. You were the most boy-crazy Jesus Freak I ever met."

"I'm still boy-crazy," Jenny said, "I'm just girl-crazy too. And, sometimes, just plain crazy I guess."

Delia shook her head. "Greedy," she said, but her smile had returned.

Once more, Jenny skated close to the edge of tears. "But yeah, it was just me and her, and then this other woman—"

"Girl, I don't need to know about your threesomes," Delia said.

"I would say that it wasn't like that, but ... yeah, sometimes it was like that. But most of the time we were just friends. And then she invited us down to California to live in this—"

"God damn it," Delia said, throwing her hands up, "it was a

commune, wasn't it? You got invited to a commune in California by a, let me guess, some white-ass hippie chick with braids in her hair?"

Jenny had to stop; her tears had turned to uncontrollable laughter. "God, how did you know?"

"It's always some blonde girl with braids and some crocheted halter top that leads you right to the devil's doorstep in the middle of the desert in California. Didn't you ever read about the Manson Family?"

Jenny held her stomach and nodded. When her fit of laughing passed, she straightened and shook her head. "Yeah, but, you know, when they come for you, you don't expect them to be in a cult. You think they're just a normal blonde girl from California with a hemp necklace and bead bracelets."

"That was your first mistake. All those girls will lead you into a cult. The boys too, for that matter. There was this tall guy, blond, of course, surfer-granola-hippie boy that was on vacation up this way two years ago, I think. He would come into the shop, flirt with me, compliment the shop, my shirt—"

"Which means your tits—"

"Of course it does, and he would just look at me with those big blue eyes. And, you know what he asked me to do?"

"I'm afraid to ask."

"Did Mr. I Definitely Have Abs Under This Shirt try to take me in the back of my bookstore after I closed? Hell, did he even try to get me to blow his mind without getting me back? No. He hands me a card for his community in God-damned California."

"Oh my God, where?"

"Down near LA. I was like, 'sir, I have a business to run. I'm not running off to be your token black woman in your self-help-sex-service cult or whatever.'"

"Could have been fun for a while."

"Of course it could have, but then what do you do?"

"Yeah, actually, that's exactly the question I'm asking right now."

"Okay, tell me everything," Delia said.

They walked and Jenny told Delia about Portland, the guy she dated, and Aurora. She refrained from saying too much about the woman who had captivated every aspect of Jenny because she feared she would send herself back into tears and bore Delia. She told her how Matina had visited Aurora and convinced them both to go with her to her community in California. Then, nervously, she told Delia about her first forays into making adult content.

"They had you do that?" Delia asked.

"Sort of. It was kind of my idea. I mean, not really, but it was an idea kind of floating around the house. And I was like, 'fuck it, I'll do it.'"

"Did you do … like did you do everything?"

"Not at first. At first, it was just kind of me, and sometimes Aurora would pose with me. It was all just pictures and a little video. But then Joseph showed up. He kind of … shit, yeah, this is going to sound bad. He was kind of like our Charles Manson."

Delia's eyebrows went up. "Didn't you think that was when it was time to go?"

"Like, when he showed up it wasn't like he had a swastika carved into his forehead. He was just this older guy—huge, tall, big shoulders, imposing, but, like, charming—and he just kind of talked to everyone and asked how they were, asked if they needed anything. And I was … I was kind of like his favorite."

"I bet you were," Delia said, giving her a sidelong glance.

"I never had sex with him, it wasn't like that. He didn't sleep with anyone in the house, as far as I know. He just kind of directed things. He's the reason I went to LA in '23. That's when I started doing like, actual hardcore stuff."

"Wow. Wow, so you really did do porn?"

Jenny nodded.

"Damn, I didn't expect the rumors to be that accurate. Are you still, like, you know, doing it?"

"Not hardcore, not with anyone else. I just have a site. Please don't tell anyone."

"When have I ever betrayed your trust?" Delia asked, stopping on the sidewalk. Jenny felt suddenly ashamed and grateful.

"You're right. I just … If Patty finds out, I'm screwed."

"Yeah, well, that woman is on her own journey. You're living with her?"

"For now. I need to get out though. But my site isn't paying me enough to do that right now."

"Well, it might be crazy, but there's a Sleep Talker position opening up. Truly fucked up what's happening with Cassandra, but it might be your answer … at least for a little while."

"You know, Barry said the same—Wait, Cassandra? I remember her."

"You don't know? Oh, my goodness"—Delia grabbed Jenny's arm—"her husband was murdered."

Jenny shook her head. "Wait, what? Patty said someone got killed, I didn't realize—"

"Mhm, someone broke into his house and killed him. They didn't rob them or anything like that. They just went in and stabbed him. Cassandra came home and found him in bed, the whole bed soaked in blood."

"Holy shit," Jenny said. "Holy shit, that's fucked up."

"I told you," Delia said.

They walked silently for a while, winding their way back across Main to the village green. Jenny ran her fingers over the bark of one of the corner trees before sitting on a nearby bench. Delia sat next to her, arms crossed under her chest.

"Do you remember John?" Delia asked.

"John ..."

"I dated him for a while when you worked for me."

"The Indian guy?"

"No that was Pat ... Wait, do you mean Indian or Indian?"

"The guy who lived in Idaho, on the reservation. Long distance guy?"

"No, that was Pat. John was Pakistani, so not Indian."

"John doesn't sound Pakistani."

"His mother was. Anyway, he was a computer guy, he redid my whole website. And then he got me plugged in with all of these other online retailers. So, since you left, the business has been kind of booming. And John still comes through town sometimes, which can be nice."

Jenny frowned thoughtfully. "Wow, that's really great. I ... Is there a lesson in there?"

"No, bitch, I'm just telling you about my life, since you didn't bother to ask."

They both laughed and Jenny hugged Delia.

"I'm sorry. I'm so fucked in the head that I can't see straight. I'm desperate for some kind of direction. I think I'm looking for signs everywhere."

"Be careful with that. If you're looking for signs, you'll find them. There's your lesson."

"Yeah," Jenny said, watching a bird fly across the cloud-streaked sky toward the falls.

"So, what are you doing with your time in town? Have you caught up with anyone?"

"Not exactly. I've had lunch with Isabella Delgado a couple of times.

I've talked to Barry a little. I might have slept with this guy Phil who works with Patty."

"Oh, I know Phil. Really? That fast huh?"

"Don't judge me!"

"I'm not judging. How was it?"

"Average," Jenny said.

"Average isn't terrible," Delia said. "But then, I guess you've been with professionals now. Hard for a small-town boy to compete with porn stars. Nice of you to throw him some."

"Shut up. It's not the same on a set and in someone's bedroom. It's two totally different … acts. I don't think they're even related in my mind."

She thought of Nolan and felt the lie.

"Well, either way, I'm sure he was happy. That going to be an ongoing thing?"

"I don't know, probably not. I'm too messed up to really connect with someone like that. And I feel like I'm too old to be doing some kind of on-again-off-again toxic bullshit."

"Well, in my experience you're never too old for toxic bullshit. But I know what you mean. Look, I need to get back to the store. Why don't you walk me back before you go do—what exactly?"

"I've been mostly hiding in the library. Patty and I had a big fight."

"Ah. Well, you know that old nook in my store is open to you. You can hide there too. It would be nice to have you around again. Plus, you can clean it out for me."

"That sounds amazing," Jenny said.

"Just don't go taking Dylan back there to deflower him, I don't think he'd recover," Delia said.

They walked back together, passing parked cars along Main.

"What is happening?" Jenny said. "Is there a movie festival at the Mist or something?"

"Wait," Delia said, stopping and grabbing Jenny's arm. "Don't you know?"

"No, what?"

"A boy went missing last night. People are starting to organize to search for him."

14
Planning

Wednesday, August 13, 2025 — Late Afternoon

ISABELLA WAS SO ENGROSSED with her work that she didn't look up when Jenny walked into the offices of Koletz Endeavors, LLC. She sat at a small reception desk a few feet inside the small, but well-appointed, office space. The company's decoration was so bland that as Jenny considered each strategically placed bit of décor—landscape painting, blue candle, green succulent, red candle, yellow rubber duck, crystal vase—she forgot them immediately.

Jenny, feeling awkward, cleared her throat.

"Mhm?" Isabella hummed, finally looking up from her screen, with eyebrows expectantly raised to greet a potential customer.

"Hey," Jenny said.

"Oh, hey!" Isabella said, her expression shifting to excited recognition.

"Hey, sorry to barge in," Jenny said.

"No, this is so retro! I love it. Come in. Sorry, he's dumping everything on me today," Isabella said, waving at her computer monitor. "Sit down." She gestured to a cushioned waiting-room chair to the side of her desk.

"Nice place," Jenny said, glancing around again.

"Thanks, it was completely empty in here before he hired me. I decorated the whole place." Isabella looked proud, so Jenny made her best 'I'm impressed' face. "So, what brings you here, visiting without texting like my grandmother?"

"Did you hear about the boy?" Jenny said.

"Oh yeah," Isabella said, leaning forward and lowering her voice. "I heard he's not a local. I think he was up with his family, and they were camping by the creek."

Jenny shook her head. "No, I mean, yeah, he's not local, but Delia told me he's part of a scouting group, and they were doing some pre-Camping Days stuff."

Isabella's face went through a contortion of expressions. First, she appeared eager for the new information, then excited to talk about Camping Days, then scared—perhaps realizing that she was talking to Jenny about Camping Days and that it was a delicate topic since Jenny probably wouldn't like to be reminded of her father's drowning. Finally, she settled on embarrassment. Jenny ignored the convulsions.

"I think we should try to help," Jenny said.

"How?" Isabella said, leaning further forward. She laid her forearms on the desk and rested her chest on them. Jenny glanced down and then back up again. Isabella wore a button-down that had the top two buttons modestly undone. Or, they would have been modest if not for her posture.

"Let's go search for him."

"Like, go out and hike through the woods and look for a missing boy?" Isabella said. The look on her face made Jenny think that Isabella thought she was kidding.

"Yeah," Jenny said, trying to keep her face as blank as possible.

"Oh," Isabella said, leaning back in her chair. "Right. I mean—Yeah, we should do that! We could make it a whole thing."

"A whole thing?"

"Yeah, I'll take the day off tomorrow. Mike won't be able to count it as a vacation day since this is so important. If he's still missing then, we can do the whole day. We can do breakfast, and I think some of the church ladies are getting together to make food for the searchers if they have to go out again tomorrow."

"Wow, they organized that already?" Jenny said.

"I'm surprised you don't—Right! Memory. Search and rescue is pretty standard up here. People go missing in the county all the time. I think there's been a search and rescue group in the area since the seventies. People are pretty on top of this."

Jenny ignored the flippant reference to her memory issues, smiled, and stood up.

"Where are you going?" Isabella asked.

"I," Jenny said, pausing and posing with one hand under her chin, "need hiking clothes and shoes, and I need to break them in a little before we're forcing our way through the forest. Do you need me to get you anything?"

"No, I've got stuff I can wear," Isabella said. "Dinner tonight?"

Jenny considered spending what might end up being twenty-four continuous hours with Isabella and didn't enjoy how that felt.

"Sorry, already have plans, but I can come over later tonight and we can get ready."

"Tonight, huh?"

"Yeah, for an early start," Jenny said, once more trying to keep her face as neutral as possible. She didn't want to give Isabella the wrong idea, but she also didn't want to offend her.

"Okay, text me. Now I need to get back to this if I'm not going to be staring at my laptop all night."

Jenny said goodbye and left Koletz Endeavors feeling like she had a real purpose for the first time in over a year.

The Quiet Rumble

Volume 10, Issue 67, Wednesday, August 13, 2025

Information

By Keith Lowry, Ed. In Chief.

FOLKS, IT'S TIMES LIKE these that I'm glad I don't have to print a newsletter anymore. I can get you this information without having to go through the whole rigamarole of physical distribution. Of course, I could ramble on and squander my digital advantages, so I'll focus on the task at hand.

As many of you have heard, a twelve-year-old boy named Carson Booth has gone missing. I'm going to give you the facts as they have been given to me by Chief Ryan. She has promised to have the police department give me updates as they come in so I can keep you informed.

First, the missing boy is Carson Booth, twelve years old. He has blond hair and blue eyes. He's skinny, 5'5", and his hair is cut short in a crew-cut. I've been told we'll be getting a picture soon.

Second, he is from Maryland, and he is out here visiting extended family. We don't have clear details on that right now—more to come.

Third, he was wearing a light blue T-shirt with a slogan on it that either said, "Cake is a Lie" or "Cake is Fake."

Fourth, he was with a camping group led by Scout Leader Thad Hill. They had set up camp a hundred yards east of Whitman Cabin, and Carson was last seen near midnight by one of his tent-mates when he went off to answer the call of nature. No one noticed he was missing until they did a head count this morning.

Fifth, it isn't known if he went missing this morning or if he never came back from his late-night journey.

Now, regarding the search for Carson. The main point of contact is the Lightning Falls Police Department and Chief Ryan. She will be coordinating the search today and if Carson isn't found, tomorrow. She's already in touch with county and state officials to get search equipment and aid as soon as possible. You can always call the police station if you have information, or just dial 911.

Tomorrow in the Mist's lobby, search parties will start organizing at 6 AM. There will be food and water provided by local churches and community organizations. I'm told that Red's will be supplying bottles of water, granola bars, and other items for folks to take with them. Searchers are recommended to bring a backpack, their own water bottle, sunscreen, and bug spray. Participants should make sure their phones are fully charged and bring a backup charger if they have one.

Those folks who cannot go hiking out near the creek or up on the High Path will be able to help with organizing and food preparation for the searchers. Anyone with a camera-equipped drone should talk to Chief Ryan.

More information will be coming down the lane soon, and I'll be sure to get it to you. Now, everyone, get some sleep, and let's get out there and get it done.

And, as always, be safe out there and take care of each other.

15
Step 2

Wednesday, August 13, 2025 - Night

JENNY KNOCKED ON THE green apartment door. While she waited, she backed up against the opposite wall and appraised Isabella's floor. The hallway carpet was faded Overlook chic with worn orange and brown geometric patterns. The powder blue walls were unevenly spackled, showing scars from dozens of tables, dressers, and bed frames moved in and out across nearly a century. A faint smell of dust and mildew haunted the narrow space, adding to the unwholesome impression. Jenny was sure she had been in the apartment building before, but couldn't recall when or with whom. The place was familiar in the way that all threadbare apartment buildings were.

The door swung open, and Isabella stood in plaid pajama pants, a black spaghetti-strap tank top, and pink-toed, white socks. Her hair was pulled up in a messy bun. Jenny thought she looked like an advertisement for dormitory living.

"Hey!" she said, scooting into the hall to hug Jenny. Jenny returned the embrace briefly, trying to naturally end the gesture by shifting the weight of her backpack. "Come on in, sorry about the mess, I'd lie and say I've been busy, but I've been cleaning for the last two hours and it's still a disaster."

Isabella wasn't lying. Her apartment was a certifiable catastrophe. Dirty dishes were piled haphazardly in and around the sink. Four pots, also dirty, stood on the four stovetop burners, two with lids stained with sauce, two without. Jenny thought the old linoleum might not have seen a broom or mop since the first Bush Administration.

If I wasn't already off the market for reasons of insanity, and we weren't wildly incompatible, this would be a deal-breaker, Jenny thought. She swallowed and nodded as Isabella pointed out that she was a chaotic thinker and thrived in a cluttered environment. Jenny believed that if that was true, Isabella must be living her absolute best life, as the living room was a complication of take-out bags, grocery store bags, dirty plates, piles of work clothing, and two pizza boxes. These were all evenly distributed across the coffee table, floor, and overstuffed gray sofa. Poking out between two sofa cushions was a rubbery, pink cylinder. Isabella followed Jenny's gaze and shrugged.

"I wish I'd seen it before you started cleaning," Jenny said.

"Oh, I didn't touch anything out here. I didn't have time. I was working in there."

Isabella led Jenny through a door into her white-walled bedroom. *I can see the floor at least,* Jenny thought. A queen-sized bed jutted out into the middle of the room, covered with an only slightly rumpled purple comforter. A consignment store clothing rack stood between a tall dresser and a tiny closet.

"Well, here and the bathroom," Isabella said. She plopped herself down on the comforter. Jenny grinned and walked over to the other side of the bed, dropping her pack on the floor. "So, what'd you get?" Isabella asked.

Jenny showed off the hiking shoes and pants she was already wearing. She also pulled out two wicking T-shirts and a new sports bra.

"They don't have hiking underwear?" Isabella asked.

"They do, I just didn't think it was worth it," Jenny said, studying her host. Isabella was pure electricity—picking her fingernails and bouncing her foot. Jenny thought she could see the woman's pulse jumping in her wrist. "So, this is nice, how long have you been here?"

"Two years," Isabella said, looking around. "As soon as I got the job with Mike. He gave me a nice signing bonus so I could move out, of course, that's the last bonus I've ever seen. I think he couldn't get anyone else to rent it, so it was kind of a win-win." She shrugged. "Still, it's nice having my own place."

"What do you do when, you know, you bring girls back here? I can't—"

"Oh, the mess? Yeah, that's not a big deal because no one ever comes back here. You're, like, my first visitor in over a year except for my parents."

"You've never had anyone else in here?" Jenny said, looking pointedly at the bed.

"Well, there's one girl in town, Chloe. We had like an on-off thing."

"And now?" Jenny asked.

"Off. Very off."

Jenny put her hands into her pockets and nodded, rocking back and forth a little, wishing she hadn't asked the question; it might imply to Isabella that she was interested. She glanced around the room and walked over to Isabella's dresser. Three framed pictures looked back at her. One was of Isabella and an older man with his arm around her shoulder.

"Is this your dad?" Jenny asked.

"What? Yeah, of course, what do you—Oh, right. Really? You don't remember my dad?" Jenny shook her head. "Well, yeah, that's him. And that's my brother Ernesto and my brother Miguel. You really don't remember? Miguel and you were in the same grade. He's out in Joseph now."

Jenny ran a finger over the picture's glass and shook her head. "I'm sorry," she said.

"No reason for you to be sorry. Miguel's going to be disappointed. He had a huge crush on you. You're going to shatter his ego when he finds out that you don't even remember him."

"I mean, it's not just—"

Isabella held up a hand, interrupting Jenny. "Believe me, his ego needs shattering."

"I did remember today, though. I found a place where I remembered everything."

"Really?" Isabella's nervous shaking stopped. Her hands lay limp in her lap, but Jenny thought that she could still see the twitching of her pulse.

"Yeah, I went to Baker's—"

"The bakery?" Isabella frowned.

"No, the bookstore," Jenny said. Isabella gave her an 'oh, right, I'm stupid' look and Jenny continued. "When I went in there, I could remember everything about it and about Delia."

Isabella frowned thoughtfully. "That's weird. Is there anywhere else in town that's like that?" Isabella asked.

"Well, I remember Barry's too. Maybe it's just that corner," Jenny laughed.

"And you remember everything about Delia, but not, like Mrs. Lundy or Miguel, or me?"

"Mrs. Lundy?" Jenny said.

"Middle school, social studies."

"Oh, Marlene. Right. No, I don't remember any of them, you, I mean. I'm sorry. I remember Patty, of course, and Delia, and Barry, and … yeah, that's kind of it."

Isabella stared down at her hands and started picking at her nails again. "Do you like, like her?" Isabella asked.

"Who?"

"Delia."

"What are you, thirteen? Do I like-like her?" Jenny asked.

Isabella laughed. "I mean, you remember her and, like, no one else."

"No, I don't 'like-like' her. She was like my second mom. She'd probably punch me for saying that. She's like a badass older sister. She's got her own business, she's got horrendous luck with guys—which I identify with—and she made a place for me where I didn't feel like I was constantly being judged. Plus, I never walked in on her giving a guy head in the living room."

"Shit, really? Your mom?"

Jenny nodded.

"Damn, the shit that goes on in a small town and no one knows. I see your mom around all the time, and I never imagined that she—"

"Don't start imagining it now," Jenny said, laughing. She sat down on the other side of the bed. "So, other than Cleo—"

"Chloe," Isabella corrected.

"—Chloe, I'm the only chick who's been in here?"

"Yeah," Isabella said. "But don't let it go to your head. It's like slim pickings here. There are a couple of other chicks, but they're already together."

"Okay, noted. So, tomorrow," Jenny said, scooting back to lean against the two pillows on her side of the bed. She started untying her shoes. "I heard that people are getting together around six to start looking."

"Six?" Isabella sounded as if she'd never heard of the time.

"Yeah, six. So, I figure we get up at five. Barry is opening then, so we can get ready and grab coffee."

"Five!" Isabella said, slapping the bed beside her. Jenny couldn't tell if she was trying to be funny or if she was genuinely offended by the early hour. She guessed that it was a bit of both.

"Yeah, so we should be getting to bed soon." Jenny pulled one shoe off and then the other.

"Okay, but … I kind of have a favor to ask."

Jenny smirked. "What kind of favor?"

"So, this is embarrassing, but I was going to start hiking and everything a couple of years ago."

"Okay, why is that embarrassing?" Jenny asked.

"Because it was for Chloe. And, like, I don't know, it's kind of a lesbian date thing, right? Big marathon dates, and we're in the middle of nature. No?"

"Sorry, I've never really been on the dating scene. I had one relationship, well, kind of two, but we didn't really do the traditional things. We just sort of—"

"What?"

"Well, I was going to say we just sort of lived together, but that's the stereotype, isn't it?"

"Wow," Isabella said.

"It wasn't like that; we lived together first and then just kind of found each other in that. Anyway, I don't know what sapphic dating is like or whatever. I even had to look some of it up on Reddit."

"I guess I'm kind of the same way. A lot of tourists come through—hikers, you know? I've gone on a few dates like that, and I've learned that some people expect this like big prolonged experience, and I'm like, 'can we just make out and stuff?'"

Jenny laughed. But the way Isabella stared at her suggested that the question wasn't just hypothetical.

"So, what do you need help with?" Jenny said.

Isabella jumped up from the bed. "This is going to sound crazy, but this one girl I met was a big rock climber, and I bought some equipment."

"Oh, I did a little rock climbing in California," Jenny said.

"Perfect! So, she showed me this knot and I need to practice it. And I thought you might, I don't know, think that it's cool."

"You want to show me knots?" Jenny asked.

"Yeah, because, I feel like every time we hang out, I put my foot in my mouth, or I come off as like shallow or stupid or judgmental—"

"You do?" Jenny did her best not to make the question sound sarcastic. She was surprised at Isabella's apparent self-awareness.

"Yeah, or at least that's how I feel. So, like, let me show you this, okay? It's something I know how to do. And maybe, I don't know, maybe it will come in handy when we're looking for the kid."

Jenny frowned. It seemed like a strange thing for Isabella to want to show her. Jenny couldn't imagine a situation where a knot would help them find Carson Booth. It felt almost like she was being cajoled into one of Isabella's kinks. But the look on her face, her slumped shoulders, and her clasped hands told Jenny that it was important to her. So, reluctantly, Jenny shrugged. Isabella ran into the other room and came back with a four-foot-long length of green and blue climbing rope.

She started with some simple knots that Jenny recognized. Then she moved on to more complicated loops, twists, and pulls. After about ten minutes, Jenny was genuinely impressed.

"Wow, I feel like you have a hell of a lot better memory than I do," Jenny said.

"I think everyone has a better memory than you do," Isabella said, turning a complex knot around in front of her, looking at it as if she knew something was wrong but she didn't know what. "Sorry."

"No, it's true. But I mean, you have a better memory than I used to. I think I learned like three knots when I was a kid, and I kind of remember them. There's no way I'd remember that."

Isabella dropped it into her lap and shook her head. "I don't think I remembered this one either." She smiled at Jenny, her brown eyes wide with mischief. "Give me your hands."

"Huh?"

"Give me your hands," Isabella said. "I want to show you another knot."

"Um, I'm not sure that's really—"

"Oh, stop. Let me tie you up," she said, laughing. She leaned forward and gave Jenny puppy-dog eyes. "I promise, just your hands. I'm not going to like tie you to the bed and have my way with you."

Jenny's smile disappeared. "Don't joke about that," she said.

"I'm sorry," Isabella said, pulling back. "Really. But seriously, it's just a funny thing, let me tie your wrists, it's kind of a joke thing."

Jenny swallowed. "I don't know. I'm not sure I get the joke."

Isabella nodded. "Okay. I'm sorry," Isabella said. "I'm really sorry. Forget about it. It was stupid. I just thought—Yeah, I'm really sorry."

Isabella stared at the knot in her lap and plucked at its ends. Jenny imagined the awkwardness that was about to follow and pictured waking up at five only to have Isabella tell her to go find Carson by herself. Then they wouldn't talk for a few days, and then maybe not at all. Under normal circumstances, that didn't seem like such a bad prospect to Jenny. But she was lonely, and she didn't want to have to infringe on Delia constantly to keep her company.

So, feeling like she had no good options, Jenny shrugged. "Okay, but like, just—"

"I'll be super quick, and I won't do it tight, you can slip out whenever you want, okay? I promise. Wait, what's your safe word?"

"Flower," Jenny said immediately.

"Wow, 'flower,' okay. You sure you're okay with this? Really, I'm not going to do anything weird, I promise. I really do. It will be five seconds. Okay?"

Jenny nodded and held out her wrists. Isabella looped the rope around three times before wrapping a complex crisscross around them and finally around Jenny's thumbs.

"That's not too tight, is it?"

Jenny shook her head, anxiety whispering in her stomach. "I'm not going to say it's comfortable, but it doesn't hurt."

"So, like, being tied up doesn't do it for you?" Isabella rested her fingers on the rope and the palm of her hand on Jenny's fingers.

"No, that's not really my thing," Jenny said. "I'm kind of ready for it to be over now."

"What is your thing?" Isabella asked, looking down at her lap.

Shit, Jenny thought. *So much for avoiding awkwardness.*

"Um, I'm pretty vanilla," Jenny said. "I mean, like, the whole BDSM thing doesn't really click for me."

Isabella scooted forward, her knees touching Jenny's.

This bitch is going to try to kiss me, Jenny thought one second before Isabella leaned in to try. Jenny leaned back, pushing Isabella's hand away.

"Hey," Jenny said. "I'm not—"

"Shit, I'm sorry," Isabella said. "I was just joking, I'm totally not into—"

"Hey, don't do that either," Jenny said. "I know who you're into, you know who I'm into. It doesn't matter. I'm just not there right now."

Isabella nodded and put her hand back on the rope. Jenny hoped it would be to untie her, but instead she just kept it there. "I'm sorry. I just … you said you wanted to sleep over, and—"

"Yeah, so we could get up in the morning and go look for the kid." Jenny studied Isabella's eyes and recognized loneliness and shame. "Look, I … I get it, I do."

"Oh," Isabella said, her eyebrows bunching, her eyes squinting, "you get it? You're so hot that everyone throws themselves at you? You get that?"

Well, Jenny thought, *kind of.* She thought of Erica and Denise at Sunrise and even Pablo, one of the nurses. . She thought of the doctor and journalist who helped her on her way from Wallowa County to the coast. She thought of how every one of them had expressed interest in her.She didn't think of herself as attractive, but she knew she'd be lying if she pretended other people didn't think so.

"No," Jenny said, choosing to lie. "I mean, I get being lonely and not having a lot of opportunities to meet people like you. I get being excited because someone new is around. I get wanting to connect. I get all of those things."

Isabella continued to stare, self-defensive scorn on her face.

"Look, I've been through so much, you can't even imagine—" Jenny stopped at Isabella's incredulous expression. "Or, maybe you can," Jenny said. *I doubt it, though,* she thought. "Either way, I'm just not in a place where I feel good about being in a relationship or hooking up, or something casual and undefined. I'm not going to be there for a long time."

"Not ready to hook up?" Isabella said, smiling cruelly. "Really? Phil?"

Fuck.

"Whatever happened between me and Phil is … Well, honestly, it's none of your business."

"Sure. I just don't get it," Isabella said. "You're home now, even if you just need a rebound, someone to take your mind off your last thing—"

"My last thing? My last thing—my *last thing* is dead. Okay?" Jenny saw rolling water and pleading eyes. She heard the nightmare splashing and her own deafening silence. "I'm done. Please. Untie me. Flower. Okay? Fucking flower."

Isabella's expression changed again. Fascination replaced scorn, which was in turn replaced by sympathy.

"I'm so sorry, I had no idea—"

"Please untie me," Jenny said.

"I mean you said people were gone, but—"

"Please fucking untie me," Jenny said, starting to cry.

Isabella pulled back and suddenly seemed to realize what she was doing. "Fuck, I'm sorry," she reached forward and started to untie Jenny's hands. "I'm so sorry, I just thought—I'm sorry, I'm an asshole. I'm such an asshole."

Tears rolled down Jenny's cheeks as she watched Isabella untie the knot between her wrists.

Twenty minutes later, Jenny quietly opened Patty's front door. Without making a sound, she took off her hiking shoes, left them in the hall, and crept upstairs. When she finally closed her bedroom door behind her, she let out a long breath.

I'm sixteen again, Jenny thought. *I'm sixteen and meeting a boy in the park. Of course, I think the boy in the park only tried to feel me up, not tie me up.* Was that a real memory? She wasn't sure. She undressed, laid her clothes out for the morning, and turned on the radio. A man with a deep voice was saying something about the night sky and the stars.

Jenny leaned back on the bed and pressed her palms into her eyes. She pictured Isabella glaring at her over her tied hands, mocking her, accusing her. Jenny couldn't understand why anyone would want to argue someone into dating them or hooking up with them. Jenny couldn't imagine doing that. The image of Isabella shifted. Nolan stood on a path near a creek. Wind tugged his short, wavy blond hair. He wore a light green T-shirt and hiking pants. His big blue eyes pleaded with her. And in the half-dream, half-imagination, she heard his voice telling her to find Carson Booth.

Don't let him die out there. Don't let him die like you let me die.

16
Early Lights

Thursday, August 14, 2025 — Early Morning

AT FIVE-THIRTY IN THE morning, the usually sleepy town was awake. Its lights were lit, its coffee pots were brewing, and its streets were, if not busy, at least not empty. Windows glowed cheerfully, and front doors swung open to release eager townsfolk. Like rivulets merging to form a stream, one person joined the next until a cluster moved ahead of Jenny toward Main Street. She didn't rush to catch them to insert herself into their community. She still felt too outside, too much like a stranger in the town she grew up in.

Her phone buzzed and she smiled when she saw Delia's name on the alert.

> ***Delia***
> Awake yet?

> ***Jenny***
> Walking

> ***Delia***
> I'm at Barry's. It's a madhouse. Good luck getting in here.

> ***Jenny***
> But coffee

> ***Delia***
> The Tim is giving it away free.

Main Street was even more uncanny in its pre-dawn glow. Shops blazed with light, crowds gathered and milled, and people wandered in and out of the diner, coffee shop, bakery, and several restaurants. Jenny saw that Delia was right as a crowd milled in front of the coffee shop. She debated waiting in line but felt too nervous and out of place. She wanted to get to the Mist as quickly as possible so she didn't miss any instructions. So, Jenny ducked into the Timber, which sported a sign with the blessed drink's name hanging from its open door. Within, Jenny found them giving away free coffee. The owner, Carl, was dressed in an old plaid flannel shirt and overalls and told everyone he'd be offering a free drink and a side of fries with dinner that evening to searchers.

He smiled at Jenny while he poured her coffee into a large cup, which she mixed with a good helping of milk and sweetener. They thanked each other for helping in the search, and Jenny felt a familiar tug in her stomach as she returned to Main Street and appraised the knots of people. She had felt a similar uplifting pull when Aurora had convinced the people at the Chico House to help at a soup kitchen a few times. It made her want to cry for a new reason, though she had no name for the elusive emotion.

Jenny followed people with heavy shirts and backpacks into the theater's lobby. Seven folding tables were set up, each with a poster-board sign taped to the front letting people know they could get information, sandwiches, fruit, maps, walkie-talkies, or other assorted things at each station. Behind the tables, posters for horror films, romantic comedies, and two superhero movies hung in plexiglass-fronted frames. One, which showed a looming building with windows that glowed faintly green, was called *The House*, and Jenny made a mental note to find a trailer for it. She scanned the tables again, spotted Patty standing behind the Congregation Church's stand, and tried to look anywhere else.

Jenny grabbed a sandwich, apple, and granola bar from the table hosted by the Lutheran Women's League. The Congregation table had apple and orange juice and an assortment of fruits and healthy snacks, like ants on a log. They all looked appealing, but Jenny judged the price of getting some celery with peanut butter and raisins was a little too high.

"Grab two sandwiches," Phil said from over her shoulder. "They made enough for everyone to get two."

Jenny felt her stomach jump and sink at the same time. She forced a smile and turned around. "Hey," she said, drawing the word out.

"Hey. Seriously, that wasn't just a clever way of avoiding an awkward 'hello,' you should take two."

Jenny reached down and took a second sandwich, holding it up for Phil to see.

"Cool. We were out for hours yesterday, but we didn't start until late morning. Today it's going to be longer." Phil pointed at the granola bars and water bottles.

"Sir, yes sir," Jenny said, taking her pack off and filling the bottom with food.

"Hey, you mind grabbing me some fruit and apple juice?" she said, trying to act like everything was completely normal. Phil glanced over at Patty's table and frowned under his light brown beard.

"Mhm," he said before striding over to the Congregation table where he and Patty started chatting. To her relief, he didn't gesture toward her or, worse, call her over to talk. He simply grabbed a plastic bag and loaded it down with drinks, fruit, and two baggies of ants on a log. Marlene stepped up next to Patty to talk to him, and Jenny turned away. She scanned the room but didn't recognize anyone else. Of course she didn't. People met her eye and smiled, but she didn't know if it was a smile of recognition or just neighborliness. They might be total strangers, or they might have been her friends, teachers, and doctors. They might subscribe to her JustBuffs page.

Jenny suddenly felt overwhelmingly alone, as if she were in a one-sided relationship with the world. People knew her, but she knew no one. And, she thought, she had no idea how they knew her. If she had been anywhere else and someone recognized her, she could have guessed why. But here? It could be for almost any reason.

"Okay, the big man has returned, having slain the terrible pear beast and a couple of minor apple fiends," he said.

"Apple fiends?" a woman with red hair said, walking up. "Please tell me you are not trying to flirt with weird fantasy references." The woman was pale, freckled, short, and fit. Her messy curls were wrangled into a bunch like Jenny's own. "Hey," she said to Jenny, taking an awkward step toward her.

"Jenny," she said, offering her hand.

The woman frowned and looked from Jenny to Phil and back to Jenny. "Um. Are you joking?"

"No, I'm sorry, I—"

"I told you she has some, you know, memory issues," Phil said, putting a protective hand on Jenny's back.

"Yeah but … shit. Um, I'm Leddy." The woman shook her hand. "That is so fucking weird," Leddy said. "Sorry. Sorry, I didn't mean to be rude, just … well, we were friends."

Jenny wanted to cry but tried to hide the sensation with a laugh. "Really?"

"Yeah, we were in the same class from kindergarten until, like, forever. We did that project about spiders in seventh grade?"

Jenny felt her chest tightening. Apparently, the feeling made its way to her face, because Leddy slapped Phil. "Shit, I'm sorry, I didn't know how—Shit, Phil, be charming."

Phil put his arm around Jenny's shoulder and squeezed a little. "Sorry about my sister, she's an asshole. I'm pretty sure that even if you remembered everyone here, you would have blocked her ginger ass out."

Jenny laughed for real, but the tightness in her chest remained. "It's not a good feeling," she forced out. "Like … I feel like …"

"Hey," Leddy said. "It's okay, I'm sorry, I just didn't think that— Shit, I'm going to shut the fuck up."

"Good idea," Phil said.

Jenny found his arm around her shoulder to be both comforting and comfortable. She hated the sensations and herself for not talking to the man for almost a week. She knew she'd have to apologize and was starting to formulate how to do that when a woman's voice interrupted her.

"Everyone, can I have your attention?" A woman in a blue button-up shirt waved at the crowd from behind the concession counter. "Hello! Hello, can I have your attention please? Hello, good morning, I wanted to thank you all for coming out to help find Carson Booth. Yesterday we were a little haphazard in our eagerness to get out there and find him. Today we're going to be more organized. Right now, there are twenty-five groups of five going out. If you're here and don't have a group, see Keith over there by the table with the maps behind him. He'll get you situated. You'll also be able to get some maps there where we've marked out the search areas for each party. Carson was last seen walking down the footpath toward Whitman Cabin, so we're going to keep looking in that direction today. You'll find packets with information, pictures, and a description of what he was wearing when he was seen last.

"There are walkie-talkies on the table over there. We're also going to be coordinating with the towers around town. The weekend Talkers have graciously offered to take turns during the day to help coordinate. I'm going to be heading over to the cabin to work with Charles, and that will be our main base of operations. We'll have some extra food, water, and batteries set up in the garden as the day goes on.

"If you find anything, whether it's a piece of clothing, a bottle, or a pop can, anything at all, radio it in and don't touch it. Take pictures and geotag it. Local law enforcement will be out to document and secure any evidence, but we're going to try to prioritize the most promising leads first."

"Who is she?" Jenny whispered to Phil.

"Chief Ryan," Phil whispered back.

"Now, I've been in touch with the county, state, and FBI. The FBI is sending their CARD team out here later today, so we'll have help with drones, dogs, and the rest. The State Police are also sending some resources our way, and a search and rescue team should be out with a helicopter soon after sunrise, but as most of you know, a lot of their resources are occupied. A few of Sheriff Northrop's deputies are here and will be lending a hand throughout the day. I'll be coordinating with all of them, so if you have any questions talk to me first.

"Around noon, we're expecting some reinforcements from the late sleepers." She was met by a smattering of reserved chuckles. "I know the high school is organizing at least three groups to go out. If we can keep them from just sneaking into the bushes together, we should be able to cover a lot of ground today." Slightly more enthusiastic laughter. "Any questions?"

A woman at the Lutheran booth raised her hand. "Do we have any idea what he was doing here yet?"

The sheriff nodded. "We have been told that Carson was visiting his cousins, the Ingrams. The Ingrams are helping with background information and getting in touch with Carson's family to get them out here as soon as possible."

A man from the crowd raised his hand, and Chief Ryan pointed at him.

"Do we know why he might have wandered off?"

The chief shook her head. "Not at the moment. Carson has been here for a week, and by all accounts he was getting along well with his cousins and their scouting troop he was tagging along with. We don't know about any arguments or conflicts and, from what we have heard, he seemed happy to be here. We have been told that he likes to explore and is interested in nature, so the most likely circumstance is that he wandered off out of curiosity and got lost. Until we have good reason to think otherwise, that is how we are approaching this."

Scattered heads nodded in the crowd.

"Also, we can expect some media here this morning. I'm not going to tell you what to say to them, but I'd appreciate it if you point them in my direction for any big questions. All right, once everyone is set, has communication, food, water, and their assigned search areas, go ahead and head out. I'll be here for the next twenty minutes if there are any other questions, then I'll be at the cabin."

17
Seeking

Thursday, August 14, 2025 — Morning

JENNY FOLLOWED LEDDY AND Phil out of the Mist. Two heavily bearded and flannelled men met them on the sidewalk as the early morning sun lit up the fronts of the shops on the west side of Main. One of the men was tall, broad-shouldered, and heavyset. The other was shorter, rounder, and had a round, red nose. She was introduced to the tall man as Earl, and the shorter as Emmett. Earl wore a trucker hat, and Emmett had a floppy cap that Jenny had always considered a grandpa hat. Apparently, Jenny had known both slightly as Phil's friends, and Jenny endured Phil's brief description of her memory issues. Earl looked worried for Jenny, and Emmett frowned heavily.

"You see a doctor?" Emmett asked.

"Yeah," Jenny said, not entirely lying.

He nodded and they left it at that.

They walked up Main Street to the edge of town. At the corner of Bankview and Main, a dirt path struck into the forest. At the trailhead, three arrow-shaped signs hung nailed to a post. The topmost read 'Whitman Cabin,' the middle, 'Kusel Bridge,' and the bottom, 'Red and Blue Trails.' Earl, Emmett, and Phil started discussing the finer points of a movie they had all just seen, and Jenny took the opportunity to retreat into her thoughts. Guilt was bouncing around her like a pinball, plinking off of Aurora and Nolan, racking up shame points in the thousands. How could she be here with these people as if nothing had happened? How could—

"Hey," Leddy said, falling in beside Jenny. "Not a fan of superhero movies?"

"What?" Jenny asked. Leddy lifted her chin toward the three men.

"Oh, they're fine, I guess. Sorry, I was just in my own world."

"Right, you were always more of a horror movie person," Leddy said.

"Yeah," Jenny said. She was about to ask 'how did you know that?' when she remembered that she had forgotten.

"Yeah," Leddy said, squinting as one of the dawn's rays broke through the trees and landed across her face. "Sorry about earlier, I shouldn't have—I'm just not really sure how that works, you know? I've never met anyone with amnesia."

Jenny chuckled awkwardly. "I don't think I have amnesia, exactly. I just … It's this town. I remember everything else except big chunks of this town." She smiled and shook her head. "I'm getting bored of this."

Leddy pulled back as if Jenny had swung at her. "I'm sorry, I didn't mean to bore you—"

"No," Jenny said, reaching out and pulling Leddy forward. "Not you or talking to you. I'm just … There's only so many ways I can think to say 'I don't remember my hometown. I remember some of it, but I don't know why I forget the rest.' I need to get one of those cards that says, 'My brain is broken, please forgive me if I don't remember you.' I'm boring myself, I guess."

Leddy nodded, bit her lips, and stared down at the path. "A buddy of mine's brain is fucked up from a bomb that went off near his Humvee," she said. "The bomb didn't hit him, you know, but it still got him. The shockwave bounced around inside the metal frame and souped him."

"God," Jenny said.

"Yeah. It's fucked. He has different issues than you, but …" She pressed her lips together, forming a straight line. Jenny thought that she was pretty. Her red hair and angular eyes made her look like a Celtic warrior woman from a movie or TV show Aurora used to watch. "What I'm saying is that I should have known better. Sorry."

Jenny nodded. "It's okay. I get it, it's super strange. So, since I'm bored by my own brain damage, I guess, tell me about you. I guess we knew each other for like twelve years, so you can rewrite the whole thing for me."

Leddy nodded. "Sure. As you've probably heard, I was your idol. More like a big sister than a classmate. You learned everything you knew from me."

"I figured that was probably the case," Jenny said.

"I got all the boys, and you got none. Cried a lot, seeing me with them after you wrote their names on your notebook with all these hearts."

"That's really specific," Jenny laughed.

"Okay, I might still be processing the fact that Adam Harris asked you to the seventh-grade fall dance instead of me. And then he asked you to go with him to watch his dad and brother at Tamkaliks."

Jenny frowned. She felt like a broken record. "I don't remember that."

"You don't remember Tamkaliks, or you don't remember Adam?"

"Adam. I remember Tamkaliks, but I don't think I've thought about it in forever. I guess I missed it this year," Jenny said.

"Yeah," Leddy said. "Next year we can go together to 'the place from where you can see the mountains.' My great-great-great, or something like that, grandfather fought with Joseph. I know I'm pale as shit, but—"

"I think I've given up trying to figure out who people are based on how they look," Jenny said. "Though, I have to say, you and Phil look nothing alike."

"Different moms. Dad got around," Leddy said, and Jenny gave her a look that said, 'I know what you mean.'

"So, was Adam cute?"

"Yeah, when we were eleven. He was also pretty cute when we were fourteen, but by then he figured out that neither of us are his type."

"Ah," Jenny said. "Maybe I turned him gay."

Leddy looked confused and then shook her head. "No, he likes fat girls."

"What?"

"Yeah, bro is into the thick ladies. You didn't turn him gay, but your stick-figure ass probably made him realize he needed more woman than either of us could offer." They laughed and for a moment Jenny felt something familiar. Then it faded. "Though, if you had had those back then—" she nodded at Jenny's chest.

"If I had had these back then I would have fallen over." She stopped and grabbed Leddy's arm. "Were we really friends?"

Leddy considered Jenny for a long moment before she nodded. "Yeah. Not all the time, we had our moments. Probably everyone does if they're stuck together for twelve years in a class of ten. But yeah, we were friends. Sometimes we were even best friends. We kind of grew apart when you went all goth-Jesus on me, though."

"Yeah, that makes sense," Jenny said.

"Part of that was my fault too. I think I was a pretty shitty kid, honestly. I was selfish, self-centered, and I didn't have a lot of time for other people's feelings."

"You seem like you figured that out," Jenny said.

"Well, the army kicked the shit out of me and salvaged something close to a human being. After that, yeah, I don't know," she said, shrugging. "I think when your older brother is a pansy-ass"—she said theatrically loudly toward the three men walking ahead of them—"you have to learn how to communicate."

"Phil's a pansy?" Jenny asked.

"Dude talks about his feelings all the fucking time," Leddy said. "Did he cry when you two hooked up?"

Jenny felt her eyes go wide and her mouth drop open. "Um … no.

I don't believe he cried."

"Good, I told him chicks hate that."

"That was one fucking time," Phil called back over his shoulder, "and I was in love with her." He turned around and walked backward. "And I was seventeen."

Leddy shook her head and smiled at Jenny. "Pansy."

The sun had not yet risen enough to reach them through the dense ponderosa that flanked their path, so they walked in predawn darkness as pine filled Jenny's nose. She heard the waterfall rumbling distantly behind her and a scattering of voices ahead. The path brought them past Whitman Cabin. Its lights were on, and the clearing in front of the building was illuminated by the headlights of two law enforcement SUVs. The pale, red-headed police officer whose name she had already forgotten stood next to a tall, black man in a crisp white shirt with a tie. Jenny thought he looked like he belonged in a movie about NASA or the stock market. The police officer waved, and she waved back.

"How many redheads are in this town?" Jenny asked.

"Four, I think," Leddy said. "I'm going to have to marry Chase, to keep the bloodline strong. He just doesn't know it yet." She waved at Chase with exaggerated enthusiasm.

"Chase, right," Jenny said and laughed with Leddy as the officer shook his head at them.

"He must think we're idiots," Jenny said.

"Chase is all right," Leddy said. "He cares too much though. Something's going to break him."

They walked the wooden bridge that crossed the Kusel, and Earl stopped to take a picture of the creek in the growing morning light. He smiled sheepishly as he lowered his phone.

"Think it might make a good album cover," he said.

Jenny considered the creek from the bridge. Fog rested on the water, which was running high because of the rain. The trees along the banks were misty and washed out as if someone had turned a knob to drain their color. It had a haunting and haunted look.

That makes sense, Jenny thought. *It is a grave, after all.*

"Our search area is at the top of the ridge," Phil said as she and Earl caught up to the group gathered on the other side of the bridge. A path snaked away and up a steep incline to the west. "We're going to go until we get to these coordinates"—he showed them a text he had gotten—"and create a base camp to search from. We can leave all our packs and coats and stuff there."

"Are we going to the outpost?" Emmett asked.

"No, not today anyway. I tried to tell Chief Ryan that it made more sense, but she wanted to do this in order. Obviously, if we see any signs that he went that way, then at least a couple of us will go and check it out. Otherwise, we stick to our grid for today."

"But there's shelter in the outpost, even if it's only a little," Emmett said.

"And the kid almost certainly doesn't know it's there," Phil said. "He's not from here."

"But if someone kidnapped him," Earl said. "They might take him there."

"I know," Phil said, "I made the same case to Ryan. She told us to stick to the grid. That being said, if someone wants to jog up there and take a quick look around then, honestly, who's going to stop you?"

Emmett frowned and nodded, and Jenny thought she saw disappointment in the man's bearded face.

"Well, let's get climbing then," Emmett said.

The hill was steeper than Jenny remembered. By the time they were half-way up, she was out of breath. To her surprise, none of the other members of the group seemed put out by the uphill climb.

I really need to start running again.

She hid her need for a break by pretending to see something. She stood off to one side, hands on hips, and peered into the trees, which were much sparser on the hillside than below.

"Find something?" Phil asked.

"Not sure," Jenny said. Then, after ten deep breaths, she shook her head. "Nope, I was wrong."

When she turned to start back up the hill, Phil was smiling knowingly.

"What?" she asked.

"Nothing," Phil said and followed her the rest of the way up.

On their way to their designated starting point, they found a beer bottle and a can of diet pop, ten feet from each other. They sent GPS and photos and put marker flags in the path to let the authorities know where to find the items before continuing upward.

"If we had more people," Phil said, "we'd have someone with us to bag that stuff right away. But we aren't really the priority right now."

"Why not?" Jenny said.

"Two girls were murdered in Enterprise yesterday and a third one is missing. So, a lot of the local resources are going there," Leddy said.

"Holy shit," Jenny said. "How aren't there more—"

"The girls were all like thirteen. So, yeah, people are going to try to find the girl who was taken by a murderer before they go looking for a kid who just probably got lost in the woods," Earl said. "It sucks, but we'll have more help soon. But that's also why we're moving so fast and not stopping unless there's something big."

"Do you think they're connected?" Jenny asked.

Leddy shrugged. "I mean … maybe? Maybe there's a sicko who's collecting middle-schoolers."

"God … how did he—"

"Shot them," Earl said.

"Fuck," Jenny said and then repeated herself several steps later.

"Yeah," Leddy said. "But that's why the whole town is out. We know that the big state resources are going to go to Enterprise."

Jenny nodded and surveyed the trail in front of them.

"Not sure if you remember the High Path, but it's a lot of holes and nooks and crannies," Phil said. "A lot of places for a kid to get lost in or stuck in. So, we'll be looking for signs of slides, scuff marks, shoe prints; things that look like they've been disturbed recently."

"Um," Jenny said, frowning, "I'm not sure I'm much of a tracker."

"Chief Phil is," Earl said, lifting his bearded chin in the tall man's direction. "He can track a crow on a cloudy day. It's in his blood." Earl let out something that sounded like a war cry. If Jenny's expression reflected her feelings, she knew she must have looked incredibly uncomfortable. "Sorry," Earl said, poking himself with his thumb. "Umatilla and Cayuse."

"Yeah, only Emmett is pure-bred colonizer," Phil said. Emmett gave Phil the finger. "But everything I learned about hunting and tracking I got from a half-Chinese, half-Australian guy named Stew."

"Wait," Jenny said, stopping and grabbing Phil's arm. "Holy shit, I remember Stew! He came into the bookstore a lot!"

The memory of the man bounced around her brain and she had to steady herself against a tree.

"He was probably reading a lot of sci-fi," Phil said.

"Yeah! He did, he was into … Dickson! Gerald R. Dickson!"

"Gordon," Earl chimed in.

"Right!" Jenny said. "Holy shit. I remember him. He was … weird."

"Yeah, Stew wasn't what I'd call a 'normal dude,' but he was a hell of a hunter."

"What happened to him?" Jenny asked.

"Stroke. Then pneumonia. He passed during the pandemic," Phil said. Jenny looked at him and felt something new and strange. Here was a man who connected to something she could remember, a person who wasn't a stranger. That somehow made Phil less of a stranger. "But he did tell me that he learned everything he knew about hunting from the aboriginal people of Australia."

"Really?"

"One hundred percent true," Phil said. "Well, it's true that that's what he told me. It was almost definitely bullshit. He told me he fucked Naomi Watts too."

"I thought it was Nicole Kidman," Leddy said.

"He might have said both," Phil said. "I think he got them confused."

They reached the top of the ridge and set their packs down. They drank, munched granola bars, and planned their search. They marked their locations on a GPS app on Phil's phone and finally started their search proper.

The terrain was uneven, rocky ground peppered with ponderosa pine trees, rocks, low vegetation, and holes that would surprise them and threaten to turn ankles. The searchers moved slowly, five feet apart, each with a stick to poke at branches, push back greenery, and overturn small rocks. Emmett found a piece of paper, but they agreed it had blown up there long ago. Still, they marked it, took pictures, and sent the information to Chief Ryan.

They swung around at the end of a half mile and retraced their path, offset by twenty-five feet, so that Jenny imagined their path looking like the track of a huge rake in a Zen garden, pulled up straight, then curving at the end, and coming back to form a parallel set of ruts. When they returned to camp, they drank water and took bathroom breaks.

"Pee where we already searched! And make sure to keep everything squared away," Leddy said to the group. "We don't want our trash to end up as evidence someone has to run down."

After hours of searching, they came up empty. They ate lunch just after eleven, sitting on the ground with their backs against their packs. Emmett didn't join them and took his lunch to hike up to the old outpost, which Jenny couldn't remember. Leddy undid her boots and took off her socks. Jenny joked that she should charge for showing her toes off, and Phil said that no one in town would pay, since they'd all seen them. The conversation continued for a few minutes, with Leddy and Phil jabbing at each other and Earl piping up to egg them both on, but Jenny didn't participate again.

Why did I say that? What am I trying to do, out myself? She felt stupid, but the conversation soon shifted, and they started to discuss social media in general. Earl was staunchly against it, and Phil teased him that he was only against it when he wasn't staring at half-naked women. Jenny bit her tongue.

Emmett returned an hour later shaking his head. "I didn't see anything, but we really should search there tomorrow if he's still missing," the shorter man said, wiping sweat from his forehead with a handkerchief. Jenny observed silently that everything about the man, from his suspenders to his floppy hat and handkerchief, made him seem older than he was. Or, if not *older*, then from an earlier age.

Before Jenny could decide when she though Emmet belonged, or anyone could comment on his proclamation, three senior boys from the high school baseball team came hiking up the hill. They were all tall, shaggy-haired, and fit. One reminded Jenny of Nolan, which pulled her guilt and shame to the surface, so she avoided them as much as possible.

With the addition of the boys, their group could cover more ground, but still, by mid-afternoon, the most they had found was an old water bottle and a flip-flop that looked like it might have belonged to a giant.

"That has to be a size fourteen," Earl said. "Who the hell is that big out here?"

"No one I can think of," Phil said. "Maybe just an idiot tourist who thought wearing flops into the foothills was a good idea."

Soon, one of the drones flew over, and they all waved as it circled them once and moved on.

"They'll be flying that out of the tower," Leddy said. "I almost tried to do that job, but I didn't have the video game skills for it."

"Shit, you do now," Emmet said.

"Jealous," Leddy said.

"You mean in the army?" Jenny asked.

"Yeah," Leddy said.

"What did you do?"

"Armored Cav, third ACR, Scout."

"What is your MOS?" Phil shouted across at her. "Tell me your damned MOS!" Earl laughed and Emmett shook his head.

"Sorry," Leddy said, giving Phil the finger. "This guy came up to me at the supermarket when I was on leave this one time. Phil had just picked me up, I hadn't even gotten a chance to change out of my ACUs, like we were stopping to pick up food and then come home, and this guy just came up and was like, 'no fucking way you're Armored Cav, what's your MOS?'"

"MOS?" Jenny asked.

"Military Occupation Specialty, it's just the job you do. There's this whole thing about people dressing up like they served so they can get fucking discounted coffee or cheaper tickets to things. And for some reason, this guy thought I was trying to get a discount on Pop-tarts or something, which the supermarket doesn't even do."

"That sounds crazy," Jenny said.

"Most of the people who do it are crazy, which is why I don't even bother looking for it," Leddy said. "But this guy, I definitely think *he* was crazy because he was just standing there screaming at me. 'Tell me your damned MOS!' So now Phil thinks it's funny to bring it up every time I talk about it."

Phil shrugged. "I don't have a lot to give her shit for," he said, smiling.

Jenny just shook her head and wondered how different their lives were from hers. She couldn't remember ever meeting anyone like them. These were people who had done serious things. At least, Leddy had. The others seemed like they were capable, though. And Jenny guessed they would all know what to do if they found themselves in a dangerous situation.

Suddenly, Joseph's face flashed in her mind. His presence, even as a memory, was overwhelming. She saw his face, his crew-cut hair, and his light eyes, and knew with certainty, that as capable as Phil, Leddy, Emmett, and Earl appeared, Joseph would be able to hurt them if he wanted to—even kill them. In her mind's eye, the older man, his face still and serene, jammed a thick branch into Phil's mouth. He grabbed Leddy by the throat and lifted her from the ground, crushing her with his thick fingers, still immensely strong despite his age. He stood over their broken bodies, ignoring them and looking at her with fatherly love. She watched herself go to him and embrace him as he wrapped those huge arms around her as Jenny faded and Venena reappeared.

"Hey, you okay?" Leddy asked, keeping her voice low so the others couldn't hear her.

Jenny realized she was crying and wiped the tears away with the heel of her hand. "Sorry, I was just … It just … My mind just followed a strange path to someone I used to know."

Leddy nodded. "Someone you lost?"

Jenny shook her head. "No," she said, wiping her cheek. "He's still alive. He's still out there."

18
Everything

Thursday, August 14, 2025 – Afternoon

BY THE END OF the afternoon, their day's search had turned up only three more items worth flagging, none of which seemed promising. Exhausted, they took their packs and trudged down the hill together. The high school boys lagged, having been put into their proper place by Leddy when she caught them looking at her ass. Jenny wasn't sure if they were bringing up the rear to avoid Leddy's wrath or to maintain a better view.

As they plodded down, Phil fell in beside Jenny. "What are you doing for dinner?" he asked.

"Probably stuffing pizza in my face while I lay in my bathtub," she said.

Phil raised his eyebrows and grinned. "Well, I wouldn't want to stop that from happening, but if you want to get something more substantial, we're going to grab dinner a little later at the Tim. You know, eat some wings, drink some beers, enjoy our free fries"—Phil slipped into a bad Russian accent—"like I hear Americans do from social media and your television programs."

"I'm not sure I'm up for something so public right now," Jenny said. She frowned and, after a few silent paces, said, "I'm sorry I didn't text you back."

He shrugged. "I kind of figured you wouldn't."

"Really? Do I come off like that much of a bitch?"

"You come off like you're in a complicated place," he said.

"Okay, yeah, that's fair," Jenny said. "How about this? I promise not to ghost you again, and you promise to understand that I might just need a few days at a time to cope."

"With what?"

"Fucking everything," she said.

He nodded. "Okay. Fair. So, can you cope tonight at my place? I'll order the pizza. You can take a bath there."

She pursed her lips and shook her head. "I'll bathe at my own home, thank you. But yes, I will let you buy me pizza."

"Perfect," Phil said, slipping back into his faux-Russian persona. "Is good, is very good."

"Just don't do that voice all night."

"Nyet," he said, "I will put on my Americanski accent for you."

"Are you always like this?"

Phil shook his head. "Only when I'm around a purdy girl," he said, slapping on a hillbilly drawl.

"You must be exhausting," Jenny laughed.

"He is," Leddy said, coming up on the other side of her. "You'll get tired of him fast. All the girls do when he's got a crush."

Jenny laughed and thought that she might be blushing.

"What's so funny?" Phil asked. "A man can't have a crush?"

"You've known me for less than a week," Jenny said.

"No," Leddy reminded her, "you've known him for less than a week. He's known you since he was a kid."

Jenny nodded, feeling a kind of temporal vertigo. "Right."

"Phil watched you blossom," Earl said in what Jenny took to be an intentionally creepy voice.

"Please don't say it like that," Phil said.

"Blossom," Earl repeated, a look of sadistic pleasure spreading across his face as Phil put his face in his hands.

They dropped their trash in big cans in front of Whitman Cabin. When they got to Bankview, Jenny split off with Earl who lived on Innich Street, a half-block past Patty's house.

"You coming back tomorrow?" Earl asked.

"Yeah, I think so," Jenny said.

"Good. We like you. You fit in."

"I … Uh, thanks. I'm a little surprised to hear you say that. I didn't—"

"Nah, you're cool. You didn't lecture us once, and you didn't just bounce around trying to get attention. You drink?"

"Not as much as I used to."

"Fair. Well, at least you aren't a total quitter," Earl said. They walked in silence for a block.

"Hey, can I ask you something?" Jenny said.

"Sure."

"What have you heard about me? Like, honestly."

She could see the big man frowning through his thick black beard. His cheeks drew up and he squinted as if he were trying to look at something far away. "Now or back then?"

"Both."

"Back then I heard you were a stuck-up, judgmental, religious chick who fucked around a lot."

"Riiight," Jenny said, elongating the word.

"Since then? Heard you died. Heard you started stripping. Got pregnant. Became a lesbian."

"All at once?"

"Yep, the Subaru driving zombie mommy stripper. I almost named my band that."

"What kind of music?"

"Folk punk," he said.

They stopped in front of Patty's house.

"You really have a band?"

"Yeah, we're called 'Jawbone's Cove,' we don't really play a lot anymore."

Jenny nodded, thinking the name sounded familiar. She couldn't remember if it was one of the stickers on Barry's counter, or if she had seen it somewhere else.

"I'm not really a hugger, so I'm going to have to disappoint you." He held his fist out and she bumped it. "See you tomorrow." He started to walk away and then stopped. "And leave Phil with some of his bodily fluids, okay? We need him to be able to help tomorrow."

"Yeah, thanks, I'll take that under advisement," Jenny said.

Jenny ducked silently inside the front door and listened. She heard nothing except the refrigerator hum from the kitchen. She sat on the stairs and unlaced her hiking shoes before pulling them off slowly. Her socks were not soaked in blood as the pain on the inside of her big toes had suggested. Instead, as she removed her socks, two big blisters appeared, puffing out from her pruned skin. She put her shoes by the door, hobbled upstairs, and stripped off her clothes. Once the bath was running, Jenny found a needle in an old sewing kit. She lanced her blisters and stared at the tub. What had she been thinking? She reached for the knob to send the water back to the shower head and paused. Her aching body cried out for a soak, but her mind and stomach revolted at the idea.

Eventually, you're going to have to be able to take a bath, Jenny thought.

"Not yet," she said to the empty room. She turned the knob, and the rush of the faucet turned into the shower's higher-pitched spray.

She first stood under the water, letting it soothe her a little, but her feet hurt too badly. So she sat, knees to her chest, and let the water drum against her head and legs and down her back. Every few minutes she shifted position to let the water massage some new part of her body. At one point, she considered leaning back and relieving her stress more completely, but she thought if she did that, she'd probably just ghost

Phil again and fall asleep alone. She realized that she might have done that if she wasn't planning to try to help find Carson Booth again the next day. So, instead, she finished her shower with a hurried bout of washing and shaving. Finished, Jenny stepped out of the tub, hoping Phil could help her relax in a way that was at least as fulfilling as what she could do herself.

She started to picture what she would wear to Phil's. She also realized that she had to decide if she would stay the night. She grabbed her phone.

> **_Jenny_**
> Hey, should I bring a bag?

> **_Treeman_**
> Do you want to bring a bag?

> **_Jenny_**
> If you want me to bring a bag

> **_Treeman_**
> You should bring a bag.

> **_Jenny_**
> I'll bring a bag.

> **_Treeman_**
> You bath yet?

> **_Jenny_**
> Just stopped bathing

> **_Treeman_**
> So, you're naked right now?

> **_Jenny_**
> No, I bath in a cocktail dress.

> ***Treeman***
> You said both cock and tail.

> ***Jenny***
> I'm reconsidering coming over after that.

> ***Treeman***
> What do you want on your pizza?

> ***Jenny***
> Fucking everything

> ***Treeman***
> Perfect

After drying off, she put on her jean skirt and a black tank top. She packed sleeping and hiking clothes and realized she didn't have any kind of toiletries bag. She tossed things into the front pocket of her backpack and wrote 'toiletries bag' on a shopping list in her notebook.

She bandaged her toes, slid on flip-flops, and threw her pack over her shoulders. Down the stairs she went, with her pack bouncing behind her like a kid going to school, and once more she was out the door and into the open air of the evening. The sun had not yet set, though it was hovering low over Wayne Butte. She walked south until she came to Library Avenue before turning right, not wanting to run into Patty. She came out onto Main Street, across from the library, and noticed people going in. She had spent several nights lounging on the building's third floor and had never noticed anyone come in past seven, let alone a group. She wondered if they had something to do with the search or the renovations she had heard about.

She continued south until she came to the Lightning Falls Museum, and she checked her reflection in the window. She didn't hate what she saw, especially for a night of pizza, a movie, and probably sex. So, she turned, crossed the street, and entered the old house that served as an apartment building.

The pizza, movie, and sex were all good enough. None were

spectacular, but they did the trick. As Jenny tried to fall asleep in Phil's bed, she did her best to let the positive feelings of the day keep her guilt and shame at bay. For the most part, they did. But as she drifted off to sleep, she found Nolan walking through her mind in the rocky foothills, northwest of town, looking for Carson Booth with sad eyes and a broken heart.

The Quiet Rumble 119

Volume 10, Issue 68, Thursday, August 14, 2025

I Love This Town

By Keith Lowry, Ed. In Chief.

TODAY REMINDED ME OF one of the reasons I love this town. When things fall apart, we work together. This past month a lot has fallen apart. Not just here, but now down in Enterprise as well. The murders of Elsa Farmer and Tisha James, and the disappearance of Polly Barro, are devastating. The disappearance of Carson Booth at the same time is heartbreaking. As a community, we know what it means to be in tension with the place we live. We know what it means to live on land that we have mixed feelings about and to work with the government that we benefit from but are also critical of.

We understand there are limited resources, though I am told more are coming. And we understand that in the face of those limitations, we have to work together. Two years ago, when the hikers went missing, we learned a lot about what it takes to search the land around us. We learned what we can count on the county, state, and federal government for. And we learned how conflicted some of us are with asking for help from those systems.

Today I saw us band together again. I stood behind a table at the Mist and watched as people young and old worked together to search for a missing boy. I watched us pick up the slack that other agencies couldn't manage because they had more pressing emergencies. This is one of the prices we pay for being in one of the most remote areas of this great nation.

I'm told that tomorrow we will have more drones, the search and rescue helicopter will be allocated to us—they apparently had mechanical issues today—and more outside boots on the ground. The high school is giving all students the day off so they and the teachers can join the search. I'm told that food will continue to be provided to searchers, and that Mr. Levi Grossman has offered to cover every expense the town incurs from this search. Now, I don't think we'll let him do that alone. I know many of us can't hike like we used to but want to help and would be glad to write a check to let our money do the walking for us. So, I want to say thank you to Mr. Grossman, not just for his generosity, but for his constant good example.

I remember when, long before many of you were born, we searched for another missing child, back in '76. That was a terrible December, but we pulled together. The streets were full then, and our little community felt, at least to me, closer than it ever had. That terrible month was, in a strange way, the time I felt most like a part of our amazing little community. Today, I'm proud to say, topped that feeling. I have faith we'll find Carson Booth because I have faith in this community. So, let's get some rest tonight, and then get back at it again tomorrow. And remember that in this age of disconnected, internet-obsessed society, we are still a town of interconnected people who do the right thing when the time comes.

19
Chasm

Friday, August 15, 2025 – Daytime

SORE AND SLUGGISH, THE party reconvened in the morning. Jenny decided to wait in Barry's line as Phil gathered more food for their day. The shop was so busy that she could only exchange cursory greetings with Barry and Delia as they hurried to serve the even larger crowd that included teachers and a few early-rising high schoolers.

She met her groggy group outside the Mist with two carriers full of cups, sweeteners, and creamer. Earl took his the same way Jenny did, sweet and light, while Phil and Leddy both took theirs black. Emmett appeared five minutes later with a box of donuts and dipped an old-fashioned into his caramel latte.

"If Phil's not doing it for you," Leddy said around a mouthful of donut, "I'll happily make you my love servant."

"Phil will always do it for me," Emmett said dryly as he looked fixedly at Phil until the taller man looked away, laughing.

"I was talking to Jenny," Leddy said.

"I know," Emmett said, continuing to stare at Phil, which made Earl laugh so hard that Jenny thought he'd spit.

"Guys," Leddy said with put-on seriousness, "we shouldn't be joking around right now, there's a boy missing."

"I'm not," Emmett said, and Jenny began to wonder if it was a bit, or if maybe there was something else going on.

"Let's go look for a missing kid," Jenny said with faux excitement.

They finished the box of donuts and plodded up Main to the path in the woods. When the men were chatting again about some aspect of pop culture, Jenny asked Leddy about the interaction.

"Oh, no—or, I don't think Emmett was serious. You've got to take everything they say to each other as a strange love language. I worry when they stop giving each other shit. And you should worry if I stop giving you shit. I'm bilingual like that."

The hike up on the second day was similar to the first, except that a search and rescue helicopter chopped the air overhead and four extra drones skimmed the sky above the forest and hills, scanning for any sign of twelve-year-old Carson Booth. The early morning air was alive and, though their group was the same as the previous day, Jenny felt like her place in the group had changed. They weren't strangers anymore, and she wondered if this was where she belonged.

Their path took them higher into the hills, cutting right at a large rock and following a narrow path up and away from the previous day's base camp. The ground remained rocky and mostly barren except where it sloped down to their right toward Evans Creek, where the trees were a little denser. To their left the ground rose sharply to a ridge about fifteen feet above their heads.

"Are we going up there?" Jenny asked.

"No good way to get up there unless you climb. That's what the drones are for," Phil said. "But it's unlikely that a kid in his bare feet would be able to get up there, or, you know—"

"What?" Jenny asked, squinting at the ridge.

"Well, it's pretty unlikely someone could have carried him up there."

They kept on until the path opened onto a mostly flat space dominated by the remains of an old stone building. The four walls, blackened in several places, especially above the windows, were half standing. Jenny guessed the tops of the walls formed the piles of rubble and burned timber scattered around the building's perimeter.

"What is this place?" Jenny asked.

"This is the old outpost," Emmett said. "Church folks built it more than a hundred years ago. They used to do retreats and stuff up here. Folks also used it as a hunting lodge until the '70s, when it burned down."

"There was a shootout here," Earl said. "You can still see some of the bullet holes." To demonstrate, he pointed to a pockmark marring the brick next to the door. Jenny wasn't sure if it looked like a bullet hole, but she didn't have any reason to doubt Earl.

"Shit," she said.

"Yeah, really wild. It's totally useless now, except for shade," Phil said.

They went in through the front door, which, without its top, was like a 'U' in the darkened stone. The perimeter of the old hall was thirty feet to a side with old floorboards, warped and dirt-strewn, curling up as if a giant had reached down into them and pulled them back, looking for the outpost's flesh under its shell. Two heavy, charred beams lay across the room's center, marred by years of weather and teenagers with knives. Names and dates cut through the sooty timber, showing lighter, less damaged wood beneath.

The remnants of a second floor poked out from the walls in three places, each a little island of old planks that Jenny thought would be safe for squirrels and birds, but little else. She saw the remains of a long bar, the foot of a wide staircase, and a stone structure in the middle of the building that puzzled her at first. Then, as she circled it, she realized it was a large, multi-faced fireplace with a stunted, long-crumbled chimney.

"I thought we were crazy for not searching this place yesterday when you guys mentioned it," Jenny said, appraising the ruin. "But I guess the sheriff was right. There's nowhere for someone to hide here. I don't know why anyone would come up here."

"Well," Earl said, "if it gets windy up here, having a stone wall at your back is a hell of a lot better than not. Remember that if you're ever wandering alone up here."

"Um," Jenny said, "I'll try to keep it in mind."

"Hey, it's happened," Emmett said.

"It might have even happened to him," Earl said.

"Really?"

"He got shit-faced and got turned around when he went out for a piss," Leddy said.

"What were you doing up here?" Jenny asked.

"We go camping. Sometimes we go hunting," Phil said.

"While getting shit-faced," Jenny said.

"No, I mean, not while we're hunting. We're not like that. But after? We are definitely like that."

Jenny crossed her arms and tried to picture herself hunting with the group. She wasn't sure she could see herself in camo and blaze orange. Still, a month ago she couldn't have imagined she'd be up here, searching for a lost kid.

"Well, I'll definitely keep it in mind if I ever get lost," she said.

They set their packs down by the ruined fireplace. Emmett, Phil, and Leddy planned their route, and they started searching. Jenny found it oddly comforting to have a building as their home base, even one without a roof or any amenities. The building made her a little sad, but it also fascinated her in the way that ruins often did. She wondered about the events that had unfolded within its walls, the drama, the joy, and the eventual destruction of the place.

"What happened there?" Jenny asked as they started their first sweep.

"There was a murder back in the '70s," Leddy said. "Some piece of shit decided to hurt this guy and tie him to a tree and leave him there."

"Fuck," Jenny said.

"Yeah, state police got involved, and it wrapped up at the outpost. Handful of people died."

"The Statie got it here," Earl said.

"No, he didn't," Emmett said. Jenny thought he sounded disappointed.

"Yeah, he did, it was that reporter guy who got away," Earl said.

"I thought they both got away," Phil said.

"Obviously," Leddy said, "no one knows what the fuck happened. I mean, I'm sure the older folks know, and we would too if we bothered to go to the library and look it up, but where's the fun in that? Then we wouldn't get to listen to Earl and Emmett argue over it."

They searched and argued for three hours before they broke for lunch. Then, once again, they were joined by a group of teenagers. However, today a handful of young women came with the boys. After they returned from their first search after lunch one of the teenage girls approached Jenny. She had long, straight, brown hair that was twisted into a thick braid, and her hazel eyes were squinted against the sun.

"Hey," she said.

"Hi," Jenny said, pulling the cap from her water bottle. As she drank, she squinted at the girl who stood awkwardly, not saying anything. Jenny lowered her bottle and gave her a quizzical look. "What's up?"

"Um, I don't feel good," the girl said.

"Okay, uh, here, come sit down." She gestured to the tumbledown stone of the fireplace and dug out an extra bottle of water. "What's the matter?" she asked, handing the girl the bottle.

"My head. And my stomach."

Jenny glanced up to see if she could find Leddy or Phil. Thankfully, Leddy was walking over.

"Maggie," she said, "what's the matter? Your head hurt?"

Maggie nodded.

"Okay, well, sit and drink the water, let me get you a granola bar. Jenny, can you give me a hand?"

"Sure," Jenny said. She joined Leddy near the ruined bar. "What's up?"

"Maggie is—she gets 'sick' a lot," Leddy whispered. "She probably just wants someone to talk to her."

Jenny looked back at the girl who was staring at her sneakers.

"You want me to just hang out with her?" Jenny said, grateful for the chance to rest her sore legs and blistered feet. Leddy nodded as she pulled a granola bar from a pack and handed it to Jenny. Then she slowly lowered herself to sit on the ground and leaned against the bar. She started unlacing one of her light tan boots.

"Would you mind? We've only got two more directions to check, and we can spread out a little more and cover the same ground, or me and Phil can take a second pass to make up your areas."

"You sure?" Jenny asked, tugging at her T-shirt to waft air against her skin.

"Totally. Honestly, you're going to have a harder time," Leddy said, glancing past Jenny to the girl on the rock. Jenny laughed. Leddy shook out her boot, pulled it back on, relaced it, and then repeated the process with the other side.

"Yeah, sure," Jenny said. She wiped her arm across her forehead. "It will be nice to sit down for a while. I'm not sure doing two days in a row was a good idea."

"What? No, you'll be hardcore in a few days." Leddy said. She looked earnest, so Jenny suppressed a laugh.

"I think I'm going to sleep for a week after this," Jenny said.

"Well, then take the chance to rest. Besides, you'll be proving how good of a person you are by talking to Maggie."

"I'm not a good person," Jenny said, shaking her head.

"Sure, you are. You're out here trying to find a missing kid. You're going to babysit a girl who probably has some fucked up home life that presents as stomachaches and headaches, and you're throwing some sympathy ass my loser brother's way. You might be the best person I know."

Jenny laughed.

"Hey!" Phil said, walking over. "We should get this next loop started."

"Jenny's going to hang back," Leddy said. "Maggie needs a babysitter."

"Oh. Huh, yeah, I-I'm sorry to hear that," he said.

"You're sorry to hear that?" Leddy said, holding her hand up. Phil grabbed it and pulled his half-sister to her feet. "Just propose already. Or you can sit next to her at the bar tonight. Come on, Cyrano." She pushed her brother away.

"Cyrano was the ugly one," Phil said.

"I know," Leddy said. She turned and mouthed the words 'good luck' to Jenny and nodded in Maggie's direction. Jenny smiled and waved before turning back to her temporary ward.

Leddy had been wrong. Leaning against her pack, Jenny found most of the hour with Maggie to be perfectly peaceful and pleasant. Though anxious and awkward, the girl wasn't especially weird or off-putting. She was a sophomore, and her parents worked from home for a big bank.

She said they weren't rich, and that people assumed that if they both worked for a bank, they must be rich. But they weren't.

She talked a little about school, which she said was mostly just fine. She wanted to do the fall play— *Our Town*—or the spring musical—*The Music Man*. Jenny asked her what parts she wanted to play, and she didn't know.

"You should try out for Mrs. Paroo," Jenny said. "I always loved her in the movie."

"I haven't seen the movie."

"Have you seen the stage version?"

The girl shook her head.

Jenny frowned. *Okay, dead end.* "How about friends? Who are you friends with?"

"I don't know, I have a few friends."

Jenny's frown deepened. *What the hell am I supposed to talk to this girl about?* She tried to think back to being a sophomore but found nothing. She tried to think about how she felt as a teen, but all that seemed to remain were the pieces she had already recovered: Patty, Delia, Barry, and Jesus.

"What do you do?" Maggie asked her after a long silence.

"Um, I'm between jobs right now," Jenny said.

"Aren't you, like, a model?" Maggie asked, looking up at Jenny with her mouth hanging slightly open.

"No ... but I've done modeling in the past. Why do you ask?"

"I heard ..." Maggie began and then trailed off.

Jenny's pulse jumped. "I'm sorry? What?"

"I heard that you're a model," Maggie said, staring at what Jenny was sure was a fascinating pile of rocks.

Her mouth went dry. She grabbed her water bottle and drank. "Where did you hear that?"

"Guys at school. They said you do, like, modeling online. Are you like a—"

"Listen," Jenny said, trying to hold back the panic rising in her stomach. "Boys—*men*—some of them will say anything about women, especially if they think they're attractive." Maggie nodded. "I don't think that's something you should be thinking about right now."

Maggie shrugged. "I couldn't do it anyway, I'm not pretty enough."

"What? You're gorgeous," Jenny said, only half believing it.

"No, I know what I look like," she said.

Jenny frowned. The girl wasn't a stunner, but what fifteen-year-old was? Everyone was awkward and strange at that age. And if they weren't, Jenny thought their parents were probably putting too much money or energy into prettying up their kids.

"Look, first, none of that matters." *Good*, Jenny thought, *lie to her*. "Second, if you saw me at your age, you'd laugh. I was so insanely awkward."

"That's what nice girls say to make ugly girls feel better," Maggie said. That hit like a punch in the gut.

"No, it's true. I was gawky and weird, and I had terrible acne. And remember the first thing I said, it doesn't matter."

Maggie nodded and plucked a twig from the ground. She started drawing in the dirt. Jenny felt like the gap between her and the teenage girl was widening. Then a thought occurred to her that, even though it hadn't been long ago that she had been Maggie's age, there was something about Jenny's experience that couldn't be conveyed to Maggie, and something about Maggie's experience that couldn't be communicated to Jenny. The things that mattered to Jenny now weren't that different. She wanted to belong, connect, and feel like she had direction and purpose. But her world was so different, her problems so foreign, that Jenny's words meant different things to her than they did to Maggie. Even if she could remember being fifteen, she spoke a different dialect of meaning than the girl in front of her.

Jenny's rumination was cut off when one of the other high school girls walked up, her face gleaming with sweat and afternoon sunlight.

"Hey," Jenny said. "Allie, right?"

The girl shook her head. "Abby."

"Right, sorry. Is everyone back already?"

Abby shook her head. "No, I mean, yeah, but not all of us. The older people are getting ready to do another direction."

"Older people?" Jenny asked before realizing that the girl meant Phil, Leddy, Earl, and Emmett.

"Yeah," she said. "You okay, Mag?" Maggie nodded.

"Are you guys friends?"

"Yeah," Abby said. "Mag, you want to play *Carilo*?"

"*Carilo*?" Jenny asked.

"It's like a battling game."

"Yeah, you want to sit under there?" Maggie said, pointing to a place where the remains of the second floor poked out to offer a little shade. Abby helped Maggie to her feet, and Jenny watched the two girls go off together and pull out their phones. She wondered if she and Leddy had ever done anything like that. How had she filled her time a decade and a half ago? Was she as much of a reader back then as she was now? Had she played video games, watched movies or TV shows, or videos online? She decided to ask Leddy later.

Content that Maggie was occupied, and nursing residual anxiety from her question about her job, Jenny decided to walk over to peer down at the winding course of Evans Creek. Rocky ground sloped down, scattered with small shrubs and sparse pines. Across the creek, stretching off to the north, green and brown grass covered the ground, and the underbrush and trees grew more abundantly and closer together. It was as if the creek were a boundary. Jenny felt like she was on the appropriate side of the stream, where life was scarce, and wondered how she could cross to the other.

Earl sidled up beside her, cracking his knuckles. "I'm fucking beat," he said. His voice was strange.

"Yeah," Jenny said, squinting up at him. "Me too."

"At least we'll get more help tomorrow," he said. His jaw jutted out, and under a low, bunched brow, his eyes gleamed with welling tears. Jenny reached out and touched his arm.

"What's the matter?" Jenny asked.

"They found that girl down near Enterprise," Earl said.

"Is she okay?" Jenny asked, guessing the answer. He just shook his head once. "Fuck," Jenny said.

"God, they didn't have to kill her. Why did they kill her? Why did they kill any of them?"

He sank onto the ground, covered his face, and wept. Jenny knelt next to him and held him as she imagined Aurora's eyes looking up at her in disbelief and terror from the waters of the creek below.

20
Devastation

Friday, August 15, 2025 — Evening

JENNY PUSHED THROUGH THE Timber's heavy front door and found herself surrounded by people filling the waiting area's benches and windowsills. Julie looked up from the hostess booth's computer screen, recognized Jenny, and pointed behind her.

"They're at the bar," Julie said.

"Thanks," Jenny said, once more feeling a little disoriented. She'd been in the Timber enough to recognize Julie, but she didn't think she'd been there long enough for the hostess to pick her out of the crowd of patrons. But her social vertigo was warm, almost fuzzy. Was this the beginning of what she could expect from life in Lightning Falls? She tried to imagine people recognizing her and her recognizing them. The normalcy her imagined picture promised felt like a novelty after Sunrise and her life in California. Maybe she would date Phil, and maybe they wouldn't go anywhere, but she could start to build a nest of friends. Of course that meant being careful with Phil. She couldn't just ghost him and pretend that everything would be okay. However things ended, she'd have to be measured and considered.

Unless he goes crazy on you, she thought. *Then all bets are off.*

Jenny circled the booth and spied Leddy, Phil, Earl, and Emmett standing at the end of the bar. Phil wore dusty, well-fitting jeans, scuffed work boots, and a pale green T-shirt with a faded logo that Jenny didn't recognize. Leddy sported daisy dukes with cowboy boots, a tan T-shirt with a fitness logo across the back, and a trucker hat. They looked like people who put in a hard day's work and were kicking back at a small-town bar. Jenny, on the other hand, felt like she was dressed for a night out in a part of LA that wished it was New York—worn-in but still bright red Chucks, a minuscule jean skirt, and a patterned, black spaghetti-strap tank top that showed bra straps that matched her shoes.

"Holy shit," Phil said as Jenny approached them.

"Hey," Jenny said.

"Don't turn around, Earl, I don't want to lose you to a heart attack," Leddy said.

Earl, wearing a Batman shirt and baggy cargo shorts, turned, raised his eyebrows, and then turned back around, fixing his eyes on the bar.

"Sorry," Jenny said. "I'm not sure what I was thinking."

"You were thinking that you didn't want to pay for a single drink tonight," Leddy said, throwing her arm around Jenny's shoulder. "And *I* am going to ride your coattails."

Jenny laughed and put her arm around Leddy's waist. She felt comfortable, almost familiar.

"Hey," Leddy said, nodding to the front of the bar, "at last, Julie has some competition now."

Jenny shook her head. "I think I might go home and change."

"The hell you will," Leddy said. "Everyone in here is going to think one of us made you do it, and they'll want to kill us. So, for the safety of my family, sit your miniskirt-wearing ass down on that barstool and wait for the drinks to roll in."

Jenny did exactly that, and it took less than a minute before Carl brought her a martini glass with clear liquid inside.

"Vodka martini," Carl said.

"Um, thanks," Jenny said. She stared at him, expecting him to tell her who it was from. He just grinned at her. "I didn't order this," she said.

"On the house. Call it a welcome home drink."

"Carl, she's been here for like two weeks!" Leddy said.

"Yeah, and you've looked familiar, but I didn't place you until you came in for coffee yesterday. I thought I remembered you from the bookstore. And then someone told me who you were, so this is overdue."

"Who told you who I am?" Jenny asked, grateful that the Timber kept its music low in the background, so she didn't have to shout.

"Oh, I don't even remember," Carl obviously lied and then begged off to serve his crowded bar.

"Well, there's drink one," Leddy said.

"It's a welcome home drink," Jenny said, sipping.

"Babe, he doesn't give vodka martinis to farmers when they come back here."

"When farmers leave, they don't come back here," Earl said.

"Carl's all right," Leddy said, holding a green beer bottle between two fingers as she leaned against the bar. "He likes what he likes, but he's not a creep about it."

Jenny turned in her seat, remembered where she was sitting, and crossed her legs. "Can we get a booth or something?" Jenny asked.

"Unlikely," Earl said.

"Phil, go do your thing," Leddy said, pushing her older brother.

"I'm not a dancing slab of sex meat," Phil said, putting on an offended expression.

"No one is telling you to dance, just go over and abuse your power over Julie to make her get us a table."

As Phil walked away, Leddy leaned over to Jenny. "That girl is in love with him. She'd have, like, ten thousand of his babies if he asked."

Jenny held her drink and scanned the bar. Leddy was right, she was catching people's attention. Some were more obvious than others, and some made her want to laugh. Two older men, clearly out to dinner with their wives, kept glancing at her. They didn't stare or give her dirty looks. Instead, she thought the expression on their faces was something like people seeing a UFO or a movie star—not sure they were seeing what they were seeing.

Jenny decided that the women of Lightning Falls should probably try dressing a little sexier every now and then so that one miniskirt didn't blow everyone's damn mind. She thought back to going out in LA and being a nobody in a crowd of gorgeous women. She wasn't sure she was comfortable with either situation.

Phil sauntered back.

"I put us on the list. She's going to see what she can do." He held his hand up to his mouth and blew on his nails before rubbing them on his shirt. Jenny thought it looked like a gesture from an old film.

"Wow, impressive," Earl said. "That girl really is in love with you."

Leddy shook her head at Phil as if he were the family disappointment before turning to scan the bar. "Who can we mooch off of? Shit, girl are your legs crossed?"

"What?" Jenny asked, looking down at her knees which were, in fact, still crossed.

"Every man in this place is looking over here. Look, see those guys?"

Jenny peered across to a booth of six men who were probably in their late twenties. They were certainly paying her a lot of attention, which didn't bother Jenny much. What did bother her was the fact that they were looking over at her, down at their phones, and then back up at her.

"Shit," she whispered as she felt the skin on her legs prickle and her heart rate explode.

"What the fuck is your problem? Stop staring and buy us a drink, assholes!" Leddy yelled, but in a way that made it seem like she was flirting with them.

"Don't—" Jenny said, but it was too late. One of the men got up and walked over. He had dirty blond hair and a week's worth of stubble over a face that looked like it had never lost all of its baby fat.

"Ty," Leddy said as the man approached, "you remember Jenny? You want to buy her a drink?"

He was holding his phone with the screen pressed against his chest. "Yeah, I remember you," he said. Jenny's mouth was bone dry. "Can I ask you a question?"

He had a cockiness about him that Jenny imagined came from a few drinks and the fact that he had his group of friends sitting at the table on the other side of the restaurant. She had seen this kind of empty swagger before, and it never had a good sequel. So, she just stared at him. Leddy put her hand on Jenny's wrist and looked up at her sharply.

"Hey, are you okay?" she asked. Jenny glanced down and saw her pulse jumping under her skin.

"Is this you?" Ty said, a shit-eating smirk cutting across his stubble as he showed her his phone screen. It showed a woman with black, curly hair tied back in a ponytail. Her eyeshadow was bright blue; her cheeks were sprinkled with light freckles. The look on her face was one of overwhelmed pleasure, and her naked body moved in rapid rhythmic sync with the blond man standing in front of her, his elbows under her knees.

"Fuck," Earl said.

"Jenny, what … Is that—" Phil said.

"Fuck you!" Leddy said, grabbing Ty's wrist and twisting it so that he dropped his phone. "Get that shit out of here, what the fuck are you—"

Jenny slid her hand into Leddy's and squeezed. Everything else disappeared as she remembered making the video with Nolan.

"If that's not her, I'm a fucking dog," Ty said, pulling his arm back from Leddy. He picked up his phone and looked at it. "That guy kind of looks like me, doesn't he?"

No, Jenny thought. *No, that man is beautiful, and kind, and giving, and would never hurt anyone.*

Was, said another voice in her head that sounded like Joseph. *He was those things. Now he's not anything.*

Leddy pushed Ty again and then turned to Jenny. They locked eyes and Jenny watched realization dawn on her face.

"Fuck," Leddy said, as the video cut back to Jenny's face. "Fuck, is that you?"

"It was," Jenny said, her voice deceptively calm. "Please put that away."

"Why? It's out there on the internet; anyone can find it."

"There are kids in here," Jenny said.

"Hey!" Carl shouted from down the bar. "Put that away!"

Ty shrugged and turned his screen off. "So, you still making this stuff? You need someone to work with?"

Phil took an awkward step forward. A few years before a man approached her at another bar and had done something similar. She had been so surprised she had no idea what to say to him. But Jenny had had years to think about what she wished she'd said.

"Fifteen dollars," Jenny answered confidently. Ty frowned. "You found my name, I'm sure you found my other site."

"The JustBuffs page? Hell yeah, we did."

"Good, then you know that it's fifteen dollars to chat with me. So, go sign up, and send me a message, and when I get around to it, I'll answer your question."

He frowned at her. "So, you're a whore?"

Phil took another step. Earl put his drink down and stepped up next to him.

"Fuck right off," Leddy said. Suddenly, Ty's friends were up on their feet and moving toward the bar. One of the men had brought his beer bottle with him. Jenny pictured the man bashing Phil with it, and Phil bleeding on the ground.

"Stop!" Jenny shouted, sliding down from her seat. "Yes, okay? I'm a fucking whore. You want to show me your dick? That's ten bucks. You want me to tell you how big it is or how small it is? That's another ten! You want to see my tits, just subscribe. Or you can watch that video over and over. But later, okay? I'm not working tonight. I'm just here hanging out with my friends."

From the look on Leddy's face, Jenny realized that that might no longer be true. She grabbed her purse.

"I don't care what you call me. I've been called everything. So there, now you know. Just subscribe, okay? Everyone who wants to see, just subscribe. I'm going to fucking need it now." She looked around the Timber, everyone was staring at her. From beside one of the dads who had been glancing at her earlier, a familiar face leaned out, mouth gaping. Jenny stared at Maggie and felt herself begin to shake.

"Shit," Jenny finally said, and turned to Leddy who had stepped protectively in front of her. "Let me out." Leddy was frozen, confusion and disbelief knitting her brow. "Let me the fuck out!" Jenny yelled. Finally, Leddy moved, and Jenny pushed past her to storm out of the bar and into the night.

Part II, Question ii, Article 1

Whether the Body and Spirit are One?

Objection 1: God has made each living thing as a soul, body and spirit, in the Hebrew נפש. Thus, the body and spirit are one.

Objection 2: No living thing is made without its spirit; thus, they are one.

Objection 3: No spirit is whole without its body, hence the coming resurrection. Thus, they are one.

I answer that it is clear that the body and spirit are not numerically one, otherwise, we could not say that the spirit continues to live once the body has died. We might instead say that the body and spirit are a whole being, as the various parts of the body, while not numerically one, make up one body. However, unless Augustine is right in his assessment that every particle shall return to our bodies in the resurrection, then it seems that the numerical identity of the body is not integral to the wholeness of the unity formed with the spirit. Indeed, if the body is instead an expression of the spirit, not merely a material union, then God may raise for us wholly new bodies from the earth. And thus, any spirit may be made whole in junction with any body.

Reply 1: No fruit is born without its tree or vine, but the fruit may be plucked and remain whole. Thus, I answer that they are not one.

Reply 2: A thing may be made whole by an equivalent to what is missing from it. Thus, a man may lack food taken from him and be made whole by an equivalent amount of the same kind of food. Therefore, a spirit may be made whole by being given a new body that is not numerically identical to the one it came into being with.

- Mikuláš Vaclavek, The Second Book of Seeings

"Tear from them that which roots the spirit through the spilling of blood in their presence. For through the mind and heart the spirit cleaves most fervently to the flesh."

-Zuzanna Cerny, The Book of Corrections

I
Preparation

Monday, February 24, 1969 - Daytime

IN A CLOUD OF sweet-smelling pipe smoke, Paul Kusel considered his notes one last time, comparing them to the bronze plate by his elbow. Photographs, rubbings, and sketches; the details were all there, but he felt that something was missing from his depictions of the relic. When he enumerated the elements, of course, they all matched. Two bearded men were etched into the bronze—one in chains, the other standing over him, his face marred by a later hammer blow. There were strange symbols—likely an alphabet unfamiliar to him—across the top of the plate. They were simple shapes, some oblong, others diamonds, boxes, or 'X's made from crude lines. A more recognizable—though, to Paul's eye, no less indecipherable—string of cuneiform crossed the plate's bottom. And there, just above the cuneiform, was a scene of a man on a throne or chair with two men flanking him.

This last element was where he felt the deficiency of his representations the strongest. While the rest of the plate bore a craftsman's fine hammer marks, this section was smooth, as if it had been pressed or stamped. His notes included a detailed description of the plate's composition, and he thought he could see a little of the difference in his photographs. But in the photographs, his fingers couldn't feel the change in the surface, or how the metal was strangely warm in that spot alone.

He reached over and brushed the bronze with the tips of his fingers. Yes, even though the plate had been sitting near a cold window, the smooth section near the bottom was still warm. He wondered—not for the first time—if that area was radioactive. He thought of Marie Curie and judged that the possibility should worry him more. But it didn't, and the idea that the plate was dangerous gave way to more practical concerns.

He could bring the plate to Iran, but what would that accomplish? Was there anything the plate could tell him that the photographs, sketches, rubbings, and written descriptions couldn't? He didn't think so. And bringing it with him meant risking its loss. His friend, Levi, had driven that point home repeatedly, for which Paul was grateful. He could not lose the relic, it was the only thing that would prove to others, and himself, that he wasn't insane. So, he opened his top desk drawer and placed the bronze plate carefully inside after wrapping it in its protective cloth.

Paul stood, closed and locked the drawer, and entered the living room. The house was smaller and plainer than the one he had grown up in, but at least it had a working fireplace. He went over to it and grabbed a poker to spread out the dying embers of his last fire for the winter, at least in Lightning Falls. He took one last puff of his pipe, knocked it out into the fireplace, and then dropped it into his pocket.

He piled his notes together with a few small books that he didn't think they'd have in Iran. Negahban, the head of the Archaeology department in Tehran, had studied in Chicago and was reputed to have a respectable library. But Paul would be more than five hours away in Shiraz. The two short volumes by Migdol were unlikely to be in anyone's collection, let alone halfway around the world. So, Paul allowed himself the indulgence of bringing them.

He went over the house one last time, turning off lights and unplugging everything. He ensured the gas range was off and the thermostat was set to fifty. Mr. Baker would be by to check up on things, take in the mail, and make sure the place didn't burn down, but he wanted the man to find it well-situated and for him to think of Paul as the adult he was. Paul hadn't been so sure of Mr. Baker's approval since he lost his job, and he didn't want something as stupid as leaving a window open to further chip away at the man's already eroded esteem for him.

Satisfied with the state of his home, he pulled his overcoat on and locked the front door behind him. One piece of business remained before he could leave for the Lewiston airport. He packed his bag into the back of his car, threw his briefcase into the passenger seat, drove three blocks to the Lightning Falls Library, and parked in an open space. Paul hurried up the stone steps and through the heavy double doors to find a young woman behind the desk peering up at him from a book.

"Good morning, Professor Kusel," she said.

"Good morning, Natalie," he returned. "Is Michael in the back?"

"Yes, professor, he's at his regular station."

Paul smiled his thanks and walked into the library's main room. The walls were hidden behind a crowd of bookcases. He had never been in a more densely packed library. The lack of open space on the first floor often turned him around and gave him the impression that the three-story building was vaster than it was. He mused that the shelves stood so high and close that anyone might imagine the space went on forever. The atrium added to the sense of special disorientation, giving a clear view of the underside of the cupola, three stories above, which sported an art-deco relief of a candle and a book.

As Paul contemplated the confusing arrangement of the shelves, he realized that he had fallen prey to the warren of books. After a moment of wandering, he found himself facing the back wall, where a metal cage encased two bookcases. A small sign read 'Rare Books,' and Paul frowned. The shelves here were the only sparse ones in the building. A collection of perhaps thirty old, dusty volumes stood on otherwise empty shelves. He shook his head and scolded himself for not contributing more to the library's paltry collection. He would have to do something about that when he returned. Perhaps he'd find something in Iran worthy of Lightning Falls' exclusive, little trove.

Mentally mapping his position, he turned left and followed the wall's perimeter until he came to the stairs. They rose to a landing and then doubled back, bringing him to a dark, wooden desk lurking in a dim corner, lit only by a poorly placed ceiling light and two green-shaded lamps. Behind the desk sat a young man with short-cropped, dirty-blond hair. He was hunched over a book and didn't notice his visitor until the man's shadow crossed the paperback's pages that he had weighed down with the ends of two formidable staplers.

"What are you reading, Michael?" Paul asked in a stage whisper, breaking the library's near absolute silence. Michael looked up and grinned. He appeared younger than his twenty years and could have passed as a sophomore in high school. Paul knew his looks didn't do him a lot of favors with the fairer sex, but he thought Michael would be glad of those boyish looks one day.

"Oh, it's ... it's just a horror book." Michael said sheepishly, his hand instinctively sliding over the pages as if he had been caught with a copy of *Playboy*. Kusel smiled and leaned over to look at the text. He squinted and then laughed.

"*Rosemary's Baby*?"

"Uh, yes, that's right," Michael said, looking confused. "How did you know?"

"I read it when it came out. Good book, great movie."

"You like horror?"

"Stories, Michael, are the lifeblood of culture. Without stories, we don't know who we are. Without stories, we don't know what to make of the world. And stories about religion, good and evil, and the devil? Well ... we've been telling those stories forever. Don't let anyone scoff at you for your interests."

"Wow, I ... well, can I ask you something, Professor?"

"When have you known me to decline a question?"

Paul, his flight time forgotten, pulled his pipe from his pocket and clamped it between his teeth. He packed it from a pouch he kept in his other pocket.

Michael smiled. "Never, I guess. Well, this is going to sound silly, but … what do you think about the Antichrist? Do you think he's real?"

"Why do you—Ah, the book! Of course." Paul puffed a little and nodded. "Nero Redivivus!" he said, more loudly than he intended. Reflexively, he glanced around; seeing no one, he chuckled at himself.

"What's that?" Michael asked.

"Nero Redivivus is an old legend that helped shape the idea of the Antichrist. But that's neither here nor there. The core of the idea of the Antichrist is that if the epitome of goodness can come into the world in physical form, then so can the epitome of evil."

"Right. But do you think … you know … is he real?"

"Well, is goodness real?" Paul asked.

"Yes, I believe it is."

"And what is evil then? Does it have its own substance?"

"No, evil is the absence or corruption of good," Michael said.

"Very good. Now, it stands to reason that while it may be that goodness, if conscious and powerful, may take on a physical form, much as we see in Hindu and Christian belief, then we might imagine a corrupted goodness doing the same."

"But wouldn't that be any goodness then?" Michael asked. "What would make an antichrist … you know, so … so—"

"So ultimate, perhaps? Well, that is the crux, isn't it? If Christianity is correct and ultimate goodness has taken on crude materiality, what would it be like if ultimate evil did the same?"

"It couldn't," Michael said.

"Why?"

"Because ultimate evil would be nothingness. To exist, something must be at least a little good."

Paul beamed at Michael. "Quite right! Thus, whatever exists is at least a little good, so there can be no true parallel between the idea of the divine entering the world—either through avatar or incarnation—and evil doing the same. Indeed, if evil did so, either no one would notice, or whatever it entered would simply cease to be."

"So, you don't think there can be an antichrist?" Michael asked.

"Well, not precisely," Paul said. "In every generation, the idea of evil works itself out in available and possible extremities. Those who are corrupted in some great way can still retain many aspects of what is good: intelligence, charisma, fortitude, wisdom. I daresay I've seen a few in my lifetime. Doesn't Saint John say there are many antichrists? There have been many, and I guess there will be many more if we don't obliterate ourselves in nuclear fire."

"But there can't be one ultimate one?" Michael said.

"Hm, if you mean, will there be one supernaturally powerful son of Satan that rules over the earth … well"—he laughed again—"I'll stay agnostic on that point. But if I were a betting man, I'd say that the odds are against it."

Michael smiled, clearly relieved by the learned man's confidence about the situation. Paul, however, while he smiled avuncularly at the college student, thought how silly the conversation was. He knew no more of the universe's workings than Michael and had seen no more of the engine that drove it. He knew they were both in the dark and knew that the difference between them was that Michael thought enlightenment came with age. Paul knew better.

The clock behind Michael's chair caught Paul's eye and brought him back to more immediate matters.

"I'd love to stay and chat about the vagaries of the concept of evil, but I do have a plane to catch," he said, patting the top of the reference desk. "Time to wing away to the land of Cyrus!"

"Right!" Michael said, "Of course, I have the research. I wasn't able to do as much as I wanted, but I think it will be helpful."

"Excellent."

Michael reached into a cubby area in the reference desk and pulled out a manilla folder stuffed with papers.

"Those are my handwritten notes, I tried to be neat. There's a bibliography there as well, just names and titles since I was working fast. I also put some articles and book names down that I wasn't able to get a hold of in time. I'm going to put in requests for those, so I can probably mail you them while you're away."

"No need for that, you can keep them here for me until I get back. This is excellent work, Michael. I trust that all of this will be useful." The older man took the folder and gave its contents a cursory glance. After a polite nod, he stowed the research in his briefcase. "So, what will you do with the rest of your semester, other than researching old Median kings and holding back the ravening hordes who demand knowledge?" Here he waved his hand at the silent library.

"Well, I can usually do both at the same time," Michael said. "One hand on my buckler, the other on the notepad, as it were."

"Very good, Michael," Paul chuckled.

"But, if I'm being honest, I think I might ask Natalie out on a date."

Kusel leaned in and touched the side of his nose. "Careful, m'boy, workplace romances rarely work. Especially when you come from such different worlds."

"We do?" Michael asked, concern sketched across his face.

"Oh yes, she's a check-out sort, and you're a reference sort. Quite different. One stays, one goes."

Michael pondered this until his concern morphed into mildly confused amusement. The change took longer than Paul would have thought.

"Very good, Professor," he said. From the tone in his voice, he still wasn't entirely sure if his mentor was joking.

"Seriously though, she's a lovely young woman. She's what, only a year or two younger than you?"

"Yeah, we're about a year and a half apart."

"Well, not so different worlds then. But the advice about workplace romances stands. Tread carefully there. Now," he said, making a show of looking at his watch, "I must away! Have a good rest of term, Michael. Take care of yourself."

"You too, Professor!" Michael said, standing and offering his hand.

They shook before Paul took his briefcase and wound his way back to the front of the library.

"Didn't find anything you wanted, professor?"

"Oh, not today, Natalie," Kusel said. "I'd never get back in time to avoid the late fees."

"Oh? Are you going on a trip?" she asked, twisting a pen between her fingers. She batted her eyelashes at him in a way that he wasn't sure was entirely innocent.

"I—Well, yes, I'm flying to Iran today. That's old Persia. I'll be participating in an archaeological dig there."

"Really?" she said, rising a little in her seat. "That's so interesting! I'd love to hear about that!"

"Well, I'd love to tell you, but unfortunately, I must be on my way, otherwise I'll miss my flight. But I'll bring you back something if you'd like that."

"I would, very much," she said, flashing him a bright and toothy smile.

"Well, I'll see what I can do," he said before wrenching himself from the conversation. He gave her a little wave and then patted the check-out desk. Then he was off, pushing his way through the front door, preparing to whistle a little tune in celebration of the young woman's smile, something that he, a little rounder than he'd like, with gray starting to show in his beard, knew would become rarer and rarer. He longed to be young again, but who didn't? Of course, his own youth hadn't been particularly happy. But he would like to go back, knowing what he knew now. He was in the process of both envying Michael the years before him and wishing him good fortune when he bumped into a tall, darkly dressed figure.

Paul would have fallen and likely torn his pants if the big man had not reached out and steadied him. Long, powerful fingers wrapped around his shoulders and held him upright.

"Levi! My goodness, I almost knocked you over!"

Levi Grossman laughed and shook his head. "I think it was the other way around."

Grossman was tall, lean, and wore a heavy beard, though it wasn't wild like Paul had seen hippies wear theirs. Instead, Levi was a man out of the 19th century, with thick eyebrows over stormy, intense eyes. He still wore suits wherever he went.

"You're right. I wasn't looking where I was going, head in the clouds."

"Oh? Are you in love, professor?" A girl's voice startled him. Standing behind Grossman, wearing a long skirt with a blouse buttoned to the neck, a narrow belt, and a small red brooch, was a girl of perhaps fifteen or sixteen years. Her hair was long, and her almost alabaster white face was unadorned by makeup. At first, he didn't recognize her, but then, after a moment, a smile leapt to his face.

"Georgina? Is that you?"

The girl curtsied.

"My goodness, you're all grown up! Where have you been hiding? I haven't seen you since, what, Harry's ninth birthday party!"

"She has been studying," Levi said, looking down at her with pride. "You may find yourself with a new colleague in a few years, professor."

"Well, that would be wonderful!" Kusel said. "Where have you been stu—"

"She has tutors," Grossman said, putting his hand on Kusel's shoulder. "I'm actually glad we ran into you. I wanted to make sure you had everything for your trip."

"Yes, yes, I'm all set up. I just needed to pick up some research Michael did for me. I'm heading to the airport now."

"Well, please, don't let me keep you."

"I wanted to say thank you, Levi, for giving me this opportunity. I know that my career hasn't been of particular note up until—"

"No," Grossman said, raising his hand, "you know the honor is mine. We're friends. Besides, the work you're doing ... Georgina, Mr. Kusel has made an incredible discovery. You should see the bronze plate he discovered in Europe."

"I would very much like to see it," Georgina said.

"I—Well, of course, when I return, I will bring it by the house, Levi. But, hopefully, by then I'll have found more than just the plate."

"Indeed!" the tall man said. "Now, we won't keep you. Go with God." Grossman held out his hand and Paul shook it. "Also, do make sure to wire me if you need anything. All right?"

"Yes, of course, my friend," Paul said. He tipped his hat to Georgina and started toward his car.

The young woman reached out and put her hand on his arm. "Professor," she said, smiling up at him. "One thing. And I'm sorry if this seems foolish. I'm not a foolish person, I promise."

He shook his head and returned her smile. "Of course not. But please, I must be going, so—"

"I ... I had a dream, and I didn't know what it meant. Maybe it's nothing, but maybe ... Anyway, not to take more of your time than I need to. I dreamed of a cave, and the ceiling was falling down. And I saw two openings. One was plain, and the other had a carving next to it. I thought it might be a lion. I'm scared of lions, so I jumped through the hole without the lion, and I was safe. And I knew, you know how you know things in dreams with no real explanation? Well, I knew that if I had gone to where the lion was, I would have died."

Paul stared at her, taking in her words.

"I know, I must seem silly, but I promise that I'm not. Perhaps it will never mean anything, but since you're going to a strange land, maybe it will mean something. And I'd never forgive myself if I hadn't told you because I was ashamed of how I'd appear."

Paul put his hand on her shoulder. "Thank you, Georgina. That was very brave, and I appreciate it. I hope that it isn't anything more serious than that you've seen too many movies. But who can say?"

He smiled once more, nodded to his friend, turned, and hurried to his car.

THE PLANE RUMBLES AROUND Paul as he reads handwritten notes and imagines a world long gone. The names are unfamiliar to a scholar of Germanic archaeology. He knows Wotan, not Inshushinak. Michael's neat timelines pull him back across ages to a people who had a writing system thousands of years earlier than the helms of Negau. He feels half-mad with discovery, anxiety, and possibility. He wonders if he will ever receive recognition for his groundbreaking work or if he will disappear in the darkness of obscurity.

II
Wonderful

Monday, March 3, 1969 - Daytime

"THEY DUG THIS FASTER than I would have thought possible," Paul said. Light slanted in behind him and a tall, lean man as they descended a steep, narrow shaft in the rocky Iranian soil.

"Well, I was told that time was of the essence. These men are experienced, efficient, and, best of all, cheap!" Vincent Millich said, patting one of the wooden support beams.

"Fantastic. Do you sink many shafts like this?"

"No, not generally," Vincent said. "We like to take our time, but with the word and money coming down from on high, I got a recommendation from Leibniz—"

"The philosopher?" Paul joked.

"Yes, I think the old fellow is better than three hundred years old now," Vincent chuckled. "No, but I think he may be a distant relative, actually. Anyway, he did some work here last year and used them. He gave me names, and a village, and I got to finding them."

"Well, they do fast work," Paul said, studying roots that poked out from the dirt above.

"You're more of a northern European man?" Vincent asked.

"Germany, mostly," Paul said.

"Interesting, is Kusel a German name?"

"No, Czech, by way of Americanization, but my ancestors lived in Germany for a while."

Vincent appeared to ponder this as they reached the end of the shaft. The tunnel revealed a five-by-six-foot area of hewn stones fitted together to form a wall with a low door. The entrance was sealed by smaller, rougher, darker stones piled on top of each other.

"Amazing," Paul said. "Utterly amazing."

"I must know," Vincent said, "how did you conclude that this was here? And how did you convince someone to pay me to dig it? Of course, I'm always happy for the funding, but you must admit it's a bit rum."

"Hm?" Paul said as he ran his hand over the ancient stone.

"Come now, don't pretend this isn't highly irregular," Vincent said. Paul detected both amusement and curiosity. "We planned, budgeted, and received approval. You know the standard song. I've done six digs now, and I've never gotten a wire telling me to hire men and sink a shaft post haste, as if 'X' were marking the spot."

"But you did it," Paul said, tracing the space between two stones.

"Of course I bloody well did," Vincent said, laughing. "Maybe your coffers are overflowing in America, but we're practically besieged for funding anywhere that isn't the Holy Land, or Greece, or Rome."

Paul nodded and grunted.

"So, you must tell me how you did it, and how you knew that if we dug here, precisely here, that we'd find this spot."

"You wouldn't believe me if I told you," Paul said, turning to the taller man.

"Oh dear, it didn't come to you in a dream, did it? I had a grandmother who dreamt the future. It was the most dreadfully unnerving thing."

"Not a dream," Paul half-lied. "I found something where it shouldn't be, and it led me here."

"In Germany?" Vincent said.

"That's right," Paul said. "In Germany. Bronze age site near Luhe. A bronze tablet with cuneiform. Elamite cuneiform, I'm told."

"That's impossible," Vincent said.

"I know. I've been told that as well. Several times," Paul said. "Have you photographed this yet?"

"Yes, first thing once they cleared it. We're ready to start removing the stones. But, since I was told to afford you every possible courtesy, I thought you might want to do the honors."

After establishing a spot to put the stones and keep them in order, Paul and Vincent began to remove the smaller rocks that blocked the door until there was a space large enough to shine a flashlight through.

"Here, take my torch," Vincent said, passing Paul his flashlight. "And be my guest."

Paul held the light to the opening, peered inside, and sighed.

"What do you see, old boy?"

"Wonderful things," Paul said. "Wonderful things."

Vincent laughed politely and said, "Indeed."

ii

PAUL STUDIES THE PHOTOGRAPHS of the plate. The shadows from the flash etch deep lines into the figures and the markings along the top and bottom, showing some features in detail, and obscuring others in darkness. Photographs without the flash show less detail, but they are less distorted as well. He longs to understand who the men are. Their dress tells him nothing, simple cloth draped over one shoulder and hung to the knee. Their beards are long but unadorned. Only the strange markings at the top suggest to him that the men might still be identified.

He pinches at the space between his eyes as the wind tugs at his tent. He is eager, and he doesn't think he will be able to sleep tonight. He wants to go down, to see the structure, to begin to catalog its treasures. There are too many hours until daylight.

III
In Situ

Monday, March 3, 1969 – Late Evening

AT THE BOTTOM OF the shaft, Paul rechecked the gas detection tubes and was satisfied that the air in the chamber was safe. It certainly wouldn't do if Vincent woke up in the morning to find his strange, new colleague dead from asphyxiation in the middle of the chamber. He hefted his pack and flashlight, swished his canteen, and took a deep breath. He knew he shouldn't do this. He knew he should just wait until morning and go in with Millich. But he couldn't help himself. His vindication was here, right here in front of him. He would just go in, look around, take a few pictures, and then return to his tent. He wouldn't touch anything. It would be like he was never there.

"Couldn't sleep, old boy?" Paul jumped at the sound of Millich's voice. "Yes, me either."

"I'm sorry, I wasn't going to … Well, that's a lie. I was going to go in," Paul said, sheepishly. "But I promise, I wasn't going to—"

Vincent put up a hand and shook his head. He was smiling. "I don't blame you. What do you think I'm doing down here? We're just two rascals catching each other in the act of stealing biscuits from the jar."

"I guess so," Paul said. "Then, well, what do you say? Shall we steal the biscuits together?"

"If by steal, you mean we'll have a good look without disturbing anything, then … well, yes, especially if it means I get some sleep tonight. This blasted chamber isn't letting me get a wink. And that's unusual for me." Paul offered Vincent his hand and they shook. "A villain's pact," Vincent said, and they both laughed. "Ms. Abimbola will have my head. She's a stickler for procedure. And, of course, usually I am as well, but— Well, what am I going on about? After you, sir."

Paul smiled, turned, and ducked under the door.

The room that met them was awash in gold, silver, and copper. Animal shapes carved from stone or molded from clay appeared under their roving lights. Drinking vessels, figurines, tablets, and other less recognizable objects cluttered stone shelves and benches. Four alcoves were carved into the side walls—two on each side. Each had an arched top, and next to each was ensconced a silver figure about the size of a hand.

"It's astonishing," Kusel said, running his fingers through the air above a stone bench covered with clay tablets and golden ornaments. "A burial chamber?"

"Perhaps, I don't see a coffin or urn or—"

"Did they bury their dead in coffins?" Paul asked, scanning the contents of a shelf.

"Some did. There are strange, U-shaped things, they look like baths. Hard to miss. Of course. Anything might be in an adjoining chamber." He knelt next to a shelf to study a tablet. "Some of this is Akkadian, some of this is Elamite."

"Oh?" Kusel asked, lifting his camera from around his neck and snapping a picture of the bench and its contents.

"Looks like administrative tablets, official records …"

"Of what?"

"Let me see … I'm just doing sight reading, and there are some words I don't know—" Vincent said.

"I understand," Kusel said with a chuckle.

"Right, here we are. On the fifth day of the month of Tammuz in the first year of the reign of King Humban-Nikash—"

Paul shut his eyes and tried to remember his notes. "That's around 740."

"Very good. Seven-forty-three BC," Millich said, clearly impressed. Paul opened his eyes and watched the man scan the text, his finger hovering over the tablet. "Sorry, some of this is just beyond my sight-reading. There's something here about an emissary from a mighty king. Ah! Ah!" Millich stood, put his hands on his hips, and laughed. "It's a list of animals slaughtered in honor of the emissary."

"Interesting," Kusel said, taking another picture. "What other years are listed on the documents?"

"Well, this is fortunate," Millich said after studying the opening lines of several of the clay tablets. "I think we can tentatively date this chamber to the first year of Humban-Nikash. Perhaps even just to the month of Tammuz. It's probably not a storehouse or a records room, there would be more variation in the dates. These are all the same. Of course, we'll have to see."

Paul pointed his flashlight toward the far end of the room. Two doors stood at either end of the back wall, and a relief stood between them. The relief showed a bearded man walking toward a group of soldiers, holding two vessels in his outstretched hands. The warriors appeared to guard another, heavily bearded and adorned man in a chariot.

"That's likely to be Humban-Nikash," Vincent said, pointing to the man in the chariot. "And that is likely the emissary whose visit this chamber was built to honor. He's bringing gifts to the king."

"What's wrong with his eyes?" Paul said, shining his light on a patch of ruined stone.

"It looks like someone struck them out. Look there, on the ground, those are the very pieces! Astonishing." His voice rose and fell in an arc of awe that tapered off into a whisper.

Paul went to the door that stood to the left of the relief. Just beyond the door to the left, another alcove dipped into the wall. To the right, a passage ran along the back of the relief. Paul could see Vincent's light peering through the other door, revealing another alcove. Paul frowned and looked from one side of the relief wall to the other and concluded that it was one big room with six alcoves, not four, and that the wall must be decorative. He tried his idea with Vincent.

"Perhaps, but it could be a ritual division of holy spaces. It may be that we are, by crossing the limits of this wall, entering into a more sacred space."

Paul nodded. "Then, shall we?"

"As long as the path is open, we will continue. The moment we meet resistance though—"

Paul held up a hand and nodded.

They went through their respective doorways and met in the middle of the passage. They stood between the chamber's real back wall and the carved dividing wall. In the middle of what Paul thought of as the genuine back of the chamber, stood another walled-up door. To their right, the back of the decorative wall depicted another scene in relief.

"What is this?" Vincent asked, shining his light over the stone.

"A man being taken away in chains," Paul said.

"Is it the emissary? I think it is, look, he is wearing the same dress, and his beard is not platted the way the rest are."

"The armor and weapons are different, though," Paul said. "Different soldiers maybe? And look, I thought the emissary was wearing something on his head. This man isn't. Different men?"

"Perhaps," Vincent said. "I expect the tablets will tell us more of the story."

They studied the relief for a minute until Paul turned his attention to the walled-up door. As his light played over the ancient stone, he drew in a sharp breath.

"Vincent, look at this!"

The Englishman turned and stood next to Paul.

"What on earth?" Vincent said.

"This plate. I've seen one just like it before. It's what led me here."

In the circle of Paul's light, on a small stone shelf next to the door, rested a bronze plate about a foot tall. It depicted two men standing beside each other, with chains next to the second man's feet.

"Look there," Paul said, pointing to a second shelf on the other side of the door. "My God, this is where the plate comes from. How on earth did it end up in Germany?"

"This is astonishing, I—" Vincent began, but his words died as he looked up. "My Lord, Paul … this is impossible."

"What?" Paul said, looking up to where the Englishman was shining his light. Above the door, a row of deep divots with strange boxy characters were carved into the stone. It took Paul a moment to recognize them as the same writing that ran along the top of his bronze plate.

"This … this is Proto-Elamite," Vincent stammered.

"Oh?" Paul asked.

"Yes," Vincent's voice was barely audible. "This is impossible," he repeated.

"Why?" Paul asked.

Vincent took a moment, swallowed, and opened his mouth. Still, another minute passed before he could speak. "Well, first, there are no examples of Proto-Elamite carved into stone. None. It is known only from tablets. Second, it stopped being used two thousand years or so before the room we're standing in was built."

"What?" Paul asked, pushing closer to look at the pale stone and its impressions. "Are you certain?"

The Englishman nodded slowly. "Yes, as certain as I can be." He raised his camera and took a picture, then, moving slightly to the left, he took another. "This is … this is astonishing. This is … Paul, this is unbelievable. This is genuinely unprecedented." He turned to the American and slapped him on the shoulder. "If this means what I think it does, we may be standing outside one of the most ancient man-made locations on Earth."

Paul frowned. "How do you know that it's not more recent, you know? Middle Elamite? Neo?"

"They just didn't use this writing system by then. It was all cuneiform. Hell, I doubt they could have read it by twenty-one hundred BC, which is when you get your first stone inscriptions from this area."

"What does it say?"

Vincent laughed. "I have no idea! No one does. We can't read this yet. But this ... the presence of Proto-Elamite in situ with Neo ... somewhere in here, Paul! Somewhere in here might be the Rosetta Stone of Proto-Elamite! Think of it. All we need is one inscription on these tablets to refer to the inscription on this lintel ... Dear God, what a find!"

Paul's heart swelled with the possibilities. "What's beyond the door?" he asked rhetorically.

"Whatever it is—I mean, it might be—It could be anywhere from forty-seven hundred to five-thousand years old. For this, we absolutely need to take our time and do everything in proper order. Let's start getting this room documented and photographed."

"Surely we're not going to wait until this whole room is—"

"Oh no, no, certainly not. But we need our people down here, doing the work. There is too much here for just you and me and Ms. Abimbola. We'll need to talk to Negahban and let him know what we've found. He'll have some good people who can help us. Once we get that in order, we'll open this room, I assure you."

Vincent stepped back and rubbed his balding head. "Good God, there goes any hope of sleep tonight." Vincent sighed. "All right, well, I suppose I should rouse Ms. Abimbola, she'll want to see this. She'll be exceedingly cross at me for this little excursion, but I suspect this will assuage her wrath. Golly."

Paul stared at the stones that filled the doorway. He felt pulled to go in, to go beyond the door into what might be the most sacred space in the structure. He wanted to batter the wall down and, if Vincent hadn't been there, he might have. But he was grateful for the check on his eagerness. He might have been a man beset by troubles, but he was still an archaeologist, not some grave robber. He swallowed.

"All right," Paul said. "Let's get your assistant and some of the workers. I won't be able to sleep either."

iii

PAUL SITS WITH COFFEE in his hands looking at the sky to the east. Pegasus reaches up from the horizon across the pre-dawn firmament, as men move lights and materials behind him. Mercury floats just above the ground to his right, and he wonders what the people who built the structure below him thought about the wanderer closest to the sun. He knows little of their mythology and none of their language. He knows that were it not for the writing on the wall, madness might be a perfectly acceptable explanation for the connections he's made. Even with that writing, his road to convincing others will be long. But as he sips from the tin cup, waiting for the dawn, he feels like he's part of something bigger than himself for the first time since he marched across Europe to push back a tide of darkness.

IV
Toast Them

Wednesday, March 5, 1969 - Evening

FIRE LIT PAUL'S FACE and throat. He had no idea what the tart alcohol was made from, but it burned in a way he was getting used to. The unnamed spirit seemed specifically designed to bolster its drinker from the cold Iranian night. He tilted the bottle down and made a face. Farhang, the chief digger, laughed expansively, and Paul handed the bottle to his left.

"And you?" Paul managed around a cough.

Gail took the drink and shook her head. Though the fire cast deep shadows onto her eyes, and lines into her cheeks when she smiled, Paul decided there was no light in which she could not have as easily been a model in Paris as an archaeologist.

"Never," she said, laughing with the digger. Her accent was strange to Paul, a mixture of upper crusty English with a hint of something else. He didn't know much about the Yoruba people or Nigeria, but Gail made him want to learn all he could.

"Professor?" she asked after taking a drink, making her own face, and handing the bottle to Vincent.

"Twice," Vincent said. "Once, on my first dig. There was a woman who lived in town, this was near Persepolis. She plied the most ancient of trades." Paul chuckled and Gail snorted.

"Certainly, that is not the most ancient of trades," Farhang said in a thick accent, also with a hint of the Queen's English.

"Oh?" Paul said, watching the man take his own hearty swig.

"Surely coin-minter is before prostitute," Farhang said.

Paul frowned at this and opened his mouth to reply, but then shrugged. "I think you may have something there," he said, taking the bottle.

"I would have thought digging was older than both," Gail said. "How long have your people been digging, Farhang?"

He winked at her, shaking his head back and forth and smiling. He was missing his top left lateral incisor, but otherwise his smile was one of the most disarmingly attractive expressions Paul had ever seen. Paul felt no sexual desire for the man, but there was a beauty in his face when smiling that drew the archaeologist in. Feeling the effects of the drink, Paul realized he hadn't expected to be surrounded by such relentless beauty of landscape, history, and people.

"We have always been diggers," he said. "Since Cyrus! Since Darius! We dig!"

"My goodness," Gail said.

"Fantastic," Paul said.

"Oh, nonsense," Vincent said. They all laughed, Farhang the loudest.

The sound of his laughter echoed across the dark open land, reverberating off ruined columns and half-buried walls under a nearly full moon and star-crowded sky. Their fire, respectable but restrained, painted their faces gold and red as they rocked back in their mirth.

"So, you paid a prostitute near Persepolis," Gail said, shaking her head as Vincent drank. He lowered the bottle and passed it to Farhang.

"No, I didn't pay her, she took me into her bed without charge. I believe I was something of an exotic to her. I was collaborating with the Italians then, and I think she found them … undesirable."

Gail snorted.

"The second time was four years ago at Susa. She was a widow. I believe she loved me."

"And the great English Archaeologist deigned to allow her to love him?" Gail said.

"No, I believe she took pity on me. You see, my wife had just died eight months earlier and—"

"My goodness, Professor, I didn't know," Gail said.

"I'm sorry, my friend. May she be worthy of heaven," Farhang said. Paul was silent.

"Well, she had been ill for many years. I would have stayed home, of course, but she insisted that I go and work. She promised that if I didn't continue my teaching and expeditions, she wouldn't survive a month. She knew I must have a life after she … well. She knew I must have one and that inventing one from thin air would have been impossible for me. I would have simply followed after her."

Gail reached over and squeezed the tall man's hand. Paul marveled at how beautiful her dark skin was against Vincent's light.

"Anyway, my wife, Anna, she endured for six long years, but she finally succumbed in '65. I was nearly done for anyway, despite her efforts to ensure I endured the blow. I tried to lose myself completely in my work." He stared into the fire for a long moment. "And, in that dark time, Mehri was kind to me. I believe she saved my life."

"Where is she now?" Paul asked, afraid he knew the answer from the look in Vincent's eyes.

"I don't know," Vincent lied.

Paul took the bottle from Farhang and lifted it. "Well then, to Anna and Mehri."

Vincent stared at him strangely, his face inscrutable in the dancing firelight.

"I—" Paul said, looking around awkwardly. "I'm sorry, I shouldn't have—"

"No," Vincent said. "Toast them. Perhaps they are laughing with each other about me out there. I don't mind that thought a bit." He gestured vaguely to the dark beyond their little fire. Paul gazed out into the night and shivered, picturing his own lost family standing in the shadows, laughing at him. They each drank to the women who had loved Vincent, and Paul watched the glassy-eyed man in the firelight and wondered how he would endure so terrible a loss. Of course, he realized, he must have something of great value to suffer so great a loss. And Paul had nothing of his own of such value, except perhaps his work.

The conversation wandered awkwardly for a few minutes before Farhang talked of his daughters, his love of whittling wood, and his adoration for the Beatles. In this last, Paul joined him. Gail and Vincent said that they preferred others, with Vincent praising Cream and lamenting their farewell, and Gail telling them about a band called 'Tyrannosaurus Rex,' which none of them had ever heard of. She, tipsy, sang a bit of one of their songs about a swan and, though they all thought she was exceedingly lovely and had a wonderful voice, she won none of them over to her musical tastes.

When the fire faded and they decided not to feed it further, they returned to their tents. Farhang and Paul walked together, arms over each other's shoulders, looking up at the stars and marveling at the fact that across the ages their people had wandered under the same lights and dreamed different dreams. As they walked through the dark camp, Paul tried to focus on the man's magnificent smile instead of peering out into the ghost-haunted darkness.

iv

PAUL SITS ON STONE quarried thousands of years ago and leans against a pillar built when Rome was a backwater. He studies the even brickwork of a wall a hundred feet to the north and speculates about the lives of the men who dug the mud, shaped the bricks, set them in the sun to dry, and laid them. He picks a single brick and tries to conceive of the day it was laid in its course. Who had laid that one brick? What had the men eaten? What did they laugh about? Did anyone remember that day, or was it lost almost immediately, with only a course of bricks to mark it? His fingers stretch and contract, as if to remind him that there is still life in him, that his story is not yet lost to the relentless turning of the earth, the wheeling of the stars, and the rising of the sun.

V
Roaring

Thursday, March 6, 1969 - Morning

"THERE!" PAUL ALMOST SHOUTED in Vincent's ear, ignoring the minor throbbing in his head from the previous night's drink. The swell of affection for his companions, the contemplation of time and its myriad mysteries, and the melancholy consideration of past losses all receded as the circle of Vincent's light revealed a low stone bench upon which a half-dozen items lay. One was a clay tablet, another a bulbous sculpture, and another a silver bowl. Among them glinted a round, palm-sized silver disk.

"My God," Vincent said. "What is it? Not a tomb, I think. It's too empty."

They stood at the doorway in the back of the first chamber and stared through a space they had cleared together, the discarded bricks stacked neatly on the ground beside them. After their first expressions of amazement, they were silent as they moved their lights left and right and up and down.

"How old do you think?" Paul asked.

"That pot certainly looks early. I can't see what kind of animal it is—"

A week earlier Paul might have asked what he meant. Now, after a crash course in Elamite archaeology, he knew that the old Elamites had been prolific crafters of painted animal-shaped pots.

"That tablet ... no, I won't venture to guess until I can see it up close, but see those little pits, like someone pressed in with the end of a dowel, not a reed? That's not cuneiform. No ... no I can't say that for sure, not yet. But, oh Paul, this is astonishing."

Paul agreed. They had, as best they could until some of the textiles were sent to the lab, dated the outer chamber to within a year of 743 BC. It was possible, perhaps likely, that they were standing in a room no one had occupied for more than 2,700 years. And they were standing outside a chamber that may have been empty for almost twice that long.

"What is that?" Paul asked, his light tracing along the inner chamber's floor. Millich turned his own light to the spot and squinted.

"Markings of some kind. Does that look like stone to you? I mean, yes, it's stone of course, but does it look worked?"

"No, other than the carvings, no. Look how rough it is." Paul said, moving his beam around as far as he could, "I think that it's a natural cave of some kind. Perhaps an ancient religious site that they adorned?”

Millich nodded silently as he traced the markings away from the bench and toward the far wall.

“That looks like it might be natural stone as well,” Vincent said. “I wonder—Wait now, is that an opening? Yes, look there, what do you think?”

Something in Paul's chest tightened and he felt sweat bloom on his forehead. “Yes?” he said, reaching his free hand to his chest. God, his heart was thundering. “It looks like a hole, maybe, four feet high? What do you think for the chamber? Twenty feet long?”

“No more than twenty-five, surely,” Vincent said. “Perhaps that's a tunnel that goes further in.” His voice betrayed an ever-growing excitement. “There may be an entire complex beyond that room.”

“Or,” Paul said, trying to breathe slowly, afraid that they were both going to let themselves get carried away, “maybe it's only an alcove like the ones out here.”

“Perhaps,” Vincent said. “But I'll wager my boots there's at least one more chamber, beyond that hole. I think this may be a tomb after all.”

“You think we'll find someone in that hole?” Paul asked, losing the battle against the pounding in his chest. His voice felt choked, and his head swam. Had they missed something with the gas tubes?

“Ms. Abimbola,” Vincent called. “Yes, Professor?” she answered from beyond the dividing wall.

“Can you go up and get me a fresh notebook? I want to record the work on this second chamber separately.”

“Of course, professor. Is it promising?”

“We shall see,” he said. Paul heard her boots on the stone floor, but paid little attention; he was too transfixed by the ancient cave and worried by the tightness in his chest.

“This is a moment we'll never forget,” Vincent said, slapping Paul on the back. “They'll write about this for decades.”

The unforgettable moment shared by the two archaeologists was cut short by the sound of two workers coming down the shaft. The archaeologists stepped back from the door into the space they had dubbed ‘the Dividing Hall.’ Paul thought it was a rather grand name for a narrow passage, but it would look good on a diagram. They went to opposite sides of the decorative wall and watched the men emerge into what they now called ‘the Entrance Chamber,’ which Paul thought was somewhat less grand than the room deserved. But, he mused, when he was the head of his next dig, he could name all the rooms.

One of the workers called out "*Ra'is*," their word for Vincent, the other pushing the wheelbarrow laden with lanterns, water, and tools. Paul's first thought upon seeing them was that they had impeccable timing. They had thirsty work ahead, and they were too impatient to leave off for something as mundane as a drink. His second thought was that the wheelbarrow sounded much louder than it should. He mused that it was unnatural for it to rumble so thunderously a moment before the first cloud of dust emerged from behind the diggers. A second later, the dim light from the shaft disappeared entirely and Millich was yelling for the men to get away from the entrance.

Before darkness swallowed the chamber, Paul's mind caught the scene as if taking a flash photograph. The look of surprise and dread on the men's faces, the plume of dust and dirt reaching out behind them, like the blast of artillery fire, and the command and poise of Vincent Millich waving the men toward him. Then black, but for their flashlight beams.

Madly, Paul thought of a paratrooper named Jimmy Gorman diving as a detonating building spit brown and gray clouds in every direction. The debris had fallen everywhere except on Jimmy, like an angel had sheltered him under the dome of its wings.

"Cover!" Vincent yelled. He dove into the alcove at his end of the Dividing Hall. Paul turned to leap into his own and noticed a detail he had missed in his excitement over the chamber. The silver shape embedded next to his alcove was that of a lion with its mouth open in an expansive roar.

Paul felt dizzy. Georgina's words outside of the Lightning Falls Library came back to him as another thunderclap sent stones hurling through the room and smashing into walls and several of the artifacts.

"For the love of God, get in there!" Vincent cried. "You'll be crushed!"

Paul shook his head and ran past the alcove into the Dividing Hall. He skidded to a stop in front of the walled-up door. Another boom shook the room.

"Vincent, come to me! We have to get through here!"

Paul threw his shoulder into the bricks. The first two courses fell inward with a clatter.

Vincent's light streaked up and illuminated the doorway. Paul stepped out again and slammed his body into the loose bricks once more. They collapsed inward and he fell into the ancient chamber. His flashlight skittered from his hand as he sprawled onto a floor carved by millennia of water flowing under what was now a desert.

Paul lay in a pile of rubble and dust. His flashlight pointed off to his right. He looked back and saw Vincent's hazy beam wave back and forth before it rose again, giving Paul the impression that Vincent was leaving his hiding place and moving toward him. *Thank God*, he thought. *Thank God, we'll be—*

Then thunder tore through the chamber, deafening Paul, as a new cloud erupted from the doorway, and Vincent's light disappeared.

Paul lay curled up in the dust for perhaps five minutes, waiting for the ceiling to collapse in on him. Twice he heard crashes that he thought would be his end, but neither affected the ancient chamber. His mind turned over the horrors of the antechamber. At least three men were dead, perhaps more in the shaft. Had Gail gotten out? Three men, perhaps more, who had woken up this morning with no expectation that this would be their last day on earth, lay crushed behind him. He wanted to vomit, but he didn't let himself. He let himself cry, however, partly because he knew he couldn't help it, and partly to clear his eyes of some of the grit that was starting to settle around him.

When the five minutes passed, Paul felt something coursing through him. It was familiar and unfamiliar, old and new. It had slumbered for over twenty-five years, but his days as a soldier awakened in his older, decidedly flabbier professorial frame. He saw Vincent standing like an officer, calling his men to him. He didn't know if the man had fought in the Second World War, but the way he had cried 'Cover!' made Paul think that explosions had not been entirely novel to the man. Paul thought of him, crushed, and pushed himself to his feet

In the reflected glow of his flashlight, he stumbled to the doorway and called out. "Vincent!" Silence. "Vincent, are you there? Can you hear me?"

For another five minutes, Paul called out for the archaeologist, the workmen, Gail, and Farhang. No sound returned to him but for the echo of his own voice. *They are dead*, he thought. *And I'll probably be dead soon.*

That thought wasn't as terrible as he might have expected it to be. Or, rather, it wasn't as terrible as Professor Kusel might have thought it would be. Corporal Kusel had been afraid of death, but after a week in Europe, he had accepted that it would probably happen, and then put the fear aside and did his job. Paul felt that same strange calm in the cave. He would likely die here, so he should try to get on with his job.

As he picked up his flashlight, Paul's fatalism felt justified. He did not expect that a room sealed for five thousand years would have a convenient egress. Still, he wagered he should look around and take stock. He removed his pack and rummaged. He had water, fruit, bread, cheese, and extra batteries for his flashlight. In a side pocket, he found almonds and some honey candy he had bought in a nearby village. Hanging from one loop was a pickaxe that would do nothing against the mountain of collapsed stone in the other room. Still, he could at the very least make a go of it for a while. He would not die curled in a corner, weeping and crying out for a mother who never loved him. If he was never again to see daylight, he could at least see things no one had beheld in five thousand years.

Paul sipped conservatively from his canteen and rinsed the grit from his mouth. Then he carried his pack to a corner in the back wall as far from the collapsed door as possible. Images of the dead men flashed through his mind and he let himself cry again, but only for a minute. Then he tried calling out, once more with no answer but his echo. Perhaps it was his location in the back corner of the cave, or the shock was getting to him, but his voice sounded strange echoing back, 'hello.' It sent a dreadful, uncanny chill down his spine.

Hoping to steady himself, he turned his attention to the room. The floor certainly did appear to have been worn smooth by running water. He concluded that the formation must be limestone, though he wondered at the lack of stalactites, stalagmites, or any of the telltale white calcification of similar caves. His light roved around the room, taking in the stone bench and several artifacts, now disturbed by debris. Resisting the urge to assess them immediately, he took in the rest of the room. When his light reached the back wall, he swore.

From his position only a few feet away, he saw that the wall was not, as they had first thought, a natural cavern formation. Instead, it was made of smooth, almost perfectly fitted, rectangular stones. Kusel knelt and ran his fingers over the surface, shaking his head.

"My God," he breathed. Suddenly he remembered the hole that had swallowed their lights. For a moment hope kicked into his gut, spurring his heart. If there was an opening, there might be a way out.

Paul tried to contain this sense of hope, to tamp it down. He didn't want to get into the habit—short-lived though it may be—of getting his hopes up. Vincent had probably been right; the door likely led to a burial chamber. Even so, he followed the wall until he came to the opening. It was rectangular and approximately four feet tall, but the edges of the stones were irregular, as if something had chipped away at them, giving them a shape more like the uneven surface of the floor. He ducked down to look inside and struggled to understand what he saw.

The opening gave way to a narrow, ten-foot-long passage. At the end stood an open, metal door that was entirely wrong for the period. Paul guessed it was iron or maybe steel. Intrigued, Paul crouched and half-walked, half-crawled toward the curiosity. He knew that a small amount of iron had been used in the bronze age, and some trace amount of steel came with iron, but a door of this size and craftsmanship seemed impossible. It looked like it had been made in the last 200 years. As he got closer, he cursed softly. He ran his fingers over the dull, gray metal and thought no tool or skill in the ancient world could have fashioned the perfectly smooth surface. The only rational conclusion was that people must have accessed the chamber recently. Paul's constrained hope grew as he pushed through the door.

The hope immediately died as he entered a tight, six-by-six stone box. He stood and felt his hair brush the ceiling. Deflated, he took stock of the room's only contents: two metal rings sunk into the stone floor. Paul knelt to study them. They weren't bronze, not copper—perhaps more iron. He bent closer. The rings' rough, dark surfaces were scarred with deep, glinting scratches. He got within an inch of the metal and concluded that the marks were some kind of writing. He had no idea what language it was, but it didn't look like cuneiform or the Elamite Vincent had identified in the outer room. Suddenly, Paul remembered the camera on his belt. He fumbled its leather case open, hoping it hadn't been damaged in the collapse.

Frustrated disappointment joined fear and despair as he surveyed a long branching crack through the lens. Paul considered throwing the camera away to be a new artifact in the incongruous cave, but thought better of it. There was still film left, and crack or no crack, he might still capture something valuable. If not, someone might still retrieve the pictures from the destroyed first chamber. He snapped two photos of the metal rings. As the flash went off, Paul noticed that the rings' undersides were brighter than the dull outsides. He ran a finger along them. They were smooth, but not perfectly so. They rolled slightly in subtle waves. He had no idea what that might mean.

He stood to examine the room more closely, hoping he had missed something, but his search of the walls and ceiling showed only smooth rock and square corners. However, when he ran his light along the floor, he thought he saw a strange indentation between the rings and the doorway. He repositioned himself around the room, crouching and standing until he was confident there was, however slight, a concave space perhaps two feet in diameter, in front of the iron rings. And, if he moved his light across it quickly, he thought the stone in the shallow indentation was darker than the stone around it.

He took a picture of the spot, uncertain that even with an unbroken lens he'd capture anything discernable. Paul considered a second picture from another angle but saw that he had only four pictures left, and the bench and its artifacts remained. If he had any chance of photographing those items, he must. Ducking low, he left the small chamber.

Once more in the center of what he now thought of as the outer room, Paul tried calling out again. Once more, his echoed 'hello' made him shiver. Once more, no other sound followed.

Fear like a stone weighed Paul's stomach. The idea of sudden death scared him, but all the more he dreaded dying of dehydration in the dark, left to ponder a life finally concluded in failure. How long would he last, nursing the monster of regret? He was sure the beast would taunt him in the silence under the earth, reminding him how close he had gotten to success and how close he had come to claiming a little self-respect. Here, at the cusp of success, the world, or God, or his guardian angel, had pulled the rug out from under him and he would be rewarded with death in a cave where no one would find him, perhaps for fifty years or more.

He tried to breathe through the fear—one long breath in, one long breath out. It took him minutes to feel ready to continue his investigation. When he felt steady enough to go on, he approached the stone bench a few feet from the collapsed door. Kneeling, he surveyed the artifacts and smiled sadly. Vincent had been right about the clay tablet; it appeared to have the same strange script that the Englishman had identified as Proto-Elamite.

Paul wondered if the archaeologist would have thought it fitting that some of the world's most ancient script should mark his tomb and that his gravestone should be written in a language no one could read. Paul's wistful smile faded when he remembered that the ancient writing was likely to mark his own tomb, and the thought gave him little comfort.

He snapped a picture of the tablet with his broken camera and wound the film. He turned to the other items. Before the collapse, a half-dozen unique items had adorned the bench, now only two others remained. One was a copper cylinder about one and a half inches long. The other was the silver disk he had observed earlier. As Paul's light played over the tube, he saw parts of the cylinder raised in relief, perhaps more of the strange Elamite writing.

Paul photographed the cylinder and the silver disk. Then he picked up the small metal tube to study it. As he turned it over in his hand his eyes grew wide. Wrapping around the artifact rose the depiction of two standing men flanking a seated man. Paul studied the image carefully, trying to confirm his suspicions in the sharp, distorting shadows cast by his flashlight. After a dozen turns of the cylinder, he felt confident that the image shown on the little metal tube had been impressed into the bottom of his bronze plate that rested in his desk in Lightning Falls.

It was a seal, or at least he thought it was. He had seen demonstrations during his undergraduate work of little cylinders like this rolled over wet clay, or in his professor's case, molding clay. As the tube rolled, it left behind a crude image and writing. The one Paul had seen had been from Israel, but he thought he remembered that such seals were common across the ancient Middle East. This one, he thought, hadn't been rolled across clay. Instead, it had been rolled across his bronze plate, and its partner that now was likely irreparably crushed in the tomb of three men.

At least three men, Paul thought. He pictured Gail and her smiling face in the firelight. Were he a braver man, he might have … what? Asked her out on a date? Or manfully tried to woo her under the stars? What did Paul imagine men who were successful with women did? Leaving aside the wisdom of such a romance during a dig, he couldn't imagine that his interest would have met with anything but laughter. No, perhaps Gail was—had been?—too kind for that. She might have tried to explain the delicate situation, even apologized for the awkwardness of her rejection of him. That, he thought, would have been worse.

He imagined her under a ton of earth, perhaps not killed right away, as he was sure—or at least hoped desperately—that the diggers and Vincent had been. The image of her reaching, gasping, trying to move and breathe was too horrible for him to bear. Paul squeezed his eyes shut and tried to focus on what was in front of him.

He bounced the cylinder in his palm. The metal was warm, much warmer than he thought likely for something held in such a cool room. Was it cool? He hadn't noticed the temperature before. No, not cool, comfortable. The room was neither hot nor cold, neither damp nor musty. It had no smell at all. Paul wondered if that was some peculiar attribute of this cave, or if perhaps his sense of smell was stopped up by the dust that hung in the air and likely lined his nose.

Paul dropped the seal—if that's what it was—into his pocket with his pipe and turned his attention to the silver disk. Crouching, he snapped another picture before picking the artifact up. It was about as wide as his palm and was thicker in the middle than at the smooth, beveled edges. It bore no marks, no writing, no images. He thought its surface, polished to a high sheen, was the mark of a master smith. He had never seen anything like it from the ancient world in any book, museum, or tomb. It was perfectly smooth and entirely without seams. If it were not for the surface's total uniformity and symmetry, he would have imagined that it had been smoothed by centuries of running water.

Paul turned it over in his hands. It too was warm. No, not warm, hot. Uncomfortably hot. He again considered the possibility that the artifacts were radioactive. He didn't know what uranium looked like and wondered if someone as uninformed as he was would mistake it for silver. Or was the disk perhaps that other strange element, one of the manmade ones? Plutonium? Was he killing himself by handling it? Even if he somehow survived, would he show the signs of radiation sickness?

He dropped the disk into another pocket and considered the other three artifacts scattered on the floor. Each could fit in the palm of his hand. One was a golden bracelet, another a bronze knife. The last was another thin, metal tube; though it was smooth, and both longer and narrower than the seal. It looked almost like a straw to him, and Paul had no idea what it was. He had two pictures left. He wondered if he had more film in one of his pack's side pockets. He couldn't remember seeing any during his inventory, but still, it was worth checking.

Paul Kusel turned from the bench toward the back of the room and almost soiled himself.

A man was standing in front of the hole in the back wall.

Paul reeled backward and almost fell over the bench. No, not a man, his own shadow, surely. There must be a new light source, something that was casting a shadow. But if so, why wasn't it stumbling while he stumbled?

"Oh God," Paul said. "Oh God, I'm going crazy. I'm going crazy like Mother."

He blinked, and the shadow remained. He squeezed his eyes tight, counted to ten, and opened them.

The shadow remained.

Regaining a little of his reason, he pointed his flashlight at the shadow.

The shadow remained.

"Oh God," he repeated. "Who are you? What do you want?"

I'm losing my mind. This is shock setting in.

He suddenly remembered the gas tubes and wondered if they had been wrong. He had known a woman who had to be admitted to the hospital for a day for carbon monoxide poisoning because one of her tubes had been defective.

He thought of his family.

That must be what was happening here. Maybe the tubes had worked, but the cave was poisoned with other gases. Perhaps the collapse had opened a vent or pocket of some kind. He needed to get out. He held his flashlight out again to try to dispel the illusion.

In the war, Paul had been afraid, but he had also been brave. He had fought when he was told to fight, had held when he was told to hold, and took life when battle demanded it. He had jumped from the sky, and he had seen death in monstrous form and number. Never once had Paul Kusel screamed and jumped like a person frightened by a mouse in a cartoon—not until the shadow reached for him, like the mummy from the old Boris Karloff film.

His scream mixed with the shattering of glass as his flashlight fell from his hand and immersed the room in complete darkness. Cowering, he raised his hand to shield his face against both the shadow-man and the broken glass. Neither touched him. He knelt in the dark for a long moment, waiting. But after his scream died, everything was still.

Oh God, I'm in the dark, he thought. *I'm going to die in a cave in the dark.*

He tried to calm himself. His first attempt failed. Was the shadow-thing still there? Could such a thing exist without light? Did shadow have its own substance? He realized his mind was trying to cope by retreating into philosophy. That was a sign of growing madness. He needed to focus on practical things, not on the esoteric library lectures his uncle used to give him.

He needed to see if he could fix the flashlight. If it didn't work, he might have an extra bulb in his pack. He doubted it, but it was possible. *But how the hell am I going to search my pack if I can't see?* It was less a real question and more a panicked reflex. Of course, with patience, he could take each item out and put it in front of him. He could do it in the room with the metal rings where neither debris nor glass littered the floor, and the room was small so it would be harder to lose things.

Paul took deep breaths and tried to calm himself, his eyes trying to adjust to the darkness. He imagined his pupils widening, hungry for even the faintest sliver of light. He stared into the perfect black of the chamber and froze.

Impossibly, he saw a pale and narrow sliver of illumination glimmering faintly on the floor. Paul stared, blinked, and turned his head back and forth to see if it was an illusion. If he could hallucinate a shadow man, he probably could hallucinate light. Carefully, reaching out in front of him, he crouch-walked over, glass cracking beneath his boots.

When he reached the beam, he put his hand out and watched as the diamond of light jumped from the floor to his palm. He followed it upward until he bumped into a wall. As he reached up and put his fingers to the source, he watched the faint beam grow sharper and then disappear as he covered a small hole.

"Oh," Kusel said, wedging his finger into the crack. "Oh, please."

He reached down to his belt for his Swiss army knife. His hands were shaking so badly, he fumbled and almost dropped it. Taking hold of it, and trying not to think about the shadow that might be lurking in the darkness, he flipped out the knife and held it in the beam. The blade glinted as he turned it under the narrow glow. His heart was galloping and sweat bloomed on his brow and ran into his eyes. He wiped it away and stuck the knife into the hole. He twisted it gently, not wanting to break the blade. Dimly he knew that if he could not escape, the blade could save him from the long hell of dehydration.

To his astonishment, the stones around the opening shifted, and the sliver grew to the size of a quarter.

Paul tried to imagine where he was in the dig's layout, and how he could possibly dig through the earth with such a meager tool. He twisted the knife until it met no more resistance. He ducked backward to let the beam of light fall on one eye.

"Oh, my Lord," he said, his mind trying to absorb and accept what he saw: a pale, cloudless, blue sky. That should also be impossible. He was at least fifteen feet underground. He reached up and jammed his thumb into the hole. The rock shifted again and clattered to the chamber's floor. The opening grew and he could see why they had not found this passage. Running up several feet on either side of the opening were jutting rocks, forming a narrow crack in the earth, perhaps no wider than his hand. From above, it would appear as a fissure only a few inches across. That wasn't ideal, but he thought he could work with it. He began to push and pull at the small stones that formed the top of the cave wall. After a few minutes, he cleared a hole big enough to accommodate his arm. Satisfied that fresh air should be less of an issue, Paul felt confident that he could at least get someone's attention by shouting up through the fissure.

He imagined the men clearing the way for him to emerge largely unscathed from the belly of the earth, reborn in the public eye as the archaeologist who miraculously survived a deadly cave-in. Perhaps the rug had not been entirely pulled out from under him after all. *National Geographic* would do an article, and so would *Life*. There would be talks, perhaps visiting professorships, and a book most certainly.

He cursed himself. Three men lay dead in the adjoining room, and he was thinking about publicity. His only defense against his self-disgust was that he was still in shock. He stepped back from the hole and peered around. The light, though bright when you were directly in it, was not enough to illuminate the large chamber. He had to go back for his pack, especially … Suddenly he thought of the small pickaxe. He took a step forward into the darkness and stopped. He could go blindly, risking bruised shins and a battered forehead, or…

Paul lifted his camera. He had two more flashes in the cube plugged into the camera, and at least one more unused in the leather case on his belt. He put his finger on the button and stopped. Fear surged again. What if he saw the shadow man again? What if, in that split second, Paul saw it walking toward him? No, not walking, lurching—like a monster from a tomb. He tried to force the idea away, but only half succeeded. Steeling himself, and terrified that he would scream again and drop his one remaining source of light, he pressed the button and watched the room light up in front of him.

It was perfectly done. He saw everything he wanted to, and nothing he didn't. His pack, the low bench, and the opening in the wall all fell into place in his mental map of the room. The shadow man was blessedly absent. Keeping an arm out, Paul walked slowly, but confidently, in a straight line ahead of him. He found the far wall, turned left, and felt his boot press into something soft. He reached down, picked up his pack, and hoisted it onto his shoulders.

He crossed the room one final time, the shaft of light beckoning him forward. He withdrew the pick and set to work. He had been right. The stone and earth gave way without protest. Fifteen minutes later, he was pulling himself through an ever-widening passage toward daylight. His pack and body scraped against stone, roaring flooding his ears, earth tumbling down around him as he pushed himself toward life and freedom.

As he pulled himself up, hand over hand, feet scrabbling first on smooth and then rough stone, he came out of the cave and into the light. He scrambled, slipping once, and almost calling out. But his self-respect demanded he do it on his own if possible. When he finally reached the top, the idle thought crossed his mind that the hand-width opening was decidedly broader than his first estimation. He wondered how the workers had missed it in their survey of the site.

Paul left the question for another time and crawled out onto the parched earth, his body vibrating. He looked across the ruins. Ten yards away, men frantically dug as a woman stood over them on a stone, commanding them in Farsi. Paul almost wept with relief. Half of Gail's body was covered in yellowish dirt, as if the collapse had painted her with one blow of an artist's pigments. She held a short pickaxe in her hand and her shirt was torn just above her belt. Paul thought no person had ever appeared more wonderful than she did upon that rock.

His body still vibrating, Paul called out in a dusty, rasping voice. No one heard him. He tried again, and one of the workmen glanced up. The man shouted and dropped his shovel. Gail turned and Paul saw the whites of her eyes go wide. The others stopped, dropped their tools, and ran toward him. Eight men crowded him and started to pull him to his feet, shouting and praising God for his survival. Farhang, tears running down his face, hugged him in a cloud of dust. Another patted him on the back, and another tried, in poor English, to ask after the other men.

Gail waited at the edge of the crowd. Through the cheering men's faces, he saw hers. Dust caked one side of her face and matted her closely cropped, black hair. Her lips were cracked, and tears had cut paths through the dirt. Her eyes pleaded with him, but Paul could only shake his head. He watched as she covered her face with her hands a moment before the vibration in Paul's body multiplied a thousand times as an earthquake rolled under them.

Farhang pointed and shouted, pulling Paul back. The others saw the earth sliding into the gap from which Paul had come and began to scramble away. Another man ducked under Paul's arm and, with the foreman, lifted the exhausted archaeologist, dragging him away as the ground flowed like water down into the opening. Gail shouted, pointed, and grabbed a man by the sleeve, yanking him toward safety. Then came terrible thunder. Stones tumbled and turned, rolling over themselves into the growing pit. All at once, the earth dropped with the force and sound of a bomb. Everyone fell. Some, like Farhang and the other digger, tumbled backward, pulling Paul away from the opening. Others pitched forward into the pit as a stream of dust and stone ejected upward, shooting into the sky.

Paul landed on Farhang, who clutched him around the chest. They watched together as the cloud of dust and sand smeared darkness across the sun. Men screamed, and Paul cast about, looking for Gail through the haze and layer of earth and stone that now coated everything and everyone. After staring at a strange shape sticking up from the ground, he realized he was looking at the top half of Gail. She was buried up to her waist in the earth, her upper body limp and blood running from her neck and arm into an ever-growing pool of black-red in the yellow dust.

Paul's hands are trembling again. The airplane's vibration is too similar to the terrestrial tumult, so he puts his drink on the tray. When he closes his eyes, he sees Vincent's face, calling for him to take cover. He sees Gail's body, slumped forward, arms hanging out and down, as if … as if her strings had been cut. Her final posture was a doll's, not a human's. He wants to drink because his eyes burn from want of sleep, but his hands shake. He wants to rest, but the plume of dust and stone keeps swallowing the two men bringing them water. He wishes he had died in the cave. He slips his hand into his pocket, and his fingers slide over the warm, smooth, comforting silver disk. His hands shake less for a moment, and he manages to take his drink.

VI
Irregular

Friday, June 20, 1969 - Afternoon

PAUL RAN HIS HAND over the upholstered cushion, stitched ivy snaking under his fingers. They trembled today, but it wasn't just combat fatigue that motivated them. He eyed his lemonade, not trusting himself to pick up the diamond-patterned glass for fear of spilling it in anger. His mouth was dry, but he didn't want the other men to see his agitation. So, he stood, took the drink, and walked to the wall of floor-to-ceiling windows. He drank slowly with his back to the men.

On the front lawn, he saw Georgina walking with a stocky man who looked like he could butt heads with a ram and come out no worse for wear. Broad-shouldered and wearing a polo shirt that was perhaps a size too tight for good taste, he walked with his head down and his hands behind his back. Paul thought he looked as if he were giving Georgina a lecture. She, in a modest gingham dress, looked as if she might have come out of a Louisa May Alcott book, he thought. He had never read Miss Alcott's books and realized he might be confusing her with Laura Ingalls Wilder.

You're escaping into pointless, errant thoughts so you can avoid the situation.

Acknowledging his retreat from the battle at hand, he sipped again and turned back to the two men on the couches. Levi Grossman—tall, thin, chestnut-bearded—was slouching in a well-tailored suit. Paul thought he was trying not to be less imposing to not antagonize the man who sat across from him: Professor Ivan Filatov, a short, balding, round-nosed man in an academic's tweed, with a leather zipper-binder open on his knee.

"I think you should try to see it from Professor Filatov's perspective," Levi said. Paul understood that his friend was trying to be as placating as possible, to limit the damage. The tall man twisted a bit of beard thoughtfully. "Two scholars and two locals are dead. You are the only survivor whose account we have access to."

"Yes, and I've told him—" Paul began, in a less conciliatory tone, but Professor Filatov looked up from the notebook in his binder and put up a hand.

"We know. You weren't in charge. No one is saying you were. But your report is irregular. Most irregular."

"How? I still don't understand," Paul said.

"Well," Filatov said, "I still think we want to know why you, an unemployed archaeologist who focuses on early Germanic studies, were in Iran on an Elamite dig."

"I thought we had covered that, Ivan," Mr. Grossman said. "As a patron of Professor Millich and Professor Kusel, I thought it might be gratifying to have them both at the same site. Academics are so cordoned off into your little corners of the ivory tower that I thought it might be interesting to have two scholars from different specialties working together."

Paul had always admired Levi's ability to be disarming, jovial, and formal at the same time. He was trying his best to admire it now when all he wanted to do was sock the self-important prig with his leather binder and matching briefcase.

"Why Iran though?" Filatov asked.

"Well, it was the first available dig," Levi continued, giving Paul a quick side-eyed glance. "I had hoped to send Vincent with Paul on one of his digs in Germany."

"But Professor Kusel isn't associated with any university currently."

"Once Paul was able to get some institutional support again, of course. Which, I thought, might be facilitated by his help on this dig."

Filatov turned to regard Grossman, and Paul couldn't see his face. He hated the small, sweaty Communist. Of course, Paul wasn't certain of the last point, but he had noted with displeasure that the number of open Reds was growing, and while he despised the idiocy of McCarthyism, he still disliked Marxists when he came across them.

"And what did you hope to achieve by this academic exchange?"

"Fresh eyes," Levi said. "A new perspective. Who knows?"

Filatov shook his head and Paul turned back to the window. Georgina and the big man were now sitting on a bench and appeared to be vigorously debating. She tilted her head when she spoke and he gestured up or down, toward her and away with wide, arcs of his large arms. Paul wanted to sit and discuss whatever they were so exercised over. He was sure it was more interesting and intellectually stimulating than this catastrophe.

"Well, there will be no new perspective, Mr. Grossman. None. Ms. Abimbola was one of the most promising minds of the next generation of Persian scholars; to say nothing of the years of excellent work that Dr. Millich had contributed."

"I'm sorry," Paul said, turning again to the men in the room. "Are you suggesting that my presence somehow caused the earthquake that killed her? Are you suggesting that the tunnel, dug by men that Vincent hired, was somehow my fault?"

"Not precisely," Filatov said. "I am suggesting that Professor Millich's schedule didn't include sinking a shaft in that particular spot. He had made no reported discoveries that would justify it, and there was no word of it in his wire from a few days earlier. So, between the time your visa was approved, and when you arrived, he had gone through the trouble of hiring untested diggers—"

"That's not true—"

"And sinking a shaft directly to the front door of the underground chamber. I'm suggesting that were it not for your unusual arrival and the break-neck speed at which he seemed to work based on information I cannot access or surmise, he would not have been in that chamber at that moment, the shaft would not have been dug so shoddily, and Ms. Abimbola would not have been standing in that place when the earthquake hit. Did you know that no other town even felt the earthquake? Not so much as a cup fell from a shelf."

Paul shook his head. Levi nodded as if thinking through Filatov's words.

The sweaty man continued. "Strange, don't you think? Very irregular. Even so, if she had been literally anywhere else, she would be alive."

"Professor Filatov," Levi Grossman said. His tone was strange, and Paul thought he detected something he couldn't quite identify. "I'm just not sure what you're getting at. This was a tragic accident, nothing more."

"We will see. I will be looking into this matter more completely, and if I find cause, I will be contacting the AIA to expel you from its ranks, Professor Kusel. I think you'll find it difficult to get new 'institutional support,' as your patron puts it."

"Please, Professor Filatov," Levi Grossman said. There it was again, something odd.

"No, I don't think we have much more to talk about here. I will continue with my investigation, and I will let you know what I find."

"Professor Filatov, I don't want to be crass, but—"

"Then don't be, Mr. Grossman. I'm aware of your generosity toward our school, especially our Anthropology Department. But I cannot allow that to affect the integrity of this investigation. Four people are dead. A site of untold historical import is destroyed. Proto-Elamite, carved into stone! Hundreds of tablets gone! The very Rosetta Stone of a language perhaps lost forever! This cannot simply be chalked up to bad luck and poor conditions." The shorter man stood and closed his binder before putting it into the matching briefcase that Paul hated. "Good day to you both, I will contact you when I know more, or if I need to ask further questions."

"Let me walk you out," Levi said, standing. He gave Paul a reassuring look and then put his hand on Filatov's shoulder. Paul sniffed and turned back to the window. Georgina and the large man were nowhere to be found. Paul walked to the small bar by the door and refilled his lemonade from a glass pitcher. He heard voices in the hall. Filatov, Levi, Georgina, and a deep voice he did not know. They spoke politely for a few seconds before footsteps preceded Georgina's appearance with the big man.

"Good afternoon, Professor Kusel," Georgina said.

"Good afternoon, Georgina," Paul said, forcing his best smile.

"May I introduce you to Percival Frei, my tutor. Mr. Frei, this is Professor Paul Kusel, eminent archaeologist."

"I'm not certain 'eminent' is the right term, but it's a pleasure to meet you, Mr. Frei."

"The pleasure is mine," Frei said, his voice as deep, and his handshake as strong, as Paul had imagined they would be. "Your family has done much for this town."

"Thank you for saying so," Paul said. "Might I ask, and I'm sorry for being nosy, but what were you two debating a moment ago? I saw the both of you so engaged that—"

"Oh, we were discussing the valid use of force to achieve moral ends," Georgina said.

"Whether might makes right," Frei said.

"Fascinating. I will refrain from prejudging who took which position," he said, venturing a tentative chuckle.

"I always take the opposite position from my students," Frei said.

"Ah, then, Georgina what did you—"

"Pompous little shit," Levi said as he entered the room, rubbing his hands together, as if to rid himself of Filatov's handshake. "Oh, I'm so sorry, I didn't realize you two had come in here."

"It's all right, Mr. Grossman, I've heard worse."

"Where?" both Levi and Mr. Frei said in unison. Paul laughed.

"I have been to the movies," Georgina said with a prim smile. "And I have read books, and it is 1969 not 1869."

Levi didn't look entirely pleased by this declaration, but shrugged. "So be it. Mr. Frei, perhaps a lesson on the proper application of uncouth language would be in order then," Levi said as he strode across the room to take up his own glass of lemonade.

"That sounds like a fine debate," Mr. Frei said. "Shall we?"

"Oh, let me get some lemonade first," Georgina said.

"I will wait for you on the back deck; some shade would be welcome. Mr. Kusel, it was a pleasure meeting you."

Paul shook the man's hand again. Levi, looking as if he had just remembered something, chased after him with long, purposeful strides.

"I'm glad they're gone," Georgina said, turning to Paul. She looked up at him with eyes that might have been brown, or green, or hazel. They were kind, intelligent, empathetic eyes. "I wanted to tell you how grateful I am that you listened to my advice."

"How did you know that?" Paul said, feeling a mild kind of awe.

"The same way I knew for you to avoid the lion's mouth, a dream. And I am ever so grateful that you took my warning." The younger woman reached out and took Paul's hand. He let her hold it between hers, feeling a strange love well up in him that he remembered from his time convalescing after a minor wound in the war. He had had the same love for the nurses, like angels from God. He had felt something similar for Farhang as the men wept together for their losses, and Paul swore to help the man if he ever needed it, for he owed him his life.

"You listened to me once, now I ask you to listen to me again."

Paul nodded, his mouth agape.

"You will doubt everything, even your closest friends. But whoever you doubt, whoever you think might be against you, trust Michael. He will lead you to where you need to go."

"Michael? I—Michael Church? Who works at the library?"

She nodded.

"But he's just—"

"He will be faithful to you, and will not betray you. Believe as you believed before. Please." She squeezed his hand in hers, and Paul's heart could not stand the pleading look in her eyes.

"All right," Paul said. "All right. I will trust Michael. And thank you, Georgina. Without you, I would be dead."

"I'm very glad you are not," she said. "Now, would you do something for me?" Once again, her eyes were huge, plaintive, and vulnerable.

"Yes, anything, what—"

"Would you mind pouring me some lemonade?" Her look changed into a wry, gently teasing grin, and Paul laughed. He poured her a tall glass and she took it with thanks. "Now," she said, "I must argue that one must never, ever use foul language so I can hear Mr. Frei make the best arguments for using it all the time," she said. Then she was off down the hall, and Paul wondered if, in reality, she belonged in a Jane Austen novel or some Greek myth about oracles.

As if trading places in a play, Levi entered as Georgina exited. He looked exaggeratedly over his shoulder back down the hall to make sure she was out of earshot and repeated his assessment of Filatov.

"He's right, though, it was my fault," Paul said.

"No, no, this is my fault, not yours. I was just so excited for you to go and, well, to see if your hunch was right. And it was, wasn't it?'

Paul nodded slowly. "Yes … but … but how?" Paul said. "How does a dream of a chamber in a place I've never studied result in a real, tangible find? I'm not a spiritualist, Levi. I'm not a believer in my family's old religion. You know that. Neither Aunt Sharon nor I are—"

"I know, I know," Levi said, chuckling. "But it's wonderfully strange, isn't it?"

Paul nodded, thinking of Georgina's dreams. Something in her words warned him from saying anything about them to Levi.

"Look, if you need an explanation, let's call it … subconscious interpretation," the tall man said.

"What?"

"You saw all the markings on those tablets, and you dreamed of a location. Perhaps, subconsciously, you are interpreting the plates."

"Levi, you are one of my oldest and dearest friends. And that—" Paul said, now making his own ostentatious display of checking down the hallway for Georgina, "is utter horseshit. How could I have surmised the exact location between the stones in that place by just looking at the plate? Horseshit."

Both men laughed.

"Horseshit it may be," Levi said, walking over to the bar. "But even horseshit is useful for some things. And if this particular dung pile helps you to not worry about one more thing, then I say let the … Well, I can't think of anything even mildly non-revolting to say after that. So, let's just have a drink of something stronger than lemonade."

Paul agreed, and Levi produced a bottle of thirty-year-old scotch. They drank and made appreciative faces.

"Excellent. Now, I think I've been patient enough," Levi said, leaning against the wall. Paul considered the younger man and admired his restraint. Another patron would have asked to see the relics immediately upon Paul's return, trauma be damned.

"You have, my friend. You most certainly have." Paul stood and reached into his pocket. He drew out a small rectangle of folded paper. Levi Grossman reached out with trembling fingers and took the taped parcel. He pulled the paper apart carefully, revealing the small metal cylinder with raised images.

"Extraordinary," he whispered, shaking his head. "Utterly extraordinary."

Paul watched the man's eyes fill with tears. "All right there, Levi?"

"What? Oh," he said, laughing and wiping his eyes. "Yes, I'm just … I'm just so proud of you, Paul. You found it."

"Found it?" Paul asked.

"A … a sign of your abilities," Levi said quickly. "Something we can both point to as a mark of your success."

"I just wish my parents were here to see it," Paul said, staring at the cylinder. "Something they could hold in their hands to know that I'm not entirely a failure."

Levi let out a long sigh. "Yes, I wish they were too." He lifted his drink. "To your father and mother, God rest their souls."

Paul emptied his glass and put the tumbler down on a coaster. "I need to unlock that little item's secrets," he said.

"How so?" Levi said, looking up from it.

"If I'm going to make any kind of case for my career, I've got to not only show that the seal and the plate are connected, which should be easy enough, but I have to do more than that. I have to translate; I have to make an argument for how the plate got from ancient Persia to Germany. That little trinket is my ticket back in. If Filatov doesn't try to ruin me, first."

"And when you're done?" Levi asked.

"Then I suppose it goes into a museum," Paul said.

"I … well, I'm embarrassed to say this, but I thought I might put it in my collection," Levi said.

"I wish you could, but that would be tantamount to grave robbing," Paul said. "Well, not a grave maybe, but archaeological theft."

"Even Howard Carter kept a few items for himself," Levi said.

"And he shouldn't have," Paul said. "But even so, this is the only thing I have from my expedition. I must work with it, Levi. I must. I wish I had some other trinket to give you."

Levi weighed the seal in his hand, furrowed his brow, and nodded before handing it back to Paul.

PAUL LEANS BACK ON the bench, his fingers gliding over the smooth metal in his pocket. He considers the oak trees that grow in the four corners of the village green and imagines their predecessors, planted far away in Pennsylvania. He wonders if they still thrive, if they have fallen ill with age, or perhaps have been cut down. He wonders if men have ever dangled from their branches, their limbs hanging like puppets with their strings cut.

In the background, the falls rumble.

He pictures Gail and wants to vomit.

He tries to shake the morbid thoughts, but can't. So, he stands and starts for the library. Perhaps, among the books, he will find a distraction from the putrid stream that has run through his mind since Iran. But, as he walks, he suspects that even in that silent place, he will still hear thunder falling around him.

VII
Worth

Saturday - August 23, 1969 - Afternoon

"WELL," MR. CECIL BAKER said, "far be it from me, as an old colored man, to tell you what to do with your white business."

Paul laughed at the voice Mr. Baker put on. It was deep, southern, and slow, a far reach from the remains of his down-east Yankee accent that had slowly dwindled over four decades in the Wallowa foothills.

"I'm asking you to tell me about my white business," Paul said.

Mr. Baker nodded and drew a puff from his pipe. He sat in an old, comfortable easy chair, his legs crossed, his white Oxford shirt unbuttoned at the collar and his sleeves rolled up. Paul thought the man looked more like a professor than ever Paul did.

"Well," Mr. Baker said, "It seems to me that you've got what they call a 'conflict of interest.' You have your loyalty to your profession, though it's shown little loyalty to you. Then there's your loyalty to Mr. Grossman, who, I confess, I've never taken to."

"I know," Paul said around the stem of his own pipe.

"It just never sat right with me that whole business with your aunt and the family's money. His riches should be yours."

"I don't know about 'should be,'" Paul said. "But I think Levi feels especially guilty about how it all turned out and he's been endlessly generous to me. I can't imagine wanting more if the money were in my own account."

Mr. Baker lifted his chin and stared down his nose at Paul with an appraising eye. "Is that so? You'd rather have another man dole out your allowance than to be master of your own destiny?"

"Well," Paul said, "even if I had all the money, I don't think I'd be master of my own destiny. Clearly, I've made a mess of it all on my own. The money is probably safer in Levi's hands than in mine."

Mr. Baker puffed and shook his head. "Be that as it may, this artifact that you found, is it worth money?"

"Perhaps some, probably not much. But its worth isn't in money, it's in knowledge."

"Then why does Mr. Grossman want it so badly that he's tried, what did you say, a half a dozen times to get you to give it to him?"

"Well, maybe I was exaggerating. I think it represents something to him. And, honestly, his persistence is wearing me down. I feel like I've gained as much information as I can from it, and ... well, now that I've lost my position entirely—"

"That little Russian fella did you in, after all?"

"Yes, that was part of the news I mentioned—"

"And the other news?" Mr. Baker asked in a cloud of smoke.

"Oh, I've met someone, her name is Gladys."

"Gladys Mansfield?"

"No, Gladys Hibbs."

"Hmm, don't know the Hibbs family. They new 'round here?" The last word he pronounced as '*hee-ya*.'

"She's down in Enterprise," Paul said.

"Oh, a southern girl," Mr. Baker said, dipping back into his fake accent. Paul laughed. "Well, God, doors, and windows," Mr. Baker said.

"Indeed," Paul said.

They sat for a while, silently smoking, thinking, and being in each other's company. Cecil Baker was just shy of seventy years old, but Paul was confident that he had less gray in his beard than Paul did. He was a broad-shouldered man who had once been heavier, but had lost much of that weight over the last ten years and now dressed in ways that complimented his trimmer physique. Paul thought that Mr. Baker had worked oppositely to most people, becoming more formal and put together in his older years than he was during his working days. Mr. Baker's way of 'letting his hair down' was to wear polished brogues and vests.

"So," Paul said, taking his pipe from his mouth. "What do you think?"

"I think you should keep a healthy skepticism, Paul. I think you shouldn't be grateful when a man, however generously, lords over you the things that should be yours by right. I think you should not hand over your principles to a patron."

Paul pursed his lips and nodded. "That is … that is sound advice."

"Good, and you take it. I don't want to waste my good advice on someone who will let it go in his ear only to be knocked back out again when he's walking home. And I certainly don't want to wake up to your mother's ghost haunting me for not trying to set you on the right path. God knows I don't need you Kusels bothering my dreams any more than you already do."

Paul sniffed and smiled. "I don't think Mother would care enough to bother."

Cecil Baker only shook his head once and puffed.

"I'm the last one, Cecil."

"Well, maybe you won't be if Ms. Enterprise 1969 has anything to say about it."

Paul nodded and grinned. "Think she'd want an old washed-up, out-of-work professor like me?"

"Only if she's gone silly in the head," Mr. Baker said. Paul nodded, agreeing. "But seriously, Paul. You need to remember what is yours, what should have been yours, and what can be yours. That man, the man who says he's your friend, has taken everything from you. Why should he get any more?"

Paul didn't have an answer except for another cloud of smoke.

PAUL STUDIES THE COLD fireplace from his easy chair, turning the hot, silver disk over in his hands. He replays the last moments between Levi and Filatov and the strange tone in Levi's voice. The silent television glows KTVR's broadcast of a high school performance of *Our Town*. A line—he doesn't remember which—spoken by an acne-faced girl pulls him to his feet, the volume knob, and the chair in front of the dark hearth.

The girl is not a good actor. Most of her lines are delivered with little grace or skill, but one line stands out. Paul doesn't have the language to describe what made the one line different, but it is worse than the others. He doesn't know how to describe it, except to say it was fake. Put on. Badly acted.

Acted. Levi had been acting with Filatov.

Paul slowly flips the disk between his fingers and scours his conversations with Levi, searching for other, performative moments. He thinks of their first meeting at his aunt's house—now Levi's home. He thinks of the conversations over drinks about archaeology and the importance of history. He remembers the night that Levi had convinced him to abandon the crowded field of Egyptology and turn his attention north, to the lands where their ancestors once lived. He thinks of the man's encouragement to pursue his theories in Iran and searches for anything disingenuous.

He can find nothing. Nothing in years of friendship.

Nothing except the conversation with the man who has destroyed Paul's career.

VIII
Delving

Tuesday, November 11, 1969 – Late Morning

"WHAT IS THIS?" PAUL asked, looking into the low, cramped, dark mouth of a cave. His heart was racing, and his palms felt damp. A chill wind blew up from the High Pass to the secluded and unfamiliar path. Paul regretted agreeing to the hike. He had hoped that getting away from his stuffy, cluttered house would clear his head. Now he felt as if the rocky ground were vibrating under him and the rumble of the falls sounded too much like the earth's quaking.

"I'm not sure," Michael said.

"What did you find?" Levi asked, emerging from behind a tree and fastening his belt.

"It looks like a cave, Mr. Grossman," Michael said.

"But there shouldn't be a cave here," Paul said.

"Why?" Michael asked.

"Because this is all basalt. Most caves are cut from limestone—"

"Lava tubes," Levi said. "The whole area is shot through with them. But I've never heard of anyone finding any up here. Let's take a look."

Paul's hand shook against the rim of the cave mouth.

"Are you all right, Professor?" Michael asked.

"I am," Paul croaked, "just give me a minute. Sorry, last time I was in a cave—"

"God," Levi said, pulling Paul back, "I didn't think. Paul, I'm so sorry, let's go home."

"No," Paul said, a jolt of rage scorching through him, "I can do it, I just need a minute. My damned heart won't slow down."

"Are you all right? Are you going to have a heart attack?" Michael asked.

"No, Michael," Levi said, "Paul is all right, it's just nerves. And he has every right to them."

"I'm all right," Paul lied, taking his hand from the rim. "Lead on, I will follow you, Michael."

"Shall I bring up the rear?" Levi said. Paul heard the jocularity in his voice and grimaced.

"As you like it," Paul said as he ducked into the tunnel's mouth.

Fortunately, both Michael and Levi had flashlights with them, and they crouch-walked their way without complication for the first twenty feet. The tunnel opened a bit at a bend and they could stand.

"I hear water," Paul said.

"Well, that makes sense. The creek that feeds the falls comes from up here. This explains why no one has ever found its source. It's been slipping along under everyone's feet," Levi said.

Paul pointed to the farther end of the lava tube. "What is that?"

Michael pointed his flashlight down the passage. "Looks like an old wooden door," the younger man said.

"Guess someone did find the creek's source," Paul said over his shoulder.

"Bootleggers?" Levi suggested as they approached the door.

"Why would they need a door?" Michael asked.

"Why does anyone need a door?" Paul asked, conflicted. Part of him wanted to run screaming from the dark space. But the rest of him was intrigued. He had wondered if his excitement for discovery had died with Vincent and Gail, but now he knew otherwise. His hands trembled, but Paul thought they were motivated by equal parts fear and anticipation.

"Endlessly philosophical," Levi chuckled. "I imagine it would be to hide their light." He directed his own light back down the way they had come. "Maybe there would be enough of a reflection off the rocks outside at night to clue someone in on their presence up here." He frowned and shook his head. "Maybe not. I don't know."

"Well," Paul said, "It's old; these hinges are hand-forged. A blacksmith did these, not a factory."

"Interesting," Levi said. "Can we try it without destroying it? The door, I mean."

"I wish someone had brought a camera," Paul said. "But yes, let's give it a go."

He pushed on the door gingerly and was surprised at its easy movement. Paul froze as a musty smell met him. The shaking in his hands grew worse. Levi, concern etching deep lines of shadow on his face, put his hand on Paul's shoulder.

"I'll go first," Levi said, slipping past Paul and crouching through the door. A second later, his voice echoed out, "My goodness! Look at this!"

Excitedly, Michael followed Levi through the door. Paul shut his eyes and saw Vincent's face as he hid in the alcove. He took a long, shuddering breath, trying to steady himself. Then the archaeologist followed the younger man. When he stood on the other side of the door, Paul found himself in what appeared to be a naturally occurring rectangular room a foot taller than Levi. Frowning thoughtfully, Paul stepped forward.

"Careful!" Levi said, grabbing his arm. "Look, holes."

Paul watched as his friend directed his light over the ground on either side of the room. Four pits, two on each side, yawned up at them. They appeared to Paul as if they were each approximately four feet across.

"Thank you," he said, feeling a rush of his old affection for Levi. "Do you think these pits are … they can't be stills, can they?"

"I'm afraid I don't know enough about the bootlegging process to say for sure," Levi said. "Huh, looks like there are two more up there. Six pits. Very strange."

Paul took a step forward, checking his footing as he went. The room was fifteen feet wide, half of which was taken up by the holes in the ground. The pits were spaced about six feet apart, which Paul roughly added up to a room close to twenty-five feet long. He stared at the far end as his companions' flashlights wended their way around the room.

"What is that?" Paul asked, reaching out for Michael's hand. He guided the light to the back wall.

"I don't … Oh, is that another passage?"

"Two," Paul said, his mouth suddenly dry. "One on each side."

He approached the back wall. Though it had no relief of an emissary, Paul knew the wall and what must lie behind it. His mind tilted. Paul felt his sanity sloshing from one side to the other like seep water in a foundering ship. He turned around suddenly, looking up at the ceiling. Nothing stirred. Even Michael and Levi were frozen in place at his sudden movement.

"Paul, are you alright?" Levi asked.

"No," Paul said, his voice cracking. "Behind that wall—" He pointed to the far end of the room.

"I'm not sure we can get behind that wall," Levi said. "I think the pits or stills or whatever are blocking the way."

"No," Michael said. "Look, there is a path. It's narrow, but we can get past them."

Paul didn't want to move. The thought of running away was powerful but anathema to him. He had come through danger too many times and in too many foreign lands to turn coward in a lava tube less than a mile from his home. Still, he dreaded going on to see what lay before him. Sweat stung his eyes and slicked his hands. Blood thudded like a desperate prisoner on the insides of his eardrums. He wanted to vomit. He wanted to soil himself. He wanted to throw himself down into one of the pits.

"Professor, do we need to go back? Do you need to sit down?"

"Water," Levi said, "give him some water." But the taller man didn't wait for Michael to comply. He took his own canteen from his side and unscrewed the cap. "Here, Paul, for the love of God, drink this."

He put the canteen to Paul's lips and Paul drank. Levi might have splashed the cool water on his face, so powerful was the shock to the professor's system. Paul drank eagerly and then sputtered.

"Enough," Paul managed. "Thank you, I-I desperately needed that."

Levi then did something Paul couldn't ever remember him doing before. He hugged Paul. "My brother, please, we shouldn't have come here. We'll find another way. We'll find another way. I promise."

Paul wanted to weep then, to cast aside all of his doubts about his friend and to go back to the way things had been before. Levi pulled back and put his hand over Paul's heart.

"Let's go back," the younger man said. Paul studied his friend's half-lit face. He wasn't sure what it was about the bearded man's expression, but the warmth in Paul's chest died as the silver disk burned his hip through his pants pocket.

"No," Paul said. He stepped back and leveled the rich man—rich with money that should have been Paul's—with a hard gaze. "No, I can go on."

"All right," Levi said, sadness bunching his eyebrows together. "Let's go on. Only a little further though, please."

Paul nodded. He didn't need to go much further. He only needed to see. He wiped the sweat from his upper lip with the back of his hand and started forward. Their boots were silent on the stone floor. The only sounds were the jingling of metal clasps and carabiners, the dull rumble of water, and the drumming of his heart in his ears.

The path between the pit and the back wall was wider than they first guessed. They slipped into the passage that Paul had known would be there. The Dividing Hall. His breath shuddered in his chest as he leaned against the chamber's true back wall and gazed along the short tunnel to where the far pit lay. For a moment, it wasn't a pit, it was an alcove. For a moment the face that peeked around the corner wasn't Michael's, it was Vincent's. Paul thought Michael might have been right about him having a heart attack.

"Paul," Levi said, wonder in his voice. "This looks like what you drew. Is this—"

"Almost exactly the same," Paul said, covering his face with his hands. "I don't understand it. How can this be? I feel like I'm losing my mind."

"Let's go back," Levi said.

"No," Paul said. "I need to see. Look, there's another door."

The three men converged on another wooden door.

"The water is louder," Michael said.

Paul nodded. Again he pushed, and the door before him creaked open smoothly. His knees gave out, and he slid to the ground despite Levi and Michael grabbing at him.

Before him stood a circular room, about fifteen feet across and bisected by the course of a running stream. Over the little canal ran a short stone bridge made of a single slab of volcanic rock. Between the men and the water was a low stone bench with smooth top. And beyond the stream, set into the rock wall, was a round metal door.

Paul felt himself slipping as the world spun around him. From a long, echoing distance, he heard Levi shouting.

"Get him up, get him out. We need to get him fresh air!"

viii

BEFORE HIS EMPTY FIREPLACE, Paul sits in darkness, turning the silver disk over and the words of Levi's message. They both burn.

> "My dearest friend, I think it would be
> best if the artifacts were temporarily given to
> me for safekeeping while you recover. Only
> until you feel better, mind you."

Safekeeping.

The little seal and the bronze plate should be given to Levi for safekeeping.

Only until you feel better.

The silver disk, so perfectly smooth, stings Paul's fingers, but he will not put it down. Levi wants the seal for his little collection. He wants the seal to show off, to display, to enrich himself once more from Paul's family. He wants the seal to … Paul doesn't know.

I was just a tool for him to use. My pain, Farhang's pain, Vincent's life, Gail's life.

Gail, so brilliant, so kind, so lovely. Dead, so Levi could have a trinket.

The silver burns in his hands.

My dearest friend …

No, Paul thinks. *No.*

IX
Council

THE THREE MEN FROWNED. Paul frowned with consternation as he paced up and down the little path in front of the reference desk. Levi leaned against a bookshelf with his hands in his pockets, a thoughtful frown buried beneath his brown beard. Michael, resting on his elbows, supported his chin with his palms and frowned as if he were considering a novel idea.

"I don't understand it," Paul said, trying to walk the line between speaking softly enough for the library and loudly enough that the other men could hear him. The shelves of any library tended to muffle sound, but the Lightning Falls Library seemed to have a particularly deadening effect on voices.

"It is certainly strange," Levi said, twisting the hair of his beard between his fingers. "Two caves, one in Iran and one here, just above the waterfall, both with multiple rooms, benches, six … well, alcoves or holes. I can't begin to—"

"Excuse me," Natalie interrupted, appearing from between two shelves as if she were a magician. She was holding a brown paper bag. "I have your lunch, Michael. It's almost two, and you haven't eaten."

"Oh!" Michael said, looking embarrassed. "Thank you, Nat. I really appreciate it."

"It's no trouble," she said. "You gentlemen aren't overtaxing him, are you?"

"Definitely," Levi said, winking. "We've been having him haul bags of coal up and down the stairs for the last two hours."

"Well," she said, shrugging, "perhaps that will thicken him up a bit."

Michael looked affronted, but it was Natalie's turn to wink.

"Let me know if you fellas need anything," she said. Then, with a flip of her dirty-blonde hair, she was gone, swallowed by the shadows.

"Please tell us that you've asked her out by now," Paul said.

"I'm still working up the courage," Michael said, opening his lunch bag.

"Don't wait much longer," Levi said, shaking his head. "She'll lose interest. If she's bringing you your lunch, this is the best time to ask."

"I agree," Paul said, feeling the strange double-pull of his feelings toward Levi.

"Listen to him," Levi said. "He's the only one of us that has succeeded in matters of the heart. How is Gladys, by the way?"

"Good. I'm hoping to see her this weekend," Paul said. He wanted to reach for his pipe, but he declined. He felt too comfortable again, and his pipe would only sink him deeper into his old habits. He found it impossible to see his old friend as anything other than his old friend in the warmth and quiet of the library. He rubbed his eyes and thought how badly he needed sleep. He had been staying up too late, drinking too much, nursing his wounded pride, and contemplating Levi's note, which he had left unanswered.

"I'll take your advice today," Michael said. "But I think we'd better get back to the matter at hand. I think we should … well, I was thinking that maybe if you showed Professor Filatov your discovery, then he would have to listen to the rest of what you have to say."

"What good would that do?" Levi asked. "A wild tale backed up by two similar caves? Lightning Falls doesn't enter into Paul's theory at all."

"I don't have a theory," Paul said. "I have pieces and nothing to connect them. Besides, other than the layout, I can't see any connection—"

"But the layout," Levi said. "An antechamber, a cave in the middle—"

"With a stone table," Michael added.

"I think it's more of a bench," Paul said.

"With a stone bench," Levi continued, "and a metal door at the end? That's enough to at least get your foot in the door, isn't it?"

Paul considered this. "Perhaps," he said. "But without any writing, or carvings, or … well, anything else at all, what good could it do?"

"Well, we can't be sure that there isn't any writing there, can we?" Levi said.

"How do you mean?" Paul said.

"We didn't exactly make a thorough investigation of the cave, now, did we? Perhaps there is writing there, or perhaps the remnants of cave paintings."

"Oh, come on," Paul said. "Do you expect me to believe that there are Elamite carvings in a North American cave?"

"Well, no, I didn't say that. I'm just saying we … There might be more there that we haven't seen yet."

"Didn't you find an Elamite plate in a German grave, Professor?" Michael said.

Levi laughed and said, "He has you there."

"All right," Paul said. "Let me give it a little thought. We can go back and take a look at it again. Lanterns, cameras, paper for rubbings, and probably a few more things I'm not thinking of right now."

"Perfect," Levi said, smiling. Paul returned the smile and took a deep breath.

"Good, maybe I can figure out if I'm going crazy or not."

"Well, that will make one of us," Levi said. "Now, in the meantime, I'm going to be a nag and ask if you've considered my note."

Paul's smile died on his lips. He blinked rapidly and felt his brow bunching. "I ... I was hoping we wouldn't have to discuss that today."

"Well, I'm sorry if it's awkward, but I do think it's important given ... Well, we're all friends here. Paul, you've been erratic lately." He held up his hands as if Paul were pointing a gun at him. "I'm not accusing you of anything, and I'm not saying it's anyone's fault. But these are important, irreplaceable artifacts, especially after what happened in Iran." Paul must have made a face, because Levi's hands went higher. "Again, that wasn't your fault. How could it have been? I'm just saying that I think, until you have some time to recover peacefully, it's best if I have them for safekeeping. I believe your future self will thank me for it."

Paul stepped back and forced his hand to not go to his breast pocket, where he kept the small paper packet. "I-I'll have to think about that," Paul said.

"Oh, come now, Paul," Levi said. "It can't do any harm, and it can only do you good to—"

The rest of Levi's words were lost in the thrumming of Paul's pulse in his ears and a strange voice that seemed to whisper in his mind. Its words burned as they slipped through his thoughts,

In those few days he will pretend to lose the seal. It will be a great tragedy, and he will make it up to you in a grand gesture. Beware.

Paul's mind reeled. He felt like he might pass out again. Roaring like a hundred tons of rock collapsing around him, blotted out all other sounds. Levi's mouth worked, and Michael stood from his lunch. Concern etched their faces as they helped him to a chair. The roaring subsided, and the world's sounds returned as if they were approaching him from the end of a long tunnel. But the roaring didn't go away entirely.

"Are you alright? Should we call a doctor?" Michael was asking.

"No, no, I'm all right," Paul said. "But no, Levi. No. The seal stays with me. And that's final. I don't want to hear about it again."

As his companions considered each other with worried looks, Paul stared into the stacks. He had the wild thought that someone else might step out of them, as Natalie had. But the person he pictured was not the young woman from the front desk, but a tall, dire man in heavy vestments like a priest, robed and hooded with a heavy metal chain clanking at his belt. Under it all, the faint rumble persisted.

ix

Paul kneels on his worn office carpet, sifting through papers. The burglars had rummaged through everything, tossing boxes and overturning desk drawers. He cannot find the bronze plate from the tomb. The thieves took it and would have taken the seal, if Paul had not kept it with him. His hand goes to his breast pocket. The paper envelope stops its warmth from reaching him most of the time. But the other thing, the one in his hip pocket, burns consistently. Paul barely notices as he curses Levi's name.

X
Decision

Tuesday, November 18, 1969 - Morning

THE SUN LINGERED BEHIND the distant, eastern mountains, and clouds brooded in the west. Paul climbed the path beyond the bridge as the smell of coming snow tinged the air. Though outwardly silent as he mounted the slope, the roar in his tumultuous mind mingled with the falls to form a continuum of distraction. Beneath the roar, three voices called for his attention, trying to pull him to their ends. The first, and oldest, voice told him to put aside his petty grievances and suspicions. Levi was his friend and patron. There were mysteries afoot, and together, they might chase them down. The second voice, quieter but just as reasonable, told him to put aside his failed career and try to begin a new life with Gladys. There were books to write that didn't require a position at a university. They could make a tidy little life together, and he might even make a significant sum with his discoveries, no less sensational for the fact that they were true.

The third voice, by far the loudest, seemed to come from elsewhere in his body. It thrummed up through his chest from the throbbing in his hip where the silver disk nestled in his pocket. This voice told him to bring Levi into the cave and push him into one of the holes. It wanted to bury the man there as Vincent had been buried in his alcove.

Paul plodded up the path, desperately trying to rid himself of the third, aching, burning voice. He thought back to Georgina's words in Levi's house and considered them carefully. Though he should doubt everyone, he should trust Michael. She had not told him to trust Levi. She had not even told him to trust himself. Perhaps the third voice was a sign that he was going mad. No, not perhaps. Its mumbling about killing one of his closest friends was a sure sign that Paul was going insane. But if Georgina—the girl who had saved his life with a word of warning—had told him to trust Michael, perhaps it was through the young man's innocence and trustworthiness that Paul might see his way through the fog of unreason.

That thought had driven him to agree to go with Michael—only Michael—to the cave to explore it with lantern, tools, notes, and his camera with its new lens. Perhaps the younger man's calming influence would help Paul decide between the first two voices or some combination of their suggestions. He could not entertain that third voice; otherwise, he knew he would be lost. Yet, even as the morning birds sang and the cold autumn air stung his cheeks, the incessant suspicion and lust for revenge rambled on in his head.

Paul's contemplations were interrupted after he wound his way through the snarl of rock and tree to the hidden place where the cave's mouth hunched under overhanging rock. Next to the dark entrance, Michael sat with his back against the stone, his coat over him like a blanket.

"Michael?" Paul said.

The young man stirred and licked his lips. He scrunched his eyes tight before yawning expansively, which knocked his coat away. Michael shivered, pulled his coat back, and slipped his arms into place as he stood.

"Good morning, Professor," he said.

"How long have you been up here?" Paul asked.

"What time is it?" He asked this as he glanced at his own watch.

"Just before seven," Paul said.

"Then not long, I think I got up here about fifteen minutes ago. Didn't think I'd fall asleep that fast. Sorry about that."

Paul shook his head. He had come upon the young man dozing in the library before, and now guessed that Michael could fall asleep just about anywhere.

"Shall we?" he said, shivering and bouncing on the toes of his boots. "It's colder than I thought it would be.

"Of course," Paul said. "Looks like it might start snowing soon as well."

This seemed to trouble Michael as he stared up at the gray sky, but his cheerful demeanor returned when Paul suggested that he lead the way.

The two men ducked into the low, straight hallway that led to the wooden door and the first chamber.

"You don't seem cold at all," Michael said.

"Well, I have a little trick up my sleeve about that," Paul said, crouching behind the younger man.

"Oh really?"

"Yes, I keep a heater on me," Paul said, uncertain why he was letting the information slip. He was sure he could trust Michael, at least according to Georgina, but why give him information that others might wheedle out of him or get him to divulge inadvertently?

"Is that the cylinder? Mr. Grossman told me that it was warm to the touch."

"Please tell me you're not interested in the seal as well," Paul said.

"Oh no, professor. Well, not any more than anyone else would be. I've never seen an artifact that old before. Let alone one that radiates heat. But I'd never ask you for it. Heck, I'd never even ask to see it." This last he said as they passed into the larger room with the six pits. They stood up straight and stretched their lower backs.

"Well," Paul said, smiling at the young man's enthusiasm. "I don't mind if you see it. Honestly, I don't mind if Levi sees it. I just think it's better kept in professional hands in the long term."

"Sure, I bet you're right about that," Michael said. "Well, when we get back sometime, I'd love to look at it if you—"

"No need to wait. The lanterns are bright enough, I hope." Paul unzipped his coat and pulled the small paper packet from his pocket. He held it out toward Michael and studied his face, waiting to see if he would make a break for it or try to argue for why Levi should have it. Instead, he simply unwrapped the paper and shined his light on the three inches of metal with a look of pure awe.

"Amazing!" he said. "And, wow, it really is warm!"

"Didn't believe us?" Paul asked.

"Well, I thought maybe you and Mr. Grossman might be pulling my leg," Michael said.

"Not this time," Paul said.

"Wow, that really is something," Michael said. He ran his finger over the impressions again before folding the paper back over the seal and giving it back to Paul. "Thank you for letting me see it, professor. That meant a lot to me. I can see why Mr. Grossman would want to keep it safe—not that I'm saying it needs to be, or that you shouldn't do it! No sir. But I think I see why now. There's something special about it. I think I'd want to see it just about as often as I could."

"Of … well, of course, Michael. You may see any of my …"

"What's the matter, sir?" Michael said.

"I was going to say that you could see any of my artifacts, but then I realized that this is the last one I have."

"What do you mean?" Michael asked.

"Well, two nights ago, my house was broken into while I was asleep in my room."

"What? Here, in Lightning Falls?"

"That's right. And, I'll be honest with you, Michael, they took a few things from me. But that's not the part that bothers me the most. I think they were looking for this." He held up the paper packet before putting it back into his pocket. "And I think Levi is the one who sent them."

"No!" Michael said.

No, Paul thought. *Don't say that.* But the third voice—loud, suspicious, accusing—seemed to have hold of his tongue.

"Yes. It's far from what I would have expected from my old friend. But then, I don't think it should have been. He's taken almost everything from me, Michael. Did you know his wealth used to be my family's? My aunt ... Well, it's rather complicated, but suffice to say, I should be the one with all the money. But he just doles it out to me as he sees fit."

"That's not fair at all, Professor Kusel," Michael said, holding his lantern up as they walked toward the back of the cave. "What do you think you're going to do?"

"I've been thinking about that a lot. I think I'm going to leave. After we do this research, I'm, well, I don't know. Maybe I'll ask Gladys to marry me. And, I suppose whether she says 'yes' or 'no,' I'm going to sell my little house and move on. There's nothing left for me here. I could never live in my family's home after—Well, you know. And there is no work for me here, and no school would hire me anywhere close to here. Heck, what even is close to here? Nothing." He sighed heavily. "Yes, I think me and this little fella are going to hit the road, as they say. And I won't be back no more, no more, no more, no more."

This seemed to make Michael sad. "Wouldn't you reconsider, Professor? Just for a little while anyway."

"No, Michael, I don't think so." Paul knelt next to the middle pit on the right side of the room. He pointed his light at the pit's rim. "Look at this, Michael. I think there is work here, someone has been at this with a chisel."

Michael leaned over his shoulder and peered down. "What is that? Is that a carving?"

"Yes," Paul said. "I believe it is. A serpent, perhaps? Yes, I think it is." He ran his finger over the small, carved shape, brushing away loose earth. "Fascinating."

He stood and pointed his light at the other pits.

"Levi was right about one thing. There are things to discover here." He took a deep breath, and suddenly, a terrible idea came to him. He turned his beam to the last of the pits on the other side of the room at the end of the little passage Vincent had called 'The Dividing Hall.'

No, Vincent didn't name this cave. That was thousands of miles away.

He walked over to it, crouched, and, with a trembling hand, wiped away the dirt next to the rim, where it looked as if someone had been at the stone with a chisel. Sweat erupted from every pore on his face, and the dull run of water from the next room became a rushing flood of blood through his head. The world rocked perilously to one side and then the other as his palsied hand brushed aside the last of the dirt from the carved face of a roaring lion. Paul reached out for Michael and found his hand.

"Help," he croaked. "I might—"

Paul didn't faint, but, nevertheless, he fell into the dark pit. It was not as deep as he had expected, perhaps only four feet. But he still cracked his head badly on the floor and felt his collarbone crack. Pain invaded him from both fronts, but his injuries were not in the front of his battered mind.

He hadn't fainted forward; the hand that had held him had pushed. "Michael … why?"

"It's not me. I'm so sorry, Professor—" Michael began.

"Shut up," another voice said. It was familiar, deep, but Paul couldn't immediately place it. "Stand over there. Where does he have it?"

Paul didn't hear Michael's answer. Instead, the next thing he heard was someone clambering down into the hole with him. Rough hands pulled him over until he was looking up at a face hidden by darkness and backlit by the glow of the lanterns above. Still, Paul could tell that the man was broad and strong. He patted Paul's chest before digging in his shirt pocket for the small paper packet. He took it and pressed it against Paul's face.

"Now," he said. "Where are the other two?"

"Wh … what?"

"The other two," the man said, his voice scratching at Paul's memory. "You know where they are. Where are they?"

"There's only one seal. I only found the one." Paul felt drunk and woozy. He thought he might have a concussion.

"Not seals. A box and a rod. Where are they?"

"I don't know anything about that," Paul said. A memory flitted through his mind, a hint of a moment in the family library, but it was gone before he could grasp it.

"Did you hear that, Michael?"

"Y-yes, sir," Michael said.

"Do you believe him? He doesn't know anything about the other two?"

"Yes, sir. I believe him. Please, he doesn't know."

"That's good," the stranger said. "You're my witness, Michael. I tried.

He doesn't know. We will do things my way then."

"Please, I'm hurt, I need a doctor," Paul said.

The man spat into Paul's face. "No Doctor for you. There are no doctors in the glow of the scarlet flame."

"Sir!" Michael yelled.

"Shut up, boy. Help me out of this pit. We have to move before the snow starts falling and we end up leaving footprints."

The stranger spat on Paul once more, and Paul reached up to wipe it from his face.

"The Brethren are finally gone," the stranger said. "Finally, the third book is burned in the red flame."

"I'm not one of them. I don't know what you're talking about," Paul said weakly. "Please help me. I can't move, my arm is hurt. My hip is on fire. Oh god, it's burning me! It's so hot!"

"Yes, the flame burns," the man said. "Still, we may consider this a mercy. Let us cut the final puppet's strings."

Paul could not see what the man was doing, but for a split second, he heard the thunder in the cave, and then he knew no more.

Part 3 – Cast Out

What lies at the end of our striving? Only Eden made anew.

- Petr Mikulášek, *The Third Book of Seeings*

If he sees far, why have we not come to the new Eden? If he sees far, why have we not found what he promised us? We are not puppets to be lifted on strings directed by his secret knowledge. We seek our own wisdom, and we are coworkers with the one who enlightens our minds.

-Zuzanna Cerny, *The Book of Corrections*

The Azure flame of Ekt and the golden flame of Lai are preserved in a painting in the house of Palamar that I observed when I visited the old priest. The other flames—crimson and emerald—are hidden behind the vast library. Yet one's mind cannot help but picture what a sight the great edifice of learning must have been to the people of Fesoro before its calamity, a beacon of burning wisdom.

- Mikuláš Vaclavek, *The First Book of Seeings*

The Quiet Rumble

Volume 10, Issue 69, Sunday, August 17, 2025

Playing Cards in the Living Room

By Keith Lowry, Ed. In Chief.

WHEN MY GRANDMA ALICE was dying, my great aunts came over to our house to help my parents. They did all the things that siblings are more comfortable with than children. They changed the bedding, helped keep her clean, and listened to her rant about how the war would ruin us all. This was in 1959, when I had just turned nine, and I understood enough about death to know that it was coming for my grandma. I also knew that there was no war on in '59. Ike's tenure may have started with war, but we were in one of those nice, peaceful lulls where our young men weren't dying overseas.

I remember my Great Aunt Dutch, so named for her blonde hair, coming out of Grandma Alice's room every day, wiping her brow with a handkerchief, and saying to her sister Molly, "Deal." Molly would dutifully get out a deck of cards, and the three sisters would play something. Maybe it was Gin, maybe Spades. I remember my mother playing with them sometimes, but never my father. My father sat by the radio, read, or typed on his typewriter. We didn't have a TV until '62.

I remember sitting on the couch, uncertain what to do with myself. A stack of comic books featuring Batman, the Flash, and Superman sat unread by my bed upstairs. Toys my aunts had brought me lay unopened in a pile next to my toybox. My bike, which I rode religiously, collected spider-webs as it leaned against our shed.

For two weeks I didn't know how to live as Grandma Alice died.

One night, after what seemed like years of sitting, praying, and feeling too ashamed to do anything, I watched Great Aunt Dutch put her cards down, get up from the table, and approach me.

"Keith-boy, what are you doing?" she said with that strange little artifact of Boston Irish remaining in her voice.

"I'm praying," I think I said.

"And how much have you prayed?"

I remember not knowing what that meant.

"Have you prayed it all? All of it? Have you said to the Lord what needs to be said?"

I think I nodded.

"And have you done what you can? Have you been a good boy, and done your chores, and made things easier for your mother and father?" I remember the 'th's' in those words as blunted 'd's,' and again, I think I nodded.

"Then you've done what you can. Stop your God-bothering and come play cards."

I wondered if such a thing was possible. Could a person really love someone and do what they were doing? Could your loved one be dying in the next room while you asked for sevens? All the evidence seemed to suggest that you could. Her three sisters, all in their eighties, had come the long distance to Lightning Falls, a place my grandpa apparently dragged her to against her better judgment in the '20s because he heard there was steady work. They changed her clothes, listened to her ranting, allowed her to misidentify and misremember them, to slander them, to revile them, and even to strike them. They did that, and every morning and every evening, they got on their knees and prayed for her. On Sundays, they drove to Enterprise, attended church, and prayed for her.

But my nine-year-old mind couldn't work out how they could also play cards.

Now, of course, I know. I know that even their card playing was a way of loving her. They were caring for the ones caring for her. They were looking after themselves so they could look after her. They wouldn't have put it that way. They would have said something like, "What can you do?" or "Life must march on."

And, of course, what can you do? Life must march on.

So, as you return to your homes, tired, perhaps dejected, perhaps feeling as if all your hard work and time are coming to nothing, I ask you not to be like I was when I was nine. Read your comics, play with your toys, tell your stories, and take care of yourselves.

Say what Aunt Dutch said, as you walk into your house and wipe your brow with a handkerchief:

Deal.

Texting

Treeman
Hey

Jenny
Hey

Treeman
How are you doing?

Jenny
I was going to write something sarcastic, but I don't have it in me. I'm not doing well.

Treeman
I'm sorry.

Jenny
Thanks

Treeman
Is there anything I can do?

Jenny
No, I think the time for helping passed right after everything that happened at the Tim. And then maybe the few days after that. Or, like, not a week later.

Treeman
I'm sorry. I was processing.

Jenny
Cool

Treeman
I didn't know what to think. I've never been with someone like you, and it was kind of a shock.

Jenny
Cool

Treeman
I just don't think I can do it. Like, I can't be with someone who is so public.

Jenny
Cool

Treeman
I'm sorry. I'm not judging, I just don't want that for me.

Treeman
I don't really know why Leddy is acting the way she is. I'm sorry about her too.

Treeman
FWIW, Emmet says I'm an idiot, and he's probably right. He's been nagging me to take you back.

Jenny
Take me back?

Treeman
Sorry, said that wrong.

Jenny
Cool

Treeman
Are you going to be okay?

Jenny
I don't know. I have to move out, so you're making the right choice, since I'll have to be even more "public" to pay rent.

Treeman
I'm sorry.

Jenny
Cool

Volume 10, Issue 71, Sunday, August 24, 2025

Dreaming Together

By Keith Lowry, Ed. In Chief.

IT'S BEEN FIFTY YEARS since the last time the Lightning Falls Library got an overhaul. Fifty years. In that time there have been changes, of course. The old Dewey Decimal System was replaced by the Library of Congress's numbering. The card catalogs were supplemented and then replaced by computers. And the collection of books has grown and shrunk annually, with our librarians curating the new purchases and culling the old herd with the annual Library Book Sale each June.

But fifty of those sales have passed since the last time the town did anything to bring the library's structure up to date. Lightning Falls erected the building in 1908 from joint donations by the Kusel, Lister, Lundy, and Cerny families. After more than a hundred years, it remains one of the most curious and overlooked architectural wonders in our town, especially in this age of digital books and endless internet video. Not many folks wander through the library doors to explore the cramped first floor or the second and third-floor galleries. Few of the younger generation know that you can go to the top and look all the way down—which, admittedly, is a fairly mundane sight of closely stacked bookcases, but still, it's a novelty.

I remember being fourteen or fifteen and standing on that third balcony, looking down at one particular classmate of mine as she did her homework at one of the carrels that hug the railing. I dreamt of what it would be like to have the courage to ask her out. A studious young woman, she was far too smart to ever agree to go out with me, and I was a smart enough young man to know it.

The things we learn at the library.

Clearing my virtual throat and remembering where I am, I repeat myself to bring this article back to its topic. Our library hasn't had any major work since 1975. And then, they only made minor changes that most people never notice.

At the top of the library is a cupola, which is usually unavailable to the public. However, the staff open it on the Fourth of July, Founder's

Day, and Valentine's Day. And if you don't know why it's open on Valentine's Day, I recommend you avail yourself of the library's history section. Look under 'Oregon history.'

In any case, workers replaced several windows in the cupola in '75 along with some flooring, some plumbing, and all of the wiring. Since then, of course, contractors have made requisite repairs, and a new roof went on fifteen years ago.

But, as some of you have noticed, the library has been getting deliveries for the last few weeks and staying open later than normal as last-minute agreements come together, plans are finalized, and equipment is stored for the big project. Starting Tuesday, the library will close until the end of Camping Days, which should culminate (if all goes to plan) with the building's grand reopening and the donation of a collection of historical books by Mr. Levi Grossman.

So, while I know that for many of you, the only real change will be the construction workers going in and out on Library Avenue, we should all still be excited about the new additions! New, beautiful (and weather-efficient) windows, a computer room, and a coffee bar with a "third-space" area, which I'm told will be for those who don't want complete silence while working or reading. Think of it as a little coffee shop without the super-fancy drinks that Barry sells.

I know that this renovation will seem ill-advised to some people. Libraries are, I think, on borrowed time. But we are a town that loves our history, our traditions, and a way of life that we think is worth holding on to. And that includes our library. So, keep one eye out for the workers and one out for the big reopening. I think we'll all be glad that we did when we can lose ourselves again in the stacks and dream our impossible dreams.

Entry 5

August 27, 2025

Oh, hey Diary, long time. I'm sorry I abandoned you, but there's a lot of that going around right now. Fuck. Okay, I'm going to try to not be dramatic, but life has been pretty shitty the last two weeks. Things were already bad with Patty, and now they're terrible. She's kicking me out. She's taken on a complete "holier than thou" thing because I'm now a bigger whore than she ever was. Honestly, I think she's happy because she doesn't have to feel like I have something over her anymore.

All of my friends are gone except Delia, who has basically been my lifeline, and Isabella, who has been really weird. She's been so non-judgmental and sweet. It's freaking me out. And I know it's a stretch to say "my friends" since I only knew them for a few days, but technically, Leddy was my friend for years. Apparently, I'm too much of an eGirl for her now, and Phil won't date someone who fucks on the internet.

I don't blame them. I don't. There are consequences to what I do. I'm just hurt that the choices I made are—I don't know. I just don't understand what's acceptable and what isn't. Every single one of those guys is going to look. And I'm glad because my subscriptions have gone up, and I need the money.

It's not like when I was with everyone in California. They protected me. I was safe. That seems insane to say now, but I was. Joseph kept all of this stuff away, and Nolan made me feel loved no matter what. And Aurora never once judged me.

God, please. I'm sorry.

21
Reset

Friday, August 29, 2025

JENNY RAN ON THE street because it was smoother, and she didn't have to dodge pedestrians. Her earbuds thumped bass-heavy EDM for her new running shoes to keep time with. A week of running had already pushed her past soreness and early exhaustion. She wasn't back to the distances she used to run with Matina, but she felt confident that she would get back there. She could almost imagine Matina running beside her, her dark hair swinging in a ponytail, her '80s punk soundtrack scoring the passing world. Silently, they had eaten miles together. Silently, they had done almost everything together. Jenny thought back to Matina's first appearance at Aurora's apartment. Dark hair, dark eyes, dark mood. She had been a figure out of Aurora's past that had demanded her attention. At first Jenny had been jealous, but soon she felt it too.

Jenny remembered the first time she and Matina had sex. It was also silent, almost solemn, not like with Aurora, who seldom stopped laughing. There had been a focus and intensity that complemented Aurora's lightness.

Jenny wondered where Matina was now. The police hadn't found either Joseph or Matina. Perhaps they were on the road, finding new people to draw into their sick little world.

Perhaps Matina was dead, and the person keeping pace next to Jenny was a ghost.

She left Main Street and went up the path toward Whitman Cabin. When the old, log building came into view, she slowed to a jog and then a walk. She circled the single-story building and pushed through the old, rusted garden gate. Rows of plants still laden with shade-loving summer produce stretched back within the bounds of low stone walls.

Jenny wandered, letting leaves slide under her fingertips. She turned the music off and pulled her earbuds out to hear the morning forest and the rushing creek, swollen by the previous week's rain. Swollen like it had been the night her father drowned trying to save her.

Everybody drowns.

She pushed the thought away with a sniff and glanced up at the sky. She shoved the impulse to cry back into a dark hole. She had cried too much for too long. For a year, she had wept silently as her roommate sobbed openly. For a year, she had lamented what Joseph had done, what

Matina had done, and what she had done. She had curled up in a ball for days after the incident at the Timber. She had to put it all away. She knew that she couldn't just get over it all, but she couldn't let the pain consume her entire existence.

And Delia's existence. I need to give her a break.

The woman had been an invaluable support, and Jenny thought she would have helped more if Jenny had let her. But she felt too guilty to impose on Delia's kindness more than every few days. She needed to find some other outlet, somewhere to put her energy.

Jenny wandered out of the garden and jogged up to the creek's bank, where she crouched. She dipped her hands in the cool flow. She wanted to dive in to let the water sweep her away or to sink into its depths. Of course, it had no depths, not even swollen as it was. She could see the bottom and wondered for perhaps the millionth time how such a thing could take a strong man's life. It was not surprising that her mind had invented slithering serpents and robed figures to supply an answer to an impossible question. It was no wonder she had to invent boogeymen to explain her father's death.

She stood and wiped her hands on the seat of her running pants. Her pulse was slow again, her breathing regular, and her mind calm.

Jenny pushed her earbuds back in, restarted her music, and ran away from Kusel Creek.

22
Retrodden

Tuesday, September 2, 2025 – Early Afternoon

"YOU OKAY?" DELIA ASKED.

"Yeah," Jenny said, looking back over her shoulder at a group of young people who had just passed them.

"Not everyone is looking at you," Delia said.

"I know, it just feels like that."

"I mean, a lot of them are," Delia laughed. "But not all of them."

"Thanks," Jenny said, sliding her hands into her jeans' back pockets.

"I want them to look; it will be good for business," Delia said, waving to a woman across the street.

"I'm glad my personal hell is going to help you out," Jenny said, taking another look over her shoulder.

"That's what makes you a good friend," Delia said. She opened the door to her shop and let Jenny go in first. "Anybody here?"

"Just me." A woman with short gray hair popped her head out from behind a bookshelf.

"Hanna, how are you?"

"Good, just looking for something shocking."

"Sex or violence?" Delia said.

"Both. Surprise me," Hanna said. Jenny walked to the back of the store and greeted Dylan. He stared at her with an even stupider slack-jawed expression than when they first met. She patted him on the shoulder and slipped past him into the back rooms. Delia's office was on the left of a short hallway that led back to the storage room. To the right was a cramped nook with a curtain for a door. Jenny slipped inside and sat down on the well-worn swivel chair. She planted her elbows on the wooden desktop and buried her face in her hands. She considered crossing her arms and trying to nap like in high school, but she didn't want red marks. So, she sat in that position while she waited for Delia to finish with her customer.

A few minutes later, Delia knocked.

"You ready to sell my books?" Delia asked.

Jenny reached back and pulled the curtain to the side. "Yes, use my face to excite people's minds for once," she said, smiling.

"I'll try. Remember, these are supposed to be cute and wholesome, so don't just start whipping your clothes off," Delia said, leading Jenny out past Dylan, who looked like a rabbit caught in a flashlight as he turned the sign on the front door so that the 'Open' side faced into the shop.

"So, you don't want me to just sprawl across the books in my underwear?"

Dylan made a squeaking sound that might have been a nervous hiccup.

"He's eighteen, right?" Jenny asked.

Delia nodded and smiled. "He's twenty. And still, no, I think for Dylan's sake, we won't do that," Delia said. "I don't want his parents suing me if he dies of a heart attack or blood loss to his brain. I was thinking cute, fun, but not—"

"Slutty, right," Jenny said, giving her a self-effacing grimace.

"Maybe flirty," Delia said. "Like, if you come into the bookstore, maybe a lady like this will appreciate that you read. Hell, maybe you'll even meet one here. God knows enough single women are haunting my aisles."

"Appealing to the ever-desirable male audience? I'm to be one more enticement for persons with penises? Must I be subject once more to the male gaze?" Jenny affected a stricken mid-Atlantic accent.

"Men don't read as much as they used to," Delia said. "So yes, let's woo that patriarchy. Maybe they'll learn something. Or at least have something more interesting to talk about on a date than Cryptocurrency or how much they understand my plight. I'd kill to have someone just tell me what they think about Algernon Blackwood so I can tell them they don't appreciate him half as much as I do."

"Right, okay. Mold me, I'm clay in your hands. Let's sell books and make your dating life better."

"Yes, please," Delia said.

They began with Jenny sitting on the counter next to the register. Dylan stacked books next to her and handed her a few to read. He also moved her hair and opened and closed the window shades. Twice, he gave good suggestions. The first time, he suggested that Jenny turn so that her back was against the wall and her feet were up on the counter. The second time, he opened a shade they wanted closed, and they both had to admit he was right. Delia immediately promoted him from gofer to photographer's assistant—asking him, as the resident straight male, what his opinion was of this or that pose, framing, or composition. Dylan, it turned out, was funny and insightful, though he remained bashful and quiet most of the time.

Jenny moved from the counter to the classics shelves and exchanged her T-shirt for a flowy, flutter-sleeve top. They swooped her hair behind her neck and back over her shoulder to fall across her chest. She leaned against the shelves and studied a green-covered copy of the *Iliad*. She sat cross-legged and studied a red-covered edition of the *Metamorphoses*. A play from Aristophanes rested on her knee as she sat against the shelves, her eyes fixed on the open pages. Finally, she peered down into Aristotle's *Metaphysics* as she lay on her stomach. Delia framed her so that she faced the camera, and her sneakers, kicked up behind her, were just out of focus.

Jenny's eyes scanned the enticing and impenetrable Greek. She wondered what it would be like to understand another alphabet, for different signs to mean the same sounds. *Or*, she thought, *maybe new sounds that I don't even use.* She sighed whimsically as Delia plucked Aristotle from her hand and told her to go change again.

A minute later, Jenny emerged in a black T-shirt that read 'The Three Laws of Robotics' across the chest, and Delia led her into the sci-fi section. Jenny found *Dorsai!* by Gordon R. Dickson in honor of Stew, who used to come into the shop. She posed like the main character on the cover, one hand up by her shirt collar. She moved from Dickson through the ABCs of science fiction. She stared open-mouthed at the exploits of R. Daneel Olivaw, smiled when she learned why "R" is for rocket, and frowned at HAL's betrayal. In fantasy, she put the flowy shirt back on and closed her eyes as the yellow-jacketed *Adventures of Dr. Esterhazy* lay open across her chest as she pretended to nap. Chin in her palm, Jenny smirked into a copy of *Swords and Deviltry*.

King, Jackson, Moat, James, and Hill surrounded and terrified her in the horror section. When they came to romance, Jenny was simultaneously tired and energized.

"Are we going to bring Dylan into these? Give me someone to romance?" Jenny teased.

Dylan, who had appeared less flustered as time passed, waved her away. "No one wants to see me."

"No," Delia said. "I think that would be fun."

Dylan's face changed from smiling to something else, which Jenny thought might be panic.

"Hey, I know," Jenny said. "Come here, sit down here with me."

They sat side by side, reading *Pride and Prejudice* and *Sense and Sensibility* together, each with a hand on the book. Then Delia had them sit facing each other, their feet interlaced. Once Dylan was looking down at his book, Delia lifted her eyebrows and her chin toward Dylan. Jenny peered over the top of her book at the sandy-haired young man as if she were interested in him. When she did, she saw him anew. He didn't look silly or shy or as uncomfortable in his skin as she thought. He looked sad. He looked alone.

"Dylan, would you be cool if we did one where I have my head on your knee? Like, I'm reading, and you're reading, and—"

Panic bloomed on his face.

"It will be fine," Delia said. And it was. They laughed when Dylan had no idea what to do with his hands, and Jenny moved him around like a puppet. They finally took pictures of them standing side-by-side, holding books up in front of each other.

"These are so fun," Delia said. "You guys are amazing."

Jenny leaned over and kissed Dylan on the cheek. "Thanks for being sweet," she said.

He stared blankly at her. "I—right, I ... You're welcome."

"Okay, I want to do a few more, and I don't think Dylan is ready for these," Delia said.

Jenny felt her eyebrows rise. "Oh, what are we thinking?"

"First, shoo, Dylan. Go take a cold shower. Come back in twenty minutes."

Having reverted to his flustered state after the kiss, Dylan stood, gathered his things, and left out through the back of the store.

"Now we're thinking sexual?" Jenny asked, standing and straightening her shirt, which had remained flowy and fluttery since the fantasy section.

"A little, but not anything crazy. Come over here."

Delia brought Jenny to the back corner where erotica filled a bookcase from top to bottom. She pulled *Fifty Shades of Grey* out and held it up.

"Really?" Jenny said.

"Really," Delia said. "There's a never-ending parade of vanilla-ass women who like to think they're kinky because they read that."

"Have you read it?" Jenny asked, turning the book over.

"Of course not. I was kinky before 2011." Delia walked over to the counter and crouched down behind it. She rustled around before popping back up a rope in her hand. "But far be it from me to deny people their 'sinful little pleasures.' So, I was thinking we could do a thing where I do a little knot around your wrists, and you hold the book up while you're tied up. You know, suggestive, but not like, having you suspended from the ceiling."

Jenny stared at the rope. "Um," she began. "Uh, do we have to do that?"

Delia stopped. "I mean, I won't tie it tight. It's just for show. I—Wait, shit, fuck I should have asked. I'm not triggering some kind of trauma, am I—"

"No, no, nothing like that. I just—apparently just having a bunch of people try to tie me up in this town."

Delia frowned; the rope hung limp at her side. "What do you mean?"

"Isabella, the night before—well, the day Carson went missing—she tied me up for like five minutes. It was really uncomfortable. I kind of freaked out."

"Really," Delia said, frowning thoughtfully. "Isabella did that?" Jenny nodded. "For five minutes?" Jenny nodded again. "Huh." She paced as she seemed to think the matter over.

"I kept asking her to stop, but she kept ignoring me."

"Right. Okay, I'm sorry that happened, and of course, we won't do this then." She tossed the rope back to the counter. "In fact, I think maybe it's a bad idea to have you pose with that one anyway."

"Really? I mean, I'll do it," Jenny said.

"No, I want to end on you and Dylan being sweet. I think you probably have too many people already thinking about you naked. I don't want to give them any more ideas."

"I don't know," Jenny said, smiling, "could be good for business."

"For you or me?"

"Yes," Jenny said.

23
First Tour

Wednesday, September 3, 2025 — Morning

A NARROW GRAVEL DRIVEWAY ran twenty feet into closely packed pines. At the end, a wide, green yard spread, bordered by the drive as it looped up and back from the front of the house. Two oak trees dominated the lawn, which was otherwise empty except for two benches. To the right, on the other side of the gravel, lay a cement platform with the rusted skeleton of a metal frame that reached six feet into the air, ending in the blunted tips of its bars like the curled fingers of an iron hand. Hedges, neatly trimmed, ran along the front of the porch on either side of wooden steps.

Two stories and an attic, painted pale lilac and trimmed light mint green, looked down at Jenny through dark windows. Two brick chimneys pointed up from the center of the house. From the taller, an antenna rose above the treetops.

"The house is a hundred and fifty years old," Link said, gesturing toward the stone foundation. "We've had the wiring redone twice, the plumbing was completely replaced fifteen years ago, a new roof ten years ago, new windows five years ago."

I'm not buying the place, Jenny thought. But she figured it was good to listen to since Link was going to be her point of contact with the town.

"The grounds get mowed once a week, though sometimes we need to gently remind the guys who do it. I don't recommend using the tree-swing."

"Why?" Jenny asked. "Is it haunted?"

Link laughed and rubbed the back of his head. "Not that I know of, but the creek that runs back there is shallow and finicky. And the branch is a little iffy, too. Though, you'd probably be fine. I'd just break the damn thing in half if I sat on it."

Jenny chuckled and wondered if that was true. Link wasn't a slim man, but his small beer-belly hadn't taken him over. She was pretty sure she'd seen him biking in and out of town in padded biker shorts.

"The front porch swing, on the other hand, is good and sturdy. If you have some fella come around looking to court you, and you want to sip some tea while talking about his prospects, that's the place to do it."

"I'm not sure if you've heard my reputation around town, but Jane

Austen it isn't."

He shrugged and scratched his beard. It was black, short, and shot through with streaks of gray, just like his closely cropped hair. "Yeah, neither is mine, but that's what this place makes me think about."

"Oh, I see," Jenny said, smiling at him, "you want me to invite you over for tea and swinging."

He laughed. "Look, I'd never say 'no,' but—Well, I should show you inside."

He led her up to the porch and showed her the swing. She wondered what he had been about to say. She was torn between thinking he had deflected her innocent flirtation because of her reputation or something else, maybe a girlfriend.

Or maybe you should stop flirting with literally everybody you meet.

Jenny didn't think much of her own advice.

"You'll have a set of keys to the whole building, except the second apartment on the first floor. If someone moves into that apartment, they'll have the same setup as you, except, well, you know, not your apartment. The other Talkers have keys to the front door," he said as he opened said door, "and all of the facilities on the second floor."

"Will they be around here much?" Jenny asked.

"So, usually folks rotate every week or so. You get four days here, then four days at the cabin, then four days at the tower, then you start over. Keeps people from getting bored, I guess. The weekend Talkers have the same deal, so you'll get to know them over time. They all have a little breakfast club at the diner. Not everyone goes every day, but since they're mostly the only folks who work the night shift in town, they keep up with each other."

The thought appealed to Jenny, but she wasn't sure if they'd accept her into their group. She felt gun-shy after her experience with Phil, Leddy, Earl, and Emmet, especially since she knew herself. She wouldn't be able to keep walls up if she connected with someone. And that, she knew, would make her vulnerable to painful rejection again.

"Here's your apartment," Link said, opening the first door on the right in the house's foyer. "This used to be a library, and that hall, where the bathroom and your bedroom are, was a sitting room or something, and then the kitchen … well, you're basically getting half of the old kitchen. The whole thing is wired up for cable, internet, whatever you need. The furniture is …" he said, patting the back of a plaid upholstered couch that Jenny figured was about forty years old. "Retro. But it's furnished. You'll need your own sheets, blankets, and pillows, of course.

And, honestly, I'd buy a new mattress too. I don't think anyone's slept on that thing more than a random night here or there for the last decade, but the guy who had this place before …" Link waved his hand in front of his scrunched-up nose.

Jenny admired the old-fashioned look of the place. Wallpaper, wooden wainscotting, and old tiles gave her the impression that she was stepping back in time. The bedroom wasn't big; the dresser, desk, and a wardrobe fit cozily around the queen-sized bed. A small closet nestled in one corner, which Jenny figured was more than enough for her current wardrobe.

"No one's lived here for a decade?" Jenny asked.

"Mhm," Link said, running the water in the bathroom sink and nodding when it came out clear. "We aren't allowed to rent it out or really let anyone stay here except in emergencies."

"Why not?"

"All part of the ordinances around this place and the Sleep Talkers, or rather 'local nighttime radio engineers,' as they are listed in Lightning Falls' ordinances. Sadly, LNRE doesn't really lend itself to a cunning little name."

"Lin-ree," Jenny attempted.

"*Liner* was one I tried for a little while," Link said. "No one knew what the hell I was talking about."

"Um, can I ask something stupid at this point?"

"Sure," Link said.

"Why do we—I mean, why do we need three people talking on the radio every night? I remember that it's kind of always been that way, but I feel like it's something no one ever talks about, and, I feel like I'm not supposed to ask."

Link laughed and shook his head. "I just figured you knew since you grew up here."

"No, I—" Jenny thought about telling him about her memory, but then said, "I don't think I ever knew."

He nodded and shook his head, still chuckling. "That's the way it is. People grow up with things and never really bother to find out why. Well, I can give you the overview. Apparently, when the Great Depression hit, Mr. Kusel, who owned the house, had a lot of money in gold. So, instead of taking a hit, he made a fortune."

"Really?"

"Yeah, something FDR did. If you had an ounce of gold back then, you'd get twenty bucks for it, no idea what that is today, but after FDR did a gold buy-back, the price jumped to something like thirty-five dollars an ounce. So, the Kusels didn't exactly double their fortune, but they sure made out."

"Okay," Jenny said.

"Right, the Sleep Talkers—sorry, I get distracted." Link tried the sink in the kitchen and nodded when it flowed clear and he had to pull his finger away when it got too hot. He sucked on his finger. "Anyway, they built the fire-watch tower and put a radio station in there. And soon after that they put one in at the cabin too. Paying jobs for people. They ensconced the whole practice in the town's ordinances and made it so that to repeal the laws, the town would have to vote unanimously to end the jobs. And that's never going to happen."

"But that's only two towers."

"Yeah, well, there was a third based out of what's now the Shonette Apartments, but it was the Lundy Hotel back then. Anyway, they moved it here in the '50s since the house was empty."

"Can someone do that? I mean, can they make a law that can only be repealed that way? Is that even legal?"

Link shrugged. "Don't know. No one's ever challenged it. It doesn't cost the town that much since the endowment subsidizes most of the equipment."

"What endowment?"

"The one that will keep your power and heat on and pay your salary, meagre as it is," Link said, checking the cabinets. "Mr. Grossman set up the endowment back in the '60s when there was some question about funding for the Liners—" he turned and pointed at Jenny. She laughed. "No? Well, for the Sleep Talkers. So, no one bothers to try to wrangle with the law. The FCC licenses are all in order, and we're not even the only funky radio stations in the area. There's another one out of an antique store down in Lostine, and then there's one out in Shaniko in a record store. Like them, we only do analog, nothing digital. So, records, tapes, that kind of thing. Though, right now, we only have record players set up in the booths. Speaking of that, let me show you upstairs. Oh, I'm going to leave this here too, just in case you need to get in touch."

He pulled a business card from his wallet and put it on an empty bookcase shelf. Jenny walked up and picked it up.

"Your name is just Link?" she asked.

"Yeah, why?"

"I thought it was short for something, like, I don't know—"

"Like Lincoln, because I'm black?" He changed his voice, made it gruffer, and Jenny had a moment of panic before he laughed. "I'm named after the damn video game character. My sister's name is Zelda, which, yes, I know, is messed up. My dad was—is—the biggest geek in the world. You like model trains?"

Jenny shrugged.

"You come over and that man will walk you through his model train collection for two hours. Then he'll show you his complete NES collection. Well, US-complete, he'll explain that part too since he's got a near complete Japanese collection …"

Link led her out of the apartment, down the hallway, and up the stairs to a short landing where they faced a closed door. He unlocked and opened it, revealing a narrow hallway with doors that marched down both sides. Framed photographs hung in the spaces between the doors.

"The changes up here were way more extensive," he said, flipping on a light. "First, they put this door in to make sure that not just anyone could get up here. Next, the broadcast studio used to be a bedroom, and the lounge and kitchen were both bedrooms as well. The bathrooms were renovated like yours, everything in here is a full bath in case someone needs a shower during their shift."

"So, I might hear people showering on my nights off?" Jenny asked, looking at the pictures. The black and white pictures showed the house and its grounds. Faces stared out at her, some serious, some smiling.

"You might, but you'll get used to it. It's just like living in an apartment building, except that you'll basically know everyone who comes in and out."

He opened the first door on their left. They stepped into a dark room. Link flipped a switch, and recessed lighting blinked on. Uneven zig-zag patterns made of something like charcoal gray foam covered the windowless walls. Against the far wall was a desk with a complicated control panel sporting knobs, lights, dials, and sliders. A laptop sat open on the desk. Next to it, a swivel-mount arm proffered a silver microphone with a pop screen. Hanging over the arm was a pair of black over-ear headphones.

"Wow," Jenny said. Next to the control panel were a bright red record player and a phone. To the right of the desk were two tall bookshelves full of records. To their right stood a small table with a metallic box. To the left of the desk, a low metal cabinet stood in the far back corner of the room. The rest of the room was empty.

Link flipped three switches, and the room's lighting changed. The recessed bulbs dimmed, and a new, warm spotlight illuminated the desk and its equipment. The board lit up, as did a few small lights on the record player.

"This will be your setup for the first three weeks, so you can get acclimated. Your weekday compatriots will just swap the cabin and tower during that time. Once you're done with your 'getting to know you' period, you can go figure out the cabin and the tower. They're less fancy, but if you learn one, you'll know the others."

Jenny nodded as she approached the control panel.

"Um, is there a manual for this?" she asked, surveying the daunting collection of knobs, switches, and buttons.

"Yeah," Link laughed. "But for the most part, you really only have to worry about five controls: Power, broadcast, volume, phone connection, and the record player." He pointed to each as he listed them. "Power comes on when you flip the second switch over there," he jerked a thumb back toward the door, "this turns the broadcast on and off, this slider here controls your volume. You want your voice to be getting into the yellow on these lights when you're at your loudest and not really dipping below here"—he pointed at some numbers next to the lights—"when you talk normally. That's your cough button. Just push it if you're going to make bodily noises you don't want to broadcast. Think of it as a push-to-mute instead of a push-to-talk." She stared at him. "You'll figure it out. There's a binder there," he said, pointing to a black three-ring binder on the desk. "Also, people *will* call in to tell you if you're too low or too loud, so you don't have to worry too much about that."

Jenny nodded.

"These will allow you to take calls on the air, and that controls the caller's volume. 'Answer,' 'hang up,' 'mute,' all labeled, but also all in the binder." He turned and moved to the record player, resting one hand on its clear plastic cover and the other on a small section of controls on the panel. "These will let you play a record on air. This switches the audio feed from the mic to the record player and back again, and if you put it in the middle, both will work. Record volume," he said, sliding another slider up and down. "And, honestly, that's pretty much it. You could get to know the rest of the controls, but I can't imagine what you'd use them for. And the other towers don't have boards this complex. They all have controls that do all the same things, but this is the fancy setup."

Jenny nodded.

"Questions?" Link asked.

Jenny shook her head. "Not yet."

"You look nervous," Link said.

"I am. I feel like I don't know what I'm doing."

"Well, really, it's just you come in, turn the thing on, and talk into it. If you're too loud, lower your volume. If you're too soft, raise it. People call in, you push a button to let other people hear them, you push a button to hang up. If you want to put a record on, you put one on and then flip a switch. Ultimately, that's all there is to it. By the third hour doing it, you'll already be a pro."

"I'm glad you think so," Jenny said.

"Trust me, you're not an idiot. I've had idiots take this job, and they figure it out. You're going to be laughing within a week about how nervous you are now. Now, the talking part ..." Link said, walking back toward the door. "Yeah, that you'll have to figure out yourself. Or you're going to just play a hell of a lot of records."

"Is that allowed?" Jenny asked.

Link stopped with his hand on the lights. "Allowed?" he asked.

"I mean, could I do that? Just play records?"

He shrugged. "Yeah. I mean, as long as you made sure they didn't have any long periods of silence, yeah. You have to keep track of what you play, but we have a deal for all the records we stock, so it's not that important. But ..." He frowned, lowered his hand, and rubbed his palms together. "I think you have the wrong idea about this. There's no 'allowed.' My job is to make sure you know what you're doing, to give you your keys, and to help with any problems you run into. But otherwise, you're on your own. You're your own boss. That's how it's always been with the Sleep Talkers, or Liners ..." He trailed off for a moment, and a wide smile crept across his face. "Or Night Whisperers."

"Night Whisperers?" Jenny said, unsure if she should laugh.

"Mhm, in the '70s, we had a couple of cool cats who thought they were smooth as silk and that these towers were their own personal funk and love connection stations"—he smiled and shrugged again—"and they decided to call themselves the 'Night Whisperers.' They played a lot of blues, funk, jazz. The name really only stuck to them, though. I don't think David Brighteye was especially keen on being called a 'Night Whisperer.'"

Jenny nodded slowly. "So, I really can do anything here? I could start an MLM, or preach a new religion, or talk about how aliens abducted me and did experiments on me?" Jenny crossed her arms and smiled.

"Well, yeah," Link said. "Really your only limit is keeping it, like, fairly family-friendly before eleven, but that's more of an unwritten rule. The audience will let you know if you're overstepping. Believe me, they will let you know. And they'll let me know, but, honestly, I can't really do anything about it. I don't have the power to fire you."

Jenny frowned. "Um, who does?"

He shook his head. "No one. Once you take the job, it's yours unless you quit. I think there's a clause in the contract that says that you automatically forfeit the job if you leave the mic unattended during the hours for a cumulative time during a certain period, or something like that. And there's something about damaging the equipment, the buildings, going to jail, stuff like that. But they worded all of that so that you're the one who is forfeiting the job; no one is taking it away from you."

Jenny stared at him in disbelief. "I skimmed the contract," she said. "I thought that was all stuff about grounds for being fired."

"Nope. Well, I mean, I guess it comes to the same thing, but no, no one can fire you. You're like a Supreme Court Justice, here for life if you want it."

Jenny followed Link through the lounge, where there were two big couches with pillows, woven patterned blankets, a TV, and a radio. The kitchen had new appliances, and the refrigerator had a stripe of blue paint tape running down the middle of each shelf. Each section had a name on a strip of the same blue tape. Link pulled the one that said 'Cassandra' off. He opened a drawer and pulled out a roll of painter's tape and a magic marker. He wrote 'Jenny' on a strip, tore it, and put it where Cassandra's tape had been.

"One side of a shelf for each person. The right is weekday folks, the left is Weekenders." Jenny saw cans of diet pop, regular pop, packets of string-cheese, cartons of milk. "You all figure that out yourselves. I think someone buys creamer every week, someone else gets coffee."

Jenny opened the freezer and saw boxes of frozen meals with names written on them. There was a good coffee maker, a kettle for tea, and a large microwave.

"I think most people eat their first meal before they show up, then have lunch during their shift, and then meet at the diner in the morning for 'dinner.' But everyone's a little different."

When the tour was over, Link stood with her on the front porch.

"So, how are you feeling about all this?" he asked.

"Okay, I think. Um, I guess I do have a question, though. If I'm here, and the other two locations are the cabin and the tower, where do the other people live?"

Link smiled. "Ah, yeah, so ... they live in town. Everyone has apartments like this except for Charles, who lives with his mother. He's a Weekender. Everyone else shares apartments in two houses in town. If Charles didn't live with his mother, he'd be in the other apartment here. So, either good or bad, you're the one person who gets to have her own place."

They walked out into the front yard and looked up at the front of the house.

"So, I can move in on Monday?"

"Yep, that's when you'll get the keys. Come by Town Hall first thing and we'll put them in your hands and you're the new permanent resident."

Despite the open smile on Link's face and the prospect of being free from Patty's constant judgment, the statement sounded ominous to Jenny.

24
Future

Friday, September 5, 2025 – Evening

CINDER'S REMORSE WAS MUCH smaller and trendier than the Timber. As she walked through the metal-framed glass doors, Jenny immediately knew what kind of bar it was. New, rustic furnishings, brushed metal accents, and bartenders with well-manicured facial hair reminded her of the nights Matina picked the destinations for their group outings. She had a thing for men with mustaches that curled at the end; long, well-kept beards had been an optional bonus. Jenny had never felt one way or the other about the faux late 19th-century style, except that she and Aurora would laugh playfully at Matina when she would lust after a slick-haired man in suspenders.

Jenny did a quick checklist in her head of what she expected to see in the dining room: exposed stills where they brewed their own beer, menus that had a story about the bar, even though it was less than ten years old, and decorations that hearkened back to the past, like miners' picks or photographs. Jenny expected to see pictures of Nez Perce, Walla Walla, Umatilla, Cayuse, gold-rush workers, settlers, and old buildings from around Wallowa County.

Oh, she thought, *and a short menu with fancy versions of standard drinks.*

The person who greeted them had short, brown hair and olive skin and wore a bow tie with their white button-down shirt.

"Hey," they said, "is this your first time at Cinder's Remorse?"

"Not for me, but for her," Isabella said.

"Great! Welcome! Do you want to sit at the bar or a table?"

Jenny decided a table would be better and followed them back into the dining room. It was bigger than Jenny had expected and featured a small, raised platform off to one side with microphones and speakers. Jenny started checking items off her list. *Stills? Check. Old photographs? Check. Tools on the walls? Check.* When the host handed them their frustratingly short menus, Jenny flipped hers over to find a brief paragraph at the bottom telling the story of Cinder's Remorse. She was almost batting a thousand.

"Do you have a drink menu?" Jenny asked.

"Of course, it's here," the host said, pulling a laminated card from a metal stand on the table.

"Ah, should have seen that. Thanks," Jenny said. She glanced at the menu, smirked, and congratulated herself for a perfect prediction.

"What's so funny?" Isabella asked.

"Nothing, just think I've been to a place like this before."

"They have great burgers," Isabella said.

They did. Jenny ordered their smash-style burger with sweet potato fries, and she had to admit it was the best burger she'd had in a long time. The conversation up to that point was also pleasant. Isabella talked about her job, how this older man had hit on her every time he came in trying to sell them software that Jenny didn't care to understand, and how the search for Carson was entering its final phase.

"What does that mean?" Jenny asked.

"So, I'm just piecing this together from what I remember, what Manny told me, and what Leddy and Phil said, but even though the search doesn't officially end, it doesn't really keep going either. Since the ground around town has been gone over twice now, and they found fuck-all, he remains a missing person. They'll be on the lookout for him, but they can't just keep covering the same ground over and over, you know?"

"So," Jenny said, "that's kind of it? Like, no one is going to look for him anymore?"

Isabella shrugged. "I'm sure Phil and Leddy and them will keep their eyes open when they go hiking, and so will a bunch of people around town, but as far as official searches, unless they find something new, yeah, I think it's over."

Guilt pushed its way up into Jenny's chest. If she had swallowed her pride and gone out on the third day to help search, maybe she would have found something. Or—more likely—Phil or Leddy might have if Jenny had helped them cover more ground. But she hadn't gone out with them; she had sulked in her room like a teenager. Sulked and made more money on her JustBuffs page than she had in a year.

"That really sucks," Jenny said.

Isabella took a deep breath and tilted her head, looking off in the distance. "Honestly, I don't think he's anywhere near here. I think someone grabbed him, and he's in some basement somewhere or in a ditch far away."

She pictured Carson shivering in a corner. The room looked suspiciously familiar, with its white porcelain, claw-footed tub. Carson looked exactly like the picture on the search flyers: short blonde hair, blue eyes, and big ears. In her imagination, he was wearing a dirty, blue

T-shirt with a faded picture of cake on the front and torn, dirty pajama pants. His clothes were soaked, and his eyes looked out blankly as he shook in a puddle of water.

"That's fucking terrible," Jenny said, trying to force the image from her mind by picking up a fry, poking it into a cinnamon-bourbon dipping sauce, and jamming it into her mouth.

Isabella agreed and sipped her coffee-flavored drink.

"Okay, in less horrible news," Isabella said, straightening in her chair and pushing her breasts out. Jenny wasn't sure if that was supposed to be flirtatious or if it was just a habit. She could never tell if the woman was safely in friend territory or if she was about to casually wander over a boundary again. "Are you ready to move into the murder house?"

Jenny shook her head and laughed. "I don't think it's a murder house," Jenny said.

"Oh, come on, four people dead! Arsenic in the tea! Really? Come on!"

"It wasn't arsenic, that's from a Shirley Jackson book," Jenny said. Isabella frowned at her, confused. "It's from a novel that—Look, the four people who died in that house probably died of gas inhalation. The whole arsenic thing comes from an article in the '70s, and people picked that up as part of the local legend."

"That is definitely not what I heard," Isabella said.

Jenny laughed. "I've had a lot of time to read up on this since I've got basically nothing else to do. And when you told me I was moving into a murder house, I took it seriously. I do not want to be the girl in the horror movie who's like, 'The house is haunted by the spirits of dead people? That's crazy, that would never happen to me!' And then she just gets freaking ghost-got."

"Ghost-got?"

"Yeah, like, the ghosts—"

"No, I get it," Isabella said, "I just think it's a cute way of saying it. Ghost-got."

Jenny took a moment to evaluate whether Isabella was flirting and then continued. "So, yeah, I read the articles from the '40s and some follow-up stuff. There was one on the twenty-fifth anniversary of their deaths and another one on the fiftieth. The arsenic thing is from the '70s where the writer says something like, 'it's our own Blackwood mystery,' and—"

"Blackwood?"

"The family from the Shirley Jackson novel. Anyway, they all died of arsenic in the book, and the reporter made a comparison. And, if you didn't know that the coroner had ruled their deaths as accidental because of carbon monoxide poisoning, you might think that he was being literal. That's where that rumor started."

"Carbon monoxide poisoning?" Isabella said, looking disappointed.

"Yeah, something about the stove or the chimney or something. It wasn't ventilated properly, and they basically just went to sleep."

"I feel like you'd notice that," Isabella said.

Jenny shook her head. "No, I had it once when I was in Portland. Our apartment had a carbon monoxide leak or something, and the building alarm went off, but we didn't hear it. It wasn't loud enough. Anyway, I just basically got this slow, throbbing headache, and we probably would have just passed out if my boyfriend didn't finally hear the alarm."

"Fuck, that's scary," Isabella said.

"Yeah, it was not a fun experience."

"Wait, so what boyfriend? I thought you were, you know, with a woman in Portland."

Jenny frowned at her inadvertent biographical detail. "I had a boyfriend for a while. We moved in together. He was—"

"A narcissistic asshole?" Isabella asked, as if the answer had to be 'yes.'

"No, I think he was just immature. So was I. We just weren't a good fit for each other. Anyway, that's ancient history. Tell me why we've never been in here before," Jenny said, looking around at the dimly lit restaurant. "It's kind of cool."

"It's mostly for tourists, hikers, people who want to feel like they are getting the real unsettled, untouched world of wild Oregon experience. You know, with simple syrup and authentic huckleberry-infused vodka, just like Chief Joseph used to drink." She said the last part in a fake commercial voice. She shook her head. "Plus, it's more expensive than the Tim."

"I wish I remembered more about that stuff," Jenny said, looking at the pictures on the walls.

"What stuff?"

"The indigenous people, the whole story of this place, the gold rush, you know," Jenny said.

"Read a book," Isabella said.

"No, I mean, growing up with it, going to Tamkaliks or all the way out to Wild Horse. I have these vague flashes of things, but I don't remember them, not really."

Isabella nodded and reached across the table, taking Jenny's hand. Jenny evaluated.

"I'm sorry. Maybe the longer you're here, the more will come back. I know I have a lot of great memories of going to Tamkaliks. I think I actually had my first real crush on a girl there. She was working at this table with her parents, and I bought a bracelet from her. I used to wear it all the time, thinking I was the shit. I loved that thing."

"What happened to it?" Jenny said, taking her hand back to grab the last part of her burger.

"Lost it in the creek, I think," Isabella said. "I can't imagine how much stuff is just—" She stopped and looked down at her plate. "We should definitely go next summer and get a replacement. Hell, maybe she'll be there, and I can get her number."

"Yeah," Jenny said before popping the last of her food into her mouth and taking her time to chew as she looked at an old black and white picture of the Kusel Creek with two men standing on its banks holding fishing rods.

"Oh shit," Isabella whispered.

"What?" Jenny said.

"Chloe's here."

Jenny lifted her chin and slowly, casually turned in her chair. She pretended to look at something on the wall, then glanced at the woman leaning against the bar. Tall, with short brown hair and a slender figure, she wore low-slung jeans, a pale-green T-shirt, and work boots.

"She's hot," Jenny said.

"Yeah," Isabella said, "she is. She's also totally insane. Shit."

Jenny turned again and saw that the woman was looking over at them. She said something to the bartender and started walking over.

"Um, you're my girlfriend," Isabella said.

"Nope," Jenny said, smiling at the new woman. Her eyes were either blue or gray, maybe light green. They were so pale that they stood out even across the room. And as Chloe got closer, Jenny felt her libido kick in hard.

"Hey," Chloe said. Her voice was deep and confident.

Jenny stood as Isabella said, "Hey, um, Chloe, you remember Jenny. She has a memory thing where—"

Chloe extended her hand. "Hey," she said again. "Chloe."

Jenny laughed as she felt the woman's grip. "Jenny."

"And I'm Isabella," Isabella said. Jenny, who had been staring into Chloe's eyes, nodded.

"Jenny, I remember you," Chloe said. "You got hot."

"Okay, nope," Isabella said, pushing her chair back. "This is going to get too weird too fast for me. Chloe is my ex-girlfriend, Jenny is my friend, please do not immediately try to fuck her."

They both turned to Isabella.

"Who?" they both said at the same time.

"Yes!" Isabella said. "Come on, Jenny, I'll pay up there. Chloe, it was really great to see you. Jenny and I were just talking about how she's moving into the murder house. Isn't that cool?"

Chloe frowned and released Jenny's hand. "The Kusel House?" Her voice was suddenly cold.

"Yeah," Jenny said.

Chloe nodded and pushed her hands into her back pockets. "Well, good luck with that," Chloe said. "Sorry to interrupt your dinner. I was just picking mine up."

"I'll text you," Isabella said as she pulled Jenny away. Chloe didn't wave; she just lifted her chin at Jenny and mouthed something that Jenny thought was 'Be careful.'

"What the fuck was that?" Jenny asked as they pushed out onto Main Street after Isabella rushed through paying.

"Chloe is terrified of the Kusel House; she had a horrendous experience there when she was a teenager."

"Really?"

"Yeah, really horrible, like police got involved. Not my story to tell."

"Then why did you say—I don't understand, why would you bring it up if you knew—"

"I was nipping that shit in the bud," Isabella said, smiling. "She is crazy, you are in a bad place for her crazy. Believe me, I could already see it. I was the same way. She comes strutting in, oozing sex, and like, next thing you know, you're doing anything she tells you to and thanking her for giving you the privilege to make her scream—"

"Yeah, honestly, that doesn't sound that bad—"

"It is, it can be, anyway. I'm saving you. I promise. Believe me, this town doesn't need its two horniest lesbians crashing into each other."

"Not a lesbian," Jenny said.

"You know what I mean," Isabella said and started walking back toward her apartment. Jenny followed. "So, what are you doing for the rest of the night?"

Jenny evaluated. "Well, I'm going to try to sneak into Patty's without letting her know I'm there. I think she has that woman over again."

"Mrs. Lundy? I always liked her."

"Apparently so did I," Jenny said. She looked up and down at the shops. "How does this town have nothing to do after ten that doesn't involve drinking?"

Isabella frowned. "What town has things after ten that don't involve drinking?"

"I mean, I guess, like there's nowhere to dance, nowhere to listen to music, during the week, I mean. I know you drink when you do those things, but the main thing is the dancing, or the music, or I don't know...."

"There's the movies," Isabella said.

"I've already seen the two movies they're showing."

"It's a small town," Isabella said. "That's why we get up to no good. You know, the boredom of youth, the malaise of wasted potential."

"I think we might be past the point of talking about the boredom of our youth," Jenny laughed. "I know I am."

"Well then, the boredom of our not-yet middle age," she said, once more reaching for Jenny's hand. "Why don't you come back to my apartment? We can clear out an area on the couch and just watch a movie or something?"

Jenny pictured the last time she had been in Isabella's apartment, her hands tied, tears running down her face. She had tried to put that moment aside since Isabella had been one of the few people in town who hadn't rejected her.

"I think I'm a little too tired for a movie," Jenny said.

"Okay, but," Isabella said, buoyant from her four drinks, "counteroffer. You need to start getting used to staying up late, since you're going to be talking on the radio all night long in a few days. So, you should definitely start staying up later and sleeping in later."

"Okay, that's not a bad point," Jenny said.

"And," Isabella said, taking a step closer, "I know ways to keep you up for hours."

"Okay," Jenny said, stepping back, "you lost me, but I do appreciate the advice. Seriously, I do need to get home and start getting things ready. I need to pack."

Isabella pouted, put her hands behind her back, and pushed her chest out in what Jenny thought was an embarrassingly obvious way. "Really? You don't want to hang out anymore?"

No, Jenny wanted to scream, *no, God damn it, why can't you take a hint?* Instead, she shook her head.

"No, it's not that. I just really need to get stuff done, but I'll text you, okay?"

When they reached Isabella's apartment, they hugged. Jenny tried to pull back, but Isabella held her close. "Sure you don't want to come up?"

Jenny smiled and shook her head. "Nope, I really need to get ready. But I promise, I'll text you when I get home, okay?"

Defeated, Isabella kissed Jenny on the cheek, lingering long enough that Jenny had to gently push her back. "Okay, you text me when you get into your apartment," Jenny said. "I don't want to think you passed out in the hallway to be eaten by cats."

"Yes, mommy," Isabella said, peering up into Jenny's face.

Trying to keep from rolling her eyes, Jenny smiled, resituated her purse, and squeezed Isabella's hand before turning to go. As she walked, she heard guitar from Cinder's Remorse and wondered if someone was putting the little stage to use. If so, why hadn't Isabella mentioned that as an option? *Probably*, Jenny thought, *because it meant potentially running into Chloe again.* Or, because she wanted nothing to come between Jenny and Isabella's apartment.

This possibility was reinforced when Jenny got Isabella's text messages. The first came five minutes later, telling her that Isabella was inside and safe. Then, a minute later, another arrived with a picture showing Isabella's low-cut dress lying over the back of a chair. The image was accompanied by the words, "I'm no good at hanging things up." A picture followed showing the lacy black bra and thong that Isabella had apparently been wearing, piled on the floor near her bed, with "see, I just leave things everywhere."

Jenny set her phone to silent and put it into her purse. She walked back up Main and turned onto Bankview. She saw a handful of teenagers smoking in Limler Park and thought two of them might be making out, but she had no interest in staring at them long enough to find out. The pungent smell that wafted from the park let her know that they weren't just smoking cigarettes.

When she got to the front door, Jenny heard Patty and Marlene talking on the back porch, and she slipped in as quietly as she could. She hurried to the kitchen and grabbed a bottle of water from the refrigerator and a granola bar from the cupboard. Then she was up the stairs, breathing easily only once her bedroom door was closed behind her.

Five minutes later, she emerged from the bathroom in her own bra and underwear, which she judged were decidedly less lacy than Isabella's. The thought reminded her that she should text Isabella back to let her know she was home safely. She pulled the phone out and found five more messages, each more suggestive than the last. The final one showed Isabella's legs from the hip down, stretched out in bed. It didn't say anything.

Jenny looked over the pictures and gritted her teeth. None of them was explicit. Isabella could have posted them to any social media without a problem, which made it hard to tell her to stop. If she did, Isabella would feign hurt and claim that Jenny was intentionally misunderstanding her. And that would mean that Jenny would once more be in danger of losing the only person who would still go out with her. Delia liked to save her money so she could spend it on her parties. Even when Jenny offered to pay, Delia had begged off anything beyond lunch. Jenny wondered if it was because Delia was embarrassed to be seen with her.

She just put you in all of her online ads. There's going to be a poster of you in her window. That doesn't sound like what someone does when they're embarrassed of you.

Jenny took a picture of her dress hanging on the back of her bedroom door and sent it to Isabella with the message, 'Home and safe. Is this a sign that I've reached middle age?' Then, before Isabella could respond, she also sent, 'Goodnight! Thanks for a great night out! Wish we could have gone dancing! Sounded like there was something happening at CR. Maybe next time!'

She set her phone to Do Not Disturb, and tossed it onto the bed.

I need new friends, she thought. Maybe the other Sleep Talkers would fit the bill. Jenny liked the fact that they all went to breakfast together every morning. The regular, sane normality of people meeting for a meal appealed to her.

She walked over and turned on the radio to hear a woman talking about a song. She wasn't sure if this was Sydney or Maddy; they had shockingly similar voices as far as Jenny was concerned. Jenny let them drone on in the background as she undid her bra and dropped it onto the top of her dresser.

She should stay up, and she should pack. But first, she thought she'd check her site, and then maybe, if someone was up and feeling like chatting, she could take a few pictures of her own and make a little money to boot. She lay down, grabbed her phone, and opened the app to find that—yes— she could, in fact, earn some money and maybe, if someone wasn't boring, enjoy herself for a bit before doing her packing. God knew she needed stress relief after Isabella.

As she began chatting with a friendly and generous subscriber, she remembered Chloe's firm grip and wondered how her hands felt other than in a handshake.

Entry 6

September 6, 2025

Hello Diary, did you also just get back from the last summer market of the year? Oh, and what did you get? Mhm … mhm … those sound amazing! I also did some devilish deals. I bought three more vintage tees that I am now in love with. One pair of flare-leg jeans that I wish were bell-bottoms but will have to do, and even a poster, because that felt like something I should have at my new place.

I'm getting a new place! Free even! I'm such a slacker. I haven't paid for a place since Portland.

Lie.

I paid for Sunrise. A lot. That's voluntary commitment for you.

But anyway, the market was good, even if it was weird being there alone. It's not Isabella's thing. I offered to help Delia with her booth, but she kind of shooed me away to "go have fun." I flip-flop between feeling like she doesn't want to be seen in public with me. Maybe I'm just Hester Prin? Prim? I could look it up, but you don't care. Do you, Diary?

25
Step 3

Saturday, September 6, 2025 - Evening

DOWNSTAIRS NOISES SLOWLY ROUSED Jenny from a long nap. Still half asleep, she reached over to find Aurora so she could slide closer to her. She wanted to smell her hair and feel her stomach under her hand and the thin, flimsy shirt she liked to wear to sleep, no matter how cold it was. Aurora was a hot sleeper. She wanted to taste the salt sweat on the skin just behind her ear.

A cold, empty bed met her groping fingers, and the world slammed back into place as Jenny opened her eyes. She immediately wanted to go back, to dwell in the fading moment. She wanted to feel like Aurora was next to her. That feeling was within her reach, even if Aurora was gone forever. She could wake up and believe she could hold her, even if she could never actually put her arms around Aurora again. The illusion was better than reality.

She sat and held her head in her hands, feeling slow and thick. She looked over at the clock and saw that it was just after ten. "Shit," Jenny said. She doubted she would sleep much tonight if she had just lost six hours to a nap.

That might not be bad, she thought. *I'm supposed to start staying up all night anyway.*

She rubbed her hands over her face and through her hair. She heard raised voices somewhere downstairs. Was Patty arguing with someone? Jenny threw her bare legs over the side of the bed and squeezed her eyes shut tight, yawning. She wanted to go back to sleep, to dwell in the lie that erased Aurora's wide, searching, panicked eyes from her memory. But her bladder grumbled at her, and the voices from downstairs sounded like they were worth her attention.

When Jenny returned from the bathroom, she pulled on her jeans, socks, and shoes. Her phone, which was nearly out of power, slid into her back pocket. She would have to remember to plug it in later. She pulled her hair back, secured it with a tie, and then opened her door silently to figure out what was happening.

Marlene's voice came up the stairs, "I don't think you have any other choice. I'm sorry to say it, but I think you're right."

Patty said something Jenny couldn't hear.

"She'll have to pack a bag," Marlene said, and Jenny imagined her standing next to the staircase, talking loudly so that Jenny could hear her. Hear her and be ready, Jenny thought. *Shit! Shit, I've been sleeping through something that I could have ...*

Her thought trailed off. She had no idea what she could have done. Maybe she was misreading the argument. She decided the best thing to do was to go downstairs and confront the situation.

The best thing to do is pack a bag just in case.

She leaned back into her room and scanned her belongings. Her laptop was already in her backpack. Her purse was next to the bed. She put them next to each other before tiptoeing to her dresser and gathering underwear, bras, and T-shirts. She stuffed them into her pack until it bulged. She ducked into the bathroom and grabbed her toothbrush and deodorant. The thought struck her that she had nowhere to go. If Patty threw her out tonight, she couldn't go to Delia's; her friend was down in Joseph meeting a guy for their third date. She probably wouldn't be home for hours, if at all. She could go to Isabella, but that was a last resort. She decided that whatever happened, she had to convince Patty to give her at least one more night. Surely Patty wasn't so mad at—well, whatever it was she was mad at—she would throw her daughter out into the night with nowhere to stay.

"Shit, I hope that's true," Jenny said to the empty room. She hefted the pack and her purse and started down the stairs, making as much noise as she thought would sound natural. She left her pack beside the railing on the second floor and made her way down to find Patty and Marlene in the dining room.

"Oh, finally, I guess you decided to stop hiding," Patty said. Jenny hadn't seen that look of condescending judgment on her face for years, not since the days of drunkenness and cruelty.

"I wasn't hiding, I was sleeping."

"Lazy," Patty spat.

"Not lazy, I'm trying to readjust my sleep pattern so I can get used to working overnight," Jenny said, knowing it was mostly a lie.

"See," Marlene said, giving Jenny a consoling look. "I told you. She's trying to make a fresh start of things."

"I know, but you're too easy on her, Marlene, and I have been, too."

"Too easy?" Jenny said. "You're too easy on me? What would it look like—"

"It would look like me kicking you out!" Patty screamed. "And that's what I'm doing. I'm so sick of this! I'm sick of being a laughingstock, or a pity stock, or whatever the heck it is!"

"You're a laughingstock?" Jenny asked, putting her hands on her hips.

"Yes, because everyone in town is watching my daughter suck dick on the internet!"

Jenny stepped back as if Patty had slapped her.

"Patty, please," Marlene said.

"Do you know what I had to see today?"

Jenny felt her mouth open, but no words came out.

"I had to see two men having their way with you. Why? Why did I have to see it? Because someone sent me a link in an email with a subject line that said 'Barbecue Spitroast!' I thought it was a recipe!"

Jenny wanted with every fiber of her being not to laugh, but she couldn't stop herself. Whoever had sent Patty the email had been mean, vicious, and—Jenny grudgingly admitted—clever.

"Is that funny to you?" Patty continued at the top of her voice. "Funny that I had to see that? My daughter a ... a ... I've run out of words. A slut. A real, actual, whore slut."

Jenny shut her eyes and shook her head slowly. She felt a strange peace that surprised her. "Patty, I found you doing a lot of those same things in this house when I was a teenager. When I was a kid. You're an adult and—"

"So, it's my fault? I'm to blame for you—You know what? I'm sick of saying it and describing it or even referring to it. It's not my fault you turned out to be rotten. It's not my fault you turned out to be what you are!"

Jenny could feel herself shaking. *Careful. Careful,* she thought.

"Patty, believe me, we all understand how you feel," Marlene said. "But I think you should calm down a little. You don't want to regret anything about this conversation."

Patty shut her eyes tight and held her fists against her face. "You're right. God grant me strength to do the right thing in peace."

Jenny stared as anxiety throbbed inside her chest.

"You need to leave," Patty said. "You need to leave right now."

"At ten-thirty at night?"

"Yes," Patty said.

"Patty, don't you think that's unreasonable?" Marlene said. Jenny thought the woman could have been a little more enthusiastic in her objection.

"No, I don't. What's the difference? You're supposed to be a night person now, right? A regular Lightning Falls Nighthawk!" She said this last with such ferocity and bile that again Jenny stepped back. "It's more merciful to kick you out at night so that I'm not interrupting your sleep cycle!"

"God," Jenny breathed.

"Don't you speak his name!" She slammed her fists on the table, and her crystal candle holders rattled.

"Jennifer," Marlene said. "Is there somewhere you can go? Obviously, your mother is … adamant."

Jenny shook her head. Jenny saw a look of relief on Marlene's face. "See, she's got nowhere to go, you can't kick her out—"

"Yes, I can! You said it yourself earlier."

"Where am I supposed to go?" Jenny asked.

"I'd say go stay with Phil, but he's too smart to have you," Patty said. "Or maybe that woman that you're involved with!"

Jenny frowned. "I'm not involved with—"

"The Delgado girl!"

"Isabella? We're not—"

"I don't care! I don't care! I don't care! I don't want anything more to do with your sordid, wanton life! You're not welcome here, I cast you out! I wash my hands of you! I knock the dust of you off my shoes! I spit you out! I never knew you!"

Marlene and Jenny stared at the short-haired woman, mouths agape. Everyone stood silently for a long moment until, mouth still open, Jenny nodded. Her pulse thrumming in her ears, she turned and walked upstairs, took her pack, and then walked back down again. She didn't stop to look into the dining room; she just yanked the front door open and pushed through the screen door out into the night.

As the screen door slammed, she pulled the straps of her pack over her shoulders and stared blankly ahead, nodding slowly as she walked. Her brain felt strange, as if someone had hit a reset button, and she was in the space between shutting down and booting up. She didn't start processing what had happened until she sat in a corner booth at the Second Wave Diner.

She picked at her food as she considered what to do. She figured she had three options. First, she could see if there was a room to rent in town. There used to be a motel, but she didn't think it was still there, and Jenny doubted she could book a room on a site at this time of night. Second, she could reach out to someone. The only two real options were Delia and Isabella. She considered Barry, but she didn't have his private number. She was sure Barry would put her up, no questions asked, but that didn't seem possible.

That left Delia and Isabella. Jenny sipped her coffee and frowned. She knew Delia would come home to help her, but there was no way Jenny would do that to her friend on her date night. Reaching out to Isabella would be awkward. Jenny didn't believe Isabella would force something onto her that she didn't want, but she did think that the woman would pressure or guilt her enough to make the situation even more unbearable. She could even picture getting into a fight with her and ending up back out on the street.

On the other hand, she could just give Isabella what she wanted. It wouldn't be the first time Jenny had traded sex for money or services. But she had never done that with someone she didn't feel comfortable with, at least not in person. Online, the interactions were completely different. Someone had to make her exceedingly uncomfortable for Jenny to stop a chat or video session. But Isabella made her feel icky, as if a creepy, self-touching old man with drool hanging from his lip were watching her. The idea of doing anything with her physically made Jenny's skin crawl. Still, she admitted, if she became desperate, it was an option.

Not for the first time, Jenny wished she had Chloe's number.

The final option was she could just stay out all night. There was always a midnight show at the Mist on Saturdays. When she was a teen, it had been *The Rocky Horror Picture Show*. She wasn't sure if that was still the case or not. The sign out front only declared a Saturday midnight showing. That would take her to about two in the morning. Then she could come back to Second Wave and drink more coffee, surf the internet on her laptop, and lounge until seven or so, when she would feel safe to text Delia and see what was up with her.

Thinking about leaving the movies at two made her realize she had another option similar to contacting Isabella. Jenny could go to the Tim and find a guy to go home with. If she did that, she'd want to do it late, so that after he had enjoyed himself, he'd just pass out and not have the wherewithal to throw her out. At least in that version of events, she would have a much better chance of ending up with someone who at least didn't make her feel skeezy the way Isabella did. She could choose. Theoretically.

Jenny took a bite of her quiche and mulled over her options. The healthiest thing to do would be to go to the movies and then camp at the diner.

Yep, that would definitely be the healthiest thing to do.

The Quiet Rumble

Volume 10, Issue 76, Sunday, September 7, 2025

Stubborn Mountains

By Keith Lowry, Ed. In Chief.

BACK IN 2017, WHICH is farther back than I want to admit, we got twenty inches of snow in a single day. That was shocking. We are accustomed to snow, the road closing, and being cut off for days at a time while plows work their way over Route 3. But twenty inches in one day?

We were unprepared.

The township plows, of which we have two, did their darndest to clear our streets. The biggest problem was, of course, where to put all the snow. For those who don't remember, the solution was to erect a new white mountain range around town. Some empty lots formed great peaks, the Everests of our new geological curiosity. Some larger yards hosted their own small chains of pinnacles that we had to account for and navigate as we returned to life over the following two days.

Once we got things up and running, however, the mountain ranges didn't just disappear. When we opened what passes for our major highway out here and goods started to flow again, the snow did not simply melt. It stuck around. There's a picture that I love. It shows Pastor Cerny, his wife Lessa, and their three children, Eleanor, Susanna, and Sarah, all sitting in lawn chairs around a meager two-foot peak of snow on their lawn. What I love about that photo is that they are all wearing swimsuits because it was taken in early June.

What's my point? Why, God help me, eight-and-a-half years later, am I bringing up the snowstorm of 2017? Because it is a parable. Carson Booth went missing nearly a month ago, and, as far as we know, no one has found any clues, tracks, or evidence of him. Scores of government officials organized and facilitated the search for the twelve-year-old boy, and hundreds of local people volunteered their time, energy, and finances to the same effort. And we, as an entire community, with the help of every level of government, found nothing.

We are accustomed to hard things out this way. We are used to the government letting us down. And, if we're old enough, we are probably used to letting ourselves down.

But we were unprepared.

Now that weeks have passed and we have returned to whatever it is that we call "normal life," we must admit that the mountains thrown up by this tragedy aren't just going to melt and go away. They will remain. We must take them into account, sometimes walk around them, and ultimately learn to sit with them as part of the world we inhabit now.

We cannot, of course, let this destroy our lives. The mountain range that has pushed its way into existence in our hearts, minds, and relationships is invisible, and I don't believe that it cuts through the center of all we are. But it's there, and we'll often walk among its foothills and, at times, have to clamber over it. And whenever we take our pictures now, they will, I think, always have a little of that melted mound sticking up somewhere in the background, even when it's summer again.

And the old-timers know what I mean. The past isn't the past, it's the present until the waves of time have so washed everything you've ever done away that you might as well have not ever been. And even then, who knows? Perhaps there is a mind that sees everything and remembers everything and might, in the end, recall it into being. And unless He does wipe every tear from our eyes, what a monstrous thing that would be to do to us.

26
From the Back of a Chair

Monday, September 8, 2025 - Afternoon

JENNY LUGGED HER THREE bags into her apartment. She deposited her suitcase, backpack, and duffel bag onto the couch next to a comforter, pillow, and two bags of unopened bedding and toiletries.

"This is really nice," Delia said, taking her purse off and dropping it onto the coffee table.

"Yeah, it's not bad at all," Jenny said, wiping her hands on the butt of her jeans.

"So, what time do you have to go on? I guess I should know that since I've been here forever, but I don't think I ever really thought about when they start. Eight? Nine?"

"Nine," Jenny said. "So, I'll be in there at eight, going over everything ten times."

"You're going to be fine," Delia said. "You know what you want to do?"

Jenny shrugged. "I don't know yet. I feel like I'm going to host some kind of night talk show, even though I've heard people do it, and that's not really how it is. I keep thinking that I need to figure out how to break for commercials, but there aren't any commercials." Jenny shook her head.

Delia nodded. "I mean, if you want to do a talk show, do a talk show. That sounds fun. You could interview people from around town. Like yours truly. Oh, is your bathroom back there? Be right back."

Jenny considered the idea of interviewing people from town, especially business owners. That sounded interesting. Of course, she could probably only do that for the first couple of hours. No one wanted to stay up past midnight to talk about their tobacco shop to the five people in town who were still awake and listening to Jenny's station.

"Well," Dellia said as she emerged from the back of the apartment, "I should be getting back to the store. Do you want a lift back into town?"

"No, I'm going to get unpacked. I'm good for dinner, though," Jenny said.

"Good," Delia said. "Six?"

"Absolutely," Jenny said, "And thank you for giving me a ride to the store. I'm not sure what I would have done without you."

"You would have just ordered it all online and waited three days," she laughed. "And you would have saved yourself some money. God, everything was so spendy!"

"Yeah, I guess so, but I didn't want to wait. And, again, I appreciate it. And for letting me stay at your place last night."

"Well, she put you in a heck of a position. I still can't believe she wouldn't let you stay an extra night before moving in here," Delia said, shaking her head. "What kind of mother—"

"Mine," Jenny said, shrugging.

Delia hugged her, told her to call if she needed anything, and said goodbye. Jenny carried her bags into her new bedroom and unpacked her clothes into the dresser and closet. When it only took her five minutes to move everything into its place, she plopped down onto the bed and said, "I need more clothes," to the empty room.

For a moment, she wondered if she'd hear a ghostly voice say, "Yes, you're a fashion embarrassment," or whatever horrifying things ghosts said. But there was nothing, not even a hint of another presence. There was only the nagging feeling that she wasn't ready for her new job.

She lay back on the mattress, which she hoped she could replace soon, and thought about the big empty house. Were there really ghosts? What kind of lives did the people live here before carbon monoxide cut them short? She suddenly wondered what kind of terrible experience Chloe had had here. She imagined that it was some kind of assault, but she pushed the thought aside. She didn't like it when people made assumptions about her, and she tried not to do it to others. She also tried to sort through the idea that Chloe, like everyone else in town, knew her in some way. Jenny drifted.

Sleep threatened, but so did her bladder. Grumbling, Jenny stood and sought out her new bathroom. She pulled the sliding door on the tub and saw a web extending from the showerhead to the soap dish on the wall.

"Did you follow me?" Jenny asked. "Or does your cousin live with Patty? Either way, this still isn't going to work."

Jenny closed the door to let the spider think about his future without an audience. Three minutes later, she was drying her hands on the back of her jeans and dropping back onto the bed. Her imagination wandered, and soon, she slept. She dreamed of walking along the creek, a dress flowing around her legs, a wide hat on her head, and an unfamiliar song on her lips. A boy was running behind her, his chubby toddler legs padding the ground damp with morning dew. Behind him, another woman in a similar dress called to the boy. Jenny turned and knelt to catch him, but he ran into the other woman's outstretched arms. As she cradled him, she smiled at Jenny and said, "Drink the tea."

Jenny woke and sat bolt upright. She grabbed her phone and saw it was 5:49. She jumped up, pulled her hair into a bunch, and ran to the bathroom. A few minutes later, she was tugging her sneakers on and hustling for the door. She stopped, grabbed her two new sets of keys, and jammed them into her backpack. Then, she was out and jogging down the driveway toward Founder's Road. She turned right and alternated between speed-walking and running for the quarter mile between the Kusel House driveway and the first houses where Founder's Road turned into Main Street. She passed the first big brick houses, saw a woman hanging laundry on a line, waved, and smiled when the woman waved back. Then Jenny turned down the first cross street and hurried to Delia's house. She arrived only a few minutes late.

"Hey," Delia said from inside the house as Jenny knocked on the screen door. "Come on in, I'm putting the cheese on now."

Jenny pushed her way in and almost ran into Barry.

"Oh, hey," she said, "I didn't know you were going to be here!" They hugged before he led her into the kitchen with his arm around her shoulder.

"The radio star has arrived," he said. Jenny laughed.

"I'd apologize for not telling you Barry was coming, but then I'd have to apologize for the other surprise as well," Delia said with a mischievous smile. She was standing in a kitchen that she might have extracted unchanged from a 1950's magazine advertisement. Muted mid-mod blues, oranges, teals, and beiges made Jenny nostalgic for a time in which she never lived. The linoleum floor sparkled, and the tiny chrome-rimmed breakfast table with its two metal-framed, teal-cushioned chairs was tucked in the corner next to a window that looked out onto Delia's back deck. A round analog clock ticked the time over the other window above the large, two-pocket porcelain sink.

Despite how much she loved Delia's house, Jenny's heart sank. Whoever Delia had invited, they couldn't be good. The only two people Jenny had uncomplicated relationships with were standing in the kitchen, and even so, she barely knew Barry. Suddenly, she pictured Delia and Barry arranging some kind of sit-down between Jenny, Patty, and every other damned person who made her feel uncomfortable. For a moment, she pictured Isabella sitting at the head of the table, moderating between her and Leddy as Leddy told Jenny what a disappointment she had been.

"Come on out back and meet everyone," Delia said, closing the oven. Jenny frowned. That didn't sound like Jenny's imagined social intervention. She followed Delia through a sliding glass door onto a raised wooden deck to see five total strangers. No, two total strangers, and three people she thought she recognized from around town.

"Everyone, this is Jenny, Delia said. "Jenny, this is Charles, Sydney, and Maddy. They are the Weekenders."

The first person to rise, Charles, was tall, dark-skinned, and dressed in a way that told Jenny that his white button-up shirt, chinos, and dark-brown brogues were his relaxation wear because his sleeves were rolled up. He wore thick, black-rimmed glasses and had a well-groomed beard distinguished by only a few white hairs. He shook her hand.

"It's incredibly nice to finally meet you," Charles said.

"Thank you, you too," Jenny said, suddenly feeling a little overwhelmed.

The next person, Sydney, jumped up and hugged her. Sydney was fair-skinned and had swooping orange hair cut longer on the top and short on the sides. She had black-outline tattoos running up both arms that depicted everything from hearts to knives to a pin-up model from the first half of the twentieth century. She wore a brown skirt with black stockings, beige, strappy shoes that reminded Jenny of a ballerina, and a brown, sleeveless top.

The earnestness of Sydney's hug disarmed Jenny. When she pulled back, which wasn't for several seconds, she looked up at Jenny with wide eyes and a huge smile.

"Oh my God!" Sydney said. "I'm in love with you!"

Jenny stared.

"Don't worry," Maddy said, putting her not-as-pale fingers on Sydney's shoulder, "she says that to most people. I'm Maddy."

Looking at Maddy was like looking back in time. The curls of her dark hair were bigger than Jenny's, and she was a little shorter, but otherwise, Maddy might have been an alternate history version of high school Jenny grown up. Her black cami top rode an inch above her black jeans that flared above scuffed Doc Martens. She wore several bracelets on her left wrist and none on her right. Her makeup was dark, heavy on the eyeshadow, eyeliner, and wine-colored lipstick. She gazed at Jenny with a strange expression that Jenny couldn't read. It might have been recognition, or it might have been appraisal.

Jenny shook Maddy's hand while Sydney clutched Jenny's left forearm excitedly.

"Okay, don't swarm her," Delia said, laughing.

"Don't worry," a big, bearded man said from his seat, "we won't be rushing over."

He did stand, however, and limp his way to her. He was tall, heavy-set, and handsome. His ruddy complexion and the white that shot his reddish-brown beard made Jenny suspect he had Irish ancestry.

"Nate," he said, holding out his hand. Jenny shook it.

"Nate is one of your weekday companions," Delia said. "Now sit down, all of you."

A combination of relief and anxiety washed over Jenny. Here was no ambush. Instead, Delia had arranged the perfect get-together for Jenny to meet her new coworkers. Immediately, she saw the genius of it. Not only would she meet them face-to-face in the company of someone she was comfortable with, but there was an upper limit to their encounter. Three of them had to be at work soon. Jenny smiled in appreciation of Delia's plan.

When everyone had taken their place, the last person raised their hand from their chair. They were short, fair, and wore their brown hair in a pixie cut. They had a T-shirt that read 'Northern Hamilton County Regional High School,' and corduroy pants. They were leaning back in their chair, giving Jenny an appraising stare.

"Hey," they said to Jenny, "I'm Linds."

"Great," Delia said, "Now you all know each other. Can I get anyone anything to drink?"

Nate, Charles, and Sydney all raised their hands while Linds and Jenny looked at each other across the table.

Once Jenny had taken her place, the conversation was slow to start.

"Where are you from?" Nate asked.

"Right here, but I haven't been home for basically a decade," Jenny said.

"Have you ever been on the radio before?" Charles asked.

"Nope, but I feel entirely unprepared, so I feel like I have that going for me."

Charles laughed. "It's nothing, really," he said.

"Everyone keeps saying that," Jenny said.

"That's because it's true," Maddy said. "There are like five things to remember, and that's it. Really, I had never done anything like it before either, and I was super nervous my first night. By the second hour, it was like nothing."

"Same," Sydney said, staring at Jenny with her chin in her hand.

"You talked for an hour and a half before someone showed up and told you that your mic wasn't on," Maddy said, shaking her head.

"I thought I was fire!"

"She had this whole persona going, like she was Smooth Sydney," Charles said.

"I was, though," Sydney said. "But, when Link knocked on the door, I was like, 'uh oh, people hate this, they hate me so much that they had to send Link.' But, when I let him in, he just walked over to the panel, pushed a button, and said, 'There, now you're live. Good luck.' And he walked out."

"He stood listening at the door for ten minutes," Nate laughed. "He does a great Smooth Sydney impersonation if you ask him."

"He won't do it unless I'm there," Sydney said, grinning. "He loves me."

"Everyone loves you," Maddy said, reaching over and squeezing Sydney's hand. Suddenly, Jenny remembered the two young women she had seen at the Market the day after she came home.

"Wait, are you two together?" Jenny blurted out.

They both shrugged and nodded.

"This is a particularly gay group," Charles said.

"Um," Nate said, "not over here."

"So he says," Charles said, grinning. Nate pointed at Charles, and they both laughed.

Delia returned with drinks. Then, after disappearing and returning, she dished out burgers, all meat, to Jenny's surprise. She would have guessed someone would have been vegan or at least vegetarian, but they all dug into the beef without objection. The conversation shifted to talking about their early days as Sleep Talkers.

"I just ran out of stuff to talk about," Maddy said. "I had to keep trying to come up with things, and I kept kind of just trailing off into nonsense." She pushed a curl back behind her ear. "I still do that sometimes, but at least now I know when I'm doing it, and I cut to music."

"What kind of music?" Jenny asked.

"I like to keep things slow and moody; I have an image to maintain." She smiled, and Jenny thought she was beautiful. "Have you ever heard of Nel and the Goretones?"

Jenny laughed and shook her head.

"They're really good. I'll send you a link to their stuff."

"I've always talked too much," Nate said, "so I think it was easy for me."

"True," Charles said. "And I didn't talk enough, but I found that when I didn't have to look at people, I could say more."

"Deep," Barry said.

"Linds," Delia said. "I've never heard any horror stories out of you."

Linds chewed a fry and frowned at the table. "I don't think I've had any real recording horror stories. And I think I kind of knew how to talk to no one pretty well already. But I grew up listening to small-town radio." Linds looked up at Jenny. "It did take some getting used to as far as taking calls, though. But, really, it's super easy. I'm not a technical person at all, and it's just second nature to me now."

"How long have you all been doing it?" Jenny asked the table.

"Ten years," Charles said.

"Six," said Sydney.

"Five," said Maddy.

"Two," Nate said.

And Linds said, "It'll be a year in October."

"And they are all amazing. And you'll be amazing too," Barry said, patting Jenny on the shoulder. "So, what's your schtick? Sultry evening host? Peppy know it all? Local news reporter?" He said this last, as if it were a new idea that he liked.

"Huh," Jenny said. "That's an interesting idea. I'm not sure if I'm cut out to be a radio news person."

"It can be whatever you want; it's surprisingly unregulated," Charles said.

They talked about the towers. Sydney gushed over how good she thought Jenny would be. Nate told Jenny that if there was anyone to ask about it, Charles and Maddy were really the experts. And though Linds was the newest, they were also extremely knowledgeable.

Dinner passed too quickly, and soon, people were looking at their watches and making their excuses. The Weekenders were going to the movies, and Nate and Linds had to walk to their towers.

"Where are you both tonight?" Jenny asked as Nate pushed back from the table.

"I'm at the cabin," Nate said, looking at Linds.

"And I'm in the tower," they said.

"How long does it take to get up there?" Jenny asked.

"It's about a half hour walk, but if you're a mountain-biker you can cut that way down," they said.

"Oh, wow, is that what you do?"

Linds nodded. "Yeah, my sister got me into it when we moved here. It's really convenient, actually."

"Huh, I hadn't even thought about getting a bike," Jenny said, smiling at Linds. "Thanks, that's a good idea."

"You'll find that Linds is the source for good ideas," Charles said, standing up and straightening his shirt. "They're kind of our unofficial leader now." Linds shook their head and frowned.

"They also don't like being called that," Sydney stage-whispered behind her hand. Linds looked away and started to study one of the potted plants on Delia's deck, and Jenny made a mental note of everyone using 'they' for Linds.

"Well," Nate said, "thank you so much for dinner, Delia." He walked over to their host and hugged her.

He was wearing a Hawaiian shirt and cargo shorts, and Jenny caught a whiff of his cologne as he shook her hand. He smelled good, and she found his voice even more soothing in person.

"Hey," he said, putting a hand on her shoulder. Jenny stood to face him. "It was great meeting you. Good luck tonight. If you need any help with anything, just give me a call on my radio."

"Same here," Linds said.

Jenny walked with them to the front door, noticing Nate's limp again. "Do you have to walk all the way there?"

"Yeah, but it's not so bad. It's more stiff than anything," he said, patting his thigh. "It's good for me to move it. I'm glad you told Linds the bike thing was a good idea; they've been trying to get me to get a bike for months."

"It would help," Linds said.

"I know," Nate said, "I just haven't gotten around to it yet."

"Thanks again for being nice," Jenny said.

"Look," Nate said, "I know how daunting this can be, but it's not that big of a deal. You'll be fine. When it gets too much, put a record on. Or five. There's no shame in setting a timer and closing your eyes while you make the town listen to your own private soundtrack."

Jenny smiled.

"And," Linds said, "really don't hesitate to call. The channels for the towers are next to the handset. I'm sure Link went over all that with you. But also, let me give you my number." Jenny got Nate and Linds' phone numbers as Linds strapped on a bike helmet. Then they were out the door as Nate and Jenny waved.

"All right," Delia said from behind them, jingling keys, "let's go, bud." Nate smiled sheepishly.

"I thought—" Jenny said.

"Yeah, I said that so I didn't get a dirty look from Linds. They're always on me about exercising."

"Do you need a ride too?" Delia asked.

"No, I'm all good. The cool air feels nice. Plus, I need to walk off some of my nerves."

Delia hugged her. "You'll be fine. I'll be listening, though! I'll call to tell you if you're fucking it up!"

"Thanks," Jenny said.

"I'll be right back, Barry, don't rob me blind!" Delia called behind her as she walked out the front door.

"I'll just be rooting through your hamper," Barry said from the kitchen. Jenny turned to see him elbow-deep in dirty dishes. The Weekenders said their goodbyes, with Sydney offering another long, tight hug. Jenny stood awkwardly in the foyer, watching them go. She felt like she should follow them, but she also didn't want to leave Barry alone to wash up by himself.

"Need a hand?" Jenny asked, making up her mind to stay for a few more minutes. She walked into the kitchen and started sorting dirty bowls, dishes, and silverware.

"Thanks," Barry said. They worked silently for a minute while Jenny searched for something to talk about. She couldn't remember if she'd ever asked him where his family was from, so she did. "Um, well, my mom was from Vermont, and dad was a bandito."

"Really?" Jenny said.

"Yeah, they met when she moved to New Mexico for some reason she never admitted to me. He was from a little town called Nogales. Bad man, did bad things. But he could tell a story."

"Wow," Jenny said. "What was that like?"

"The times I saw him? They were few and far between, but they were interesting."

"I'm sorry to hear that," Jenny said, holding a plate.

Barry pointed to a cabinet with a soapy hand. "Not a big deal. Mom married a musician from Dana Point a few years after she had me, and he was great. He had a huge family, so I grew up basically in a big community near the ocean."

"Oh, wow, that sounds nice," Jenny said, unsure of what else to say.

"It was. Honestly, I was kind of hopin' to find something like that up here, but, you know, the mountain variety. I didn't exactly find that though, you know?"

"Well, there's Delia? I didn't know you two were so close."

"We aren't, really," Barry said. "I mean, we work next to each other, and we try to promote each other's stuff, and she invites me to some of her parties."

"Then …" Jenny said, looking around the kitchen, "what's all this? I thought—"

Barry looked at her and shook his head, smiling. "All this is because of you, dude. After—well—after everything you went through, we figured you needed some people on your side. Dinner was Delia's idea; inviting the other Talkers was mine," he said.

"Oh," Jenny said, gripping a bowl in both hands. "I—Wow, I don't know what to say."

"You don't have to say anything," Barry said, and Jenny's mind inserted a *'man'* at the end. "Which is, I know, an incredibly trite thing to say, but really, it wasn't a big deal. And it was fun. I kind of wish we could make it a regular thing. Especially as the nights are getting colder, I love sitting outside by a fire and—" He stopped, and his eyes went wide.

"What?" Jenny said, looking over her shoulder as if there might be someone behind her.

"I totally forgot!" Barry said, running the water and rinsing his hands. He dried them and hurried into the living room. He returned with a bag that said 'Fashion Backward' on it. "This is for you, kind of a house-warming, break-a-leg kind of thing."

Jenny took the bag. "Wow, you didn't have to—"

"Don't feel bad, it wasn't expensive, and I thought you might like it. Plus, I know everyone complains about how chilly the booth in the house is, so I figured you'd need it."

Jenny opened the bag and pulled out a forest-green cardigan with wooden buttons. It wasn't exactly her style, but it was nice, in a small-town-girl kind of way. It looked as if it would be tight on her. She held it to her face and sniffed. What was that? Perfume, light and familiar. Sandalwood? Whatever it was, she liked it, though she was surprised that any store would sell something that they hadn't thoroughly cleaned.

"Thank you," she said, trying to sound genuine.

"Try it on, I don't want you pretending it fits if it doesn't."

Jenny wasn't sure she'd ever had a man tell her to put more clothes on. She slid her arms in and buttoned the sweater. It was tight, but not uncomfortable, and it certainly was warm. She looked at herself in the hallway mirror and admitted that she made the rather dull-looking sweater look at least a little hot.

"What do you think?" Barry asked.

"It's cozy," she said, smiling. Jenny turned her head down and to the side. She sniffed.

"Oh no, does it smell like mothballs or something?" Barry asked.

"No," Jenny sniffed again. "It's perfume. It's … familiar."

"Really?"

"Yeah, something that—" She sniffed again. "I don't know, maybe a friend used to wear? Or maybe something I tried in high school? It's not bad, I like it."

"Well, I'm sorry about that. I figured they would have washed it before putting it on the rack. Let me take it back and have it dry cleaned," he said, looking embarrassed.

"No, it's fine," Jenny said. "I—I don't know, it makes me feel—I don't know, but it's not bad. It's good."

"Are you sure?" Barry said, giving her a skeptical look. "I don't think I'd take a gift that wasn't clean."

"No, it's really okay," Jenny said, though she wasn't sure why. Barry was right; it was weird and should have grossed her out, but it didn't. It was almost like there was a picture in her head of the woman who had worn it before, and she felt strangely close to her.

"If you're sure. Honestly, I'm embarrassed. I thought I had given it the sniff test, but—"

Jenny shook her head and hugged Barry. "No, it's great. Thank you. And thank you for thinking of inviting the others here. That was a big help. I'm going to feel a lot less awkward meeting them at the diner now."

He hugged her back and kissed the top of her head. "Whatever you need, you let me know. I know what it's like to be here without much support."

"Damn it, Barry, I'm gone for literally five minutes and you're trying to seduce this innocent young woman?" Delia said from the foyer.

"No, it's the other way around, I swear," Barry said over Jenny's head.

"It's true, I put this on to stoke his fiery passions," Jenny said, turning and modeling the sweater.

Delia stopped and looked from Jenny to Barry and back again. For a moment, there was an expression on her face that Jenny couldn't read. A smile quickly replaced it.

"Oh, that's cozy," Delia said. "And now I feel like an idiot for not getting you something."

"Really," Jenny said, pushing the sleeves up to her elbows, "you did too much already. I really appreciate dinner, and honestly everything you've both done for me. I wouldn't have this job if you both hadn't pushed me to do it, and I wouldn't know anyone without your help, and, yeah, I don't know, you are, like, really awesome."

"'You are, like, really awesome?'" Delia said, shaking her head. "You spent way too much time in California. But, before this turns into some kind of overblown lovefest, you should probably get back home; otherwise, you *will* need a ride."

Jenny pulled her phone out and looked at the time. "Shit, you're right. Thank you again!" She hugged them both and then hurried out the door into the night.

27
Again, Finally

Monday, September 8, 2025 – Evening

A DRIZZLE BEGAN AS Jenny left Main Street and started down Founder's Road, toward the old Kusel House. Pines crowded to the edge of the road, leaving no room for a sidewalk beyond the edge of town. Jenny looked at her watch and saw that she still had over an hour before she had to start, but even so, she hurried. Something about dinner had changed how she felt. She was still anxious, but now there was a strange eagerness mixed in. She could see herself flicking switches and turning dials. She could hear herself speaking into the microphone. Soon, Jenny was crunching up the drive toward the front lawn. Everything was dark, and she realized that she hadn't left any lights on for herself. Technically, sundown wasn't for another half hour, but the mountain to the west and the tall pines brought early darkness.

The house's windows, black and empty, chilled her. She thought about the articles describing the four bodies slumped together in the drawing room for days, waiting for someone to find them. Jenny wondered if their ghosts remained—if there even were such things as ghosts to remain. It didn't matter really; she knew her mind would make up for any missing spirits every time the empty house made a sound.

She felt suddenly dizzy and took an awkward step just before the porch. She took hold of the railing and steadied herself, thinking that she needed to calm down. Everyone was right, the job wouldn't be difficult. The trickiest thing would be thinking of things to talk about for hours on end. She took a deep breath and felt herself suddenly calm. She took another breath for good measure and thought, perhaps, Aurora was smiling at her from somewhere. She had always told Jenny to breathe, and that everything would be okay.

"Breathe, the world is one, there is no pain, there is no death," she would say, stroking Jenny's head.

She was wrong, Jenny thought. She pictured Aurora trying to breathe as splashing, rolling water filled her lungs. Jenny once more shoved the image out of her mind and took the three porch steps in a single leap before pulling both sets of keys from her backpack. She tried the first set, found that it was wrong, and grabbed the other. She pushed her way in, clicked on the hallway light, and breathed deeply the smell of rain and dust.

She went into her apartment to make sure everything was where it should be. She had no reason to think anyone would have been in her space, messing with her things, but she felt a compulsion to go over everything. Of course, there wasn't much to go over—her laptop on the desk, her clothes in the drawers, a few books on the top of her dresser. The space felt alien and empty. There wasn't another human for a quarter mile, which, she realized, didn't sound far. But with the pines surrounding the vast empty house, she might as well have been the only person in town.

Jenny thought about writing in her journal but decided that she would wait until after her first evening. She didn't need to capture her pre-work jitters. Instead, she considered how she looked in the mirror with her new sweater, unbuttoned the top three buttons, and gave herself an appreciative frown. She thought she could make it work. Wasn't that a thing seventy-five years ago? Sweater girls. She thought she had heard that somewhere.

Stop, you're going to be on the radio, no one cares how much décolletage you show.

Feeling cute despite there being no one to see, Jenny shrugged and decided that it was time to stop stalling. She glanced around the room, trying to decide if there was anything she should bring with her. She grabbed her charging cable, remembering how panicked she had felt going home with the nice man in the wee hours before the sun rose on Sunday morning, when her phone had only three percent power. Thankfully, she hadn't had to call for help, and he had let her use a cable to power her phone.

Despite his kindness, Jenny tried to forget as much as she could about the encounter as she closed her apartment door, locked it, and went up to the second floor. She didn't mind casual encounters, but every time she thought about it—or any experience with a man, for that matter—she had the nasty habit of picturing Nolan standing in the corner of the room. He never watched. He just stared at the wall, his clothes dripping.

The upstairs hall was dark. Jenny slapped the wall a half-dozen times looking for the switches. Finally, the hallway and breakroom lights snapped on. She ducked her head into the lounge, saw the refrigerator, and let out a frustrated moan.

"Fuck me," she said, realizing that she hadn't gotten anything for her lunch. In all her preparations to try to be ready for the evening, it had entirely slipped her mind to have a meal ready for the half-way point. She would have to broadcast for eight hours without a real meal. She walked into the room and looked around, seeing a loaf of bread on the counter. On top of it was a sticky note that read 'Eat me 9/6,' Jenny pulled open the cupboards and soon found one with a large jar of peanut butter that had a best-by date of six months in the future.

"Thank God," she said. She confirmed a jar of huckleberry preserves in the refrigerator as well. They had no name on them, but whoever's they were, she'd happily give them two jars in replacement for the teaspoons she'd be using. A couple of PB&J sandwiches for her first night at the job sounded just about perfect to her. She had some cans of soda in the fridge downstairs, so things were looking up.

Jenny walked back across the hall to the broadcast room. She turned a knob and light flared. She rolled it back and the room dimmed. She studied the controls and found the little spotlight that Link had used during her tour. After tinkering for a bit, the room glowed with a warm, early morning light that comforted Jenny. She closed the door behind her and strolled over to the broadcast desk. Labels covered everything, and she admitted that it all did seem fairly straightforward. She tried a few different buttons and watched needles jump up across illuminated readouts for power and the volume of different inputs. The ones she was most concerned about—the microphone, phone, and record player— all responded to her experimental fiddling precisely as she hoped they would.

Satisfied that the correct needle jumped when she talked into the microphone, another sprang to life when she played a Beatles album, and yet a third shot up when she spoke to herself after calling into the tower on her own phone, Jenny felt most of her anxiety ebb away. That left only the eagerness. Perhaps meeting the other talkers had stirred something in her. Perhaps it was their confidence in her. She didn't know what caused the sudden desire to sit down and broadcast, but she liked it.

A high-pitched tone startled her and made her jump. It took a moment for Jenny to realize that the sound was coming from the hand-held radio in the corner. She walked over, picked it up, and pushed what looked like the talk button. But nothing happened. She studied the device, turned a knob from 'alert' to 'talk' and then pushed the button again.

"Hello?" she said.

"Hey, it's Nate. You doing okay over there?"

"Yeah, thanks, I think I'm ready."

"Great," he said. "Good luck tonight. If you need anything, just give me a call. If you can't figure this thing out, just text me."

Jenny thanked him, put the handset back into its cradle, and decided to pick out some albums for the evening. She pulled randomly at the spines of the records, exploring them to get a sense of their organization. The left case was almost all rock and roll, stretching from the '50s to the early 2000s. The bottom shelf had electronic music that started in the '70s and ran up to a bright yellow album cover that looked new. Jenny stared at the woman on the cover, her thumbs hidden under the collar of her primary-red jacket, her tattooed abs and long brown hair eliciting a physical reaction from Jenny. The brightness of the colors and the woman's beauty were almost mesmerizing.

"I'll come back to you later," she said, patting the album back into its place.

The second case of records started with jazz at the top and worked its way through blues, funk, and hip hop. This made her uncomfortable, and she wanted to start pulling albums from the shelves and rearranging them in some other way, maybe chronological, with the blues or jazz first, then rock, then hip hop, then techno. It wouldn't be perfect, but at least the shelves wouldn't seem so segregated.

She thumbed her way through the jazz and found herself returning to a pink album with a picture of a smiling black woman in black and white in the bottom right-hand corner. The title read, 'The Bessie Smith Story.'

Jenny flipped it over. She didn't know who Bessie Smith was, but something about the album appealed to her, so she set it on the desk. She grabbed three more blues albums, picking them mostly by their covers. She set the record player up so that it would play for a little over an hour with one disk on the turntable, and three stacked on the spindle, ready to drop, one by one.

Her watch buzzed.

Ten minutes until she had to be on.

Jenny walked to the light controls and changed the room from a warm morning to a cool blue evening. She wished she had a window so she could look out onto the town. She realized she wasn't high enough for that but wondered if the fire-tower would give her that imagined vantage. She pictured herself in the tower, her face illuminated by the control panel, the town's yellow lights twinkling in columns and rows below her. She could imagine herself happy there, flipping switches and talking into the darkness. The image felt warm, cozy, almost familiar.

Suddenly, an idea struck her. She had to broadcast at nine, but no one told her that she couldn't start before that. Maybe, if she could get a few minutes of practice before people started tuning in, she'd feel a little less nervous. It was better than just waiting for eight minutes with nothing to do.

So, Jenny sat down on the chair, pulled herself close to the desk, drew the microphone arm nearer her lips, donned her headphones, and pushed the broadcast button.

"Good evening, Lightning Falls," she said, feeling the words slip out of her mouth. "I'm your host, Jenny Berger, and this is the Kusel House Tower."

28
Back in the Saddle

Monday, September 8, 2025 – Evening

THE BROADCAST LIGHT GLOWED a soft, comforting, anxiety-inducing green. Jenny stared at the microphone as she heard her voice repeating through her headphones. The voice meter shot up almost to the level that Link had told her; she turned a knob.

"So … I'm completely new at this," she said. The needle rose to the appropriate level. "So, forgive me if I'm a little, I don't know, slow? I mean, not like—*slow*—but I've never done this before. I've never been on a podcast or a radio station, I'm much more of a—"

She stopped herself from saying, 'I'm much more of a video person.' She didn't think that would help her reputation.

Then again, how much more could it hurt?

"Um, so I guess I should tell you something about myself. I'm twenty-nine and I was born here in Lightning Falls. Well, you know, not in town, but in Enterprise, at the old hospital. Um … I lived here until I was nineteen, and then I moved to Portland, because that's what you do, right? And then … um … I went down to California for a few years … and now I'm back here."

She took a breath, unsure of what to say about herself next. While she tried to choose between going into further detail about her distant past or her more recent time in town, the phone rang.

Jenny picked up the phone and put it to her ear. "Hello?"

"Hi." The caller sounded like a teenage boy whose voice hadn't fully deepened yet. There was something unfinished about it. "Am I on the radio?"

Jenny paused. "Uh, actually, hold on," she said, taking the phone from her ear. She heard him say "no, wait," but she didn't wait. She pushed the button with the 'broadcast phone' label over it and saw the corresponding light blink green.

"Okay, hi? You're on the air now, I think. Who is this?"

"Um," the young voice said, "uh, you've got big—um—"

Jenny frowned, waiting to hear what the adolescent boy might say. She was sure it would be about her breasts, which, honestly, would have been a strangely innocent kind of harassment. No one knew Jenny's body better than she did, and he wasn't telling her anything she didn't already know. She thought it might be a good teaching moment to not react, not hang up. She wanted to ask him what he hoped to achieve. But, instead of continuing with his commentary, he hung up.

"Wow, that was ... riveting. Look, I—" She searched for the words to address this strange start to her time in the broadcast room. "Okay, maybe right out the gate is a good time to mention this. Though, I'm guessing I'll probably have to say it a lot. My name is—"

She froze. She was about to say something else. What had it been? A chill ran through her as she thought that maybe she had been about to introduce herself as 'Venena,' the name she had used while living in Chico. The name Joseph had given her.

Why the fuck were you about to say that?

"My name is Jenny, and since I was fourteen, men have been making comments about my body. So, I'm used to it. I don't love it most of the time, but I'm used to it. But ... no, that's not really what I want to say. Shit, you really can't take things back here, can you? You just say them and then they're out there. Um, also, I guess I can curse? I don't know. Maybe not? Link didn't say anything about cursing."

She felt like she was already losing herself in a word jumble.

"Um, no, that's not what I wanted to say. I wanted to say that you don't have to approach women—anyone, really—like that. If you appreciate that someone looks good, then it's probably okay to tell them, but not in a weird way. I think it's about what you're—"

What are you hoping to achieve, my love? Joseph's voice in her head.

"About what you're hoping to achieve. So, if you call a woman to tell her on the radio that she has big ... eyes, let's say, then what are you hoping to achieve? Maybe you're sitting there—"

Maybe he's sitting there, thinking about how he ruined things with you. Maybe he's sitting there smelling a shirt you left behind. Maybe he's sitting there with another woman, telling her that you were crazy. You can't control any of that, Joseph said as he stroked her hair. *You can only pity him or forget him.*

"Maybe you're sitting there thinking that your friends will find it funny. Or maybe you're hoping that by talking to me that way, that you'll get the courage to talk to other girls that way. But you shouldn't want either of those things," she said.

The phone rang.

She looked at the board and realized that she still had the phone patched in. She pushed the 'answer' button.

"Hello, you're on the, um, Kusel House Tower Radio Station."

"No one wants to hear you lecture them on morality," a woman's voice said. "Believe me, there isn't anyone in this town who is going to learn the difference between right and wrong from you."

Jenny took a deep breath. Her heart was racing. She wanted to hang up, to shut the woman up. But, like a defense against the impulse, she could almost feel a heavy, comforting hand on her shoulder.

Take it easy, don't panic, don't get mad. Just put her in her place, Joseph said.

"Ma'am," Jenny said, "I can't imagine that's true. Do you know how much I've been through? Do you know how many men I've spoken to?"

"And much more, I'm sure!" the woman said.

"Yes, and much more. I am experienced. I guess you might call me a 'slut,' if that's the kind of person you are. I'm not going to pretend I'm innocent. But since I've had so much experience with men and women, yes, clutch your pearls, ma'am, I'm bisexual—"

"I don't care about that, I—"

"Don't you think both young men and women would benefit from my experience about how not to talk to people? How not to become one of those creeps on the internet? How not to make some of the wrong decisions that I've made?"

"I'm pretty sure they can learn all of that without talking to you," the woman said. "I don't know why the town let you get on here, but you can be sure we won't be listening to your channel in my house."

She hung up.

Fuck her, Joseph's voice said in her mind. *Does she think you're selling ad time? Oh ... were you thinking about doing that?*

Jenny took a deep breath and pushed the phone button. She looked at the clock. It was still three minutes before nine. She hadn't even officially started yet.

"Well, I guess we're off to a great start," Jenny said. What was she doing? She wasn't here to moralize at people. She wasn't here to teach the youth about the dangers of the world, sex, and relationships. But what was she here for?

To put a roof over your head, my dear, Joseph said. She shut her eyes and shook her head. What was this? She'd gone months without hearing his voice in her mind. He had been like a well-buried corpse. And here he was, unexpectedly climbing his way out of the grave.

"I ... I'm sorry, everyone. They both kind of caught me off guard. I signed on early to try to get my feet under me before I was officially supposed to be on the air. But—yeah, I guess that was maybe a bad idea. Or maybe not, I don't know. At least now I can start at nine with a pretty clear expectation of what this is going to be like.

"You know," she said, cradling her forehead in her hands and taking a deep breath, "I guess both of them were just sitting there, waiting for me to come on so they could call and say those things. Are there more of you out there waiting to do the same thing? I mean, what happens in one minute when I'm supposed to be on? Do I just get a flood of those kinds of calls?"

She watched as the clock ticked down.

"I guess we'll see in thirty seconds. Anyway, thanks for joining me for this little pre-show experiment. I guess we'll get started for real here in a second."

Jenny hugged herself and felt the soft fabric of the sweater under her fingers. She thought about Barry's kindness. A part of her said that maybe he'd want something in return later. Even if that turned out to be the case, it was one of the few nice things anyone had done for her since she'd gotten to Lightning Falls. She focused on that thought, on Barry's kindness, and on the sweater.

As the clock ticked to exactly nine, she leaned forward and spoke: "Good evening, Lightning Falls. I'm your host, Jenny Berger, and this is the Kusel House Tower."

Okay, I've got that part down pretty good.

"Tonight, I have a heck of a show lined up for you. I'm—" The words started to roll out naturally until they didn't. She stopped, unsure of what to say next. "I—Sorry, I was trying something there and it didn't quite work out. Guess I'll have to keep working on it. Anyway, that was my second attempt at getting things started. If you've been here for the last ten minutes, you know that it's been an interesting launch for me. Still, here we are, and at least I'm not stumbling over every word."

What are you doing? She thought. *Stop talking about yourself.*

"I—um, I'm not really sure what other people do here. I've listened to some of the other Sleep Talkers, and I know that Sydney does stories, and Charles likes to debate, but I'm not really sure what my style is going to be. Maybe I'll leave that up to all of you."

The phone rang. A knot of anxiety tied itself together in her stomach.

She pushed the 'talk' button.

"Hello, you've got Jenny!" she said. She immediately frowned and shook her head at herself.

"Hey," a familiar voice said. "I have a question. Oh, this is Isabella Delgado, by the way."

"Hey Isabella," Jenny said, a mixture of relief and anxiety rolling together in her stomach.

"So, first I want to say that you're doing an amazing job," Isabella said.

"Thank you," Jenny said.

"Second, I think your show should be about you. You know, about what you think about things, what you like and don't like. I think that would be an effective way to draw people in, you know? Talk about movies, or books, or music. Like, what are you obsessing over right now?"

Jenny frowned. She didn't think she was obsessing over anything. That kind of talk had always left her feeling cold. "Um, I did just finish Glen Moat's new book," Jenny said.

"Really? How was it? I love his movies."

Jenny wanted to correct her, to tell her he didn't have any movies, that there were only adaptations of a few of his books that other people had made into movies. But she didn't. For the moment, Isabella was her lifeline.

"Um, it was good. I feel like I need to read it again to really get everything out of it. But that's how I am with most things. I need to try them more than once before I know what I really think about them. So, like, I usually need to watch a movie twice, or read a book twice, or—"

"Oh, wow, yeah, I don't think I've ever read the same book more than once," Isabella said. "Well, that's not true. I read stuff in high school that I've reread since then."

Jenny wasn't sure what she could say to that. If something was worth reading once, then it was probably worth reading again. "Yeah," Jenny said, "well, some of that stuff they assigned us in school kind of went over my head until I read it again. A lot of it probably still does. But I'm glad I got like my first experience with it in school, to like, I don't know, prepare me for it later."

"Yeah, totally," Isabella said, but Jenny could tell she didn't mean it.

"Um, but yeah, that's a really helpful suggestion. Maybe I can talk about different movies and books that I've seen, and I guess if other people have seen them and want to talk about them, they can call in."

"Exactly," Isabella said. "And then, if you want to do news, or gossip, or something like that—"

"Not sure I want to do gossip," Jenny said. "I feel like that wouldn't be great. Maybe I'll leave that to someone else."

"Oh, maybe you could have me come in and I'll do it," Isabella said.

Jenny frowned thoughtfully, wondering if that was allowed. "That's an interesting idea," Jenny said. "I wonder if I could have someone come in and do a segment or something."

"Sure, it would be so much fun to do that together." The inflection in her voice changed just enough for Jenny to get the point. Isabella wasn't trying to help, precisely. Instead, it was just an excuse to be alone with Jenny.

Why couldn't someone else volunteer for the job? She thought of Phil. She thought of Chloe.

"I'll think about that," she said, trying not to let on how uncomfortable the idea made her. "I should probably figure the job out first before I start inviting other people to do it for me."

She almost said something about pay, and how Isabella would be working for free, but then she imagined the innuendos that would follow, and she swallowed her words.

"You've really given me a lot to think about," Jenny said, trying to put a lilt of flirtation into her voice. She figured that it might balance out the flat, uncomfortable tone that had seeped in as her knot of anxiety tightened. "I appreciate you calling, Isabella. I really do."

That part, at least, was genuine.

"No problem, girl, I'm here for you," Isabella said. "I'm always down to talk about movies, and books, and music, and shit," she said. "Oops, sorry, maybe I'm not supposed to curse."

"Actually, I think it's okay," Jenny said. "But I guess I'll have to get back to you on that."

"Cool, I hope the rest of your show is as amazing as you are," Isabella said.

Jenny thanked her, told her she'd talk to her later, and hung up.

"Thank you again to Isabella for being the first nice person to call in tonight." She looked over at the record player. "Since it's been an insanely eventful first twenty minutes of me sitting here, I'm going to immediately turn to some music. So, why don't we start with some blues? I haven't actually heard this person before, but I love the album cover. I'll be back in a bit after I've—" She didn't know what to say. *After I've cried? After I've reconsidered my life choices yet again?*

"After I've had a chance to process all of this. All right, be back soon."

She pushed the record player button and then remembered to turn off the phone feed. She turned the record player on and put the head onto the outer rim of the first record. A piano started slowly, reminding her a little of a down-tempo version of an old song she couldn't remember the name of. Then a woman's voice rose with the music, lamenting how hard it was to love someone if they don't love you.

Jenny pushed the microphone button and set a timer for forty minutes to come back and check. She took her headphones off, hung them up, pushed herself back from the desk, and rubbed her eyes. That had felt like a hell of a lot longer than twenty minutes.

As she got up to go find the bathroom, she suddenly wondered where Joseph had gone. He had been so present when the first two people had called, but then he just seemed to fade into the background when she talked to Isabella. As inexplicably as he had appeared, he had vanished.

The fist of anxiety in her stomach throbbed as she wondered what awaited her when she came back from her break.

29
Six Pictures

Monday, September 8, 2025 – Evening

JENNY WALKED OUT INTO the hallway, and it struck her for the first time that the entire house and its grounds were open to her. She could go anywhere, do anything, and no one would stop her. She could do the show naked, dressed as a clown, or while hosting a party. She imagined herself as a DJ like one she had seen in an old video of a spring break with people drinking and dancing in the background. She could have the party people of Lightning Falls shaking their asses to music while she interviewed them one by one about who they were when they weren't drinking heavily and making bad life choices.

She walked to the bathroom and was surprised to find its walls crowded with framed flyers from Camping Days gone by. Perfectly eye-level as she sat was a red one-sheet that read, 'Come Shelter in the Swelter! Camping Days 2023!' Jenny wondered if she might do something for Camping Days with her show. Maybe people could call in and talk about their experiences.

Sure, and have them all dance around the fact that your father died during Camping Days over twenty years ago.

Maybe she could use that. Maybe she could talk about that event and what it meant to her, and that would let other people talk about their experiences.

What are you going to tell them? Hi, I'm Jenny. I couldn't cope with the guilt of my dad drowning because I wouldn't take 'no' for an answer, so I invented boogeymen and sea serpents that I still see in my dreams.

When she walked back out into the hall, the framed pictures that lined the walls caught her attention. They were all black and white, and Jenny thought one or two of them might have been from the 19th century.

She stopped at one that showed a frontiersman in a wide-brimmed hat that shaded his squinting eyes as he stood next to Whitman Cabin. He wore a white shirt, plain trousers, and suspenders. He had a broad mustache that hid his upper lip. A rifle stood beside him, its butt in the ground next to his boot, its barrel gripped firmly in his fist. The cabin's sign and power cables were missing, but otherwise it looked almost exactly the same. Jenny wondered if it was the first picture ever taken of the building. Unfortunately, there was no information placard.

She moved to the next photo and found a group of serious-faced people standing together in front of the Kusel House. Jenny saw a man she thought could be the frontiersman from the first picture, only much older. His hair and mustache were white, wilder, and longer. Only his eyebrows remained thick and black. He still squinted. His hand rested on an elderly woman's shoulder, and her hand rested on a bearded middle-aged man's shoulder.

The bearded man bore a strong resemblance to the frontiersman behind him. Jenny guessed that the younger man was the son, and the older couple were his parents. From his neat appearance, she imagined he was a banker or businessman of some kind. The banker also had a woman next to him, and in front of them were two girls who looked like they were a few years apart. The younger might have been six or seven, the older maybe ten. Jenny wasn't sure when the picture might have been taken, maybe the 1920s. But it could have easily been ten or twenty years before or after. There was no car in the driveway, but that meant nothing. Jenny didn't know enough about clothing to guess what the high-necked shirts or modest dresses might say about when the people had stood together on the lawn.

She went to the next picture and found two couples in front of a gazebo. The women wore wedding dresses, and the men wore suits. The brides looked so similar that, at first, Jenny thought they might be twins. But as she studied the picture, she realized that it was their identical makeup, jewelry, dresses, and hairdos that made them look similar. One was a little taller and broader with wide, open eyes. The other had a thinner nose and squinted just like the man with the mustache.

Jenny stared at the two women and then back at the group picture. She focused on the two girls. One had a birthmark on her neck, and … yes, there was the same birthmark in the wedding photo. *Well,* she thought, *we have a timeline: Grandpa, the frontiersman, with his gun, his son, the banker, and his whole family, and then the little girls all grown up and getting married … on the same day.*

Hoping to find the next stage of their lives, Jenny stepped to her right to survey the next photograph. Here was a picture of the woman without the birthmark and her husband, standing in a well-appointed room. She was holding a baby, and they both looked immensely proud. Their dress, especially her headband, suggested the 1920s to Jenny. If so, perhaps the group photo was fifteen years earlier.

"So, you had a baby," Jenny said, running her finger over the glass. She had never felt much desire to have children. But she envied the look of joy on the woman's face.

The next picture showed the other woman with the birthmark, perhaps in her forties, standing next to a man in a soldier's uniform. She didn't know much about wars, but he didn't look like pictures from World War I. Doing a little mental math, she guessed the photograph was from the 1940s. She felt a strange pull in her core, not exactly nostalgia or longing, but a weird twisting that made her feel dizzy. She felt like she was flying a thousand feet above the ground, taking in whole swaths of time in big gulps.

Jenny side-stepped to the last picture. Here, once more, was the woman with the birthmark on her neck, now in her mid-fifties. Jenny recognized the front porch and its swing. The woman was posing with a tall man. Jenny returned to the wedding photo. She didn't think he was the same man who had married birthmark-woman. This older fellow had a thin mustache, jowls, and a belly. He stood next to her with his arm around her shoulder, his hand dangerously close to her breast. Jenny felt strangely jarred by his presence, like he didn't belong.

Her mouth felt dry as she went over the images again, realizing that almost certainly some of these people must be the ones who died in the house. But who? Four people, two elderly parents, a woman, and her husband. Jenny peered into the misty past and found that she could discern frustratingly little. Yet, what she could see was strangely comforting. The ghosts of the Kusel House, if ghosts there were, seemed less dreadfully faceless. These people, whichever ones had lost their lives here, were comfortingly normal. For the most part, they looked happy. She sensed no diabolical secrecy, no closed-in cultishness, no gothic brooding. Well, not in the girls, nor the women they became. And not in the family picture either. She went back to it and looked at the rest of the—she counted—twenty people depicted. Some of them were downright smiling, others looked kindly, many looked simply at peace.

She touched the picture frame and wondered at the idea that all those people had lived their lives from beginning to end. They had today after today until all their todays were gone. If Jenny guessed rightly about the date, every person in that group picture was certainly dead. Jenny took in all of the photographs in order again until she came to the last one, which showed the sister with the birthmark and the strange, serious older man. Finally, she went back to the wedding picture of the two couples laughing together in front of a gazebo.

"What happened to you?" she asked the four happy people.

30
Ancient Meaning

Monday, September 8, 2025 – Night

JENNY SPENT MOST OF the next hour on the couch in the lounge. She could have gone downstairs and into her own space, but it felt right to do what everyone else did when they were working here. She wanted to know what Charles did when he was in the house by himself, or how Sydney entertained herself. She pictured Maddy reading a book or, which seemed just as likely, playing a video game on a handheld system.

She tried to picture Nate limping slowly up the stairs and felt bad for him. She wondered why he had picked a job that involved walking around so much. Jenny wondered if he'd be happier with work that kept him in one place, instead of having to hike up a mountain four nights a week every third week.

He has his reasons, Jenny thought. *Just like everyone else does.*

She tried to picture the last member of her new little community, Linds. She had a tough time remembering what they looked like, except that they had short hair and had worn a high school T-shirt. It had been a long name.

Northern Hamilton County Regional High School.

The name came to her surprisingly easily. She frowned, not certain if that was right or if she was just making it up. Maybe, she thought, it just had a rhythm to it that made it easy to remember. She ran the words over in her mind again. *No,* she thought, *it didn't.* And yet, she felt confident that she was remembering it correctly.

Jenny thought about her own high school years and found them blank. How many teachers had she lost? How many friends had simply disappeared because of … what? Was it what Joseph had done to her? Had that damaged her brain in a way that she didn't realize until she came home? It was strange brain damage, however. Its erasure was oddly selective.

As she pondered, her mind wandered, and she dozed.

"The word 'tower' doesn't mean anything," Joseph said. "It's ancient, from before Latin, from before Greek. The meaning is lost."

Jenny looked up at him from where she reclined naked on a towel, a grape held between her fingers, a glass of wine at her elbow. It was just before dawn in the community house's courtyard, and the fountain burbled peacefully behind her. Joseph wore only a pair of white linen draw-string shorts, his white hair in the same crew-cut she imagined he'd worn since he was a child. Jenny's eyes were black with kohl, and she wore golden bracelets around her wrists. Behind Joseph, Nolan stood nude, tanned, and visibly aroused by Jenny's state of undress. Beside him stood Aurora, also naked, but draped so heavily in golden necklaces that her nipples barely poked through the confusion of plate, disk, chain, and rope. Every strand of hair on their naked bodies was golden, as if each had been dipped in precious metal. Both stood still and radiated the light and warmth of the early morning sun.

Jenny looked at Joseph, who was as tan as ever, his skin dotted with age spots, his belly protruding and round, the white hair on his arms, shoulders, and legs forming a kind of wispy nimbus about him. He reminded her a little of Marlon Brando in *Apocalypse Now*.

"I made you watch that movie," he said as she stared at him. "That's why you're comparing me to Brando."

Jenny popped the grape into her mouth.

"I love you," he said, smiling down at her. She knew that if she let him, he would ravage her time after time. And a part of her wanted it. Not the sex, but the connection, the approval, the 'yes' of it all from him. She wanted to be the one into whom he poured his desire and from whom he received satisfaction.

"And I love you," she said, pulling another grape from the bunch that lay on a plate before her, inches from her breasts.

He swallowed.

"If only … "

"If only what?" she asked.

But he didn't speak. He only looked at her with love and regret.

"If only I were another man," he said finally. "Not the man who turned you into this."

Jenny tilted her wine glass back and drank it to the bottom, feeling it trickle down her chin, neck, and arm. She breathed deeply the scents of honeysuckle, jasmine, and rain. Jenny lowered the cup and laughed. She rose to her knees and crawled to him. She put her hands on his knees and looked up into his gray eyes.

"I can be whatever you want me to be. I am yours to command. Tell me to change. I want to change. I don't want to be frozen anymore. Tell me to change, I want to change again."

"No," Joseph said. "You are not. My Jenny is gone."

Behind him, the sun rose, and in that golden disk she saw her reflection.

"Who am I?" she said, recognizing nothing in the woman who looked back at her.

She looked at the sun again and, for a moment, the unfamiliar face faded and another, strange and brooding visage appeared. This one opened her mouth to speak.

But before she could, Joseph answered her, "A thing," Joseph said, his voice hitching and his hand going to his eyes to cover them. "A thing."

Jenny screamed and almost fell off the couch. Her sweat soaked her clothes, and her hands ached from being clenched so tightly.

"Shit, shit," she said, sitting up and pulling her damp shirt away from her. "Fuck, no, no thank you!" she said to the house. "No thank you, please!"

She stood and stretched, twisted, and stretched again. The couch was uncomfortable, and if that was the sort of dream it produced, she decided she'd do well to avoid it.

"Get out of my head, Joseph," she said.

From the other room, music was still playing. Jenny looked at her watch. Almost an hour had passed, though it felt much longer. Her mind was foggy; she needed caffeine. She found the coffee maker in the kitchen and decided to have her first nighttime coffee in probably five or six years.

The first of many, she thought. *Probably.*

As Jenny made her coffee, she thought about the dream. About Nolan and his arousal, about Aurora and the far-off look in her face, and about herself and how alien she'd been to her own mind. She tried desperately not to think about Joseph, and even more desperately not to think about what she had been offering him at the end of the dream. What the hell was wrong with her? Why couldn't she dream of him as the monster she knew he was?

She wanted to cry, but the feeling wasn't there. Instead, the only thing she felt strongly was a desire to return to the microphone.

After I change clothes, she thought. Five minutes later, she pulled herself back into place in front of the desk, wearing a dry shirt under her new sweater. Jenny pushed the button for the microphone, let the playing song end, and then pushed the button for the record player. For a moment, the image of the sun appeared in her mind, burning above Joseph's head. In its impossible brightness, a face looked back at her.

Jenny felt dizzy as the words tumbled out of her.

"Good evening, folks, welcome back to Kusel House Radio. I'm your host, Jenny Berger, and have I got a show for you."

Entry 7

Tuesday, September 9, 2025

Hey, bestest friend, Diary! So, I'm awake! Very awake. Night one is officially* done, and now it's a quarter after five. My brain is on fire, and so is my voice, so I'm not saying anything out loud until I get to the diner.

What was my first night like, you ask? Well, first, a pervy teen called in, then a very angry lady who, now that I think about it, didn't seem angry at the kid calling in to tell me about my body. I guess she figures that if I put it out there, I should expect comments. And, ma'am, I do expect comments. I do. That doesn't make them any more pleasant or appropriate! I wish I had said that. Next time. That's the good thing about this, there's always a next time to prepare for.

Let's see, the second stretch went super well … except that I can't remember any of it. No, sorry, that was the third stretch. The second one went fine, and I DO remember it. But there's one section where it's all blank, except for the feeling that it was going really well. It was sandwiched between some freaking deep sleeps so, maybe I wasn't even totally awake the whole time. That's good, if I can do this show asleep and be a rockstar and then not have to remember it, maybe that's a good thing? Probably not. Probably if that keeps happening, I should see a doctor.

I should probably see a doctor anyway about my memory. But, you know what, Diary? I'm tired of doctors for a while. Okay?

Um … Oh, sections four and five were also good. A guy named Mike called in. He works overnight, too. He's a caretaker. And let's see, he also subscribed to my JustBuffs page, so that's … interesting. More on that in another entry, I think.

Oh, I just put an asterisk next to being done, because (technically) I'm not done. I have to go up and turn off the music. I said goodbye at five. I hope my voice gets used to talking all night.

Okay, time to shower, and then go to *Second Wave*. I'm really glad Delia had her dinner last night, otherwise, I'd be super nervous right now. But I'm not. The other Sleep Talkers aren't my friends yet, but they aren't total strangers either, so, yeah, that feels nice.

31
Wherever You Are

Tuesday, September 9, 2025 – Morning

JENNY SHOWERED, APPRECIATING THE excellent water pressure. She made a mental list of everything she needed to buy to make the bathroom feel like her own. She had gotten by with the bare minimum at Patty's, though she wasn't sure why. Maybe it had been her frugality; maybe it had been the nagging fear that Patty would throw her out when she learned Jenny's secret.

Well, at least my judgment isn't entirely broken.

She rinsed, wishing she could stay in the hot water a little longer. The mornings were getting colder fast, and Jenny thought about all the winter clothing she'd have to buy. Reluctantly, Jenny turned off the water and reached for her towel. She dried herself off, turned on the bathroom fan, and padded barefoot into her new bedroom. She frowned, thinking it odd that she'd just showered and was about to get dressed for only a few hours before going to bed.

I have to change my thinking. I need to shower when I wake up in the afternoons. I wonder how many more things I'll have to rearrange to make this work.

She threw on her clothes, picking a pair of jeans and a blue sweater. She put the green sweater Barry had given her on a hanger. She sniffed it and then walked to her notebook and added a line to her to-do list: 'Dry clean Barry's sweater.' She returned to the bathroom to find that though the fan was doing a good job of dispersing the steam, the mirror remained fogged. Jenny reached out and wiped it with her hand and screamed.

The eyes that looked back at her were not her own.

No … no they were. She blinked and stared, trepidatiously leaning in. Yes, they were her own, normal, gray eyes. But for a second, she thought she had seen someone else's face.

"Fuck," Jenny breathed. "This is the first sign. Either I'm going crazy, or this house is haunted. Shit, this is where I'm supposed to leave. Like, a rational person would just leave, right?"

Instead of leaving, she wiped the mirror with a towel and stared at her reflection until her pulse slowed. Nothing else strange happened, and Jenny's mind began rationalizing and justifying what she had seen. The most convincing to her, however, was that she really had seen a ghost or some psychic memory of someone in the house. She knew it was more likely that the distortion of fog, water, and distraction had made her mind process the image incorrectly. But it felt wrong to her if the Kusel House had no ghosts. Jenny just hoped they were friendly, or at least not murderous.

She continued her morning toilette and finished by pulling her hair back into a messy bun of curls as her phone alarm buzzed. She ran upstairs to see that the final record was on its second-to-last song. A minute remained of her first night.

She faded the music down and leaned into the microphone, breaking her promise to rest her voice until she got to the diner.

"Okay, everyone, that's it for me on my first night here. I … I need to come up with a good sign-off for this thing. So, maybe …."

A picture of her father tucking her into bed bloomed in her mind. He kissed her on the forehead and turned out the light. Then, as he closed the door, he leaned in. In a gravelly voice, he said, "Good night, Miss Calabash, wherever you are."

Jenny never understood it, and now, remembering it for the first time in years, she felt it tug at something in her chest.

"Um, how about this? Good morning, Lightning Falls, and goodnight—"

She couldn't think of anything; her mind was blank.

"Sorry. Sorry, I was just trying something there. Well, maybe you all can call in tomorrow to suggest some good sign-off lines. For now, let's just finish with: Good morning, Lightning Falls."

She pushed the 'broadcast' button and felt stupid. She hoped that no one had been listening at the end. She powered everything down, put the records back in place, and locked the broadcast room behind her.

Booth. It's a booth.

Her phone buzzed.

> **_Nate_**
> Everyone's wrapping up and heading to the Diner. You coming with?

> **_Jenny_**
> Yeah, grabbing my jacket and heading there now.

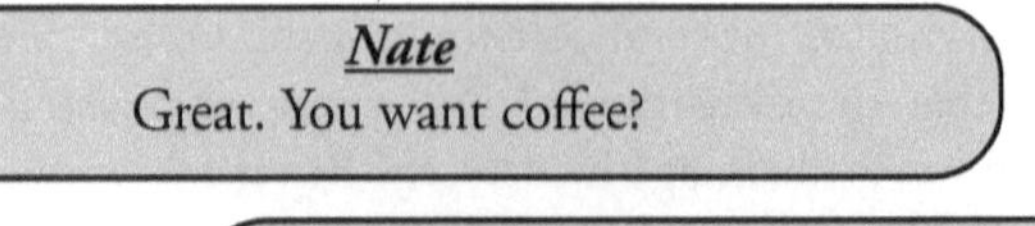

Five minutes later, Jenny looked around her new apartment, decided that she had so little there that there wasn't anything to fuss over before she left, grabbed her jacket and keys, and locked the doors behind her.

She felt like she was replaying the previous night in reverse. Her mind was ablaze with the new experience and the new people she had met only hours before. Part of her wanted to run back, to get her things and go back to Patty and beg her to let her stay. Part of her wanted to rent a car and drive back down to Chico to see if anyone was still living in the community house and settle back into her life there. Part of her even wanted to drive past Chico, down to LA, to connect with the few people she had considered friends there. All options seemed strangely safer and more familiar than this new, nocturnal life she had started in earnest less than twelve hours earlier.

Jenny pushed the ideas aside as untenable—except maybe returning to LA—and put her earbuds in. She swiped through her phone and clicked on her music app. In the broadcast room, blues and folk had felt the most appropriate, but in the cool predawn darkness, she wanted something else. Her mind was too awake, too alive, too peppy...

She thought of the yellow album cover and the beautiful woman on it. What had her name been? The cover had two words on it. She looked them both up and found her and the album.

The artist's name was Lights.

She hit play. A tone began, and the woman, whispering and haunting, sang about ghosts. She walked up the road, hands in her jacket pockets, feeling like the main character on a TV show with her own oddly perfect soundtrack. A feeling of wellness rose within her as the pines swayed in the wind. The streetlights of Lightning Falls glowed gold and white before her, and the faint base of the falls rolled under the music in her head.

32
Second Wave

Tuesday, September 9, 2025 – Morning

MUSIC GUIDED JENNY UP Main Street as dawn lit the eastern-facing buildings in pinks, purples, and oranges. Jenny checked both ways and, seeing no cars, walked out to take a picture. It looked idyllic, perhaps like every Main Street in America wanted to look. She wished she could remember growing up in such a beautiful place.

She smelled bread baking as a few stray drops of rain pattered the pavement and longed for an older, purer time. She thought of what Aurora would have said to that, that the evils of the past weren't pure. Jenny knew that. But there was something lost, something that the world once had that was now gone. She didn't know why the little street with its fire station, library, and movie theater made her feel so strongly, but she wanted to somehow chase after the feeling. To try to fulfill the longing. But she had no idea how to do that.

We follow the best we know, and sometimes it leads us into dark places.

There was Joseph's voice again, but this time it was simply a memory.

We are all looking for the same thing: a perfect world. The problem is that no one can agree on what that looks like.

She hadn't thought much about the idea of a perfect world since Joseph destroyed hers. He had held forth sometimes for up to an hour on the idea of a perfect world. Those had been times when she had felt like she barely knew him. He would pace and lecture and take on a professorial tone. And when he finished his lecture, he'd laugh at himself and call her to him. She would sit on his knee as if she were a child, and he would hold her close and stroke her hair.

My perfect world has you in it, darling.

Jenny swallowed, looked over her shoulder, and got off the road.

Rain tapped the sidewalk, and Lights sang in her ears.

She pulled the diner's front door open and stepped in. Despite the quietness of Main Street, the Second Wave Diner was bustling. To her left, two men with white hair were playing an old arcade game. Beyond them, a middle-aged woman with excessive makeup took menus from a plastic holder and led a young couple to a booth. A wall of pale-green block glass divided the waiting area from two rows of booths and a counter that sported three glass cases, one with doughnuts, one with pies, and one with cakes. Jenny pulled her earbuds out, checked her messages, and wandered back. In the back-left of the diner, she saw Nate and Sydney waving their hands from a large corner booth.

"Good morning," Charles said, lifting his coffee cup in greeting. He wore a sports jacket and a checked button-up shirt. Maddy and Sydney sat on either side of him. Sydney wore another sleeveless shirt showing her many tattoos, and Maddy wore another black cami, possibly the same one she had on the prior evening. Jenny internally shook her head at herself as she judged that both were attracted to her. Linds sat next to Maddy and was wearing a flannel shirt with the sleeves rolled up. They were sipping coffee as Jenny approached the table and nodded at her over the mug. Nate, who was sitting in one of the two chairs on the outside of the table, stood and extended his hand.

"How's it going?" he asked, offering her the chair next to him.

"I never sit with my back to the door," Jenny said, looking down at the chair. They all stared at her. "That's how Buffalo Bill got it."

Sydney gawked, Charles looked thoughtful, and both Nate and Maddy stared blankly. Only Linds smirked.

"Sorry, just a thing my dad used to say," Jenny said, plopping herself down in the empty seat.

"Was he serious?" Sydney asked.

"Well, I think he meant Wild Bill," Charles said.

"Shit," Jenny said, "Yeah, that's what he said. I got it wrong."

"Actually, now that I think about it, Buffalo Bill also got it from behind," Charles said. He grinned. "Kidney failure. Though I doubt his seating had anything to do with it."

"Charles knows everything," Sydney said.

"I do not," Charles said.

The waitress arrived, flirted with Nate, took their order, and scooted away.

"You should ask her out," Charles said. Nate shook his head.

"Why not? You two would be so cute," Sydney said.

"Well, first, she's like, ten years younger than me," Nate said. "And second, what if it goes bad? Then, five days a week, it's going to be awkward in here."

"Just don't be an asshole and it won't go bad," Sydney said smiling sweetly.

"That's only half of it," Maddy said. "What if she's an asshole?"

"Kelly? No! She'd never be an asshole," Sydney said. Charles leaned back to allow them to talk over him.

"Neither would Nate," Maddy said. Sydney gave Nate a sympathetic nod that said that she didn't entirely believe that.

"So, how was your first night?" Nate asked loudly, turning in his seat to face her.

"Weird," Jenny said. "It started off … not great, and then it kind of smoothed out."

"Oh my God, that boy!" Sydney said. "Oh, we were listening from the beginning."

"You had it on early?" Jenny asked.

"Kind of, we just turned it on and waited for you to start. When you got on early, we already had it on."

"You did fine," Maddy said. "Better than me on my first night."

"Did you listen, Charles?" Sydney said.

"No, I thought it more polite not to listen to the first night," he said. "No one needs everyone remembering all of their first fumbles."

"Well, I'm flattered that you all either listened or didn't listen," Jenny laughed.

"You should have listened," Maddy said. "By one, she was a natural. You sounded like you'd been doing it for years."

Jenny thought back, still trying to remember the third stretch of her night, and still drew a blank. Sydney spared Jenny a recounting of her half-asleep radio broadcast as she stood and waved enthusiastically toward the front of the diner. Maddy also raised a hand. Jenny turned in her seat to see two older women shuffling in, knit caps on their heads, white hair sticking out from under them. They both waved back as the hostess led them to a booth toward the front of the diner.

"Who are they?" Jenny asked.

"You don't know?" Charles said.

"Sorry, I have a memory thing. It's not … I just don't remember a lot of people or stuff from town. Like, honestly, other than Barry and Delia, and my mom, I really don't remember anyone. So, if I knew any of you—"

Everyone around the table shook their heads.

"Linds and I are new," Nate said.

Charles said, "I don't really make it my business to get to know teenage girls in town."

"We were like, thirteen when you left," Sydney said, sitting back down.

"Wait, how do you know when I—"

"You're pretty popular around town right now," Maddy said. "And that was Anna and Hanna, they're kind of popular too."

"They're our idols," Sydney said, reaching in front of Charles to grab Maddy's arm.

Jenny stared, confused.

"Lesbians," Charles said, straightening his silverware on his napkin. Suddenly, Jenny thought back to Patty's whispered comment at the summer market.

"Oh," Jenny said. "Huh. I never knew Lightning Falls was so queer."

"It's not," Charles said. "This town has two thousand people in it. If five percent of the population is queer, then statistically, we should have about a hundred people in town who fit the bill. I know of a dozen, and half of them are in this diner right now. You just found a little pocket in an otherwise fairly conservative town."

"Well, I know two more," Jenny said.

"Oh, who?" Sydney said, leaning her elbows on the table.

"Um, I guess I don't want to out them if they aren't," Jenny said.

"You hang out with Isabella Delgado," Maddy said.

"Uh—"

"You're popular," Sydney said. "Everyone talks about you."

"Maybe Jenny would like to talk about something else?" Nate said.

"And Isabella dated Chloe—"

"Like, what it's like to live in a haunted house—" Nate said.

"Wait, is it haunted?" Jenny said, turning to him. He shrugged. "Because I'm pretty sure I saw something this morning."

Jenny described the moment she saw another woman's eyes in the mirror. Sydney said that she saw a tall, dark-skinned man standing on the gazebo in the backyard one morning.

"There's a gazebo?"

"Yeah, haven't you been in the back yard yet?" Nate laughed.

"No, I just, well, I just moved in yesterday, I guess."

"You should probably explore the grounds, it's a cool, old house," Maddy said. "Syd would happily give you a tour."

The other young woman practically bounced in her seat.

"Honestly, that sounds like a fun group activity," Charles said. "Touring the old Kusel Mansion."

"Is that something we're going to do? Because I love that idea," Sydney said.

"We should have Mrs. Bellarmine give us the tour, and put the town's historical society to some good use," Charles said.

"Think she's up to it?" Maddy asked.

"She gets around faster than I do," Nate said. They decided that a tour of the house and grounds would be a good bonding experience and a way for Jenny to get to know her new home.

"And know where all the ghosts are," Sydney said. The young woman pushed her orange hair back behind an ear and stared at her with big, earnest eyes.

Shit, Jenny thought, staring back, and feeling mesmerized. *I might be in trouble here.*

"Syd, do you need Jenny to do anything for you at the end of the week?" Nate asked. "As far as the booth and lounge are concerned, I mean."

"Um, probably not. Just don't drink all my energy drinks, okay? You can have some until you're all set up, but I'm going to pass out if I don't have caffeine."

"Oh, I wouldn't—" Jenny said. "Oh, are you at the house this weekend?"

"Mhm," Sydney said, smiling broadly.

I'm in a lot of fucking trouble, Jenny thought. She hadn't considered the specifics of the three Weekenders in her new house. Sometimes it would be Charles, and he seemed like he would be interesting to chat with over coffee. But he was safe. Other times, it would be Maddy or Sydney who were both looking at her with interest. Jenny felt her pulse racing.

Nate put his hand on Jenny's forearm, perhaps sensing her unease.

"Plenty of time for you to figure things out," he said. "We should all hang out on Friday if you're going to be free. It's kind of weird being up all night when the rest of the town is asleep, and you don't have to work."

"Yeah, I've been trying to figure out what I'm going to do with my time," Jenny said. "So, hanging out sounds great."

The waitress returned with their food, and conversation slowed as they all dug into omelets, pancakes, and sausages. They chatted a bit more about ghost sightings. Linds and Nate were silent and just shook their heads when asked if they had ever seen anything in the Kusel House. Before Charles could answer the same question, Sydney veered off in another direction, wondering if ghosts had relationships. Breakfast ended soon after, and they poured out onto the sidewalk together, with Maddy pulling out a vape pen and Nate taking out a pipe.

"Wow, how old are you?" Jenny asked.

"Used to smoke cigarettes. I tried one of those," he said around the stem, nodding toward Maddy, "but it just didn't do it for me. So now I do this. I think it makes me look stately."

"It doesn't," said Charles at the same time Maddy said that it did. They all laughed.

"Um, what are you doing right now?" Sydney asked.

"I'm probably going to go home and sleep," Jenny said. "I'm not used to this life yet."

"Oh, yeah, that makes sense," Sydney said, her excitement slightly diminished. "Well, maybe we can all hang out tomorrow."

"Come on," Maddy said, taking Sydney's hand and pulling her down the street. She looked back over her shoulder once and said, "It was good to see you again. Congratulations on finishing your first night."

"Thanks," Jenny said and waved as Maddy practically dragged Sydney as the orange-haired woman walked backwards and waved.

"Shit," Jenny said as Nate and Charles both chuckled.

"Just so you know, they're open," Nate said. "So, if Sydney decides to try to climb all over you, she's not betraying Maddy."

"Well, there's that at least," Jenny said.

"Still, probably smart to steer clear. Could make breakfasts more awkward than they sometimes are," Nate said.

"That's your standard philosophy," Charles said.

Nate shrugged. "You want to join us for dinner? We usually eat at Cinder's Remorse around seven."

"Yeah, that sounds great," Jenny said.

"You want a ride home on Linds' pegs?" Nate joked as Linds pulled their helmet on and swung their leg over a scuffed blue ten-speed bike.

"What?" Jenny asked.

"I don't have pegs," Linds said, grinning and shaking their head.

"Kidding," Nate said. "Just … for a second, this felt like some kind of kids on bikes story. I figured you'd ride on the pegs and then we'd all go down to the old stand-pipe to see what kids have gotten eaten recently."

Jenny shook her head. Then, a second later, it clicked. "Oh!" Jenny laughed.

"Yeah, probably shouldn't joke about that with Carson Booth still missing," Charles said.

"True," Nate said. "Sorry, sometimes my mind just goes to dark places."

Behind him, Linds nodded.

"Do you need someone to walk you home?" Charles asked.

"Thanks, but I'm all good. It was nice seeing you both again. And thanks for making me feel welcome."

"Well," Nate said, "any time, especially if you don't want to feel as welcome as Syd seems like she wants to make you feel."

"And I'll make you feel even less welcome," Charles said, grinning.

Jenny laughed and turned to head back down Main Street. She waved, put her earbuds in, and started walking. As she restarted the last song, she glanced back over her shoulder. Nate and Charles were lagging behind her. Nate limped along, and Charles kept a slow pace beside him. They talked as Nate looked up at the sky and Charles looked thoughtfully down at the sidewalk.

Jenny smiled, turned her music up, and strode past stores slowly opening as the sun rose over Lightning Falls.

The Quiet Rumble

Volume 10, Issue 76, Thursday, September 11, 2025

By Keith Lowry, Ed. In Chief.

DESPITE THE DATE, I won't write about September 11, 2001. If I'm still kicking next year, I'll do a twenty-five-year look back at how that day changed everything for all of us. And if I'm not still kicking, I'll leave it to the living to look back on their own past.

Today, I want to talk about our quietly famous little cadre of radio personalities, the so-called Sleep Talkers. In my time, these fine folks have gone by many different names. When we were kids, we called them the "Tower Jockeys" since we thought that sounded cool and a little bit like fighter-pilots and test-pilots and disc jockeys. A lot of us wanted to grow up to be Tower Jockeys, and I suppose that listening to George Harfolk read the newspaper and talk about current events on weeknights instilled in me a love of communication. Even though he died of a heart attack New Year's Day, 1964, his voice stayed in the back of my head almost every day until I retired from doing real journalism a decade ago and settled into this palaverous retirement of musing about the past online.

Our Sleep Talkers, Tower Talkers, Night Talkers, Night Whisperers, and, when October rolls around, I've also heard "Ghost Talkers," are a group of six people who have been serving our town for almost a century. Now, it's my job to remember things about Lightning Falls, but my memory fails concerning the historical connections between the Tower Jockeys and Brethren of the New Settlement. I know there is a connection, or at least that's what I've been told, but how it all fits, I don't know. What I do know is that Jeremiah Kusel had the fire-watch tower built in the 1930s to serve double duty: keep an eye out for flames and smoke and host the first all-night local radio station for our little berg.

The origin of our local radio stations in the fire-watch tower is, incidentally, why we call them Tower Talkers, despite the fact that two of the radio stations are not in towers. It would probably be more accurate to call them "House Talkers," but that's so much less cool. The Kusel House tower was once in the Lundy Hotel, but that was relatively short-lived, though I guess maybe a four-story building back then could have been considered a "tower."

Anyway, over the years, dozens of people have taken up the job of talking to us at night. They lull us to sleep, welcome early risers into new days, and keep the few night-birds among us company while the rest of us slumber. They do it for a small salary and housing. That was the deal from the beginning. That was Mr. Kusel's plan and philosophy: to give people decent work and help them make their way. It's a philosophy we have so little of in our world today.

I've heard people ask what the point of the Tower Talkers is. Why do we still spend money on them? Well, we don't spend much since there's an endowment and donations. But if you want the answer, I would tell you to look around and ask yourself what makes Lightning Falls different. Is it that some folks have such a hard time finding us? Is it that we get to have a little anonymity, being so far removed from the world? Or is it our history, rooted in religious refugees who believed in egalitarianism, dignity, and a better future?

I think it's that last one, and though much of what the Kusel family hoped to bring to this place has disappeared, the Tower Jockeys remain. They are part of our essential culture, the thing that makes us who we are as a community. So, I think we should be grateful that they exist, and they keep doing their work.

So, thank you, Tower Jockeys. Thank you for whispering us to sleep, for waking us up in the mornings, and for sitting with us during the long, cold watches of the night.

And, since we have a new Talker joining us, welcome. I hope you find a home among a group of wonderful people who I think are among the best we've ever had.

Entry 8

Friday, September 12, 2025

Well, Diary, what a week! I think I'm just about settled in on my new sleep schedule, and I can happily report that I have not seen any more ghosts around the house. Though maybe that will change once we've done the house tour, which doesn't happen for a week, but that's okay, there's plenty of time for the ghosts to communicate directly with me before then.

(Also, reminder to self, get something to wear for Delia's 1920s party next Friday.)

But that's the future, what of the past? Well, workdays 2-4 went … fine, I guess. To date, I have had four calls from horny men/boys, ten new sign-ups for my website, and two angry calls about how much of a whore I am. I have also talked to a dozen or so people from town, learned a little bit about the blues, and generally settled into a good pattern.

It's weird to work a job with a schedule again, but it's also kind of cool to be able to just go upstairs and work and take breaks across the hall or sleep in my own (NEW!) bed.

Speaking of my new bed, I got new sheets, new pillows, and a pile of new clothes, about a third of which I have to return. I got a few new books in the delivery as well, since I'm almost done with the new GM book. For some reason, I have a hankering for history, which isn't normally my thing, so I got a couple of books on American history. We'll see how that goes.

Okay, as is my new habit, I'm going to go freshen up before saying good morning to Lightning Falls and heading to the diner.

33
Forward

Friday, September 12, 2025 – Evening

"IT'S STRANGE," JENNY SAID, "having the night off."

"You get used to it," Maddy said from across one of Cinder's Remorse's brushed metal tables.

"I'll be there," Sydney said around a small clump of fries she was shoving into her mouth.

"Maybe that's what makes it weird," Charles said. He sat to Jenny's right, across from Sydney, who picked up one of her fries and threw it at him. She missed, and it skittered across the floor. He gave her a look that said, 'Are you five?'

"No, I think it would be weird no matter who was there. I just don't really know what to do with three days off. They aren't really, I have other things I need to do. I definitely have a lot I can do with the apartment, and I have my other work."

At that, Sydney's eyes lit up again after glowering at Charles. "Really?"

Jenny had thought long and hard about the topic and had decided this was the best course of action with her new group of friends.

"Yeah, I've got a bunch of new clothes I can wear for shoots, and I need to put some new content up to keep all the new people happy. So, yeah, I'll probably spend some time shooting photos and videos."

"What does that entail?" Maddy asked. Unlike Sydney, Maddy looked intellectually interested.

"Well, a tripod, some lighting, me fighting with my makeup for an hour, and then taking a couple hundred photos so that I can find twenty that I can put up with. Then I have to edit them, watermark them, and finally post them. Then I have to go on a bunch of websites and post samples and stuff. It's a whole process."

"Maddy's a good photographer, she should shoot your pictures!" Sydney said.

"Really?" Jenny said.

"I'm okay, I'm not great. And I've never done portraits. Just kind of whatever I see that I think is beautiful."

"I'd like to see your pictures sometime," Jenny said.

"You should, she's being modest," Nate said. "She's really good."

Dinner continued until the Weekenders had to head out to their respective destinations. The weekday group, alone together for the first time, looked at each other awkwardly across the table. Nate ordered a round of beers before excusing himself.

Jenny moved over to the seat next to Linds.

"So, how do you like being home?" Linds asked. Jenny thought they looked like it pained them to make small talk, so she decided to forego shallow conversation.

"Honestly? It's been pretty bad. I'm waiting for the next terrible thing to happen."

Linds nodded slowly. "What do you think the next bad thing will be?" Linds asked.

"That all of this will fall apart," Jenny said, waving at the three pushed-together tables. "When I got here, I thought I was making friends, and then that fell to shit pretty fast. Before that, I thought I made some friends, and that fell to shit, but it was slower. And before that—" Jenny drank. "Well, that ended a lot worse."

"I guess I know what you mean," Linds said.

I seriously doubt you do, Jenny thought. Before she could follow up, a hand touched her shoulder.

"I *thought* that was you!"

Jenny turned and saw Isabella standing over her, wearing a tight burgundy dress.

"Hey," Jenny said, trying to sound excited. She stood, and Isabella hugged her.

"Oh my God, so, how was your first week?" Isabella practically yelled with an effusiveness that made Jenny's skin crawl.

"Oh, right, yeah, I'm sorry I haven't been texting, I'm still getting used to being up when everyone else is asleep and, you know, the other way around."

"Totally! I completely get that. But how is it?"

"It's good, it's strange, but it's good." Jenny looked past Isabella and saw a short-haired woman standing with one work boot kicked up on the bar's foot-rail and one elbow on the bar, facing in her direction. A stool was open next to her.

"Are you here with Chloe?" Jenny asked.

"Yeah, just a girls' night thing. I'm keeping her from pouncing on the tourists. You know, public service."

"Oh, um, Isabella, this is Linds." Jenny turned to include Linds in their conversation. Linds extended a hand, and Isabella shook it.

"I listen to you most nights," Isabella said. "So, sorry if I geek out a little.”

“No worries,” Linds said, giving Isabella an appraising look that Jenny thought bordered on the confrontational. Isabella didn't seem to notice.

“Anyway, we should get together for dinner. Maybe Sunday night?”

“Yeah, sure. Somewhere other than the Tim would be great.”

“Oh, let's go to the Mexican place, I heard they changed their menu.” She turned to Linds. “I don't know if you tried it before, but it was terrible.”

Linds shook their head.

“Well, let's do it then. I'll text you,” Isabella said before hugging and kissing Jenny on the cheek. “It was incredible meeting you!” Linds nodded. Jenny watched Isabella strut back to Chloe, who raised her drink toward Jenny. Jenny once more admired Chloe's easy confidence, sighed, waved back, and dropped into her seat.

“She's annoying,” Linds said.

“Yeah,” Jenny agreed. “Wait, do you know her?”

“She hit on me when I first got to town,” Linds said.

“Who did?” Nate asked, pulling up a chair across from them and pushing empty plates away onto the other tables.

“Isabella. And tonight she acted like she didn't even know me.”

“Well, you're incredibly forgettable,” Nate said, and raised his chin as the waitress came over with their beers.

“This is true,” Linds said. They toasted to the Sleep Talkers, past and present, before drinking.

“Wait, so Isabella hit on you?”

“Yeah, she couldn't get it through her head that her gaydar was malfunctioning.”

“That's really interesting,” Jenny said.

“Is it?” Nate said.

“Yeah, she kind of won't leave me alone either,” Jenny said.

“That seems to be a big problem for you,” Nate said.

“What do you mean?”

“He means Sydney,” Linds said.

“Oh, yeah, right.”

“And by now she's in your house, maybe picking your locks and hiding under your bed,” Nate said.

“Stop fantasizing out loud,” Linds said.

“So, what are you going to do about Sydney?” Nate asked just before he tried his beer.

"I have no idea," Jenny said. "I can't pretend to be asleep all night. There's nowhere to go in town. God, I wish the library were open twenty-four hours."

"Well, why don't we catch a movie?" Nate said. "We all have basically the same problem, which is time to fill when it's dark. So, why not do like our ancient ancestors did and go to a public place together and watch actors pretend to be someone else?"

"Okay," Jenny said, looking at her phone. "Let's go see a movie."

34
Too Late

Saturday, September 13, 2025 - Early Morning

> **_Jenny_**
> Hey, I'm on my way home. I'm going to make myself some tea. Do you want me to make you one too?

> **_Syd_**
> OMG yes! Thank you ♥

> **_Jenny_**
> Cool, I'll let you know when they're ready. I'll be in the lounge.

THIS IS MY BIG *strategic plan*, Jenny thought as she strode down Main Street at a quarter before two. They would hang out in the lounge. Jenny would spend her time in the lounge, work in the lounge, and do everything she could in the lounge. That would keep Sydney from just wandering into her apartment, where she could stare at her with those big eyes.

Sure, Jenny thought, *it's not like the whole house is empty, and we could do literally anything anywhere on the grounds in the dark without anyone even knowing. She could have her way with me under the stars, and it would be just as private as my bedroom. So, where's the safety in this plan?*

Jenny shoved the images out of her mind. She found that the more the excitable woman crept into her imagination, the more Jenny liked her there. Of course, her imagination was a crowded place. Chloe's sharp jawline and dark eyes also enjoyed hovering above Jenny with powerful masculine energy that Jenny hadn't found attractive in a woman before. Sydney and Chloe felt like such different magnets for her apparently unrelenting libido.

When did I get so fucking horny? Jenny thought.

Don't lie to yourself. Nolan's voice whispered in her mind. *You've always been like this. That's part of what I loved about you.*

"I'm sorry, babe," she breathed into the crisp night air. "I'm so sorry.

I feel so fucking terrible."

His imagined voice didn't reply. Her subconscious could not fabricate him telling her that it was okay. She knew it wasn't and suspected that it never would be. She could never make Nolan tell her it was all right; she could never imagine Aurora telling her she forgave her.

Aurora's last thoughts weren't forgiveness, they were confusion and terror. Jenny had no right to append them to make herself feel better.

Her mind flowed back, before the end. She pictured Aurora playing the guitar, her brown eyes looking up at Jenny as she played a folk song that used the four chords she knew. She pictured Nolan mowing the lawn, shirtless, while the women of the house catcalled him and drank sangria.

She pictured Joseph taking Nolan under his wing and having their private meetings.

She had never asked what they talked about. Hell, Joseph and Nolan might have been getting hot and heavy by themselves, and she wouldn't have known. But she knew that wasn't true. Well, she was pretty sure it wasn't true. She couldn't imagine both of them lying to her so completely as to hide something like that.

At least not Nolan.

She thought of Matina and her dark hair, dark eyes, and deep-maroon lipstick. She stopped on the path just before the porch steps. Maddy. Maddy reminded her of Matina. Hell, their names were even similar. Was that what was happening? Was she drawn to the same patterns over again? If Maddy was Matina, then was Sydney… Aurora? No. Aurora was too cool, too much of a hippie. There was maybe more of both Matina and Aurora in Maddy. Then was Sydney …?

"Shit," Jenny said and sat on the step.

Sydney was Nolan—young, eager, and enthusiastic.

"Shit."

What are you doing, Jennifer? Now, it was Patty's voice in her head.

She was repeating the same shit with new people. Or, if not repeating, then at least echoing and rhyming with it. She couldn't do that. She had to grow at least a little as a person; otherwise, what the fuck was the point of her surviving what Joseph had done to her?

She wrestled with her revelation as she stood and turned to look at the house. The second-floor hallway light was on. Jenny jumped up the porch stairs and went inside. Once in her apartment, she started hot water and prepped two coffee mugs in the kitchen with tea bags. She checked and saw that they expired in a month. She added tea bags to her shopping list on the refrigerator, hanging from a Valley Park magnet that showed the theme park in cartoonish cameo with a roller coaster mounting over.

When Jenny finally took the two cups of tea upstairs, she set them on the small coffee table and picked the overstuffed chair instead of the couch where Sydney could sit next to her, their knees touching. Boundaries. She texted Sydney and wondered how long it would take her to bounce out of the room and into the lounge.

It was less than a minute.

Sydney practically ran toward Jenny. Jenny stood to hug her, fearing that if she didn't, the younger woman would fall into her lap.

"Hey!" Sydney said. "How was the movie? Oh, thank you for this," she said, backing away and looking down at the cup that Jenny had set near the couch, "I'm dragging! I'm not sure this has enough caffeine in it to matter, but every little bit helps. Um, is this black? Good, I don't like green. So, how was the movie? I've been wanting to go to the movies, but nothing has really grabbed me recently. Oh my God, I used to love going when I was a kid, but like, my parents couldn't afford it a lot, so sometimes when I was a teenager, we'd sneak in. It was hard, though, because, you know, it's such a small theater, but I think the owner sometimes just let us watch because he knew we couldn't afford it. Is it less expensive here? I mean, it's not as bad as the city. I think it's crazy how much they charge for tickets. Ow! Okay, that's definitely still too hot. But yeah, so, how was it?"

Sydney sat cross-legged on the couch, and Jenny got the impression that she wanted to bounce in place but was holding herself mostly still by sheer willpower. She also marveled at the young woman's capacity for talking so much after doing her job. Maybe this was the perfect job for Sydney.

"It was okay. A lot of action, not really my thing. I like detective stories. They don't really make a lot of those anymore."

"Oh my God, right? Everything's all CG now. So did you guys go to the diner after?"

"No, I figured I'd come back here and make something. I got some cans of soup."

"Yeah, better to save some money. Still, I'm so jealous! I hate this whole weekend/weekday thing. I wish we were all on at the same time and off at the same time, so we could all hang out."

"Well, we get to do this. I guess we'll get to hang out like this, every three weeks or whatever, right, since we rotate."

Sydney nodded, picked up her tea, held it close to her mouth as if she forgot that it was hot, and then, once reminded, put it back down again.

"Yeah, totally. I mean, this is so much better than working at the tower or the cabin. It's amazing to have someone here while I'm working. It can get kind of creepy all by yourself, you know?"

"I do. It was kind of freaky all alone in here by myself this week." She immediately regretted her words.

"Oh no! We should come and hang out here some nights! You know, just like, be here so you can have someone around."

"I mean," Jenny said, "that would be cool sometimes. But I'm kind of all over the place, I wouldn't want you just sitting in here wondering when I'm going to come out."

"Believe me, Maddy and I can entertain ourselves. Oh, speaking of, we wanted to ask you about your other job. You know, the website? Do you think we should start one?" Sydney asked, leaning back on her palms and pushing her chest out. "Like, the two of us together? Me and Maddy, not you and me. I mean, you'd be welcome to—you know, but like, for me and her. I feel like we could … maybe we could make some extra money and get out of here sooner, you know?"

"Oh, um, well …" Jenny frowned, folded her legs under her, and rested her chin in her palm. "I guess there's a lot to consider."

"I think I'd be good at it, but Maddy is kind of, I don't know, she's more of a behind-the-camera person, not that she's not super-hot, I just don't think she'd be down with all the attention, and I don't care. But what's it like for you? Is it all just dudes sending you dick picks? Tell me, I want to learn."

They talked for forty minutes about the pros and cons of Sydney's idea. When it came to the practical aspects and the downsides, Sydney was surprisingly thoughtful and took her time working through different aspects and implications of the work. Jenny was impressed.

"Have you done something like this before?" Jenny asked.

"Not officially," Sydney said. "But there were definitely people who DM'ed me looking for pics, and … you know? Why not make a few bucks?"

"How were those experiences?" Jenny asked.

"You know, some were pretty okay, others were kind of creepy. I kept it out of town, though, no one here knew. I made a social media profile and made my hometown New York City, and like tagged my stuff for there."

"Smart," Jenny said.

"Thanks. I've had some bad experiences here," Sydney said, looking down at her cup. For the first time, Jenny thought she saw something deeper, more serious under her energetic exterior. "I just want to try to avoid encountering that stuff while I have to live here."

"Yeah," Jenny said, "I know what you mean."

"I know," Sydney said. "I didn't mean to bring up your bad shit."

Jenny smiled and shook her head. "Believe me, the stuff that's happened since I got back is not my bad shit. It's uncomfortable, at least some of it, and I'm pretty sure all of you will stop being my friends pretty soon, and I'll be alone again."

"No," Sydney said, putting her empty mug down. "No, I won't do that. No one will do that. You're one of us now."

Jenny opened her mouth.

This is it; you're going to say it, and then she's going to pull back. It's going to be like Isabella when you first met, but worse. It's going to be like Leddy at the bar or Patty when she threw you out.

"Shit," Sydney said as her alarm went off, "I need to get back." She jumped up and hurried around the coffee table to Jenny. Jenny rose to hug her again.

"When are you taking your next break?"

"Oh, I probably won't take another long one until I'm done. So, should I grab you when we walk down for breakfast?"

"Yeah, just text me. If I don't reply, knock really loud. Six?"

Sydney nodded, waved awkwardly, and hurried from the room.

Jenny picked up the mugs and carried them back downstairs, feeling like a tornado had just swept her up and spun her around. She washed the mugs and felt a wave of sadness sweep through her. A snippet of a song floated with the melancholy, and Jenny put the sponge down to try to catch the words. A song by the color ... the Colourist, a band Aurora had loved.

"*I don't want to love you ...*" Jenny tried. That wasn't right. "*But I'm afraid ...*" No, that was wrong.

She pictured Aurora with her guitar, half-whispering, half-singing the song. Her hair fell in big, looping rings down over her shoulders as a rare sunbreak shot through their apartment window before Matina, Joseph, and Nolan, back when it had just been the two of them. Jenny sat on the bed while Aurora serenaded her. Light counted the little hairs on her arms, her stomach, and the small of her back. It danced on the bracelets that hugged her wrist, the lace of her pale bralette, and on the folds of her long skirt.

Suddenly, words poured from Aurora's lips, and the hand of longing reached into Jenny's stomach and pulled. Jenny let out a low moan as sorrow flowed like water from a deep well, too long choked with stones. She collapsed onto the kitchen floor and wept while her fingers sped across her phone's screen until she found the song. Through bleary eyes, she stared at the words "Stray Away." She hesitated, afraid to press play, knowing that the bottom of her well of sorrow opened into an ocean, which Jenny suspected had no bottom. Even so, with her back to the counter, she pressed the button. As the guitar started, she let her phone rest on the floor, hugged her knees to her chest, and screamed silently into the empty apartment.

When it ended, she pictured Aurora looking her in the eyes, singing the final words, and she didn't think there was any greater sorrow in the world than hers. She couldn't conceive of feeling more pain or longing than she did for the woman who had loved her so innocently and completely. Her fingers clawed at the floor, her hair, her jeans. She thought of how the people in the Bible rent their clothing, and how that seemed right. She wanted to tear at her shirt, to rip it apart. She wanted to crawl outside and pour dirt over her head. She felt like she would start hyperventilating, like she would have a heart attack. Her feet kicked, her mouth worked, and her back arched.

"Oh God, give her back. Oh God, please, please, please give her back!"

But God did not give her back. God let her kick and moan and plead with sighs too deep for words. When she emptied herself and the well once more collapsed, mercifully blocking the flow of grief that threatened to drive her mad, Jenny dragged herself to the couch and lay on it, empty and scraped out. She felt nothing but exhaustion and the dull, throbbing presence of Aurora's absence.

As Jenny drifted on the edge of merciful sleep, she realized that along with every other feeling, the ever-present serpent of anxiety that coiled in her guts had loosened and seemed to slumber. Jenny experienced a strange calmness unlike anything she had known since the night it all happened. She rubbed her stomach and realized that she didn't feel anxious. It was strange. Her anxiety had been a constant companion. As Jenny drifted to sleep, she did so with real peace for the first time since the night that Joseph had killed the two people she loved most in the world ... before he also killed her.

Proposition: In that place, there is no time. It is eternal.

Answer: As the master of the sentences says, "Eternity may only be properly ascribed to God."

Objection 1: None are born or die there.

Objection 2: Those perishable things do not perish in that place.

Objection 3: The finite is not diminished with use.

I answer: There is time in that place, though it is distinct from our own. There, the standard measures of temporality do not obtain. However, I observe four means by which time may be measured there. The first is the index of the enumeration of repetitions that, if known, acts as a measure of time. Second, the wanderers, who, though they do not precisely exist in as linear a fashion as our world, do, nevertheless, rear, raise, and bury their children. Third, the great powers who have wrested for themselves strength enough to process outside of the curse to greater and lesser degrees. They, by being free of stagnation, are subject to time. Fourth, the interaction between that place and worlds beyond itself, and those who sojourn within from without.

Answer 1: Birth and death are not the only measures of the passage of time, for before God made life, time existed.

Answer 2: Just as fruit may be frozen in ice and not perish, so too may things be frozen by other means and not perish. Thus, the imperishable attribute may be given to the perishable without removing its temporal nature.

Answer 3: The Lord demonstrated that the finite may be multiplied without logical contradiction or the stoppage of time. When he multiplied the loaves and fishes, he showed that such perpetual fecundity is not contrary to the passage of time.

- Mikuláš Vaclavek, *The Second Book of Seeings*

The Brethren are to grow within a world unchanging. Though rulers rise and fall, though ages wax and wane, the fallen world changes not. We must strive forward as wanderers in a stagnant world, though pulled back by the murky frozen waters, we must swim ahead while all others sink in the filth of waste. Let us heed the words of the master and be sojourners in a world unchanging.

- Petr Mikulášek, *The Third Book of Seeings*

I
Waters Unnamed

Wednesday, October 8, 1828 – Late Morning

MICAH'S BACK HURT HIM something awful. It throbbed and spasmed, causing him to jerk back in his saddle. Between pangs, he slumped forward, too tired to remain upright for much longer. Soon, he guessed, the spots would appear.

Then I'll be goose-buggered.

He was sure the damned nag that had led him off the path and set him to wander for the past three days would be glad to be rid of him. And, if he was honest with himself, after days of half-conscious meandering through foothills devoid of life, fodder, or familiar sign, Micah thought he might be glad to be rid of himself. The only thing that kept him from sliding from his saddle voluntarily to die in the dust was the image of his cousin that haunted his fever-stirred mind. Each morning, Ruth, her round face framed in auburn curls, seemed to rouse him from slumber and beckon him to eat and ride.

He had hoped persistence would have led him to a river by which he could lie himself down either to recover or die in a place where men might find him and send word of his demise back to his cousin. But here, in these scrabble-bound hills, he imagined that none would discover him for a hundred years, unless some Indian should happen upon his bones.

He prayed that the Lord should comfort Ruth, and that if she should marry, it would be to a good man. Then he prayed for a place where he could fall from his horse without breaking his neck. He looked around and, seeing the steepness of the slope, thought that his second prayer might require angelic intervention. He reached out weakly to push a pine branch away from his face, but it slipped and smacked him in the eyes, stinging and blinding him.

"Oh, Jesus!" he cried, his words half-curse and half-supplication. His back spasmed, and he nearly fell from the saddle. There weren't many jerks left in his spine before his legs gave out, and he'd be eating dirt as his last meal.

This was not what he had hoped for himself. He thought maybe he'd make a tidy little pile of silver trapping beaver skins for the Hudson Bay Company. He had hoped he might join Ogden's party, a man who had made a name in just that employ. But Micah had found that the famous trapper had gone south to explore a lake. Still hoping to join a larger party in the future, Micah had struck out on his own against the advice of the men camped around Fort Nez Percés. He hoped to get some experience under his belt to show himself a worthy American among the expert French Canadians and British. But now, he would be bones on the earth, perhaps just another twenty yards down this slope.

Rain began to fall, tapping the stones beneath his unnamed horse's hooves. His hands were clammy, his skin damp under his buckskin blouse. He wondered how long it would be before wolves, or bears, or perhaps more fittingly, beavers would eat his body.

"I hope they choke on me," he said, barking out something that was supposed to be a laugh. But pain so twisted the sound that it echoed out of him like a howl.

The nag turned right and around a tall, wide, straight fir. Faintly, Micah thought he heard the sound of death. A low rumbling that was too steady for thunder rolled toward him from somewhere off to his right. He leaned forward against the horse's neck and groaned.

He drifted and felt himself slipping before his legs spasmed tight and held him upright a little while longer. The roaring grew louder as he wandered back and forth across sleep's border. Finally, when the sound was almost unbearable, and the rain had begun to fall so hard that it seemed to come up at him in a mist, the pain won out. He arched and grabbed at the small of his back. Micah slid from his saddle and expected to crash into the ground and break his shoulder, or perhaps bash his head into a tree and break his neck. Instead, two feet of water cushioned his fall and shocked him awake.

Pain curved his back once more and pushed his head under the surface. He sputtered and splashed, trying to breathe. He flailed, found purchase, and finally pushed himself onto his knees. Blinking, he wiped his eyes and saw a bank a few feet away. Had he found a river? Was this salvation? He dragged himself halfway up onto dry ground, coughed water, and kicked feebly to push himself up a little further. Above him, thunderheads rolled as heavy drops of rain smacked his face. Closer, water fell from stony heights, foaming and angry. Then it seemed that the sky and the earth met, fused as light flashed between the precipice and the thunder clouds above. The air exploded, and a tree on the ridgeline lit up like a candle.

As flames danced in the rain, Micah felt himself fading. He blinked once, wondering if the engulfed tree's flames would spread, and if smoke would take him before the pox did. He blinked again and pondered drowning in the rising pool. Blink. As unconsciousness took him, he wondered if the man standing on the ridge line would kill him.

MICAH DREAMS OF A dark, ramshackle tenement huddled in the streets of New York. He can't remember the names of the streets that crossed nearby, nor those of his two older brothers who died before he learned to speak. He remembers his cousin, Ruth, and his Uncle Zebulon, who took them from the city to a farm where Micah learned to shoot. He remembers a book that Ruth put before him to teach him how to read, and how poorly he had taken to it. He dreams that she is waiting for him over the hill where the sun rises, the wind pulling her auburn hair from her bonnet, and tugging the flowers in his hand that he has plucked for her wedding day.

II
A Moment

Monday, October 13, 1828 - Midday

THE SUN BURNED SCARLET through his eyelids. Someone was touching his head. Micah reached for his knife, drew it with a shaking hand, and held it up before him.

"Get back," Micah said through dry lips. "Plague."

He opened his fluttering eyes and saw a man crouching over him. The sun behind him, he was a shadow. His fingers roamed Micah's face and tugged gently at his beard. Then, he rolled Micah onto his side and slid a flat rock under his head. Micah's new vantage put the base of a tree in front of him where the stranger took his seat, crossing his legs. The man was tall, dark skinned, wore buckskin similar to Micah's, and was laden with ornaments. Red paint covered the bottom half of the man's face, and his hair was shaved on one side. Micah's vision wavered, and he struggled to focus. He didn't have much experience with any of the tribes in the area. He had seen Nez Perce and Cayuse at the fort, but he hadn't been there long enough to learn to distinguish them.

The man spoke in heavy, truncated syllables, almost every word sounding to Micah as if they ended in a soft 'e.' To Micah, it might have been any language. The man was calm and seemed unperturbed by the knife in the sick man's hand. His words flowed like smooth waters and reminded Micah of a musical instrument.

"Sick," Micah managed. "Don't touch me. Please. For your mother's sake."

He did not want to be responsible for this man's death. He had taken a life, and he swore never to do it again if he could help it. He had seen the man disappear at the end of his knife, replaced by human-shaped meat in the space of one drunken minute. No wrong any man had ever done him weighed as heavy on him as the wrong done by his own hands. He did not know this painted man, could not understand his words, had no comprehension of his meaning, but he did not want to go before his maker as the author of another man's death.

The stranger rose and strode out of Micah's sight. He returned a moment later with a shallow, wooden bowl, which he set on the ground. The man propped Micah up and lifted the bowl to his mouth slowly. Micah drank water gratefully, sputtered, and drank again. Three times the man went and returned, and three times he propped Micah up and then laid him back down again. The final time, he took a small skin from his belt and folded it beneath Micah's head and spoke in his deep, resonant voice.

Micah's eyes closed, but he didn't sleep immediately. Instead, he drifted in a half-dream as snow fell in big, fluffy flakes around him. He swung an axe, cutting through the base of a tall pine until the towering trunk leaned and crashed. Then he stripped its bark and dragged it alongside dozens of other logs.

This will make a good home, he thought. Then Micah slept.

ii

MICAH DREAMS OF THE painted man binding his wrist with a long hemp rope. The stranger throws the end over a high branch, letting it dangle near the ground. Then he does the same to the other wrist. The painted man pulls the ropes, and Micah stands, his arms moving with each tug. His legs are bound as well, though he doesn't remember the stranger tying them. The painted man moves his arms and legs up and down. He pulls one rope for his mouth, another for his neck, and another for his heart. The stranger looks pleased, staring at him from eyes that split, and split, and split, until they swarm like bees across his face.

III
Hitilettu

Wednesday, October 15, 1828 - Afternoon

EACH BREATH WAS RASPING fire. Micah's back was a furnace, his throat a chimney. His skin burned and itched, and he wanted to die. He wanted to stop drinking water, to stop pissing himself, and to stop the damned Indian from bathing him. But the stranger remained with him day by day, keeping him from death. He had made a litter from skins and poles upon which Micah slept, and upon which the stranger brought him to and from the water.

The stranger bathed Micah's marked skin and let him dry in the bright, cool air. He kept a fire burning and made broths of roots and fish, which Micah sipped. He made a paste of meat and berries which neither Micah's palate nor stomach could endure. Thankfully, he also made a fine stew that Micah could eat. He cooked other things that he did not feed Micah, but instead rubbed onto the burning, itching spots. The dark-skinned man rubbed cut roots onto Micah's temples and sores. These felt like nothing until several minutes later, when the itching would subside.

Not a stranger.

Hitilettu.

That was his name.

The man said the word and touched his chest with an open palm. Then he would say a longer, more complicated word and touch Micah's chest. Micah guessed that the complication of hard consonants and wide vowels was the Indian's name for him, but he never learned it.

Hitilettu never seemed to worry about catching the pox. Perhaps, Micah wondered, his people were especially resilient to the plague, or he had already suffered through the disease. Perhaps some magic protected him. Or, Micah considered, maybe the man was just a fool and soon he would be lying right next to him, moaning and dying in his own waste and pus.

But he didn't. Day after day, Hitilettu nursed Micah Whitman. Day after day, Hitilettu remained untouched by sickness. When he was not tending to Micah or hunting, he would sit on a large stone with a flat top, legs crossed, eyes raised to the top of the waterfall. As Micah passed to the other side of the worst of his sufferings, he started to wonder if one of the man's gods lived up there. He didn't know anything about native religions, but he thought they were pagans who had as many gods as the Greeks. Perhaps, Micah thought, at the top of the water was a demon, or some nymph of legend. Perhaps Hitilettu was wooing her with his silent stares.

When the pox finally dried, scabbed, and fell from him, leaving his skin a pitted waste, Micah Whitman rose and bathed himself in the stream that flowed from the waterfall's pool. Hitilettu watched, and the tall, dark-skinned man looked pleased, but did not smile.

He never smiled.

Micah walked on unsteady legs back to the fire. He sat and pulled a buffalo skin, the origin of which he did not know, over his thin shoulders and let the heat dry him. He looked at his new companion and saw that Hitilettu was once more looking up at the top of the waterfall.

"Who's up there?" Micah asked, scratching the back of his neck, and disliking the uneven skin he found.

It's better than being dead, he thought.

He smiled at Hitilettu and waved. The man lowered his gaze and regarded the trapper with a blank look. His eyes were strange. They were golden, unlike any Micah had ever seen, and they seemed to reflect the sun in the day and the fire at night—like a beast's eyes. Then he spoke once more in his indecipherable language. Though he did not grasp the meaning, Micah still enjoyed listening to the man talk. His voice wasn't just deep, it was melodious, almost like someone blowing over a wide reed or a glass bottle top. Micah closed his eyes and felt himself sway a little under the heavy skin and the fire's warmth.

Beneath his closed eyes, Micah saw the creek running out from the pool, straight and cold, until it turned and met another water that flowed down from the mountain. Where they mingled, three rocks jutted up, making white water, and Micah judged that a man with a small boat could take his craft close to the right bank and avoid the trouble. Then, beyond the meeting, the water smoothed out again, running swiftly past tall fir trees. Like a bird, he flew above it all with the sun overhead. He saw an opening among the trees near where the waters met. He saw himself standing in that place and digging a hole wide and deep.

Hitilettu stopped speaking, and Micah opened his eyes. "You are a medicine man," he said. "Or a witch. But I owe you my life. Do you want me to dig?"

The man nodded his head once, slowly.

"Then make me some more of that stew, and when I'm strong again, I'll dig."

THE FIRST FLAKES BEGIN to fall. Micah wonders how he will survive in the mountains without shelter. The old nag is gone, and Hitilettu has not built so much as a lean-to for him. As he spoons the fish into his mouth and drinks the hot broth, he believes he will soon be strong enough to chop wood, but he has no axe. Perhaps, he thinks, he survived the plague only to freeze to death at the foot of the waterfall.

IV
Pantomime

Tuesday, October 21, 1828 - Morning

MICAH SCRATCHED AT HIS beard and plucked out a small, crawling bug. He frowned at it and flicked it into the fire. The snow was gone, replaced by rain, which, in turn, made way for clear, dry skies.

"I suppose now is as good as any to try to find my way out of here," he said to Hitilettu, who was chipping a stone arrowhead with a smooth creek rock.

The Indian put his tools down onto a deerskin and looked up toward the top of the waterfall. He spoke, pointing to the source of the water and then down to the pool. Though the sun was not high above the trees in the east, it still shone in his golden eyes. Micah listened and discerned none of his meaning as the man pointed, gestured, and waved his hand back and forth.

"I understood about none of that," Micah said. He sniffed.

Hitilettu pointed at Micah and said the long words that the white man took to be his name, and then pointed at himself and said his name. Then, with slow, ponderous pantomimes of walking, sleeping, and eating, he conveyed to Micah the idea that they would leave the place together and come to a place that was full of other men.

"Fort Nez Percés," Micah said. "Should be four or five days from here if we knew where in creation we were. I think I rode for three days from there before I ended up here, and I was on horseback—"

Hitilettu pointed at the sun and held up four fingers.

"That's right, four days," Micah said. "You understand me a heck of a lot better than I understand you, don't you?"

The painted man nodded.

"Well, that's something, at least. Fort. Do you know where the fort is?"

Hitilettu stared at him, showing no sign that he understood Micah's meaning. Micah had an idea, and he gathered up a bunch of small sticks and began to break them. He fashioned miniature models of buildings, the twigs laid like logs on each other, only a few rows high, but enough to convey that he meant a place with multiple buildings. Then he put two squares of sticks around the buildings to represent the fort walls. Finally, he dug in the earth with his fingers next to his model fort.

"Fort Nez Percés," he said slowly, pointing to the model. "River. The Columbia River. I think it's west, but I'm not sure."

Hitilettu drew in the dirt a wavering line and another connecting with it where it bent. Micah understood it to be the place where the two creeks met. Hitilettu broke another stick and held both halves up. One he held to himself, and the other he held toward Micah. Then he moved them from the place next to his dug-out streams and brought them to Micah's model.

"That's right, we want to go to the fort."

Hitilettu then took a stone and put it with his two sticks and brought the stone and sticks back to his plot.

"You want to come back. With what? Supplies? I'll confess, this may be as good a place as any to trap beaver, and there doesn't seem to be any of my people or your people here, but I spent most of what I had on my supplies, and they walked away with my horse. So did the rest of my money."

Hitilettu frowned and looked at Micah for a long moment, studying him.

"No money. No wampum!" Micah said, unsure if the word would mean anything to the man, or even if he was using it correctly. He had heard men use the term in the east, but the country was vast, and he had no idea if the idea translated. "Money," Micah said again. "Trade."

This, Hitilettu seemed to understand, and he nodded. He put the stone back at the fort.

"Right, we need to give them something for tools and food and—"

Micah stopped. Hitilettu had pulled something new from a pouch and put it between the two stick men. He carried this new thing with them to the fort and left it there, returning with their stone. After his performance, he held it up and lifted his chin, as if asking for approval.

"Yes," Micah said, staring with wonder. "Yes, that will do."

Hitilettu put the new thing into Micah's hand and looked pleased.

Micah Whitman was also pleased.

iv

MICAH FOLLOWS HIS COMPANION along the side of the waterfall's pool and to the foot of the rockface. He watches the man in buckskins clamber over one wet stone and then another until they hide him from view. Then Micah follows over slick rock, scrabbling to hold on to sharp edges and rough moss. He finds himself sheltered under an overhanging rock at the bottom of a rising path. His companion goes before him, and they ascend the hidden track. When they reach the top, Micah finds himself in a strange, stone room. Three solid walls box the men in, and a jagged, shoulder-high wall faces outward, hiding the space from anyone looking up from the pool. It is a hidden place with old, brown pine needles carpeting the floor and a wide shaft of morning light slanting in through the strange, uneven, wall-length window that looks east. Hitilettu points to an opening in the western wall. Though the sun grows dimmer as they enter the cave, the walls gleam with reflected light.

V
Fort Nez Percés

Monday, October 27, 1828 - Morning

HITILETTU APPEARED CONFIDENT AS they trekked for four days across the mountain and down into the uneven, rocky plains beyond. From the western foothills, they struck north and west until they came to a wide river that Micah Whitman hoped was the Columbia. They followed its banks north and met mounted Cayuse who conversed freely with Hitilettu, though Micah had the impression that they did not greet him as one of their own. The native men confirmed that they were on the right path and that they would see other white men soon, which they did. This made Micah nervous, for he believed that if any discovered what they carried with them, their lives would be in great danger. He doubted anyone would attack them on the well-traveled road to the fort, but he suspected that things might get tricky when it was time to do their trading.

Those travelers they met going north were courteous enough and brought bear, elk, and deer meat, as well as skins, on the backs of horses or on sleds. Those they met coming south had rifles, smoked new tobacco, and bore prized adornments. They kept the wide, south-westerly running river on their left, and Micah thought he recognized the brown, sloping rise of the far bank.

On the morning of the fifth day, they came to the tree-crowded mouth of the Walla Walla River. A strip of green spread for a quarter mile on either side of the water's sloping banks. A little way up from where it ran into the Columbia, they met two men who operated a ferry. One was a scruffy-looking Scotsman, and the other a palaverous Umatilla who went on constantly in his strangely accented English, a mix of non-native and Scottish pronunciations. Hitilettu conversed with the Umatilla in a conversation that was three-quarters indecipherable to Micah. They paid for their journey with a small leather pouch, the contents of which Micah never learned. Once they had crossed on the large wooden raft, they walked north, and soon the fort's walls came into view.

Perhaps a hundred feet across on all sides, the wooden fort stood ten or twelve feet tall. From their southerly approach, they could see a bastion at the southwest corner, rising on wooden legs and overlooking the sparse milling crowd of men and horses. A gate opened in the western wall through which a queue of men and their mounts wound. Micah and Hitilettu followed the line through the gate and found themselves in a narrow wooden passage. Walls pressed in close, smelling strongly of pine. Micah imagined that if someone attacked the fort, the defenders would use the narrow passage to hem them in and make them easy targets for pitch, bullets, and stones. A second passage disgorged them into the fort proper.

A vast, grassless courtyard spread before them, with a dozen stone buildings clustered along the northern and western sides. A corral for horses stood to their right on the southern side of the open space. The line of traders snaked to a large building with a window. When he got closer, Micah saw a man standing at the window, dealing with a pair of white men in heavy furs. When they were finished, another pair replaced them.

The fort smelled of horse and smoke, and there was a constant, low buzz of conversation. The longer they stood in the line, the more Micah's anxiety grew. The object in his pocket was not large, but any amount might prompt a mob to ask where it came from. The trick, Micah knew, was to pay and move on without drawing attention to himself.

They stood in line for an hour as Micah pondered his plan. He would collect provisions and return with his companion to ... what? Collect pelts? They seemed like small beer now. No. He was returning to mine. Mine and then what? He wasn't sure. He supposed he would figure that out. He wondered what Hitilettu's goal was. What did the man want out of their partnership?

"What are you trading? Do you have so many furs that you store them somewhere else? Do you need labor to bring them? We can provide this to you." The voice, thick with a French accent, interrupted Micah's contemplations and came from a tall, towering man with a long, brown beard. He wore a woolen cloak and a fur hat. Beside him stood a shorter man with heavy mustaches and only one eye. Micah shook his head.

"I am buying, not trading."

"Ah!" the big man said. "Are you part of a party? Who are you with? You are not with Ogden, surely. Who then?"

"No," Micah said. "I am alone. Or rather, I'm with my companion. He hasn't yet led me to any beavers, but if he does, I will return, and if there are enough for us all, I will let you in."

Micah hoped that this would be enough to satisfy the man.

"Perhaps better that we should go with you. These savages are not to be trusted, eh? They will likely cut your throat in the wilderness when you are alone and take your horse. Come, let us make a go of it together.

We have many supplies already, and with this, we shall make a good start. We have left our party to strike out on our own. We will be glad of a new friend." He gestured to a small cart piled high with skins.

"No, thank you, though," Micah said. He wanted to leave the line and let the men go before him so that he could do his business in front of less nosy people.

"Next," the man at the window called.

"Your turn, my friend," the big man said. Micah looked from his new acquaintance to Hitilettu and back again.

"Why don't you take your turn first, I—"

"No, of course not," the man said, putting his hand on a long bone-handled knife at his hip. "Do your business so that the rest of us may get on with ours."

Hitilettu looked pleased, and Micah shook his head. "Of course."

He walked up to the window and listed the items that he needed. The man took note of the pickaxes, saws, axes, bark strippers, mounts, saddles, tack, blankets, and provisions of food, feed, whisky, and more. When he had tallied the amount, Micah looked over his shoulder to find Hitilettu wandering among the buildings with an appraising eye. The large man and his companion were closer than he was comfortable with. But the goods required payment, so Micah drew a handkerchief from his pocket and uncovered the stone lumps as surreptitiously as he could.

"I'd be obliged," he said to the man who stared at the rocks, "if you were discreet in your response to my tender."

The man at the window thought for a moment before he nodded. "I'll have to weigh it." He spoke with an accent, maybe Scottish, though Micah could no more discern the British Empire's accents than he could one Indian dialect from another.

"I understand."

The man went away.

"What is going on?" the big man said from behind him. Micah looked back and saw a strange, greedy look in the man's eyes.

"He is seeing to a matter, I'll be done soon," Micah said as affably as he could. His hands were shaking. He wished Hitilettu could understand him and stand in the space between him and his overly interested new friend.

"Your face," the big man said, "have you had the pox recently?"

"Yes," Micah said, "and the good Lord saw fit to bring me through alive."

"Hm," the man said. "Perhaps you should have been here when you had it, to help pass it around to these heathens."

Micah turned on the man, giving him a hard look and forgetting the delicate nature of his position. "That is a mightily unchristian thing to say," Micah said. The man shrugged and spat.

"Sir, I have the balance of your payment," the man in the window said. Micah turned and received back his handkerchief, somewhat lighter than before. "Here is your receipt. You can pick up your horses and provisions by the main gate. They'll be packaged and prepared for you. And, if you will allow me, I would like a word."

"Is there something wrong?" Micah asked.

"No, sir, I would just like to speak to you."

Micah nodded and touched the brim of his hat.

"Come and see me before you leave," the big man said. "We can do business, I think."

Micah touched his hat again and walked quickly over to the main gate. He watched the man in the window hold up a hand and step away. A younger man replaced him a moment later. A door opened in the trade building from which the clerk appeared. He produced a cigar, lit it, and then walked over to Micah in a cloud of smoke.

"Good morning, sir," he said. He had long sideburns but was otherwise clean-shaven. Tall, tanned, and well-muscled, he appeared formidable, despite Micah assessing him as close to fifty years old.

"Good morning. Is there a problem with my order?"

"What is your name, sir?" the man asked in his thick accent.

"Whitman," Micah said, shaking the man's proffered hand.

"Whitman, I'm sure you understand that in this area our main currency is beaver skins. White men and red men bring us those skins, and in return we give them many of the same things you have requested. Many, but not all. We don't have a heavy stock of pickaxes here, as few are needed in the fur trade."

"Yes," Micah said, "but you need them to clear ground and make way."

The man nodded and puffed his cigar. "That's true, and that's why we have the supply we do. And when a man arrives and asks for two pickaxes, I care nothing about it. That is, unless he arrives bearing the kind of tender that you did today."

Micah feigned confusion and then bemused understanding. He had thought long and hard about how to answer the question if it should come up. He spoke the words as he had practiced them over the campfire every night on their journey as Hitilettu watched impassively.

"Ah. Carolina, sir."

"Carolina?"

"Yes, North Carolina, my father was there and dug himself up a bucket full of the … *tender* that I brought today," Micah said, looking uneasily over his shoulder.

"That was nearly thirty years ago," the man said, cocking an eyebrow.

"Yes, sir, and what I handed you today was most of what I had left. I admit to having a little more, but I hope to return soon with your more common currency."

The man rolled his cigar between his lips and nodded, looking out at the Columbia River. "Hard times then for your family? If so little is left, I mean."

Micah thought of the ramshackle building his mother had lived in, his dead brothers, and the hard-scrabble plot of land his uncle had taken him to. "Yes, sir," he said, looking across the river to a rise of land that brooded over the far bank.

"My name is Samuel Black, I'm the chief trader here. We do not have many independent white men working in the area, and even fewer Americans. You're aware of the rules for trapping in the spring and summer?" he said.

"Yes, sir, but there's a good many months before spring, I think."

The man nodded, frowning thoughtfully. "So, there are. But will you try to trap beaver in the winter? The Cayuse will not. Might I suggest adding a rifle to your provisions?"

Micah stared at the man, baffled that he hadn't thought of it himself. "I—well, yes, I'd be very obliged if you could provide me with one, and as many bullets as the winter will want."

The man sniffed. "I've already put it down. May I risk overstepping myself and suggesting that you remain with us until the Lord's Day?"

"That's generous, sir but—"

"You would be wise not to travel alone after dealing as you have here. We have the service read on Sunday, and men are less likely to do murder when they're hard on hearing the Lord's words. Besides, those who have seen how you paid will likely be on their way by then. They will want to get back out, as the trade has waned over the years," Black said.

"That is kind of you, sir. But I am also eager to get away to begin."

"How did you arrive without a horse?" Black asked.

"Pardon me, sir?" Micah said, looking over his shoulder again. The big man and his companion appeared to have concluded their business at the trading window and were now watching him. Hitilettu was nowhere to be seen.

"A man doesn't walk from North Carolina to these territories on foot," Black said.

"Oh, it wandered off one night, or was taken, I reckon."

"Your second guess is more likely. The Snakes have been taking horses. Where about were you?"

Micah frowned, looking down the Columbia again. "About four days downriver. I met my companion there; he helped me find my way back here."

Black sniffed again. "Well, he would be welcome to stay as well," Black said. "The Indian house is there, and you could stay in one of the bunk houses."

"I think we will be moving along. I do thank you for your concern, though."

Black reluctantly accepted Micah's decision and had one of his men bring three horses out, packed with their provisions.

"We deal primarily in Made Beaver," Black said, "so the rate of exchange is perhaps not as precise as I first measured. I have added some extra grain and feed. I can also send for any specific provisions you might want."

"I can't think of anything for now," Micah said, checking his new purchases against the list in his head. Satisfied, he turned to call for Hitilettu but found him standing close by. He was smoking a pipe and looking at Micah with eyes full of the sun.

"I beg you to reconsider your decision," Black said. "These French and Americans … No offense intended," he said, shaking his head. "For your safety."

Micah wasn't sure why he decided to decline Black's offer, except that he felt an overwhelming anxiousness to return to the place where the lightning had set the tree aflame. "No, but again, thank you. And God bless you for your charity, sir."

Black shook his hand again before Micah and Hitilettu led their horses away.

THE PATH IS DRY and without grass, and Micah is glad for the feed for his horses. As the beasts walk together, he thinks of the sparse grass and low bushes that will provide for them when they reach the place where the waters meet. He hopes his companion knows somewhere better suited to their steeds than the pine forest and dry, rocky earth. The future occupies his mind, but his hands grip the wood and steel of his rifle against the dangers he imagines behind him.

VI
Upon the Earth

Monday, October 27, 1828 – Before Midnight

MICAH CRADLED HIS RIFLE in his arms, his back against a narrow patch of smooth rock as night insects chirruped around him. The smell of gunpowder still lingered after his two test-fires, and he hoped the shots would encourage him if he had to use the weapon and discourage anyone from approaching. When Micah and Hitilettu had ridden away, the big Frenchman and his companion had joined a knot of six or seven other men outside the fort. Their group had watched as he and Hitilettu rode south to the mouth of the Walla Walla. When Micah surmounted the rise on the south side of the river, he thought he spied the party riding south toward the ferry.

Hitilettu tended the fire and cooked salmon on an iron grate with simple meal cakes. They drank water from tin cups and sprinkled the salmon with salt from a pouch. Micah praised his companion's cooking when they ate, and the man looked pleased in the firelight that glowed in his eyes.

"We may be goose-buggered," Micah said to his companion, raising his chin toward the surrounding darkness. In response, Hitilettu spoke in his low, melodious voice. As he listened, Micah fought the urge to close his eyes for several long minutes. Soon, however, his lids drooped, and his body slid down the rock.

He dreamed of words he knew to be English, but did not understand. He dreamed of them coming from his mouth, and, confusingly, from his fingers. With the words came ideas, and with the ideas came a new sight. The words rolled through his mind like a wave of fire, burning and transforming everything. They roared about him, transfiguring the sky, mountains, earth, and sea, rebinding them in new, uncanny relationships. He thought of Ruth, and unfamiliar words sprang to life, embers dancing up from his dry mind. He saw her fear of men and her desire instead for the demanding work of the ground and the crafting of beautiful shapes with her hands. He saw her, and the world and himself on fire, but not destroyed.

Infused. As fire dwells in iron.

A noise woke him. It sounded like a wounded animal. Micah opened his eyes to almost complete darkness. The moon, more than half full, was still low in the sky to the east, and a bright star gleamed red near the horizon to the southwest. The fire remained only as embers. Micah sat up and threw pieces of driftwood onto the smoldering coals.

He reached for his fallen rifle, found it, and pulled it close.

"Hitilettu," he whispered. There was no answer, only the strange, muffled sound of some prey animal in a trap. Huffing, mewing, and a deep syllableless hucking rode the air from somewhere to the west. Trembling, he rose, his weapon gripped hard in sweating hands. Micah stalked around a boulder and tried to see what was before him. Faint moonlight traced the outlines of several hunched forms that might have been rocks.

If they are rocks, he thought, *then why do they move?*

And they did move in slow, lumbering jerks across the ground. The rifle started to slip from his sweat-slick fingers. The sounds were all around him now, shallow breaths, soft whimpers, and wet throats closing and opening.

Behind him, the logs caught, and fire rose, flaring orange light across the ground. Before Micah, a large, shape lumbered, and the firelight showed the familiar face of a man with a long beard and huge, terrified eyes under a fur hat. About him hung a woolen cloak, smoothing his form into the trundling lump that Micah had mistaken for a stone. It took him another second to understand what was wrong with the man's mouth. It was wide open and gurgling with strange sounds. There was something in it. Only when the man turned his head did Micah perceive that the dark shape protruding from between the man's open lips was the handle of a knife, and from the corners of the man's mouth, black blood flowed freely. A moment later, his pleading eyes rolling, he collapsed onto the earth to writhe feebly in the dust.

Micah watched as, one by one, eight men ceased their movements on the stony earth as Hitilettu sat above them, cross-legged on a rock. And though the light did not reach his eyes, they glowed an amber orange, and he looked pleased.

vi

MICAH SITS UNDER THE moon alone, pondering the lives of men. He drinks whisky from an unsteady tin cup and when that fails him, he drinks it from the bottle. He considers the lives of eight men and wonders at the manner of their deaths. He cannot construct in his imagination how the prelude to his arrival had unfolded. He cannot imagine how its sequel continues as the sounds of heavy things slide and crunch in the space beyond the rock against which he sits and drinks. He sees the large Frenchman's face staring up at him from the dust, mouth full of bone, metal, and wood.

VII
Where the Waters Meet

Monday, November 3, 1828 - Morning

SNOW FELL LIGHTLY AS Micah set the tip of his shovel against the earth and pushed it down into rocky soil. He had found the clearing near the bend in the creek that he had seen in his dream. He and Hitilettu had cut and set four logs as boundaries for the house. Now, Micah began to dig in earnest, stopping once an hour to gather stones from the plot and set them to the side to provide for the foundation. Others, Hitilettu brought from the banks of the creek. When midday came, they ate fish and berries; when evening came, they ate elk and bread.

Hitilettu trapped beaver for Micah and returned from hunting once a week with fresh meat. He caught fish in the stream and snared birds and other small creatures. He rode the horses east to graze them on the rolling hills beyond the pine forest, and at times he would return with goods he had traded. One day added a sack of corn to their provisions, another brought a second good buffalo skin. At night, he would speak while Micah whittled strange figures that flowed from his hands—imperfect spheres with eyes carved on all sides looking out. These he burned, finding their finished appearances troubling. But though they troubled him and haunted his dreams, his hands refused to carve anything else when Hitilettu spoke by the fire, his eyes aglow.

Three weeks of digging produced a hole almost four feet deep. Micah found bedrock and cleared the area, leveling it with dirt. Then he began to lay stones for the foundation. The walls went up, day after day, until they stood two feet above the rim of the hole. Then he applied a mixture of clay, horse dung, ash, and dried grass, smoothing it with a wooden board until the walls were even and waterproof. Then he dug a trench around the foundation and applied his earthen mixture to the outside of the wall. Finally, he sealed and leveled the top of his foundation with the mixture.

When he finished with the basement, Micah began to chop. He felled tree after tree until seventy lay stripped of branches and bark. He laid them across the cellar opening and on stones and smaller logs to keep them off the ground. They covered the trees with skins when rain fell and exposed them when the sun shone. They made the cellar their home as winter came on, and Micah slept under a roof for the first time in months.

One day, two weeks after they started living in the unfinished cellar,

Hitilettu returned with a new, strange item. He handed Micah a leather satchel. Micah shook its contents onto the dirt floor near the fire and frowned.

"I can't read," he said, lifting the cover of one of a half-dozen books. The letters on the cloth cover were familiar, but he could not force them into any meaningful collaboration. Hitilettu nodded and touched one of the books while pointing at Micah's head. He said something, and Micah frowned, wishing he could understand. He had tried to work out a shorthand with the man, a shared vocabulary of simple words, but the painted man would not oblige him. Micah wondered if the man thought Micah could read the books to him to help him learn English. Far from home in a strange and wild land, Micah would have rather learned Hitilettu's tongue, as he thought it would be useful to him in the days to come.

That night, Hitilettu spoke while Micah carved, nodded, and slumbered. He saw the eyes on the wooden orb in his hand glow an amber-gold as a voice whispered into his ear. He was suddenly sitting against a wall of sandstone bricks. A desert of rolling dunes and smooth, dipping valleys spread before him. In the distance, a tall man approached on foot through wavering air. He wore a satchel over one shoulder, and the dark skin of his bald head gleamed. He came on slowly. Hours passed under the unmoving sun. When the man finally drew near, he knelt before Micah. His clothes, a simple skirt of light cloth and a sash about his forehead, were alien to Micah. The stranger reached into his bag and produced a wooden rod one cubit long and made a mark in the sand. He spoke a word, open and airy. He wiped the symbol away and made it again, repeating the sound. Within Micah's mind, a door opened, and he reached for the rod. He then made the symbol and spoke the word.

The stranger's eyes glowed a deep yellow.

Micah woke in the morning to the smell of mint brewing in the pot. He rose, rubbed his eyes, and saw Hitilettu sitting cross-legged in a shaft of dawn light that lanced through their log roof. He was looking at a book that lay next to Micah's bed of furs and branches. Micah shook his head and picked up the volume.

"I can't—"

He stopped. Five filigreed gold stars ran down the brown leather spine between six gold crossbars. The space beneath the top star was red and displayed a single gold-lettered word.

"Ho-bo-mok," Micah sounded as his eyes traced the letters. His mind blazed with confusion and doubt. "Hobomok." He had never heard the word before; it seemed like nonsense to him. Surely, he thought, this could not be what the letters meant. He opened the cover. There he read, 'Hobomok, A Tale of Early Times. By An American.'

He wanted to vomit as the world spun around him.

His finger traced the text at the bottom of the page, and he read it aloud, *"Then all this youthful paradise around, and all the broad and boundless mainland, lay cooled by the interminable wood, that frowned O'er mount and vale. Bryant."*

He looked up sharply and saw Hitilettu staring at him. "How? How can I read?"

Hitilettu spoke in his strange language. And Micah understood him.

"I see," Micah said, feeling dizzy. His vision blurred, and the world darkened. Micah closed his eyes against the twisting darkness.

Hitilettu looked pleased.

vii

MICAH AND HITILETTU LIFT the end of the log and walk it up with their hands as they pass under it. It rises above them, and its end touches the top of the wall. They continue to walk under it, lifting it and sliding it up and over its perch. Then, leaving his companion to hold the beam in place, Micah climbs to the wall and guides the aged wood as Hitilettu walks toward the other end of the building's frame, turning the log on its pivot. Micah guides it into place with metal hooks before clambering over to help Hitilettu place the far end. The year-dried wood fits well. They repeat the process, layer after layer, until they stand before the roofless structure.

Both men look pleased.

VIII
Entry 1

August 4, 1830

The sun has finally shown its face again. Clouds have hidden the sky for the last two weeks, though I have noticed it little as I have spent most of my time in the cave with my axe and barrow. Hitilettu returned two days ago with more provisions and told me that Mr. Samuel Black is no longer at Fort Nez Percés. A younger man named Barnston has taken his place. Hitilettu has said nothing particular about him. I am curious to meet the man myself, if only to put a face to the name. Though I look forward to my next journey to the fort, I do not know when that will be.

I have most of what I need here, and so I find little reason to travel. We have crafted a fine pine bed, the desk at which I write, and the chair upon which I sit. A three-legged stool sits by the pool where Hitilettu spends his mornings contemplating the waterfall. We have built a narrow bridge across the stream to the rocky western slopes. We built another that connects to the flat pine-land to the north.

In two years, I have encountered no other living man than the one I see in the water's reflection. I cannot call Hitilettu a living man, for I do not believe him to be such. He is not a spirit, whatever that word may mean, for his hands are firm and his breath puffs smoke. What manner of being he is, I dare not guess. He is uncanny, and his presence sometimes makes my mortal flesh quake. I fear him and do not fear him at the same time. I believe he knows my thoughts about him.

Whatever his nature may be, it has been a boon to me, and I dare say it will be an even greater boon when our work here is complete. I now need fear no highwaymen nor thief in the night. When our work is done, I shall take a horse and ride north to the fort to purchase a wagon. Then, we shall load it down with good provisions and return here. Then we shall load it down further with our prize and ride away from here, east to Ruth. I have sent her one letter a season since my companion put letters into my head. She, in turn, sends me a half dozen in the same period, which Hitilettu gathers from the fort. I am a poor cousin, for I often lose track of time in my daily routines and forget to correspond with the only person whom I love.

However, though it may help my memory, I believe the purpose of this little book is to serve another end entirely. Hitilettu brought it with ink and a supply of steel nibs from England and set it down next to one of the carvings my hands insist upon making. I took his meaning to be that I should transcribe the strange things that I see in my dreams, in which eyes often take such a prominent part. I do not believe the ink he has brought will be sufficient for the task, though I can see, though I know not how, a method of making more ink with berries, charcoal, and a bit of pine sap. I believe this insight, like the many things that come into my head, is from my companion.

The first record of my dreams must wait, I fear. For I find that though my spirit is willing, my flesh is weak. My hand cramps at this first attempt at writing, so I will conclude this entry here with the promise to write more of my dreams, which more often than not feature the man in chains whose eyes beckon me forward.

MICAH DREAMS OF THE man writhing before a column of fire. His arms, bound by ancient iron, pin him to the smooth stone floor. The air about him resonates with heat, darkness, and inexorable madness. Micah feels himself drawn forward, seeking, longing to understand what the bound man possesses. He knows that the prisoner holds within him something golden, something of immeasurable value. He has, Micah knows, a secret to tell.

IX
Entry 35

December 1, 1831

Winter snow has begun to fall, and I find myself in an age of repetition and preparation. Each morning, I wake just before sunrise and break my fast on porridge with meat and berries. Then, if the snow is not deep, I make preparations for the day, drawing water, cutting wood, seeing what fish are in the weir or what creature may have been caught in a snare. I clean the catches, hang any furs, and then, finally, walk to the path that leads to the cave. There I work for the rest of the day. I have taken to eating my midday meal on the ledge before the cave's mouth, where I may, with some obstruction, look out over the forest and onto the plains beyond where the horses graze. There, I see mountains in the distance and feel a great longing in my chest. I believe it is for reunion with my cousin.

Our three horses remain, neither increased nor diminished in number. Neither stolen by Snake nor swollen by strays from the herds of the Nez Perce or Cayuse, they have stayed close. I believe this is due to some quality that Hitilettu possesses. He commands the beasts, and they obey him.

I continue my work until an hour before sundown and return with my barrow down the hidden path.

Then Hitilettu appears and together we eat. He speaks and tells me stories of a world I can barely imagine. I cannot tell if his stories of betrayal and loss are legends, myths, or his own experiences. He tells many tales, but they all follow a similar pattern. There is a great warrior, or medicine man, or lore-master, and he is sought out by another who wishes to be a warrior, medicine man, or lore-master himself. The acolyte earns the master's respect and becomes the master's prized pupil. At some point, however, the pupil betrays the master and becomes his enemy. They challenge each other for many years, but in the end, the master overcomes the student. The instrument of victory is always the same: foresight. The master always sees farther than the pupil, and thus knows the land better, or knows where and when roots will grow, or learns more of the past in order to appease those who seek wisdom.

He is always one step ahead of the treacherous pupil.

I wonder if these things have anything to do with the dreams I have of the man in fetters, many of which I have recorded within this text. Could the bound man be the master? Or, since he is bound, perhaps the defeated pupil? Or am I trying to relate two things that have nothing to do with each other? Or might they have some relationship that I cannot yet see?

Or, perhaps, am I the pupil? Does he warn me not to betray him? I cannot imagine ever attempting to turn on him. Even if I had the inclination, which I do not, I know he is far mightier than I, and I would fare poorly in such a contest.

Of course, I ask Hitilettu these questions, but I receive no answers, only more stories.

Because snow is falling, I believe my work on the morrow will be to shovel the pathways. I shall luncheon here, then, in the warm cellar, instead of at the cave. Or, perhaps, I will simply sleep the morning away, as I believe I have caught a chill of some kind.

I should save a little of my mind's vigor to write Ruth a letter. It has been a month since my last.

ix

The light of that conflagration will fade away; my ashes will be swept into the sea by the winds. My spirit will sleep in peace; or if it thinks, it will not surely think thus. Farewell."

He sprung from the cabin-window, as he said this, upon the ice-raft which lay close to the vessel. He was soon borne away by the waves, and lost in the darkness and distance.

The last words of the book sting his watery eyes. He reads them over again, despite the pain. Then, closing the book, he reaches up with a trembling hand and sets it onto the shelf next to the first two volumes.

His skin is wet, and his back aches. He believes he will soon collapse as he did years before, though now he has a bed of furs and pine branches to break his fall. He wonders if this will be the last book he will ever read. He wonders if it is fitting. Is there some parallel between himself and the doctor? Or is he the monster, created by Hitilettu, alive but not alive—a man made from the dying body of another man? Is Hitilettu the Modern Prometheus? Is Micah Sisyphus? He has dug, and wheeled, and dreamed, but perhaps for naught. He stares into the fire of the stone hearth and feels his legs weaken.

X
Prepared

Friday, February 14, 1834 – Before Sunrise

MICAH COUGHED. PAIN ROLLED out from his chest through his spasming arms and legs. His bowels emptied in the stream as he trembled with cold and terror. He lay naked upon the bank and stared up at the looming, cloaked figure. *This*, he thought, *must be Death himself.* He did not look as Micah had seen him in art, except for his cloak. Instead of a scythe, the figure held a cage of iron from which emerald flame rose, painting the world in an eerie, green ghost light. The figure's skin was silver-white, and it wore tattered layers of brittle, stained cloth. Above its nose, its skin was smooth and eyeless. Below, the mouth was open and worked, spilling writhing worms upon the earth, which slithered and dug their way toward Micah.

He wanted to scream, but his throat cracked and rasped. The sores across his face and chest had burst and festered, piercing him with sharp needles every time he moved. They looked out of him like red sockets, staring in all directions. A thin, cracking sound wheezed out of him, and he felt the words that Hitilettu gave him slipping away, his mind reeling, tumbling in dumbfounded incomprehension.

Something large whispered out of the water behind him and slithered against his back.

The door to his cabin opened, and Hitilettu stood, framed in green light. In one hand, he held Micah's journal, and in the other, a chunk of the dark rock Micah had broken from the bowels of the earth.

Micah blinked as the world blurred. Something was wrong with his vision. Hitilettu's eyes, which glowed gold even in the ghost-light, began to split and multiply. Soon they covered the top of his face and roved in every direction, looking at everything in the world except Micah Whitman.

And in his many-eyed searching, Hitilettu looked pleased.

Then the thing behind Micah began to slither over him. Heavy, smooth, and slick, it coiled around his neck and pulled, lifting Micah's head from the ground slowly, almost gently. Hitilettu held up his prizes for Micah to see one last time before turning on his heel to disappear into the cabin. Micah's bowels released again as the slick, living cord began to tighten. He wanted to say one final word, to speak one last defiance or benediction into creation.

Instead, he let out a thin whine that died as the dark thing constricted about his throat.

X

Part 5 - Dancing

"I answer that there are various modes of being, and to each mode is given various affinities. That which is spirit and dwells in the desert place may cleave to flesh for a time with ease, for flesh it once had. But that which has a flesh of its own may not cleave with ease, for it is possessed by its own physical manifestation. Nor may it be displaced with ease, for it is within its own natural form."

- Mikuláš Vaclavek, *The First Book of Seeings*

"Why does the Fourth Book reveal only the path to passing communion? Why does it hide the secrets of full union? It is because the secrets do not fall within his sight. He sees less than the puppets claim. Yet we have begun to discern these hidden ways. We have, with help from the one who seeks knowledge, taken the first steps toward filling new wineskins with old wine."

-Zuzanna Cerny, *The Book of Corrections*

35
Devotion

Saturday, September 13, 2025 - Morning

SOMEONE SHOOK JENNY'S SHOULDER.

"Hey, you alive?" A voice whispered. Jenny rolled over onto her side and blinked bleary eyes. Light haloed a dark face looking down at her.

"Ror?" Jenny said, reaching up to touch her soft cheek. Her fingers traced the curve of Aurora's smooth skin. "Did I oversleep?" She pulled her closer. Her breath was sweet, and Jenny wanted to pull her down—

"Um—" Sydney said, her voice nervous.

Jenny snapped awake, reality rolling over her like an avalanche. "Shit! Sorry," Jenny said. "I was dreaming, I think."

"Damn," Sydney said, sitting back on the carpet. Her eyes were wide, and her lips parted in what Jenny took to be a confusion of surprise and excitement. "Wow. Who's Rory?"

Jenny took a deep breath and pushed herself upright. "Sorry, she was—she was a friend."

"Yeah," was all Sydney said.

Jenny rubbed her eyes and yawned. "Shit, I didn't mean to fall asleep. How did you get in here?"

"The door was open. I knocked and I saw you lying here."

Jenny frowned. She was sure she had closed and locked the door. "Really?"

"Yeah, I promise, I didn't, like, pick your lock and stare at you while you were sleeping." Sydney laughed. Then her face darkened. "I really didn't. I feel like that kind of sounded like I did."

Jenny laughed and yawned again. "I think I'm losing it. What time is—Oh, you're done?"

"Mhm," Sydney hummed.

"Okay, let me pee and then let's go get breakfast."

"Cool," Sydney said, crossing her ankles and hugging her knees. Jenny once more noticed Sydney's tattoos and made a mental note to ask her about them sometime.

Jenny felt Sydney's eyes follow her as she rose and walked to the bathroom. She closed the door behind her and leaned against it, letting her tears flow in an aftershock of her earlier grief. She wrapped her arms around herself and slid to the floor, the well of sorrow momentarily reopening. Jenny held her face in her hands and shook. She cried as quietly as she could, not for shame but for privacy. She didn't want to have to tell Sydney about Aurora, at least not today. She didn't want to make Sydney feel bad either. She gave herself a minute and let the pain roll through her like a seizure, taking hold of every part of her, as every part had been Aurora's. A minute wasn't enough. A minute was cheap and insulted her love. But a minute was all she had.

When sixty seconds passed, she sucked in a huge breath, put her palms on the cold floor, pushed herself up, and plopped herself down on the toilet.

Two minutes later, face rinsed, hair readjusted, Jenny stepped out of the bathroom and grabbed her jacket.

"You'll need something heavier than that soon," Sydney said.

"I know, I ordered one, still waiting for it to come. Ready?"

They went out the front door and across the lawn.

"Have you been hiking yet?" Sydney asked as the drive crunched underfoot and the pines closed in around them.

"Only when we were out looking for Carson Booth," Jenny said.

It's called a booth.

The voice in her mind startled her.

"Oh, right," Sydney said. "I—well, I was wondering if you maybe wanted to go hiking after work one day. You know? Instead of going to the diner? Before it gets too cold."

"Like as a group, or …?"

Sydney was silent for several steps.

"Ah," Jenny said, trying to find the right words. "So—"

"No, I mean, it's totally cool, we can go as a group," Sydney said. "I mean—"

"No," Jenny said, "look, we barely know each other, but I already love hanging out with you, I really do, I—"

"I get it," Sydney said, smiling bigger than ever, "It's cool, I understand."

"No, you don't. I … just want to … Look," Jenny stopped and took both of Sydney's hands. "I don't want to go into details. But before, when you woke me up and I said a name—"

"Rory," Sydney said, peering down at her feet.

"No, *Ror*, that was her nickname. I really loved her—*love* her. I love her. And I'm just not in any place to be more than friends with someone, no matter how beautiful and energetic and wonderful they are."

Sydney gazed up at her, her face scrunched in frustration. "If you still love her so much, why aren't you two together?" Sydney asked. "She must be—"

"She's dead," Jenny said. "She died. She was murdered. About a year ago."

Sydney's hands slipped from Jenny's and covered her mouth. "Oh my God," she breathed into her fingers. "Oh my God, I'm so sorry. I'm so fucking sorry!" Sydney wept and hugged Jenny hard, harder than anyone had since she had come home. The crush of her arms surprised Jenny, and so did the ache that welled in her. Afraid of opening the depths she had so recently purged, Jenny stood still and let Sydney hold her.

When they parted, Sydney took Jenny's hand.

"I can't even imagine what that must be like. If Maddy—God, I couldn't do it. I'd die."

"I know," Jenny said. "And it—Well, I guess I don't really want to talk about it right now. But please know that I think you're great, and it's because of that, because we have to work together, because Maddy is—"

Sydney shook her head. "Nope, you don't have to explain. I understand. I am one-hundred-percent here for you. So is Maddy. Can I tell her? Not like it's some exciting thing, but like, so she understands. I feel like I need to—"

"Yeah, you can tell her. But please don't, you know, talk about it a lot with other people."

"No!" Sydney said, aghast. "I wouldn't! I promise!"

"I believe you," Jenny said, smiling to reassure the younger woman.

"Okay, good. Friends then! But don't be mad at me if I think you're hot and maybe I stare at you sometimes."

Jenny laughed out loud. "Same," Jenny said.

And Aurora—no, *Sydney*—smiled sweetly and grabbed Jenny's hand. They walked, hand in hand, up the street to the edge of town, and soon Sydney was pointing at things in store windows and Jenny was stopping her in front of the bakery so that they could both breathe in the morning bread. When they came in sight of the diner and saw Maddy talking to Charles and Nate, Jenny felt suddenly awkward until Sydney left her to wrap Maddy in a huge hug and kiss.

"Um, how's it going?" Nate said, glancing back and forth between the couple and Jenny.

"Good," Jenny said, self-consciously brushing a strand of hair behind her ear.

"Linds is going to be a little late, which is not unusual for them, and I'm starving. So, let's get inside," Nate said, opening the front door. They filed in, one by one, and were met by the early-morning smells of bacon and coffee.

The Quiet Rumble

Volume 10, Issue 77, Sunday, September 14, 2025

Rain

By Keith Lowry, Ed. In Chief.

I'M GOING TO SHOCK everyone by saying that I don't remember the last time it rained so much in Lightning Falls. I know, I can hear the out-of-date "You've Got Mail" ringing in my ears already declaring the arrival of messages that contain some variation of "But, Keith, remembering things about Lightning Falls is your job!"

Indeed, it is, Dear Reader. Indeed, it is.

I remember a rainy year in '69, and again in '76, and I'm fairly sure it rained like the dickens in '99 right before Y2K. But since then? Well, I know we've had them, but I guess nothing important enough has coincided with the weather to stick it in my memory. That's how it goes for me, I think. Certain events are memorable, and then other facts—details that surround them—glom on and become part of what I remember.

There was a terrible car accident on Route 3 in '84 that killed two families, the Schillers and the Margates. Eight people dead—four parents, four kids. Monstrous. We had no idea what to do with ourselves. I remember the song that was playing on the radio when Leo Volker came in and told me about it. There was snow on his buttoned-up trapper hat, and he had only one glove on. I was smoking, drinking cheap whiskey, and putting together an article on some nasty business involving embezzlement in a local business. On the radio was Dolly Parton and Kenny Rogers's "Islands in the Stream."

I have no idea what music I listened to yesterday.

I remember that I had the best eclair I've ever had from Lost Boys when I sat in the library and read about a building collapse in 1908 that killed the children of two of the founding families of our town. And I remember Lily Krenshaw was wearing the best possible pink sweater a human can wear as she walked past me in my carrel. She leaned down with those shocking gray eyes that everyone saw a year later on that local soap commercial, smiled a smile to unmake a man's heart, and said, "You have cream in your mustache."

Those were the only words she ever spoke to me. Now, I believe, she lives on the east coast.

I remember as much as I do because the moments are important to me. The rain doesn't seem to have played much part in the notable corners of my life over the last twenty years. Maybe, if I'm lucky, something wonderful will happen over the next week or two, and we can all remember when it was so rainy in '25, when one of our high schoolers cured cancer, or landed a role in a big Hollywood movie.

That would be lovely, wouldn't it?

Now pardon me while I go to see if I can find an old soap commercial on the internet.

36
Seeds

Monday, September 15, 2025 - Night

AFTER A WEEKEND AWAY, Jenny was eager to return to the recording booth. To her frustration, however, the rows of buttons and knobs confounded her when she finally sat down. She fumbled with which buttons to push, talked into a powerless microphone for three minutes before she got a call letting her know that she was sending out dead air, and accidentally started a record when she didn't mean to. An hour in, she had shaken loose the fast-forming cobwebs and was rolling along. The only real difference was that she found herself looking at the clock constantly and was hyper-aware of the time. At 10:08 precisely, she took a call.

"Hello, this is Kusel House Radio. I'm Jenny. Who is this?"

"Hey, this is Pete Ingram." Pete's voice was high, and Jenny pictured a tall, thin man with awkward features.

"Hi Pete, what's on your mind?"

"Um, first, I just wanted to say that I think you're doing a great job. I've been listening since last Monday."

"Thanks, Pete," Jenny said. She braced for his next compliment or confession that he had joined her website.

"Um, I heard that you went out looking for Carson the first couple of days."

Frowning, Jenny nodded at her microphone and then remembered—for perhaps the twentieth time—that the caller couldn't see her. "Yeah, the first two days I was part of the search. Well, not the first day, but the first two days that the whole town went out."

"I just wanted to say thank you. And I was wondering if you'd let me thank everyone who went looking for Carson."

"Ingram … Oh, wait, you're—" Jenny stammered.

"His uncle. He was visiting us when he went missing."

"Oh, wow, I'm so sorry. How are you all holding up? I realize that's kind of a stupid question."

"It's very hard, we still go out searching for him every day."

"God, yes, I guess I would too. And yes, please, say whatever you want to say. And if there's a way people can help, please tell us what it is. Do you need—"

"We don't need anything, we just want to say thank you to everyone, and to ask people to keep their eyes out for anything. I know the official search is over, and the town did amazing things. But we're just asking that if folks are hiking or camping or doing anything out in the area around town, to just keep Carson in mind."

"God, yes, that's so important. I … I'm sorry, I feel like a heartless radio person just saying the things that someone says when they see real horror. But I'm not, Pete, not heartless, I mean. I know what it means to lose people, and please, I want you to call in whenever you want and let people know what they can do to help."

"I really appreciate that," Pete said, his voice catching.

"I want to tell you that it's going to be okay, but … yeah, I think that's kind of a lie. I do think it's important to say that there are a lot of us out here who are where you are. We ended up in a place of sadness, and we're still here. You're not alone."

Silence met her on the phone, but in her head, her voice mocked her.

Are you not alone because other people have lost people? Did they know Aurora? Did they know Nolan? Is their loss the same as yours? Is your loss the same as theirs?

She pictured Nolan and tried to think of him as just an interchangeable partner, a complementary object, a man to a woman. She tried to think of Aurora that way: one object in a relationship with another. When you lost your object, you understood other people's losses of their objects. Was that how it worked? Something deep in her gut told her it wasn't. Nolan hadn't been an interchangeable piece, and his loss wasn't like the loss of anyone else in the world. She might go through the same stages of grief as everyone else for Aurora, but the loss of Aurora was unique. She was, in fact, alone in her grief for them, for no one loved them like she did. They were not objects, they were people, and people were something else entirely. It felt cheap to think of them as unique. That wasn't the point. It wasn't the point that there just happened to be one Aurora. Her very being, her very personhood, made her loss categorically different. Jenny didn't know how it was different; she didn't have the words to express the mystery she felt herself facing. But she could feel its contours and sense its depth and breadth. She realized that the very shape of her loss hinted at a vast and unnamable mystery.

Dead air lingered on the radio. Mystery or not, she had to fill it.

"I guess I mean, I can't tell you it gets better because I haven't just moved on from what I've lost. I can't stand on the other side of it and say, 'one day you'll be over it.' I don't know if that helps, but I guess for me, knowing that I'm not just part of some inept group that hasn't figured out how to get over my hurt yet is helpful. God, I'm sorry, I'm rambling and I—"

"No," Pete said, "I appreciate it. I do. And I appreciate you letting me talk. I have to go. Please keep up the good work."

"Thanks, Pete," Jenny said and pressed the button. She pictured Carson Booth wandering among the foothills, lost and scared. Though the boy she imagined didn't have the face from the flyers. Instead, he had Nolan's face. She thought that Carson probably resembled Nolan when he was thirteen. She wanted to help him, but had no idea—

No, she did have an idea.

"Hey, everyone, I just thought of something. I know it's probably kind of crazy, but if you work in a shop, or you take people out for hikes, or canoeing down the Kusel, I guess if you do anything with tourists who don't know about Carson, maybe let them know. There are so many people who explore the butte and forest that could be keeping an eye out, but they won't know what's happened if they just showed up two days ago and are staying in someone's spare bedroom. So, please, just let folks know what happened to Carson and to, yeah, I don't know, I guess keep a lookout for any signs of him. I feel like that's something we can do."

The phone rang.

"Hello, this is Kusel House Radio. I'm Jenny. Who is this?"

"Hi, this is Chris Newman, and I'm sorry, but I don't think that's a good idea."

"Oh. Okay, why not, Chris?"

"Do you want us to tell the people who are paying to be here that we lost a kid? Do you think that's good for the health of our town? People come here for vacation; they don't come to look for missing kids."

"I mean, sure, but don't you think that—"

"How many families come through town? Do we want to tell all the parents, 'hey, we lost a kid, but don't worry, yours are fine?'"

"I don't think we need to say it—"

"People won't want to come here if they think their kids are in danger. People already have a hard time finding us, and now you want to wave them off even more? I think you should be careful about telling people what to do. You aren't even mildly qualified to give advice like that."

"I ..." Jenny started, but the words faded before she could say them.

"That's right," the man said. "Anyway, please don't give advice about things you don't know about. Yeah, that's all I have to say."

He hung up.

"Right," Jenny said.

The phone rang again. Anxiety welled in her stomach. Jenny pushed the button.

"Hi, you're on Kusel House Radio, this is Jenny."

"Hi," a woman said. "I agree with Chris. If we do what you're saying, we're going to scare people away from town."

"Okay," Jenny said. "But if they just look up the news in town—"

"No one does that. Do you do that? When you take a vacation, do you look up the local news?"

I haven't been on a vacation in over a decade, Jenny thought.

"I don't know."

"Well, most people don't, and if we just start dragging visitors into this, we're going to hurt the town."

"Okay, thanks for your call. I'm sorry, I didn't get your name. Hello?" The line was dead, and the call button blinked again. Jenny answered it.

A young woman's voice replied, "Hi, I'm Mercedes, and I think you're completely right. People not only have a right to know what happened here, but they'll want to help. I think if I visited a place and found out later that I could have helped a missing kid when I was hiking, I would be really upset. Like, I don't think I'd change anything I did except that I would just be on the lookout, you know?"

"Yeah," Jenny said. "I do. I agree with you, Mercedes. Oh, and do you think it would hurt the town?"

"No, and if people don't want to come here because something bad happened, I think they could try to find somewhere where nothing bad has ever happened, and they won't."

"Right," Jenny said. "Thank you."

Four more calls came in rapid succession: two told Jenny she was an idiot, one told her that they sympathized but that it was a bad idea, and one told Jenny that she was right.

"Besides," the last caller said, his voice sounded old and tired, "we owe it to the tourists. If something bad did happen to Carson, you know, something nefarious, then we owe it to parents to tell them to keep a closer eye on their children. God forbid something else happens and we didn't warn them."

After the caller hung up, the call button continued to blink.

"Okay, everyone, I'm going to stop the discussion right there, for now. I think a lot of people are getting upset about this, and I think it's a good idea to let it all cool off for a bit. So, I'm going to play some music and I'll be back in a little over an hour. If people still want to talk about it, we can."

The clock read 10:53, and she was about to take an hour-and-a-half break. Jenny guessed that few people would want to debate after midnight on a weekday. She put on a collection of folk albums, stood, stretched, and meandered out to the break room. She grabbed some grapes from the refrigerator and her copy of *The Shaded Lane* by Glen Moat from the coffee table. There was something about his writing that always brought her back. He wrote about the tiny details of town life, and she wondered if the places he wrote about were real. She hadn't ever bothered to look them up. As far as she knew, the town of Weeping Cedars might have been as real as Lightning Falls, or as fictional as Derry, Maine.

She read for an hour, added another record to the pile, and read until she started to feel guilty for leaving the audience with only music. When she returned to the broadcast room, she found she had been right to let the argument cool off. No one wanted to keep debating the issue in the wee hours of the morning, so she decided to talk about reading and the books she enjoyed as a kid. She described lying in bed while her father read to her about Aslan, and her mother scaring her with the red-spined stories of T.R. Malcroft. She talked about reading stories of Sam and his Faithful Friends in books with big color pictures of Virtue Vista Valley. She reminisced about how she loved reading *Princess Emerald's Endless Adventure* books, where she got to choose what Princess Emerald did.

A man named Joe called in to talk about how he bought the entire *Endless Adventure* series for his daughters and how they had loved them. An older woman phoned and, between painful-sounding coughs, told Jenny how she used to illustrate children's books.

When the conversation dwindled, she flipped her records over. When an hour of her workday remained, she said farewell, put on the last stack of records, and pushed back from the desk. She didn't have the same nervous excitement as the previous week, but she still felt good, tired, and full, like she had done something valuable. She went into the lounge and focused her satisfied energy on straightening up.

Her checklist reminded her that she had dry-cleaning to pick up after breakfast. She also had to do grocery shopping. As she put boxes from the counter back on their shelves, she thought to herself that she was starting something she hadn't had in a long time—a routine.

That made her smile.

37
Fitfully

Wednesday, September 17, 2025 - Evening

JENNY CARRIED HER LAUNDRY basket down creaking, wooden steps into the poorly lit basement, a thrill of goosebumps rolling up her legs. She felt like a child, hurrying to the washing machine and jamming everything in as quickly as possible. When she slammed the door, she jumped. Laughing nervously at herself, she started the machine and threw her basket on top. Her laughter grew as she remembered one of the first videos she ever did at the Chico house, sitting on a washing machine and pretending that it was more enjoyable than it actually was.

Mildly embarrassed by the cliché, she turned and appraised the requisite creepy basement. Stone walls? Check. Inadequate lighting? Check. Small, dirt-caked windows? Check. Shelves of indeterminate items of indeterminate age? Check. Dark alcoves that led either to places unknown or simply hid shadows in their shallow recesses? Check.

She opened her mouth to say something into the darkness, hoping to make a glib contribution to what felt like another cliché, but she decided against it. Instead, she set a timer and hurried up the steps to get ready to broadcast.

Two hours later, she was pining for the spooky basement.

"I'm sorry you feel that way," Jenny said to the empty line. "Well, folks, that's another vote for not letting tourists know to keep an eye out for Carson Booth. And I honestly feel like I'm just mostly hearing the same thing over and over again. So, I'd like to make a request. If you're going to call in, please either keep your statements short and sweet, letting me know which side you're on, or, if you have something new to add to the conversation, I'd love to hear it."

People didn't have new things to add, nor did they keep their statements brief. Jenny did her best to keep her temper in check as person after person called in to tell her that she was potentially ruining their town's businesses. As the conversation heated up, the room grew colder. After one particularly passionate plea for her to just shut up about it, Jenny flipped the phone broadcast switch to the 'off' position.

"Okay, folks, I need a few minutes to change my laundry, get a soda and a blanket, and just take a breather. I'm not shutting the conversation down; I just need about ten minutes. So, I'll throw a couple of songs on and then I'll be back, I promise."

Two minutes later, she was skipping down the old wooden basement steps under a flickering bulb. She pulled everything from the washer and pushed most of it into the dryer. One flimsy T-shirt—whose integrity she was unsure of—and her mesh bag of bras in hand, she turned to run back upstairs and froze.

A man stood near the wall.

He was there, out of the corner of her eye, not looking at her. Instead, he was staring at the wall, his hand resting on the stone. A second, taller, darker man stood a few feet away, looking up the stairs. Jenny jumped, turned, and screamed.

She blinked.

No, there were no men. No tall, lean figure wearing a suit, his fingers stroking the stone; no man in a loose button-up shirt with the sleeves rolled up. There was only a pile of chairs, half covered by an old drooping sheet. Jenny couldn't believe she had mistaken the strange pile for a human form; they looked nothing alike.

But I must have, right? No, that's what the ghosts want you to think.

Not wanting to hang out in the dark chill under the house any longer, Jenny ran up the stairs like a five-year-old and slapped the light behind her, not daring to glance back for fear that she'd see the face of the mustachioed man.

Wait … did he have a mustache?

She slammed the door behind her, locked the sliding latch—whose presence she found ominous—and hurried to her apartment, trying to think about anything else. Once inside, she hung her bras over the rims of her dresser drawers and remembered Nolan joking about how much space she needed for them.

"Sorry, did you want a flat-chested girlfriend?" Jenny had asked.

"Doesn't matter to me," Nolan said. "If I did, though, maybe I could save money by buying a smaller house, so we don't have to have an extra room for your huge—"

She had thrown one of the bras at him, and it had slung over his head like a hat. When he saw himself in the mirror, they both laughed. When she had gone to retrieve it, he had pulled her down onto the bed and shown her how much he appreciated her body, just as it was.

The memory throbbed, and she tried to think about something else. She pictured Nolan's face in the bed, then Nolan's face among trees, hiking. Nolan became Carson, and Jenny's present situation replaced her memories. She thought about the continuous phone calls and wished she had just kept her mouth shut about Carson Booth.

No, I don't really mean that. I just don't know what to tell these people.

Jenny went to her closet and tore open one of the plastic dry-cleaning bags. She took her new, green sweater out, sniffed it, and was happy to find that the smell had gone. The smell hadn't been bad; she had even kind of liked it. But the fact that it was gone reassured her that she wasn't wearing someone's dirty laundry. She pulled it on as she went to the kitchen, where she poured herself a glass of diet soda. Deciding that there was nothing else she had to do that would justify her prolonging her break any longer, she headed back upstairs.

As she pulled the wheeled chair up to the desk, a wave of fatigue washed over her. She hadn't done hours of talking like this before without at least an hour's break.

I'll have to get used to this if I'm going to keep being so controversial.

She let the current song finish, hit the mic button, and had to catch herself from nodding off.

"Wow, okay, I'm back. Sorry, I think this constant debate is really taking a toll on me. But I promised," she yawned, "that I would keep it going. So, feel free to call in."

Blinking light, button, greeting.

"Hi, this is Thad Meecham. I coach the Nighthawks—"

"Oh, the high school team!"

"Football, that's right," Thad said. "And I want to tell you that I understand what everyone is saying, I really do. We rely on the few tourists that we get to help prop our town up. We don't have a big factory or anything like that, and most of my players' parents work from home, doing remote jobs, or they drive out of town to work on farms or at businesses over an hour away. We need tourists to keep Main Street alive."

Jenny nodded and put the back of her hand to her mouth as she stifled another yawn.

"But I want to say that even so, we need to do the right thing. I try to instill in our players a sense of civic duty. I think that's something that's sorely lacking in our society today. And I hear all my neighbors calling in and telling you to be quiet because doing the right thing might make life more difficult. But that's the point of the right thing, right? If it were as easy to do as the wrong thing, well, no one would ever pick the wrong thing, I guess."

Jenny wasn't sure she agreed with his assessment. Sometimes the wrong thing just felt good.

"I … yeah, I guess I never thought about it that way."

Yes, I have, she thought as she tried to keep her eyes open.

"Well, I bet you have, even if you didn't use those terms, since you're obviously sticking to your guns despite all these people calling in to tell you that you're wrong. That's real Nighthawk spirit."

"Nighthawk spirit," Jenny said, the words thick in her mouth.

"That's right—" Thad's voice slurred and bent in her ears, and she felt herself falling forward. Her last thought, before sleep overcame her, was that she was going to bump into the microphone, and that would be embarrassing.

She dreamed.

She sat before the broadcast board, and the words slipped smoothly and quickly from her lips.

Good evening, Nighthawks.

She wasn't taking calls. No, she was telling the town what she thought.

If a boy goes missing, then we pull together. That's what people do. We don't turn on each other, we don't break down and get scared. We are a community, and that community comes together and weathers the tough times. That should be all we need to say about that. Anything more borders on the shameful. All right, let's move on to the next news story.

Local police arrested teenagers for defacing private property on Bankview today. Two boys, one sixteen and the other seventeen, were captured on a doorbell camera on Sunday night spray painting the word "Buffs" on a house's front door. The owner of the house, Patty Berger, said that she didn't want to press charges, but only wanted the boys to pay for the repainting of her door.

And that's the kind of thing I'm talking about, folks. That's the kind of mayhem that I think we need to avoid. We all know that Patty's daughter is a disappointment. Who wants to see their child grow up to be a prostitute? Yes, I know that she calls it something else, but really, that's what it is, isn't it? If you get money for sex, that's what you are. And, I'm not saying if that's good or bad, but it shouldn't be forced on everyone. And, clearly, our young people know all about it. And that's horrible. When I was that age, I knew … Well, I guess that doesn't really matter. What does matter is that instead of being considerate of her situation and Mrs. Berger with respect, these boys thought it was funny to try to shame her. Why? Who knows?

But let's stop it, all right?

Okay, let's talk about something a little more uplifting.

Preparations proceeded today for Camping Days as piles of scrap wood, donated by Tek's Hardware, have started to appear by the path to Whitman Cabin. The wood collection—

Deeper sleep swaddled Jenny, pulling her down and down.

She swam in darkness, drifting, bodiless, a mist on the wind. Deep within her, a nameless longing ached, and beyond the unseen horizon, something huge threatened to rise.

She woke.

A kink in her neck panged as she sat up. She was on the couch. Her head hurt, her mouth was dry, and her throat scratched. She rubbed her itching eyes and surveyed the lounge. How had she gotten here? She looked at her watch.

"Fuck me!" she croaked and stood up too quickly. Her head swam, and pain roared. She checked her watch again. How in the world could it be just after four in the morning? That wasn't possible. How long had she been asleep? How long had the radio been silent?

She stumbled across the hall and into the booth to find the record player working its way through a stack of records. The top one was familiar. It had a red label and said 'Columbia' across the top. Jenny saw the sleeve standing behind the record player. It was pink and showed a woman in black and white in the bottom right-hand corner. The words 'The Bessie Smith Story' were stylized in black across the top.

Jenny felt the floor rock under her, and she pulled the chair closer, letting it catch her as her knees buckled.

What the hell had just happened? Based on how much of the first record had played, it appeared that she had only left the booth ten minutes ago. That was impossible. The last thing she could remember … Thad. She remembered Thad, the football coach. And that was when? Around eleven. Five hours ago.

Five hours.

What the hell had happened for five hours? Jenny did quick math. If a full stack of records usually gave her about an hour, she'd go back on just after five. That would leave less than an hour for her to talk. But her throat was so scratchy, her head so painful, she didn't think she could do it. She decided that unless she was miraculously better in forty-five minutes, she'd just flip the records over and let Bessie Smith finish the night out for her.

No, go back on.

The thought was powerful—*hungry*—but she pushed it away and pressed her palms into her eyes where a new pain was lancing through her brain. Her stomach turned, and she dashed to the bathroom. She made it just in time to throw up into the toilet. She pulled her hair back with one hand and held on to the sink with the other as she knelt on the cold tile floor, vomiting up unfamiliar food.

I had lunch? I got up, made lunch, and I don't remember it at all. Oh God, what's wrong with me?

She knelt until her stomach was empty and the need to vomit had passed. Her head continued to throb. When she felt steady enough, she rose and went to the couch. She set her alarm and fell into restless sleep.

She ran through dark cobblestone streets closed in by old, hunching Victorian-style rowhomes. A too-large moon brooded full behind sluggish clouds, tracing ramshackle roofs and crumbling brick. Her feet splashed in water that reflected green gas-light lamps hung from creaking, rusted hooks on high posts. She ran toward darkness and watched as a pinprick of light rose in the distance and hovered overhead until a new emerald light bloomed above a hunched figure in whose hands a hooked pole wavered. He turned to her, and his waxen face grinned stupidly as his mad eyes fixed on her.

He bowed.

Jenny screamed and sat up. She threw up again on the carpet as the alarm on her watch vibrated.

"Oh God, help me," she groaned as lightning bolts seared from the back of her eyes along her skull. She peeled off her sweat-soaked sweater and jeans.

Another heave and she knew her stomach was empty. She spat and rose, vowing to clean the mess after she flipped the records. She had a job, and she would do it, even if it was confined to turning albums over. Head on fire, she accomplished her task and returned to the lounge. She found acetaminophen and popped two into her mouth, chasing them with pop. She hoped the caffeine and carbonation would help ease her discomfort. Then she set to work with paper towels, a sponge, and a bowl of water to clean her mess.

Twenty minutes later, the roaring in her head was a dull rumble, and her breakdancing stomach had slowed to a mild jitterbug. The floor was as clean as she was going to get it, and she left the supplies on the coffee table to remind her to finish the job when she felt better.

Then she was down the stairs and into her apartment, stripping her remaining clothes off in her living room and leaving them in a little pile. She tested the shower water until it was warm enough and then into the spray she went, letting it wash over her as she shivered uncontrollably, feeling as if she had the worst case of flu of her life.

Entry 9

September 18, 2025

Diary.

Kill me. Really, I'm over living. I feel the worst I've ever felt in my life. Literally. I feel worse than when I died. It's like there's a knife in my head and a hand in my stomach. Please, if you don't mind just making me not exist anymore, that would be fantastic.

Okay, nope, focusing on the page makes me dizzier.

Bye.

38
Support

Thursday, September 18, 2025 - Morning

"I think you're just stressed," Delia said, squeezing Jenny's hand. The two women sat across from each other at a wrought iron table in front of the coffee shop. Barry sat between them to Jenny's right, and Sydney and Maddy to her left. "We've all been stupid and absolutely irresponsible with you. You've been through so much, and we just let you go live on your own without a support system. We're all going to change that." Delia scanned the table, receiving nods from everyone present.

"She's right," Sydney said. "You need help."

"I really wish you'd go to a doctor," Maddy said.

"Maybe, but you feel better now?" Barry asked.

Jenny nodded again. She did feel better. In fact, she mused, she felt better than she had in a long time.

"I think if it happened again, I'd get checked out. But right now, with all the stress you're under—the change of living conditions, the change of sleeping patterns, the, as Delia said, lack of support, going off to live on your own without anyone else around … I just think that you need some normalcy."

"Should I stop working as a Sleep Talker?" Jenny asked. The idea made her tear up, though she wasn't sure why. She liked the job, but she'd been doing it for less than two weeks.

"No!" Barry said, laughing and adding his hand to Delia's. "No, I want you to have normality, consistency, and yanking you out of there seems like the opposite of that. No, I think we should do everything we can to help you build your nest, make you feel at home. I think we should at least have someone in the apartment next to you, don't you think?"

"Yes!" Sydney said. "That's a great idea!"

"I don't know," Jenny said. "That feels like asking a lot of someone."

"Not really," Maddy said. "Maybe people might like a little change of scenery a couple of nights a week. Like a local? I don't know, advertise it as co-working with a bed? Sorry, that sounded bad."

"*Oh my God!*" Sydney shouted. "What if that apartment was a little, I don't know, library or study hall, or reading room or something! That way you'd never be totally alone!"

"Um," Barry said, "I love that enthusiasm, but there are a lot of things to consider, since it's not really our house to do anything with.

Like safety, for one—"

"We don't want a bunch of randos walking into Jenny's house," Delia said.

"But maybe we could do something just for the Sleep Talkers," Barry said. "We'd have to loop Link in on it, see what he thinks. I'm not sure Charles would be much help, since he has his mother to take care of, but maybe he'd appreciate a night or two away if someone helped him out."

The tears that had threatened at the idea of leaving the Sleep Talkers suddenly broke out. Sydney leaned over and put her head on Jenny's shoulder, hugging her. Barry reached behind Jenny and rubbed her back.

"What's the matter?" Delia asked. Jenny shook her head.

"No, it's just that this is the best," she said, laughing at herself through her tears, "you guys are the best. I didn't expect this. You don't have to do all of this for me."

"Yes, we do," Maddy said. "You're one of us, and we need to take care of each other."

A part of Jenny's brain noted how trite that sounded, but she pushed the thought aside.

"I'll talk to Link," Barry said. "And we should see what Linds and Nate are cooking up on their own."

"Are you sure you don't want us to talk to your mom?" Maddy said.

"No, definitely not," Jenny said. "I don't want her involved in my life anymore."

"Don't you think that you'd—"

"She threw her out, Mad," Sydney said. "Like onto the street with nowhere to go."

Maddy nodded and leaned back in her chair.

"Look, we have the party tomorrow night, and we're all going to have a great time," Delia said.

"You're all going to have a great time," Sydney said, pouting. "We're going to miss most of it."

"Actually," Delia said, "I have a surprise about that. I talked to Link. Technically, for special occasions, only one radio needs to broadcast at a time. You know, if people are sick or there's an emergency. So, I got Link to agree to letting you all have the night off."

"Wait," Maddy said, "how does that work?"

"Well, originally, I was going to have Jenny host the party at the haunted house—No, don't worry, I scrapped that idea for a lot of reasons. The biggest is that Charles said he'd be happy to come early, get his fill of music and food, and then leave so he can broadcast from the cabin."

"But I'm at the cabin this weekend," Sydney said.

"Do you want to come to this party?" Delia asked, peering at her from under raised eyebrows. Sydney opened her mouth, closed it, and nodded. "Good. Charles will take the cabin for one night, and we'll send him off with snacks galore. The rest of you will be at my house. Do you have your outfits?"

"I have something that's at least semi-appropriate," Barry said.

"We bought stuff two weeks ago," Maddy said. "Syd insisted on having our own fancy dress up if we were going to miss yours."

"Is yours black?" Jenny asked, smiling.

"No," Maddy said. "Dark blue. I'm going to be sunny for a change."

"I bet you'll look amazing," Jenny said.

"She does! I've seen it! I'll be in green! I always wanted to be a flapper!"

"You almost have the hair for it," Delia said. "Jenny?"

"I got something, but I don't look like a flapper in it. I don't really have that slender-boy look they were going for back then."

"Neither do I," Delia said. "But that's not the point. I'm sure you're going to be knocking fellas on their keisters! Oh, and I forgot, I have a little accessory for you, so I hope you didn't spend a lot on jewelry."

"None at all," Jenny said. "I hadn't even thought about that. I'm not much of a jewelry person."

That was Matina, Jenny thought. *She was the jewelry girl.*

"Great, why don't you come over tonight then, before your show, and I'll give it to you?"

"It will have to be early. I have dinner plans," Jenny said.

"Oh?" Sydney said, sounding both interested and jealous at the same time.

"Isabella roped me into getting together. So, tonight we're back at Cinder's. I am *not* looking forward to it."

"Poor baby is too popular," Delia said. "But no rush. It can just wait until before the party tomorrow night."

"If you ever get tired of the pretty women of this town throwing themselves at you," Barry said, "you could redirect a few my way."

"I'll keep that in mind, Barry," Jenny said.

"Hey, I know I can't offer what you can, but, you know, free coffee for the rest of their lives," Barry said, lifting his cup and winking over it.

"Honestly," Maddy said, lifting her own mug, "I might take you up on that offer."

"Is that transferable to partners?" Sydney asked, flapping her eyelashes at Barry.

"Yes, I guess it would be," he sighed, playing defeated.

"Good, then you can move in with Barry three nights a week," Sydney said.

"Wow," Maddy said, "whoring me out that fast for coffee?"

"*Free* coffee!" Sydney said. "Plus, I know you have daddy issues, so it won't be that bad—"

"That bad?" Barry said, laughing.

"You all can discuss your arrangement tomorrow night at the party. Barry and I need to get to work," Delia said. "Jennifer, if you need anything, you call me."

Everyone else around the table echoed the sentiment.

"I will, I promise," Jenny said.

The Quiet Rumble

Volume 10, Issue 78, Thursday, September 18, 2025

What We Leave Behind

By Keith Lowry, Ed. In Chief.

TIME MAKES EVERYTHING AND destroys everything. Without it, we don't exist, and with it, we lose everything we have. Cheerful, no?

Well, it's that time of year again to wax philosophical and build our shelters. The days are coming when the young people of Lightning Falls will slap together bits of scrap wood and pile their sleeping bags with extra blankets. They'll fish, cook, hike, and canoe for a few days at the beginning of October, like their parents did. They'll do it all and wonder what the big deal is. In the age of endless streaming videos, it seems quaint. But there will come a time when most of the people who participate in this year's Camping Days will look back fondly and remember what it was like to get away from it all and connect with classmates, parents, and the older folks in the community. They'll look back and wish they could time travel and take from these days something intangible, something they've lost. They don't know that they have it right now, and they won't have a name for it when it's gone. But they'll suspect that it dwells here, in these coming days.

If only, they'll think, *we could get back into them.*

The shelters we build by the waters have ancient origins. They go back to the Bible and make their way into our town through a roundabout path through different religious groups. It's not particularly obvious in our town, where the Jewish population is essentially zero, but Camping Days, which culminates on the first Saturday in October, often lands fairly close to the holiday of Sukkot. This year, they are practically back-to-back. But my understanding is that we didn't get our tradition from the Jewish religion directly. Instead, our founders had their own traditions that they borrowed from European Jewish communities.

Now, I'm not a global or religious historian, so I don't have much to say about that. What I can say is that the shelters are, and always have been, temporary. We build them, not to last, but to shelter us for a little while. Then, like mandalas, we unmake them.

The shelters that I made in my boyhood were pretty good. I built them with the skills I learned from my father, and they never fell down. In fact, I never heard of a shelter imploding until I was well into high school. I guess we really did build things better back then, since we have a few collapses every year, now. Maybe wood has gotten worse, or the nails aren't as pointy as they used to be. But I suspect it may be something else: something we left behind and lost in the past.

I don't believe that the world gets worse year after year. Some things do, and some things get better. I also think it's a fool's errand to try to hold on to the things you think you'll lose. First, it's impossible. You cannot grab time by the tail and hold it back. Second, none of us has the foresight or the language to understand or name what we will lose. We don't know what that thing is that we will leave behind when we tear the boards apart and throw them back into the scrap pile. Perhaps it's innocence. Perhaps it's ignorance. Or, perhaps, it's just being. Perhaps what we lose is a little of our own existence, and that's what the shelters are there to teach us. Once we are old enough to leave them behind, we've learned how to lose parts of ourselves to the past. But as children, we don't know how to do that yet.

So, maybe, when folks tear down their shelters this year, the thing that will remain within them, locked forever in the unchanging past, will just be ourselves. And, if I'm right, I have absolutely no idea what we're supposed to do with that knowledge.

39
Eye Contact

Thursday, September 18, 2025 - Evening

AS JENNY DRESSED FOR dinner with Isabella, she wondered why the town didn't record the Sleep Talkers' broadcasts. She didn't think it would take much in the way of hard drive space, but then she didn't really know. She guessed that in the days before MP3s, it would have been cumbersome to record three people a night for nine hours at a time. She understood why they hadn't done it in the past, but she still wanted to hear some of the Sleep Talkers that Link had mentioned. She wanted to hear recordings from her strangely missing teenage years. But, more pressingly, she wanted to hear what she had said during the missing hours of her own broadcasts. Or, at least, part of her wanted to hear them. Another part admitted that the idea of listening to herself say things she couldn't remember sounded terrifying.

Jenny chose a cute corduroy skirt and dark brown boots and considered herself in the mirror. She wondered if the jewelry Delia had for her would go with her outfit. Unsure of her appearance, she considered the pile of skirts and shirts on the bed. She wasn't a jewelry person, but she was a clothes-horse. That was something she had shared with Matina. Clothes, running, lust, and Indian food. For all Aurora's bohemian lifestyle, yoga, and incense, she had never liked pakora, saag, or curry. Matina had introduced her to a small, hole-in-the-wall Indian place two miles from their house in Chico, where there were only three tables and a small back patio. They would come back smelling like coriander and cumin, and Aurora would leave them to themselves. Jenny had never planned on spending the night with Matina after their dinners, but she almost always had.

I won't be spending the night with anyone tonight, she thought as she did her makeup. She wanted to walk a fine line. She wanted Isabella to find her attractive, because that felt gratifying. But she also wanted her to be cool about it and respect the boundaries Jenny had set up. It was, she knew, a dangerous tightrope to walk. Or, if not dangerous, then potentially annoying.

After fixing her makeup, she pulled on a vintage Cranberries T-shirt and gave herself one last look before grabbing her purse and hurrying out of her apartment. As the soles of her new boots crunched gravel, she tried to understand her need to keep responding to Isabella, to keep seeing her, and to keep impressing her. None of it made any sense. She had thought that doing her work as a Sleep Talker and making new friends would have relieved her of any need to maintain her friendship with Isabella. But oddly, her desire to see the woman was stronger than ever. She didn't understand herself at all.

Once in town, Jenny crossed Main Street and smelled weed wafting from the Village Green, so she hurried past. There was something about its pungent odor that felt out of place here, in the small town in the middle of nowhere. She knew Aurora would have told her that was ridiculous. Weed is nature; nature belongs in nature. But the association for Jenny wasn't with nature; it was with people acting foolishly and laughing at things they shouldn't laugh at.

She had used drugs several times at the prodding of others in the Chico house, and had hated the way they made her feel. Jenny remembered leaning against a wall, staring up at Joseph with big eyes, her limbs languid, her lips open and hungry. She would have let him do anything. She remembered his gaze that said he would have liked nothing better than to have done all the things with her, but not while she was in that state. Desire and regret, proximity and distance had vibrated between them. His eyes had told her that if anything were to happen, it would be while she was in her right mind. He didn't like sultry Jenny, Jenny on pills, Jenny smoking weed, or Jenny on mushrooms. That Jenny, who she came to realize at Sunrise, was Jenny in coping mode, wasn't the real her. That was Venena.

She pushed those thoughts aside when she saw Isabella standing in front of Cinder's Remorse and waving a vape pen. Jenny waved back, and when she reached her, they hugged.

"You look amazing! Where did you get that skirt? Oh my God, how old is that shirt? Is that a band? Do you want a hit? Let's go inside. Look, don't hate me, okay?" Isabella said as she pulled open the front door.

"Why would I hate you?" Jenny asked, suddenly sure that Isabella and Chloe were back together.

"Well, I brought some friends."

Jenny had been right, but Chloe was only part of the story. The woman lounged next to Isabella's empty seat, one arm thrown over the back of her chair, the strap of her tank top squeezed between a well-developed shoulder and her slender neck. She cocked a smile and stood when Jenny approached.

"Good to see you again," Chloe said and pulled Jenny in for a hug. She spoke directly into Jenny's ear, her breath tickling her skin. "This is so fucked up. I told her not to ambush you. You're in for a hell of a night.

Sorry about that." As she pulled back, she gave Jenny a sympathetic smile.

Jenny understood immediately; Chloe wasn't the only other person at the table. Taking up four seats were Leddy, Phil, Emmett, and Earl. Jenny felt anxiety shoot up from her stomach through her chest. She tried to force a smile.

"Hey!" she said. "This is a surprise. How are you all?"

Everyone got up and gave her perfunctory hugs except Emmett, who squeezed her tightly before holding her at arm's length and staring at her intensely.

"How are you doing?" he asked.

"Um, okay," Jenny said. "Just getting used to my new situation."

He nodded, frowning concernedly, and surveyed her as a doctor might. "You eating enough?"

"Yeah, Dad," Jenny said, shaking her head and smoothly extracting herself from his grip.

"Sorry, I just … yeah, sorry, I've been listening."

"We all have!" Isabella said, lifting a red cocktail. "You're amazing!"

"Thanks," Jenny said.

"No, really, you're awesome," Phil said, waving at their waiter. "I'm kind of a huge fan of what you've been doing the last week. With Carson."

"Oh," Jenny said. "I kind of thought you'd be upset with me."

"Why?" Phil asked. He turned to the waiter. "Hey, can we get a round? Whatever people want."

"Daddy Warbucks," Leddy said. "Everyone good with Margaritas?" They were, and Phil ordered pitchers.

"So why would I be upset about Carson Booth?"

"I figured, with the hardware store—"

Phil shook his head. "What? No, there's a kid missing. Who cares if a few tourists are upset?"

"Besides," Earl said. "Not many tourists come into the hardware store, so it's no real danger to them."

Phil shrugged. "Even so, I think what you're doing is important, and I hope you keep doing it. I know it can be tough. Some of these people are assholes."

"I think you sound hot on the radio," Chloe said, fixing her with intense eyes.

"Um, thanks," Jenny said, trying not to smile like a kid who has just been told they are good and smart and make their parents proud.

"Oh yeah, you definitely have a great radio voice," Isabella said.

"And the face for it," Earl said.

Jenny wanted to cry because she wanted to laugh. Just like that, she slipped back into the dynamic of teasing, affirming, serious, playful banter that she had tasted for two days when they searched for Carson Booth together. It was comforting and disorienting at the same time.

These are your people. Stay close to them.

The words in her mind were strange, foreign, and familiar. She remembered the first day she met Joseph when he came to the house in Chico, and Matina introduced him to everyone. She remembered him asking her to walk him back to his car. As he stood in the driveway, he fixed her with his light eyes and said, "These are your people. Stay close to them."

But his words had felt different than those in her head. He had been … What? Comforting? This voice, lacking Joseph's southern twang, had been desperate. It felt like some lonely part of her mind was echoing his sentiment. She didn't understand why, though. She was in a good place, at least socially. But maybe that desperate voice was some part of the old her, the her she had forgotten. Maybe the idea behind it was that these were her people in a way that no one else could be. They had known her for longer than anyone, even if she couldn't remember a thing about them.

Chloe interrupted Earl as he was talking about a new song he had written. "Don't you need to go?" She held up her phone. It showed 8:28. Jenny had lost track of time.

"Shit, yeah, I should get back."

"Fuck, did we make you late?" Isabella asked.

"No, I've got a half hour. No big deal."

"I'll walk you out," Isabella said.

"Me too," said both Leddy and Chloe.

"You boys discuss Superman or whatever," Leddy said. The three men said 'goodbye' as Jenny led her quartet past the bar and onto Main Street.

On the sidewalk, under a light drizzle, Isabella and Leddy pulled out vape pens.

"So, really, how have you been?" Leddy asked. She leaned back against the wall and put one booted foot up.

"Like I said, it's been an adjustment," Jenny said. "I'm still getting used to the hours."

"Yeah, I bet that's tough. Look, I know we all tried to act like everything was cool in there, but we owe you a real apology. So, I'm sorry. Everyone's sorry. I admit, it caught us all off guard."

Jenny nodded, not sure what to say.

"Look, this is a small town, and all of us like you. Hell, I know you don't remember me, but I've known you for kind of my whole life, and I don't want this shit to be like this festering thing that just drags on, okay? Maybe we can't be great friends or whatever right away, but we definitely don't want there to be bad blood."

Jenny nodded. "Yeah, I—Yeah, okay. I mean, you're right, I don't think we're going to be best friends right away, but I do appreciate you apologizing. I'm sorry too. Sorry, I freaked out so bad at the Tim that night."

Leddy laughed. "No, that was great. I'm not sure if you heard, but Phil and that guy got into it right after you left, and then one of his boys jumped in and Earl grabbed him and, like, threw him. It was almost like the Big Brawl."

Jenny smiled. "Because of me?"

"Well, yeah, kinda. Anyway, you need to get to work. But I hope we're cool, you know? I hope that we can all do this again soon."

"Yeah," Jenny said. "I think I'd be down for that."

Leddy smiled and stepped tentatively toward Jenny. They hugged, and Isabella clapped.

"Cool, I'd better get back. Good luck with your show tonight," Leddy said.

When the door closed behind her, Isabella hooked Jenny's arm in her own.

"Come on, we'll walk you to the edge of town," Isabella said. Chloe fell in on Jenny's other side, but didn't take her arm. Instead, she shoved her hands into the back pockets of her jeans, and Jenny idly wondered what those pockets felt like. As they walked, Isabella put her head on Jenny's shoulder and hummed to herself the tune of one of the songs that had been playing at the restaurant. "Oh, look," she said, pointing across the street.

Jenny turned and saw Maddy and Sydney walking out of the sandwich shop. Jenny waved, and they waved back. Sydney almost tried to cross the street, but Maddy pulled her back.

"God, they are such an interesting couple," Isabella said. "I thought about asking Maddison out at one point, but she's a little too goth for me. I feel like she's too goth for Sydney, though, too."

"I think they're kind of perfect for each other," Jenny said.

"They are," Chloe said.

"Do you know them?" Isabella said.

"Kind of," Chloe said.

"Okay, keep playing Miss Mysterious," Isabella said, exasperated. "She's so aloof, like the less she says, the hotter she is."

You might give that a try, Jenny thought.

"Isabella is trying to play it cool," Chloe said. "Like she's not going to take me home and make me—"

"Shut up!" Isabella said. "Do not say another word."

Chloe gave Jenny a half-cocked smile. "Can I ask you a personal question, so I can get it right?"

Jenny frowned, confused.

"Chloe, shut your fucking mouth, right now," Isabella said.

"When you go down on someone, do you look up at them, or are you like, fully focused on the business in front of you? You know? Like, eye contact or no eye contact?"

"Don't you answer that," Isabella said.

"Don't you want the authentic experience, baby?" Chloe said. "She loves your JustBuffs page, by the way. She visits it nightly."

Isabella stopped in her tracks and stared at Chloe. "I do not. You fucking bitch," she stammered. "I—I don't even know what to—"

Jenny wondered if a human was capable of feeling more socially awkward than she did right then. "Um, I should probably get back … My job …"

Chloe smiled, took Jenny's hand, and pulled her into an embrace. "She's crazy," Chloe whispered in Jenny's ear. "Seriously, do yourself a favor. And I'm sorry about all this."

She kissed Jenny's cheek and pulled back.

"Have a great show tonight! Hurry home, it's getting cold." Her voice was sing-song and overly cheerful. She was right, but it wasn't just the cold that raised goosebumps all over her legs and arms. Jenny turned to Isabella, who was blushing and not meeting her eyes.

"Hey, um, text me, okay?" Jenny said.

"I don't—" Isabella started.

"Look, I am going to leave this for you two to discuss," Jenny said. "I'll talk to you soon."

Jenny took an awkward step toward Isabella, stopped, turned, and walked away as the rain fell harder and colder.

40
Taken

Thursday, September 18, 2025 - Night

JENNY STARED AT THE control panel. The clock read 8:55. She hugged herself and rubbed the soft material of her sweater, feeling the awkwardness of her encounter with Isabella and Chloe transforming into anger. Isabella had made her feel uncomfortable time after time. Now, if Chloe was telling the truth, or—Well, she hadn't explicitly said it. What had Chloe implied? It had seemed obvious in the moment. But now, Jenny wasn't sure she had understood her. What was it? Would Isabella visit her site, and … and what? Have Chloe pretend to be her? Or would she fantasize about Jenny while she was with Chloe? Was that what Chloe had been suggesting?

That was … sick? Jenny tried to give Isabella the benefit of the doubt. Maybe Jenny misunderstood. No, she didn't think so. Maybe Chloe was joking. No, if that had been the case, Jenny could imagine how Isabella would have reacted. She would have laughed at it, acted scandalized, even smacked Chloe's arm for embarrassing her. But she just stood there and got genuinely angry, as if Chloe were betraying a secret.

"She's crazy. Seriously, do yourself a favor. And I'm sorry about all this."

Chloe's words, breathed into Jenny's ear, repeated in her mind. What was Jenny supposed to do with this information?

Jenny's phone buzzed.

> **_Isabella_**
> I'm so sorry. Chloe made a bad joke, and it caught me totally off guard. I'm sorry about how I reacted. I was just so floored by what she was implying.

> **_Isabella_**
> NONE of that was true.

> **_Isabella_**
> NONE of it.

Jenny stared at her phone.

Two minutes to go.

The voice in her head was excited. Jenny didn't feel excited. She felt tired. She thought about texting Maddy and Sydney to see if they would come over. Didn't Delia say that she'd have people around her all the time now? Well, maybe not all the time, but it was probably a solid idea so soon after she blacked out for five hours.

One minute to go.

> **_Jenny_**
> Hey, I kind of had a terrible experience just before I got home. Any chance you guys could come over and keep me company? I know it's kind of insane to ask right now. Totally understand if you can't.

Get ready, get ready, don't let everyone down.
Jenny's phone buzzed.

> **_Syd_**
> OMG! Yes! We'll be there soon. We'll be in the lounge when you take your break. Want us to bring anything?

> **_Jenny_**
> Thank you!!! No, just yourselves. I love you two!

> **_Syd_**
> We love you back!

Jenny pushed the button.

"Good evening, Nighthawks! This is Sleep Talker radio, and I'm your host, Jenny Berger. Have I got a show for you tonight! We're going to talk about the weather, which has been wetter than usual, some town news, and then maybe take some calls."

The words rolled out, fueled by nervous energy. She could feel her hands vibrating.

"So, first, the weather. It's been raining here in Lightning Falls … a lot. More than I can remember it raining since … Well, since the second worst day of my life. Or maybe it's the first worst. I guess it kind of sucks to have so many terrible days that they're competing with each other. Anyway, from what I heard on the real radio, all three creeks are rising and … Well, yeah, I guess take it from me, you don't want to go canoeing when the water is this high, especially at night."

No, this is wrong, Jenny thought. *Don't make light of that. Don't be so glib. What am I doing?*

"All right, let's dive into some news. Everyone is getting ready for Camping Days and … Oh, no, I've stumbled on that topic again."

This isn't me.

This isn't me.

Stop.

Stop.

Help me.

Help me.

"I'm—I'm sorry. Everyone, I'm sorry. I'm not feeling well. I have a headache that's killing me."

No, please, don't stop.

"I need to take a break. I might need to be off tonight. I—"

The phone light was blinking. Jenny's hand reached out and pushed it.

"Hello, you're on Kusel House Sleep Talker Radio, this is—"

"Jennifer?" Patty's voice came through her headphones like a slap to the face.

"Mom?"

"Jennifer, are you okay? Do you need a doctor?"

"No, M—Patty, I'm fine, I just have a migraine. I think, I'll be fine."

"Do you need medicine? I can go—"

"No, I'm fine. I have to go lie down."

"Jennifer, I can come over and—"

"No, you wouldn't want to be here, it's a house full of lesbians," she almost yelled.

"Jennifer!" Patty said. "Why would you say that to me?"

"Because it's true. Thanks for calling. I appreciate your concern. Good night."

Jenny pushed the button.

News, I have to do the news.

"No," Jenny said into the microphone, "No, I have to take a break. Let's put on some rock and roll to—"

She stared at the record on the record player. No. She had prepped the first four Led Zeppelin albums. But staring up at her was the Bessie Smith album.

"What the fuck?"

Her hand reached out and turned the record player on as her phone buzzed.

> **_Delia_**
> I'm coming over.

Bessie began to sing.

"I have to go," Jenny said. She pushed the mic button. The phone button flashed, but she ignored it.

Jenny rose on unsteady feet. She was burning up; sweat was pouring from her forehead and neck. She lifted her hair to waft air against her skin, and she unbuttoned her sweater. The room lights blinked.

What the fuck is happening to me?

Jenny pulled the sweater off and threw it over the back of the chair. She stripped off her T-shirt as well and left it on the floor. Her skin glistened as she took one tentative step after the next toward the booth door. She made it out and across the hall to the lounge. Then down onto the couch she fell, her head throbbing. She thought she might drift away then, out into the darkness. But she didn't. She simply lay, her head pounding, until she heard feet running up the stairs.

Sydney's momentum almost took her past the lounge.

"Maddy and Delia are right behind me," she said before charging into the room and collapsing to her knees on the floor beside Jenny. "Are you okay? Can I get you anything? What's wrong?"

"Migraine," Jenny said. "Just a bad migraine, I think."

"Did you take anything yet?" Jenny shook her head. Then Sydney was up and running to the bathroom. She returned with pills and water as Maddy and Delia came into the room together.

"Sorry for the show," Jenny said.

"It's okay, Nate and Linds are still broadcasting," Maddy said.

"I think she means that her tits are out," Delia said. "Nice bra, where'd you get it?"

"Online, I'll send you a link," Jenny said as she took the medicine and water from Sydney.

"Did you pass out again?" Delia asked.

"No, just … I felt like I was going to. Like I was burning up."

"Hence the stripping," Delia said.

Jenny nodded, took the pills, and downed the water. "Thanks," Jenny said to Sydney, handing back the empty glass.

"What can we do for you?" Maddy asked, sitting on the old easy chair's arm.

"I—" Jenny began and then felt silly. "Probably nothing."

"I know," Maddy said, "when I have a migraine, I like to have a damp cloth over my eyes and for Syd to stroke my head."

"Is that a service that's available?" Jenny asked, uncomfortable with asking for that kind of familiar affection.

"Of course," Sydney said.

"We'll go in shifts," Maddy said. "Just, don't let Syd know if you're feeling better; she has Roman hands if she thinks the headache has passed."

"I wouldn't!" Sydney said.

"Mhm," Jenny said, patting the couch behind her. Sydney sat, and Jenny put her head on her friend's lap.

"I'll make sure everything is running for the show tonight," Maddy said.

"No, we can take turns with that too," Sydney said.

"You guys are amazing," Jenny said, feeling tears well.

"Not that amazing," Maddy said, backing out of the room and throwing up finger guns. "I'm just here for the show. And I also mean the toplessness."

"She's not great at innuendo," Sydney said after Maddy had left the room. "Or, like, talking sexy."

"Are you good at talking sexy?" Jenny asked.

"Nope, but I know it. I rely entirely on being adorable."

"Should I leave you two alone?" Delia asked.

"Nope," Sydney said, "It's good to have a chaperone."

"I'm getting chilly," Jenny said.

"Let me grab you some clothes," Delia said.

"My T-shirt and sweater are in the booth."

Delia returned five minutes later with a fresh, long-sleeved shirt. "Here, your other clothes were soaked. I put them in the hamper."

"Thank you," Jenny said as she pulled the fresh shirt on.

"Well, this is less interesting now," Sydney said.

"I'm sorry, I'll have to keep you interested with my riveting personality," Jenny laughed.

"Eh, pass," Sydney joked, and then leaned down and kissed Jenny on the forehead.

"We're all set for the next hour," Maddy said as she returned. "I didn't know you were such a blues fan."

"I'm not," Jenny said. "Or, like, I think it's fine. But, yeah, I don't know." She rolled over onto her side. "I'm tired."

"Close your eyes then," Delia said. "We've got you. I'm going to order some pizza, so you all have something real to eat later."

"Are you sticking around?" Jenny asked.

"Yeah, for a while, to make sure I don't need to drive you to the hospital. And to make sure that the house full of lesbians doesn't take advantage of your diminished state."

"Did I really say that on air?" Jenny said, covering her eyes.

Maddy laughed. "Yeah, you definitely did."

"How did you hear that? Weren't you already waking over?"

"I was listening on this," Maddy said. Jenny peeked between her fingers to see Maddy pulling a small device from her pocket, wrapped in a white headphone wire.

"You have a portable radio?" Jenny laughed.

"Yeah, it's retro," Maddy said, as if that ended the matter.

After Jenny thought about it, she realized that it did.

41
Concern

Friday, September 19, 2025 - Just After Midnight

Coffee toasted the air as Jenny woke from a pleasant dream about sitting in a café and talking to an old man she had met the first time she went to Powell's in Portland. He had been just the right amount of gruff and funny. He'd also helped her find a book. In the dream, he was talking about his grandmother and her favorite soups. A vacation feeling of calm and wellness had laid over the scene.

When Jenny opened her eyes, Maddy's thigh was under her head.

"Morning," she said to the younger woman, who was reading a small hard-backed book.

"Hey," Maddy said. "Syd's on the radio. There's coffee."

"How long did I sleep?"

"Almost two hours. How are you feeling?"

"Fine, actually." Jenny sat up. "Delia left?"

"Yeah, once you were totally out and the pizza came, she called us vampires and went home. I took it personally."

Jenny studied Maddy's face, trying to figure out if she was serious or just had a dry sense of humor. "Really?"

"Really, she said it, not really that I took offense," Maddy said, giving her a reserved smile. Jenny felt a strange, pleasant incongruity between the woman's demeanor and that of her excitable partner.

"Right, sorry, still waking up. Coffee, you say?"

"I do say."

A finished cup of coffee later, Jenny felt downright chipper. Her headache was gone, she felt better rested than she had in a week, maybe two, and she was enjoying the quiet of having Maddy with her.

So, is this what it will be like when she works here? I wonder what Charles is like as a ... What would you even call it? Space-guest? House-mate?

She thought 'space-guest' was funny. She imagined Sydney one weekend, Maddy the next, then Charles, who she guessed might try to teach her some things, which wouldn't be terrible, since he seemed like he had a good sense of humor and knew what he was talking about. The idea of having some idea what her days and nights would be like, and that she liked the people involved, bolstered her sense of wellness.

She wondered how long any of it would last.

"Hey, you're up!" Sydney said, popping into the room with a *you won't believe this* look on her face. She quickly crossed the room and hugged Jenny, who put her coffee down and hugged back.

"I am up. Thank you for the cuddles."

"Literally any time," Sydney said.

"What happened in there?" Maddy asked.

"Oh!" Sydney said, backing up and taking a seat on the arm of the couch between the two dark-haired women. "You won't believe who called in asking about Jenny! Mr. Grossman!"

"Seriously?" Jenny asked.

"Yeah, he was really concerned about you. He offered to have a doctor come over. I told him thanks, but you were sleeping off a migraine, and that you'd be okay. Was that the right thing to say?"

"Yeah, totally," Jenny said. "I feel great now. If I keep feeling like this, I think I'll go back to work as soon as the break is over. I'll take it slow, a half hour at a time," Jenny said, seeing the look of concern on Maddy's face. "And you two will be here to catch me if I fall."

They both looked at her and nodded. But Jenny didn't fall. When she got back to the booth, she felt … normal. Entirely normal. A few regular callers rang in to see how she was doing. The fourth caller, however, had an unfamiliar voice.

"Jennifer?" The voice was old, tired, and raspy. Immediately, Jenny could see the man's long, bearded face.

"Hi, you're on the Kusel House radio station. This is Jenny. Who is this?"

"This is Levi Grossman, Jennifer. I'm calling to see how you're doing. You've had a rough few nights this week."

"Hello, Mr. Grossman. It's really nice of you to call. Syd—Sydney told me that you called a little while back. I really appreciate your concern. I'm feeling really good. I think I just had a bad migraine."

"I see. And it's gone now?"

"All gone," Jenny said.

"I'm extremely glad to hear that. Extremely glad. I would like to make sure everything is okay at the house. It's been so long since anyone lived there that I fear something might be loose, a pipe or valve or something. Especially, given the house's history."

Jenny blinked and felt stupid. "Right. Right, of course," Jenny said. "I … I really appreciate that, Mr. Grossman."

"Do you have somewhere else you can stay for the day? I will have an inspector come out tomorrow. I don't want you to sleep there any longer until we've had the air checked. We were entirely remiss for not having an inspector go over the house thoroughly before you moved in. I guess we figured that since people have been working there consistently, there was nothing to worry about. And I guess we would just keep assuming that if you weren't getting sick."

"I … Yes, I have somewhere to sleep. You can have an inspector out tomorrow?"

"I can get a lot done when I set my mind to it, Ms. Berger," he said, chuckling. "And when it's important, I can usually get it done in a few hours."

"Thank you, sir. That's really … Thank you."

"Of course. In the meantime, crack a window and tell that young woman, Sydney, that she is a joy to listen to."

Jenny thanked him again, felt her alarm buzz on her wrist, and put a new stack of folk albums on. When she returned to the lounge, a chilly breeze wafted in through a cracked window while Maddy and Sydney leaned against each other under a blanket for warmth.

42
Roaring

Friday, September 19, 2025 - Early Evening

JENNY MARVELED AT HOW organized Delia's bedroom was. The books, jewelry box, and photos on her dresser were neatly arranged and dustless. Her bed was immaculate, with wrinkle-free pillows laid over a neatly folded-down sheet that capped her plaid bedspread. Delia's vanity appeared set up for a photoshoot, with each box and bottle in an aesthetically-pleasing symmetry. Jenny hoped that the closet door hid a jam-packed, piled mess.

She doubted it, however, as she surveyed Delia's stunning green and gold sequined dress, silk headband, silver shoes, and black stockings. She wasn't a large woman, but neither was she slender. Jenny thought she looked like she enjoyed her life, and Jenny envied that.

"You know my family moved here illegally?" Delia said, taking a small gift bag from her vanity and handing it to Jenny.

"Really?" Jenny asked.

"Mhm, we were one of two black families that came here when anyone who wasn't white was forbidden from moving into the state."

"Shit," Jenny said, "I didn't know about that."

"Yep, I don't think they really enforced it—I think only one person ever got arrested in the like sixty years that it was the law of the land—but still, not exactly a welcome sign, you know?"

"But your family came here anyway?"

"Mhm," Delia repeated. "My great-great-grandfather figured the town was so remote that no one would notice. He visited first, though, to make sure it wasn't a sundown town."

"Wow," Jenny said, sipping her drink.

"But the Brethren were rabid egalitarians; men and women, black, white, Indian, Chinese, didn't matter."

"That's amazing," Jenny said. Delia nodded.

"Yep, if seeing other humans as human is amazing, it's amazing." Jenny frowned, but Delia turned to her. "The history of the human race is humans not seeing other humans as people," she said contemplatively. "So, yeah, it is kind of amazing. Still, you know, it's fucked up that it's amazing. Now, I'm not telling you this because I want you to have some deeper understanding of me as a person, not that you ever ask."

Jenny frowned, knowing Delia was right. "I'm sorry—"

"Oh, shush, I don't go prying into your past either, do I? No, I wanted to tell you that, because I wanted you to know how wonderful the gift is that I'm about to give you. My great-grandfather worked as a hard laborer, with no outlet for his creativity, but my grandfather worked as a gardener. He should have been a scholar, and by the end of his life, he was. You know he wrote a book about Lightning Falls? I gave a copy to Maddy the other day. Anyway, he was a gardener at the house you live in now."

"The one with the carbon monoxide leak?" Jenny asked, trying to put as much sass into her voice as possible. She had been angry all afternoon after she awakened to messages telling her workers had discovered and fixed a small leak.

"That's the one. He took their garden and the one by the cabin and made them bloom. He worked there for decades, planting, picking things, choosing what the family would eat, and cultivating the beauty of their land. He met my grandmother there. She was the cook."

"Wow, I didn't know. And I didn't know because I didn't ask because I'm a terrible racist."

"That's right," Delia said, grinning over the small silver gift bag. "But the Kusels were not as monstrous as you, and they treated my grandparents like they were family. Not like that aunt/uncle bullshit they did in the South. They spent Christmas together, were at the birth of each other's children. Mr. Kusel helped build my grandfather's house with his own hands."

Delia's eyes were glassy.

"He was a kind man; the whole family was kind. When they died, Grandpa and Grandma never had to work another day in their lives. And when my grandfather left, he took a few things from the house to remember the family."

"Oh?" Jenny said, wondering what secret treasure Delia had hidden in the bag.

"I know you said you're not a jewelry person, but, well, I want you to have this. If you don't like it, you can give it back after tonight."

She handed the bag to Jenny as a tear ran down her cheek.

"Thank you, Delia," Jenny said. She reached inside the bag and pulled out tissue paper. Under it, she found a small black jewelry box. Inside, a simple silver star pendant lay on a fine silver chain.

"It's beautiful," Jenny said.

"That belonged to one of the daughters. The Kusels were wealthy, but they didn't flaunt their money except to help people. So, my grandfather said that most of the jewelry was like that, simple, silver, and elegant.

Nothing too spendy. He said that other than their engagement rings, the women never wore diamonds or other kinds of jewels."

"Thank you, this is so lovely. Help me put it on?"

Jenny turned her back to Delia, and her friend pulled the chain around Jenny's bare shoulders and clasped it. Jenny stood and considered herself in the mirror. Dangling strings of beads crossed her silver-blue dress, and her headband was a silver ribbon with an Art Deco sunburst pattern on the side supporting a dyed blue flower. The silver necklace was the most elegant and real piece of her costume.

"You look gorgeous, like you always do," Delia said, hugging her from behind.

"We look gorgeous together," Jenny said, and put her arm around her friend.

They went into the living room where Barry was arranging food on the dining room table. When he saw them, he clutched his heart and feigned falling backward. He was wearing a nice suit, though nothing about his outfit particularly screamed the 1920s. In the background, jazz played on an ancient iPod. Jenny, who wasn't usually one for jazz, found it surprisingly catchy.

The people came in steady trickles. Soon, Delia's living room, kitchen, dining room, and back deck were full. Jenny marveled at the mechanical awning that Delia extended when rain began to fall, and then laughed at herself for letting simple technology mesmerize her. She didn't recognize most of the people at the party, so she hung close to Sydney and Maddy. They both looked amazing, though Sydney's dress didn't quite fit, and she had to keep pulling the top up for fear of flashing the whole party.

Charles appeared with two bottles of unmarked, clear liquid.

"Moonshine," he said as he handed it to Delia. "It felt time appropriate."

"This will not make us go blind, will it?" Delia asked.

"No, ma'am, I've tried some of this vintage myself. I know a couple that shines out in Joseph."

Jenny shivered at the name, but no one seemed to notice.

"Well, this is very thoughtful. Thank you, Charles," Delia said. "Now, get yourself a plate, and when you are ready to go, I'll wrap you up a plate as well."

"Yes, ma'am," Charles said before heading toward the food with a purpose.

A few minutes later, Charles wandered over to the little knot of women with a plate of ham, deviled eggs, and celery filled with cream cheese flecked with tiny red dots. Sydney stole one, tried it, made a face, and handed it to Maddy. Maddy did the same and handed it to Jenny. Laughing, she tried it and smiled.

"Pimentos," Charles said. "Anything else you'd like to take, Sydney?"

The younger woman was still forcing herself to chew and holding a hand over her mouth. She shook her head.

"Good," Charles said, popping a deviled egg into his mouth. Once he swallowed, he turned to Jenny. "How are you feeling?"

"Much better," Jenny said. "Apparently, I've been poisoned."

"Apparently so have we all," Charles said. "But I can't say that I've ever had any adverse effects from working in there all night. Still, now that I think of it, I suppose sometimes I do get queasy now and again."

"Thank you for working tonight," Maddy said. "I guess we could take turns if you want to hang around the party longer or come back."

Charles shook his head. "No, I think a couple of hours at a shin dig is more than enough for me. I know it's a surprise to look at me, but I'm not much of a party animal."

"No, that's exactly what I would have thought," Sydney said, giving him one of her endearing looks. Jenny wondered if she was taking out her adorable, innocent wrath on him for not warning her about the pimentos.

"What would you have thought?" Nate asked, approaching with a tumbler of clear liquid.

"Moonshine?" Charles asked, nodding toward Nate's glass. The larger man nodded and lifted the tumbler.

"We were just talking about what a partier Charles is," Jenny said. She scanned the room. "Is Linds here?"

"Not yet, but I think they're on their way."

The conversation turned back to the Kusel House and its deleterious effects on them all, and before long, Linds walked through the front door wearing the most authentic tweed herringbone suit at the party. They removed a heavy overcoat, disappeared upstairs, and then reappeared a moment later. Jenny surveyed Linds from head to toe and shook her head.

"You look like an entirely different person," Jenny said.

"Thanks," Linds said. Nate raised his glass and his eyebrows. Linds nodded, and Nate headed for the bar. "Is everyone still alive?"

"Yes, despite being poisoned," Maddy said. "Where did you get that suit? It looks amazing."

"I have a friend who has a tailor. I thought I might, I don't know, get something that I could actually use for occasions."

"Well, shit," Jenny said, "You're out-classing everyone else here. I just got mine off of Amazon."

"Same," said Sydney and Maddy in unison.

When Nate returned with a drink for Linds and his own tumbler refreshed, Maddy spoke up, "You know, I learned something interesting about the Sleep Talkers from this book Delia gave me. They're old. Like, really old."

"What do you mean?" Linds said.

"So, Delia gave me a book her grandfather wrote about Lightning Falls. And they were around before radio."

"Really?" Charles said. "How so?"

"They had these platforms around town, and people would sit up in them at night and, well, talk to the ghosts."

"Fuck me," Nate said into his glass. Jenny wasn't sure if he meant anyone else to hear him.

"Ghosts?" said Sydney.

"Really?" Jenny said.

"Mhm, they would sit up at night to talk to the ghosts or spirits to keep them calm. All night. It apparently went back to when they settled the town."

"Great," Nate said, downing the rest of his drink in one gulp.

"I mean, obviously that's not what we're doing," Sydney said.

"No," Maddy said, "At least I'm not. Anyone else talking to ghosts?"

"I think I have ghosts in my house," Jenny said.

"Sure, and I saw a ghost in the cabin once," Charles said.

"Really? You believe in ghosts, Charles?" Sydney said.

"I don't know if I believe in them or not, but I saw an old man with a long brown beard walk in the front door, pick up a shovel, and walk back out. There were two feet of snow on the ground outside the door. That was in June, six or seven years ago, and there was no shovel there before he opened the front door. I thought I was going out of my mind."

"Wow," Jenny said.

"I'm going to get more of this ham. Can I get anyone anything? Pimento celery, Jennifer?" Charles asked.

"Yes, please," Jenny said.

Sydney asked if anyone else had seen ghosts, but both Linds and Nate had started paying attention to something across the room that Jenny couldn't quite pick out. When Charles returned, the music sped up, and Sydney and Maddy pulled Jenny to dance. Jenny watched Sydney's short, red hair swing from side to side, and she felt herself slipping. For a moment, it was Aurora before her, her long hair moving in slow motion. Maddy's dark eyes met Jenny's, and Jenny felt drunk. Then Maddy was gone, and Matina danced in her place, her shoulders bare, her lips dark, music and light moving her.

Please, God, help me, Jenny thought as reality jitterbugged its way back into place and painful longing yawned open within her. *Please, it hurts too much, just stop this. Stop the party, stop the world, stop the music, it's too much.*

But God let the music play.

43
Second Tour

Saturday, September 20, 2025 - Morning

LINDS, DRESSED ONLY SLIGHTLY less dapperly than they had hours earlier, biked up to the Kusel House like a European delivery person from a period piece. They wore chinos, a button-up shirt, a floppy cap, and a tweed jacket. In one hand, they clutched a paper bag with grease-stained corners. Their bike tires scattered gravel in front of the porch where Charles and Nate stood chatting while Charles smoked his pipe. Jenny sat on the porch swing, smelling the sweet aroma of the pipe. Linds propped their bike against the stair rail and smiled up at Nate.

"What's this new look?" Nate said, taking the bag from Linds.

"I don't know. I felt good last night, and I wanted to kind of keep the train rolling. Does it look bad?"

"You look amazing," Nate said. "I wish I could pull that look off."

"What did you bring us?" Charles said, reaching a hand out toward the bag.

Nate playfully slapped his hand away. "Not for you, this is my love language."

"The pastries are for everyone," Linds said. "Morning, Jenny."

"Morning. Thank you for the pastries, if we can get any inside," she said, leveling a withering look at Nate and Charles, who were having a silent battle of wills over the newly arrived sweets. Jenny ducked, reached out, and plucked the bag from behind Nate's back, where he was hiding it from the taller man.

"Damn it," Nate said, and Charles nodded approvingly.

They entered Jenny's apartment. Delia greeted them as she came out of the back with a cup of coffee. Jenny slipped past her with the bag. She returned a minute later with a serving dish full of pastries.

"I didn't buy this," she said, putting the flower-patterned plate down. "It was in the cabinets. I'm not sure I'm at my party hosting stage yet."

"I think that was Cassy's," Nate said.

"It predated her," Delia said. "I think it's been here since the '80s at least."

Nate frowned thoughtfully, snatched a chocolate croissant, and began munching. Sydney and Maddy wandered in from the back of the apartment.

"Where were you two?" Charles asked.

"Doing girl things in girl places," Sydney said, then, seeing Linds, she almost screamed. "Oh my God! You look amazing!"

"Um, thanks," Linds said, clearly unprepared for Sydney's enthusiasm so late and so early.

"Oh no, Nate, you'll never be the fanciest boy in the group again," Maddy said dryly.

"He never was," Charles said. "You sure you don't mind?" he asked Jenny, waving his smoldering pipe.

"No, I love pipes," Jenny said. "And whatever pipe tobacco you use is … I don't know, it reminds me of something, and it makes me happy. I might just have you come over and smoke in the living room every day."

"Well, I'll be sure to indulge whenever I'm here then," Charles said, clamping the stem between his teeth.

"There are candles," Maddy said. "We'll get you one. When's your birthday?"

"April," Jenny said.

"Well, there's Christmas," Sydney said.

"Wait, how do you all do Christmas?" Jenny asked.

"I sit at home with my mother and listen to John Lennon guilt-trip me," Charles said.

"And we just do ours together," Sydney said.

"I go to my parents' place and spend it with them and my sister," Linds said.

"I just wake up late and play video games," Nate said.

"I … We should do something together," Jenny said. "Like, maybe Christmas Eve or Christmas night?"

"Night would work for me," Linds said.

"And you could come over to our place in the morning," Sydney said.

A warmth that had been building in Jenny since her last migraine had passed, brimmed up and over, and she laughed out loud.

"Or not?" Sydney said, abashed.

"No, I want to do that. I was just … I don't know, happy, I guess."

The doorbell rang, and Jenny went to answer it, feeling light and full.

Mrs. Vivian Bellarmine was a tiny woman in a yellow slicker and matching hat. She wore old green galoshes, black pleated pants, and a crocheted burgundy sweater with big wooden buttons. She smiled thinly at Jenny. "Miss Berger?"

"Yes, Mrs. Bellarmine, please come in!"

The woman hurried in and doffed her cap and coat, hanging them on pegs in the hall. Jenny realized that she had spoken to her once before at the summer market when Patty had tried to make a joke about underwear.

Did I see everyone at that market? She wondered. Then, suddenly, the red-haired police officer flashed into her mind. What was his name?

"Is everyone here?" Mrs. Bellarmine asked.

"Yes, they're all inside. There are pastries and coffee if you'd like some."

"After the tour, thank you. Do you have tea?"

"Yes," Delia called from inside the apartment. "About six different kinds."

"Perfect. Well, why doesn't everyone come out here, and we can begin? Is the second apartment open?"

Everyone gathered in the foyer in front of the stairs. Jenny liked how they felt like a middle-school class, hands clasped in front of them, ready to learn.

"The building," Mrs. Bellarmine said, starting in without an introduction, "was built in 1881, a year after the stockade was taken down. The stockade was erected in 1877 during the Nez Perce War and remained through the Bannock War. Things settled down after that, so in 1880, they pulled down most of the stockade, though you can still see some of the old stone wall on the far side of Hitchman's Creek. The house was built by Elisha Kusel. Some people have asked me if his son Jeremiah helped with the building. Of course, Jeremiah was only eight at the time, so perhaps he carried a rock or two, maybe a board. But he'd do plenty of building around town after that, even if his beginnings were humble."

Here she chuckled, as if on cue. Jenny got the impression that the woman was reciting a script from memory. She spoke fast and had taken on something close to a mid-Atlantic accent.

"This front area was and remains the foyer. To the right of the front door, we have the old library where, yes, the Kusel family was found in 1948. To the left is a parlor. The house is divided down the center from front to back, which made it rather easy to convert into apartments and the radio station. Now, come with me."

She led them into Jenny's apartment and asked permission before going into her bedroom. She described the dining room as it once was, and Jenny couldn't remember if her description matched what Link had told her. Then she led into the kitchen at the back of the apartment.

"This was split in half, as it was originally large enough for feeding ten or more people regularly. Besides the family, there was a cook, gardener, and driver. Once Mr. Jeremiah Kusel became the head of the household in 1900, he endeavored to keep as many people employed at the house as possible."

"Did Elisha Kusel die?" Maddy asked, tentatively raising her hand.

"Not by 1900. That was the year Mr. and Mrs. Kusel had their first daughter, Tabitha. To give them space, Elisha and his wife, Karolina, moved to a smaller house in town."

"Oh, can we see that?" Sydney asked.

"No, it burned down in 1955, sadly. This house is the last of the Kusel family houses, proper. Though, of course, other members of the family lived in other houses around town. Those are not open to the public, however. Now, the Bakers, aptly named as Caroline Baker was the cook, were, of course, Ms. Baker's grandparents. Of course, that was not her last name when she became the cook, but fortune makes do."

Delia gave a slight bow. Sydney's mouth gaped as if Mrs. Bellarmine had just revealed Delia's secret identity as Superwoman, and Nate wore an appropriately interested expression. Charles simply nodded, as if he knew the whole story.

"There was also a gentleman named Patrick Gambol who was the driver. His family also still lives in town. You may know them. They run the record store."

Mrs. Bellarmine continued her narrative about the first floor and led them into the other apartment. It was empty of all but the most basic furnishings, which, Jenny guessed, no one had updated since the '80s. She spoke of restrained, tasteful parties and long hours worked by the three men of the household. She talked about the women's philanthropy and the businesses they invested in.

When she took the group outside, she led them through light rain to the gazebo and stood under its roof, describing the day of the double wedding, on which both Tabitha and Sharon married their respective beaus. She spoke of the small dock that jutted out into Hitchman's Creek, of which little more than a few stumps and rotten boards remained. They came back into the house and went upstairs, as she enumerated which rooms were which. Then she brought them to a locked door at the back of the main hallway.

"Oh," Sydney said. "I didn't even notice this was here!"

The hallway continued beyond the door, with two more rooms on each side.

"Wow," Jenny said, "it's huge."

"Guest rooms and the master bedroom," Mrs. Bellarmine said.

Jenny touched a doorknob and felt the world tilt as she pictured the room beyond it. A large, four-poster bed in which the parents slept jutted out into the middle of the space, with two large dressers, a vanity, two wardrobes, and an old spinning wheel in the corner, collecting dust.

"Was there no housekeeper?" Jenny asked, suddenly.

"There were several, but none stayed for more than a few years. The Kusels had a mind that their housekeepers should get an education and then find better jobs. Two went on to be journalists, one ran a small dress shop in town, and two others became secretaries and moved away."

"What about the rest?" Maddy asked, counting up years on her fingers.

"I don't know. They probably just got married and raised their children."

"So, no old chatty housekeeper to spread gossip?" Charles said, puffing his pipe.

"No, Mrs. Kusel liked them to be young, smart, and to keep them moving. Pardon me, Ms. Berger."

Jenny stepped back from the door she had been touching and felt a thrill of panic as Mrs. Bellarmine unlocked it. Confusingly, part of her was terrified that the room would look exactly as she had pictured it and part was afraid it wouldn't. Mrs. Bellarmine flipped on the light, and Jenny froze in the doorway.

A four-poster bed jutted into the middle of a room with two dressers, two wardrobes, and a vanity. And in the corner, a sheet lay over a shape that suggested an old spinning wheel.

"What the f…." She let the words out in a breath.

"What's the matter?" Linds asked, stepping up behind her.

"I … Sorry, serious déjà vu."

"Interesting," Linds said. "Do you get that a lot here?"

"No, never before now," Jenny said.

"Interesting," Linds said again.

Jenny entered the room and felt a sudden jolt of longing. Unable to stop herself, she walked over to the object in the corner and pulled the sheet from it.

A small table with an old vase and photographs appeared in a cloud of dust.

"Please don't pull things apart," Mrs. Bellarmine said.

"Sorry, I … I didn't mean to," Jenny said, letting the sheet drift back down over the table.

That doesn't look like a spinning wheel at all, Jenny thought, studying the outline of the frames and vase under the draped white cloth. Sydney cooed over the vanity, and Delia joined her. Maddy sidled up next to Jenny.

"You okay?"

"Yeah, just having a ghosty moment, I think."

Maddy nodded and took Jenny's hand. Jenny looked down at their intertwined fingers and smiled. The brimming warmth rose again and righted the tilting world.

Their guide led them up a narrow set of stairs to the attic, where they found dozens of old boxes.

"The township uses this for storage, though there are some of the family's old things still here. Records, books, old toys, silverware."

"Clothes?" Maddy asked.

"No. All of the family's clothing was destroyed. There was some fear of contamination immediately after their deaths. That, of course, turned out to be incorrect."

"All of their clothing?" Jenny asked.

"Every last piece," Mrs. Bellarmine said.

"I—Wait, you had some clothing at your booth during the summer market. Was that—"

"No, those belonged to a woman named Constance Lister who passed away in the 1940s. Her family donated some of her clothing to the local museum since they were one of the founding families of Lightning Falls."

"It seems weird to have your clothes on display for everyone a hundred years after you wear them," Sydney said, considering her own outfit. She was wearing ripped jeans and a white cami under a white lace, long-sleeved shirt. Jenny tried to picture the outfit on a mannequin a hundred years in the future. It made her sad to think that all someone might know about Sydney was an outfit.

"Did they burn the bedding and curtains as well?" Charles asked.

"Yes, every piece of cloth in the house. It was all done poorly, however, since there was no infection, only a carbon monoxide leak, which I guess you all know about now." Everyone chuckled. "Would you like to see the basement?"

"Is there any history down there?" Sydney asked, rubbing her arms.

"Well, no, except that you can see where they had the boiler that leaked."

"It's strange that there's a basement, isn't it?" Delia asked. "Not many houses here have basements."

"If they were built before 1940, they do," Mrs. Bellarmine said. "But you also can't dig that deep here; the soil is only three or three and a half feet deep before you hit bedrock. They took the earth they dug and put it around the foundation, building it up a bit to give them a full floor below ground. That's why there's a slope down from the house to the creek."

Everyone except Linds, Nate, and Charles passed on seeing the basement. Jenny had already seen it, and no one else found it particularly riveting. By the time the party returned from the depths, Jenny had tea brewing for Mrs. Bellarmine. They all sat in the living room, munched pastries, and sipped hot drinks.

"Are there ghosts here?" Maddy asked Mrs. Bellarmine, glancing briefly at Jenny.

"Oh yes," the older woman said. "I've seen a few."

"Really?" Sydney asked.

"Indeed. I believe I've seen Mrs. Kusel twice over the years, and pardon me for saying so, Ms. Baker, but I think I've seen your grandfather as well, in the garden."

Delia frowned thoughtfully. "Did he say anything?"

"No, I was in the kitchen in the other apartment, not this one, and I was looking out the back window on a bright summer day. I thought, 'My goodness, that garden is in bloom,' which was a surprise because I had only ever seen it in a state of overgrowth, and then he popped his head up, shears in hand, smiling and waving. Well, I waved back and then went out to see who it was. When I opened the back door, the garden was in an entirely different state of affairs, and there was no one there."

"Hm," Charles said into his coffee cup.

"Jenny saw someone in the mirror!" Sydney said excitedly.

"Oh?" Mrs. Bellarmine said.

"It was nothing. It was my first morning here. I thought I saw someone else's eyes. I just—I was adjusting. It was nothing like what you described."

Mrs. Bellarmine seemed like she was concentrating, trying to remember something. Then she shook her head. "No, that bathroom wasn't there back then, and I don't know of anyone else who's seen something in a mirror. Was there anything else to it?"

"Not at all," Jenny said. Then she thought of the men in the basement and decided not to say anything.

"Maybe you should change what you read," Delia said, holding up *The Shaded Lane.*

"Moat? Interesting," Linds said.

"Yeah, I like him a lot. Why? Do you read him?"

Linds and Nate shared a quick look. "I used to. I don't anymore. Hits a little too close to home."

Jenny smiled and said, "Oh, really? What about you, Nate? Do you read horror?"

Nate shook his head. "No, I'm a *Twilight* kind of guy."

"Really?" Sydney asked. Jenny thought she seemed half-bemused and half-skeptical.

"No," Nate said. "I like history, like—"

"World War Two," Linds and Jenny said together.

"Yeah, I like World War Two, among other things," Nate said defensively. "I like reading about rockets, too."

"That's so dad of you," Sydney said before jumping up and disappearing down the hallway.

"Just what I like to hear," Nate said, scratching his beard self-consciously.

Volume 10, Issue 79, Sunday, September 21, 2025

The Jazz Age

By Keith Lowry, Ed. In Chief.

I KNOW IT WILL surprise some of my youngest readers, but I was not alive in the 1920s. I didn't get to see the victory of Women's Suffrage. I didn't witness America marvel at the rise of automobiles, movie theaters, or radio. I didn't get to hear Jazz in its first blush or read the first editions of F. Scott Fitzgerald's works. It would be decades before I first read *Bernice Bobs Her Hair*, and even longer before I think I understood it.

I wasn't there for all of that, but golly, I wish I had been.

Before we started focusing on only the bad parts of our history, Americans tended to look back to the 1950s as the best decade of the 20th century. The Korean War happened, but that didn't cast nearly the shadow over our nation that Vietnam would in the '60s and '70s. People liked Ike, housing was affordable, and children expected that they'd do better than their parents had. Yes, there was racism and Jim Crow, and the Ruskies had the bomb. All of those things are terrible, and I wouldn't try to even hint that they weren't. Yes, America had a lot of growing up to do (and we still do). But there was a sense of hope, a sense that the future would be better than the present. And, of course, you can't have that hope without acknowledging that the present has its problems.

But for my money, the '20s are the decade I would have liked to have lived through the most. Yes, there was prohibition and the evils that came with it, and yes, that great evil of racism was perhaps even more present than it would be in the '50s. But, even so ... the art! The architecture! The burgeoning innovations! The music! Who wouldn't want to experience that?

I'm not a man who believes that the music of his youth is the best music ever made. I do think that some great muse breathed her spirit upon rock, folk, and blues in the late '60s in a way that has left us all wishing she'd come back. But I don't think that it was the greatest music ever made. I suppose if I had to pin that down, I'd have to look to the most obvious, and perhaps most boring answer, and say that that honor broods on the work of another muse-beloved man by the name of Beethoven. But for the 20th century, give me Jazz. Not the strange experimental stuff that is only accessible to the most secretly initiated, but the raw, swinging music of the clubs when people still wore suits to go out and enjoy themselves.

It's great to dance to, drink to, and smoke to. And, depending on the piece and the partner, it's pretty good to do some kissing to, as well.

Now, I didn't get a chance to experience all that jazz firsthand, but I did get to dress up and go to a party on Friday night hosted by perhaps our greatest local party-thrower, Delia Baker, who runs Baker's Books. And while I was there, I saw, ate, and drank things that made me long for those heady days of hope and prosperity. I saw art like we don't make anymore—as a culture, as a movement. I saw clothing that was both sexy and artistic, and it further undermined that lie that less is always more.

But most of all, it brought into focus the fact that I have never been to a '90s party or an aughts party. I don't think there will be 2020s parties fifty years from now. I do think that people will still be having 1920s parties, though, well into the next century, because there's something still so wonderful about it all. So, I don't know what Delia has planned for her next soirée, but I'm putting my vote in for next year to do this again. It's nice to take a little trip into the past, even for one evening, to remember what was good and bring a little of it into the present.

44
Such a Sweet Thing

Monday, September 22, 2025 - Evening

ADVICE DOMINATED THE CONVERSATION at Cinder's Remorse as the Sleep Talkers gathered for dinner before Jenny's first night in the fire-tower.

"The baseboard heat does a great job, sometimes too great," Charles said. "It can feel like an oven. But if you turn it down, you're freezing."

"There isn't really anywhere to go when it's cold, so you definitely end up feeling more cooped up than anywhere else. Even in the cabin, there are two other rooms you can go in," Maddy said.

"The High Path is super windy," Sydney said. "Wear layers."

"During the winter, it's ridiculous; you'll feel really penned in. It's pretty great during the summer, though," Nate said.

Only Linds remained silent as the group talked about the pitfalls of working in the tower between bites of burgers, salads, and flatbreads. In the corner of the bar, a young man with a guitar strummed slow versions of old pop hits.

"The walk up can be a pain in the ass," Maddy said. "So, give yourself a little time."

"Maybe you'll love it," Nate said. "And you'll want to always be in the tower."

"He said disinterestedly," Charles said.

"Who am I to keep someone from their favorite tower?" Nate said, and the men laughed. Jenny shook her head. She thought she might be glad to help Nate never have to trudge his way up to the tower again, or at least make his journeys up there fewer.

The young man with the guitar finished his song and said something to the patrons that Jenny didn't catch. Then, before he touched his guitar again, he let out a breathy, longing, "Ahhh," followed by three pairs of chords. It took Jenny a moment before her memory summoned the name of the song: Crimson and Clover. Sydney's eyes went wide.

"I *love* this song, dance with me!"

Maddy glanced from her burger to her greasy hands to her crumpled dirty napkin. Then, smiling apologetically, she stole Jenny's. Hands cleaned, she and Sydney walked out into a little, open space between the tables and danced slowly. Jenny watched and longed. She wasn't sure whether she longed for one of the women, or both of them, or to just dance like that with someone who loved her as much as they loved each other.

"Come on," Nate said. Jenny peered up, about to decline the invitation, but Nate was not extending his hand to her.

"That's how you ask someone to dance with you?" Linds asked.

"No," Nate said. "That's how I ask *you* to dance."

Linds shrugged, took Nate's hand, and joined the dancing pair.

"Do you expect me to ask you to dance?" Charles said, staring at Jenny over the rim of his glass.

"No," Jenny said. "But I've just decided that I'm going to ask you."

"Well, that seems very fine," Charles said. He folded his napkin, put it on his plate, and stood.

He held her confidently, and his cologne—something masculine and sweet—tickled her nose. He was a good eight inches taller than her, and she could feel how fit he was through his dress shirt. She wondered how he stayed in shape as he led her in something that reminded her less of the middle-school slow dance that Nate and Linds were acting out, space between them as they stepped awkwardly left and right, and more of something she'd seen in the movies. They fell into a box-step, and Charles smiled.

"You're a good dancer," he said.

"I have no idea how," Jenny said. "I've never done this before."

"You've never danced? Or you've never slow-danced?"

"I've done both, but it was a lot more like them," Jenny said, nodding at Sydney and Maddy pressed body to body, heads on each other's shoulders, as if they were two people in a snowstorm, huddling together against the cold and sneaking kisses to warm themselves.

"Well, you're a natural," Charles said and pulled her a little closer.

For a moment, Jenny felt scandalized and thrilled. What would people think? She imagined the other patrons in Cinder's Remorse commenting on the differences in their skin colors, women whispering behind napkins, men frowning disapprovingly over their whiskies. The thought felt foreign, slipping in from some strange pit in her mind. Lightning Falls was an overwhelmingly white town, but she had never seen or experienced anything that would make her think that their dance would scandalize the town's citizens. She also realized that she had never asked Delia what her experience was like in town.

She tried to tell her mind to shut up and enjoy the dance, but she suddenly felt self-conscious and guilty. She closed her eyes, trying to block the thoughts out and just enjoy the moment with a man whom she thought might end up being a good friend one day. And, through brute force, she managed to focus on the flow and feeling of the moment. Nothing about Charles drew her back to her old life; nothing about him made her think of the terrible things that had happened to her. In his arms, under the canopy of the song, she allowed herself to be present. And, though the young man drew the song out, it ended too soon.

"Thank you," Jenny said, giving what was perhaps her first curtsey.

Charles laughed and bowed. "And you. It's been a while."

"Well, you were fabulous," Jenny said.

"You all danced!" Sydney said, trotting up to them, ready to burst.

"Everyone, please, a hand for our amazing Sleep Talkers."

Jenny froze at the guitar player's amplified voice. She felt herself blush as a round of polite applause rolled across the room. Sydney turned and raised her hands in an ostentatious wave. Maddy, Charles, and Nate all responded less theatrically, but still acknowledged the crowd. Linds gave a perfunctory nod and a swish of their hand. Jenny felt unable to move.

"She's shy," Nate said, putting his arm around Jenny, and laughter replaced the sparse clapping. Nate led her back to the table.

"What was that?" Jenny asked.

"You don't know? We're kind of famous," Sydney said.

"'Famous' is a strong word," Charles said.

Jenny glanced around the room. People were looking over at them and smiling. She wanted to crawl under the table.

"They're all staring at us," Jenny said, feeling old, familiar anxiety push its way up and into her chest.

"Yes," Linds said. "But they won't for long. They know who we are, especially as a group, but we'll fade into the background soon enough."

Linds was right. The musician played a passable rendition of "Across the Universe," and one of an Elvis song that Jenny didn't know the name of. When he took a break, Jenny surveyed the room and found no one taking any interest in her table.

"You okay?" Nate asked.

"Sorry, I just—That was weird. Not, like, terrible, just weird. I know I feel like we're a little clique or whatever, but I guess I really kind of felt like that was an internal thing. You know, like any group of friends or people who work together. I didn't really think about everyone else seeing us as a group from the outside."

"We go into their houses every night," Charles said. "We are something old, something that barely exists anymore. We are like stylites, sitting on our posts, speaking into the night."

"Stylites?" Sydney asked.

"Holy people," Charles said, "at the periphery of the community, up on their poles looking up and down."

"Well, I'm not holy," Jenny said.

"In the most ancient sense of the word, you are. The holy was that which was set apart, separate from everything else. We are set apart, alone in our towers, and yet in everyone's homes. They know us, but we don't really know them."

Jenny frowned, uncertain of what she thought about Charles's take, and not sure if she had her own. She surveyed the people at the table and saw the group anew, not just as a group she was part of, but as something within the town, a community that had its own identity before her and would remain after her. She pictured it changing over time, person by person, a new dynamic forming every few years.

A regular Ship of Theseus.

Jenny frowned as the unfamiliar thought bubbled up, and she wondered if she had heard the term somewhere.

45
Third Tour

Monday, September 22, 2025 - Evening

BY A QUARTER AFTER seven, the sun was already down; Jenny was glad to have Linds at her side as she started off for the tower. The rain that had peppered the town all day had finally relented, and they walked among dripping awnings and signs under a cloudy, dark sky. Their feet splashed in puddles while Linds' bike made a pleasant, low ticking sound as it rolled.

"So, which is your favorite tower to work in?" Jenny asked as they were passing under the Mist's marquee.

"I guess if I'm being honest, I don't really like any of them," Linds said. "But if someone made me pick … I don't know, the fire-tower, I guess."

"Really? Huh. The house's room is so nice."

Linds shrugged. "The house just feels wrong to me. Maybe it would feel better if I weren't always alone there. But it just feels kind of, you know, creepy. Does it feel like that to you?"

"It did at first," Jenny said. "But not really anymore. Of course, I'm not really alone a lot now. But yeah, it's definitely better when other people are around. What's it like living next to Nate?"

"He snores loud enough that I can hear it in my apartment, but otherwise it's kind of like living next to anyone. There's good and bad. It's nice to have someone water my plants when I'm not there, and to bring in my junk mail. And it's nice to be able to help him out when I can. I don't think I'd like living next to a stranger as much, so I guess it's more good than bad."

"I wish I had someone in the apartment next to me," Jenny said.

"Well, I lucked out with Nate. We'll probably end up living near each other forever unless he decides to finally start dating again."

"Why doesn't he date?"

"Trauma."

"God, if that were the case, I'd be a monk for the rest of my life."

Linds nodded slowly. "Well, you might ask Sydney about her—"

"What about the Cabin? What don't you like about that?" Jenny said.

Linds stopped and put their hand on Jenny's arm. "Hey, look, I don't want to be weird or rude or anything, but I've been meaning to ask you about something. Has anything strange been going on with you? I mean, other than getting sick."

Jenny stopped and stared at Linds. Jenny thought they looked concerned, but she found it hard to read Linds.

"I mean … yeah," Jenny said. "A lot of weird stuff. That whole thing at Cinder's Remorse was pretty weird."

"No, I guess, I mean … uncanny. Like, spooky stuff. Have you … I don't know, been seeing any dark, robed figures lurking in the shadows, or maybe been visiting an old gothic dark city in your dreams?"

Jenny felt her mouth hang open as she racked her brain for an answer. She had had strange dreams, but she couldn't remember any about a dark city. No, wait, wasn't there one? One with something strange about the lights. She couldn't remember.

"No robed figures," she said.

Suddenly, she was back in the canoe, paddling, and a figure stood on the bank, dark fabric hanging from his form, a lantern held high, his mouth writhing with worms.

"You sure? You looked like—"

"No, sorry, just a weird fantasy I had as a kid. It's a coping mechanism. I haven't seen any robed men."

"Okay, well, that's weird, right? What's the fantasy?"

"It's just a thing my brain does because of something horrible that happened to me. It's not something I really want to talk about."

"Okay," Linds said, nodding. "So, no more ghosts? No dark cities?"

"I don't know. I think I saw one more ghost that I didn't tell anyone about, or like a pair of them. But it was just something out of the corner of my eye. Two guys in the basement. Neither of them was wearing a robe; they looked totally normal. One was in a suit, the other, I don't know, just a shirt and pants. And yeah, maybe I had one dream about a city. And I'm going to say right now that that's fucking weird that you're asking about a dream I had, and I might actually have had it. What the hell does that mean?"

Linds shook their head. "I'm not sure. It's just—I've seen some really weird shit, and, well, some of the stuff that you're saying on the radio when you've been kind of out of your mind sounds familiar to me."

"Out of my mind?" Jenny heard sudden anger creep into her own voice, but she wasn't sure why. Linds was right. She had gone out of her mind a couple of times.

"Yeah, sorry, what would you call it?" Linds asked.

"I don't know. I think I'd call it 'carbon monoxide,' and 'being super stressed out and dealing with trauma you couldn't understand.' I get that

Nate has trauma; everyone has trauma. But I don't think most people's damage quite measures up to what I've been through."

"I think I unders—"

"No, you couldn't." The anger bubbled up from somewhere, and she couldn't understand it. She felt like she was a bystander to her own growing rage. She wasn't angry at Linds. Nothing Linds had said should make her angry. Yet here it was, gushing up and out. "And I'm trying to adjust to this new situation, and I guess trying to find a place where I don't feel constantly judged—somewhere I feel at home, you know? I would have thought that if anyone would understand something like that, it would be you."

"Why would I understand that?" Linds asked, staring at Jenny. "Wait, do you think that I just go around being judged by people because I'm … Do you think that the fact that I identify like I do or that I'm not interested in sex affects most of my interactions with people?"

Jenny thought about her own social interactions and shrugged.

"You'd be surprised how little it comes up," Linds said. "Even with the people who probably think I should fuck off and just be a girly girl. Most of them just treat me like anyone else, too."

"I—" Jenny started, realizing that she had a heap of assumptions about Linds that she hadn't tested because she'd never sat down alone together and talked. She had made such easy connections with Sydney and Maddy that she had projected that easy relationship onto everyone in the group. But Linds had been distant, and Jenny had been okay with that.

"I'm sorry," Jenny said, trying to rationalize her reaction. "I think I got defensive because … Did you know I was in a mental health facility before I came here?" Linds shook their head. "I was. It was called 'Sunrise.' I guess I got kind of triggered because you asked if I'm going crazy."

"I didn't ask if you were going crazy," Linds said, keeping their eyes on Jenny. "I asked if anything strange has been going on with you other than the times when you clearly aren't yourself. That's strange enough in itself, you know? People don't just start talking differently and forgetting what happened for hours at a time just because they're having a hard time. Or because they got carbon monoxide poisoning. It's strange. So, I'm asking if there are other strange things on top of the already obviously strange things."

Jenny recognized the reasonableness of Linds's words, but her anger and hurt bubbled back up and stuck themselves to the parts they could twist. Again, she felt like the words flowed out of a part of her she didn't know. "I resent the idea that I'm strange because I deal with things differently. I probably have brain damage, okay? You have no idea what's happened to me."

"What do you mean?" Linds asked.

"I mean I died." The words reverberated in her ears, tripling back on themselves like an echo in a tiny room. She felt wild, unhinged, both distant from herself and infinitely close to her pain. In the strange vertigo of the echo, she struggled to remember how she died. Her memory of the terrible event was confused and hidden, folding back on itself.

Someone I love killed me.

No, someone I didn't know killed me.

No, it was someone I love. And they killed the people I loved.

Yes. Yes, they did.

The words hummed in her mind, blurred and twisted. She blinked. She blinked. The world and her memories snapped back into focus.

"I drowned. A man held me underwater until I stopped breathing, and then he pulled me out and gave me CPR. I don't know how long I was dead for, but I was dead. And now I can't remember shit. I can't remember anything about this town—"

"You're not the only one who can't—" Linds tried.

"And now I'm having episodes. I should go to the doctor, I guess, but I don't have health insurance right now, and—"

"You make enough that it doesn't make any sense that you can't get—"

"Shut up. Just shut the fuck up!" Jenny said, losing control again. She heard Patty's voice in her own, and she froze, scared by her sudden outburst. She felt her eyes go wide and her hands slap themselves over her mouth. The fountain of anger—was that Patty's legacy to her?—collapsed in her mortification. "Oh God, I'm sorry. I'm so sorry. I don't know why I'm so upset right now. I'm … I just …"

Linds peered at Jenny passively, unfazed. "It's okay," Linds said. "I'm sorry I asked the question like that. I was wrong."

"No," Jenny said, feeling the cavity where her anger had been filling with embarrassment and shame. "I'm so sorry. You don't have to walk the rest of the way up with me. I wouldn't blame you if—"

"What? No," Linds said. "Look, I know I say shit wrong. My sister tells me that all the time. I'm kind of bad at the whole easing into sensitive topics thing. And I know you don't believe it, but I've been fucked up too. Unlike you, I really can't tell anyone about what happened to me."

"No one?" Jenny asked.

"My sister knows, and this guy who was part of it knows, and Nate knows a little, but that's it."

"You don't have any other friends who know?" Jenny asked.

"I did, but they're … gone," Linds said. Jenny watched as Linds's face contorted, holding back tears.

"I had friends, too. They're gone too. I'm really sorry," Jenny said. She wanted to hug Linds, but they didn't look like they'd appreciate the gesture. Instead, they just nodded.

"Come on," Linds said, wiping their eyes, "I should show you the tower."

They retreated into small talk as they reached the edge of town and started through the pines toward the creek. Linds talked about how they had moved to Lightning Falls with their parents a few years earlier.

"It's a nice house, but four adults in one place is too many," Linds said as they crossed Kussel Bridge, talking loudly so Jenny could hear them over the rush of the falls upstream.

"Why here?" Jenny asked as they reached the far side, where stones lined the path, birds called in the darkness, and the trees moved around them in a relentless, restless rustle.

"My mom … She wanted to live in Washington. She had some idea that it would be perfect for us. But the first place we rented didn't feel right, and the second place was too busy, and the third place—"

"How long were you in Washington?"

"Six months. We kept moving. She kept losing her damn mind everywhere we went. We kind of thought she might have actually lost it for real. But then we drove down here for a long weekend, well, not here, but to Lake Wallowa. Anyway, we passed the turn off, and she got all excited and wanted to see the waterfall."

"How did she—"

"The invisible sign."

Jenny shook her head.

"None of us saw it but her, but she *really* saw it, if that makes any sense. She made Tom, my dad, stop and turn around. Even when he did, and we were sitting like twenty feet from it, it still took us all a minute to actually see it sitting there in the shrubs."

"I don't understand. Is the sign old?"

"You don't remember? Oh, right, sorry, your memory thing. Apparently, it's a town joke. The sign that's supposed to let people know we're here is impossible for a lot of people to see. People just drive past over and over, searching for the turn-off, and they swear they never see a sign. It's strange. But it's there, and I can attest that you can stare at it and not see it. I have no idea why."

Jenny studied Linds under the moonless sky, phones lighting their way, casting campfire flashlight shadows onto their face. Jenny couldn't read their expression, but she didn't think that Linds's claim of ignorance sounded genuine.

"And she fell in love with it?" Jenny asked. "The town, I mean."

"Yeah, right away. I kind of knew she would. We come from a small town in the woods, so it made sense. The fact that Main Street is pretty well stocked, and the fact that there's a coffee shop here, and that there's almost no traffic, yeah, she pretty much wanted to move here right away. Of course, that hasn't stopped her from buying other houses."

"Wow, must be nice."

"We got kind of a huge settlement because of what happened to our house. And my parents had some other money, and—Yeah, anyway, they bought a place down in Enterprise and one in Joseph."

"Why?" Jenny asked.

"Honestly, I have no idea. Maybe to rent? Right now, they're both kind of empty. My sister is squatting in one."

Jenny gave an interested "hmm," not sure of what else to say.

The trail that led to the High Path was treacherous in the dark. Divots in the dirt threatened to grab the toe of her shoe, and stray rocks promised to trip her if she wasn't careful. Branches reached out to snag her shirt and hair or slap her in the face. The steep climb got her heart pumping, and despite the frigid wind, Jenny was sweating by the time they reached the top of the rise where the path split. To her right, the trail went higher up onto Wayne Butte and the old Outpost ruin. To her left, the path followed the ridge that overlooked the town below. She hadn't come up here since she had searched for Carson Booth with Phil and Leddy.

Linds led the way. "It's pretty flat from here, except for the stairs."

"How does Nate do this with his knee?" Jenny asked.

"He has hiking poles that he keeps at the cabin," Linds said. "But yeah, I'm not sure how much longer he can do it. I wish he'd take better care of himself; I think that would make it easier for him."

"I'd think all the walking would help."

"Honestly," Linds said, fishing for keys in their pocket, "it's not that much. Check your watch one day. I don't think I get 10,000 steps most days unless I try. Of course, I'm usually biking, so it's going to be less.

Still, it's a small town, and it doesn't take much to walk around Main Street and out to the cabin or your house. It's only another, what, ten or twelve minutes to get here? And that's mostly because it's uphill. Here we are."

Jenny stopped short, almost running into a chain-link fence. Linds unlocked a gate, swung it open, and waved for Jenny to go first.

"I have questions," Jenny said as Linds closed the gate behind them and locked it. They propped their bike up against the fence. "First, am I supposed to have a set of those?"

"Yeah, did Link not get you one?"

"Nope," Jenny said.

"You can borrow mine for this week, then, or I'll get the other set from Link."

"Thanks," Jenny said, following Linds towards a large, dark shape. Her flashlight traced four steel legs that grew up from the rocky earth and leaned in toward each other, meeting twenty or more feet above them in an amorphous blob against the black sky.

"I didn't think it would be this dark out here," Jenny said. "I know that's ridiculous, but ..."

"The house is a lot more, I don't know, *normal* than the other stations. This is a fire-watch tower they built for double-use in the '30s. So, technically, when you're up here, your second job is scanning for fires."

"Ominous," Jenny said.

"I saw one once, last summer. You have to call it in. There are instructions on the wall. So, it's different like that. Also, other people staff this place during the day. There are a few hours when no one is up here. So, if you're a secret arsonist, that's your window, from six to eight in the mornings and evenings."

"I'll keep that in mind," Jenny said, following Linds up the metal staircase that wrapped its way around the tower. "Why is it locked?"

"Hm?"

"Like, why the fence? Does it go all the way around?" Jenny asked.

"Yeah, a full perimeter mostly to keep out vandalism. The tower is in kind of a shitty position where it's far enough out of town that no one can see it most of the time, but not so far out of town that kids won't come here."

"I thought someone was here most of the time," Jenny said.

Linds smiled in the ghoul-light of their phones. "Wait until you're up there. An army could surround this thing, and you'd never see them.

Visibility out toward town is great, but visibility straight down is terrible, at least at night. So, people could kind of do whatever they want down here while you're up there, and you'd never know."

"And the gate stops them?" Jenny said, glancing back at the way they came and feeling suddenly uneasy.

"You probably couldn't see it, but the fence is eight feet tall. And there's barbed wire at the top."

"That seems like overkill to stop kids from spray painting things."

"Well, it also ends the High Path," Linds said as they reached the top step. They produced their keys again and stepped up onto a metal catwalk. "The path used to go all the way to the top of the falls, but people would get hurt up there, or jump off and get hurt or killed."

"Wow, people are stupid. They'd just jump off?"

Linds flipped the light on. "I've heard a lot of kids did it before they put the fence up."

For a second, Jenny had a flashing memory of falling through space, water spraying her back, her legs straight down, her fingers pinching her nose.

"When did they put the fence up?"

"I'm not sure, in the late '80s, I think. Before either of us was born." Linds stepped into a large, rectangular room. Windows ran along the top halves of the walls above wood paneling. The floor was metal with three thick rugs covering most of it; only the area immediately around the central desk was bare.

"Broadcast board is there," Linds said, pointing to the center of the wall opposite the door. "Records there, refrigerator, hot-plate, microwave, cabinets." They pointed to the left of the broadcast desk and followed the wall to the corner and around along the left-hand wall. They stepped deeper into the room and turned to point at the wall to the left of the doorway. "Radio, same kind you have at the house, map of the area."

Jenny followed and surveyed the radio, map, and a bulletin board laden with flyers, business cards, and old typed letters hung with pushpins.

Linds continued on the other side of the door. "Nightstand and lamp, bed"—then around to the last wall—"books, TV with antenna since there's no cable up here, VCR, DVD, and an old Xbox." They returned to the broadcast table. "Record player, phone, etc. The heat is baseboard, and the thermostat is there, next to the door. Drop your bag down and come back down. I'll show you the bathroom and the generator."

Linds showed Jenny the small cinderblock outhouse, which thankfully had its own light, though Linds warned her to still check for spiders and snakes. The generator was near one of the tower's legs, under a metal awning on two thick and two thin wooden posts. Linds demonstrated turning it on with the turn of a key and a few button presses.

"The manual is upstairs in a drawer in the desk. All the manuals are, even for the TV. In case you don't know how to use a TV."

"Thanks," Jenny said as she walked Linds back toward the gate.

"No problem," Linds said, pulling their bike's handlebars out from the chain links. "If you have any questions or problems, let me or Nate know. And, by the way, you won't need nearly as much of a tour for the cabin. It's a three-room cabin with indoor plumbing, so you'll be good. There are water bottles in the fridge and some granola bars if your lunch doesn't hold you over."

"Thanks again," Jenny said, trying two different keys before getting the right one for the gate. Linds stood on their peddles, put their helmet on, and flipped on a headlamp.

"Good luck tonight, it can get stuffy in there," Linds said. They waved, and without another word, Linds was peddling down the path fast enough to make Jenny anxious. Then, swallowed by the darkness, Linds was gone. Shivering under a cold wind, Jenny locked the gate, visited the outhouse, and then hurried up the stairs to get ready.

46
Settings

Monday, September 22, 2025 - Night

JENNY ALTERNATED BETWEEN SWEATING and freezing.

Well, she thought, *at least everyone was honest with me.*

The baseboard heating in the tower seemed to have only two settings: full blast and off. She grabbed a hoodie from her backpack and pulled it down over her T-shirt, ten minutes after she turned the heat off for the third time. This would have been the perfect time for her new sweater, but she hadn't been able to find it since she had her last migraine. She would have to dig through the closet next to her hamper again before she saw Barry next. She didn't want to admit she lost his gift. Not that he'd care, Jenny realized. He'd just be glad she had gotten some use out of it.

Within ten minutes of her donning the hoodie, her breath formed faint clouds.

God, what is it like up here in the winter?

The windows started to fog over. Jenny switched on a dehumidifier that sat in the corner. It seemed to keep the humidity at bay when the heat was on, though it didn't do much when the temperature dropped between sauna sessions. It wasn't until two hours in that she found a happy medium by keeping the heat on and cracking the door.

Having the door open also opened some mental barrier against going outside. She slipped in and out of the booth during her breaks and walked around the catwalk to look down at Lightning Falls. The town's lights lay below her as she leaned over the railing and remembered how she used to lean out of her bedroom window in Patty's house. Back then, she could only see the east side of town from her third-floor perch; now she commanded a view of the nearly perfect grid of the town's crisscrossing streets. Main Street ran like a thread of light through the town's center. Off to her right, mostly hidden by the pines, the Kusel House stood alone to the south. And, though she couldn't see them in the distant night, she pictured mountains rolling in successive peaks and valleys out thirty-five miles to the Snake River and the Idaho border.

Over the scene, the falls rumbled to the south, loud enough that Jenny imagined the spray misting up to her. She considered hiking to the top of the falls after sunrise to get a view blocked off to most people by the fence. But, after a quick check of her phone, she discovered that the sun wouldn't come up until well after she left for the diner.

I guess I'm walking home in the dark, Jenny thought. That was a new idea, and one that brought with it a complex of uncomfortable possibilities. The forecast called for more rain around the time she'd be plodding back down the High Path. That seemed inconvenient enough. But what about when it snowed? Would she have to dig her way out? That would be impossible.

I'll be gone before then.

The thought echoed in her mind like the others had, but it felt more like a memory. Had she left Lightning Falls in the autumn? She didn't think so, but it was fuzzy. She had hitched a ride out on Route 3 from a truck driver. She remembered him, a chubby man with a week's worth of stubble and an old flannel shirt. He had been fifty, maybe, and kind. He hadn't offered to trade his pleasure for a ride; she had. She could remember that part. It had been chilly, and she was wearing a coat. She had slid into the seat and introduced herself. He offered her his hand, dry and calloused.

And then I offered him mine, Jenny thought, laughing at herself. She remembered almost everything about the interaction, and how the man kept insisting that she didn't have to. Jenny couldn't remember why she had made the offer in the first place, and why she had insisted that she wanted to. Had she? She hadn't found him remotely attractive, but he hadn't disgusted her either. She remembered not caring one way or the other about the act, only the look of disbelief on his face when she went through with it.

Had that been in the autumn? She thought it was spring, but other than that exchange, and the other men who drove her across the state, only one of whom she repeated the exchange with, everything about leaving Lightning Falls was a blur.

She tried to retrieve her earliest memory after the journey. She remembered the hostel in Portland with eight bunk beds to a room. She remembered a guy with a shaved head and a woman with a tattered backpack. She had had enough money to stay for a month, and she had gotten lucky with a job at a coffee shop. Then her first roommates, a strange, silent girl who was obsessed with anime and a guy who was never at their apartment. She couldn't remember their names, but she didn't think that was because of her memory loss. They weren't memorable; they had just been there.

She wondered if there were people in her world now who would be unmemorable. Would she sit here in this tower ten years from now and try to recall someone's name that she now took for granted?

I'll be gone before then.

The thought kept coming back. Maybe she would be. She pictured her friends and shook her head. No, the desire to leave was a remnant—a relic from her youth in Lightning Falls. It was a Pavlovian response to the town. Lightning Falls was, to Jenny, the place you wanted to leave. But why? What was out in the world that she was looking for? What would she have out there that she couldn't have here?

Nothing. Everything I ever needed was always right here. But it doesn't matter. I always go.

Jenny shook her head again at the thought that felt both foreign and familiar. She faded the music down, hoping that her intrusive thoughts were wrong.

September 24, 2025

Oh, hi there, Diary! It's been a few days! So, how are you? I'm better, thanks. No more migraines now that they've fixed that pesky poison gas leak in the house. You know, the same one that killed 4 people 80 years ago? I mean, probably not the exact same one, right? They put new carbon monoxide sensors in. I guess they hadn't tested the old ones for years. So, that's super safe, now, right?

I'll be honest, I didn't think it was carbon monoxide at first. I remember what that's like. Super killer headache, but it didn't give me an actual migraine. Still, "the proof of the pudding is in the eating," as someone's English great-grandmother used to say.

Um, my first week at the fire-watch tower is going well. It sucks having to walk out and back in the dark, but I keep reminding myself that I don't have to do it for another two weeks after Friday morning. Though I feel bad for Sydney, who will be there this week- end. I wonder how long us being synced up like that will last. Wait, maybe I'm confusing myself. Week one, I was home, and Syd was there on the weekend. Week two, I was home, but that was a fluke, and then Maddy was there on the weekend. Syd was in the cabin in week two. Week three, I'm in the tower, so is she, and Charles will be at the house this weekend. THAT will be interesting!

So, what, then? I'm in the cabin next week, and then Charles is in the cabin next weekend? Then I'm back in the house and so is Syd. I'm so confused. I guess they aren't on the same rotation as we are. Do we even stay on this rotation? I feel like I should put some clever math equations in the margins, like that meme with the blond guy whose eyes go wide, and all the numbers fly across his face.

Anyway! Time for bed, this sexy lady is tuckered out. I need to get up in seven hours, go run this breakfast/dinner off, and then get ready for another dinner/breakfast and do it all over again. The hum-drum of workaday life!

47
Choice

Thursday, September 25, 2025 - Evening

JENNY STUDIED HERSELF IN the mirror on the back of her bedroom door. She felt conflicted as she stood in her underwear, her running clothes piled on the floor next to her. She had made progress toward her goal of getting back to her ideal weight, but there was something about her body that felt wrong. She turned, examining herself from every angle, and couldn't pinpoint what it was. She felt too tall, which she thought was ridiculous at five feet five inches. Normally, she felt short, especially without shoes on.

But other things felt strange as well. Her breasts felt too big; her hips too wide. She put some of that down to feeling like she still had a few pounds to shed, but it went beyond that. She could picture herself at the fittest she'd ever been, just before everything had gone horrifically wrong, when she'd been proud of her two baby abs and her ability to do six pull-ups. That image still felt too curvy, too voluptuous. She wondered if Sydney and Maddy were getting to her. They were both so slender, and both were at least two inches shorter than her. Maybe if she had spent more time with Isabella, she wouldn't feel so out of sorts with herself.

That's hardly a reason to subject myself to her, she thought as she walked to the bathroom to shower.

An hour later at Cinder's Remorse, she picked at her salad as she listened to Nate and Charles debate some historical point about tanks. Sydney was talking about a mystery movie she'd just seen, and Maddy kept interjecting to correct her about the plot. Jenny watched them and wondered if and when she would give in and express interest in one or both of them openly.

But I'm not interested.

Jenny shut her eyes and tried to understand the intrusive thought. Was that true? Was she really not interested? She didn't think so. She wondered if the words were a defense mechanism. Did Sydney remind her too much of Aurora, and Maddy too much of Matina? That might have been it, but the comparisons were so shallow. Syd and Aurora were both enthusiastic, but Aurora had been nothing if she wasn't an old soul. It was as if someone had plucked a hippie from the late '60s and dropped her unchanged into Jenny's life. Sydney … well, Sydney was Sydney.

"Hey, you alright?" Maddy asked, putting her hand on Jenny's arm.

Jenny opened her eyes. She felt the sudden double desire to kiss her and to push her away.

"Sorry, just having one of my moments," Jenny said.

Maddy squeezed. Love and something like revulsion pumped together in Jenny's veins.

She's not Matina, she tried to tell herself. But the feeling of discomfort remained. *She's not. But she's not Phil either.* Jenny suddenly remembered the feeling of his long, strong legs against hers in the dark. The alarm on her wrist buzzed, dispelling the sweaty, close memory. Jenny jolted to her feet.

"You in a rush to get to the tower?" Nate laughed. "You must love it up there. You know, it's all yours if you want it."

Jenny forced a laugh. "No, you were right, it kind of sucks up there. But, you know, I'd be happy to take one of your nights if you want me to."

Just don't miss me when winter comes.

Jenny put her hand to her chest and took a deep breath.

"You good?" Nate asked.

"Indigestion," she said. "I need to get up and move around."

"You want us to walk you up?" Maddy asked.

No, I want you two little sapphic pixies to give me some space.

"Yes, please," Jenny said. "Charles, I look forward to seeing you tomorrow. Is there a book I should read or a documentary I should watch beforehand?"

Charles smiled wickedly and said, "Yes, perhaps Kant."

Jenny opened her mouth to say that she had heard the man's name, but her mouth surprised her. "*The Critique of Pure Reason, The Groundwork of the Metaphysics of Morals,* or something else?"

Charle's smile transformed from mischievous to appreciative. "Have you read Kant?"

"Yes, but he spins my head around and I don't know up from down when I'm reading him."

"He is dense," Charles said, leaning forward and putting his elbows on the table. He frowned into his clasped hands. "I'm curious to hear who you *do* like reading. So, no assignments from me."

Jenny smiled weakly, her lips and tongue suddenly back under her command.

I really am going crazy, she thought.

"Um, great! Then I'll see you … I guess I'll see you at the Mist in the morning. Good night. Good night, Nate, Linds. Have a good show."

Jenny turned quickly and hurried to the front of the bar to get her coat from the wall.

"Jenny!" Barry called, taking her wrist lightly as she almost rushed past him. She turned and hugged him, grateful for an uncomplicated interaction. His plaid shirt smelled of coffee, with a hint of cologne.

"Headin' up to work?" he asked.

"Yeah, up to the tower this week," she said.

"Getting cold at night, hope you brought your sweater," he said, taking in Jenny's sleeveless turtle-neck.

"Actually, I've been scared to tell you, but I can't find it. I'm so sorry. I've looked everywhere and I just can't figure out where it went."

She felt an arm go around her waist and glanced down to find Sydney grinning at Barry.

"Hey, coffee man!" Sydney said. "Maddy will marry you."

Barry's face contorted through several emotions in rapid succession—first, anger, then puzzlement, then concern, then amusement. "Really? You proposing to me through your girlfriend?"

—*Dudette?* Jenny added to his question, which made her smile.

"She's willing to sell me for free coffee, so yes," Maddy said, also coming up beside Jenny and putting her arm around her back. It felt like the most natural thing in the world, and Jenny wanted to run away. She didn't run; instead, she let them hold her while they bantered with Barry. Then she made her excuses, told him she would look for his gift some more, and led her friends to the coat rack.

Once outside, Sydney took Jenny's hand, and Maddy shoved hers into her jacket pockets.

"When did you lose your sweater?" Maddy asked.

"What? Oh, um, the night you guys came over. It ended up in the hamper with my other sweaty clothes."

Maddy nodded slowly. "Um, I don't want to creep you out or anything, but the guys came over the next day to check the house for gas and stuff, right?"

"Yeah, why? You think some gas-leak inspector stole my sweater?"

"Maybe," Maddy said. "You never know, those guys are pretty local. They might even subscribe to your site. Would it be the weirdest thing someone has done?"

Jenny thought back to her last interaction with Chloe and Isabella. "No, definitely not," Jenny said.

"Have you checked your underwear drawer? Maybe they took some," Sydney said.

"I doubt they'd take clean ones," Maddy said.

"Ew!" Sydney almost squealed. "Men are disgusting. I don't know how either of you likes them."

"Wait, I thought—" Jenny started.

Maddy shrugged. "I'm with Syd now. But I've been with guys. I'm not really in a guy era right now, though," Maddy said.

"Are we still saying 'era?'" Jenny asked, half to herself.

"I know what era she's in," Sydney said in a sing-song voice.

"It's the same one you're in," Maddy said.

"What is that?" Jenny asked, laughing.

"Our Jenny era," Sydney said, squeezing her hand.

"Oh," she said, smiling down at the pavement. "I … don't know what to say to that."

"You're the shyest porn star I've ever met," Maddy laughed.

"I hate that term. It's like the only industry in the world where you can start working and immediately claim to be a star. Like, if … What's Earl's band's name?"

"Jawbone's Cove," Maddy said.

"Right, if they did as many shows as I have done videos, they would be, like, regionally popular. But they wouldn't be rock stars."

"Okay, what term do you prefer?" Maddy asked.

"A professional visual sensual assistant," Jenny said in a mock English accent.

"Definitely not," Maddy said.

They joked about Jenny's work along Main Street, through the woods, and over the bridge. She described awkward moments and surprisingly comfortable ones. She talked about everything except the parts that mattered to her.

"Did you ever, like, totally fall for someone? I mean, you're there, naked, and like, doing it, there has to be chemistry sometimes!" Sydney said.

"Doing it?" Maddy said. "You are such a child." Sydney stuck out her tongue. Maddy gave the forest an 'Is anyone seeing this?' expression that Jenny would have found endearing if Nolan hadn't been looking at her across the gap of death.

Jenny took a deep breath and nodded. "Yeah, you get chemistry with people. And you get the opposite, too. Sometimes, within a few seconds, you realize that you aren't going to enjoy any of it with someone, and you just want to get through it. Other times, you're like, 'wow, this person is awesome, I kind of want to hang out with them, and yeah, cool, now we're making out and having sex.'"

"I think that's the part that's kind of strange to me," Maddy said. "I mean … I'm not a prude, like, I like sex, and when I dated guys, I didn't wait a long time to …" She trailed off.

"To what?" Sydney asked, drawing the words out.

"To *do it*," Maddy said, rolling her eyes. "But the whole thing of like, 'hi, how are you, oh, there's your dick,' just … I don't know, it feels … empty to me?"

"Yeah," Jenny said as they started up the incline beyond the bridge. "It can be. And at other times, it's kind of just cool, and now and then, it's amazing. So, I guess it's kind of like any other job that way."

"Tell me about when it was amazing," Sydney said. "Was it with a woman?"

"Well, actually, kind of. But that was when I was doing stuff with people I knew. I didn't do much in LA with women. A few times, and they were fine. But mostly it was with Aurora and Matina. That was just sort of us being us and one of our housemates filming it."

"Oh," Sydney said. "I knew you had, like, a thing with someone, but, like, threesomes?"

Jenny laughed. "Yeah, it was just kind of the vibe with us."

They walked in silence for a minute before Sydney said in a small voice, "Would you ever do that again?"

"Make porn with people I love?" Jenny asked.

"No, or, I don't know, maybe. But, I mean, be with two women again?"

No, I wouldn't.

"If I cared enough about them," Jenny said, pushing the thought back. She squeezed Sydney's hand.

"Like as just a physical thing, or—"

"No, I … look, I'm not saying I don't do just physical things. But what I had with them was something more, and I think I'd want something more. I don't want just sex, at least not with people I care about. I'm not in *that era*," she said, mimicking Maddy's tone from earlier.

Maddy reached down and took Jenny's other hand.

This isn't what I want.

Yes, it is.

Jenny forced the doubt out of her mind. She had no idea how things would work, or whether they'd work, but she chose to leave her fears behind and move forward. She squeezed the hands in hers and led the two women toward the gate.

"What era are you in?" Maddy asked.

"I think—" Jenny said, knowing that the words about to come out of her mouth were corny and deeply cringeworthy, but she pushed herself to say them anyway, "I think maybe I'm in my Syd and Maddy era."

Part 6 - Tabby

Part I, Question vii, Article 2

Whether All Times are One

Objection 1: It seems that all times are one, as the first mover is one, and thus the first movement is one. All things that follow from this first movement are thus of the same time, and thus all times are one.

Objection 2: As there is one eternity coterminous with the divinity, and one act of creation, so too, then, must time be one.

I answer that, on the contrary, all times are not one. Thomas Aquinas assumes in his discussion of Aevum that time is a unity due to its unified first movement. This is true only within the confines of a singular world or cosmos. Yet not all worlds are one. [Article 6] The first moments of many times set forth many worlds before them. It may be said that within each world, time is a unity, and thus Thomas is correct, but the worlds are a plurality with each possessing its own time. Some may be said to relate to each other, and therefore have an overarching time which governs their relationships, and thus it may be said that their times are ultimately one. [Article 9] But others may exist apart, and thus not come into relationship except through the relationship essential to all existence: the foundational being of their Maker. [Article 10] As divinity is not temporal, these cannot be said to be under the governance of a single time, and thus time is not one.

Response 1: This is only true if there is only one first movement. As the answer shows, a single first movement is only required within a single world. But there may be many worlds, and thus it is not required that there be only one first movement.

Response 2: While there is eternally only one act of creation, for the eternal is one in both act and being, it does not follow that there is only one object of creation, for, evidently, there are a plurality of objects which have been created. Thus, as there are many trees, people, and stars, so too may there be many worlds in which a first movement may obtain.

- Mikuláš Vaclavek, *The Second Book of Seeings*

TABBY'S FLESH STILL TREMBLES as she tells her parents and uncle all she's seen. Only slowly, when she finishes, does she become still. The adults consult with each other, and her uncle goes to dress. He will go into town after sunrise. He says he knows which family can help them. Her father puts her on his knee and strokes her hair while her mother goes to heat milk and chocolate. They sit together under the moon, looking out at the night and marveling that such wonders should appear in their time.

II
Relief

Saturday, March 13, 1926 - Evening

THE WHITE STONE RELIEF showed a man and a woman in short tunics, welcoming the morning with raised and open hands. They faced each other with the sunrise behind them, its rays flashing out in all directions, illuminating a geometrical landscape. No animals roamed the sparse, abstracted, oblong trees, nor did birds wing above the equilateral mountains. The sea was likely devoid of slipping serpents and frolicking fish, though its placid, featureless surface hinted at neither a hidden fecundity nor a vast emptiness.

Tabby, holding a cigarette in one hand and touching the points of her silver sunburst necklace with the other, reclined on one of the Harkman Hotel's gleaming red-leather lobby couches, contemplating the two barefoot figures and wondering if they were meant to be Adam and Eve, or perhaps just prototypical "Man" and "Woman." With the length of her tunic and the bob of her hair, Tabby guessed that the woman was the "new" woman. If so, perhaps the man was the "new" man, though she didn't know what that would entail. Perhaps it meant only that the great striving masculine side of nature withdrew a little, allowing the ancient, and perhaps primary, feminine aspect of creation to live without domination, strength not overwhelming beauty. Was not the Sky the child of the Earth in Greek myth? Surely, she had read that in Bulfinch. She wondered if the great Life Force that moved through the world ever contended with itself, and then immediately realized that it must. What was Darwinism if not the striving of the *Élan Vital* with itself to accomplish its own goals? In so striving, it worked within itself, perhaps in a Hegelian dialectic. Or was that Fichte?

She sighed and shifted, pulling her feet up and curling like a cat on the soft leather. Winston, the hotel clerk, glanced at her, and she wondered what he thought. Did he merely delight in her beauty? She knew she was beautiful; everyone told her. They complimented her dark hair and darker eyes. Without vulgarity, they complimented her figure, the grace of her movement, its symmetry, its perfection: her lips delicate, her hands elegant, her neck statuesque. If Winston merely glanced and appreciated her appearance, then Tabby would have preferred that he stare. Let him put his elbow on the desk, his hand under his chin, and let drool run from his lip. At least then she would know he was not asking himself how she could be here, a married woman with a newborn at home, almost 2,500 miles away.

She knew how she could be here, but not *why*. She could no more explain 'why' to Winston than she could the difference between Fichte and Hegel. Something about formality, being, and nonbeing. Something wild and something ordered.

Tabby put her cigarette out in the standing ashtray next to the couch and sighed again. She wondered how Lawrence was getting on with their son. He had all the help he could want. Her parents, three grandparents, Sharon, and Sharon's husband Archie would all dote on the little fellow. Sharon especially. Tabby knew the two would have a special relationship. As she considered that fact with a dull pang in her stomach, she pulled another cigarette from the small metal case in her clutch and tried to light it with shaking fingers. Finally, on the third snap of the lighter, it took, and she drew in a deep breath of fire.

Her fingers shook a little less.

She wanted to be in Lawrence's arms, but tonight she would take a lover, that was, if her friends would ever come down from their rooms. She felt as if she were always waiting. Waiting for trains, for friends, for men, for time to move on. She wondered when it would all be over, and then chided herself. Of course, she knew all that. There were no real surprises to come. Well, perhaps there were a few, like when her friends would finally come down.

As if summoned by her thought, the elevator door opened, pouring Conti, Jinks, and Leopold into the lobby in a swirl of chatter, laughter, and smoke. Tabby forced a smile and waited for them to come to her before she stood.

"Well, you all look fabulous," Tabby said, staring at the gold, green, and black they wore.

"So, where to tonight?" Leopold asked.

Tabby didn't know or care. She only wanted to move, to dance, to drink, to let the jazz wash the world away. And of course it would. That was the promise of the one who saw far. And He was always right.

ii

Tabby laughs, her head back, mouth wide, eyes closed. Her hair is black and waves under the band of sequins, a feather bobbing, a cigarette burning from fingers straight out, pointing in the same direction as her pale, slender forearm, her elbow cradled in her other elegant hand, her other forearm crossed against her flat stomach beneath tastefully small breasts. She is laughing not because she thinks the man is funny, but because she's supposed to laugh. Some men are funny, but the tall man with the short, straight nose and cleft chin isn't. He thinks he is, and he's rich enough to expect people to laugh. Tabby doesn't need to laugh because of his money, her family is also rich and immune to whatever spiteful reprisals such a man might marshal against those who offend him. But she laughs anyway because it's something to do. It's more interesting than standing and staring, and the music is too loud for her to bandy words with him about Romanticism, Suffrage, or German Expressionism.

So, she laughs.

III
Desire

Saturday, March 13, 1926 – Late Night

THE DOORMAN OPENED THE Harkman's heavy glass door, letting Tabby and her three friends in behind her. She thanked him and put her hand on the arm of his overcoat, feeling the wool slip beneath her fingers. She winked at the tall, olive-skinned man and laughed with Conti and Jinks while Leopold frowned apologetically.

"Good evening, ladies, sir," Winston said from behind the hotel's front desk. He had slicked black hair and a thin, waxed moustache. His eyes flicked to Tabby. She thought he must be judging her, but for the moment, she didn't care. The jazz and gin had swept the world away. Now she floated on its flooded surface and wondered if there could be anything to worry about in the depths below.

"Good evening, Winston," Conti said, prancing up to the desk and leaning over it. She kicked up one heel and offered the man her cheek.

"Miss Lister, as I've—"

"Oh, give her a kiss or she'll sulk all night," Tabby said, stopping in front of the elevators. "That's an order, Winston."

Winston gave them a 'what can you do?' look, smiled, and leaned in to kiss Conti on the cheek. At the last second, she turned her head and planted one on him good.

"Miss Lister, my wife—" he began, but the blush on his cheeks and the smile on his lips belied the protest in his voice.

"Oh, you don't have to tell her a thing," Conti said, running her thumb over his mouth to remove the smudge of red. "Marry, me, Winston."

"I—"

"Agree to it," Leopold said, walking up behind Conti and taking her by the shoulders. "She'll leave you first thing when she wakes up."

"I will not," Conti said, her platinum hair gleaming gold in the warm lobby lights.

"Miss Lister, if I could marry you, I would," Winston said. Tabby believed him. Of course, Winston was a fool for meaning it. He would bore Conti in an hour, unless he convinced himself that he was happy to sit at home at night while she Charleston-ed and fox trotted her way across half the cities in America. But then, he didn't make enough money to be so bored with life as to get his kicks from his young wife running around with other men. A moment later, she regretted that thought.

"Come along, Conti," Jinks said, pulling a cigarette from her silver case and pushing the elevator's call button. "If you still love him tomorrow, it's meant to be."

Leopold pulled Conti away, her sequined, green dress sparkling. Conti reached out for Winston as if he were a love torn from her by the injustices of an uncaring society.

"Winston," Tabby said, stopping in front of the desk. "We have some friends who will be stopping by. Will you send them up when they get here?"

"Of course, Mrs.—"

"Ms.," Tabby corrected.

"Ms. Kusel," he said, forcing the words out. "How will I know they are your guests?"

"It's Garvey Henderson's set, as well as—what's his name, Jinx?— Right, Percy Anderson's party," Tabby said.

"Henderson and Anderson," Winston said.

"That's right. Send them straight up to us, if you would," Tabby said.

Winston said that he would, avoiding her eyes.

The elevator door slid open, and a man with skin as black as volcanic rock smiled at them.

"Good evening, Ms. Kusel, Ms. Lister, Ms. Shaw, Mr. Navokov."

"Good evening, Henry," Tabby said. "I apologize for Conti's being in rare form tonight."

"Not very rare," Jinx said, not looking at the elevator operator.

"Winston, I love you," Conti said as the doors closed. Then she turned to her companions. "Why won't you let me have any fun?"

"Because the kind of fun you want to have will get Winston fired and wreck his happy home," Jinx said. She touched her beaded headband that wrapped her bobbed brown hair.

"What do you think, Henry?" Tabby asked. "Do you think we should let Conti have her fun with poor Winston?"

"I couldn't say, Ms. Kusel," Henry said, looking straight forward.

"Diplomatic," Leopold said.

Tabby frowned. She felt lightheaded. A little of it was the gin, a little the jazz, and a little the sweat she knew was waiting for her, either with Garvey or with Percy's friend, Alejandro. She didn't have a preference, and she knew that either was possible. She would wait for the nudge, the hands on her shoulders, the whisper in her ear.

"Henry, are you married?" Conti said.

"No," Jinx said. "If you want to have your way with someone, there are plenty of men coming by. Or stop torturing Leo."

"*Leo?*" Conti said, dragging his name out.

"Yes, Conti," Leopold said, looking down at her. His square jaw was set under stark gray eyes. As Tabby looked at him, those eyes split and then split again until hundreds, of darting, seeking orbs of every color covered the top of his face. She blinked and the vision was gone. The Man was toying with her.

Next, he'll put his eyes on Jinx or Conti.

She hoped the vision didn't portend anything ill for Leo.

"Will you comfort me in my bereft state, abandoned by every other man I see?"

"You mean, will I be your last choice?"

"Yes," Conti said, giving him a sly smile.

"Far be it from me to be picky," Leopold said.

"Fourteenth floor," Henry said as he pulled the elevator lever, and the car came to a smooth stop. He opened the doors.

"Good evening, Henry," Leopold said, gently pushing Conti out of the elevator.

"Nighty-night, Henry," Conti said.

Jinx walked out after them.

Tabby turned to the elevator operator. "I'm sorry, Henry," she said. "I shouldn't have done that."

"I'm sure I don't know what you mean, Ms. Kusel," Henry said, looking down. She noted that he had never mistakenly called her by her married name.

"You do. I was careless when I asked you about Conti. I put you in an impossible position, and I'm sorry." She put her hand on his arm. "I won't do it again."

"You have nothing to apologize for, Ms. Kusel." But when he looked up at her, his eyes said something different. Tabby watched them to see if they would split. Instead, they remained steady and firm. She wanted to give him the kiss of peace, but this was Chicago, not Lightning Falls.

"Have yourself a good evening, Henry," Tabby said, slipping a five-dollar bill into his jacket's breast pocket.

"Thank you, Ms. Kusel. And you, as well."

Jinx was waiting for her in the hall as Leopold fumbled with the keys to the apartment while Conti hung on his arm, making mooneyes at him.

"Why do you do that?" Jinx asked.

"Do what?" Tabby asked.

"Talk to him like that? It's not right."

Tabby shook her head at Jinx. "I don't get you Jinxy. You dance to their music, drink at their clubs, and you can't find it in your heart just to be kind?"

Jinx shrugged and walked down the hallway toward the penthouse. Around her, the wallpaper was gold-green, the light fixtures sunbursts, and the floorboards dark horizons where verdant dawn met the carpet's sea, which wore scallops of light blue against a dark, royal blue field. Jinx, in her gold dress, sashayed across the depths like Aphrodite clad in sunlight. Tabby watched her go, beautiful and sullen. She knew that if Jinx had more to drink, which she certainly would, the woman would once more confide in Tabby how sad she was that the Ku Klux Klan had fallen to pieces recently after such a promising rise in Oregon over the last few years. Tabby wished Jinx's family had accepted the invitation to join the Brethren. If they had, perhaps she'd see how backward her thinking was. But then, beyond their egalitarianism, what did the promise of the New Settlement have to offer?

Love, fear, doubt, sex, wealth, she thought. *More and less than I could ever want.*

She followed Jinx as frozen waves lapped beneath her feet.

Tabby lies in the bed with the sheet pulled up over her high, goosebump-dimpled chest. Her nipples are so hard that they ache, and her eyes burn with smoke and sleeplessness. She lingers on the edge of choice, either to rise or to rouse both the man beside her and his desire. She cannot decide if she would feel more alone walking through the moonlit silence of the Harkman's penthouse or in the man's arms again. Perhaps they would feel the same. Some nights she sleeps well next to her lovers. Some nights she enjoys them enough that she carelessly casts sleep aside. Tonight, she wishes sleep would take her, for tomorrow she travels.

IV
Station

Wednesday, March 17, 1926 – Early Afternoon

TABBY KICKED UP DUST as she stepped off the passenger car into the footprint-scattered earth of the Enterprise train station. The large white building always reminded her of a barn, with its gambrel roof. She had had four days to adjust from a Chicago mindset to one more appropriate to one of the most remote parts of the country. Still, even after four days, she still found it jarring to walk out into the small community where the only car in sight was her family's black Oldsmobile Model 30.

Conti followed after her, pursued languidly by Jinx. They had exchanged their fashionable city clothes for less assuming frock dresses, yet they still appeared too glamorous for Enterprise's dusty station.

"Well," Jinx began, "at least the …" She faltered.

"What?" Conti said.

"I don't know," Jinx said. "I was hoping I'd find something to be optimistic about, but I couldn't come up with anything."

"Oh, why do you even come back if you hate it so much?" Conti asked. Tabby sympathized with the frustration in her voice.

"Who would I pal around with while you two till the soil of the old homesteads? Leo?" Jinx asked, pointing to her bags as a short man with a gargantuan auburn mustache hurried up to them. He tipped his cap and nodded as he picked up Jinx's two large suitcases and two hat boxes.

Tabby's frustration with Jinx was simmering. She took a deep breath, reminding herself that a few days apart would allow them to all heal from the little bumps and bruises of living in such proximity for weeks. Still, she wanted to tell Jinx what she thought of her haughty attitude and incessant racialism. But, to keep the peace on the car ride home, she held her tongue.

"I'm going to have to sit up front, aren't I?" Conti said, pouting at the car.

"Well, it's Tabby's car, and you're the least—"

"No, I'll sit up front, Conti," Tabby said. Then, giving in to an impulse, she leaned over and kissed Conti on the cheek. "And we will drop you off first."

Tabby could tell that Jinx disliked the arrangement. The order should be Jinx first, as her father had the greatest wealth, then Tabby, then Conti. Of course, Tabby would be last because she never wanted Gambol to do more work than he needed to, and, in social ranking,

Tabby's father, not Jinx's, stood first. His father had founded the town, and their family had built it. And, Tabby mused, in keeping with that logic, Conti should rank before Jinx, as her family was one of the few remaining from the first settlers who had come across the Atlantic. All Jinx's family had was an accumulation of wealth earned from fortunate investments.

The three women were uncharacteristically quiet as Gambol pulled the car onto the road. Tabby thought Conti's seemingly unflagging energy had reached some indefinable limit after so long in the same company. Tabby couldn't remember Conti being so quiet the previous March when they came home from Portland. But last year, her friends had been with her for only two weeks, not two months.

Or, she thought, *maybe she's preparing herself for the final jolt of change.*

The trip home was always an easing out of the continual social life of this or that city, though the last leg of the journey from La Grande to Enterprise was always a shock. Before that, their party still met interesting people. This year, there had been an inventor and his wife, a dozen businessmen traveling alone, and two dozen adult children of wealthy families, bound for Portland or hopping off on their own small regional lines back to the country. Each night, the number of interesting people shrank, and each day, their society became less metropolitan. They spent more time reading or talking quietly about less frivolous things, such as the proposal to open a Normal School in La Grande, and the possibility of the state finally repealing the Free Negro prohibition. And, of course, their secret stores of booze dwindled on the dry trains that arced across America's vast fruited plains.

Tabby knew that when Conti and Jinx returned home, they were different people. Their families would not approve of their lives in Chicago, Portland, or San Francisco. She felt sorry for them, but also wondered what it was like for them to return to the small town. Did they have to break habits and change their way of talking? Certainly, Conti couldn't profess her love for the clerk at Cerny's Druggist or the movie projector operator at the Silver Ring Theater. Lightning Falls was too small for that, its people too conservative. Gone were the days of the New Settlement and its ideals of unbounded love. The last twenty years had seen too many who belonged to the Congregation Church and the Baptist Church come into town with their traditional views for Lightning Falls to remain the New Eden that its founders had envisioned.

Tabby looked out the window and thought about how strange the world was. Rolling fields of dry-land grain slipped past as the foothills of the Wallowa Mountains rose and fell, alternately concealing and revealing the mountains to the east. Scatterings of single pines stippled the hilltops or clustered in close copses. Here, farmers drew life from the dry soil, bidding the land to be fruitful whether it would or not. Tabby felt a kinship with the land that slipped past her window. They were both pulled forward by the great force of life that wove its way through the world. It commanded the dust to rise and walk, the stones to bear children, the corn to live and die so that others might live and die, and the sky to weep so all might drink. Tabby drank, she bore fruit, and she waited to die so others might live.

"We've ruined this country," Jinx said, looking out her window. No one responded.

After fifteen minutes, the forest appeared, first in smatterings of trees and finally in a swath of ponderosa pines that closed in on both sides of the road. The land rose on either side of State Road Three, and they could see little except the ever-denser forest that broke only here or there to show, once more, the rolling land beyond them. Ten minutes on, they passed the two stumps cut as a warning that the turn to Lightning Falls was coming. Not even a sign at either end of town had remedied the prevalence with which travelers missed the turn. Folks sometimes even found themselves down Molosh Road, to the cliff where John Molosh would take the town's refuse and cast it over.

Gambol slowed the car and turned into what appeared to be a sure collision with the forest. Instead of plowing through trees, they drove along a narrow, well-kept road that ran for more than a hundred feet before curving to the right. Then, though trees still closed in on both sides, they saw the first houses of their hometown peeking out in the bright light of a cloudless day.

Tabby looked to her right to watch her family's driveway slip past, and felt her heart lighten as the trees gave way to Main Street and the big brick houses and businesses that ran up the center of town. Gambol pulled the car up in front of a large home with blue shutters and an imposing oak tree in the yard. Tabby and Gambol both got out. The driver opened Conti's door and went to get her bags. Tabby waited for her friend to come around so she could hug and kiss her.

"When shall we get together again?" Tabby asked.

"Oh, I don't know, the day after tomorrow? Do you want to come over for lunch?"

"Yes, but let's have a picnic if we can, in the park, would you like that? We can play at being respectable."

Conti laughed weakly.

"All will be well," Tabby said, and kissed her friend again. They clasped hands and walked up the path with Gambol in tow, toting Conti's luggage. Once her friend was safely inside, Tabby and Gambol returned to the car.

Tabby took her seat next to the driver again, leaving Jinx alone in the back. They went up Main Street, passing busy people in hats and overcoats, and turned onto the second-to-last street, Whitman. From there, they drove several blocks until they reached the corner of town where Whitman met Hitchman's Creek Road. They stopped in front of another large brick house. This one sported green shutters and a large hedge that ran around the front yard, effectively hiding the whole first floor from view. Tabby pictured the wide yard and beautiful covered deck that looked down to the banks of the street's eponymous creek. She hated how Jinx's family hid their property from the rest of the town. Then, thinking about how the forest almost entirely shrouded her own family's home, she chided herself for being a hypocrite and opened her door. Tabby embraced Jinx and kissed her lightly on the cheek.

"Well, when shall *we* meet again?" Jinx asked, and Tabby thought she detected a hint of accusation, as if Jinx suspected that Tabby would no longer want to associate with her now that they had returned to town.

"What's the matter? Why are you talking like that?"

Jinx was silent.

"How about on Saturday for lunch or tea?"

Jinx looked up at her family's house. "I don't know how much longer we'll be here," Jinx said flatly.

"Oh?"

"Father is growing bored with small-town life, and the lawyers have cleared up the complications back east." Jinx's words were stilted, as if she were reading them from a card.

"Then we must make sure we see each other as often as we can before you go," Tabby said.

"You'll be glad when we're gone," Jinx said, turning her dark eyes to Tabby. "So you can have your little Negro-loving Eden back, am I right? Easy to love them when they aren't here," she said.

"I—" Tabby stuttered, so shocked by the incongruous turn that she didn't know what to say.

"Father says you will go the way of the Shakers."

Tabby took a step back. "I thought we were friends," Tabby said.

Jinx shook her head. "No, I don't think we are. You're a vapid tramp. I don't know why I agreed to go with you. You don't want what is best for this country, for Oregon, for Lightning Falls. You certainly don't want what's best for your own family. I don't know why I have associated with you."

Tabby felt her mouth working, but no sound came out.

"I don't think we are friends," Jinx continued. "You and that silly girl were the closest thing to society in this pit, so you were a lifeline, and I appreciate that, I suppose. But I don't think I'll have to stay here much longer. So, no, we are not friends. I think it's best that we skip lunch on Saturday and every lunch after that as well. So long."

Jinx turned and walked through the gate into the closed bastion of her family's, apparently temporary, sanctuary.

"Shall I hurl her baggage into the creek, Ms. Kusel?" Gambol said, blank-faced as he gazed up at the imposing house.

"I would like that very much, Gambol. But no, bring her bags up as you should. We can daydream on the way home about them floating down the water."

He nodded and carried Jinx's bags through the gate. Tabby looked up at the house, shook her head, and climbed back into the front seat.

"Ms. Kusel, the back seat is open," Gambol said when he returned.

"Oh, fiddlesticks on the back seat, Gambol. Please just take me home."

"Yes, Ma'am."

iv

The houses slip past her window, and she blinks as each moves out of view, her mind festooning each frame with the *ratta-tat-tat* of jazz-club drums. She blinks between the beats, and life after life flashes in the little moving pictures running left-to-right, sliding frozen tableaus, her eyes open only long enough to catch branches mid-sway and doors mid-swing. Forward she goes, backward the world. She touches her lip with one unsteady finger, the tip of her tongue tasting the salt of her skin as the sky, soft and bright, frames solitary disconnected scenes in the staccato silence of her wandering mind.

V
Reunion

Wednesday, March 17, 1926 – Early Afternoon

TABBY STEPPED THROUGH THE front door to find her father, Jeremiah, coming out of the library with a book in his hand. His face, drawn and contemplative, was transformed by the light of love. He wrapped her in his long, strong arms and kissed her cheek.

"My darling daughter is home," he said.

"Hello, Papa," she said, holding him tightly. Before they could say more, her mother, Eliska, called her name. Then they were hugging. Footsteps on the stairs followed, then it was Sharon in her arms, and the world was a heaping of affections, greetings, and tears.

"You look so beautiful," Sharon said. "City life always suits you."

"Hotel life suits me," Tabby said.

"Miss Tabitha," a voice said from behind the little family cluster. Tabby leaned around Sharon to find the cook, Mrs. Caroline Baker, holding the baby.

"Caroline, how are you?" Tabby approached the woman and kissed her on the cheek.

"I'm very well, Miss Tabitha, and so is he."

Tabby looked down at the chubby-faced baby and allowed herself to cup his chin in her palm. "Yes, he is looking very well. Thank you for looking after him."

"Oh, I'm not the main culprit," Caroline said. "Your sister and mother have been doing the good work."

"Caroline is being modest," Eliska said. "We'd be entirely lost without her help. It's been too long since I had babies to contend with."

"Would you like to hold him, Miss Tabitha?"

"No, I shouldn't. I don't want to confuse him."

"Don't be silly," Sharon said. "You're his mother, it won't confuse him."

Tabby struggled to speak, holding down her tears by main force. However, Larry and Archie saved her further protest when they came in, looking dapper, wind-blown, and flushed. She hugged and kissed Archie before turning to her husband.

"Hello, sir," she said, feeling suddenly nervous.

"Hello, lady," Larry said. Then he kissed her. Warmth bloomed out from her core as she touched his clean-shaven face. She wanted to take his hand and lead him upstairs immediately.

"Look at us," Jeremiah said, "all together again. Tabby, please tell me you don't already have dinner plans."

"Of course she does," Sharon said, "you can't expect her to put down the heavy work of social life for us country bumpkins."

"No," Tabby said, smiling and staring into Larry's eyes. "I most certainly do not have plans. In fact, my social calendar is devoted only to family until the day after tomorrow at luncheon, when I am meeting Constance Lister for a picnic."

"Oh, that sounds fun," Sharon said.

"You should come, I'm sure she'll want to hear all the local gossip from someone who knows how to sift the grain from the chaff," Tabby said.

"I'll be at her service," Sharon said, giving a playful curtsy.

"Do we have our own lunch on the horizon?" Archie asked. "We're ravenous."

"I'll happily trade you a lunch for a baby," Caroline said. Eliska chuckled and picked up her grandson. "I'll go finish with the sandwiches. Would you like anything special, Miss Tabitha? I have egg salad, but I can whip something else up."

"No, whatever you're making is wonderful. Gosh, I've been looking forward to your cooking again, Caroline."

"That's a kind lie, Miss Tabitha," she said before returning down the hall.

"What have you strong men been doing?" Tabby asked. "Wrestling bears? Sailing boats up and down the creek?"

"No, something far more heroic," Archie said, "we've been trying to get one of the old dock legs up without hurling ourselves into the mud."

"Well, you look clean as a whistle," Tabby said, looking both men up and down.

"We've been successful at not hurling ourselves," Larry said, "but not nearly as successful at removing the leg. I'm afraid the two might be mutually exclusive."

"Well, after lunch we'll put on some rougher threads and come out together to figure it as a quartet, won't we?" Sharon said.

"That's a grand idea, perhaps you'll come too," Tabby said to her parents, "and we can have Caroline and Cecil as well, pointing and pulling and slapping themselves with creek mud."

"That sounds like a grand time. May I join in?" The voice, deep and resonant, came from the library doorway. Tabby turned to see the slender figure of her uncle with his pipe in hand.

"Uncle Peter! I didn't know you were here!" she cried.

"In the flesh! I thought I might finish my chapter while you all fell about in desperate affection," he said in a cloud of blue smoke. She went to him and kissed his cheek. "Hello, Tabby dear," he said.

"Hello, Uncle," she said, feeling her joy was almost complete. If only her grandparents were present, she'd feel perfectly at home. She asked after them, and her mother told her they would be by for dinner.

Luncheon was a fine, light affair full of laughter and storytelling. They spoke of the town, the house, business, family, and the baby. Peter talked of matters foreign and domestic, and Tabby told them of Chicago, the jazz clubs, and her strange interaction with Jinx.

Peter and Jeremiah wore identical frowns that would have told a complete stranger that they were brothers.

"Well," Jeremiah finally said, "the Shaws have certainly contributed financially to the town, but I admit I'm not sorry to see them go. They never really believed in what we're doing here. I am sorry about your friend, though, Tabby."

"She is—*was*, I suppose—never a very good friend," Tabby said, laughing lightly.

"I'm not surprised either, the collapse of their interests in the state—" Peter began.

"They were involved with the Ku Klux Klan's recent political successes here," Jeremiah said to Archie, who was leaning forward with obvious interest.

"Ah," Archie said. "I met some of those people in Portland. Terrible people, not the sort who would have much in common with the Brethren in any way."

"Indeed," Peter said. "I wonder, since their house will be for sale soon—"

"Uncle Peter, you're always prospecting," Sharon said, smiling.

"Well, I was prospecting on your behalf, my dear," Peter said.

"Oh, but Archie and I have our home, we're very happy," Sharon said.

"I know, Dear, forgive me. I, well, I was thinking about Mr. Bartos. I know he's unhappy with his current home."

Sharon froze in the act of lifting her cup to her lips, her smile wilted. Archie scowled at Peter.

"Why would you mention him?" Archie asked.

Peter looked from Sharon to Archie and back again. "I'm so sorry, my dear, Archie, my mind is always ticking along like a heartless machine.

Of course, that was insensitive of me to mention. Will you both forgive me?"

Tabby studied Peter's face. He looked genuinely stricken. *No one works harder to maintain the intricate and delicate balance between the family's happiness and its duties than Uncle Peter,* she thought. *Except perhaps me.*

"I—yes, of course, I forgive you, Uncle Peter," Sharon said.

"Archie, I am aghast at my insensitivity—"

"Think nothing more of it," Archie said, but his face remained dark for the remainder of the meal.

After another minute of awkwardness, the conversation renewed. Twenty minutes later, they adjourned to put on rougher clothing to remove the last vestiges of the old canoe dock in Hitchman's Creek. Tabby learned that this was the first step in the men's plans to erect a new launch in its place. They toiled for an hour and finally succeeded in pulling the rotted wood out from the mud with a wide sucking sound that left them all in stitches. Muddy, they lay laughing on the lawn in the afternoon sunlight while they drank lemonade served by Caroline, who had declined the invitation to pitch in. Her husband, Cecil, however, reclined on the grass between Tabby and Sharon, waggling his hand over the baby, who reached to grab the gardener's fingers.

Then, shedding drying mud with every step, they broke into cohorts and undressed in the mud room. The women went first. Cecil returned to his gardening, as he was the least dirty and the least put off by a few spatters of mud. When the women had shed their soiled clothes, an impromptu race began. Wrapped in towels over their undergarments, they ran down the hall and up the stairs.

The sisters outpaced their mother down the hall, their big fluffy towels billowing, their bare feet stamping the wooden floor. Tabby felt like a child again, her hair streaming behind her, laughter ringing out as if she were made of bells. When they ran up the stairs, pushing for first place, she rolled on the hallway carpet, her knees against her chest as Sharon comically pushed her aside to cross the well-established finish line that lay in the boundary between Sharon's room on the right and Tabby's room on the left.

Her sister stood over her, panting, cloth clutched at her collarbone, while Tabby lay upon her unclasped towel, like a sunbather.

"You look quite glamorous," Sharon said, brushing a lock of hair from her sister's forehead.

"I am quite glamorous, haven't you heard?" Tabby said. Then she took Sharon's hand and kissed it. "Please," she said, "let us be friends until the end. Even when we cannot. Please."

The shadow of her hair hid Sharon's eyes as she looked down at her sister, so Tabby could not see her expression. For a moment, Tabby was afraid Sharon would lift her head to reveal eyes that split and split and split. But she brushed her hair aside, and her two gray eyes remained.

The catch in Sharon's voice told Tabby everything. "I will always be your friend, no matter what they make me do. No matter what." She pulled Tabby's hand back to her and kissed it in return.

"Ready or not, the men are coming!" their mother called, taking the stairs much more respectably than her daughters had. The women laughed, and Sharon helped Tabby up.

They snatched up the towel, and the women heard the men whooping below, one, perhaps Peter, but it might have been Jeremiah, calling, "Olly Olly oxen free!"

"Oh," Sharon said, "who will bathe first?"

"We have our own tubs," Tabby said.

"Ah, the boiler's been lounging a bit," Eliska said. "Tabby, why don't you go first?"

"Or," Sharon said, dragging the word out, "perhaps Tabby and Larry haven't seen each other in three months, and they might want to bathe after a little time catching up."

Tabby opened her mouth, closed it, smiled, and nodded.

"Good then. Mother, you go first. I think I may have a few things to discuss with Archie as well."

"I'm offended," Eliska said, "as if I would have nothing to say to your father after he looked so fine pulling on that rope."

The men's voices approached the foot of the stairs.

"Poor Uncle Peter," Tabby said, and they laughed together. "Someone should tell him he can bathe first."

TABBY LEANS OVER HIM, gasping. Her hair, long and damp, tangles in his hands. She presses her palms into his chest, his coarse and curling hair looping over her arched, tense fingers. Her eyes, wide and unblinking, study his face, which, like hers, is open and alert.

She imagines herself upon a great undulating sea, her hair wet with spray, the wind buffeting her as the deck of her vessel rolls. Here she is captain, though, like a captain, subject to the elements. She is great and she is small, and somewhere beyond the horizon lies the morning isles where hope and dread brood together.

She presses her knees against his sides, her feet sliding against his sweat-slick thighs, and she knows only him, and he only her. She longs to kiss him, longs to remain like this, longs to stay, and yet she reaches out and forward toward the impending culmination without which this moment would be incomplete. She wonders if there is a world in which the consummation is the act, and the act is its consummation.

VI
Waxing

Wednesday, March 17, 1926 – Afternoon

LAWRENCE LAY WITH HIS head on Tabby's stomach and traced the line between her hip and her knee. His fingers would sometimes detour through the hair just to the left of his well-established path. Tabby smoked and ran her hand through the dark curls on his head.

"I wish I could stay here with you," she said, "like this. You are wonderful."

"Do I rank favorably against your many conquests?" Larry asked, his finger rounding the acme of her knee.

"I would never call them 'conquests,' my love," she said. "And you don't compete with them. And they can't compete with you. They are beasts of another evolution entirely."

"Beasts," he mused, "I'm sure they are. Regular bulls in season, I imagine."

"Your imagination is too generous. You should replace your bulls with mostly confused and over-eager boys who happen to occupy the bodies of men."

He rolled over onto his side and looked up past the rise of her breasts to her smiling face. "So, no Romeos to speak of?"

"Romeo was a lovesick teenager who would likely be as adept as the fumblers that I encounter," she said.

"Then no Casanovas?"

"Ah, a better fit. You may turn back around and continue what you were doing, by the way; I was enjoying that."

Larry smiled and obliged, his hand running back up to her hip and over and through.

"Yes, that's the spot," she said. "Casanovas? You'd think so, at least from how they talk when gin is in their hand. But no. The world is still too stifled by—oh yes, darling, that's it precisely—the old limitations for anyone to be particularly good at it. It makes one wonder how you honed such fulfilling skills."

Larry shifted. "I have always had a talent for listening, adapting, and improvising, my love."

Then he spoke no more until Tabby lay entirely limp and staring at the ceiling. Satisfied at work well done, he climbed to her side, and she leaned into him.

"I do not deserve you," she said.

"You do," he whispered, pushing a ringlet of hair behind her ear. "You deserve happiness, my love. I don't know why you deny it to yourself."

"I don't," she said, nestling deeper under his arm. "See? Here I lie like Aphrodite, as satisfied as a cat."

"I mean … I mean with our son. You could be so much happier if you'd just—"

She pulled back and saw the concern and love written on his face. She wanted to respond in kind, to touch that face and tell him that he was right. But the pain that tightened her stomach was too great.

"Please," she said, "don't ruin this. I love you, I love this, and, in my own way, I love him. But I cannot be … I can't let myself …"

"Let yourself what?" he asked, putting his finger under her chin. "Be happy? Hold him? Kiss him? There is still so much time, Tabs. So much time."

"No, there isn't. There isn't. Twenty years? What is that?"

"Twenty-three," he said.

"Twenty-two," she said.

"You're right," he said.

"Twenty-two years. But before then, we'll lose Archie, then we'll lose Sharon, and then we'll lose everything. He won't, though. He'll still have her. They'll have each other. And how could I endure that? How could I ever go through all of that if I'm his mother? How can I live every day knowing what will happen and go on like we're a normal family?" Tabby said. She had pulled completely away from him and now sat alone on her side of the bed, her back against the headboard, her knees pulled to her chest.

"My love," he said, his hand resting on her foot, "twenty-two years is more than any person ever can be sure of. Don't you see? This is a gift! Yes, there will be dark days at the end. Don't you think that Archie lives with that shadow over him? Don't you think that Sharon lives with it? And yet they love each other, don't they? They love, they laugh, they care for one another, knowing that he will go, and she will … well, she will do what she must."

"They are stronger than I am," Tabby said. "I can't do what He wants if—Please, my love, please don't ask me this again. I want to be happy with you, I want us to have this"—she waved her hand at the bed and his body—"for the time we have left."

"How can you manage our love if you know it will end? How does anyone? Are you being asked to do much more than anyone else does? More than any widow who sits alone for ten or twenty years after her husband dies? You, at least, will be spared that." He spoke with a tenderness that nearly swayed her.

"I know. And I can manage it because I know that when I go down into the darkness, you will be by my side. I know that I will never have to live without you, even if we must be parted every year. I know that I will come home and you will be here to kiss away the person I pretend to be out there. I know that because He sees far. I know that because you love me. There is no shadow over us, my love. When we come to the end of our path, we will come to it together. We will jump into the abyss as lovers, not as strangers. But when I go, Sharon and I will be …"

She covered her face with her hands. Larry closed the gap between them and stroked her hair. She twined her legs with his.

"Please, I'm begging you not to ask me this again," Tabby said through her fingers.

"I can't promise that," he said, kissing the top of her head, "but I will promise this. I will ask only once a year."

"Why?" she sobbed. "Why must you ask me?"

"Because my heart breaks seeing you deny yourself the happiness you could have now. Because my heart breaks knowing that I cannot share the raising of my son with his mother. Because, for as much as I love you and I will lie between your thighs until I die, we are missing something that we might have together, moments of love and joy that are of a different species than Eros. And poor advocate that I am, I still must make my case once in a while for those other loves whose tables we might feast at together before the end. For there are meals uneaten between us that I believe would bring you joy."

She looked up at him, her body shaking between laughter and sorrow. "You wax poetic, my sweet," Tabby said.

"You arouse poetry within me," he said.

Then her eyes followed the line of his tall form down, and her sorrow fled. "You wax in other ways as well."

"You arouse many things within me," he whispered. And they fell into each other once more.

TABBY DOESN'T BOTHER TO wipe the tears from her cheeks as the car takes her out of the forest and past fallow fields of gathered grain. The hills that rise around her are already bleakly barren under the first light snow of late November. The road before her is empty but for the frost, and Gambol takes his usual caution, keeping his speed low. Perhaps, she thinks, it is out of care that he goes so slowly from the forest, down to where the train will take her far from home. But perhaps, she hopes, he wants to linger a little while longer. Perhaps he, like her, aches in her leaving.

VII
Dignity

Saturday, August 4, 1934 - Midmorning

TABBY KNOCKED ON THE door of the ramshackle little house. Its simplicity and smallness suggested that it had been built before the great reunion swelled the town's population. Tabby wondered if that meant that the occupants predated the Congregation's arrival. The name on the mailbox read 'Gallo,' and Tabby pictured a man with threadbare clothing by that name who had done work for her father years before and wondered if this was his home. She shifted the weight of the basket that hung from her arm and waited. A half a minute later, a man in his shirtsleeves came around the side of the house, wiping his brow with a handkerchief.

"Can I help you?" he asked. He wore a flimsy old cap and had a respectable gray mustache. Tabby wasn't sure if this was the man she remembered.

"Mr. Gallo?" she asked.

"Yes, that's me. Who are you, Ma'am?"

He lifted the brim of his cap. She wasn't sure if he was showing her courtesy or merely adjusting the sweat-damp cloth to see her better.

"I'm Tabitha Kusel," she said.

"Oh, my goodness, you certainly are," he said, adding his cupped hand to the cap's brim to shade his eyes. "Forgive me, Ma'am. Of course, I know you. What … what brings you out here? How can I help you?"

Mr. Gallo shifted from one foot to the other and wiped his hands with a handkerchief he produced from his back pocket. He looked around at his overgrown lawn, unruly bushes, and faded house paint.

"Forgive the state of things, Ma'am," he said, appraising his own unkept appearance. "And my state as well. I was just mowing the back lawn. I guess I should have done the front first."

"Nonsense, Mr. Gallo. Please, forgive me for showing up unannounced."

"Nothing to forgive, you and your family are always welcome. Please, can I get you something? Some coffee or …" He trailed off, his face searching for anything else to offer her.

"Actually, Mr. Gallo, I've come to make you an offer, if you'll forgive me. First, I wanted to give these to your wife."

"No, Ma'am, that's too kind of you." He dropped his eyes, and his mouth and nose twitched like a rabbit's.

"Nonsense, it's only a few jars of preserves, a little coffee and tea, and a fresh loaf of bread from Field's."

Mr. Gallo didn't speak; he only nodded.

"Is your wife home?"

"Yes," he managed. "Yes, I'll go get her. Please, I—"

He looked around, and she realized that he was looking for a place for her to stay while he went to fetch his wife.

"Actually," she said, hoping to spare him, "why don't you take this to her and take your time? Perhaps we can meet for lunch at the diner. Would you be free at eleven-thirty?"

The man reached into his pocket and produced a scuffed, round pocket watch that was missing its chain. He flipped it open and nodded.

"Yes, Ma'am, I can meet you then. Might I ask what it's about?"

"My father needs some work done, and he is looking for men he can trust who have shown their worth in the past. Are you available to work, Mr. Gallo?"

"Oh, yes, Ma'am!" he said.

"Very good," Tabby said, offering the basket to him. "Then I will see you at eleven-thirty for an early lunch. Please bring a pencil and paper, Mr. Gallo."

He agreed, tipped his cap again, and almost bowed as she turned and walked back down the path toward the street. Once on the sidewalk, Tabby surveyed the houses around her and thought that in the nation's desert of want, the Life Force had made an oasis of plenty. Here it bubbled up like a fresh spring, and in that, she thought, the old dream of the New Eden was evident. Even the poor in Lightning Falls worked and ate; even the worst off did not go without. This, she thought, was worth every journey, every lover, every winter spent away from Larry. Precisely how her adventures fashioned these wonders remained a secret known only to Uncle Peter. But she trusted, for the Man With Many Eyes saw far.

She strolled on, smiling to herself, and exchanged a morning greeting with a woman sweeping her front porch. A man passed on the other side of the street in a light suit and wide hat. She turned to him to say 'good morning' when he stopped and lifted the brim. Thousands of flitting, glaring, ogling, dreaming, hazy, burning eyes spread across the top of his face. Tabby's step faltered, and she almost tripped. She looked down to make sure of her footing, and then back across the street. The man was standing with his hand raised, but he only had two eyes that looked at her with concern.

"Are you all right, Ma'am?"

"Yes, sorry, I lost my balance there for a moment. I'm fine, thank you. Good morning!"

Heart pounding, she marched on, back toward the car and Gambol. She fished a small handkerchief from her handbag and dabbed her upper lip. She tried to remember the last time she had seen Him. It had been three years ago, when she was in Portland. He had changed the face of a tall man with light blue eyes and a thin scar that traced the curve of his chin. He had appeared and gone just as quickly, and, just like today, she had faltered. The tall man had caught her, and when she looked into his natural eyes, she had accepted his invitation to dinner.

Their conversation had stumbled until they started to speak about philosophy. The man had been an inveterate Platonist, but utterly uninterested in Plotinus' modifications. They had argued playfully and then made love playfully. The next morning, the man told her that he loved her, and she told him that she could not love him. He had broken a bottle of her perfume and stormed out in an overwhelming cloud of sweetness.

She looked across the street to where the man was watching her. She had no desire to talk to him in that manner, or any man in Lightning Falls who wasn't Larry, for that matter. She bid him good morning again and moved on. She wondered what the point of the appearance was. Was it just to scare her? To remind her that He was always watching? Or that He was everywhere?

Or was He looking for credit? She had been attributing her work and the good that her family was doing to the great Life Force. Had He appeared to remind her that she should lay the credit at His feet? She didn't know. He had not spoken plainly to her since she was a child. Since then, He had doled his will out in whispers, hints, and the voices of the dead.

The voices of the dead. She wondered if that was what the meaning of His appearance was. Did He have something to say? Perhaps she should speak to her father.

Gambol was leaning against the door, smoking and sweating. "Where to, next, Miss Kusel?"

"I have another basket to deliver a block down, I'll just walk. Then we'll go up to Bankview; there are two more there," Tabby said, forcing a smile. "Then I have lunch at eleven-thirty at the diner."

She made her deliveries and three sets of plans for lunch, each on successive days. Her father would find work for them all around town, sometimes with each other, sometimes alone. Mr. Gallo would be the most help, however, as he was a strong laborer. They needed people like him to help them take materials up for the fire-watch tower.

Over the previous five years, the town had transformed as her father, husband, and brother-in-law racked their brains to find projects to employ the people of Lightning Falls. They had brought the whole town over to municipal water and had helped lay the connections to Wallowa Falls Hydroelectric Plant. They had torn down buildings and raised buildings, and they had shored up the banks of Kusel Creek and Hitchman's Creek while diverting other smaller waterways to fill them. They had restored the old cabin and put the radio tower next to it. They had worked and worked, and her father had endeavored to make sure that if there was any whiff of charity, it clung only to the baskets full of preserves, coffee, and tea. He insisted that men and women should earn their money with their hands. There, he said, the people of Lightning Falls found more than just their pay. There, they found their dignity.

She wondered if that applied to the Kusel family as well. There was no lack of money, Tabby knew. In their lives, they would never know even the slightest pinch of need. Though the world languished in darkness, Lightning Falls remained a lamp hidden under a bushel. They were in want of want, and that, she knew, was the difficulty. Men like Mr. Gallo were not skilled, and there would always be work in the fall and spring, preparing roads and fixing roads, but there were only so many works in such a small town, especially when half the town's men were on the job.

After lunch, which Mr. Gallo insisted on paying for, she returned home with a number in her head. She found her parents sitting side-by-side in the library, reading.

"Good afternoon," she said, sweeping in with a flourish of her skirts and curtseying. Her father gave her a serious half-bow from his chair with a twinkle in his eye.

"Good afternoon, Mother," a voice said from off to her right. She saw her son sitting by the front window, a copy of *Robinson Crusoe* propped on his lap.

"Good afternoon, my dear," she said. He smiled up at her, and she returned the gesture briefly before turning back to her parents.

"How did the visits go?" Jeremiah asked.

"Well enough, Mr. Gallo will happily help with the tower. Also, please put an extra two dollars and seventy-five cents into his pay. He bought me lunch."

"That was generous of him," Eliska said.

"Yes, I thought so too. But I don't want him—"

Her father held up an understanding hand, and she nodded.

"Why don't you pick yourself up a book and sit with us?" her mother said. She glanced at the boy in the chair.

"No, I have to—" Tabby said, "I have—"

"I believe Larry was looking for you," her father said.

"Larry can find her in here," her mother said.

"I think he's upstairs," he said.

Tabby smiled gratefully and left the library. She found Larry in their room with suitcases out. She felt her body begin to tremble.

"What are you doing?" she asked. "Do I have to go? It's not time yet."

He looked up at her and smiled. "What? No—well, yes—I hope you will go, but with me. Though not just yet. I'm just checking these. I was thinking you and I could go on a trip together while there's time."

Tabby took a long, relieved breath. The quaking in her limbs subsided. "Ah! Where will we go?"

"I was thinking Europe, but we could also go to South America, perhaps Brazil. Where would you like to go?"

"Oh, I do want to see Europe. You've been and I haven't, and that's beastly unfair," she said, plopping herself down on the bed in a pantomime of pique.

"Well, when I was in Europe, it was a bit out of sorts, my love."

"I know, but—"

"And it will be out of sorts again soon enough. We should go while we can."

She nodded. "Will we go alone?"

"Yes, I was hoping we would," he said. "I don't want anyone taking a moment of your time from me."

"That sounds utterly wonderful," she said. She looked up at him coyly. "You won't be beastly, will you? You won't send me off like you always do to be prey to the lusts of other men?"

"Only men?" he asked, a twinkle in his eye.

"That was twice," she said, and shook her head at him. "And it's not for me. But perhaps Paris will change my mind. Who knows, maybe it will change yours as well."

"Far be it from me," Larry said, sitting next to her, "to say 'no' to anything I haven't tried. But it was my hope we might be more—I don't know—*traditional.* We have given up so much to see your family's vision through. I thought this might be just for us."

"Yes," Tabby said, "yes, I want that. Let's do that. You and me, Larry, like a normal husband and wife."

He kissed her.

She pulled back, suddenly remembering her encounter in the street. "What is it?"

"I—I saw him, Larry. Today, while I was out delivering baskets."

"Who did—" Larry's eyes widened with understanding. "Did he say anything?"

She shook her head. "But I think he wants to speak to us."

"Poor Sharon," Larry said.

"Yes, so we'll have to do something nice for her when it's over."

"She's not coming on the vacation," he said, laughing.

"No, but perhaps she and Archie could see us off in New York."

"That I can agree to," Larry said. "Whose clothing shall we get out of storage?"

Tabby shook her head. "I don't know. Let's have a meeting and see what everyone thinks."

vii

TABBY WATCHES AS HER mother pushes Sharon out the front door. Her father reviles her sister with words deep and cutting. Sharon's eyes are wide with pain as Archie takes hold of her hair, pulls back, and then propels her forward with a thrust, down the porch stairs. She falls into the gravel, her hands scraping, her dress tearing. Tabby storms down the stairs and feels her sorrow, resentment, and anger throbbing in her veins as she kicks her sister's leg and scorns her under a full moon.

Larry belittles her, Eliska spits upon the ground, and knocks her shoes against the porch steps. Only the boy does not speak. He stands, his eyes shut tight as his father holds him in place and his aunt scrabbles on the ground to protect herself.

As Sharon gains her feet, she stumbles once before scurrying across the lawn into the dark. To their left, light glows down on them from the window of the little shelter overlooking the yard from its perch on four metal legs.

VIII
Purposes

Friday, November 13, 1936 - Evening

"AND I WOULD RATHER be with you," Larry said. "But we must do what we must—"

"But why? Why Larry? What am I accomplishing out there? I'm not spreading the good news of the New Settlement. I'm not winning the hearts of men to fill our coffers. I'm not keeping untamed wanton lusts fulfilled. So, why am I doing this? I am told I must be out there, but don't need to be," Tabby pleaded.

"Yes, you do," Larry said, picking up a small jewelry box from her vanity and putting it in her bag. "And you know that better than I do. You were told that this is part of the plan. And your health—"

"My health? Because I wheezed in the cold weather as a child? There is cold weather in Chicago, and New York, and Portland, Larry."

"But the mountains—"

"This is nonsense," she said, balling her hands into fists. "How do we know it's right?" Tabby dropped onto the bed and pushed her bag aside.

"Because everything else he told us has happened," Larry said. "From the passing and repealing of prohibition to the Great Panic to the rise of this man in Germany. All of it is happening. Every last bit to the date. He sees far, Tabby, and his vision is true."

She knew this, of course. She had made the same argument a score of times, both to herself and to Sharon over the years.

"I'm not young anymore. The men, they don't—"

"Stop it, you remain one of the most beautiful women on the face of this planet. You are a goddess of light, and I can't believe any man would not long for you."

"You don't know what it's like," she said. "You don't know what—"

"I know," he said, sitting down next to her and putting his arm around her, "that I miss you terribly when you're gone. And I know that it torments me to know that other men get to touch you and be with you and make you feel all the things I want to make you feel—"

"But they don't!" she insisted. "Not one, none of them. They can't make me feel what I feel for you or with you, don't you understand? I'm not out there enjoying myself. I'm nothing more than a prostitute for this monstrous dream that will never come true."

"Don't say that, please—"

"No, Larry, it's true. If the dream were going to come true, it would have by now. *The Brethren journeyed across the world,*" she said in a sing-song, remembering the words from her childhood. "But then what? We found a book, and a body, and a basement, and we thought that meant we had come to the right place. And then what? A boy in a piece of old clothing told us the future. And we've believed him—"

"Because it's all come true—"

"But can't you see? There are so few of us left now! Conti's family, the Milers, and us. That's all that's left of the Brethren, Larry. That's all. Three families, and we will … we'll be nothing soon. Twelve measly years. What is that? It's nothing. Twelve years and we'll all be gone."

"No, we are more than that. Since the reunion, there are so many of us," Larry said, stroking her hair.

"They are not us, my love. I know you think they are, but they aren't."

He squeezed her, and she wept. They went on like that, back and forth, until the pain in her was all used up and she felt scraped out and empty. Then, her eyes blank and resigned, she packed her clothes. The next day, Gambol drove her and Conti back to the train station in Enterprise, where they waited for their duty to take them far from the quiet streets of Lightning Falls.

"Will Leo meet us in Chicago?" Conti asked when they finally boarded and were away.

"No," Tabby said, watching houses give way to fields, forests, mountains, and streams.

"Why not?"

"He married in the spring, don't you remember?"

Her friend was silent.

"I … I loved him," Conti said.

"I know," Tabby said. "Thank you for coming with me early this year."

"I'll have to go back for Christmas," Conti said, dabbing at her eye.

"I know," Tabby said. "I understand."

"It always makes me sad that you have to spend Christmas alone."

"I'm never alone," Tabby said, her breath fogging the window. She poked at it, making little spots in the mist, over and over until it was full of little circles, like moist, staring eyes.

STRANGE, STRONG ARMS HOLD her on the dance floor as three men play a slow serenade. Shadow hides the man's face, and she muses that he is the same unseen man who holds her each time the winds blow cold, and she descends from the bright foothills into these dark rooms full of smoke and sound. She longs for a wide country where winds do not whip themselves up through the canyons of tycoon-built towers. She aches for the man who waits for her there, and the warmth of family as the unseen man lifts her chin with a finger and brings his mouth to hers.

IX
Generation

Tuesday, July 25, 1939 - Afternoon

TABBY STRODE ACROSS THE lawn toward the gazebo where Peter reclined, his eyes staring out past Hitchman's Creek.

"Papa told me you just got in," she said, extending her hands to the tall, white-haired man. "You've lost weight!"

"One must keep light on their toes while avoiding Herr Hitler's devotees," Peter said, standing and offering his arms. She hugged him and kissed him. "You are looking very well, my dear. My goodness, you haven't aged a day since you turned thirty."

"Well, I would have liked to have heard twenty-five, but I accept your compliment nonetheless," she said, kissing him again on his clean-shaven cheek. "You have shrunk, but your mustache has grown!"

"Ah, yes, well, it seems that the smaller your lip-rug, the bigger your ego. So, I'm trying to go in the other direction."

"Oh, I despise that expression," she said, sitting next to him on the cushioned bench.

"I do as well, but I am compensated all the more when I see you wrinkle your nose. Now, tell me all about your life for the last two years!" He put his hand firmly on top of hers and shook it with affection.

"What is there to say? I serve at our master's decree."

"Oh, come now," he said, pulling and pushing her so that she turned in her seat, the way he had done when she was a girl. Then she had laughed as he ruddered her back and forth, the next best thing to a carousel, she'd say. But, so many years later, little of the old delight remained. Still, she did not protest. "It's not so bad, is it? You come and go as you please, you enjoy the lives of both a married woman and a rich eccentric spinster, and you do so with the knowledge that you are doing it all to support your family's work."

This, she also did not protest. She had learned that that was the easiest thing. "You're quite right," she said, forcing herself to smile. "Tell me, what brings you out of the dark recesses of the doomed Nazi Reich?"

"Success," he said, smiling self-contentedly.

"Really?" Tabby said, reaching out to take his hand, genuine excitement replacing her discontent. "You've really found it?"

"Oh yes. Of course, it took some doing, and some doing of dirty deeds as well, I might add. But I was perfectly splendid in my sordid affairs."

"Did you leave a mess behind you?" she asked, feeling suddenly as if she were ten years old again and he was telling her stories of the gentleman thief who stole both jewels and affections.

"Broken necks, broken hearts, broken locks," he said. "Not … precisely in that order."

"Uncle Peter!" Tabby said, her voice a high and giddy giggle. Before the laughter died, she pulled herself up short, frowned, pulled back, and looked at him. "I'm sorry, I don't know why I said it like that."

"A moment of childlike glee is nothing to be ashamed of; it keeps us young," he said.

"No, I … I just haven't been feeling like myself lately. I get giddy when I shouldn't, and sullen when I should be happy."

He frowned sagely and nodded. He put a finger under her chin and lifted her face for his study. "Are you getting enough sleep?"

"No, not really," she said. "That must be it."

"Tell me, why aren't you sleeping?"

"I dream … disturbing things," Tabby said.

"Tell me about them." All laughter was gone from his face, and he looked at her solemnly.

"I wish I could, Herr Freud, but I don't remember them."

"What *do* you remember? Surely you must remember something."

"Amber," she said. "I remember amber, glowing as if infused with broken light. Shards of amber, falling through space."

"And that's all?"

"And something moving, something titanic, dark, scaled, and slithering!"

She buried her face in her hands. Peter put his arm around her and shushed her gently. "And where is this great twisting beast? Under your bed? Or in it?"

She shook her head and released something that might have been a laugh if it wasn't so bestial. "No, below the horizon, to the east."

Peter nodded and squeezed her shoulder. They sat like that for several minutes, listening to the water ramble over the creek stones and Cecil trimming a hedge. They drank in the pine-spiced air and thought about what their dreams portended.

When Tabby calmed, she sat up straight and looked at her uncle. "Will you come inside and show me your prize?"

"That is an excellent idea," he said. "You can help me hide it!"

"Hide it? But don't we need to—"

"Always better to be one step ahead," he said, tapping the side of his nose with his finger and winking. She laughed and took his hand. They returned to the house, and Tabby waited for him in the library. When he appeared again, he held a small wooden box. He handed it to her.

"Now, that isn't its original form, of course," he said as she lifted the lid and revealed a crudely fashioned brooch—a simple ring of iron with the accompanying metal pin. "It was refashioned by Celts of some clan or another, perhaps three thousand years ago."

"But this is iron," Tabby said.

"Yes, quite right. But they could smith iron here and there. This, as well, is especially pure and workable iron. They wouldn't have had to smelt it or really do anything but heat it and beat it." He laughed and seemed pleased at his little rhyme.

"It's so light," she said, weighing it in her fingers. "I assume you'd gather the cloth through the ring and then slide this under?"

"I assume you're right," Peter said.

"Nothing decorative about it." She turned it over in her hand. "What's this?" She pointed to a faint impression in the back.

"I don't know," he said. "Perhaps the blacksmith's stamp."

"Do you think they had such things a thousand years before Christ?"

"Well, who am I—Oh, well, hello, my boy!"

Tabby felt her stomach drop. She turned and saw her son, his brown hair mussed and his long-sleeved shirt muddy.

"What have you got there, Mother?" he asked.

"Just something your great uncle snatched from Germany," she said.

"Come and take a look," Peter said. Tabby handed the box back to her uncle and walked over to study one of the shelves of books.

"Here you go, have a look now. Don't be afraid, you can't hurt it. Except to make it into something else, there's no power on earth that could destroy that."

"Isn't that true of everything?" the boy said.

Tabby smiled as she examined a two-volume set of books by Howard Carter.

"Well, yes, I suppose it is. Nothing is ever truly destroyed," said Peter.

"Except memory," Tabby said. "And dreams."

"But they are immaterial," the boy said, "and perhaps the least subject to destruction."

"You have been reading Plato, I think," Peter said. "That is very good."

"Is it?" Tabby asked, remembering the man who broke her perfume bottle.

"Do you not like Plato, Mother?"

"I—Well, it doesn't matter what I like."

"Here, tell me what you make of it, young man," Peter said. Tabby waited, staring at the volume-crowded shelves, but not seeing them. In her mind, the lad was staring down into the box with wide-eyed wonder, taking the metal tremulously into his hand, and turning it over and over. She dared not look, lest her little walls come tumbling down.

"It's three thousand years old?"

"That's right," Peter said.

"How do you know that?"

"It was found among other objects from the same time period. That is how archaeologists date things."

"But how do they know how old those objects are?"

Tabby heard Peter walk toward her.

"Pardon me, my dear," he said, reaching past her to the shelf and pulling the two-volume set down. "These," he said, "are a bit beyond your current level, but I think you'll catch up quickly enough."

"These are about King Tut," her son said.

"Quite right, they are. And you know, have you ever seen pictures of your mother and your aunt from around when you were born?" A moment of silence. Tabby pictured him nodding. "Did you ever see them wearing those fancy headbands with the feathers? Yes? Well, they were all trying to look like queens from King Tut's time. Oh yes, Nefertiti, Ankhesenamun, Cleopatra."

"Wasn't Cleopatra much later?"

"Well, look at that, perhaps these books won't be beyond you at all."

Silence followed, and Tabby wished she had a cigarette.

"What's it for?"

"The brooch? Well, magic, of course. We're going to cast a spell," Peter said.

"But magic isn't real."

Peter tutted and tsked, and Tabby imagined he was shaking his head and pulling out his pipe. A moment later, she smelled the sweet scent of his tobacco. She knew now that the Socratic method must follow, and he would be calling her son 'my dear boy' before long.

"It is an endless shame to me that boys no longer believe in magic. Do you believe in the Incarnation?"

"Yes, I suppose so."

"And the Resurrection?"

"I suppose so."

"What is that, but the magic of God? What is life but the magic of the great Élan Vital that moves through us? In fact, my dear boy, one must ask not whether magic exists, but whether we could even ask questions were it not for magic? How can we, but moving atoms and colliding energy, reason and wonder? Was it all contained in the first moments of the universe, thrumming on inevitably until we came to this moment here? Does the very pattern of cause and effect contain within it the mindless mind that must ask and answer its own questions, all meaninglessly as rock to rock, mimicking the sounds of reason in a reasonless existence?"

"I—" the boy began.

"Such must be our belief if there is no magic. We must imagine that our universe looks as if there are minds within it, looks as if there is life and vital thought, looks as if there is Eros and Philia and Logos, indeed, looks just like a universe filled with such things, but is not. We must imagine that we live in a counterfeit so perfect as to fool the wisest of us, and yet remain a counterfeit against which no true universe of magic might be compared."

The boy was silent.

"Don't you think?" Uncle Peter said, clamping his teeth down onto the stem of his pipe loudly enough that Tabby could hear it from across the room.

"I ... I don't know," the boy said.

"Bravo!" Peter exclaimed excitedly. "Perhaps you have been reading Plato after all!"

Tabby turned and saw, for a moment, a strange double-vision. There was her son, tousle-haired and muddy, with a small wooden box open and resting on a pile of books he held between his hands. There, too, was the man he would become: intelligent, curious, and sensitive. An ache radiated from her core, and she felt she would begin to weep if she didn't leave.

"My dear," Uncle Peter said, as she started out through the back of the library, "are you quite well?"

"I've just become very tired," Tabby lied. "I thought I would lie down."

"Oh? I'm sorry to hear that. I had hoped for your help with this."

"Perhaps someone else can give you a hand," Tabby said.

"Yes, that is a good idea. Do you mind calling Cecil for me before you put yourself to bed?"

Tabby didn't mind at all.

That night at dinner, she didn't talk much. Afterward, Larry asked about her health, and she told him that she wanted to go on another vacation. He told her he wanted to, but he didn't think they could until the autumn. She told him she understood, smiled, and wept silently into her pillow after the lights went out. Soon after, she slept.

She dreamt that she was walking down the hallway of the Harkman, her feet splashing in the blue carpet waves. The green-gold of the walls glowed around her as a strange breeze buffeted her from the elevator's open doors. There, in a smart burgundy elevator operator's uniform, Henry stood with one hand on the handle and the other on the glossy leather brim of his cap.

She smiled and approached him, feeling languid and liquid, her legs like those of a lioness, lifting and lilting forward, each step upon the toes of her arched foot. The sequins of her dress glinted in the weird morning light that welled from the walls. The band on her head was tight, and she could feel the feather that jutted up from it bounce with every step. She could hear no saxophone or trombone, but even so, music seemed to vibrate through the hallway.

When she reached the elevator and stepped inside, a sudden giddiness clambered up from her stomach, through her chest, and out over her lips. She laughed, and it seemed to take a year for the sound to bubble up from her throat and over her tongue as Henry pulled one lever to close the doors and another to start their descent. She laughed in slow, rolling waves that moved across her like an outgoing tide. The thought, whatever it was, made her heart feel light and free, though a moment later she couldn't remember it. Tabby sighed and felt her shoulder rise in a gesture of dismissal.

The elevator stopped, and Henry opened the doors. The hallway that lay before Tabby might have been the Harkman, but only after a century of neglect and decay. The carpets were dirty, the walls and doors painted dull off-white, and the light fixtures were unremarkable and spotted with dried paint. In the middle of the hall was a hurrying, scuttling girl-creature with long brown hair and strange clothing. She wore a flat-brimmed cap, denim pants like a farmhand, a man's tan undershirt, and shoes of some style Tabby couldn't identify. She moved like Charlie Chaplin in one of the pictures where he sped around for comic effect. Then the strangely dressed girl saw her and her face contorted with manic speed into a rictus of horror. For one second, the two women stood staring at each other, then the weird girl sped away through a door.

Henry looked over at Tabby and shrugged, slow and sleepy. Tabby laughed again, and the doors of the elevator closed. Down they went, for what felt like ages, until finally they stopped. She turned to thank Henry, but he would not look at her. Instead, he stared straight ahead, his mouth gaping in a silent, shaking scream.

The doors of the elevator opened, and Tabby stepped out into a dark, dripping cave. In one hand, she felt the cool metal of the brooch. In the other, she held a block of dark, smooth-grained wood. She held them up and examined them.

"Hello?" a voice said from somewhere in the darkness. It sounded like a musical instrument, without breath or flesh. She had only ever heard one other voice like it. "Is someone there?"

Tabby stepped forward, peering into the cave, aware that she must be careful, for the floor fell away on either side of her.

"Come here," the voice continued as she took another step. "I want to tell you a secret."

Tabby woke as she took the next step, the shadows of the cave dissolving into the unforgiving reality of the room around her. And, between blinks, she glimpsed the outline of a figure sitting in the chair by the window, his head tilted to one side, the moon reflecting from his thousand eyes.

RAIN AND SNOW SCATTER against the train's window. Tabby thinks to herself, *This is the last time I will return home to find Archie there.*

She dreads the meeting. She knows that many have returned home to say 'goodbye' to a loved one, but she knows that this farewell portends more. The cold, but comforting, cycle of years, season to season, cracks. The winter land's cacophony threatens to scatter the steady, reliable heartbeat of her summer country.

The Life Force, which has pushed her forward for so many years, swells, and soon, she knows, it will crest and all she loves will go down into darkness, tumbling, battered forever to sand beneath its rolling waves.

X
Cleave

Sunday, October 8, 1944 - Morning

SHARON'S FINGERS DUG INTO Tabby's arm so hard that Tabby was afraid she'd hurt one of them.

"God, I don't want to," Sharon said, her muffled words almost lost against Tabby's chest.

Tabby couldn't decide if this would be the third most difficult day of her sister's life. The day Archie died had been monstrous, as had the weeks that led up to it. They had all known it was coming and that it couldn't be long. But they hadn't known the exact day or hour, and so everyone found themselves behaving strangely. Some, like her mother and Larry, had doted on Archie. Others, like Caroline, wept when they thought no one was looking. The men had gone on a camping trip a month earlier, and then spent days fishing on the pier or working together on one project or another. Cecil and Caroline had made sure Archie's favorite meals were on regular rotation and set aside special desserts for him. Jeremiah had mixed his favorite drinks, and Cecil finally lost a game of chess to Archie, brilliantly making it seem as if the man had really outsmarted the gardener.

Sharon, on the other hand, had begun to withdraw, and for the first time in their lives, the sisters truly understood each other. Tabby had comforted her sister nightly as Sharon had pulled away from her doomed husband.

Archie, for his part, had been a man of immaculate and admirable stoicism and even humor. This, Tabby believed, had hurt Sharon even more. He had been the one condemned, and he had been such a scoundrel by being so beautifully brave. And, though he had followed Sharon's lead and did not press her, his affection and care for her never diminished, up to the afternoon they had walked into town together to see *Arsenic and Old Lace* at the Silver Ring Theater. He had held her hand and kissed her cheek as they strolled along Main Street, and she stared straight ahead.

Tabby pictured their little group walking together, block after block, until they came to the edge of town and the stretch of road that led to their home. It had been windy all day, and when they came to their drive, they saw that one of their lawn umbrellas had rolled all the way around the house, up the drive, and across the road. Archie, without thinking, ran across to pick it up. When he turned to come back, they saw the truck, careening around the corner, swerving in the lane.

Tabby believed her brother-in-law could have leapt out of the way. There was time. Instead, he looked at them with an expression that had haunted her every day: gratitude. Archie's eyes were not resigned, not peaceful, not panicked; they were thankful and full of love as his cheek twitched up in that lopsided grin of his and he closed the umbrella.

Then he went under the truck and tumbled head over heels, an expression Tabby had always thought of as an exaggeration. But Archie had gone head over heels twice before his body lay broken and still on the road. The truck had swerved once more and crashed into an old pine, throwing its driver through the window and into a pile of broken limbs.

Everyone had gone to Archie's side then, except Tabby. She had walked calmly to the truck and the man who lay, blinking and gurgling, on the ground. She had crouched down next to him and pulled a branch away from his face.

"I know how you feel," she had said as the world tilted and rolled around her. Then she had stood and kicked him in the face a dozen times until he was silent.

She wished it had been two dozen.

Now, as she sat, comforting her sister in her white wedding dress, Tabby wished she could kick someone else—maybe Arthur, Sharon's groom-to-be. She pictured his nose breaking the way the driver's had, his teeth coming loose, but not quite out.

"My dear, it's time." Jeremiah stood in the doorway of Sharon's bedroom, wearing his best suit.

"She needs another minute," Tabby said. "We both do."

"Of course," he said, walking over to sit on Sharon's other side. He put a hand on her back, and she turned to him, pressing her face into his shoulder.

"Daddy," she said, "please, I don't want to do it. I don't. I hate him. I hate them. I hate everything they've done to us. I hate it all. Tabby was right. They're foul, monstrous, dark things. Please don't make me."

He patted her head. Tabby leaned forward and lay across Sharon's back, pressing her cheek just below her sister's neck. Jeremiah wrapped them both in his embrace. They breathed together, and Tabby thought about sitting in the gazebo in their bathing clothes on hot summer days after splashing in Hitchman's Creek, their towels around them and their father singing songs of peace and hope with Uncle Peter. That had been before Sharon had ever spoken to them with a stranger's sneering face; before she had, with an unfamiliar voice, told them of many years of joy and trouble, of the world's convulsions, and their own coming catastrophe. Then there had been only the simple, natural hopes and fears that accompany most lives.

She wanted to go back, to live one more day in that hope, or at least one more day before Sharon would have to leave them forever. But then, she had lived that day yesterday, and it hadn't lasted. She hadn't been able to slow the hours, hadn't been able to keep this moment from coming. The Life Force surged on, thrumming through the universe at its own pace, measuring its own steps. She was just a vessel. So were they all.

"My dear, it is time," Jeremiah said finally.

Tabby squeezed harder and then let go. She leaned back and wiped her eyes. She looked at her sister and realized that this was the last moment she could truly think of her that way. This woman, Sharon Jolette Kusel Alden, would soon add another name, one that meant nothing to Tabby except that this man, Arthur, would never be a brother to her or Larry, and never a son to her parents.

She stood and took Sharon's hands. "Come, it's time to be brave."

"That's all that's left," Sharon said, letting Tabby pull her to her feet. "Days of bravery. No more days of joy."

Tabby smiled as best she could. "Oh, I don't know about that. I think they'll sneak up on you."

"Not for years and years," Sharon said, closing her eyes and hanging her head in shame.

"Perhaps. But don't think that this is all gloom. He sees far."

Sharon nodded and wiped her eyes again.

"Come, dear," Jeremiah said, "time lingers not in this place."

Sharon took her father's hand and let him lead her to the door. Then she stopped, looked back at her sister, and said, "This is the last time we'll all be together."

Tabby wanted to correct her. But, as she looked past her sister into the hall where the Man With Many Eyes stood, his mouth a solemn, straight line, she decided to allow her sister's lie to hang between them. Certainly, it was better that this should be the last time than to acknowledge the future's monstrosity.

After the minister of the Congregation Church performed the ceremony, Sharon left the house for almost the last time. She wore a smile so perfectly practiced that even her new husband, who had made a study of her before their betrothal, had no idea that it was false. Tabby stood with Larry, her parents, and Uncle Peter in the driveway and waved them farewell.

When the car turned left, heading out of town on their way to the coast, her parents and Peter went inside. Only Larry remained with her.

"Are you all right, my love?" he asked.

"Yes," she said, staring after where the car had been. The world tilted again, and a man stood at the far end of the gravel drive. He was too far away for her to see his face, but she knew it swarmed with eyes. "I—"

"What is it?"

"I don't know, I need to think about things. Come inside, it's getting cold."

That night, she sat at her vanity, rubbing cold cream on her face as Larry stood near the bed, pulling at his tie. She stared at him in the mirror's reflection and saw, past him, the Man lying on their bed, looking at her. He wore a threadbare suit, though it looked richly made. His shoes were elegant but scuffed. He folded his hands across his stomach, and upon each finger he wore bands of silver and gold, each adorned with an orange-gold stone of polished amber. Of the two men, she wasn't sure which she hated more.

"I'm leaving again tomorrow," she said.

"Tomorrow?" Larry asked. "So soon? We have another month and a half before—"

"Yes," she said, unclipping her earrings. She expected the Man to disappear after she looked down to put them into her jewelry box, but he remained on the bed, watching her. "Tomorrow, and tomorrow, and tomorrow."

"My love, you don't have to—"

"I do. There isn't much time left, Larry. We've got to get it all in before the end, you know? We have to do our parts, and my part is ending soon."

He sighed loudly and began to unbutton his shirt. "Tabby, you don't have to—"

"I don't have to what? You've been telling me for years that I must go out, I must meet other men, I must take them into my bed. You've never told me why, because you don't know *why*. None of us know *why*—"

"My dear, Peter knows—"

"But Peter's not telling, is he? He's coughing and sputtering up his lungs, but he's not telling. He'll be in the grave before any of us, and not once has he sat us down to say, 'This is what I alone have been told, this is the hope, it's not all for nothing.'"

"I know, and I know it's frustrating; it's a test. It's all a test, like Abraham and Isaac," Larry said.

She coughed up a short, harsh laugh. "Nonsense. It's nonsense what they say about that monstrous story, and it is nonsense that we're being tested. Why would God or—" she looked at the Man on the bed, his eyes roving, "or anyone who 'sees far,' why would they need to test us? It's a story for children that we've decided is worthy of adult approval."

Larry took a deep breath, held it, and then let it out. "I understand that today was upsetting for you. It was upsetting for us all. This is an upsetting season."

"It's not the season that is upsetting; it's the age. We have entered an age of ice, my love, and now everything is dying."

"Not everything," Larry said, crossing the room to stand behind her. He looked at her in the reflection. "We still have each other for years—"

"Don't say years like we have years and years. Three. Three years, Larry. three and then no more. How can we act like three is anything when twenty went by like a flash? How can we act like there's anything that can be done in three years that's worth it?"

"I don't know what you mean. We move through life in minutes and seconds, in mornings and afternoons. And of those, we have thousands."

"Of minutes, perhaps. But not mornings. A little more than a thousand mornings. And every day we wake up, we must tick another one off."

"Oh come, you don't know the precise date any better than we did with Archie—"

"Enough," she said. "I can't. I need to go. I need to feel a man's arms around me who doesn't just accept his fate. I need to feel skin against me that doesn't think it's a slave and that I'm a slave."

Larry looked at her, perplexed. "A slave?"

The Man on the bed sat up and turned, swinging his legs over the side. He stood and walked to the door, sliding one olive-skinned, long-fingered hand up the door jamb. She didn't know what to make of it. He hadn't appeared to her for this long since she was a child.

She closed her eyes, squeezing them shut, and then opened them again. Finally, the Man was gone.

"Oh," she said, tears welling, "I'm sorry. Go back to whatever you were doing. My mind is on fire right now, and I'm boiling over. Ignore me. But I will be leaving. Maybe not tomorrow, but soon. I'm fairly certain of that."

He nodded slowly, squeezed her shoulders, and leaned down to kiss her. But, finding her cheek covered in cold cream, he descended to her shoulder. She watched him in the mirror and wished she could take back everything she had just said. But that was the thing about time, it countenanced no reversals, no do-overs.

So, she was silent as he returned to taking off his clothes, and she returned to taking off her face.

X

Tabby lounges in a room of roving lights. Their colors, yellow and red, blue and green, rotate and roam over and across her long, lean legs. Though others crowd the loud, smoky room, she knows that only she can see rolling colors that skitter up her stockings, across her hips, and over her chest to her neck, where they glide across her lips and against her tongue, where she tastes their strange savors, light and tropical. A hand traces fingers over her bare shoulder and tugs at her necklace. A knee cradles her head, and a woman runs an ice cube along the path between the crook of her elbow and her wrist. She looks into the woman's eyes and wonders what her light tastes like.

XI
Christmas

Thursday, December 25, 1947 – Just Before Sunrise

TABBY WOKE FROM A dream she could barely remember. Impressions from another time lingered and faded like sun-scattered mist: Sharon helping her get ready on their wedding day, pulling an old log from the creek, running through the house. A tear ran down her face and onto the burgundy pillowcase of the Harkman's penthouse master bedroom. The man who lay next to her snored softly, his naked body still well-muscled from his service. He had been a colonel, and though he seemed to want to forget it, every tenth man they had met the night before wouldn't let him. Salutes, thanks, drinks purchased, drinks shared, all while Tabby stood beside him, stroking his arm, and agreeing with the men that he was a hero, and with the women that he looked ever so fine.

They had stayed up well past midnight, kissed under the mistletoe, and drank too much champagne. He had passed out before she could love him. She expected he would wake up with a terrible hangover, though Tabby felt no ill after-effects. She rarely did. Conti had been like that. They would wake after a raucous night and eat an early breakfast together, chatting about music and gossiping about who was cheating with whom. But now Conti was gone, thrown from a horse a year ago, the last scion of her family snuffed out by a mount she had trusted for years.

We Kusels are the last of the Brethren, whittled down to a bitter mote.

Tabby stood and considered her robe, but her modesty wasn't her concern. How could it be? How many men had she slept with? How many men knew not just what she looked like, but what she felt like, sounded like, tasted like? There were five men in the penthouse that Christmas morning, and three of them had seen her like this. So, she left her robe and strode out into the living room.

The space was both cozy and impersonal. The couches, set in an L-shape, were warmly upholstered. A Persian carpet stretched across most of the hardwood floor, with spindly-legged tables pressing their clawed feet into its ornate plush. Framed photographs of fields, forests, and mountains hung from the two full walls. The far wall was only half-height and served as a breakfast counter for the kitchen, and the last was made up of floor-to-ceiling windows and a sliding door that led out onto the balcony.

In the corner stood a Christmas tree, tastefully hung with lead tinsel and colorful, shiny, bright ornaments. Beneath it, piles of neatly wrapped and stacked presents lay in festive paper tied in ribbons. Next to the tree stood a stand-up bar with the crèche on top. Tabby padded over to look at the ceramic shepherds, sheep, woman, and man. The wise men and the camels would not arrive for another twelve days, but there was one piece missing that Tabby wanted to add, as it was Christmas morning, and they had all been a bit too in their cups to remember the night before.

She cast about, looking for the small ceramic child.

"You know," a voice said behind her, "it was nothing like that."

She turned, her hand to her heart, expecting to see one of the men from their party. Instead, she saw the Man, standing by the window, bouncing something in his palm. His eyes, a multitude searching and staring, gazing, and longing, turned toward her. He waved his hand across his face like an adult changing their expression for a child, and only two eyes remained to regard her with piercing and domineering amber light. She wanted to ask him what he meant, but she had trouble getting moisture into her mouth.

Even so, he answered her unspoken question, "No manger, no journey to Bethlehem, no star in the east. A boy born to a couple like any other."

"You were there, I suppose?" Tabby managed.

"Yes," he said.

"Did you know he was special? Or … or just that people would make him special?"

"Yes," he said.

"Is he … you know? If you were there, then—"

"I don't know," he said, bouncing the small object in his hand.

"I would have thought that you would know, since you're … well, I guess since you see far."

He nodded slowly. "If he is who … who even I hope he is, then he is beyond my nature as much as he is beyond yours. He is deeper than my being, and I cannot look upon his essence, no matter what your theologians like to say about it."

"What are you?" she asked, forgetting her nudity and taking a step toward him. He wore the same dark gray suit she had seen him in every time since she was a child, though the cut always changed to keep up with the times. Was he vain, or was it a trick of her own mind?

"What are you?" he asked in return.

"I … I'm a human," she said.

"But what does that mean? You think you know. But it's all whispers and pantomime. You think you know how the body works because some of you know how many organs are in it. You think you know how the mind works because some of you have dissected it, and others have played with psychology. You think you know where you come from because you've dug up fossils and started telling a story that connects them to you. You think you know what a soul is, or that you don't have one, because some people have told you things that they don't fully understand, or sometimes even half-understand themselves. You sum up the vast mystery of your existence into a neat little word that means almost nothing. You do this with everything. You package mystery into neat sounds like *human*, and *reality*, and"—he looked down at his hand—"*Messiah*."

She swallowed.

"He hated the idea," he said, his voice like a wide wind over a deep valley.

"What?"

"The idea of Messiah. The warrior king, or the one who would purify the religion. *Hosannah* is a political cry, not a spiritual one. He hated it."

"Because you were there," she said, taking another step toward him.

"I was there. I was looking on, desperate to see. I longed to look into his mind, to know, to see whether he was—"

"What? God? The Son of God?"

He shook his head. "No, true. I wanted to see if he was true. Like a sword is true. His people had long said that the Word of God is true, and I wanted to see if it dwelt in him."

"And did it?" Tabby asked, nearer again by a step.

He shrugged, his fierce eyes staring at his palm.

"Then," she said, feeling a mad question coming into her mind, "do you celebrate Christmas?"

"Yes," he said. "But not as you do."

"Then how?" she asked.

"I live in hope," he said, though his eyes looked anything but hopeful to her. She saw in them horrors and despair, torments and conquest, loss and domination.

"What do you hope for?"

"Apokatastasis," he said.

"What's that?"

"A dream," he said. "The best dream. A dream of which I am not worthy."

"Well, whatever it is, why don't you, you know, make it happen? You see far, don't you?"

"I do. But not that far. In fact, the extent of my sight is coming to its end. At least for today."

"What does that mean?" She was almost next to him now.

"When my sight ends for this day, I will see again, anew, and far."

"So … tomorrow?" She didn't think that sounded very far at all.

"My tomorrow, not yours. As each of your days passes, my sight grows shorter. My day is nearing its end. For me, it is soon. It is always soon. For you … I yet see far. But a new day will come. And once more, I will see far."

She didn't understand. Her head was swimming. She touched his arm. He looked up at her finally, and his eyes blazed as they took her in.

"Do you feel lust?" she asked.

"Oh yes," he said. "Long have I lusted after the flesh of the daughters of men."

"Do you lust after me?" she said, bringing her hand to his shoulder.

"If I did not, you would not dare approach me," he said. And for a moment, she saw him, not as she always had—as a man uncanny—but as a fire that raged and burned in a pillar of black light, rising up from the bottom of a great pit, ringed by wide balconies of enthroned flames. At the sight of him, she wanted to fall to ash, to disintegrate into a mist, and resolve herself into a dew.

"Oh," she whispered, "oh God."

"No," he said, and then his hands were upon her.

When she woke upon the floor, he was gone. She explored herself and found that though she remembered the culmination of his lust, there was no evidence that she had been with a lover except for scratches upon her back. She stood, her thoughts jumbling one over the next, with memories of his body and the flashes of dark flame that accompanied his alien passion. The world was unreal. Her body felt like it belonged to a stranger. She laughed but couldn't remember what was funny. She wept but couldn't recall a single sad thing in her life. All was well; all was broken. Her hands ran over her skin, and she thought about returning to her bed to wake the officer and get him to do what the champagne had kept him from before they had fallen asleep.

Yes, she thought, *that's what I'll do.*

But there was something she had wanted to do first. The memory of her encounter faded like a dream, leaving her with only the impression of lust and of being possessed by someone far stronger than herself, than anyone she had ever known. She wanted that feeling again.

But first … something. She had been looking for something. She wanted to—her gaze rested on the nativity set. There she saw the little blonde baby resting in the straw-filled cradle. She wondered who had put him there. She noticed something else that she must have missed the first time: an angel. It hung upon the manger's pinnacle and held a banner in its hands that read, *'Spes.'*

Tabby frowned, giggled, and felt suddenly ashamed of her nudity. She shivered, though the room was warm. She should cover herself. She should go back to bed. Back to bed into the man's arms. She was excited, and though laughter bubbled up here and there, a petite frown pouted her lips as she tried desperately to remember the name of the man she was returning to or the man who waited for her in Lightning Falls.

XI

HER EYES ARE CLOSED, her lips pressed tightly, and she folds her fingers under her chin, her elbows against her bare breasts. Her knees rest upon the bed when he is not lifting her with his enthusiastic thrusts. He holds her in place with strong hands high on her hips. Each movement shouts across her body, calling from one nerve to the next, but building toward nothing but his moment of climax.

She, under the dark vault of her mind, watches as each wave rolls over, tumbling her against the sand and among broken planks. She intuits that once the shattered wood was something more, something that belonged to her. But now, here on the shores of the morning isles, she can only remember waking in the foam of the sea, born naked as if from the blood and seed of some slain titan.

XII
Consummation

Thursday, June 17, 1948 – Early Afternoon

TABBY CLASPED HER SEQUINED headband behind her head and wondered if she should forgo clothing entirely. Why shouldn't she meet her death as she met her life, with a heaping of scandal? Larry would never allow it. It would amuse her father, and her mother would shake her head, but Larry, ever more careful with her as the years had gone by, would want to cover her, less out of modesty and more out of some sense of … what? Regret? Guilt?

She didn't care any longer. She wanted to go into town and find one more lover to help her feel like herself. She didn't feel like herself, and that wasn't good. You should feel like yourself on the day you're going to die. It wasn't good to pretend to be someone else at the end. A person should unmask in the face of death. And to do that, she needed a tumble, someone to make her feel like the Tabby she was, the languid feline who loved every tom.

She wondered idly if Cecil would come over, or maybe old Gambol.

She stood and smiled into the mirror, baring her teeth. Her face was perfectly powdered, rouged, shadowed, and lined. Her mascara and dark red lipstick were without fault, and her hair, cut precisely as it had been twenty years earlier, tugged an aching longing from her for days long gone. She pushed the feeling aside. It was useless. Let others drink the wine of regret; she would abstain. Today, she would soberly face the dying of her light.

As she glided down the stairs, Tabby again considered simply stripping off her dress when she came to the living room. She pictured the ones who would come, the ones who would find them in their chairs, and wondered what they would make of Tabitha Kusel sitting in the buff at tea with her family on an idle Saturday afternoon. What would they think? What lurid tales would arise of the family's wanton and taboo habits? What would the rumors be, and how long would they live after her? She wondered if she would be immortal then, reported on in every newspaper. A family dying of gas inhalation was one thing, but when the eldest daughter sat in nothing more than a two-decade out of date headband and simple silver necklace, then even the papers in Europe would take notice. They'd whisper of madness, bestial practices, cultish secrets, and devilish sorceries hidden behind the forest's walls.

Or, perhaps, they'd just assume that there was foul play. And, of course, there were those who couldn't have that. So, even if she did decide to slip away in the altogether, they'd likely stuff her into something presentable. That saddened her. She didn't even have control over that one last little joke.

She came to the foot of the stairs and turned left. There, sitting together, she saw her mother, father, Larry, and Sharon in the library.

"Oh, Sharon, you're already here," Tabby said. "How wonderful."

"Tabby," Sharon said, her face hard, her chin quivering. She stood and walked over to her and tried to hug her. Tabby, however, kept her at arm's length, leaned in, and kissed the air next to Sharon's cheek.

"You look so matronly! How wonderful for you! A mother without a child, but a mother nonetheless! How is my son? How has he adjusted to life after the war?"

"He is well," Sharon said. "Please, Tabby, won't you hug me? I-I can't stand it if you don't."

"Hug you? Oh, of course, of course, but be careful, this dress is a menace, and you might scandalize my husband. Shhh," she said in a stage-whisper, "of course he won't be scandalized. You know he sent me out like a woman of the night for years to scream in other men's beds? He's the scandal, did you know that?"

"Please, Tabby," Larry said, standing and walking over to her.

"Go away, Larry, I must hug my sister," Tabby said. Then she made a show of raising her arms and putting them around Sharon. "Oh, sister, I love you so much! You know, I think I've loved you best, even though you've gone away. You know, I remember ..."

"What?" Sharon asked, hugging Tabby tightly.

"I ... oh, I don't remember what I remember. It's good that I don't, or I'd be sad. Come now, we are all here, let us get on with it. Time lingers not in this place."

"My dear," her mother said, "come and sit, we do want to spend some time together before Sharon does what she must."

"What you must," Tabby said, shaking her head. "Oh, how I envy you! You get to kill us all and leave it all behind, my love! You get to go on without us in your lovely house looking over the creek, just like ours! It will almost be like we never existed."

"Please don't say that," Sharon said, weeping. "Please, Tabby, I love you. The last three years have been a living nightmare for me. That man! That man and ... oh, God, Archie! I miss Archie so much. And I've missed you all so much. Please, Tabby, don't let our last moments together be like this."

Tabby smiled and stroked her face. "This is your winter now. I have had mine year after year. Only, instead of having to leave your home, your home will just die. No bother for you."

"But she has had to leave her home," her father said. "Tabby, don't be heartless, we've all sacrificed. We've all suffered."

"For what?" Tabby said, laughing and walking into the sitting room. "What have we done it for?"

"For the New Eden," Larry said. "A new world where no one else has to suffer."

Tabby laughed. "Tell me how this will bring that about."

"He sees far," Larry said.

Tabby's face hardened, and she folded her hands in front of her like a girl about to give a recitation. She nodded. Her eyes scanned the room and stopped on the rolling bar. It stood behind the large, stuffed chair her parents shared like two young lovers. On the cart stood several bottles, including one she didn't recognize. It was small and had a cork stopper. It looked as if someone had gotten it from the druggist.

"You're right. I'm sorry," Tabby said. "He does see far. Come, I'll make us a drink. And we will sit, and ruminate, and reminisce."

Tabby made five scotch and sodas while the others breathed a collective, though tentative, sigh of relief. They began to talk of happier times. They even dared to laugh as they remembered summer mornings at the creek, weeklong trips to the coast, and comical mix-ups during the construction of the Congregation Retreat House beyond the High Path. They remembered when they tore down the last of the old night shelters, and the last time they built their huts down by the creek that bore their family's name.

This last sobered them as they realized that all their legacy would one day be tallied in the name of a creek and a street.

"Not all," Sharon said after a long, contemplative silence. Tabby didn't look at her.

"Larry, are you all right?" Jeremiah asked, yawning and reaching across the gap between his chair and Larry's. He nudged his son-in-law's shoulder. The man looked fast asleep.

"Tell me, sister, did you block up the heater's exhaust yet?" Tabby asked.

Her mother, catching the impulse, also yawned.

"Yes," Sharon said, "though it will take hours for the air to become poisonous. That's why I brought the—"

She froze, looking over at the bar. Then she looked down at her glass.

"Oh, no," Tabby said, "I didn't give you any. I didn't give myself any either. Larry, I'm afraid, got a double dose."

"Tabitha!" her mother said, trying to rouse herself, but her voice was thick.

"Why?" Jeremiah said, looking down into his own drink. "We … we were supposed to—"

"To what? Sit and reminisce for hours? To cry and laugh and remember the good days until the sun went down?" Tabby asked. "To remember Uncle Peter, who took his secrets to the grave? To remember Conti, who never knew that her time was short? To tell stories of poor Gambol who must mourn us all?"

"Eliska," Jeremiah said, holding his wife against him. "Eliska, I love you. I love you more than words. Please, my love, don't go without knowing that."

"I know," Eliska said. She looked up and kissed her husband before laying her head on his chest. "I love you, too. Don't be afraid, my love. Sharon, don't be afraid, my darling." She closed her eyes.

"We were going to say goodbye," Jeremiah whispered. "To say … I don't know."

"It won't matter in a moment, Father," Tabby said. "In a minute, it will all be precisely the same as if Larry and I said our farewells with tears in our eyes. What difference does it make when Larry is now nothing, and soon I'll be nothing?"

Jeremiah shook silently as he held his wife's body. "Sharon, I love you. Tabby …"

"I love you too, Father!" Sharon put her drink down and went to his side, hugged his head against her, and kissed his temple. "I love you, too, Father! Mother! Oh God, Tabby, why?"

"Don't worry, dear. I didn't do all of your work for you. You still get to kill me."

"What?" Sharon wept.

"I didn't want to deny you all of it. So, you still may kill me."

Sharon was shivering, her lips pressed against her father's slack face. She reached down and brushed her mother's hair. She leaned down and kissed Eliska's head, sobbing. Then she brushed the tears from her hair and left her parents in each other's embrace. She turned and lifted Larry's head and kissed his lips. "Goodbye, Brother," she said. "I'm sorry."

Sharon stood, straightened her dress, and looked long at Tabby. Finally, she walked over and picked up her sister's glass and took it to the bar.

"What happened to you?" Sharon asked, mixing the drink slowly.

"Everything," Tabby said. "Nothing. I barely exist. I'm a mote. A speck of light scattered before the dawn, a glimmer of starlight before the sun rises. Life pulses on, but I may as well not be here."

"That's not true," Sharon said, turning. Her hand was shaking badly.

"It's the only thing that's true, Sharon. And it's true of you and all those people who think you are one of them. It might even be true of Mr. Eyes."

"Who?" Sharon said, holding the glass in both hands to keep the liquid from sloshing out as Tabby took it.

"Mr. Eyes. That's what I called him when I was a girl. When he first appeared to me. He is full of eyes. And he does see far. But far enough that it matters? I don't know." She lifted the cup to her lips and downed its contents in one gulp. "And I don't care. I have overstayed my welcome. I was nothing but a body, nothing but something for men, or the family, or the great unending Life Force to use. I've never been more than that." Sharon shook her head, but Tabby went on, "It's all right. How should the pot say to the potter, 'Why have you made me thus?' I am dust to be trodden underfoot. Now, goodbye, Sister. Kiss me if you want. It will be no different to me in a moment."

Sharon did kiss her. She kissed her, hugged her tightly, and sobbed. "I'm sorry for what this has done to you," Sharon whispered.

"So am I," Tabby said. She put her glass down on the table. "Now, goodbye, dear one."

Then Tabitha Kusel sat on her dead husband's lap, closed her eyes, and said no more.

xii

I
Vouched

Sunday, June 14, 1908 - Night

TABITHA OPENED THE FRONT door and stepped out onto the porch. The moon was huge in the western sky above the trees. To the left of her family's front drive, warm, dim light glowed from a window several feet above the earth. Inside the small wooden room, a young man, whose name Tabitha didn't know, spoke to the spirits. Even on the quietest nights, she could never hear what the people said. Usually, the forest's voice, loud with insects, birds, and Hitchman's Creek, drowned out the tower's low and steady whisper. But tonight, even those sounds disappeared under the incessant roar of the waterfall.

Most of the time, the rumble of the falls was low, distant, and lost under the sounds of radiators, horses, tea-kettles, and Mama and Papa speaking in the next room. Usually, Tabitha would have to close her eyes and concentrate to hear even the faintest suggestion of the mountain stream that tumbled over the cliff, at the end of the High Path, into the pool below. But tonight, it was louder than normal, and no matter how she folded her pillow over her ears, she couldn't shut it out. So, Tabitha thought she might come out and have a talk with it, like her grandfather supposedly did when he founded the town. She had never tried talking to the waterfall before; she had been too scared because in her grandfather's story, it had talked back. But she was eight now, and by her reckoning, that was too old to be scared of the waterfall, especially since her mother told her that the story was just made up.

Tabitha walked over to the edge of the porch and looked out toward the butte, which wasn't very tall, and so she couldn't make much out except the tops of trees. She put her hands on her hips the way she had seen a woman do in town, and she tried to make her voice sound as stern and grown-up as she could, so that the old waterfall would take her seriously. She thought that if Jesus could calm the storms, and if she was one of His little sisters, as her father said, maybe she could, if not actually silence the waterfall, at least get it to quiet down a bit.

"Now you listen here," she said, doing her best impression of the woman from town, "you're being too gosh darned loud, Mr. Waterfall. You need to let a girl sleep. I can't be staying up all night listening to you grumble on like that. If you've got something to say, come on out and say it so we can all get our forty winks!" Tabitha felt nervous, as if the waterfall were about to talk back to her. "And ... and how do you like that?" she added.

"He can't hear you," a man's voice said behind her. Tabitha jumped around to find a man rocking on her grandmother's old rocking chair. He wore a dark suit and a wide-brimmed hat pulled low to hide the top of his face. She thought about screaming or running. Then she thought of the young man in the little tower, and wondered if he could help her.

"It's all right, I'm not here to hurt you," the man said. His voice was like an instrument, something like a trumpet, or maybe a trombone. It breathed, but not through the same kind of mouth that she had. He pushed himself back and forth on the chair with a polished black leather shoe and folded his pale hands in his lap. His suit looked like one her father owned.

"Are you friends with my papa?"

"Yes," the man said in his strange woodwind voice, "I know him. I know your grandfather and grandmother, too. They are all my people."

"Your people?" she said, half turning away from him, ready to sprint if he should rise.

"Yes, they are my people. Just like you are. You are mine as well."

Tabitha frowned; she didn't like the sound of that.

"You know who else is mine?" he said. Then he lifted his chin just a little to the west.

"The waterfall?" Tabitha asked.

"That's right."

"How can a waterfall be one of your people?" she said, unconsciously squaring her shoulders toward him, the idea of fleeing fading.

"That is hard to explain," he said. "And it's not important to you. What is important is that I want your help, Tabby."

"My name is Tabitha," she said.

"I know you think that," he said. "But it's Tabby. I need your help, Tabby."

"If you want my help, then call me by my real name," she said. She could feel her face getting hot, and she wanted to go up to the man and slap him the way that woman had slapped the old man in town.

"I am. Now, come here to me and let me whisper something to you."

"I think you can tell me from here," she said.

His mouth opened in something that might have been a smile, but it reminded her more of the chimps she had seen at the zoo in Portland. "Come here," he said. She obeyed, her arms and legs moving without her consent across the porch boards.

She stood in front of him, her heart pounding, her eyes watering.

"What?" she asked with quivering lips.

"I want to tell you a secret," he said. He leaned forward, putting his pale, thin hands onto her shoulders, his long fingers arching over them onto her back. He did not smile, did not try to comfort her. Instead, he leaned in and whispered in breath that smelled like cigarettes, alcohol, and her mother's perfume.

"Tell your uncle I am calling him. I am calling him through Jan Tomasek. Tell him to open his ears and bind the knot."

Tabby's body shook, her chin bouncing up and down, her dark hair falling into her face. She wanted to ask him why he couldn't just tell Uncle Peter himself, but her teeth were chattering too badly. Still, he answered her unspoken question.

"Only you can see me, Tabby. Only you can hear me. You are special. Now listen."

One of his hands slid up behind her head and pulled her close to his chest. He turned her so that her ear lay over his heart. There she heard a strange rhythm that entranced her. She had heard her mother's and Sharon's hearts, but this sounded nothing like them. It seemed to pound out in heavy and light beats a strange and syncopated rhythm. It made her want to dance. She wondered how he could be alive.

He wrapped his arms around her and held her.

"The time is coming, dear one. Your life will be a light to those in darkness."

Tabby didn't understand. She wanted the man to let her go. She wanted her mother. He released her.

"Now go, wake your uncle. Tell him what you've seen. Hurry, time does not linger in this place."

Tabby stared at him, her mouth working silently. Then, not certain why she did it, she reached up and lifted the brim of his hat and screamed.

Part 7 – Hymn

"I have taken what was not mine and made it mine. I have dwelt in a shelter not my own. For the seeker after knowledge has shown me this way. What has the Bear found that I have not found? What has he done that I have not done? I have slain, and bound, and cast out, and adorned my shelter with that which is mine. Has the Bear done more? Am I not master?"

-Zuzanna Cerny, The Book of Corrections

"In that tower, I beheld one whose beauty and sorrow exceed my ability to describe them. Her dark hair, amethyst lips, and sapphire eyes so entranced me that I forgot my wife. So lovely was she that I stood long in the doorway and pondered the might of the Creator who could make such radiance. My wonder was all the greater as I perceived how diminished by sickness she was. In that cursed place, it consumed her without end, neither allowing her to succumb nor overcome. After I stared long at her doomed beauty, I fell to my knees and did her proper worship, vowing to serve her as my meagre powers would permit."

- Mikuláš Vaclavek, *The First Book of Seeings*

48
Existing Situation

Friday, September 26, 2025 – Afternoon

JENNY WOKE IN DARKNESS to the sounds of two people breathing. One snored lightly, and the other sniffed once and then fell back into a deep, slow rhythm. Jenny checked her watch. It was almost five. She knew Maddy's alarm would go off soon, so she snuggled up behind her and breathed in faint remnants of shampoo. Maddy scooched back against Jenny, took her hand and ran it around her stomach.

The snoring went on, and Jenny leaned in to kiss the skin behind Maddy's ear. She stopped, remembering that she used to do the same thing to Aurora. She felt dirty at the idea of repeating the same intimacy with someone new. Instead, she leaned down and kissed her shoulder. Maddy squeezed Jenny's hand against her skin. They lay together under the blankets, breathing, until the alarm on Maddy's phone buzzed. The snoring behind Jenny stopped, and Sydney let out a low grumble.

"I don't want to," she said.

Jenny rolled over and put her hand on Sydney's arm.

"Me either," Jenny whispered. Sydney froze.

"Oh my God," the younger woman said. Then she was crawling on top of Jenny and hugging her like a koala bear.

"Don't worry, she calms down with that after a while," Maddy croaked. Jenny felt her sit up before she snapped on the bedside lamp. Jenny glanced over and saw Maddy taking a long drink from a glass while Sydney clung to Jenny. Maddy put the glass back down and turned to stroke Sydney's hair.

"It's okay, Syd, you can let go. She's not going to run away. Um, right?"

"No, I'm not going to run away," Jenny said.

Sydney squeezed her again and then reluctantly detached herself. She slid down next to Jenny and put her head on Jenny's stomach. "I can't believe you're actually here," Sydney said.

"I can't believe my lips aren't sore," Jenny said. "I'm not sure I've made out for that long since high school."

"I love kissing," Sydney said, peering up at Jenny from under a stray strand of red hair. Her eyes went wide, and she sat up. "You weren't like, expecting more, were you? I mean, with your, um, experience and—"

"No," Jenny laughed, "I wasn't expecting more. I don't know what I was expecting. But kissing and cuddles feel totally right to me."

"Okay, good!" Sydney said and collapsed back down onto Jenny.

"Oof, but right now my bladder could use fewer cuddles," Jenny said. "Three chicks and one bathroom—"

"Two bathrooms. Syd's apartment is right across the hall," Maddy said. "But you can use mine. I can wait."

Ten minutes later, Jenny was pulling her socks and shoes on as Maddy poured coffee into three big mugs.

"I'm surprised you two have kept separate apartments," Jenny said.

"Why?" Sydney said.

"Um, stereotypes?" Jenny laughed.

"I mean, we live together," Maddy said. "It's like one big apartment that just has a hallway down the middle. Why give up free space and an extra bathroom?"

Jenny took a mug from Maddy and frowned thoughtfully. She surveyed the living room and was impressed by how tidy everything was. A modest flat-screen TV stood on an entertainment center against one wall, and two bookcases stood against another. The books were almost entirely fantasy and horror, and their spines were all lined up evenly with each other.

Another bookcase stood by the hallway. This was lined with shorter, narrower books that ran in groups with nearly identical spines except for volume numbers a third of the way up. Ten volumes of blue books with white bottoms sat next to each other before twenty or so covered an entire shelf. These had different color spines and little boxes with different comic characters drawn near the bottoms. Another group had pastel covers, and another black with red lettering.

"Wait, I know those, those are …" Jenny started.

"Manga," Maddy said. "Japanese comic books."

"*Right*," Jenny said, drawing the word out. "One of my first roommates in Portland read a lot of them."

Sydney came in through the front door and scooped up her coffee before settling on the couch next to Jenny. "So, are you coming back over tonight?"

"Syd," Maddy chided.

"Um, I don't know," Jenny said. "I guess maybe. I don't know what the rules are."

"There aren't any rules," Sydney said.

"Right, I guess," Jenny said, staring into her cup. "I guess I should kind of put it out there that I'm here for this, but I'm also still kind of raw. Like, I need some time to adjust, you know?"

Sydney nodded.

"And so do we, Syd," Maddy said, taking a seat on the floor in front of them. "We need to feel out what feels good as a group, not just automatically dump Jenny into our whole setup as if it isn't going to change things."

"I know," Sydney said, pouting comically.

"I think," Maddy said, "that we should plan some dates. Like, real dates. All of us together, but also one-on-one."

"Wow, that's a really good idea," Jenny said. "So, like just you and me?"

Maddy lowered her eyes bashfully. "Yeah, if you want."

"Yeah, I do."

"And I get one too, right?" Sydney said.

"Yeah, of course," Jenny laughed.

"And we should do one too," Maddy said, looking at Sydney. "It's important for us to, like, have our own time as well."

"Have you done this before?" Jenny asked.

"No, but I've been reading a lot about it," Maddy said, smiling. "I wanted to be ready."

"Wow," Jenny said, shaking her head. "You've been studying to be ready for me joining your—"

"Our love nest!" Sydney said, almost squealing.

"Wow again," Jenny said.

"It is not a love nest," Maddy said. "Well, yeah, actually, Syd's side is kind of a nest. But we don't have a love nest. And we should try to be adults about this and take things slowly. There's no need to rush."

"I want you to move in right now!" Sydney said, smiling up at the ceiling. Jenny pictured Snoopy dancing.

"Syd!" Maddy said, rolling her eyes.

"I know, I know, it's a bad idea. Still, I want to sleep like we did last night all the time."

"I don't know about all the time," Jenny said, "but I enjoyed myself thoroughly, and I'm down to do it again tonight at least."

That was good enough for Sydney, who agreed to allow everyone out of her sight long enough to shower. This meant reluctantly letting Jenny return home after promises from both Jenny and Maddy that they would all see each other again at dinner. Maddy walked Jenny to the front door and awkwardly leaned against the wall.

"She's going to love bomb you, but if you survive that, I promise, she calms down."

Jenny laughed. "I don't know, it's nice to have someone excited to see me instead of, I don't know, whatever I get from other people."

"Well, just know that I'm excited to see you, even if I'm not, like, giving off SpongeBob vibes."

They hugged before Jenny stepped out onto a drizzle-wet Main Street. She took a deep breath of petrichor and wanted to feel good. Instead, anxiety and a deep sense of discontentment rose from where they had been lurking since she woke up. She wanted to scream and smash a rock through a window. Why wasn't she happy? Why did she feel immediately put off by what had happened last night? Especially since, as far as things went, not much had happened. She tried to locate the feeling, to pin it down and interrogate it.

I don't want to do that again. I certainly don't want to go further with them.

The thought was so intrusive that she pictured someone else jamming it into her brain. She pictured herself finding the thought, taking a knife, and cutting it out of her head. What did the thought mean? Did it mean that she wasn't into Syd or Maddy? Did it mean she wasn't into women at all?

Chloe flashed in her mind, and her visceral attraction to the woman nixed that second idea. So, was it just Maddy and Sydney? Sydney seemed younger than she was—so excitable, so breakable. Maddy was firmer, more adult. But she was with Syd, and what did that say about her? Maybe nothing. Maybe it meant she had a saint's patience. Or maybe it meant that she wasn't ready to be in a relationship with someone who had serious trauma like Jenny.

Or maybe I'm just not into them.

Jenny squeezed her eyes shut against the storm in her brain and risked a few blind steps down the sidewalk. When she opened her eyes, she stopped and stared into the front window of the Lightning Falls Art Gallery. Staring back at her was a painting of a woman in a diaphanous white nightgown being pulled in every direction by disembodied hands that grabbed at her from the darkness. Jenny wondered if the hands were meant to be ghostly, or metaphors for society, or maybe the woman's mind.

If it's that last one, I'm with you, sister.

Jenny continued past the gallery's front door and paused when she found what she took to be a companion piece. A man lay on the ground, his face pressed against the earth. Feet crushed him as his hand groped for the handle of some tool that lay obscured by the surrounding darkness. The feet were bare, booted, and heeled. Jenny returned to the first painting and studied the hands. Some were big, others small, some were hairy knuckled, and others immaculately manicured. Finally, she saw the titles of the paintings and their price tags. Both made her want to cry. If she wanted the set, they'd set her back a cool $10,000. She wondered if anyone able to afford them could relate to the set that the artist named, 'Eve & Adam.'

49
Severance

Saturday, September 27, 2025 - Evening

DELIA ROSE FROM HER seat and raised her glass.

"To all of you, who I've gotten to know a little better since Jenny came back to town."

The Sleep Talkers and Barry raised their glasses around Delia's dining room table. A glass baking dish of lasagna lay mostly empty, and a devastated basket of garlic bread sat between Nate and Sydney. The group drank. Then Barry stood as Delia sat.

"And, like, I want to propose another toast," he said. "To the person who brought us all together like this. To Jenny Berger, our prodigal returned."

Everyone toasted again, except Jenny, who blushed. Sydney was predictably enthusiastic, which both flattered and disquieted Jenny. Finally, Nate stood and toasted Delia, which Jenny reacted to with Sydney-levels of enthusiasm.

"Well," Delia said, "now that our love-feast is complete, who wants to help me clean up?"

Barry bolted up and started scooping up plates. Linds grabbed the baking dish, and a general flurry of passing and taking commenced.

Delia sat back in her chair and watched with a pleased smile. "I could get used to this," she said.

"You should get used to it," Charles said, piling flatware into a salad bowl. "We should do this regularly. Not that you should have to do the cooking every time."

"I don't mind the cooking if you all do the cleaning," Delia said.

"That suits me just fine," Charles said, taking his collection into the kitchen. Everyone agreed and repeated their agreement when Nate brought out dessert.

"You made this?" Sydney mumbled around a bite of cheesecake.

"Yeah," Nate said, cutting a piece for Jenny. "Let me know what I can do better next time."

Linds took a tentative bite, and then another heartier one.

"Make more of it," Delia said. Everyone agreed.

"Well, I still have a lot to learn about making—" Nate began, but he was cut off.

"Make more of it," Maddy said.

Once more, everyone agreed.

Too soon, the Weekenders gathered in the foyer and pulled on coats. Jenny joined them.

"It just keeps getting colder," Charles said, pulling on a knit cap. "I don't remember it being this cold at the end of September, for … Well, I don't know if I ever remember it being this cold."

"Oh, speaking of the cold, Jenny, did you ever find that sweater?" Barry asked.

"I'm so sorry, no," Jenny said. "But then I haven't had a lot of chance to look for it. I'll definitely look today, though. I'm sure it's just in the closet."

"Didn't you have it last?" Sydney asked as she scooped a forkful of the last piece of cheesecake into her mouth. She was looking at Delia. "Did you put it somewhere to dry?"

Barry gave Delia an appraising glance.

"I just put it with the rest of your laundry," Delia said. "Check your closet, I'm sure it's there."

"Unless the inspectors took it," Maddy said.

"Oh, yeah," Jenny said. "That's the running theory. I still haven't checked my other clothes yet."

"We think they might be panty perverts!" Sydney stage-whispered.

"Well, let's not shame anyone for their little predilections," Delia said. "I dated this man who loved a good pair of—Sorry, that is too much information."

"Did he like stealing them?" Maddy asked.

"No. Right! Right, stealing is the thing. Bad. It's a bad thing," Delia said, holding up a finger as if she were proclaiming something in an old musical.

Jenny laughed. "Yeah, well, if they didn't steal my grandma sweater, I'm sure it's around somewhere. Oh, sorry. I do love it."

"It's cool, I know it's not super fashionable," he said, throwing his hands up. But there was something in his voice that Jenny had never detected before. His affability sounded almost forced.

"Okay, we should go so you all can get to your towers and Barry can try to erase this conversation from his memory," Jenny said. Hugs were shared, as were promises of reunion after work. When they parted ways, Charles stood next to Jenny on the sidewalk and pulled out his pipe.

"You don't mind?" he asked under one arched eyebrow.

"I insist," Jenny said.

"You want to walk a bit? I need to move to feel like I'm working off some calories," Charles said as he bit his pipe's stem. Jenny agreed, and they started down the sidewalk. The sun had set, and the pale streetlights glowed misty above them. Charles lit his pipe and puffed. Jenny thought he looked handsome in his wool overcoat and stylish scarf.

"Can I ask you a personal question?" Jenny said.

"Yes," Charles said. The tone in his voice said he was wary.

"Do you have a boyfriend?"

"No," he said. "And now, you're about to ask me, 'why not?'" He puffed contemplatively for a moment. "I don't have a boyfriend because I don't have what you have. I don't have a pool of immediately compatible partners at the ready. I know all the openly gay men in this town, and we aren't good fits."

"Why not?" Jenny asked.

"Well, they are either too old, or too young, or too married, or being single is their hobby. Besides, I'm no one's dreamboat."

"I find that hard to believe," Jenny said.

"I am stuffy, cantankerous, I live with my mother, which either labels me as gay or Irish Catholic, and I work a night job. And I smoke."

"But," Jenny said, "maybe that's someone's thing."

"Maybe it is, but if it is, they are not my thing, at least not here. Oh, I've met a few people over the years, mostly tourists. I've even kept in touch with one or two. But I don't really have time for something serious."

Jenny nodded. "What about in Enterprise? Or maybe—"

Charles stopped and stared at her under that one raised eyebrow. "Jennifer, I find conversations about my love life to be boring. I recognize that you are a creature of such social interactions, but I hope that you can recognize that I am not."

"Right," Jenny said, clicking her teeth shut at the end of the word. "Sorry."

"No need to apologize. I imagine romance is front-of-mind for you right now. And I'm happy for you, even if your world is an impenetrable mystery to me."

"My world is an impenetrable mystery to me, too," Jenny said. They walked in silence for another block. The first few steps felt uneasy, but Charles poked his elbow out, and she hooked her arm into it.

"We should go dancing again," he said.

Jenny was about to agree when she noticed a sound rising from somewhere. She cocked her head, listening. "Is that singing?"

"Yes, the Congregation Church has its Saturday evening services. Sometimes I like to walk by to hear their hymns. They do the old-school style, none of that rock-band mega-church nonsense. Give me 'A Firm Foundation' or something by Charles Wesley any day over some of what I hear coming out of the Baptist Church."

"Didn't know you were religious," Jenny said.

"I was when I was younger, now … I don't know what I am. Still, I like a good hymn now and then—from a distance."

Jenny didn't know the hymn that the Congregation Church was singing, though the people sounded enthusiastic. She caught only the line "For the world to see!" as they passed the stone building. Stained-glass windows glowed warmly in the foggy evening, and Jenny saw the familiar symbols of books, scrolls, and flames depicted in bright reds, blues, yellows, and greens.

"What kind of church is it?" Jenny asked.

"Protestant," Charles said. "Probably just an offshoot of some offshoot of the Baptists, or Lutherans, or Presbyterians, or Methodists."

"Thanks, that clears it up," she laughed.

"The history of American religious divisions is not my forte," he said.

They are monsters. They aren't who they pretend to be.

Jenny blinked at the strange thought as it pierced her sinuses. She pulled her arm from Charles and pressed her hands to her eyes. A picture flashed through her mind.

"What's the matter?"

"There used to be a stable here," Jenny said.

"What?" Charles asked.

"Sorry," Jenny said. She dropped her hands and blinked away the dark spots that remained. Surveying the intersection where the church stood, she said, "I don't know why I said that. I just had this impression, like I could see it. Horses, and stalls, and saddles. That was so weird."

Jenny glanced up and down the street and felt vertigo tugging her to one side and then the other. The street appeared as normal and familiar as any other street in Lightning Falls, but it also felt wrong. It felt like it should look different.

It's too crowded.

Jenny squeezed her eyes shut again and shook her head. The feeling passed.

"Are you alright?"

"I don't know," Jenny said. "I think so. I just had this weird feeling. That was really strange."

"Well, let's get you home. Do you want me to call Delia? She could drive us."

"No, I just need to keep walking. I didn't sleep amazingly last night. I probably need to just crash for a bit."

"By last night, you mean a few hours ago," Charles said, offering her his elbow again. She took it.

"Yeah, it's strange how we have to talk now. Last night means ten in the morning. It's weird."

"You'll sort of get used to it, but most people won't let you get too comfortable with your nocturnal vocabulary."

"Ah, the day people," Jenny said, forcing a laugh.

"Indeed. Now, I'm curious about what you said the other night, about Kant."

"Yeah," Jenny said, "I'm going to be honest, Charles, I have no idea why I said that. It just came out."

Charles puffed and scowled. "Have you read any Kant?"

Jenny shook her head.

"Do you know someone who does? Take a course in Philosophy at college?"

"I didn't go to college, and no. Nothing. I'll be honest, I'm not sure I ever really heard of him before you mentioned him. I—yeah, I still don't actually know who he is."

"Then how did you know that he wrote *The Critique of Pure Reason?*"

"I don't know, maybe Jeopardy?"

Charles nodded slowly. "Maybe. But what about *The Groundwork of the Metaphysics of Morals?* That one isn't much of a trivia question. I didn't even recognize it when you said it. I had to look it up."

To that, Jenny had no answer. She kept her silence for most of their walk back to the Kusel House. Jenny continued to feel that each street she saw was wrong, packed with too many buildings. Some of the bigger houses felt like they should be there. But most of the smaller houses felt off, as if she were seeing the wrong versions of them. It was like reading a book she had read before, only to find that it had changed. There was something terrible in it, and something familiar.

Places change. That's okay. But it's not how I remember it.

Once more, her thoughts felt alien to her. It was only when they reached the gravel drive that the feeling of unfamiliarity faded, though not entirely. Unlike the rest of the town, she felt a nagging certainty that the area in front of the house was less crowded than it should be.

50
Strengthened

Sunday, September 28, 2025 - Evening

JENNY KNELT ON HER bedroom floor and tossed the last of her clothing into a pile at the foot of her bed. Her hamper lay upside down, and the hangers hung empty. Jenny wrinkled her nose in frustration. Sighing, she stood and took a step back from the mess. She held up her phone, took a picture, and sent it to Barry.

> ***Jenny***
> I guess there's a house inspector with a new green sweater. I'm sorry. I really appreciate the gift!

It took Barry twenty minutes to reply with his usual water-off-a-duck's-back attitude.

> ***Barry***
> It's okay. Things happen. I'm glad you got some use out of it!

Jenny felt guilty as she rehung her clothes and dumped her dirty laundry back into her hamper in heaping armfuls. She'd gotten three gifts since returning to Lightning Falls, and she'd already lost one of them.

Then, Patty's voice rose unbidden in the back of her mind, *"I've gotten three gifts," but how many have you given? I raised such a selfish whore.*

Jenny felt the thought like a knife in her ribs. She had been selfish. Hadn't Delia been telling her as much?

"Well, I've kind of been dealing with remaking my entire fucking life," Jenny said to the imaginary Patty she pictured in her bedroom doorway, arms crossed, foot tapping. Imaginary Patty said nothing more. Of course, she had no comeback to that. Why would she? Her job wasn't to be reasonable; it was to judge and harass Jenny at every chance.

Guilt forced Jenny to check her watch. It was 7:38. She didn't have time to run down to Main Street and go on a shopping spree. But she could do a little browsing to get some ideas for gifts. And she still needed to get her early-morning lunch. She pulled her boots on and a big fluffy sweater, popped her earbuds in, and walked out the front door, sliding her arms into her coat and pulling a thick white knit hat down over her hair. She felt surprisingly free, as if leaving the spontaneous, imaginary Patty behind. But there was something else in the freedom. Except for her running excursions, Jenny hadn't gone out alone for weeks. She certainly hadn't walked up Main Street without plans to see anyone. Every day had been a blur of work, scheduled meals, friend dates, real dates, and the one-off photoshoot. The idea of going into a store by herself and browsing, and maybe making small talk with a store clerk, sounded refreshingly novel.

Pep played in her ears. She pictured Aurora learning the songs and singing acoustic versions of them back to her. Jenny missed her terribly. She imagined them walking together, arm in arm, and sharing the earbuds. She could almost feel her there, and her stomach ached.

But the image didn't last. The ghost beside her morphed and grew into Nolan's tall, gorgeous form. His presence was so strong that when she closed her eyes, she believed he was there, just an inch from her. The feeling was so intensely real that she started to cry. She didn't understand what was happening. It was like the music was opening—A door? A window?—something that let her almost get to Aurora and Nolan. She couldn't touch them, see them, or hear them, but … but almost. Almost. The strange, brimming experience didn't fit into any familiar emotion, so it overflowed into all of them. She might have laughed. She might have danced. She might have stomped her feet and spun in circles with her arms out. Whatever she was feeling, whatever the music was channeling, her body needed to respond. So, she wept and laughed and hugged herself.

If this is what it means to be haunted, Jenny thought, *then let me always be haunted.*

The haunting lasted only for a minute. When the song ended, so did the overwhelming. The next song began, and an echo of the impression wavered for a few beats, but then it was gone. She felt full, and she didn't know what to do next. It was as if there was no reasonable sequel to the experience.

"What was that?" she said into the cold night. She breathed the scent of pine deeply and laughed as she exhaled. But her laughter was cut short as a discouraging thought came to her.

I feel better after walking with the imagined ghosts of my two dead lovers than I do when I wake up next to two living people I care about.

Were they imagined? Could her imagination do that to her?

She wondered if people really had souls or spirits, and if those souls were immortal, what Nolan and Aurora thought of her. They must hate her, she concluded. She had let them die. She had let Joseph push them under the water and hold them there while she watched. She had believed he would bring them back, just like he said he would. But he hadn't. He let them die.

"After you go in and come out, I will bring you all back," he said. "But we have to be quick."

With their bodies cooling on the floor, she had let him put her under the water. Dying had been monstrous. She couldn't remember most of the physical sensation of it, but her panic, her certainty that this was the end, and the repeating memory of her father screaming for her to swim, all remained with her. She had gone down into the darkness, accompanied by his remembered cries. There she had lingered for what felt like a lifetime, and there she had felt a huge, thrumming presence in the distance. Then Joseph's lips had touched hers, and she coughed and sputtered as he pumped his palms against her chest. When she regained herself, she lay on her side and saw Aurora's empty eyes staring up at the bathroom ceiling. She turned and saw Nolan lying behind her, face down, unmoving. Joseph had stood, wiping his hands and smiling at her.

"Well, look at you. Back to life. Get her clothes," Joseph had said. Matina, standing in the doorway naked, wore an expression that might have been fear, wonder, or lust.

"Help them," Jenny had choked, taking Aurora's hand. Aurora's fingers, heralds of love and peace, made in the very image of God, were then cold and still, never to move again. Jenny had pulled herself over and lay on top of her, trying to restore life the way that Joseph had. She had breathed into her, pressed against her chest, and failed. She had climbed to Nolan then and tried again, with the same result. Then Jenny had screamed as she clawed at the bodies of her beloved, impotent to change what she had let Joseph do to them.

So, they must hate me.

Nothing felt right. The strange sensation of fullness remained, as did the feeling of freedom that had come over her as she left the house. But so too did shame, and with it a sense of dread. She had no right to any of this happiness. Hatred and spite were all she deserved. She wanted to see them, wanted to tell them that she was sorry, and she knew they must despise her. She wanted to tell them that that was right, and that for what she had done, for what she had let happen, she accepted it. She would sit before them in some endless limbo, accepting their hatred if that's what God demanded. She would do it without a second thought.

She didn't understand how this feeling of perfect self-hatred and almost dance-inducing freedom could live together in her chest. Like an impossibly complex knot, it seemed to pull and tighten, and she wished someone could undo it.

Her mind was so wrapped up in her strange world that she didn't notice an uneven patch of sidewalk. She tripped and almost fell. She caught herself on a lamppost and paused. She needed to get herself together. She was liable to run into someone or get run over crossing a street if she was so wrapped up in her fucked up navel-gazing. She took a long, slow, deep breath and let it out. She focused on the house in front of her, trying to put herself back into the real world of people and things. She breathed again, and again. Then she set off, trying to put the heavy thoughts behind her. But it didn't take more than two blocks before she started wondering what she was going to do about Sydney and Maddy. How could she continue to be with them if all she felt was uncomfortable? How could she be with them at all after Aurora and Nolan? She didn't understand any of it.

"Hey," a voice said, tearing her from her renewed contemplation. Earl stood against the wall outside of Sharko's Sandwiches. Emmet stood next to him, smoking.

"Hey, guys," Jenny said, wiping at her cheeks. "What are you doing?"

"Dealing drugs," Earl said.

"Really?" Jenny asked, trying to remember what Earl had said his job was.

"Yeah, we've got all the old ladies in this town addicted to D's," Earl said.

"Fuck me," Leddy said, walking out of the sandwich shop with a brown paper bag. "Don't ask him to finish that thought."

"What are D's?" Jenny asked instinctively, her mouth moving faster than her mind, which agreed with Leddy.

"Deez Nuts!" Earl shouted triumphantly. Emmet snorted and cracked half a smile. Jenny stared blankly for three seconds before shaking her head and turning to Leddy.

"I'm sorry I didn't listen to you. Are they twelve?"

"Every man will be twelve years old if you let him," Leddy said. "What are you up to?"

"Just taking a walk before everything closes. You guys?"

"Sandwiches, we're going to play some games tonight. You want to come over? I think we can get another TV set up," Leddy said.

"No, it's okay, I'm not a big gamer. Thanks, though."

"Phil is getting drinks," Earl said, answering Jenny's unspoken question.

"Gotcha. Well, you guys have fun," Jenny said, reflexively looking over her shoulder to see if the taller man was approaching.

"Sure we can't get you hooked?" Earl asked.

"On the video games or D's?" Jenny laughed.

"Either/or," Earl said, stifling a laugh.

"I'll pass," Jenny said. "Night all."

She started to walk away, but Leddy caught up and grabbed her arm. "Hey, um, I don't know what your situation is right now, but maybe text Phil. He's been talking about you a lot."

"Really?" Jenny said. "I'm kind of wrapped up in—Yeah, I'm not sure if I'm in a position right now to—He kind of told me he didn't want to be with someone like me."

"I know, and I told him he's a fucking idiot. Either way, I did my sisterly duty. We should do something soon."

"Yeah, I'll text you. Or you text me. We'll do something," Jenny said.

"Let's go hiking. Or there's a pool hall down in Enterprise. You play pool?"

"It's been forever," Jenny said. "But, yeah, that sounds great."

"Just you and me. No one who wants to fuck you," Leddy said, walking backward down Main.

"Honestly, that sounds amazing," Jenny said.

"Perfect, let's make it happen," Leddy said, pointing at her with both hands in a gesture that made Jenny think of a used-car salesman. Jenny laughed and walked away, her head spinning.

The Quiet Rumble 505

Volume 10, Issue 81, Sunday, September 28, 2025

Useful Myths

By David Greenly, Contributing Author.

I WAS REVIEWING THE demographics of our towns in Wallowa County the other day, and I saw something that depressed me. It didn't surprise me, of course, I know how overwhelmingly white this area is. And, before I lose any of you, I'm not here to tell you you're bad for the color of your skin. I'm not here to call you names or berate you for the things that were done a hundred and sixty years ago. But Keith did ask me to write a little something for Camping Days because he thought the tradition should involve some teaching about this land and the people who once lived here. People who, according to the demographics, do not live here anymore.

My great-great-great-grandmother was, as people say, 'full-blooded' Ni Mii Puu, the people known by French fur trappers as the Nez Perce. She married a farmer in Idaho, and so on down through the generations, my ancestry includes French, English, Scottish, and Irish. We think there might even be a little Italian in there. So, again, my readers, I'm not here to shake a fist at you. My ancestors are your ancestors.

But I do want to say something to you about this place and the stories we tell about this place. We tell stories for a lot of reasons. Sometimes we tell them because they make us laugh. Sometimes, to scare ourselves. But I think most of all, we tell stories to locate ourselves in the world. We speak our reality into existence through our stories. Part of that process is telling tales that make us feel like we belong somewhere, to justify our presence in a place. You see this a lot with people who claim Native American ancestry. They say, "Somewhere back there my ancestor married an Indian, and so I have Shoshone blood, or I'm part Apache, or I have Iroquois in me." You see this among people of the American South, and as far as I can tell, it's a myth that grew up around the Civil War. White people claiming Indian blood to give them a native claim to the land. Or, perhaps, to identify with tragedy, which carries with it sympathy, and to some degree authority. Or maybe they just thought of what bad-ass fighters the native peoples were, and they wanted to feel connected to that.

The fact is that very few people truly have the blood of the Navajo, Blackfoot, or Umatilla in their veins. Most of the stories are just stories with no real historical basis, though they do serve a purpose. They justify and they obscure. They keep people from wrestling with the hard truth of the massacre of the native populations across the continent that cost millions of people their lives and continues to cost lives today. They shield people from asking some very basic questions about how they should live in the context of that reality.

Lightning Falls has an especially pernicious form of this kind of myth in the story of Micah Whitman. This story tells of how a fur trapper with an especially coincidental name (we are in Wallowa-Whitman National Forest, after all, named after perhaps the most famous/infamous missionary in the area). This fur trapper is not only befriended by an Indian, but encouraged and led by this stoic character who, essentially gifts him the land. The native man, who is conveniently never named in the stories, has preternatural gifts and never laughs, exemplifying the stereotypes of the mystical, stoic Indian. By his good graces, Micah Whitman survives the winter—a reworking of the Plymouth story—and is aided in his building of a permanent home. Our Micah Whitman is the exact opposite of Marcus and Narcissa Whitman, who were killed by Cayuse men. Micah's helpful Indian nurses him back to health, teaches him the ways of the land, and helps him build his home.

The intention of this myth is obvious. It justifies the existence of Lightning Falls. It even suggests that our helpful native is complicit in the replacement of his people. It allows the people of Lightning Falls, whenever someone brings up the fact that the land the town sits upon belonged to the Ni Mii Puu, to nod their heads and say, "Yes, what a tragedy. But we, of course, were invited."

It's not a true story, but it is useful.

I'm not writing this to tell people how to feel, or what to think, or how they should respond to this viewpoint. I'm writing this to give people a new tool to use in their thinking. I'm asking people to ask themselves whether or not the stories they tell are helping or hindering them from recognizing their relationships to the world. And, of course, as most of the men I know will tell you, more tools are always good. So, while this might be an uncomfortable edition of The Quiet Rumble, please accept it as a gift to add to your toolbox for this year's Camping Days. One more hammer to build a sturdier shelter.

May you build well with it.

Texting

> **_Jenny_**
> Hey.

> **_Treeman_**
> Hey, long time.
> I know, that's my fault.

> **_Jenny_**
> What are you doing?

> **_Treeman_**
> Getting my ass kicked in Call of Duty. What
> are you doing?

> **_Jenny_**
> Lying here.

> **_Treeman_**
> Really?

> **_Jenny_**
> All by myself. Just lying here.

> **_Treeman_**
> Um
> What are you doing all by yourself?

> **_Jenny_**
> Wondering what you're doing.

> **_Treeman_**
> Should I come over?

Jenny
Yes.

Treeman
Right now?

Jenny
Right now.

September 29, 2025

Fuck.

Why? Why do I do what I do?

Fuck me.

Fuck

Me

51
Conflict

Monday, September 29, 2025 - Morning

JENNY SHIVERED ON A small boulder as water rushed past her boots. The rumble of the stream over the edge and into the pool below made her wonder why the founders didn't call the town 'Thunder Falls' or 'Grumble Falls.' She couldn't remember the last time she saw lightning here.

"We should have done this after sunup," Maddy said, stepping over a fallen branch.

"No, I like it," Jenny said, watching the water slip past in the light of their phone's flashlights. "It feels like a different place up here in the dark. I don't know … It's kind of ethereal, especially with all the mist and fog."

"It's spooky," Sydney said, walking over and taking her place on Jenny's other side. "But I kind of like that. I don't like it when I'm alone, though."

"How do you guys do it?" Jenny asked. "Like, when it's snowy and freezing, what do you do with the tower?"

"If it's really bad, the tower just doesn't get used for a few days until the town can plow the path. Then we just rotate who gets a night off. But most of the time it's not too crazy. We don't usually get this much precipitation. And it's not usually this cold this early. I'm expecting it to snap back warm again, at least for a little while," Maddy said.

"I hope so, I'm not ready for winter yet," Jenny said.

"I am," Sydney said. "It's my favorite season."

"You like it because you can't go anywhere and you get to just snuggle under blankets," Maddy said.

"Yes," Sydney said. "That is a non-controversial position."

"Do you want to hike up a little more and see the cave?" Maddy asked.

"The cave?" Jenny said.

"Well, it's just the opening where the water comes out. You can't go in it."

"Sure," Jenny said, glancing at her watch. "Then we should probably head back down. We'll be late for breakfast."

As they followed the water up along the shelf that formed the High Pass, Jenny kept an eye out for stones, roots, and anything else that might trip them up along the way. She used her role as the group's pathfinder as an excuse to go out in front and not take anyone's hand.

Why am I like this?

Because you got what you really needed a few hours ago from Phil. And they can never give that to you.

Jenny wanted to kneel next to the water and throw up. She despised the intrusive thought.

"There it is," Maddy said, shining her light up the rambling water to a horizontal cleft in the rock face.

"Wow, that's dramatic," Jenny said, frowning appreciatively.

"Yeah, like Moses in the desert," Maddy said.

"What now?" Jenny said, laughing. Maddy just shrugged. "Well, it's really cool. Thanks for showing me this."

"Oh! We should go camping in the summer. We can put our tent near here one week when you're at the tower," Sydney said. "And you can do your show at night, and we can sleep in our tent during the day, and we can live off the land."

"I feel like that would be really sweaty," Jenny said. "And not in, like, a fun way."

They turned around and talked about past camping and hiking trips. Sydney talked about her father taking her with him during the summers before she got to the fourth grade. Jenny was curious about Sydney's family, but didn't think she was in a great headspace for details she would want to remember. Her mind was preoccupied with the twin serpents of memory and regret. She hated that she had invited Phil over specifically to have sex. She hated that she had felt better after their encounter than she had after making out with Sydney and Maddy. She hated the fact that the feelings that had built up inside her seemed to have disappeared entirely the moment she gave in to them.

Who even am I?

Jenny pondered the question and half-heartedly contributed to the conversation as they descended the slope.

"What do people want to eat? I'll text Nate," Maddy asked. They relayed their orders to Maddy, who sent them in. Jenny let Sydney go on about future plans until they reached the Second Wave Diner and slipped in through the front doors.

As they made their way back through the booths, Jenny saw an unexpected, familiar face in one of the seats. Delia was cutting into a stack of pancakes and chatting cheerfully with Charles. Nate was actively listening, and Linds had their head down. Were they praying? No. As Jenny got closer, she saw that Linds was bent over a book.

"Morning," Sydney said and practically bounced into her seat. Maddy sat next to Linds and immediately leaned over to read over their shoulder. Linds made room by putting their arm over the back of Maddy's chair without looking up. Jenny sat between Delia and Nate. Delia was finishing a story about her father. She reached over and rubbed Jenny's arm.

"My father was nothing like that," Charles said, grinning. "He would have told me to go look it up and then left me to my own devices to find out how to look it up. I think he wanted me to have a library card early so he and my mother could have some time alone."

"As good a reason as any," Delia said.

"Perhaps. Though it did not make me popular in school."

"Who was popular in school?" Delia asked.

Everyone was silent for a moment until Sydney piped up, "Maddy was. She was one of the popular, pretty Christian girls. You know, hot for Jesus?"

"Don't say it like that," Maddy said, looking up from Linds's book.

"No, I didn't mean like you were horny for Jesus—"

"God, Syd, don't—"

"I mean you were like, a hot girl looking good for the big man in the sky," Sydney said.

"Please don't say any of that like that," Maddy said, turning away from Linds, who was trying to hide their laughter by focusing on their book.

"No, I don't mean, like, you wanted to get down with—"

"Sydney stop!" Jenny, Nate, and Maddy all said at the same time.

"What?"

"Well, beyond Maddy," Jenny said, "I don't think anyone was popular in school."

"You kind of were," Delia said.

"I was?"

"Yeah, in that same Goth-for-Jesus kind of way," Delia said.

"Right!" Sydney said! "You were like Maddy's role model—"

"Syd, please!" Maddy said, obviously embarrassed. Jenny frowned and glanced back and forth at the young women, one in dark clothes, one in light. Suddenly, it struck Jenny who Maddy sometimes reminded her of. She pictured herself, looking into the attic bathroom mirror, trying to perfect the balance of her makeup between dark and light. She stared down at the table, embarrassed and flattered.

Mercifully, the waitress arrived with the second round of food.

Jenny's omelet, Sydney's breakfast sandwich, and Maddy's waffles all looked amazing, and everyone said so, pouring words into the awkward silence. The waitress refreshed their drinks and disappeared into the back.

Jenny turned to Linds. "Whatcha readin'?"

"A book a friend sent me," Linds said.

"What kind?"

"American History," Linds said. "Some stuff about my hometown."

"Cool," Jenny said. "Where did you grow up again?"

"Upstate New York," Linds said. "Small town like this one."

"Nowhere is like Lightning Falls," Sydney said.

"They are more alike than you think," Linds said. Delia nodded, though Jenny wasn't sure if she was just observing how all small towns are alike, or if there was something more in the gesture.

When they left the diner, Delia took Jenny aside. "Hey, I was hoping we could do some girl time tonight, just you and me. You know, dinner and a movie or something?"

"That sounds great, but I think I'm a little restaurant-ed out."

"I can bring General Tso's and we can just hang out," Delia said.

"Yes," Jenny said, "that is a deal."

Jenny hugged her friends, put her earbuds in, and walked home to sleep alone as a mass of guilt, shame, desire, and regret writhed in her stomach.

Entry 12

September 30, 2025

I'm the worst, Diary. Judge me all you want. You can't judge me worse than I judge myself. I spent two nights in a row with Maddy and Sydney, and then the hour I get on my own, bam! I fuck Phil. Now, tonight, I broke dinner plans with Delia.

We rescheduled for tomorrow night, so, it's not the worst thing ever, but what am I doing? I feel like I'm losing my mind, Diary.

Help me!

52
The Cabin

Monday, September 29, 2025 - Evening

ONE LAST FIRST TIME, Jenny thought. Rain pattered against her knit cap as the lights of Main Street glowed golden in the hazy evening. After tonight, there would be no more surprises; no more new places to explore. By morning, she would have experienced all the so-called 'towers' and would be fully initiated into the world of the Sleep Talkers. The idea was both comforting and depressing. While it had been nerve-wracking at times, she had enjoyed discovering the facets of her new job. But, with tonight's broadcast, the novelty would end.

Maybe that wasn't entirely true. There were sure to be elements of the job she couldn't foresee. And at some point, one of the Sleep Talkers would leave, and then a whole new dynamic would follow. If Jenny didn't go first, then it would probably be Nate or Charles. She hated that idea. She wanted their group to stay together. Jenny wiped a trickle of rain from her cheek as two images formed in her mind. In the first, Nate left, his knee bothering him too much to continue walking out to the cabin and house, let alone the tower. In his place … who? She couldn't picture it. She would be sorry for Linds in that scenario. But what if it was Charles? She imagined the group's dynamics wouldn't change much if he left, and she was immediately ashamed at the thought. Charles was so kind, smart, and funny. But, she had to admit, he wasn't close with others.

The second scenario involved Jenny leaving first. That idea formed a pit in her stomach. It made her think of the Sleep Talkers as a group that didn't care if she was a member or not. There had been a time before Jenny, and there would be a time after her. If she left before anyone else, she would be nothing more than a blip, a phase that the Talkers went through, barely worth mentioning.

She thought about who they must have been with Cassandra, and what might have been different. She couldn't imagine Sydney would have been nearly as flirtatious with the older woman, but then she didn't know. Thinking about the Sleep Talkers with someone else in her place gave her the same strange ache that picturing Aurora with her previous boyfriend had given her. She didn't have a name for the feeling, only that she didn't like it.

Tired, she opened the door to Barry's coffee shop and stepped in. The bell tinkled above, but Barry wasn't behind the counter. Instead, she saw Mr. Grossman and another stocky, unfamiliar man standing in front of the counter.

"—taking too long. We may need to do something more direct," Mr. Grossman said loudly enough that Jenny guessed he was talking to Barry in the next room. The broad-shouldered man, who wore a dark, rain-wet jacket and blue baseball cap, touched Mr. Grossman's arm and lifted his chin. The white-bearded old man turned and smiled when he saw Jenny.

"I don't think we need to do that, Mr. Grossman," Barry called from the back. "I think we just need to put things back the way they're supposed to be and everything will take care of itself."

"I wish that were the case. But we still don't know what we need to know, and Camping Days starts soon."

"Now—" Barry said, coming through the back door. His eyes fixed on Jenny, leapt to Mr. Grossman, then the stocky man, and finally back to Jenny. "Hey, Jenny," he said. "How are you doing?"

"I'm damp," Jenny said, pointing at her head and grinning. "Please tell me you have some kind of anti-rain magic tea back there."

"Hmm, you want that old sorcery. I'll see what I can do. Give me just a minute. As I was saying, I don't think we need to do anything other than we're doing, Mr. Grossman."

"Good evening, Ms. Berger," Levi Grossman said.

"Hi," Jenny said. "Sorry to interrupt."

"Not at all, we were just discussing how poorly the renovations are going with the library. We don't even know whether they're going to be able to make the modifications to the rotunda in time for the reopening on Saturday."

"That sucks. Is something holding it up?" Jenny asked.

"So many things!" Mr. Grossman said. "Still, Barry is ever the optimist that things will right themselves. Personally, I think we need to take a stronger hand with the person in charge. Let's have a woman's perspective on it. What do you think we should do?"

"You mean, leave them alone and hope they get it done on time, or light a fire under their asses?" Jenny asked.

"In so many words," Mr. Grossman said, clearly amused at her turn of phrase.

Jenny's first thought was to tell them to let the workers do their jobs, since they probably knew best. But instead, she said, "You should probably talk to them. If they haven't managed to do it right up until now, then you probably shouldn't trust that they'll get it done without some, I don't know—"

"Shepherding?" Mr. Grossman said.

"Yeah, sure," Jenny said.

"Good. That is what I like to hear. Let's be assertive. Would you like to take the reins on this, Barry, or shall I?"

Barry pursed his lips and glanced at the stocky man. Then, staring at the top of the counter, he said, "No, I'll talk to them."

"You will?" Mr. Grossman said.

"Yeah, I'll do it."

"Excellent. Now, give this young woman whatever she wants; it's on me. Go ahead, get one of those triple mocha candy-cane crunch lattes," he said.

Jenny laughed. "That's not for me. But I will take an extra-large dirty chai with skim milk," Jenny said. Barry obliged.

"How do you like working here?" Mr. Grossman asked as Barry was preparing the drink.

"It's a little confusing. Sometimes it feels like home, like it's exactly the thing I'm supposed to be doing, but other times—I don't know. I feel like I'm still adjusting." She almost said that she didn't feel like herself sometimes, but that felt too personal to share with Mr. Grossman, no matter how kindly he was. She also didn't entirely like the look of the stocky man who was stealing furtive glances in her direction.

I wonder if he's a subscriber, Jenny thought.

"Everything in life is an adjustment," Mr. Grossman said. "I'm just glad we adjusted the darned pipes in that house before they carried you off like the Kusels!"

It wasn't the pipes.

Jenny stared at the man and frowned as the thought kicked its way into her mind.

It wasn't the pipes then, and it wasn't the pipes now.

"Are you all right, my dear?"

"Yeah, sorry, I zoned out for a second. I was just thinking about that house and how dangerous it is," Jenny said. "With gas leaks and such."

Mr. Grossman nodded enthusiastically. "It is! And that is all the more reason I'm a fool for not keeping a better eye on things. My dear friend … well, he lost his family in that house. But that was a long time ago."

"You knew one of the Kusels?" Jenny asked, leaning against the counter.

"Mhm, I certainly did. As did my wife, Georgina. As did Mr. Frei's father." Here, the stocky man nodded and gave her a constrained smile. She returned the greeting. "But then, this is a small town and I'm a busybody," Mr. Grossman said, laughing. "Still, the blame rests on my shoulders for not making sure things were maintained. I will make certain that we don't have any more oversights."

"I appreciate it, I'd hate to wake up brain dead or something," Jenny said, chuckled, and immediately thought it was a stupid joke.

"No one wants that," Mr. Grossman said as Barry handed Jenny her drink.

"You sure I can't get this?" Jenny said, holding her paper cup up.

"No, it's on me. For your advice. You see, Barry, the younger generation isn't so much of a pushover. A firmer hand! That's good advice."

Jenny thanked Mr. Grossman again, nodded to Mr. Frei, and waved to Barry. Then she was back out on Main Street. She crossed Adams and saw the light was on in Delia's bookstore. She stood before the window and saw Delia and Dylan at the counter together. She considered ducking inside to apologize for skipping out on dinner, but she thought better of it. She didn't have a real excuse, and Delia would see through any nonsense story Jenny made up. It would be better to just make it up to her tomorrow night. Jenny continued on, music playing, sipping spices from her cup, and ducking under shop awnings to avoid the rain.

When the shops gave out, she crossed to the other side of Main Street and hurried past the last few blocks of houses. On the corner of Main and Bankview, she started up the path into the forest. The pines were lousy cover against the steadily increasing rain. She hurried up the path and was grateful to see that the cabin's external lights were on. She fished for keys, fumbled them, found the right one, and then pushed her way into Whitman Cabin.

Linds had been right. The cabin was downright cozy compared to the lookout tower. Jenny hung her wet coat and hat on pegs near the door, and she put her pack down next to the sofa in the main room. According to Maddy, it was a pull-out—though not worth the effort. An old desk stood in the corner, and an open door to her right showed a full bathroom. A corner of the main room served as a kitchen, and an old entertainment center took up another corner with a small flat-screen TV standing on two plastic legs.

Jenny ducked into the broadcasting room and found no surprises. Within moments, she had the full lay of the cabin, turned the radio on, checked the shelf of records, and put her lunch into the fridge. One shelf was full of diet pops with a note that read 'Everyone enjoy! – Link.'

Jenny checked the time. It was 8:46. She got up, used the bathroom, turned on the two space heaters, and sat back down. She hit the broadcast button.

"Good evening, Lightning Falls. This is Jenny Berger, and I'm here, finally, in the old Whitman cabin. I hope everyone out there is having a good night. We have more rain, which is annoying, so let's all try to stay safe, warm, and dry. It's Monday, which means that most of you started your work weeks today, just like I'm starting mine. So, if you want to talk about your jobs or how you hate Mondays, why not give me a call?"

The phone did not ring as Jenny forced herself to ramble on about some of the jobs she'd had in the past, avoiding any mention of her website. After a few minutes of boring herself, she tried another tack.

"As you all know, it's Camping Days later this week. As a kid, I remember loving Camping Days ..." She trailed off, unsure of how she had stepped back onto that landmine.

I'm dying out here.

Jenny pictured her father dying, drowning under dark water. She pictured the robed figure with the green flame in its lantern cage that brooded over his death in her memory. She wondered how much more therapy she'd have to get to make that figment disappear.

Her phone buzzed.

> **_Sydney_**
> You good?

"Sorry, everyone, I'm just not on my game tonight. I think being off for a few days makes me rusty. Or-or maybe I'm just bad at this. There was this moment at the beginning where I felt like everything was going well, you know? I would jump on and know what to say. But now ... I don't know, I feel like I just don't know what I'm supposed to say tonight."

> **_Sydney_**
> Do you want us to come by?

> ***Maddy***
> Hey, if you need us to, we can pop by and hang out in the lounge, we don't mind. Maybe being alone in the cabin isn't any better than being alone in the house. No pressure, just let me know if you want us to do that.

"Sorry, folks, I'm quiet because my friends are being awesome and texting to see if I'm okay. I think I am okay, it's just a little bumpy start. I'm not really sure why I'm worrying so much about getting used to doing this, though. I'll be gone before Christmas."

Jenny frowned at the microphone. Where had that come from? Was she having another one of her … what even were they? Migraines? Residual effects from being drowned?

"I mean, they'll probably fire me for being so terrible at this. I just want to try to do my best before they get rid of me, I guess." She tried to laugh, but it wouldn't come. "I …"

Vertigo tilted the room. Jenny suddenly wondered if she was completely delusional. She pictured her room in Sunrise. Was she still there? Were Lightning Falls, and the Sleep Talkers, and her friends all figments of her shattered mind? Was she as crazy as Grace? Were they quietly laughing in a corner together, completely disconnected from reality?

No, she thought. *No, just breathe.*

"I think I need to just calm the hell down and take it easier," she said. "Link tried to tell me how chill this job is, and I haven't treated it that way at all. I feel like I've been trying to be someone else, like some kind of DJ, and that's not at all me. I don't even know where I got that idea from. So, maybe that's not how I do this. Maybe I'm the person who plays her favorite music and shuts the heck up most of the time. Maybe I'm just going to start reading books that are in the public domain over the radio. Oh, that's a fun idea, what is in the public domain now?"

She pulled a list up on her phone and scanned through it.

"Hmm, *Winnie the Pooh*, *A Farewell to Arms*, *The Great—*"

The words died on her lips. She pictured a man with light hair parted down the middle, sipping gin with fruit juice and gazing stoically out a window at a party in—where was it?—Philadelphia. A slender, dark-haired woman who moved like a ballerina laughed and teased the sullen man.

She was mad, like me.

"Maybe I'll read *The Great Gatsby*," Jenny said, dreamily. "And, maybe we should have some jazz."

53
Desert Place

Monday, September 29, 2025 – Late Night

THE VINYL TURNED AT thirty-three revolutions a minute, and Duke Ellington's fingers danced. Saxophones, trombones, and trumpets called across decades, bidding Jenny to rise and move. But it was the drums, beating like a heart uncanny that pulled her from her chair. In thick woolen socks, she danced across the carpet in unfamiliar steps that she knew better than walking. She turned on the balls of her feet, kicked, and held her arms out in front of her as if she had a partner. She could see him, a tall man in a gray suit, peering at her from under the brim of a hat.

The arm of the record player lifted, and the second album fell.

What am I doing?

Her body was too big. She didn't know the dance. She was too tall. Where did she learn to move like this? What was she wearing? What was she thinking?

Jaunty piano began a song Jenny didn't know.

Yes, I do. It's James P. Jordan.

Fire lapped Jenny's thoughts.

What is this?

Her mind felt cloven down the middle.

My dear, it's the Charleston.

The world bent and twisted, rotating like the record, spinning, and spinning. The cabin tilted, and she almost stumbled. She kicked and kicked, turned, and turned. Her mouth opened to scream, and smoke billowed out with the taste of gin and the smell of men's cologne around her.

God, please. God, please. God, please.

The log walls tumbled down and were replaced by darker, smoother, richer wood that closed in on her until it stood, foursquare about her, chrome running up between the boards, and bursting in rays of silver sun. The man next to her wore a deep burgundy suit with black lapels, and a soft cloth cap with a leather brim. His black skin was hidden almost entirely by long sleeves, white gloves, and a high collar.

His name is Henry.

"Where are we going tonight, Ms. Kusel?" he asked, his hand on a lever.

"Down, Henry," Jenny said in a voice that wasn't her own. "All the way down."

And down they went.

Jenny felt like she was standing behind someone, her hand on their shoulder, following as they led. When her lips moved, it was as if someone else moved them. When her legs shifted her weight from one slender hip to the other, it was because someone else put their hands on them and positioned her like a doll. When the doors opened and she stepped out into the music and smoke, she felt like a puppet hitched to strings.

She walked to the bar and ordered a martini as piano, saxophone, and bass transported the people from the world above to the one below. Jenny watched as people danced and held each other in the shadowed underworld where they shed the guises Olympus demanded they wear.

Here they are themselves, she thought. *But not me.*

Hands on her shoulders turned her and pushed her through the door before her drink could arrive. She stumbled out onto the gravel drive of her home under a full moon. She surveyed the yard, noting the shelter off to her right with its window glowing yellow in the night. On the porch, her father rocked slowly in the old chair. She shook her head as the thrumming music mingled with the low rumble of the falls. She took a step, and the front yard was replaced by the family library where four people waited for her, their eyes unseeing, their skin eaten by worms. She walked over to the rolling bar and poured herself a drink. Before it could touch her lips, her uncle strode smiling into the room, his arms wide. He embraced her.

"Finally!" he cried and wrapped her in a crushing embrace. A wind rose as he held her, whipping her hair up in a fury of curls and waves.

I never bobbed it.

The bookshelves broke as sand bit through them, feasting on their pages and cardboard covers. The four corpses, stripped of their flesh by the blowing grit, fell to bones and disappeared under rising dunes.

"Don't be afraid, they're all here," her uncle whispered.

When the wind had done its work and the house was no longer about them, they stood together under a twilight sky. The air was cold, and the sand gave off no heat, having long ago radiated away the day's fire. Jenny peered down at her body, which was wrapped in brittle strips of cloth under a loose tunic and dark cloak. Her uncle wore the same. Their feet were bound in the same desiccated strips but were otherwise bare.

"Come and see," he said.

He led her by the hand over a low dune and down into a shallow valley. Then up again they trudged until they surmounted a ridge three times Jenny's height. When they came to the top, she took in a dry, cracking breath. A path appeared before them, striking its way up through a blasted land of lifeless rock along the side of a mountain.

"Come and see," he said. She followed him up the path for what might have been hours. Along the way stood broken pillars and fleshless skeletons in twisted and obscene postures. Narrow paths branched off the main trail, ending in small buildings that jutted out from the rockface. Their stone walls rose under gabled slate roofs, reminding her of mausoleums. At the corners, carved into the stone, smooth vertical lines with rounded tips reached up like stalagmites and down like stalactites to meet in the middle. Where they met, golden suns burst with triangular rays. Where the roofs touched the walls, borders of undulating onyx gleamed. The buildings' tops, longer than their bottoms, slanted back to meet the mountain's slope, as if one might enter the front door and follow whatever rooms lay within deep into the bedrock. Jenny imagined vast halls dug into the stone, festooned with gold, silver, and volcanic rock.

Her mind tilted.

I'm crazy. I'm in Sunrise. I'm still drowning. Dad. Dad, save me, I'm drowning.

The man led her up past dozens of buildings, pillars, and skeletons until they finally surmounted a sharp ridge whose bitter stones Jenny thought would slice her to pieces if she took a wrong step. However, that fear was quickly overwhelmed by the sight of what lay below her in the bowl of what she thought had once been a vast volcano.

A low city filled the ridge-rimmed depression and climbed its sides. The squat, sand-color buildings ran in straight, ordered streets, and from them fluttered scatters of the pale cloth that covered her body. Five low towers, square and flat-topped, stood evenly spaced around the center of the town. All was strange and alien, but her eyes were drawn to the city center where a pit yawned, perhaps a mile across. Its rim was a thin line of pale brown sand, and below it, stone ran down in striations of dark and light, gray and tan, with rare bolts of gold and silver glinting in the dim light.

Jenny wanted to know where she was, but she already knew. As the question formed in her mind, it was answered. She stood on the Mount of Seeing. Here she had lived for decades in the dry dark, waiting for morning.

No, I've never been here before.
Her mind burned.
Yes, but I have.
The voice was distinct and clear. A woman's voice, not her own.

"Look and see, remember and be strengthened, for the time is not yet at hand."

"Who am I?" Jenny asked.

The man gazed at her and shook his head.

"No one," he said. "And I will teach you each how to be no one in your turns. And I will teach you both how to overcome. He sees far."

Jenny wanted to ask what that meant, but the wind rose suddenly and pulled her cloak into a billowing plume behind her. Sand skittered over the rocks and then took flight, pricking her skin. The wind gusted, and she felt her brittle clothing torn away. With it went her skin and sight and heart and—

54
Suspended

Tuesday, September 30, 2025 — Morning

JENNY PULLED THE MICROPHONE close and waited for the final song to end.

"And that, folks, was Louis Armstrong, finishing us up. Tomorrow night I'll be back, and I think I'll take some calls to see what people think of this format, where I mostly play music and only do a little bit of talking. So, give it some thought, and I'll do the same. Until then, good morning, Lightning Falls!"

She pushed the broadcast button, pulled her headphones off, shut the control panel down, and turned off the record player. After returning everything to its proper place, she started toward the cabin's main room. As she crossed the carpet, she faltered, a dream coming back to her for a moment. She was walking up the side of a dry mountain. There had been a city, too, or had that been a different dream? She couldn't remember. Was it the dark city that someone had asked her about? Who had that been? Right! She remembered. Linds had wanted to know if she had dreamed of a dark city. But the city she visited didn't seem dark, exactly. Or, she didn't think so. But then she wasn't sure. She should try to remember as much of the dream as she could so she could tell Linds about it later.

After straightening the couch cushions and packing her things, Jenny checked her phone and waited. A handful of minutes passed before the first knock came. She opened the door, and Nate stomped in, wearing a translucent plastic poncho over his coat. He stamped his feet and shook the plastic while Jenny stood back.

"It's really coming down. Do you have anything to keep dry with?"

Jenny looked at her coat and hat and shook her head.

"I thought that might be the case," Nate said and dug into his coat pocket. He produced a small plastic square, which he handed to Jenny. She tore it open and shook out her own poncho.

"Oh, this is sexy! No one has bought me anything see-through in a while," she said.

"I shop at only the finest of plastic lingerie stores," Nate said. He turned and opened the door when the second knock came. Maddy and Sydney barreled into the room, splashing as they came. They were both wearing bright yellow raincoats with hoods.

"You look like you should have a red balloon in your hand," Jenny said, pushing Sydney's hood back. The younger woman gazed up at her with damp red hair framing her face. Jenny's desire reasserted itself, and she kissed Sydney's cold lips.

"Well, okay," Nate said, looking mildly embarrassed.

"Sorry," Jenny said, smiling.

"No, it's just not every day I get someone see-through clothing and then they turn around and kiss someone else."

"Oh, does Nate need a kiss?" Sydney said.

"I'm okay," Nate said, holding up his hands. He went into the broadcast room and switched off the light as Jenny pulled her coat and hat on. Then, parka crinkling into place, she opened the front door and let the group out in front of her before she stepped out into the downpour. They plodded up the path, their feet splashing in deep puddles, water drumming on their hoods. It was too loud to talk, so they walked in silence. Head down, Jenny watched her feet under the path lights, and pictured them wrapped in dry cloth, making deep divots in the sand. What had the dream been about? She had climbed a mountain and ... what? A man had taught her something.

He taught me to be no one.

Aurora had told her about a strain of Buddhism that sought pure nonexistence. The Self, she had said, was a lie. We must learn not to be. Jenny wasn't sure if that was what Buddhists really believed, or if it was just a West Coast American interpretation, but it hadn't seemed particularly appealing. She didn't like the idea of not existing.

As they emerged from the path and crossed over Bankview, Jenny noticed a strange reflection flickering on the wet earth. Blue, red, blue, red.

"What's going on?" Jenny asked, almost bumping into Nate.

"No idea. Police. Hey, were they there when you two walked down?"

"No," Maddy almost yelled over the thudding rain.

"Are they in front of the diner?" Sydney asked.

"I don't think so," Nate said. "Come on."

They hurried to the east side of the street and past blocks of houses. As they got close to Cunningham Avenue, they could see that three police cars were blocking the street in front of Adams, forming a ring around the front of Delia's bookstore.

Everyone ran except Nate, who hurried as fast as he could. Sydney sprinted and outpaced them, reaching the nearest police car and stopping as she passed its hood. Jenny watched as Sydney peered into Delia's shop, covered her mouth with her hands, and collapsed to the ground, her head bowed to the earth. A pit, dark and monstrous, opened in Jenny's stomach. Her breathing stuttered, and her heart started skipping beats. She thought she might be having a heart attack as she stumbled to a halt against one of the car doors. She bent to comfort her friend, but her eyes flicked into the bookstore, and she saw what Sydney had seen. Maddy came up beside her, paused, and then grabbed Jenny and tried to pull her back.

"No," Maddy said, "don't look! God, don't look!"

But Jenny did look. Jenny had been there when her father drowned. She'd watched two of her friends drown at the hands of a man she trusted. She had seen the pleading look on Nolan's face and the look of confusion and horror on Aurora's. She had known the immeasurable and indelible ache of knowing she would never speak to them again, never kiss them again, never love them again.

Even so, she'd never seen anything so monstrous as what hovered in the middle of Delia's bookstore. Three police officers stood around an object, their flashlights picking out pieces of it, showing dark skin, a leg, a foot, an arm, a breast, all hanging limply—elbows lifted away from the body, head hung forward, and blood, black and gleaming, running everywhere.

"Delia!" Jenny screamed. She ran forward out of Maddy's grasp as one of the officers turned and held out a hand. She saw his face, young, pale, and terrified. Some part of her brain recognized him as the young, red-headed officer she had seen at the summer market and spoken to in the Timber.

She pushed her way past him through the door, where she found her friend seemingly floating in the middle aisle. No, not floating, hanging from something almost invisible—was it fishing wire? Her elbows were wrapped in it, her arms bulging and swollen where it cut into her. It encircled her wrists and cut into the skin under her armpits. Police flashlights glinted off dozens of strands that rose from behind her. Jenny's gaze followed the strands up to where they were tied to two metal bars that crossed over Delia, spanning the store's central aisle, and resting on the tops of two bookshelves.

"Miss, please," the stricken officer said, tears running down his face as he stepped closer to Jenny. "Stay back."

Jenny screamed as the image burned into her mind: Delia hanging naked, blood slowly dripping from a finger, nipple, and toe. Blood over her neck and chest from the deep cuts in her face, where her mouth had been widened on both sides. Blood running down her leg. Blood on the floor of her store.

"How? Oh God! What the fuck is this? What the fuck is this?" Jenny screamed, tearing back the hood of her parka. The red-haired officer's attempt to move her away from the scene was less a push and more of a hug. He wrapped his arms around her and tried to walk her back. She could hear him crying, feel the shudder of his chest against hers as he begged her to step back. But she moved away from him, tearing herself from his grip and circling Delia, skirting behind the bookshelves to get behind her.

"Chase, stop her!" another officer shouted.

Chase, that's his name. The thought drifted through her mind, untethered from the horror around her. Chase didn't need to stop her, however. Jenny stopped herself. From behind Delia, Jenny could see what had happened to her friend. Fishhooks ran across her back in a checkerboard pattern. Two dozen or more pinches of skin, each with a trickle of blood, puckered her back. Each sprouted a fine line that hung taut from the poles above.

Before Jenny could see more, her hands were pulled behind her back, and handcuffs were put on them.

"Get her out!" someone shouted.

Jenny let herself be guided backward the way she had come, out the front.

"What are you doing?" Maddy shouted as Jenny came out with the officer behind her.

"Will you stay out?" Chase asked. She nodded as shock rolled across her body, turning every muscle to liquid, voiding every emotion. He removed the handcuffs, put one of his hands on her shoulder, and then turned away. She heard him speak into his radio, something about ambulances, but he sounded like he was a hundred miles away down a well. She felt her legs give out, and she slid down the side of one of the police cars. Sydney was by her side immediately, her arms around Jenny's shoulders, the softness of her chest against Jenny's cheek. Jenny hung her head, her hair like a curtain drawn down to hide her from obscene reality. She screamed her lungs empty, sucked in air, and screamed again. She screamed until her voice broke. Jenny felt someone take her hand. Maddy leaned in and put her forehead against Jenny's, and she started to pray.

Jenny quaked in Sydney's embrace and under Maddy's supplications. She trembled as Nate stood over them, staring and crying silently, his hands clenching and unclenching. For a moment, they were alone together in their horror. Then Linds was at Nate's side, and Charles was kneeling next to Maddy.

"Get her up, get her inside," Charles said. "The diner, now."

Jenny let Charles put his head under her arm and lift her, his strong hand around her waist.

"She's dead, Charles. Delia's dead." Jenny said, her voice strange in her mouth.

"I know," he said. "God help us."

Then other people's screams rose. A crowd formed, and its undulating offense and nightmare insistence grew with it. People called for the scene to be covered. They called for answers. They called for a clearer view.

Charles led Jenny away from the growing tumult, and Sydney ran ahead, waving at the waitress who stood in the Second Wave Diner's open front door, craning her neck. The waitress moved out of the way, and Sydney opened the second door. Charles led Jenny in. Then Maddy and Sydney opened the inner doors, and Charles guided Jenny past the front counter and back to their table. He helped her down into her seat and nodded at Sydney.

Coffee came. Charles, Nate, and Linds stood in front of the table as Maddy and Sydney sat on either side of Jenny. People came into the diner talking loudly, but they hushed when they saw the three people standing, facing them from the back corner. Jenny stared straight ahead, seeing everything from a desolate, detached place.

Lights poured in through the diner's large windows. Jenny sipped coffee from a trembling mug, but she declined food. She wasn't hungry. Still, the manager brought bread, fruit, and French fries for the table. He offered his condolences. Jenny could see that he, a heavy man with small, kind eyes, had been crying. She covered her face and shook.

"I want to go home," she said after sitting for the better part of an hour.

"Okay," Maddy said. They helped her from the booth seat. Maddy spoke to Charles in a low voice for a moment before Charles turned to her.

"Delia was our friend, but you were closest to her. I know it won't make it better, but we're here for you. We'll come by with food and whatever you need."

Jenny nodded, her eyes empty.

How do I become no one?

Soon we won't have a choice, the other voice in her head said.

Sydney wanted to hug Jenny all the way home, but Maddy pulled her back and asked Jenny what she wanted. "Just hold my hand," Jenny said. Sydney did. Jenny felt her phone buzz two dozen times or more as they walked. She imagined Isabella texting her, maybe Patty if she had been woken up by some prayer-group chain. Phil, Leddy, perhaps even Earl, would be reaching out. Maybe the whole world was messaging her. It struck her that she would be able to tell who on her JustBuffs page was from town if they sent her condolences through the site. Of course, that assumed that people knew her well enough to connect her to Delia.

Of course, they would. I'm all over Delia's email ads. Sitting there stupidly reading books in the place where someone would hang her up on fishing wire.

When they got back to the house, Jenny was shivering. She had lost her parka somewhere, probably in the bookstore, when Chase tried to save her from herself. Despite her hat and coat, her hair and clothes were soaked. She stumbled through her apartment and dropped each piece of wet clothing on the floor, leaving a trail behind her. She went into the bathroom, threw up, rinsed her mouth, and retreated into the bedroom, shivering.

"Here," Sydney said, grabbing a piece of clothing from the corner of the bed. "It's dry."

Jenny let Sydney guide her arms through scratchy wool. She sat still as Sydney buttoned the front of the sweater.

"I didn't know you found it," Sydney said, hugging her.

Jenny stared down at the green wool and ran her hands over it.

"I didn't," Jenny said dreamily. "Can you plug my phone in? And then just hold me?"

Sydney did as Maddy sat beside them, stroking their hair.

59
Out of Order

Tuesday, September 30, 2025 – Night

"FUCK, MY HEAD!" JENNY croaked. Her throat was raw, and her skull pounded.

There isn't time to hurt; you have to help. Open the door. Let them in!

"I can't, I can't do anything, oh God, make it stop!" Jenny said, curling up on the floor. Fire raced through her eyes, and acid down her tongue. Her ears were an endless siren. She put her fingers to her mouth and tasted dirt under her fingernails.

Let me then. Let me do it. Just let go and let me. If I don't, Sydney dies. Maddy dies. Charles—

"Yes, yes, please, just do it—"

Darkness.

Warmth. Pain and warmth. Wet on her cheek, sounds, shouting, arms around her, voices talking, noise, pain, noise and movement, pain, searing pain.

"Bring her over here—" someone said. Arms around her lifted and moved her, and then down on something soft, the voices a blurring and throbbing murmur.

"Get her water. There! The door—"

"Locked! Stay away from the windows!"

"They could just burn it down with us in it!" A voice—high, loud, and panicked.

"Good luck to them in this rain," said another, calm, close, strong. "Jenny. Jenny, it looks like you're in a lot of pain, but I need you to look at me."

She tried to open her eyes, but they felt glued shut. She thought there must be crust over them, so she reached up and wiped, but there was nothing. She blinked and saw the face of a person she could barely recognize.

"Where am I?"

"The cabin," the person said.

"What's happening?" Jenny said.

"We have no idea," someone else said. She knew that voice—Maddy. "What is going on, Jenny?"

"Is she sick?" Sydney asked.

"I don't know," the person in front of her said. The person. Jenny recognized them … or did she? Who was this woman … no, not …

Jenny was confused. Her head was a marching band running through John Philip Sousa's greatest hits.

A snap of thunder and shattering glass. Was that a bullet?

"Shit, get inside!" A man—Nate—Nate's voice was urgent. "Where the fuck are the police?"

"You called them?" Charles asked.

"Yeah, when we got here, and the door was locked."

"Maybe they're the ones shooting at us," Maddy said.

No one said anything to that. Even in her pain and stupor, Jenny knew that if that was the case, whatever was happening was hopeless. She blinked and saw the broadcasting room of the cabin, a room with no windows, and no way out. Glass shattered again in the next room.

She wanted to throw up and then pass out.

"Get that open," Charles said.

"What?" Sydney said.

"The basement door," he said, and his heavy footsteps crossed the room.

"There's a basement door?" Sydney asked.

"Yeah," Maddy said, "how did you not know that?"

"I don't know I—"

Creaking—loud and painful. Then a slam and wood rattling.

"Shit!"

"Fuck!"

"Come on," Nate said. "I don't think they can do anything to that door short of cutting it down with an axe, but I don't want to wait for them to try."

"Come on," the person in front of her said. "We need you to get up. Can you get up?"

Jenny nodded. That was a terrible idea, as burning pitch rolled through her skull. They helped her up slowly, arms on all sides.

"Put your back against the door," Sydney said as it rattled in its frame.

"What, so they can shoot me in the back through the door? No thanks," Nate whispered from against the wall. He had put his boot against the door's corner. "Charles, go down after them! I'll go down last."

"You sure about that?" Charles said.

"Yeah, go."

Charles followed Jenny down the stairs, every step a clatter of pain behind her eyes. Jenny heard him say, "Now, come on!"

A loud scraping tore across her hearing, a slam and rattle, and then heavy, uneven footsteps. Another slam and darkness.

"Do we have some way of locking that?" Charles asked.

"I don't think so," Nate said, "but let's look around."

Phones lit up the box of a room with its plastered walls and dirt floor. Wooden crates lay stacked on wooden pallets, and a metal cabinet stood in the corner next to metal shelves. Maddy walked over and picked up a rusted rake.

"Good idea," Nate said, hobbling over beside her. His limp seemed worse. He grabbed a tool and handed it to Sydney.

"I need to sit down," Jenny said. Sydney led her to a crate and helped her sit. The pounding in Jenny's head was a little less now, though it was still hard for her to focus on anything. The other person walked over to Jenny and crouched down in front of her.

"Tell me what's going on," they said.

"Who are you?" The question pushed itself out of Jenny's mouth, like a person shouldering their way through a crowd.

The person frowned and looked at Sydney for help. Jenny saw a look of terror and confusion on the red-haired woman's face.

"My name is Linds, do you remember me?"

"Lindsay?" Jenny asked.

"Linds," Sydney said. "They're your friend."

Jenny studied the person in front of her and tried to remember. No, that was also a terrible idea. Remembering seemed to tighten the barbed wire net around her skull. She put her face into her hands.

"I'm sorry, my head, I just—"

Above them, wood crashed, and a rain of small objects pattered on the basement ceiling.

"Shit," Charles said.

"Here we go," Nate said, hefting the haft of a broken farming tool. "Phones off! Now," he whispered. "Get behind those boxes!" Linds and Sydney helped Jenny move. Before the lights went out, she watched Charles take a position under the stairs, and Nate push Maddy back with him against the wall, holding her rake like a spear.

"Maddy," she whispered.

This is my fault, Jenny thought. *We're all going to die, and I don't know why, but it's clearly my fault. What is happening? Please, I don't want to die here. I don't want Maddy or Sydney or Charles or—*

Someone wrenched the basement trapdoor open, and light slanted down the stairs. The first heavy boot clomped on the top step, followed by another.

"Shit," a deep voice said. "I can't see anything."

The voice was familiar, but Jenny couldn't place it. Her mind was tearing itself apart with every new thought.

"Use your flashlight," another person said. Their voice was also deep and familiar. Why couldn't Jenny place them?

"I have a shotgun," the first voice said. "I didn't bring a tactical light attachment for my fucking shotgun."

"Fine. I'll hold the God-damned light, and you kill them."

"Who is that?" Sydney whispered, pulling Jenny farther behind the crates. She was crying, her voice was shaking, but she put her back against Jenny's chest, putting herself between Jenny and the men.

"No," Jenny tried to say, but her mouth was barely working. She needed water. She needed sleep.

"Okay," the second voice said. "Go. Wait, you reloaded?"

"Yes," the first said. Jenny thought they sounded annoyed with each other, like an old married couple. The thought would have been amusing if they weren't coming down the steps to kill her and every remaining person that she cared about in the world.

"Okay, go."

One footstep, then another.

"Oh, God, please," Sydney whispered.

Then there was thunder, and Jenny fell into darkness and oblivion.

60
Waking

Wednesday, October 1, 2025 – Early Morning

"SHE'S … NOW," A voice.

"—her up," another voice.

Jenny felt herself lifted and moved, floating. Voices, all different, all tumbling over each other, drifted through a thin, fuzzy veil.

"—me in! I'm her—"

"—'am you'll have to wait for the EMTs to—"

"—Chase, let us in, we—"

"This is a crime scene. Someone tried to kill them; you need to step back."

"Chase, please, it's us, we know her." Leddy. That was Leddy's voice.

"Please just let the EMTs do their work." Jenny knew that one, too. The police officer she had met, the one who had talked to her at the Tim, the one who had tried to push her away at Delia's. Light flared into Jenny's eye as someone lifted her eyelid.

"Ow, fuck," Jenny said.

"She's talking, she's awake," a voice above her said too loudly.

"Fuck, my head," Jenny said.

"Miss, can you hear me? What's your name?"

"Tab—Jenny Berger."

"What is your name?"

"Jenny Berger," Jenny said more forcefully. "Please stop shining the light in my face."

"Are you injured? Have you been hurt at all?"

Jenny ran her hands over her body and shook her head, and daggers tumbled between her temples. Someone handed her a bottle of water. She drank.

"No, I have a hell of a headache, but other than that, I'm okay. Please, stop with the light, I'm okay. That light is the only thing that's hurting me."

"You need to take her to the hospital." That was Patty's voice. "She wasn't acting like herself at all. That wasn't my daughter."

"I'm okay," Jenny said. "I think I had another migraine. I just—I don't know, but I'm fine now. Really, please, I'm okay." Jenny pushed her way up and past the two EMTs. They were outside under a dark, cloudy, rainless sky. "Look, other than what's left of my headache, I'm fine."

"Jennifer, you need to go with them. Go to the hospital, get yourself checked out," Patty said, her voice desperate.

"No, Patty, I'm not going to the hospital. And even if I do, it won't be in an ambulance. I don't have that kind of money."

"I think you should go too," Sydney said. She stood next to Maddy, both of their eyes dark with concern.

"Unless the police send her," Linds said, "she doesn't have to go."

"I might do that," a woman said, walking up to face Jenny. "I'm Sergeant Kellaher. Can we talk?"

The sergeant sent everyone else away and asked Jenny about the evening.

Let me answer. Let me take control.

Jenny felt a hand on her shoulder pulling her back. She resisted for a moment and then, looking into the sergeant's eyes, she nodded. The world flew up and away, as if Jenny were falling into a deep well. Then it rushed back, and she was standing in front of the sergeant, who was shaking her head.

"So, you came here to do your broadcast, you got one of your migraines, and then you blacked out."

"Yeah. The migraines have been so bad that sometimes I black out," Jenny said. "I need to get medication, I guess."

The sergeant frowned and rubbed the side of her nose. "Did you recognize the men who broke in?"

"I never saw them," Jenny said.

"Did you recognize their voices?"

"Maybe? I was so panicked, and my head was so bad, that I don't think I could say for sure."

"If you had to guess?"

Jenny stared out into the dark pine forest and thought. She tried to recall the voices, but she couldn't. Phil? Was it Phil who had come to kill her? Earl? She tried to picture Earl coming down the stairs to murder everyone in the cabin. She couldn't do it.

Jenny shrugged. "I'm sorry."

"Miss Berger," the sergeant said. "I understand that this has been an extremely confusing and scary night. I need to urge you to do two things. First, go to the hospital. Let them check you out. I'm a hair's breadth from taking you into mental health custody, and the only reason I'm not is that you didn't hurt anyone, you don't appear to be a harm to yourself, and you seem calm. But please, for everyone's sake, go."

"Take her in now," Patty said, stepping closer to them. "Can't you see she needs help?"

"Ma'am, under OSR 426.228, I can't do that. She is not an immediate danger to herself or others. And while I agree that she needs care, the need doesn't appear to be immediate to me."

"How?" Patty yelled. "How is it not immediate?"

"Jenny didn't do anything," Leddy said. "She was the victim here. She didn't hurt anyone."

"Miss, I don't—" Patty began, but Phil stepped up and put his hand on her shoulder.

"It's okay. We're going to keep her safe. Everyone here wants her to be safe. Okay? We'll make sure she gets to the doctor when she's ready." Patty turned, hugged Phil, and started to cry against his chest. The incongruity of Patty and Phil hugging added to the surreality of the situation.

"Second," the sergeant began, "if you will not go to the hospital now, then I need you to go somewhere safe. Officer Gadke scared the men away, and we're looking for them, but I think it's best for you to sleep somewhere other than the Kusel House tonight."

Jenny took a deep breath and nodded.

"We'll take care of her," Linds said.

"No, she has to go to the hospital," Patty insisted.

"Where?" Jenny said, turning toward Linds.

"We'll talk. I know a place. I don't want to say anything here." They gestured to the crowd of people, and Jenny nodded.

"Well, that's good then," Sergeant Kellaher said, standing. "I will want you to come in tomorrow or the next day and give a fuller statement once you've had a chance to get yourself together. Do you understand?"

Jenny nodded. "Yeah, I do. And I will."

"Good." She closed the flap of her metal clipboard. "Go to the hospital."

"I will, soon," Jenny said.

The sergeant nodded.

"Thank you," Jenny said.

"You're welcome, but you should be thanking Chase. They almost killed him."

Jenny turned to where the sergeant nodded and saw Officer Chase Gadke with gauze taped to his cheek. He was staring into nothing that lay a few inches beyond his toes.

"Hey," Jenny said, walking up to him. He lifted his head slowly and smiled.

"Miss Berger," he said. "How are you doing?"

He's not bad, not too skinny. Skinny for the fuzz, and skinny for me, but if you're looking to thank him for his gallantry, I'll go along. The voice in her head sounded sleepy.

"I'm … sore. My head is still trying to wrap itself around everything that's happening. I wanted to say I'm sorry for this and thank you," Jenny said.

"You don't have anything to apologize for. Those men tried to kill you. I just—" Chase started.

"Sergeant, um—" Jenny interjected.

"Kellaher," he said.

"Sergeant Kellaher said you almost died helping us. I can't—" Jenny felt her chest start to shake.

What is this? Oh, the damsel in distress routine? I know that one. I can do that one.

Stop it, Jenny thought back at the voice.

"It's all right. My brother got me worse with a branch one year, scraped me up a lot better than this," he pointed to the bandage on his face. "Is it true what they say, chicks dig scars?"

Not face scars, darling.

Jenny reached up and touched his face.

"Yeah, pretty much," she said. "Did they shoot you?"

"No, they tried. This is just wood splinters."

"Did you get them?"

He smiled sadly. "No, they … they got away. But I'm glad I got here in time to scare them off."

"They were on the stairs," Jenny said.

"Yeah, I kind of made them change their plans," Chase said. "And then your friends made things difficult for them. So, they fought their way back out, past me. I'm sorry I didn't get them."

Jenny tried to picture it, and found it hard to imagine people shooting in the cabin, and armed men being chased out of the basement by—what?—rakes and shovels? Of course, she'd never been in a gunfight, so she didn't know how confusing and intense it could be.

"Is it okay if … I mean," Jenny said, glancing around. "Can I hug you?"

"Um, yeah, I … yeah," he said, like a deer in headlights. Jenny put her arms around him, and he hugged her back surprisingly hard. She thought for a moment that they both might start crying, but he pulled back before the waterworks could start. "Thanks, I needed that," he said. "How are you doing?"

"I have no idea," she said honestly. "My brain is … yeah, I have no idea."

"You have somewhere safe to go?" Chase asked.

"Yeah, I think so," Jenny said.

"Then go there and stay there. The people you were with tonight, stay close to them. They were brave. They have your back."

Jenny stepped back and wiped her eyes. "I will, I promise."

She took Chase's hand and squeezed it. Then she turned back to her friends, who were waiting in a semicircle.

"You had somewhere we could go?" Jenny asked Linds.

"Yeah, I think I do. Come on, while Patty isn't paying attention," Linds said.

61
Refuge

Wednesday, October 1, 2025 – Before Dawn

LINDS OPENED THE FRONT door and stepped into the house. Jenny stood on the front yard path, surrounded by her friends.

"Hey!" Linds called. "You here?" They turned and tilted their head. "Come on in, she's probably gone back to sleep." They followed Linds into an empty, brightly lit foyer. "Take off your shoes, please, my parents don't want shoes in the house."

Jenny slid her backpack and duffle bag onto the floor before taking a seat on the third-to-last step of a wooden staircase. Sydney sat next to her as she started to unlace her boots. Maddy took a place on the bottom step. When Sydney removed her sneakers, she put her feet on Maddy's back and dug her heels in.

"Oh, yep," Maddy said, arching her shoulders back. "That's exactly the spot."

"Is there a sign-up list for that service?" Nate said, struggling with his boot on his bad leg.

"If you're looking for volunteers," Charles said, smiling.

"Hell, I'm not going to turn anyone down," Nate said. "But you're going to have to go all elbows and knees on me, I'm like a big knot."

"Do we want to talk now, or—"

"I'm exhausted," Jenny said.

"Same," Nate said. "I think I'm having a post-adrenaline crash."

Everyone seemed to agree.

"All right, let's get some sleep if we can. Charles, do you mind the couch?" Linds asked, smirking.

"Actually, I prefer the floor. Just a pillow and a sheet are all I need," Charles said. "It will be like the good old days."

"I can do a little better than that, but cool. The guest room has a queen-sized bed," they said. "I'm thinking Sydney, Maddy, and Jenny will take that."

"Yes, please," Sydney said.

"Nate, we are taking the kids' room."

"Kid's room?" Nate asked.

"Yeah, bunk beds," Linds said.

"I'm offended," Charles said. "I don't get a bunk bed?"

"I think your feet will dangle off the end. And when you hear Nate snore, you'll be glad for the distance. I'm used to it. Besides, there are a few things Nate and I need to talk about. Of course, you can have my bunk, and I'll sleep on the couch," Linds said.

"No, no, I know when I'm being cast into the outer darkness," Charles said, but he was smiling.

When they had broken up into their rooms, Jenny found herself nestled against the wall with Sydney in the middle of the bed and Maddy on the outer edge. The room was warm. Sydney fell asleep almost immediately and started to snore lightly. Maddy leaned up on her elbow and peered at Jenny, streetlight reflecting in her eyes.

"Are you okay?" Maddy whispered.

Jenny shook her head. Maddy reached across Sydney to take Jenny's hand. Jenny brought it to her lips and kissed her fingers.

"Thank you," Jenny whispered. "You were so brave. I was completely out of it, but I saw how brave you were."

Maddy shook her head.

"Are you afraid now?" Jenny asked.

Maddy nodded. "Are you?" Maddy asked.

"Terrified," Jenny said.

They kissed and then lay down, their fingers falling slowly apart as sleep took them.

When Jenny woke, sunlight flooded the guest room. Sydney was still gently snoring, but she had slid to fill Maddy's empty space. From the way her foot was pressing into Jenny's leg, she was trying to take Jenny's spot as well. Jenny found the situation both annoying and charming, and considered trying to mold Sydney into a more comfortable position for them both, but she knew she'd never be able to fall back to sleep in the bright light. The room was not equipped with the blackout curtains common among the Sleep Talkers. She peeled back the covers and climbed gingerly over Sydney. After finding the bathroom and tugging her hair into a moderately presentable bunch, she followed the sound of voices downstairs.

She stopped after three steps as the previous day came crashing back to her: Delia hanging in her bookstore, people trying to kill her and her friends, the police officer who almost died. It was only by pure luck or divine intervention that no one had been seriously injured or killed.

Except for Delia.

She remembered her friends taking up gardening tools to protect her from men with guns, and Sydney, crying, putting herself bodily between Jenny and certain death. She pictured Maddy disappearing into the darkness with Nate and remembered fearing not only that she would never see them again, but that they might have to endure the same hell she had known before—watching their loved ones die in front of them.

Jenny slumped down onto the stairs and wept into her hands. She felt so broken, so poisonous, so impossible to understand. She had no idea why anyone would want to try to kill her. Was it something to do with her website? Were the men obsessed fans? Were they religious fanatics trying to kill the local whore? Was it Phil and Earl? Or Earl and Emmet? Was it Barry? Maybe it was Chase, and he had staged the whole thing. She thought back to the guy at the Tim who had outed her and wondered if he had come to finish destroying her life.

Was it Joseph? Had he come to Lightning Falls to take revenge on her for going to the police?

"It's okay," Nate's deep voice startled her. She felt him ease down onto the step behind her, his bare feet resting outside of hers. His hand pressed comfortingly on her back, and she folded over to her side, burying her face against his knee. The heavy weight of his hand moved slowly back and forth between her shoulders.

"I'm sorry," she managed between sobs. "I don't know what's happening to me."

"I know," Nate said. "And don't be sorry."

"I don't understand. I don't … You almost died last night."

Nate, to her surprise, laughed. "Yeah. Thanks for that, by the way."

Jenny looked up at him and saw that he was smiling genuinely. "What?"

"It was … interesting," Nate said. "I haven't been in that kind of situation for a long time. It was nice to know that I haven't become so much of an old man that I just, I don't know, fell apart."

"Fell apart? From what I remember, and I was pretty out of it," Jenny said, wiping at her eyes, her pain forgotten, "but you were all amazing."

He smiled. "I don't know about amazing, but no one shamed themselves, that's for sure. Those girls," he said, glancing up toward where Sydney slept, "sorry—*women*—are amazing."

"Charles—"

"Pfft," Nate said, almost laughing, "Charles is an old-school badass. He was a wrestling champ in the Navy, and here in town, he once held off three men who wanted to beat his cousin to death. If there was anyone I wasn't worried about, it was him."

"I didn't know that about him. I don't really know anything about any of you. Especially … um," Jenny stared at Nate and felt fear rising in her stomach. The other person. The one Maddy had talked about last night. She couldn't remember the other person's name. She felt her mouth moving and the place between her eyebrows scrunching in the effort.

"Linds?" Nate asked.

Relief and horror flowed through her.

"Yeah, Linds. I'm sorry. My … my brain. I can't think right."

"Stop apologizing. But also, I don't think this is what you think it is."

"What do you mean? I'm sorry," she said, leaning back from him and shaking her head, "I'm just like, groping your leg here.

"Believe me, I don't mind it. The day I complain about a beautiful woman hugging me is the day that—Actually, yeah, that day doesn't exist."

Jenny laughed and hugged his leg again.

"Look," Nate said. "Why don't we go downstairs, get you caffeine and food, and we can start to talk? Linds and I have been going over a lot of stuff over the last few weeks, and I think … Yeah, we should all just talk together."

Jenny didn't understand what Nate meant, but coffee and food sounded amazing. She used his hands to push herself up and then helped pull him to his feet. Jenny started down, and Nate followed slowly after. She turned, but he waved her on, one hand on the railing as he favored his knee. She waited for him at the bottom of the stairs, partly out of consideration, and partly because there was a voice from the next room that she didn't recognize. For a moment, she was afraid that it was Linds's voice, and that she had forgotten even what her friend sounded like. But then Linds spoke, and while the two voices were distinct, they were also curiously similar.

"Through there," Nate said, reaching the bottom. "Coffee's not bad."

He led her down the hall and into the kitchen, where four people gathered around an old square farmhouse-style table. Facing Jenny, Maddy sipped from a big yellow mug that read, 'Ikan—' over 'Coll—' in dark blue lettering that wrapped out of sight. To her left, Charles sat with paper in front of him and a pen in his hand. One more seat around showed her the back of Linds's head, which Jenny, thankfully, recognized. In the last place, across from Charles, a woman who looked like she was around Jenny's age, half-stood and half-knelt in her chair, with one foot on the floor as she leaned over the table and pointed at whatever Charles was writing. She had long, straight brown hair, the same color as Linds's, though she was dressed in lighter, more colorful clothing than Linds's muted grays and current bulky brown sweater.

"Hey," Nate said.

Linds turned in their chair.

"Hey," Linds and the long-haired woman said together.

"Morning," Jenny said.

"This is my sister, Gina," Linds said.

"Oh, hey," Jenny said.

Gina straightened and smiled. "Hey, how's it going?"

"She got shot at last night," Linds said.

"I know," Gina said, "but you know, how are you this morning?"

"Well, I was just crying on the stairs," Jenny said, pointing her thumb behind her.

"Yeah, that makes sense," Gina said. "You want coffee?"

"Please," Jenny said.

After Jenny had been given coffee, a bagel with peanut butter and huckleberry preserves, and a few minutes to eat, Gina put her hands on the kitchen island and said, "Okay, so, are we going to talk?"

"You want me to grab Sydney?" Maddy said.

"Yes," Charles said.

"I'm here," Sydney said, and they turned to see her standing in the doorway from the hallway.

"You look like you got stuck in the dryer waiting for your step-bro and fell in and went through the tumble cycle," Maddy said. Jenny and Gina laughed; no one else did.

"I kind of feel like it," Sydney said. "Without the fun part. Oh, bagels! Is there coffee?"

When Sydney had gathered her breakfast, Gina led them into the living room, where there was space for them all to sit. Once again, Maddy and Sydney flanked Jenny as Sydney licked dripping butter and honey from her fingers and slowly nibbled her way through her food. Jenny noticed that Charles was the only other person sitting. The rest, Linds, Gina, and Nate, stood before them, as if they were going to give a class presentation.

"Oh," Jenny said suddenly.

"What?" Maddy said.

"I … I think I know this. This is like a Glen Moat book. They are going to tell us that there's like a vampire in town—" Jenny started.

"That's King," Charles said.

"No!" Maddy said, "I mean, yeah, that's *Salem's Lot*, but it's also *Red Street* by Glen Moat. But yeah, I know what you mean. You guys, there isn't a vampire, is there?"

Sydney, who had been studying a bit of honey on her fingers, lifted her head and said, "Wait, what? vampires?"

"No," Linds said. "As far as I know, there aren't vampires."

"Like, in general, or here in Lightning Falls?" Nate asked. He seemed earnest.

"In general, but who knows?" Linds said. "For all I know, Dracula is real and out there living his best life. But no, as far as we know, no vampires. And no, we're not going to explain to you what's going on, because we have absolutely no idea."

"Okay," Charles said, "then why do I feel like I'm in a lecture hall?"

"Because this morning I heard Jenny say something she shouldn't have. And, honestly, with the things that have been going on the last few weeks, I thought we should probably talk over what we know."

"Okay, so what did you hear?" Jenny asked.

"You started to tell the EMTs that you were someone else," Nate said.

Oh no, they heard! The voice in her head was almost giggling.

"What did I say?" Jenny said, her head suddenly aching again, she squinted her eyes against the room's light. She was having a hard time remembering her encounter with the paramedics.

"You okay?" Gina asked.

"My head, it's just … Sorry, I feel like my head is going to burst open. Like last night … Shit, shit, oh God my—" Pain overwhelmed her, and Jenny felt herself falling forward. Somewhere, faintly, she felt sticky fingers grab her arm as she slipped down into darkness.

"Among those various early religious influences on Weeping Cedars, the most enduring was the Second Great Awakening through its reshaping of American Protestantism. Out of this movement came many new traditions which have uniquely shaped the American religious landscape, such as the Church of Jesus Christ of Latter-day Saints. Though Mormonism, as it is popularly called, has had little effect on Weeping Cedars, other, smaller, more ephemeral communities have left their mark. One thinks of the ecstatic preacher Lionel Quincy and his poetically minded herald, Roger Godman, who, incidentally, is a distant relative of the author. Though their religious teachings took little root in Weeping Cedars, their families have left an indelible mark on the community. One also must mention, at least in passing, the Brethren of the New Settlement, whose community in West Virginia was in contact with the three founding families of Weeping Cedars for a time in the mid-nineteenth century. What direct influence their teachings of equality, peace, and polygamy had upon the founding families is unclear, especially given the families' penchant for racist and xenophobic stances throughout that period. Though it may be that we can find traces of their humanity in the work of Dr. Henry Kunicki and his empathy for those suffering mental distress."

- Under the Shaded Cedars, Kathryn Goodman, Ph.D.

"One is reticent to criticize Dr. Goodman's work given the nature of her passing, but it must be said that her conflation of the offshoot community in West Virginia with the Brethren of the New Settlement proper is incorrect. One must distinguish these two communities as firmly as one distinguishes between the Anglicans and Methodists, or the Roman Catholic Church and the Lutherans. However, unlike with these exemplar communities, we have no written records of this rebellious or protesting community's teachings. It may well be that it was precisely the egalitarianism of the Brethren that drove the West Virginia community away. Without further data, one cannot say with certainty what the nature of their influence was on Weeping Cedars or any other community that they communicated with."

- "Religious Communities in Goodman's Work" by Celeste Byrd, Ph.D. in *Reflections of Light, Essays in Honor of Kathryn Goodman.*

I
A Dying Dream

Tuesday, December 24, 1743 – Night

Herrnhut, Upper Lusatia

WORRY TROUBLED JAN'S STOMACH like sloshing, sour ale. He plodded beside his father, Tomas, as heavy, wet snowflakes descended on Herrnhut. Long, three-story tall, white buildings with red gambrel roofs loomed simultaneously welcoming and sinister under Jan's swinging lamplight. Tomas hummed a hymn that Jan could not place as, step by step, they drew closer to the Married Couples' Choir House. The younger man brushed snow from his nose and considered how he should approach the confrontation that lay before him. He could not rely on his authority, which no one in the community recognized, nor his father's, which had diminished over the years. Gone were the days of his grandfather, Petr Vaclavek, a soft-spoken man with eyes too large for his head. No one had ever doubted him. No one had ever laughed at him. He had never needed to rely on dreams to lead him, at least as far as Jan knew.

"Beautiful night," Tomas mumbled, interrupting his humming. Jan looked at him and forced a weak smile.

"Are you looking forward to the gathering?" Jan asked.

"Mmm," Tomas replied. The sound was tentative, and Jan knew what it meant. His father was less focused on singing hymns and more interested in the Lovefeast. There he could indulge, and on this night, when many were joyfully celebrating the Incarnation of the Light, they would not look so suspiciously at Tomas's love of beer and wine.

Jan's sour stomach threatened revolt as they neared the Married Choir House. He bid a blessed Christmastide to a group of young men who passed them heading to the Single Men's Choir House, and he envied them the lightness of their steps. He took deep, coughing breaths, hoping to settle his nerves, and stopped before the large, red chevron-patterned wooden doors.

"Best we go in and get out of this cold," Tomas said.

"Yes, father," Jan said after a long pause. He opened the door slowly.

They stamped their feet, knocking the snow away in little piles and leaving runnels of water glistening on their boots before removing their hats and cloaks to hang them on pegs. Merry voices echoed out of the kitchen and the dining hall. They checked in on the wives, and Jan saw

Ana stirring something on the stove. She glanced up at him and gave him a cool, though not hostile, look. That, at least, was an improvement since their afternoon argument. He breathed deeply the warm kitchen scents, and Tomas clapped a hand on his shoulder.

"Shall we?"

Tomas's red-rimmed eyes peered at him from under thick eyebrows raised in an expression that might have been openness, surprise, or drunkenness.

"Yes, of course, Father. Lead the way."

Everywhere, men and women bustled about discussing the spiritual meaning of Christ's nativity. Jan moved through small crowds offering greetings, but found that his stomach would not allow him to contemplate the appearance of the Word of God in the flesh of men. Instead, he felt he must conduct his business before he lost his nerve. He searched the clusters of conversationalists for Karel the Miller. The man's wide, jowl-lengthened face had loomed large in Jan's dream, looking at him with wonderment and worship. Jan didn't believe that Karel had ever turned that wobbling face of his toward him with anything other than condescension, and he had no idea how he would transform the man's regard for him. But Jan knew he must, or he would lose all.

Jan's heart faltered when he found Karel standing next to Ondrej and Jiri, the other men who had featured in his dream. He could see their faces floating in the darkness above a stooped old man, his face plaintive and his arms laden with thick, clanking chains.

Jan was unsure what to make of the man's pitiable state or the three faces that hovered above him in the darkness. Jan thought the old man might represent their community, Herrnhut. Or perhaps the chains symbolized Herrnhut, and the old man represented his family. Or, rather, he represented Jan's family and those who had come with them to this place, seeking freedom. That might make more sense. Jan thought of his family as ancient, going back to Mikulas Medved, with each generation of men leading and guiding their small society. So, perhaps the old man represented all the Poutnici his grandfather had brought to dwell with the Unitas Fratrum under the protection of Count Zinzindorf. And now, perhaps it fell to him, Jan Tomasek, to free them from these chains.

Perhaps.

Jan admitted that he had little of the Spirit's gift of interpreting dreams. Nor did he have his great-great-great-grandfather's gift for interpreting spirits or the meanings of symbols. No one since Petr Mikulasek had—but then, as far as Jan knew, none of his other ancestors had received dreams and visions. None had needed to interpret. They had only to read the Three Books and follow their little communal devotion.

As Jan caught Karel's eye, he saw both recognition and dismissal there. That look redoubled his fear that he would disappoint his ancestors and become the last of his line to lead the Poutnici. Of course, his leadership was merely titular now. If their once tight-knit community within the Unitas Fratrum had any leadership, it dwelt among the three men who were trying to look deeply engrossed in their theological discussion as Jan approached them.

"The Savior is born," Jan said, finding a space between Ondrej and Jiri that they had neglected to close.

"Blessed be the day of his birth," Jiri said, and the other two men echoed his sentiment.

"I passed by the kitchen on the way in, and the bread smelled wonderful," Jan said. "I believe the wives have quite a treat for us."

A rousing round of mild nods and pursed lips followed. Jan's stomach turned.

"I am pleased to find you three gathered together in this way," he said, pushing on. "I ... well, I was hoping we might all talk about the future of our community."

Ondrej opened his mouth, as if interested, and then closed it. Jan saw in his expression a moment of confusion, followed by recognition, and, as the man turned to Karel, expectation.

"I take it," Karel said, "you mean our particular community, and not the Brethren in general."

Jan nodded.

"I see," Karel said, and both Ondrej and Jiri gave him solemn nods that reflected the miller's somber tone. "This is a good idea. It has been too long since those who wander have gathered together, and I think coming together one more time would be profitable."

One more time? Jan thought.

"One more time before we prepare ourselves to move on from this place," Jan said, smiling hopefully. The other three men looked at each other and then back towards Jan. Their expressions were a mix of apology, condescension, and embarrassment.

"I believe that we should meet after the Epiphany, perhaps the first Saturday following," Karel said.

"Yes, I think that would be fitting," Jiri said.

"It will give us time to contemplate and pray for the future of our community," Ondrej said.

"All right," Jan said. "But I do beseech you all to take it into your hearts to prepare to go from this place. We have sojourned with the Brethren for many years now, but they are not our people, nor is this place our home. Good as they are, they are frozen like the rest of this dark city, and we must labor forward as best we can. I—"

Karel glanced about the room before reaching out to lay a heavy hand on Jan's shoulder. "Come, why don't we take the air for a moment? The room is close, and the smell of food is distracting me, weak glutton that I am. Will you join me, Brother?"

Karel's face bore a sternness and a species of pity that brought Jan close to despair.

"Of course, Brother. Will you gentlemen join us?" Jan asked hopefully, thinking that perhaps of the three, Ondrej might be kindest to him.

"No, I think you and I should speak together," Karel said. Then Jan knew his position was hopeless. This man, who did not descend from Mikulas, was about to take him outside and tell him what his future would be, and there was nothing Jan could do about it. Perhaps there wouldn't even be a meeting after Epiphany. As the two men went to the pegs and took their cloaks and hats, Jan steeled himself to endure his humiliation as Karel put his hopes down like a lame horse.

When they stood together under the falling snow, they looked up at the star-strewn sky and let the flakes fall and melt on their clean-shaven faces. Jan thought this was as good a place as any for his family's dream to die. And if it were to die, Christmas Eve was a better time than most. Was it not true that the seed must fall into the earth and perish before it could grow anew? So then, perhaps, the hopes of his ancestors must go into the earth and wait for the grace of the child Christ to make something new of them.

"How old were you when we came to this place?" Karel asked.

"I was thirteen," Jan said.

"Ah, yes, I forget that you are older than you appear. Your face is so youthful. So, you remember Bohemia and our village."

"Yes," Jan said.

"And you remember the persecution? The pressure to bend the knee and to conform to the Papist idolatries? Purgatory? The false worship of saints?"

Jan took a moment, blinked away a snowflake that landed on his eyelash, and nodded. "Yes, I remember."

"Forced conversion, theft of our property, burning our books. The limits upon what we could say or do, the hiding, the secret meetings, the fear ... Do you remember?"

Jan nodded.

"Some of us imprisoned, many of us fined and impoverished. I am ... let us see, I was twenty-five when we came here, so I am twelve years older than you, Jan. I remember my brother in prison. I remember that they removed my uncle from his position. Yes, there was a moment of hope, but the dream of Frederick flew from us, and all that remained for us was to find our hope in other lands. And this we have done. We will not return to the kingdom to suffer, and we have no cause to go out from this place where we are welcome, warm, and well fed. Unless, of course, you think we should go to one of the new settlements, like Bethlehem." He looked at Jan and smiled. The smile was not warm, but it was understanding. He knew that that was not what Jan wanted. "Do not think that I let go of our fathers' dreams lightly. But, for the good of our wives and our children, we must. *You* must, Jan. The days of wandering are done, and the Three Books ... well, is there anything worthwhile within them that is not encompassed by the teaching of Christ? Do we not skirt the very limits of the same idolatry we accuse the Papists of?"

Jan stared, his mouth slack, his heart beating so loudly that he struggled to hear Karel's words. The miller went on for a time, expanding on his view that the life of Christ was more than sufficient to inspire them and their community for centuries to come. They did not need the Three Books, nor did they need to separate themselves any longer.

"We have found our Eden, Jan. Look around. Rejoice. The love of God is among us; it is here, in your father, your wife, your boy. Rejoice and be glad that this dream has been fulfilled, and we have found the home Petr promised us."

Jan, unable to speak, found himself unwillingly comforted by Karel's words. The miller, he could tell, saw the struggle on Jan's face. The older man smiled at him, for the first time without condescension. Jan thought he saw something like true brotherly love.

"We will meet after Epiphany. Then we shall sing hymns and pray together. We will say goodbye to this dream, and we will recommit ourselves to this community that the count has made for us. Then you must give up your pride and become like the rest of us, just one more brother among the brethren."

Jan felt the man's heavy hand on his shoulder again before it slapped him heartily on the back.

"Come, take a moment, and then join us. I hear the first hymn, and you were right, the bread smells wonderful. Eat and drink with me, brother. Let us praise the Light that is coming into the world."

With tears in his eyes, Jan watched Karel stroll lightly back to the choir house and through the front door. He watched him stand aside and give a little bow as Tomas exchanged places with him. Jan blinked as his father approached, an enameled glass in his hand, sure to be full of wine.

"Father, I have failed," Jan said. The older man frowned at him, perhaps not entirely comprehending his son's meaning. "Those who wander will wander no more. I have failed Mikulas, I have failed Petr, I have failed grandfather, and I have failed you."

Tomas's face was a relief of sorrow, deep lines carved into his brow, cheeks, and chin. He reached with his free hand for his son's shoulder and wept. "My son, you have not failed. It is I. I failed our dream. But think of how merciful the Lord is! We have failed here, in this place, among these good peo—"

He stopped. His face went slack, abolishing the deep crevices of lament. Slowly, an expanding expression of wonder widened his eyes and opened his lips. Fear lanced through Jan as he thought the older man was suffering apoplexy. But Tomas's eyes focused on Jan, and the rest of his body neither shuddered nor seized.

"My son, your face," Tomas said.

"What? What is it, Father?" Jan said, reaching up to touch the snow-wet skin of his cheeks.

"Light … like Moses, like Christ at the Transfiguration," he said.

Jan could not understand what the man was talking about. He cast about, searching for the meaning of his father's words. Then he saw a light, off to his left, in the eastern sky. He turned, and his own eyes grew wide. Close to the horizon, he beheld a blazing star that bathed the whole landscape in a silver-gold light. It rose a little, and beside it, Jan watched the moon appear.

"Father, there, the Christmas star!"

His father turned and shook his head. "I see nothing, only light from your face."

"Look, the whole world is bathed in its light. Oh, Father, behold the star in the East! It guides us!"

"My son, I see no star, but perhaps I see its light upon you." Tomas's voice was stronger and more joyful than Jan had heard in years.

"Father, the moon rises next to it, and look, it changes. From new to half, and now to whole, and look, it diminishes again!"

"I see no moon, Jan," Tomas said, his hand squeezing his son's shoulder so tightly it hurt. But Jan paid the pain no mind.

"And again, the moon comes, and again it goes, and oh! Look, the star is splitting! Behold, it leaves behind it a great tail, and there … six fans I see! Six tails to this great star! What can it mean?"

"My son, the light dances on your face, and I see it, six points in your eyes, no, seven!"

"The star itself and its tails, seven, the sign of perfection, the number of the Lamb! Father, I … No, look, it is fading—"

"And so is the light on your face. Oh, Jan, the vision is ending, hold the moment if you can, for it will not come again."

"Time lingers not in this place, Father! Look upon me and I will look upon it!"

And they both watched as the light faded. Then, again, they were in darkness.

"What … what could it mean, Father?"

"I do not know, Jan. But we will discern it together, yes?"

Then Tomas embraced his son, and the two of them wept together under the falling snow.

JAN SITS NEAR THE fireplace, writing, while Ana sleeps in the bedroom. From the corner, he hears his name, and he turns to see the old man from his dream sitting in a chair, his hands no longer shackled, his face no longer twisted by need. His eyes lead Jan to a chain that lies across the floor, snaking its way to a darkened corner where Jan thinks he sees movement in shadow unnaturally deep.

"Write, boy," the old man says. "And help me break this chain. In return, I will show you what will come, and how you shall find the new Eden."

Jan stares at the dark corner, his eyes searching for whatever hides at the end of the chain.

"How—" he begins, but his voice fails him. He swallows and tries again. "How will you do this?"

The old man regards him impassively with eyes that burn with the reflected firelight.

"I see far."

11
In the Watches of the Night

Saturday, January 11, 1744 – Evening

Herrnhut, Upper Lusatia

FIFTEEN PEOPLE STARED AT Jan. Their faces told him different things. Some clearly thought he was desperate, others seemed to think that he was about to tell them that he was making a joke, and still others thought that he had genuinely lost his mind. One was angry.

"I see," said Karel the Miller.

"A new star?" Ondrej asked, one eyebrow lifted, his thinning hair falling over his tanned forehead. He turned to the rest of the group, perhaps for confirmation that he had heard Jan correctly.

"Yes, and you will all behold it. The whole world will behold it. I have written about it here," he said, touching a small stack of newly printed books. "I have had one printed for each of your households."

"This is pure distraction," Karel said as he rose to his feet. "This is the talk of a desperate man. You have not had a vision; you have panicked. We spoke on Christmas Eve, and—"

"Yes, brother, we did, and immediately after we spoke, God granted a vision to me, and one to my father. I saw this new star, and he saw— Well, I will let him say what he saw."

Tomas stepped forward with his hands clasped before him. The assembled couples, single men, and single women looked at him with wonder. Here was Tomas Petrick, son of Petr Vaclavek, clear-eyed, steady, and sober in a way most had not seen him in years, and others had never seen him at all. He pursed his lips and took a great chest-shaking breath.

When he opened his mouth and described his vision, the crowd met him with an alloy of wonderment and disbelief. Some, like Pavel the Beermaker, Maria of the Single Sisters Choir, and Ondrej, took his sobriety as a seal of truth upon his testimony. Others, like Jiri the Cartwright and Karel, looked on with deepening suspicion. This second group did not hide their incredulity but kept their peace until Tomas finished speaking.

Karel then turned and encompassed the assembled families with a sweeping gesture of his long arms. "Do you expect us to believe you?"

"Yes," Jan said, "for it is the truth."

Karel nodded solemnly. "You suppose that we know nothing of the human heart? We are simpletons who cannot see what you are doing,

Jan?"

"What is my son doing, Karel?" Tomas asked.

"Here your family stands at the precipice of your pride, destined for the fall that must, as the Word of God declares, follow after it, and you hope to stave off your just correction by the means of false visions and false prophecies? What are we? Children? What shall you say when the vision does not come to pass? That we lack faith? That we who do not admit to seeing this invisible star are blind? Will that be your recourse, Jan, when those of us with clear minds and clear eyes see no six-tailed star? How shall you dupe the gullible then? Tell them that we are of the dark city, unable to go forward, unable to progress because we linger, frozen under the sway of the curse?" He looked around. "We have heard such preaching before. Do you not see it? Can you not hear it coming? If we do not behold his imaginary vision, we will be reprobate. He will cast us out into where there is weeping and gnashing of teeth. Only those chosen few who will uphold this ancient and threadbare dream of his madman ancestors will he deem worthy to remain among the Poutnici."

He shook his head, and Jan knew that if they had been outside, he would have spat.

"I suppose I can say nothing more, nor, I suppose, do I care to. Perhaps you will mislead some away from this place of love and gospel, perhaps you will, like so many before you, mislead their daughters into your bed, you whom God supposedly speaks to, and lead them to places where they will be hated, impoverished, ostracized, and tormented. But I warn those of you who would go with him that that path is wide and goes down into destruction. Do not sell your birthright for this man's proud pottage. Cleave to the promise of the Risen One! Cleave to the good people of Herrnhut! Cleave to that which you know to be true."

Karel took his wife's hand and led her out of Jan's house. The assembled families followed, and only Maria of the Single Sisters Choir remained next to Ana, Jan's wife. Once everyone else had left, she stood and walked over to Jan.

"I dreamed last night of a star with six tails, and I saw you standing beneath it, leading us home." She kept her eyes down.

"Why didn't you say something?" Ana demanded. "You let them—"

"A voice told me to tell no one except those who remain. And … well, here we are."

"Did the voice say anything else?" Tomas asked.

"I was told … 'the knock will come before dawn,'" Maria said.

Jan smiled at the younger woman and took her hands in his. "Thank you, sister. You have strengthened our hearts. Let us believe and have patience, for the dawn shall rise upon all of us." He looked at Ana. "You shall see. We all shall see."

Once Maria and Tomas were away, Jan went to bed, hoping that he would rise before the sun and that knocking would wake him.

It did.

Ondrej and his wife Eva stood before his door, wrapped in their woolen cloaks, lightly dusted with snow. "We have come to apologize," Ondrej said, his eyes downcast. "We rose for our hour of prayer, and when we … Well, come and see."

Karel's incredulous words echoed in Jan's memory as he walked with the couple under small, melting flakes to the great courtyard in the community center. Several people stood, looking at the sky to the east, their eyes wide with wonder. Ondrej pointed. As more doors opened and more people pulled on cloaks to come out into the winter morning, Jan saw the first faint appearance of the star. Still small and pale, he knew that it would not remain so. It would grow, and as the weeks passed, so did the number of people who returned to his home. Finally, when the six-fanned tail appeared in March, Karel came and knelt before Jan and Tomas and begged forgiveness.

Their community agreed that they would separate themselves from the Unitas Fratrum and return to Bohemia for a time. They would become a community unto themselves. After a time, they would travel to the New World and find for themselves a new Eden. This was the teaching written in Jan's book. There were hardships ahead, journeys and losses; the first would be their separation from Count Zinzendorf's people. But they need not weep, for the division would not endure, and for a time they would sojourn beside the Unitas Fratrum again in the new world. Until then, they would grow in numbers and faith.

So, the people prepared to set out in spring to return home and wait for another sign.

ii

NINETEEN ADULTS OF THE newly anointed Brethren of the New Settlement stand with their children and belongings and make sorrowful farewells to the people of Herrnhut. They clasp hands and make vows of brotherly love. They pray for safety and future reconciliation. The count himself kisses Jan on the cheek and promises him a place should they wish to return. Jan, for his part, swears that their peoples shall meet again in friendship. Then, as the spring rain dapples the earth, one Brethren leaves another to make their way in the world.

III
The Fourth Book

Tuesday, August 22, 1780 – Just Before Dawn

Rajská Údolí, Moravia

JAN TOMASEK, WHOM THEY called *Kouzel*, was dying. His son Tomas, named for Jan's father, knew that Jan's end was near, but he could not make himself believe it. Had the old man gone soft in his head? Perhaps. But dying? It was hard to conceive.

The softness in his head had been particularly evident the prior evening. Gasping, he had instructed Tomas to find Dorota Marinova, perhaps the most beautiful young woman in their community, and subject her to strange, humiliating degradations. Tomas pictured the look on her face, her eyes welling with tears, her parents clasping each other as Tomas followed Jan's instructions to revile the woman publicly, chase her, spatter her with mud, and finally, push her with the sole of his boot, out past the village limits. He pictured her mother and father, weathered and stricken, doing as they had been ordered: hesitatingly scratching mud from the earth and throwing it, if not at her, then near her. Then, when Dorota had fled, they turned, spat on the ground near his feet, and returned to their home, weeping and befuddled.

Heeding Jan's words, he had carefully chosen the direction of her expulsion. He had driven her northeast, and now, as morning brooded over the eastern hills, he hoped he knew where to find her. Tomas followed the path through the forest, smelling honeysuckle, as the morning birds trilled the impending dawn. Above the horizon, two lights, brighter than the stars about them, hung beside each other. He took this as a good omen. He would find the girl and bring her back, and then, perhaps, she would warm his father's bed and restore him. He had heard of such things practiced among the pagans of old and wondered if Jan's visions had foreseen the beautiful young woman's restorative powers. He was uncertain why her expulsion had been necessary, but, again, the man was old, and his mind was not what it once was. Still, he had seemed lucid enough and had been insistent enough to demand obedience.

Tomas followed the bending path and finally came to the small hunting lodge. It was no more than a square of masonry, a little taller than he was, with a thatched roof. Hunters used it for storage and sometimes for shelter in bad weather. But he guessed that the person inside was no hunter.

He stood at the door and pondered what he should say to her. He scrunched his wide face and tried to make his brain produce something reasonable. But what was there to say that would be reasonable? They had cast her out of the community for no reason. He had insulted her, harangued her, and spat on the ground where she lay. He had forced her parents to say terrible things. What explanation could he offer when he did not understand it himself? He thought he might try to make something up, but he had never been imaginative, nor a good liar. So, he knocked and hoped for the best.

"Please don't come in," a woman's voice said.

"Dorota, it is Tomas. May I speak with you?"

"Do not come in! Why have you come? To torture me further? Or have you come to kill me? Or will you take me now for your wicked pleasure since I am alone?"

"No, I have come to welcome you back," he said. Silence followed. "Dorota, it is hard for me to explain, but I will try. Jan is dying. He is dying, and he has asked for you." Something shifted inside the hut; he could not tell what it portended. "He is calling for you and wishes for you to be restored to the community, and for nothing more to be said about the matter." He paused, and an idea came to him. It wasn't a very inspired idea, but it seemed reasonable. "And he wishes that I should offer you my deepest apologies."

The door swung open, and before him stood Dorota, just as he had imagined her. Hair wild, dress muddied and torn, scratches on her arms and right cheek. Her state of disarray, however, barely diminished her beauty. Indeed, the rage in her eyes was fey, and he thought that such a state must reflect the beauty of the wrath of God. It was hard not to love such a woman.

"Your apologies?" she whispered, though her voice rose in volume with each word. "What do I want with your apologies? I am shamed forever. You tied me! Why? You spat upon me! Why? You exiled me! Why? I can never return home!"

"No, this is not the case. Please, come with me, and you will not only be restored but ... but elevated. I swear it, for Jan has chosen you by name to come to him."

"Oh," she said, her volume rising even further, "am I to be his bedthing? The lust-toy of an old goat? Am I to be grateful to him for saving me from this devastation that you have laid upon me? And what choice do I have? To wander the ways without protection, hoping not to be taken up by the first passing scoundrel? Is this his idea of love, that he should send you to strip me of all I have so that I might come crawling back to his generosity, wanton for what I possessed only yesterday?"

Tomas' mouth moved, but he could not find the words to fill it. He suspected she might be right about Jan's hopes. Finally, he shook his head. "I do not know," he said. "I do not. But what would you have of me? Forgive me. I must bring you back."

She lifted her chin and crossed her arms. Then, after he thought she would refuse, he watched her shoulders slump and her head fall.

"So be it," she said. "What can I do but go with you? If I refuse, I will be devoured by man or beast. At least if your father is to consume me, I perhaps can return to my parents afterward. If they will have me."

Dispirited in his victory, Tomas led the young woman back to the village as the sun rose over the eastern hills. The streets, blessedly empty, led them to Jan's house, where they entered to find the old man lying on his bed, his eyes closed.

"Is he dead?" Dorota asked, hopefully.

In response, Jan coughed first weakly and then loudly. A great, wracking, cluttering hack moved him up and down and back and forth under his blankets. Once the fit had let go of him, he spat into his chamber pot and peered up at them, smiling. His face was old and sagging. The lines around his eyes were deep, and his hair was sparse. He considered them from under thick, wild, white eyebrows.

He gestured at her with the flick of his hand.

"What does he want?" Dorota asked.

Jan shook his head and beckoned her to come closer. He tugged at her torn dress. She stepped back defiantly, but Tomas was behind her and halted her flight.

"Will you trap me here?" she asked as the old man reached out to tug at her dress again.

"No," Tomas said. "But where will you go?"

"You will let him do this to me?" she asked, eyes pleading. But Tomas was silent. She sniffed, and in the sound, Tomas heard the judgment of God upon him. He would be damned for this. He felt his body tremble as the woman once more lifted her chin and removed her dress. Standing in her long shift, she moved to take it from her shoulders. Finally gathering a shred of manful dignity to himself, Tomas resolved to stop her, to stop all of this … whatever it was. But before he could intervene, Jan waved his hand and shook his head.

"What?" Dorota asked. "You do not want me to remove it? Will you do it yourself then, you old pig?"

Jan's eyes danced at the insult, and he threw his head back to laugh. All that escaped him was a wet, wracking spasm. He gathered himself and once more shook his head. Then he pointed to the foot of his bed. Tomas and Dorota turned together to find a shirt of light-gray wool folded and lying on the corner of his blanket. The old man gestured toward it and then toward her.

"You want me to-to wear it?"

Jan nodded, his gap-toothed smile wide and leering.

Dorota took a tentative step toward the end of the bed. She spun to regard Tomas with a look of confused scorn. "What is this? What perversion must I endure?"

Tomas, weakly, shrugged his shoulders. He didn't understand, but he had resolved to stop her from stripping, not putting more clothes on. So he watched as she shook her head at him and turned once more toward the folded clothing. She lifted the too-large shirt before her. Tomas recognized it as the shirt that Jan wore when the weather turned cold. She let it fall over her head and arms and presented herself to him.

"What would you have—" Her words ceased as the old man took hold of her wrist. Her body convulsed once, and then she sat slowly and awkwardly on the bed next to him as he caressed her arm.

Now, Tomas thought, *he will send me away. He will send me away, and I will have let him corrupt her. What will I do? Oh God, help me! Make me brave!*

But Jan did not send him away. Instead, the old man peered steadily at his son, his heavy brow drawn low, his mouth a twisted crescent of a smile. Long had authority worked within him and bent the nervous youth he had once been in Herrnhut into this hungry, sly old man. Tomas forced himself to meet his father's gaze impassively. He could not bear to peer into Dorota's eyes, afraid of the judgment he would find there. Yet, she drew his gaze as her face contorted, and her head dipped.

Tomas stepped back, his heart suddenly thundering in his chest. What was this before him? The woman, a vision of beauty a moment before, now leered at him with the same crooked, hungry smile. Her brow bunched low, her shaded eyes held him with the same leering stare he endured from his father's face. Indeed, like twin gargoyles, they regarded him, their breathing in time, their blinking synchronized, and their countenances one in motion and expression.

"Write, my son; the Fourth Book is not complete. Hurry. Time lingers not in this place."

He was wrong. They were not one in motion, for while Jan's mouth remained still, Dorota's lips formed the words that issued forth in the old man's voice. Trembling, he stumbled back, nearly knocking over his desk. He gripped the door and thought his chest would give way under the hammering of his heart. Sweat bloomed across his body, and the room swam.

"Do not fear me. Take courage and write. I am dying, and I go to the Great Pit to await the Dawn. Take up your pen and heed my words."

Tomas blinked and wiped sweat from his brow. He nodded, sucking in deep, shuddering breaths. He staggered forward and collapsed into his father's chair, where he reached for the pen. His right hand was still vibrating, so he gripped it with his left to steady it. He gulped air and tried to look anywhere but into the face that was both Dorota's and his father's.

He nodded to himself. This had been what he had wanted. Not this precisely, for his imagination could never have borne this, but for as long as he could remember, he wanted to see a wonder like the star that his father had seen in his vision. He would have been satisfied to see even its reflection as his grandfather had. This, though uncanny and unlooked-for, was an answer to his years of prayer. He was seeing a sign, and he must not turn away. He steeled himself to receive his father's words.

"I-I am ready, Father," he said. He dipped the quill into the ink well, watched as the tremor in his hand steadied, and then tapped the loose ink free.

"*Behold the vision of Jan Tomasek, descendant of the great Bear. Here it is shown to me concerning the sheltering of spirits,*" Jan said through Dorota's mouth.

She spoke, and he wrote. An hour later, as her voice grew weary, he called for beer, bread, cheese, and fruit. Tomas gave her food and drink, and she ate like his father, heartily and with much smacking of the lips and licking of the fingers. Tomas could not eat, for his stomach revolted at his father's features and voice distorting the woman's beauty. But he could drink, and he did. When they began again, they did so with a flagon of ale next to each of them, for her voice and his nerves.

Morning became afternoon and wheeled to evening. Evening gave way to night, and still she spoke. As midnight drew close, Tomas's hand hurt terribly, and she looked tired and worn.

"Now," she said. "Go to the stream and fill this flagon and return with it." She offered the pewter vessel, which had held her ale. He stood and took it, his legs stiff, his back aching. He stepped out into the night and saw a cluster of people sitting on the porch of the house that faced his. Among those who sat there, he recognized Dorota's parents. He raised his hand to them.

"All is well," he said. "All will be well soon. She shall be returned to you, unharmed and whole."

They did not speak but only looked at him from the complication of shadow and light that their little oil lamps cast. He walked out of their sight, hoping that he was telling them the truth, down the small path and around the bend, to where the hill dipped down to the stream. There he took the three stone steps to the bank and knelt. The moon was high above, a little over half-full and bright. The cool water felt good on his cramped and burning fingers. He let the stream flow and flexed his sore muscles beneath the surface. Then, not wanting to leave either his father or Dorota in their current state any longer than necessary, he took the filled flagon and stood.

Though he had become accustomed to the strange partnership between his father's mind and Dorota's body, his heart still sped up as he approached the house. He imagined that when he opened the door, he would see something monstrous. Perhaps Dorota would be upon his father, performing some indescribable coupling of a man with himself. Perhaps she would hunch like a witch, sneering at him from under the shadow of her long hair. Perhaps she would be gone, his father's mind within her, lost in the night like an *upiór*.

He was grateful that the flagon's lid did its work, for his hands were once again shaking as he opened the door. His legs almost gave out as relief flooded his chest. He did not find the two engaged in some unspeakable act, nor did Dorota wear the face of a demon, nor was the bed empty. Instead, Dorota remained exactly where she had been when he left. Her face had not changed, her fingers had not moved, the folds of his father's night-shirt were untroubled.

"My son, you will pour that water upon her head. When you do, you will repeat the words, 'be opened,' three times. Then I will go. My body has already given me up."

Tomas's body jerked in an involuntary reflex of fear, sorrow, and revulsion. He looked at his father's hand, which had gripped Dorota's wrist, and saw that the wrinkled, sun-darkened fingers lay still and easy upon her smooth, pale skin.

"When you free her, you and I will not speak again until you come to the Great Pit to dwell with me and prepare for the morning. But the time will come when I must speak again. You have written my instructions, but I have more yet to say that you must not write."

Then Jan Tomasek spoke strange and troubling words to his son through the lips of Dorota Marinova. And when he had finished, Tomas stood before the young woman and kissed his father farewell by pressing his lips to Dorota's forehead. Then he poured the flagon over her head, saying, "Be opened. Be opened. Be opened."

Blinking, she looked up at him and raised her hand to her throat.

"Water," she said, her voice cracked and dry. "Please."

Though Jan's brow no longer rested above her eyes, and his grin no longer bent her lips, Tomas could not help but see his father in her face. He fled from her and brought the flagon to her parents, whom he bid to go collect her and bring her happily once more into their home.

THE SHIP RIDES LOW in the waves, and the wind bends the great sail above them. They crowd the deck, peering west under shaded eyes. The cry has gone up, but they cannot see what the man in the crow's nest sees. They pray for a wave to lift them so they can gaze upon the land that waits for them. Salt spray dampens their faces as the sailor calls out again.

"Land!"

Then comes the wave, and they rise. Clinging to each other, they mount the ocean's great hill and see for the first time with waking eyes the emerald thread of land stretching across the horizon. Praises ascend, perhaps winged to their Creator by the gulls that circle above. The Maker of all things receives thanks, the Incarnate Word receives blessing, the Spirit of Love is adored.

And so, too, is the one who has no name. They do not know what to call him, and so they repeat only that which they are certain of, ringing out together the refrain they have learned from prophecy given and prophecy fulfilled.

He sees far.

He sees far.

He sees far.

IV
Shelters of Wood

Friday, October 5, 1804 – Night

Gilgal, Pennsylvania

JANA KUSEL WATCHED RAIN gather on the nub of a shorn branch until, too fat to hold itself up, it plopped down onto a bed of pine needles within her little shelter. But for this one leak, her woven roof of pine branches did its work well. Her wool blankets, one over her crossed legs and one over her shoulders, kept her warm. She had built her shelter around a flat, tall stone against which she sat while she read under the light of the little oil lamp that hung from her low ceiling. As her eyes moved across the pages, she contemplated those who wander forward while the world remained frozen in a cursed stillness.

We must consider the meaning of the wandering people and what the darkness of the city represents. We must see and understand, listen and comprehend. For the dark city is the world, and its perpetual night is the great adumbration of sin. All are stultified. All are held. Even the wanderers, those few that Mikulas describes as free to progress, do not charge forward beyond all about them, for they are not entirely free. They, too, are pulled back repeatedly by the stymying lethargy of the world's torpor. Unwilling to go forward into joy, the world—here represented by the dark city— draws the wanderers back and back even as they struggle forth. However, though the world slows them, they progress. But though they progress, they do so in an immobile, cursed, and crystallized world. So even their progress falters.

Thus, Mikulas writes in the First Book, "there I saw an oddity among the many cursed. For one group, though poor and ragged, cleaving to the mind and will of the one who first laid the enchantment, were capable of wonders matched only by the very great. They, alone but for the powers of that city, were capable of change. Only in the Keeper of Books, the Queen of Light, and a small handful of others did I witness that capacity. The Wanderers, as they name themselves, then, are the only ones not among the mighty who have slipped the full fetter of the halting conjuration that lies over this place where time lingers. Thus, I shall approach them and sojourn with them for a time to learn from them, perhaps to the benefit of my beloved."

From this allegorical passage, we learn how we, his beloved, must wander in the world, ever striving forward, but allowing for the fact that we may backslide, pulled down by the weight of the benighted world. Though still, we make progress, where others, overburdened by Papal, Monarchical, Lutheran, or Calvinistic deceptions and delusions, remain ever in the same place. Thus, we must not burden ourselves with shame and guilt. We must cast off the darkening conception of mortal sin and think instead of those times we stray as inevitable moments in which the world, its sooty fingers grasping, pulls us back. We must remain conscious that neither lust of the flesh, nor gold, nor wrath, nor hearty appetite can long keep us in its thrall. Should we be taken by any of these, we shall lift it to our Creator to be used as a prod or a glory to His final purpose.

Therefore, husbands, look to your wives, wives to your husbands, and hold them lightly, for great is the might of desire. Children, look to your parents, and parents to your children, and hold each other lightly, for though mighty is the bond of the hearth, so too is the danger of the world. You dwell now in shelters of wood, like the Hebrews in the desert. When a new settlement comes, you shall dwell in shelters of gold, and diamond, and adamant. So, hold not jealously these shelters of wood, and weep not for their movements and ecstasies. Be of great joy that you are free to move forward, albeit slowly, while the world lingers behind in its own everlasting shadow.

Jana closed her eyes and long pondered the words of the Third Book. She thought of the blacksmith who dwelt in Emmaus, the town to the north. He was of the Unitas Fratrum here in the New World, in this commonwealth of Pennsylvania. She thought of his strong arms, his calloused hands, and the way his eyes lingered upon her. She thought of how her husband, Vaclav, saw the blacksmith's stares and made no comment. He, too, knew the Third Book, and he, too, took for himself pleasures of his own liking. They were not the pleasures of her flesh, except when performing his husbandly duty. And even when he did press into her, she thought that his mind wandered to other faces and bodies. She did not begrudge him this fancy, for her mind also wandered out and forward, north to the heat and smoke of the forge.

Jana slid down onto the bed of needles and pulled her blankets over her. She folded a small scarf behind her head. She wanted to let her hand and her mind wander, but no door covered her dwelling place. Though the autumn rain provided some privacy, she put her desire aside and merely rolled to her side and squeezed her knees together, smiling under the warmth of her blankets. She dozed as the rain fell.

When she woke, the shower had stopped, and the moon was high. Her breath misted in the light of the little lamp. Curious, she sat up, regretting the movement immediately as freezing air rushed against her back. She looked at the lamp and saw that someone had come and refilled her oil. She guessed it would have been Ana, or perhaps Veronika. Both were devoted to her. Neither would have liked the idea that she would wake in darkness. She wondered if they would have enough of their own oil for their long nights on the platforms.

She crawled from the warmth of her hut and drew her woolen cloak after her. She lifted her lamp and surveyed the bank of the stream that ran along Gilgal's edge. Up and down the little creek hunched the low, rectangular shelters that her people built each year. A few let slip slivers of light between their woven branches, but most were dark. She could hear low voices here and there, and she wondered whether her husband was among them, whispering and telling stories of the land they had left behind, and of Jan Tomasek and his six-tailed star. Or was he with the young man who entertained his familiar passions? She hoped that if he was, *they* had at least had the foresight to add a curtain to the front of their little tabernacle. The Brethren of the New Settlement were permissive, but even they found such couplings uncomfortable.

She needed just such a covering, she decided, less for privacy and more to husband the little warmth of her hut. She decided to return home and find a cloth fit for the task. Then she would find Ana and Veronika and thank them. And, in so doing, perhaps ease their lonely burdens a little on this cold night.

Her trek home was brief and profitable. She not only found the very cloth she had in mind, but two small nails that would allow her to hold it in place. Their ends were blunt, so there was little fear they would mar the cloth permanently, and she could push them between branches, tucking the end in to form a little door. She didn't know why she hadn't thought of it when she first built her shelter, except that the days had been so fine and warm and the evenings so mild. No one had thought that a storm would bring a chill autumn with it so immediately and absolutely.

She strode quickly from her house and came to the first platform by the walnut tree, where she climbed the ladder to the little porch and knocked on the door. Rustling followed, and a long moment later, the door opened. Veronika stood in the doorway, her hair mussed, and her pouting lips pinker than usual. Behind her sat Ondrej, a man a year younger than Veronika's twenty.

"Good evening," Jana said. The young man was clothed, though in a state of obvious excitement. His eyes were alight, his mouth open as if thinking of the right thing to say, and his clothing was, if not disheveled, at least not in a state fit for walking about the village. Jana smiled.

"Good evening, Mrs. Kusel," Veronika said. "Would you like to come in out of the rain?"

Ondrej looked as if he wanted nothing less than for the married woman to come in and interrupt their conversation. Jana wondered if the possibility that she might let him kiss her passed through his mind. She thought not. To him, her thirty years must seem like old age. She did long for a kiss, however, and she thought that she might demand one as payment for Veronika shirking her duties of keeping watch and speaking to the spirits in the night. Jana might make such a demand, but then she would feel shame, not merely for exacting a kiss not freely given, but for the fact that she would carry with her the weight that the only kiss she could procure was one wheedled under threat.

"No, thank you, the porch roof is keeping me dry. I wondered if perhaps you refilled my lamp oil earlier this evening," Jana said.

Veronika shook her head. "It wasn't I, Mrs. Kusel. I'm sure it was Ana; she said she intended to do so earlier this evening. Though if she hadn't, I would have."

"I believe you," Jana said. "You have always been so attentive. Be you also careful." Here, Jana glanced at Ondrej and then down. His eyes grew wide, and he drew his knees to his chest. "Our neighbors would not abide us if early children visited us in great numbers and frequently."

Ondrej blushed deeply in the lamplight and did his best to look anywhere but at Jana. Veronika, on the other hand, regarded her thoughtfully.

"Of course," the younger woman said, nodding and pushing a curling strand of dark hair behind her ear. "That is very wise, Mrs. Kusel. Rest assured, there is no danger of early children."

"Well, that is reassuring," Jana said. "And thank you for telling me about Ana, I will visit her straight away."

"I believe she is with Zuzanna," Ana said. "They are speaking together."

"Mrs. Kusel," Ondrej said, as she turned to go. She stopped and turned to regard him with raised eyebrows.

"Yes, Ondrej," she said.

"I—Well, we were talking about the spirits—"

"Yes, I'm sure you were," she said, trying not to smile.

"We were, and I wondered if it was true that they are most attentive to us when we build our shelters by the water."

She couldn't tell if he was asking because he genuinely wanted to know or if he was attempting to give her the impression that there had been a real conversation before she appeared at their door. She decided to humor him.

"The spirits listen at all times when we speak to them at night, but it is true that they are more attentive, as you put it, when we build our shelters by the water. They are closer, you might say. The water brings us to them, and they to us. And so, they can hear our words more clearly."

"And we can hear them?" he asked.

"No," she said. "To hear the spirits, we must do as Jan Tomasek has shown us, and then, only rarely. Still, it is a comfort to know that once a year, the spirits can hear the whole community without hindrance."

"But they can hear the ghost talkers," Veronika said.

"Oh yes," Jana said. "But the ghost talkers speak from their own shelters every night." Ondrej looked confused. "There are times when we want to hear the spirits, and for that, we have been given instructions. But there are also times when we want the spirits to hear us."

The look of puzzlement remained on his face, and Jana found herself at a loss. She also didn't have a particularly good understanding of why they would need the spirits or ghosts to hear them more clearly. That was something she might ask her husband about later. Hoping not to be backed into a corner where she would have to admit her ignorance, she nodded to them both, kissed Veronika on the cheek, and left her to her young man. Down the ladder she went, careful not to slip on the slick rungs. Then, pulling her cloak more tightly about her, she walked up the winding path to the little hill that rose next to the creek, turning Ondrej's question over in her mind. Up she walked and up she climbed until, once more, she knocked at the door of the little platform.

Ana opened the door, and, just as Veronika had predicted, there sat Zuzanna with a tin cup of coffee in her hand.

"Good evening, Mrs. Kusel," both young women said in unison.

"Good evening, ladies all," she replied.

"Please, come in," Ana said. She was tall and had to duck to stand under the platform's low roof. Her light brown hair was long and straight, and her face was narrow and sharp. Her brown eyes and thin lips always made her look like she was thinking, which, Jana knew from experience, was more often true than not. The silver band on her left hand, though small, looked outsized on her thin finger.

"How fare your Josefs?" Jana said.

"Both are well," Ana said, gesturing to a small chair. Jana hung her cloak on a peg and sat. The room was warm, heated by a little iron stove in the corner. "I believe they are enduring the cold heartily together. And how is Victor?"

"He is well, thank you. His shelter is falling down around his ears, but he is well. I don't think his father helped him with it at all."

They all laughed.

"Would you like some coffee?" Ana offered.

"Yes, thank you. I'm afraid I fell asleep early and now am pulled in both directions. It would be nice to wake up a little."

Jana took coffee and they chatted for a while. She thanked Ana for her kindness, and soon matters turned from the polite to serious theological considerations.

"What did you think of Magdalena's testimony last week?" Zuzanna asked. She did not look at Jana but instead stared into her cup. Ana also began to study the color of her coffee. Jana shifted in her seat and nodded slowly.

"I found it to be ... fascinating," Jana said. "But I'm not entirely certain I understand what she meant. Perhaps one of you could illuminate me."

Ana frowned and shook her head. Zuzanna, however, looked up with eager eyes. She had the most perfectly symmetrical features Jana had ever seen. Her small nose and mouth made her round face seem larger than it was.

"I think she was saying that we have been led astray," Zuzanna said.

"Oh," Jana said. "By whom?"

"By Petr Mikulasek," Zuzanna said.

"The author of the Third Book has led us astray?"

"Yes," Zuzanna said. Ana gave her a sharp look, and Zuzanna quickly added, "That is, at least, what I took Magdalena to be saying."

"And how has Petr Mikulasek been leading us astray?" Jana asked. She wasn't sure if she should show either of the two emotions struggling within her. She could laugh, but then she might offend and silence Zuzanna. Or she could let fly the anger she felt at the young woman's presumptiveness, but that would likely have the same result. She wanted to hear what the woman thought, so she kept her expression as still as she could.

"He has misread his father's works. Mikulas did not mean for those who wander to be an allegory for us, or an example for us; he wanted us to ascend to be like the mighty ones."

A week earlier, Jana had gleaned the same meaning from Magdalena's testimony in the meeting hall. She had discussed it with Vaclav, but her husband had dismissed it as a passing fancy. Jana wondered now if he had been wrong.

"What do you think of that interpretation?" Jana asked.

"Well," Zuzanna said, putting the tin cup down on the floor next to her. "I have been rereading the First and Second Books. And I think—"

"Hush now," Ana said. "Do you presume to tell the first woman in our community how to read the Four Books? Do you think that you should insult the very founders of our society? Not only insult, but accuse of devilish deception?"

"No," Zuzanna said, holding up her hands, "I was not—when I say that we have been deceived, I do not mean—forgive me, Mother Kusel, that isn't what I meant. I meant that errors were made, not deceptions, I … I misspoke. And because errors were made, we were led astray."

"Do you believe you understand the First and Second Books better than Petr Mikulasek?" Ana asked, her thin hands clenching into fists. Jana found it easier to keep a calm exterior when Ana was mad enough for both of them.

"I … No, but I think Magdalena sees the truth," Zuzanna said, "or at least she may. I don't know. You're right, I don't know more than Petr Mikulasek."

Jana laughed. "Oh, come now, Ana, don't be so angry. No harm is done in such contemplations. It is good! We should return to the Books anew and let them speak to us with open hearts. When we do that, we may find that new mysteries unfold before us. We may also find"—here she offered Zuzanna a maternal smile—"that we can make mistakes.

And there is no crime or shame in making mistakes."

"But Mother Kusel, your family—" Ana began.

"My family can stand a little questioning," Jana said. "We can endure a little examination and reconsideration. Do you know why? Because I am confident that when such examinations and considerations come, we will find together that our path is the right one, and that, though we may have made small errors along the way, the interpretation of the books is sure. Do you know why I feel this way?"

"Because He sees far," Ana said.

"Because He sees far," Jana said.

And on that rainy October night, Zuzanna voiced her agreement.

ZUZANNA STANDS WITHIN THE hall and gives her testimony. She proclaims the error of Petr and his Third Book. She calls him a moralizer, a fable teller, and one given to the sins of analogy and allegory when the plain meaning of the text is clear. She holds up the books of Mikulas and cries out for the people to read them again, forgetting the layers of dross that hide their true, silver shining meanings.

The people in the hall look at her blankly, but she can see passions rage behind their eyes. For some, she is an apostate and therefore must be truly cast out, not merely in the manner of the ritual. For others, however, her words ring true, and they long to rise and affirm her. But first, they must meet and discuss.

When she leaves the hall, they whisper in her ear, and soon, under the cover of night, they meet to speak of what might be done against those who have poisoned the message of their ancestors.

V
If He Sees Far

Wednesday, May 8, 1822 – Morning

Gilgal, Pennsylvania

"IF HE SEES FAR, why have we dwindled in number? If He sees far, why are we cloven so?" Zuzanna's words rang across the village green. Those assembled, more than forty, Victor guessed, moved like pendulums, looking first at her as she stood in her heavy green cloak, her arms waving passionately, and then back to him and his mother. Jana stood beside him with her hand resting comfortingly in the center of his back. He wished his father were still alive, not to comfort him, but to see the man he had become, the man that the community would soon behold for the first time in his true capacity as leader of the Brethren of the New Settlement.

Victor kept his peace and let her speak, his mind working like a steam engine, turning, whistling, and puffing as he waited for the right time to refute her.

"We have been led astray by false faith in counterfeit authority, like the Papists before us! I, for one, do not doubt the words of Mikulas Medved, for he has shown us the great mystery of the City of Night. But his son, Petr, wrote of that which he did not know. He fashioned for us moral chains and earthly fetters! Instead of learning the lessons of the Dark City, we repeat them! We follow one of the mighty because He sees far, and he promises us a new settlement where Eden may begin again. But many are the promises of new Edens! I contend that He Who Sees Far does not care for us. For what has he done but tear our community from our homes three times? First, we sojourned with the children of Hus. Then we left them, and for what?

"Then we came across the sea to live here in this fine land, but we are not to stay here. No, we are to go on again in the coming days. When? We do not know. And for what? The promise of a paradise? I tell you, paradise has been waiting for us, but it has been ignored because we have been satisfied with the errant promises of four paltry books. Why? Why should we be content with this meagre serving of knowledge when much more awaits us? The First and Second Books are only the beginning, and they should not have been restrained so by Mikulasek! Let us therefore do away with the Third Book and throw open the doors to new knowledge. Let us make a collection of it, and from that knowledge, make for ourselves a new Eden."

The crowd met this proposal with silence. They turned to look at Victor. The hand on his back pushed him forward gently. He opened his mouth and drew a deep breath.

And though he spoke passionately of his family, of the hardships they had endured, and the long journey and the many signs promised by the One Who Sees Far, his speech did not have the effect he desired. He could feel the crowd dividing as he spoke. He could see scowling, accusing, ungrateful faces turning from him. And when his words failed him, he watched the crowd disperse in silence, and Zuzanna's triumphant eyes blazing from beneath her bonnet.

Four days later, Victor stood before the assembled families and the community's elders. The crowd numbered sixty in total, almost half of the Brethren. He fought back both tears and the urge to pick up a stone and batter Zuzanna into the ground. *Let her collect knowledge with her brains scattered across the earth*, he thought. But he kept his face placid as each person presented themselves to the community's elders. Each testified that they carried with them only their clothing, coin, and food for their journey. If they were to leave the community and seek new forms of knowing, they would have to entrust themselves to their new mistress and her wisdom. They would take none of the Brethren's possessions or knowledge with them.

This restriction had not bothered Zuzanna, who told him that she knew one who would impart hidden knowledge and draw them into the circle of his wisdom. They would dwell within his flock, and he would provide for them. Victor believed none of it. He felt confident their community would starve or dilute itself within a generation. Then there would only be one remaining community of the Brethren—one New Settlement, one true Eden.

Each member of the departing assembly passed into the Kovar household, where they stripped and received new, clean clothing for their journey. Under the watchful eye of the Kovar Matriarch and Patriarch respectively, women and men demonstrated that they had secreted no book, scroll, or scrap of the visions of Mikulas, Petr, or Jan. When they appeared from the back door, they received back their old clothing, a loaf of bread, and as a group, two horses and a wagon to carry what little they possessed.

"Where will you go?" Jana asked over her silent son's shoulder.

Zuzanna regarded her for a long moment. "Don't you know?"

the woman asked, her round face bounded by a tight and voluminous bonnet.

"No," Jana said.

"I thought your master sees far."

Jana said nothing.

"Perhaps he'll tell you. Now, we must be away; time lingers not in this place."

"No, it does not," Jana agreed. Then she stepped forward, past her son, and embraced Zuzanna. "Be well. I hope ... I hope that one day we might be reconciled, if only for the sake of Mikulas and his vision."

"You and I never shall," Zuzanna said, "but perhaps our children's children will welcome such a day." She returned the embrace. It was formal, with no love in it. But Victor appreciated that it was better than sending their former brethren away with slight, slap, or slander.

When the horses had drawn the wagon away and the people who were no longer among the Brethren of the New Settlement were out of sight, Victor turned to his mother.

"What are we to do now?"

"I do not know. But we will learn. Has Maria been found?"

"Yes," Victor said. "Maria," he called. A girl of fifteen stepped forward, her eyes downcast, her clothing soiled with mud, her sleeves torn. "Come with us," he said.

Maria followed Victor and his mother to the stone hut. They ducked under the low door and into the darkness within. The squat square building smelled of earth and smoke. Jana went to the corner where a cedar chest sat and lifted the lid. She drew forth a light-gray woolen shirt.

"Remove your dress, but nothing more," Victor said to the girl. Her eyes never met his as she nodded and took off her dress.

NICOLAS STARES AT HIS father's hand as the stream tugs the man's fingers and runs over them like little rapids. He cannot bring himself to look at Victor's eyes, which are red pits, plucked by crows. His father's leg, tangled in a thick branch, points down and away from his body as if a giant has twisted him like a stubborn drumstick left to dangle for some choicer meat.

"This is what comes of venturing too far," his mother says. "Within the community, we accept such behavior, but outside—" She nods at the knife protruding from his father's corpse as if to finish her thought. "Learn what he would not. Do not think yourself stronger, or cleverer, or wiser, or greater than you are."

Nicolas, twelve years old, crouches and touches the toe of his father's boot.

"Yes, Mother," he says. "I will learn."

VI
Indwelling

Wednesday, May 2, 1855 – Night

West Virginia

THE HUSBAND AND WIFE rode west to Harrisburg under a full moon, then southwest to Cumberland. There, they set out on the great National Road toward Cumberland and on to Wheeling as the moon crooked Jan's grin at them. At each town, they stopped and stayed for a night at an inn where they ate, danced, and spoke with locals and fellow travelers alike. They paid for private rooms and made love when they thought others would not hear them. Upon reaching Wheeling, they met the taciturn young man who led them south, first on wide roads, then along tracks where two could barely ride abreast. Finally, as they wound their way over hills and beside valley streams, they followed foot and deer paths under pine, oak, maple, cherry, ash, and elm.

Following the youth under a newly full moon, Nicolas and Marketa Kusel finally emerged onto a wider road where they could ride side by side. Their guide, whose name was William, led them up a final wooded hill. They passed between pickets that stood four feet high and half a foot wide. On their flat sides, unfamiliar letters were carved deeply into the wood. Marketa guessed that they belonged to the benighted city, and she whispered as much to her husband while William rode ahead. Nicolas offered only a grunting assent.

Nicolas's gelding and Marketa's mare snorted as, upon turning a corner in the winding path, wavering lights came into view above a wooden palisade. They approached, and over the sound of their mounts, the faintest hint of singing floated down to them. A chorus of voices rose together somewhere beyond the wall, lit by hanging lamps. Imposing gates stood closed before them. When William led the couple forward, doors opened on creaking hinges, though the young man made no discernible sound or sign.

The doors were large enough that they did not need to dismount, so they rode under the gate lintel and surveyed the hilltop town. The main street ran away from them for perhaps a quarter mile. Buildings rose on either side. Most were wooden and either one or two stories tall, their windows dark and sullen. Two taller stone buildings stood out under the full moon's light. One, with lanterns hung from its steeple, appeared to be a church. The other, whose windows glowed faintly green or blue, stood at the far end of the street, and from their distance, Marketa could not tell its purpose. Though both of the stone buildings were lit, they somehow managed to appear more melancholy and more bereft than the rest of the street.

Marketa looked up and saw one more cluster of lights brooding high above them, as if a large house or tavern looked down upon them from its perch on a hill above the town. As they progressed further up the street, those distant, floating lights were hidden by trees and buildings. But Marketa never lost the feeling of being watched from a high and all-seeing vantage.

William led them toward the singing, which grew louder as they approached the church. He dismounted but made no indication that they should do the same. He tethered his horse and opened and entered the doors to the narrow building. A dull glow seeped out onto the dirt street along with the words of the song.

"... where the sun doth ever shine!

Lift them high! Lift them high! Lift them high!"

The people's voices were so boisterous and their number so great that Marketa expected to see a community of a hundred strong leave the church in a cheerful, loving throng that belied the grim character of the town. Instead, what issued forth from the church's doors was a crowd of thirty stoic, solemn-faced people who emerged silently in measured steps. Marketa glanced at her husband, who returned a furtive, concerned look. The small crowd, which Marketa believed could never have made the noise they had just heard, gathered before them in two groups that flanked the church's doors. Finally, five more people emerged and clustered before Marketa and Nicolas.

One was tall, lean, and middle-aged. He held a lantern before him, revealing a face given to sagging jowls. The next was a stocky man with a long black beard who wore a ring of red metal that cinched it near his chin. The third was a dark-haired man whom Marketa marked as Italian, Spanish, or Portuguese. The final two stood more than a head shorter than the tall man, were pale, and looked like twins. One was William, who had led them in. The other was a frail-looking young woman who leaned into William's crooked arm. She wore a plain, pale blue dress under a heavy green cloak.

"Good evening," Nicolas said. "I am Nicolas Kusel, and this is my wife, Marketa, and we have come from Gilgal to extend a hand of friendship to our divided brethren. We have come at the behest of your—of—" He searched for the right word.

"We are here at the invitation of Zuzanna Cerny," Marketa said.

The young woman started to cough so violently that Marketa feared she might harm herself. Her concern transformed into a species of dread, however, when she realized that the girl was laughing. Short, harsh, barking laughs that wracked her thin frame. The girl's dark, sunken eyes peered up at Nicolas as her mirth faded.

"You look like your father," she said, grinning lustily. "Like he looked on the day he banished us from the Brethren with nothing but our clothing. Only, you look more like a man than he was. Are you more of a man?" She stepped forward awkwardly, her bony hand grasping up at him. His gelding backed away from her, and Marketa could tell why as the first whiff of the woman's rot reached her.

"Stay back," Nicolas said. "Who are you?"

The girl laughed. She could not have been more than fifteen years old. If she had been thirty, she would not have been present on the day of the schism. If she had been thirty-five, she would not have remembered it. Was this woman forty? No, it was impossible. *Someone must have told her*, Marketa thought. But she didn't speak as if she had learned it from another. She spoke as one who knew.

"Who am I?" the girl asked, indignant. And then she repeated the question, turning to the boy who accompanied her, her face a mask of fear and bewilderment. "Who am I?"

"You are our mother," the boy said in a hollow, sullen voice.

"Your mother ... I ... William, I ... I am your mother. I am mother to you all."

The girl's face spasmed, stretched in a great yawn, and then scrunched up as if she were making a stage appearance of anger. She smiled and laughed, and wept and moaned, and she writhed in ecstasy, all in the span of ten long heartbeats that filled Marketa's veins with ice.

Finally, when the girl's contortions ended, she looked at them with sagacity and slyness beyond her years.

"I am their mother. I am the one who has called you here. I am the one you have come to see."

Nicolas's horse took another two steps back. Marketa blinked, her confidence wavering.

"Where ... I ..." Nicolas began. Then Marketa watched his face progress through his own series of contortions from confusion to disbelief, to fear. "Do I speak to Zuzanna?"

"You do not merely *speak* to Zuzanna, boy. I am Zuzanna."

"They have summoned her," Marketa said.

"No," the wasted girl replied, "I am Zuzanna, and you behold me now as I am. I welcome you to our community." Marketa felt her fingers and toes go cold with fear, and her stomach churned. The girl who called herself 'Zuzanna' leveled her with an appraising look and said, "Don't be afraid. You will be unharmed here," she said. Then, after gazing up and down the street, she said, "By my people, at least. I vow it."

Then, true coughing bent her over, and both William and the dark-haired man who stood next to them took hold of her. The tall, jowly man stepped forward, and his voice was deep and calm. "Our mother is still learning to live in her new shelter. Come, she would treat with you, but not in the Shadow. Will you dismount and speak with us as the brothers and sisters we are?"

"What is happening?" Nicolas asked. "What does she mean that she *is* Zuzanna?"

"Our mother means what she has said; she is present with us. Please, I entreat you, join us for a meal. You are safe here; none of us will harm you, though you may see many strange things." This he said with a glance at the stocky man with the ring in his beard. The bearded man gave him a dark look before turning on his heel. He strode up the road to a building next to the church and opened the front door. Red light tinted the man's body, giving Marketa the impression that the man was covered in blood.

"Stranger than this?" she asked, steadying her dancing mare as the man entered the red light and closed the door behind him.

"It is possible," the tall man said. "Please, I am Isaac, and you are welcome here."

"Yes," the girl wheezed, "you are welcome here and safe. Come with us."

Marketa stared at her husband, hoping to convey her desire to leave, but he either did not understand or did not accept her silent plea. He dismounted and bid her to do the same.

"We will stable your horses and bring your bags to your rooms," the dark-haired man who steadied Zuzanna said. He had a thick accent, and Marketa guessed that he was from Spain.

"We only need one room," Nicolas said.

"Very well," the man said. He passed the girl to William and came forward. As he took her horse's reins, he looked up, and Marketa followed his gaze to the top of the building that the bearded man had just entered. A red candle glowed in a round window on the third floor. She was almost certain that the candle had not been lit before. Isaac waved to them with, it seemed, some urgency. "Come, let's eat and drink and find some comfort together against the dark of the night."

The tall man led them away from their mounts and into a tavern which, despite the town's drear, was well lit and warm. A fire filled the hearth, and lamps hung throughout the common room. They served good, strong ale, and lamb stew with carrots and potatoes. Marketa sat close to her husband, her hand testing the draw of the knife on her belt while avoiding the eyes of the girl who named herself Zuzanna. The meal seemed to restore the wan girl's strength, for as she ate, color bloomed in her cheeks, and she sat up straighter.

When she looked as if she could speak, Nicolas addressed her. "How…?" he asked. "How is it that this is your … your being?"

"We have learned more than the Fourth Book teaches," the girl said. "We are no longer restricted to summoning the spirits for only a moment. To tie and loose, to cast out and reclaim, to adorn and summon. We may now remain without end."

"How?" Nicolas asked. "Where have you learned this?"

"We have studied under the master that your master has libeled. We have wandered in the Shadow, where knowledge dwells, and we have learned. We have walked where Mikulas walked, and we have beheld what he beheld." She smiled terribly, first at Nicolas then at Marketa.

"You have been to the Dark City?" Marketa asked, disbelieving.

The girl nodded.

"How?"

"One of the mighty has revealed to us the way. He led us to this place of power and has taught us to build a door."

"And so now you may go and come as you please?" Nicolas scoffed.

"No, not yet, and not here. The door is not complete, nor is our power. But the time will come, little brother, when we shall build a door, and our power will be sufficient."

"What do you mean, 'not here?'" Marketa asked, but the girl did not answer her. "To what purpose would you want to build such a door to that accursed place?"

"Knowledge," the girl said. "Knowledge to overcome the limitations of what we now know. For you can clearly see that my possession of this shelter is not without difficulty. We still must learn."

"But why?" Nicolas asked. "What are you seeking?"

"Is it not plain?" Isaac said. "We seek the only answer worth knowing—how to overcome death."

"No," Marketa said. "That isn't the purpose of Jan's book. We live in the hope of the Resurrection, not in fear of death. We speak to the dead because they can guide us, counsel us."

"These are the words of puppets," the girl said. "Puppets pulled by the strings of their unfaithful master. Tell me, what has he told you to bring me?"

Marketa and Nicolas looked at each other. She longed for a moment alone to confer and comfort each other. But she only received a short, furtive nod.

"He sees far," Nicolas said.

"Yes," Marketa said. She turned to the girl. "He told us to bring you a book."

"So it is," the girl said, wheezing. She took a drink of ale. "Did the Seeker After Knowledge not tell us that this would come to pass?"

"He did," Isaac said. William, who stood behind them, repeated the words weakly.

"Come then, let us receive this gift as it was intended."

Nicolas reached into the bag at his side, but Isaac raised his hand. "No, not here. Let us go to the library together and receive it there. But first, finish your meal."

They ate what remained of their stew and drank their ale to the bottom. Then, fortified, they rose. Joined by the man Marketa now thought of as 'the Spaniard,' they left the tavern as a party of six, with the girl leaning on William's arm again.

"If you are truly Zuzanna, how have you done this? Have you simply not completed the ritual?"

"No," the girl said. "To not complete the ritual is to invite madness in both the spirit and the shelter. One must sever the bonds more completely. And one must make space. Even now, the process is not perfected. Even now, we have much to learn. I do not expect to remain in this shelter forever. I will choose another, and we will learn more."

"And what will become of the girl?" Nicolas asked.

"What remains of her may gibber out the rest of its days in forgetful madness," the girl wheezed with a dismissive shrug.

"You do not care? I thought you called yourself their 'mother,'" Marketa said.

To this, the girl said nothing.

They walked down the grim street under newly lit lamps. Several paces in front of them, a man carried a long pole with an ember at the end. As he stood under blooming light, Marketa saw that his dress was elaborate. He wore a heavy, high-collared cloak and a tall hat. Tall boots came to his knees with buckles of the same bright metal as the buttons on his vest, perhaps brass. His face was long and gaunt under the shadow of his hat's brim, and stubble peppered his lean jaw. He did not look up as he passed, but the girl who called herself Zuzanna bowed her head in his direction.

"Such are the strange ones who walk among us now in this Shadow," she said once they had taken a dozen paces past the lamplighter. Marketta turned to regard him once more, but the thoroughfare was empty behind them.

"What is this?" Marketa asked, seeing, as she turned, figures in windows, backlit by pale green light. Their hidden faces conveyed to her a sense of desperation and dread. She took Nicolas's hand tightly as they approached the looming building at the end of the street.

"We have dwelt in the Shadow and learned firsthand what you have only glimpsed through your four books. Here we live under the eye of the Great Master, and at his feet we abide."

"What master?" Marketa asked.

"They serve the Unfaithful Student," Nicolas said. "One of the Accursed."

Zuzanna spat on the road.

"Unfaithful Student … bah," she said. "Calumnies."

"I don't understand," Marketa said. "The Unfaithful Student is a … a story. He is a symbol of the pride of the intellect, as the Radiant Queen is a symbol of the pride of beauty. The Mad Doctor signifies pride of man's command of nature, the Pale Lord is a sign of the pride of wealth, and the Lonely—"

"No," Zuzanna said, "such are the tales of children. Such are the feeble digestions of a spiritualizing mind. Here we stand in the Shadow of the City itself, not some churchman's allegory."

Marketa felt Nicolas's hand take her elbow.

"Here, they do not accept the Third Book."

Zuzanna spat again, and Marketa gasped.

"I don't—How can you read the First and Second Books without the Third? How can you discern the spiritual meaning of Mikulas' visions if—"

"There is no spiritual meaning," Zuzanna said. "There is only the City and the lie of Petr Mikulasek."

Though the night was cold, Marketa felt sweat bloom across her forehead. Within her gloves, her fingers felt slick. "Nicolas," she said.

"Be still, my love. Remember the words that were given to us."

She thought back to the boy in the small stone hut who looked at them with a crescent smile and leering eyes. She tried to recall his exact words.

'You will see for the first time and you must not fear, for I have long seen these hidden things.' Or had it been, 'I have long beheld these hidden secrets?' She wasn't sure, but the meaning was the same. Nicolas and Marketa would see what Jan Tomasek had seen, and he had told them not to be afraid. She was finding his command extremely difficult to obey. Her limbs trembled at the thought that she walked in a place that was full of realities she had believed in only as symbols and just-so stories.

Marketa had the disorienting impression that, if she survived, this journey would divide her life into the years before and after. She would enter the tall, dark building as herself, and another woman would leave. She wanted to run back to her horse and gallop away to preserve herself. She did not want to be someone who had peered into the living darkness. She thought that such a person could never be truly happy, as she and Nicolas had been happy. And yet, she continued forward, following the young woman to the great double doors of the building she took to be the town's library.

The doors opened into a small room with desks set against the walls on either side. Lamps hung from hooks, though unnaturally deep shadows shrouded the corners and spaces below the desks. Marketa had the impression of entering a different kind of space than any she had known. Paintings hung from the walls in soot-blackened frames. Their dark oils suggested gothic cathedrals, low, rambling, benighted cities, and dire figures, tall and fell. They were too dark for Marketa to make them out with any certainty, but the impression they left upon her was one of hoary drear and ancient dread. Cursed and blighted were the places and figures depicted there, and she understood that she was in the presence of some vestige or foreshadow of the place which Mikulas called the 'City of Madmen.'

"This way," the girl said, gesturing for the others to follow. Marketa swallowed and then again, trying to resist the urge to run or throw herself into her husband's arms. She turned to him, hoping for so much as a comforting word, but dread contorted his face. She wondered if she wore the same look.

As Zuzanna led them into the library's main room, Marketa's mind revolted, and vertigo threatened to topple her as her vision blurred and the room incongruously stretched out to titanic dimensions. In one step, they moved from the close dimness of the vestibule into a colossal, groaning space. The air was heavy with the must of ancient paper, wax, and unknown spices. Shelves rose above them to impossible heights and beyond the limits of her sight. Walkways of wrought iron hung one above the next, rising through the gargantuan towers of scrolls, codices, tablets, and all manner of recorded knowledge. The moaning of the vast space came, it seemed, from those metal paths as they swung, never still, under the feet of low, robed, scuttling things that hurried with lights in their hands up and down the paths and around hanging spiral stairs that led into immeasurable darkness.

Every book ever written must be here, Marketa thought.

The disorientation sent Marketa to her knees, her hand reaching out to steady herself. She did not find the wooden frame of the door. Instead, her fingers met a cold rail. She gawked as her eyes traced a cable of twisted metal thread from beneath her hand to an iron grating below her feet. Through that grating, she could see an endless plunging down of shelves, books, walkways, and small scuttling figures.

Marketa knew that she was going mad, and she nearly lost her dinner. She heard a noise and saw that Nicolas had given in to the same impulse and was vomiting over the side of the walkway. The thought of his sick falling below them was almost enough to overcome her self-control. When she thought she could control her body no longer, the vision rolled up like a scroll, and she found herself kneeling on the wooden floor of a crowded, but mundane, room of bookshelves, lit with simple lamplight.

Marketa's attention was split in three directions. First, she saw Nicolas doubled over. She moved to put her arm around him. His eyes remained shut, and she didn't know if he was aware of the restitution of the sane world, or even if, were he to open his eyes, he would see the same close and sanely proportioned space that she did. Second, the sickly young woman's face had taken on a wild, hunted, desperate look, and she started to cling and scratch at William, mumbling and pleading with him. And finally, as she comforted her husband, she surveyed the cases and saw nary a volume anywhere on dozens of shelves. The cases were empty.

"Please," the girl said, "please, stop this, stop it, she's killing me, she's in me, please kill her, please kill me, I can't anymore, I'm bent, I'm mad, the worms in my mind, I lay in heaps, I am in pieces, I puzzle, I puzzle, please kill me, brother, I will do anything, I will do anything, unmake me, unmake … Oh, oh, no, no, please, I-I can't remember, I can't remember. I can't remember—"

Here, the girl broke off and began to choke and retch. She made noises like a beast caught in a trap—violent, monstrous, gasping, bleating sounds. She flung herself to the floor and writhed like a woman on fire, or like a beetle with two of its legs pulled off. Her back arched, her mouth gaped, she stuck her tongue out long and serpentine as her eyes rolled back and her fingers curled into arthritic claws. Sweat bloomed, and her hair, which shook in her convulsions, stuck to her pale skin.

Nicolas, shaking, pulled Marketa close as the girl flailed on the floor. When Marketa was certain that the girl's frail body must snap under the power of her spasms, she let out a cry and fell flat, her head lolling to one side so that her weak eyes fixed on Marketa's for a brief moment.

"I am empty skin and rotten meat," the girl said. Then her face underwent a contortion of emotion that seemed to Marketa to be a devil's mockery of the ecstasy she shared with Nicolas. When the tremor subsided, the person who looked at her from the sunken eyes and trembling lips regarded her with detached contempt.

Nicolas squeezed Marketa's hand. He was staring up and around, and from the expression on his face, she guessed that he now only saw the barren shelves of the little community's earthly library.

"What have you done?" Nicolas said.

Zuzanna sat up and brushed the hair away from her damp forehead. "What do you mean?" she asked.

"What have you done to that girl? What have you done to this place? What devilish bargain have you made?"

She laughed. "We have sought wisdom, like Solomon. And I have done nothing to this girl that you have not done to many of your own."

"No," Nicolas said. "No, that is not the way. Our ritual is momentary, this … this is monstrous. This is the ravishing of a mind, this is possession, you are a devil, you have become as the Evil One!"

Zuzanna laughed again. "You understand nothing of what we do, nor of your own ways and dealings, Nicolas Kusel." She stood, grinning. "Here we delve into mysteries beyond your pitiful aspirations and childish dreams to restore an Eden that never was. Here we peer into the void that sits at the heart of all things and learn the ephemeral emanations that vibrate into being across the worlds and realms of the mighty who wrest from that unending void the only thing worth possessing—existence. While the pitiful throngs seek their happy heaven, and you seek a thin and worthless respite in your 'New Settlement,' we stand against the coming darkness by sitting at the feet of one who has overcome the endless march of decay. He, not you or your cursed and cursing master, will endure and stand when all else has fallen."

As Zuzanna spoke, she smote her breast with her fist, and Marketa saw her standing on a vast field of night under weak red stars. She wore tatters, and her diminished limbs were bruised and wasted, her ribs and hips protruding like those of one wasted by famine. A scattering of teeth clung to the inside of her mouth, and snatches of hair stuck to her scalp. Like a living corpse, she stood upon a barren expanse, unliving and undying. The vision was not overpowering, as that of the library had been. It did not replace her waking sight, but lay over it, transposed and translucent, a kind of double vision.

"We stand against the Nothing that devours all, and our master has taught us much in this great struggle," Zuzanna said.

"Where?" Marketa said, finally finding her voice. "Where are these teachings? I see only empty shelves. You are mad! You have built Bedlam!"

"You see shelves that wait," Zuzanna said. "But they shall be filled, and that work has already begun. Come! I came to receive your gift, and I shall. But I want you to also see the fruits of our labor. I want you to return to your community in the knowledge that your books are not the only ones that have come from the Great City."

Marketa rose with Nicolas, and with their arms around each other, they followed the girl and her companions deeper into the library. Though the library was minuscule compared to the overwhelming vision of unending space, it was not, by rational standards, small. The community had built a hall with three floors. The second floor was open in its center, allowing them to look up through it. The third floor was also open, and drew back further than the second, and reminded Marketa of the receding balconies of a theater. As they passed through the center, a pale blue light descended from somewhere above, showing the floors above them and the glass ceiling through which distorted stars twinkled. The stars sent a tingling terror over her skin, for, though she didn't know how she knew, she was certain that they were not the same stars that had looked down on Marketa since she was a girl.

They wound their way through the warren of shelves until they came to the back wall, where five more floor-to-ceiling bookcases stood out from the rest. Their wood was darker, almost black. Looping, disorienting knots were carved into the four corners of the cases, and beaten silver capped the front edges of the shelves. These, too, were empty except for one. On the middle shelf of the centermost case, stood five cloth-bound books.

"Behold," Zuzanna said. "Behold the wisdom we have accumulated in thirty short years."

Marketa stifled a laugh, partially to avoid antagonizing their host, and partially because the laughter that stirred in her chest was manic, wild, and disjointed. It threatened to knock her to the floor, to tear her clothing and her hair, and to drive her out into the wilderness where she would go about on all fours and hurl herself into fires.

"It may seem paltry to you," Zuzanna said, "but in two hundred years, you have produced only one worthy work." She raised a hand to Nicolas's open mouth. "Do not claim the writings of Mikulas for yourself. He did not write in order to send your people out on your doomed journey. He was a wanderer, a delver into mysteries, and he wrote what he saw. And he left you. You never tell that part of the story. Your Petr Mikulasek was an abandoned son with an abandoned mother. To fill his gaping soul, he founded your false faith with his so-called Third Book, a confusion of half-truths at best." She spat again. "Only the Fourth Book is of any value, for the Cursed and Cursing spoke it through the fool Tomasek. And one day we shall place it here, beside these works, and learn more completely his secrets." Her hand went to the volumes on the shelf, her fingers trembling as they stroked the unbroken spines.

Marketa looked at Nicolas and shook her head, her breath shuddering in her chest. She saw the conflict in his face and watched as he shut his eyes tight, as if trying to block out some overwhelming, unseen light. Zuzanna seemed too enrapt by her dream of one day possessing the writings of Jan Tomasek to see Nicolas reach down to open the bag at his side and draw out a small book bound in red cloth.

"Sister," Nicolas said, his eyes still shut, "that day is today. We have been sent to offer you this as a gesture of reunion."

Marketa stood by, helpless, as he proffered the book. She wanted to reach out and grab it, to take it with her and run. She wanted to dig a hole and hide it where no one would find it before weather and worms could wear it away. But she knew why Nicolas held the book out to the frail girl possessed by a mad woman: they had been instructed to by the man who had written the book. He had ordered them, and they must obey. For the one Jan Tomasek served, the one they served, saw far. And this, she tried to believe, was part of what he saw.

Marketa clenched her fists at her sides as Zuzanna reached out with shaking hands to grasp the proffered volume. Greedily, like a person starved for words, she opened the cover and read the first page. Then she flipped pages, scanning them, her mouth mumbling and wet with saliva as she gibbered quotations in snatches, plucking seemingly random passages, beginning in the middle of sentences and moving on before their ends. Finally, satisfied that what she held was no counterfeit, she looked up with wide and searching eyes.

"Tell me why. What reason did your ghost give?"

"As I said, it is a gesture of reunion. And one," Nicolas said, "that I hope you take. For no matter what has passed, you remain our brethren. And we live in hope that you will rejoin us, and our wandering people will be whole again."

She gazed at him for a long moment before again staring at the book. She slid her fingers over the scarlet cloth. Then she turned and put the book on the shelf next to the others before letting out a weak cry and collapsing on the floor.

"She is well," Isaac said as William and the Spaniard lifted her. "We thank you for your gift and pray that your hope of reunion is realized. Now come, your room awaits, as does more ale. This is a dry place, and you must be thirsty."

They left the library. As they proceeded toward the inn, Marketa felt her skin grow cold. Beyond the gate wall rose a hill in the place of the slope they had climbed not an hour earlier. Upon that mound stood a house made entirely of glass, from which a bright and roving light went forth. So bright was the glare that Marketa could not look at it directly. But when she peered down at the street and the buildings around her, no light from that house reached them. No one spoke a word about whether they saw the vision, and Marketa kept her silence.

When they reached the tavern, they ate bread and beer before Isaac showed them to their room and handed them the key to the door.

"Do not wander," he said, "for you have already seen strange things, and they abound all the more as the night grows older."

Then he was gone, and Marketa fell into her husband's arms. He, for his part, leaned upon her and wept. She believed she might have stood there for hours, holding and being held. However, before long, a knock at their door cut their comfort short.

Trembling, Nicolas asked who it was, and William's low whisper came to them, "Please, sir, will you help me?"

Marketa shook her head, fearing for their safety, but Nicolas pulled back from her and opened the door.

William stood, his eyes red, his mouth screwed down in sorrow. "Please, sir, will you help my sister? I cannot do it."

"What do you—" Nicolas faltered. Then, after a deep and shaking breath, he spoke again. "Where?"

"Our house is just across the way. Come, no one will see. They have retreated to their homes and barred their doors and windows. We lie under the Shadow here."

"All right," Nicolas said, his hand going to his knife. "My love, you must stay here."

"I will not," Marketa said. "I will go where you go, and you will not leave me alone in this place."

Nicolas nodded, apparently relieved she was wiser than his attempt at nobility. Then, together, they followed William. He led them down the stairs into the main room, which was now lit only by a dying fire. Nothing moved or made a sound where, only minutes before, there had been light, life, and conversation.

"Do not look at the things you see," William whispered as his hand rested on the front door's latch. "Do not touch them and do not speak to them, lest you join them in their city."

Gripping Nicolas's hand, Marketa fixed her eyes on the ground and followed William out into the street. Where previously there had been dirt underfoot, now cobblestone spread before her. She dared not shut her eyes, but she did all she could to keep herself from gazing at the tall buildings that rose about them, or listening to the lamenting voices that rose like a discordant chorus. All had changed—all but the building next to the church, which remained three stories tall, with a red candle in the window. Before it, tall and wavering, stood a spindly-legged form in her periphery. She dared not look directly at it, yet she could not disregard its uncanny figure. At first, she thought it might be draped in loose, light material. As they passed it, however, she saw that it was bare and pale, its skin sagging and fluttering in the unmoving air. A thin, whiplike appendage extended from its center, holding a lantern aloft, its flame crimson.

They hurried past and sped in through a door. William shut it quickly and quietly behind them.

"We must be as silent as we can," William said.

"Are your parents here?" Nicolas asked.

"No, Zuzanna made my sister kill them before she took her. But we must be silent, so we do not wake Zuzanna. Come."

He brought them into a back room where the girl who had called herself Zuzanna sat at a small table. She was looking at a candle and biting the nail of her right thumb. She glanced up when they entered.

"I thought you said—" Marketa began.

"Zuzanna sleeps, but my sister is awake," William said.

Nicolas squeezed Marketa's hand once and then strode over to the girl and knelt silently before her.

"Lady, what is your name?" His voice was barely loud enough for Marketa to hear, so she stepped forward.

"I don't remember," she whispered. "I am food and eaten."

He took her hand and kissed it. "What would you have me do?"

She lifted her chin and shuddered. "I will not scream. I will not wake her."

Nicolas bowed his head, and Marketa could see his shoulders shaking. She wanted to go to him and comfort him, but that time would come later. Instead, she watched as he stood, taking the girl by the hand. He led her to a bed and had her lie down. Nicolas gestured for his wife to approach.

"Comfort her," he said. Marketa looked down into the girl's eyes and saw there a mixture of madness and fear.

Marketa knelt beside the bed and took the girl's hand in both of hers.

"Please," the girl said. "Before she wakes."

Weeping, Marketa kissed the girl's hand. Nicolas, his eyes brimming with sorrow, took one of the pillows and held it before her. She nodded. He lifted it and then lowered it, shaking.

"I cannot."

"Please," she said again. "Please, I puzzle, I puzzle, I burn and float. I am empty, I am empty."

William spoke in a low, whispered voice. "She is only a beast for her to ride until she breaks. Then Zuzanna will find another."

Nicolas nodded. He leaned down and kissed the girl, not, Marketa thought, as she had seen him kiss lovers, or friends, or even their own child. Instead, St. Paul's admonition came to her, and she wondered if she had ever before seen a true kiss of peace. Then, his countenance cloven by sorrow, he put the pillow over the girl's face and pressed it down over her nose and mouth. He pressed and pressed, and in Marketa's hands, she felt the girl squeeze and squeeze. Then, after too long, she felt the girl's grip shift, as if no longer grasping, but groping, feeling, searching. They were the fingers of a blind person in the darkness, trying to discern their surroundings.

They were Zuzanna's fingers.

Then, with one last spasm, they grew limp.

She watched as Nicolas shifted, but she shook her head.

"Not yet. Not yet," Marketa said.

Nicolas nodded. He held the pillow firmly against the girl's face for two more minutes, and only then, when Marketa was sure that no pulse had twitched in the girl's wrist for a count of one hundred, did she nod and free Nicolas from his ghastly duty.

He fell back from the bed and sat in a corner of the room, sobbing into his hands. Marketa took the pillow and lifted the girl's head, putting it under her. She straightened her hair and pulled the covers up over her, taking her arms and laying them over her chest. Then she went to her husband and cried with him. William strode across the room and took the girl's green cloak from the back of a chair, and brought it to the fireplace. He threw it in and stood before the flames until they died down.

"Come, I will bring you back now," William said.

"No, we should leave," Nicolas said. "They will find her and know what we've done."

"No," William said. "You are safe, not even the servants of the crimson flame will harm you after Zuzanna's vow. Even so, I did this. You must think of it as one more monstrosity when they tell you in the morning. Then fly from here and do not return."

He led them across the street, and the tall, pale thing wavered once more in the corner of Marketa's vision, its red light bathing the cobblestones underfoot. William left them in their room, and Nicolas locked the door with shaking hands. Then into each other's arms they fell, weeping themselves to sleep.

In the morning, Isaac roused them. He joined them in the common room to break their fast together. Marketa asked after Zuzanna, and he said nothing for a long moment.

"She will not see you again before you leave," he said.

"We would like to be on our way quickly," Nicolas said around a mouthful of cheese. "Will William be guiding us?"

"No," Isaac said, sniffing. He rose suddenly and fixed them with a morose gaze. "Alejandro will guide you to the road to Wheeling. And then, who knows when next our two peoples will speak again?"

They finished their food and small beer. They took their bags and walked out into the street to find a sparse crowd gathered in front of the church. At the head of the group, the short man with the long beard stood, looking gravely upward. Nicolas grabbed Marketa's hand. She took a long, deep breath, steadying her stomach as she tried to feign surprise at William's body. Suspended before the church on ropes that wrapped his elbows, he hung like a doll, limp and lolling.

"What happened?" Nicolas demanded as the Spaniard, whom Isaac had called 'Alejandro,' led their horses out onto the street.

"Zuzanna has ordered it. The spirit clings to the world through those it loves. By removing them, we make the natural spirit cleave less fervently to the body. His death is unfortunate, but necessary."

They mounted, and Marketa once more tried to keep her eyes downcast as they followed him. Once they were beyond the gates, she turned and considered the foggy, tree-draped hills. High above, she saw lights burning hazy red and remembered the building that brooded over the town. She wondered if it was the same glass structure she had seen blazing with light, but … no, that had stood here, where they were riding, or at least she thought it had. These red lights glowed dully, high above and far away, and, though they discomforted her, there was nothing uncanny about them. She considered asking their guide, but decided, instead, to know as little as she could about the cursed place.

They rode in silence for an hour until finally, Marketa could take the clamor of her thoughts no longer. "Tell me, sir, how is it that you came to associate yourself with the people of the village?"

"My dreams," the man said. "They led me here to join these blessed people."

"Blessed?" Marketa asked.

"Oh yes, they are a holy flock. I was drawn from across the sea to join their numbers."

"How is it, Mr.—"

"Delgado," he said.

"How is it that you dreamed of this place and found it, Mr. Delgado?"

"I was shepherded here, Mrs. Kusel," he said. "That is what a member of the flock does, is it not? Allows themselves to be shepherded?"

Marketa thought he must be right, but didn't say anything more until they left him.

vi

SOBBING, MARKETA SPEAKS INTO the insect-buzzing night, telling the ghosts what she's seen. She's never done the work of a ghost-talker; she doesn't know where the ghosts are. So she stares out the little elevated hut's window at the old oak tree and pours her words into it. She wonders if the words, soaked in the Shadow, have hurt the tree that stands in the corner of the village green. She hopes that her years of weekly recitation have not poisoned it, but the things she says are so foul, she cannot imagine they have had no effect. Still, she can think of no other way to release the darkness from her soul. So, she speaks of the dead woman, the dark streets, the vast library, and the towering, pale thing that held its red flame.

VII
A Word Before Leaving

Thursday, May 1, 1873 – Before Dawn

Gilgal, Pennsylvania

ELISHA WALKED PAST THE stone hut and let his fingers slide along the piled slate. He had only entered the stone hut twice, and both times the voice within commanded that the Brethren travel. The first time had been nearly twenty years ago, when the voice of Jan Tomasek had come out of Amos Lister and ordered his parents to go on a journey that would leave them forever changed. Then, a month ago, the same voice spoke from a different boy's mouth, ordering a new voyage. Reuban Swant had hunched forward in the old, worn, too-large woolen shirt. His hands had rested on his splayed knees; his ankles crossed under him. He had reminded Elisha of Amos, his mouth curved in the same way, like the crescent moon. Reuban had tilted his head forward just like Amos had before his parents went to see Zuzanna. But Reuban hadn't told them to go and come back. He, leering and mad, had wanted them to take one final journey.

"Lament," the boy had said, "for the days of division shall not be ended in your lifetimes."

Elisha stroked his beard and squinted in the darkness.

"But they will end?" his wife, Karolina, asked.

"Yes, He sees far," the boy said.

"How must we go forward then?" Nicolas asked, mimicking his son's gesture, running his hand along the course hair of his gray beard.

"The Brethren must go west to the place where the waters meet and the lightning falls. There, you will establish a new settlement. There you will find a new Eden."

"Who will show us the way?" Karolina asked.

"He will walk with you when you near that place. He will show you the sign."

"When should we leave?" Elisha asked. Shadows trembled between the walls' stacked stone. The low roof gathered smoke that wound through woven branches wet with evening rain.

"You should take your belongings and travel on the fifth day after Epiphany. And, know this, that though you travel with them and arrive, son of Victor, you shall not see another Christmas."

The boy turned to Nicolas, his dark eyes regarding the older man for a long moment.

"So, I will be dead within the year," Nicolas said.

The boy had nodded. "Then you shall come and dwell here, with me, and prepare the vessels of morning."

"I will be ready," Nicolas said, bowing his head and reaching out to take the boy's hand.

"We will be ready," Elisha had said, putting his hand on his father's shoulder.

Elisha remembered emerging from the hut when the ritual had concluded and rewarding Reuban Swant with the promise of his very own apple pie. The boy had asked if they would permit him to share it with his sister. The thought still made Elisha smile. The Brethren were doing something right if their children's first thoughts were of generosity.

Elisha let the memory go and walked up the path, surveying each of the houses one last time. He knew that he would not see this place again, and it made him sad. He knew that sentimentality was not a terribly useful trait, and he believed that they were going to a place that would be at least as beautiful as Gilgal. But he would miss these stone houses and their neighbors to the north—the 'Moravians,' as they were known. They did not always see eye-to-eye, but they had lived in neighborly charity, and when conflict had arisen, they had dealt with each other out of mutual respect and brotherly love. The joy of those conflicts, almost more than the joy of their reciprocated kindness, had made him believe that perhaps this place was to be the new Eden they had been promised.

He continued up the path and spied the lookout in the village green. They would have to build new lookouts. They would have to speak to the spirits on the trains and on the ship that would take them north along the west coast. They would have to adapt to many changes in the days to come.

Hands pressing down on his knees, he took big steps up the rise, where one of the four oaks grew next to the platform. When he came to the ladder, he took two rungs at a time, pulling himself up swiftly to the top, where he clambered onto the small porch before the door. He listened and heard a voice. Then he knocked.

"The morning is coming; the sun is about to rise. Your labor is complete. Come, and welcome the new day," he said, putting his mouth close to the door.

The voice stopped, and feet scrambled against the floor. A moment later, the door opened, and two young women looked up at him with bright, smiling faces.

"Has the night truly passed?" Nadia asked. She was the older of the two, having just celebrated her twenty-third birthday. She smiled so genuinely that he was transfixed, and believed for a moment that their sojourns were over, and the true sun had arisen.

"Yes," he said, "truly."

Nadia stood on tiptoe and kissed him on the cheek. He touched the place where her lips had been and smiled. Then she and her sister Zdena slipped past him and hurried down the ladder. He watched them go and wondered who would marry them in their new land. Perhaps they would find young men in nearby towns. He prayed Nadia would find someone soon, otherwise—Well, he would rather not think about otherwise.

The community already suffered the effects of too few men. Without men to preserve their names, young men from outside Gilgal brought new and strange-sounding names to the Brethren. When the Pekar girl was married, then came the Swants. When Ana Havel married, so joined the Listers. With Elizabeta's marriage to Jonah, the Svecs became the Cunninghams. Only the Kusels, Zemans, and Kovars preserved their family's old names.

The changing names were not his primary concern. If the Brethren continued, what did it matter what they were called? His concern was for his own soul. He loved his wife deeply, but in his heart, he had never been a chaste man. He had never strayed in the flesh, though he knew many members of the Brethren had. But he respected the limits of the strength of his will. He wished for more men in the community for many reasons, but sometimes, like this morning, he wished for them most of all so that the women had other men to look at and desire. He knew he was not handsome, but he also knew that authority robed plain men in gold and gave natural men an unnatural appeal. He prayed that the paucity of husbands would not endure beyond his ability to resist temptation.

The journey will help, he thought. There were no secret places for people to go on a crowded train or ship. No place for him to give in to his desire.

He hoped.

A foolish thought. The voice was in his head, but it also came from the shadow that hid the back of the rocking chair in the corner. He saw himself with Nadia alone in an empty compartment, her lips on his, her bare breasts beneath his hands. He saw them on the deck of the ship under the stars. And he saw Karolina unbothered. *I can make it so. I can whisper into her ear and she will not only not mind, but encourage you.* The chair moved back and forth once, and then again. Elisha turned and fled from the platform and never returned there again.

vii

THE TRAIN IS NOT as crowded as Elisha wants it to be. Two doors down, the compartment is empty and private. He kneels beside the bed in his cabin, asking for the strength to resist the temptation in his loins. His wife kneels beside him and puts her arm around his shoulders.

"Go to her," she says. "Go and be glad. This is our way, and I would not deny you."

"No," he says, "for I would not share you, and I would not be a hypocrite."

She looks up at him. Her eyes reflect the lantern light. "Would you stay with me then? Stay and enjoy my comforts?"

Her eyes split. Four circles of brown stare up at him. They split again.

"I have many comforts, if you prefer."

They split again, and again, and again. Though a scream wells in him, he does not let it out. Instead, he pushes away from her and scurries from his cabin into the hall. She follows him, her face trembling with a thousand eyes, the lace of her bodice slipping under her fingers. He reaches for the latch of the first door he finds and fumbles it open. Nearly falling, he pushes his way in and slams the door against the vision. His fear-wracked mind registers that this is the empty compartment.

But it is not empty.

Nadia rises from the bed to greet him, her clothes piled neatly on a chair in the corner of the small room. Her hand goes to his, and she draws him to her.

He hates himself as he loves her.

VIII
Settled

June, 1873

Oregon

THE BRETHREN OF THE New Settlement followed the Wallowa upriver until it scattered into a many-fingered fan on a wide plain stretching to a rim of low hills on the eastern horizon. To the south, mountains rose before tapering off as they jogged toward the rising sun. To the north, foothills rambled on out of sight. Here they waited for three days, fishing and gathering, waiting for the sign that the old ghost had promised them in a hut three thousand miles away. Then, on the morning of the third day, a man in buckskin on a fine roan mount approached them. The bottom half of his face was painted red, and the side of his head was shaved. He looked no older than twenty, and his eyes reflected the dawn. He did not speak but instead pointed north. The Brethren took their horses, wagons, and packs, and followed him up a stream that leapt with fish. He brought them between two rises of earth and then steadily along a valley that ran through the low hills.

They followed the stream north for half a day until the barren hills took on, tree by tree, a slow and growing forest. Then the people rested under the shade of the pines and ate, sharing their food with their guide. He brought them fish from the streams and spoke to them in a language they could not understand. Yet the sound of his voice, like a breeze across reeds, entranced them. They slept under the stars, and though a thunderstorm brooded to the north, they stayed dry.

In the middle of the night, their guide came to each of the leaders and roused them until six couples huddled together in the cool night air. He led them up a rise where they could watch the storm flash and crack. He held up his hand against the moon and raised three fingers. Then he pointed north again. A lightning bolt smote the sky. He put down a finger. Another followed, cleaving the darkness. He put down a second. Then another flashed. The man put his hand down, and the thunder rolled in, wave after wave. He kept them there for another five minutes before he brought them back to their camp. They saw no more lightning that night.

Before they slept, they conferred with each other, and all agreed that the lightning appeared to strike the same place three times. They wondered what it portended, and if perhaps they would find a settlement already in place, with some tall steeple in the center of town, its pinnacle set with an iron rod to attract the lightning. Worry and hope wrestled within each of their breasts that night as they drifted fitfully to sleep, picturing the Indian with his hand raised and the three bolts that came, seemingly at his command.

In the morning, he took them up the same path he had brought the leaders the night before, and they struck north again along the valley's western ridge. They traveled for another half a day among the pine trees, straight and tall, their branches wide and hanging with clusters of needles that looked like bunches of fallen snow. Between the trees, a thin pillar of black smoke rose to the north. Finally, the land to their left rose into the foothills of a low, flat-topped mountain that peeked at them from between the trees. Another mile along their path, and their guide struck west to bring them by winding paths to the roaring foot of a tall waterfall. The people pointed up at the pines along the ridge beside the falling water. Three trees were blackened by fire, and smoke drifted from their bare, smoldering boles.

The people fell to their knees and praised God for bringing them to the place where lightning falls. Their guide sat upon a flat rock near the pool and looked up at the top of the waterfall.

He looked pleased.

viii

IN THE WATER'S SPRAY, they cut down trees that have wandered close to the pool. Their axes bite into the wood, sending splinters and chips spinning, and cutting deep V's in the boles. Down the trunks fall, one by one. The first shelters of new wood will not last. They must cut and dry their lumber, dig their cellars, and clear their ground. The years will forget these first steps, as no pen records the people's labors.

IX
The Body

Tuesday, June 17, 1873 – Morning

Oregon

ELISHA AND KAROLINA STOOD before the cabin with their guide beside them. He had roused them before the sun rose and led them alone along the creek that issued from the pool at the waterfall's foot. He pointed to the closed, moss-covered door.

Well-made against the weather, the building nonetheless looked badly damaged by decades of neglect. The rusty hinges protested as Elisha pushed with his shoulder. Karolina followed him apace into the cabin. The room that met them was lit by only a few slanting rays that leaned in through cracks in the roof and shutters. Karolina raised her lantern. Though it had given way in some places, the roof had stood the elements well. Water had soaked through and damaged the floor to the right of the doorway and in the room's back-right corner. The rest of the cabin, however, looked dry and sturdy.

To her left was a door, and before her, against the back wall, a desk. She picked her way carefully across the floor, testing each board before she put her full weight upon it. Atop the desk was a leather-bound book and a dark rock. She shook the piece of old furniture with her free hand and found it solid. Setting the lantern down, she carefully opened the book's cover. Footsteps sounded behind her. A door opened, and Elisha thumped through into whatever lay beyond. Karolina gingerly flipped pages filled with faded, but mostly legible, writing. Dates told her the age of the journal, and she guessed that if they had arrived a decade later, the ink would have been almost invisible. Letting the pages fall, she picked up the rock and held it close to her lantern. She sucked in a short, shallow breath. Then she lifted it into one of the slanting beams of sun, and her heart sped.

"There is a dead man in the other room," Elisha said as he came back through the door.

"Look at this," she said. Karolina drew her husband close and guided his hand to hers. Together, they studied the glinting gold that clustered like grapes out of the dull rock.

"Is there more of this?" Elisha asked. She could feel his body tense in excitement.

"I don't know. Let me read."

An hour later, Karolina rose from the desk chair and walked outside to where Elisha sat on a fallen log, smoking with their guide. She regarded the painted man cautiously.

"Hitilettu?" she said, trying the word out loud for the first time. The man took his pipe from his mouth and nodded. The sun burned in his eyes. Then he rose, spoke not another word, and mounted his roan. Looking once more toward the waterfall, he rode away.

Karolina watched him go as her heart thundered in her chest. The book had told her he was not a man, and she believed its author. Elisha watched the not-man go and then turned to her with a quizzical look on his face. Karolina stood silently for a long moment, gathering herself. Then, when she felt ready, she sat beside her husband and put a hand on his knee.

"The man inside is named Micah Whitman," she said.

"What was the word you spoke to him? Why did he go?" Elisha asked, peering over his shoulder to where the horse and its rider had disappeared into the pines.

"His name. Come, you should read the book yourself. But, before that, we must … well, I think we must look at something."

She led him back inside and into the side room where the body lay. In the corner, under a faded and moldering blanket, she found a coiled rope, took hold of it, and pulled. Slowly, a square of boards rose and revealed a stairway beneath. She tried each step carefully and led Elisha down into a wide, musty space. As he descended, she hung her lantern from a hook in the ceiling. The light, wavering and bright, sketched the room around them.

"Is this—?" Elisha began.

"Yes," she said. "I believe it is."

Before them, filling almost the entire space but for a narrow path, stones lay piled, each like the one they had found on the desk, each gleaming with the same bright yellow streaks of precious metal.

"We will have to tell the community about this," Elisha said.

"Yes. But remember that it was shown to us alone."

"The people will understand that," Elisha said. "But they will not understand if we keep it from them."

"There is more," Karolina said. "More in the mountain for us to take. With this, we may build a new place, Elisha. We can finally bring about a new Eden."

She took his face into her hands and kissed him. There was fumbling and pulling and lifting, and then, there was love among the metal and stone and must.

That afternoon, they led each of the Brethren's leaders into the cabin and down into the basement. As each person stared in wonder and praised God and the One Who Sees Far, Karolina wore a small, private smile as she mused that while all shared in the awe and joy of the gift, none received quite the celebration she had shared with her husband. After sober minds returned in the wake of the shock of such wealth, each leader agreed that the treasure had been vouchsafed to the Kusels. In turn, the Kusels promised that each of the founding families would receive a fair portion. Once all had seen the stones, the body, and the book, the community pulled rocks from the river and dug a hole to form the corner of their first temporary building. Elisha stood upon a prominent flat rock by the waterfall and spoke to his people.

"Today, I proclaim our new settlement founded. This is where the lightning falls," he said, pointing to the water, "for our guide showed us three bolts from the sky that landed here as a sign. So, we shall dwell here, and make for ourselves a new home, a new community, and a New Eden upon the earth. When we began, we called ourselves the Wanderers, for so taught Petr Mikulasek. But we wander no more. Here we may finally rest."

Jeremiah holds the girl in his arms and imagines her future. He pictures her standing upon Proclamation Rock, passionately encouraging the dwindling Brethren to take heart. He weeps as he cradles her in the drafty little lookout platform and holds her up to show her their family's house through the window. He wishes he could give her something more than a dusty main street with a dozen houses and a meager corner store. But the One Who Sees Far brought them here, so he tries to trust. Yet, though He Who Sees Far has led them across land and sea in safety, and they have gold aplenty, their numbers dwindle. He pictures his daughter standing on Proclamation Rock, but he cannot picture people around her. He wonders if all that will remain will be the crowd of pines to listen to her words.

X
The Great Welcoming

Tuesday, June 17, 1902 – Afternoon

Lightning Falls, Oregon

JEREMIAH WATCHED THE WAGONS approach from the south, rolling along the dusty road from Enterprise. They were two dozen in number, each bearing with it the goods and hopes of a single family. Over a hundred and fifty people walked and rode to meet the remaining population of Lightning Falls. Zemans, Kovars, Listers, Cunninghams, and Swants stood around the Kusel family on the sunny spring afternoon, trepidatious but hopeful.

When the first wagon reached them, the Kusel brothers stepped forward together and raised their hands in greeting. A tall man with a long, dusty, sweaty face approached them and removed his hat. He wiped his brow with a handkerchief.

"Good afternoon," he said. He was young, perhaps only twenty years old, but he had an air of authority about him.

"Good afternoon," Jeremiah said. "Welcome to Lightning Falls. I am Jeremiah Kusel, and this is my brother Peter."

The tall man took a step toward them and extended his hand.

"I am Jacob Grossman," he said. "I am the temporal head of our congregation." Jeremiah looked from Grossman to Peter and back again. The brothers Kusel shook the man's hand.

"The temporal head?" Peter asked.

"Yes, our minister is coming up now, he—" Here Jacob laughed self-consciously and looked down at his hat. "The road has not treated him well." He looked back over his shoulder. A man approached on a horse, a handkerchief held to his head, a riding coat flopping about him as he sat heavy in his trotting horse's saddle. When he finally came to a halt in front of them, he clumsily lowered himself to the ground and gave an awkward bow before he resumed wiping the dampness from his face.

"May I present Minister Cerny?" Jacob said.

Jeremiah and Peter exchanged another look and then shook hands with the minister.

"Thank you for extending this gracious olive branch," the minister said. "Too long have the wanderers wandered apart. I dare say that this is the happiest day of my life." Jeremiah nodded solemnly, though the minister's pallid complexion and unsteady gait undercut the weight of his words.

"We, too, are exceedingly glad," Jeremiah said. "Shall we lead you in?"

"Not just yet, I think," Jacob said. "I think it is better that the leaders of your community and the leaders of ours break bread together. Something of a love feast in memory of days long gone."

"I can think of no better idea," Jeremiah said, and meant it.

The heads of Lightning Falls' six founding families joined ten members of the newly arrived congregation. They brought tables and the people ate bread, cheese, and fish. They drank wine and toasted to each other's health, their reunion, and the future of their community.

Jeremiah found himself sitting across from Jacob Grossman, who, it turned out, was not yet married, and a beautiful woman with dark hair and blue eyes whom Jeremiah found enchanting. Beside her was a big man with a wide, friendly face.

"May I also present Mr. Jasper Lundy?" Jacob said. "He is a pillar of our community, and I expect he will be a great boon to this town."

"It's a pleasure to meet you," Jeremiah said.

"And you, sir. Your family's name is well-known to me. How edifying it is to meet you in the flesh! And how humbling to break bread with you."

"You are far too kind, sir," Jeremiah said, his eyes flicking to the woman.

"This," Jasper said, his big hand resting on the blue-eyed woman's hand, "is my betrothed, Mary Cartwright."

"So many new family names," Eliska, Jeremiah's wife, said. "We have the same phenomenon, as we've had a rash of girls instead of boys."

"Oh, well," Jacob said. "That is true, we have had many come in from the outside. There will be, as you say, many new names. But Mary's from another branch of our community in New York. She has returned home to us, so to speak. But soon, a Lundy she'll be."

Mary smiled at Jeremiah and met his gaze.

"Well," Jeremiah said, sipping his wine, "we are blessed to have you among us."

"We are all blessed in each other," she said. "I hope I am as much a help to this community as I'm sure my future husband will be."

"I am certain you will be," Jeremiah said, finally taking his eyes from her.

"As am I," Jacob said, and raised his glass once more. "Let us drink once more to this happy reunion and this circle of blessed friendship."

ELISHA WALKS DOWN MAIN Street beside his wife, Karolina. He marvels at how much has changed in the twenty-four years since the Great Welcoming. The cane in his hand is light and does little work. At eighty-five, he is still spry, and today he feels an even greater spring in his step. His granddaughter Tabbitha has returned from her yearly travels, and he is eager to see her with her new son. He thinks how cruel it is that fate should separate a mother from her child. But, of course, the one they serve sees far.

A young woman in a plain dress pushes open the druggist's door and steps out in front of him. She sees him and apologizes. He tips his cap and feels Karolina pause at his elbow. The young woman, with long dark hair, holds the door open for another, much older woman in a nice, but threadbare dress.

"Grandmother, please be careful," the dark-haired woman says.

The old woman nods impatiently. Then she sees Elisha. She stares at him for a long moment.

"Mrs. Gallo," Elisha says.

"Mr. Kusel," the woman says.

Karolina steps forward to take the woman's hand. "Nadia, how are you? You are looking so well."

"As are you, Karolina. But the doctor says I am not well. So, he sends me here. They are in cahoots! Ah, well, home I shuffle to drink my tonics. The Listers tell me their daughter is coming home today. Will Tabby be with her?"

"Yes, we're on our way to see her now," Karolina says.

"Wonderful. Send her my love."

Elisha blinks and nods.

"Of course we will," Karolina says.

"Good afternoon, Mr. and Mrs. Kusel," Nadia says. There is no pain in her voice, no resentment, no hint at her years of trouble. But as the woman shuffles away, there is no spring in her step. Elisha puts his hand on the granddaughter's arm.

"Would you permit me," he says, drawing her close, "I would like to put the medication on my account."

The woman stares at him for a long moment, studying his face. Then she nods once. "That would be very kind, Mr. Kusel. Thank you."

His cheek twitches, he nods, and then she is away.

"Come, Elisha," Karolina says. "Tabby is waiting."

"Master Mudri was the first to open the door, two years before I journeyed to Zadar to study under him. He was well known as a master of philosophical and mathematical mysteries. The man I met, however, was not the professor of repute. He was wild-eyed and gibbering, and I believed that I had come to the home of a man whose mind was irrecoverably shattered and incapable of teaching me anything. However, while I dwelt in the house of Mudri, a man brought his sick child to the master and bade him to make her well. Mudri did so with a stone he held against her head. Her body, which had been alternatingly hot and cold, limp and spasmatic, calmed, and before my eyes her skin dried and her eyes opened. The man wept and promised Mudri a fine reward, but the master seemed uninterested in the man's gifts. Instead, he wanted a bit of cloth from the girl's dress. He cut one inch of rough-spun, which he then dropped into a boiling solution that he constantly fed in a pot over his fire.

When he ladled some of this mixture into a bowl, I feared he would make me drink it, or that he might even drink it himself. However, he let it cool. He dipped a bundle of reeds into it and daubed the black accumulation onto the handle of a door. He then bid me to open the door, which I did.

Before me stood the streets of perpetual night, their stones wet with unfallen rain. I spied Pelilac and his long pole, though I did not know him then. Mudri introduced me not long after. He stood behind me, his hand on my back, and said, "Behold Gradludi, the city of madmen." And, though I trembled, I stepped through the door. For here was philosophy far beyond that of the academics."

- Mikuláš Vaclavek, *The First Book of Seeings*

"We may be divided by many things, as some follow the secret sapphire flame, and others the roaring crimson, but together we will work the work of our master so that he may bring us beyond the emptiness of death."

-Zuzanna Cerny, *The Book of Corrections*

62
Unpacking

Wednesday, October 1, 2025 – Noon

JENNY SCREAMED HERSELF AWAKE. The room was too dark, and something heavy was on her eyes. She tried to sit up, and the wet covering slipped away, down onto her hands in a little pile of cloth as she blinked the room back into view. Jenny glanced down at the washcloth and then around at the worried faces.

"Jennifer," Charles said, reaching out to touch her forehead with the back of his hand. "Are you alright?"

"Oh God," she said, memories flashing through her mind like overexposed films at five-times speed. "Oh God, what's happening to me?"

"She has to go to a doctor," Charles said. "I have to insist. Whatever we were hoping to accomplish by bringing her here will be better served at the hospital."

"Does she have a fever?" Gina asked, walking calmly into the room with another mug. Jenny marveled at how many mugs the woman owned.

"Not that I can feel, but the cloth—"

"It wasn't on her cheeks or her neck or the rest of her," Nate said.

"That means literally nothing," Charles said, turning to look at Nate. "Can't you see that there's something wrong with her? She could have a tumor, or brain damage, or some kind of embolism. She needs a doctor."

"You might be right," Gina said, putting the cup on the coffee table before Jenny. "But we don't think so."

"Excuse me for asking it this way," Charles said, turning to the woman, "but are you a doctor? What qualifications do you have to say that?"

"No, I'm a software engineer—"

"Then what is the basis for—"

"Because she tried to tell a police officer her name was Tabitha Kusel this morning," Linds said. "And as soon as we started talking to her about it, she passed out. Does that seem normal?"

"No, which is why—"

"Also," Linds said, "I had a dream."

"You had a dream," Charles said. He was clearly trying to keep his tone neutral, but failing. His voice was thick with skepticism.

"Yeah. I don't really dream anymore. But two nights ago, I had a dream."

Charles reached up and pinched the bridge of his nose. "This is starting to sound insane," he said. "Please, I don't want to be the voice of reason in a group of people I have generally seen as reasonable up until now." He took a deep breath and then sat down next to Jenny. "Maybe I'm going about this all wrong. Look, I know that for probably everyone else here, last night was the first time you've been shot at—"

A chorus of voices met him.

Linds said, "No—"

Gina said, "Well, shot at, yes, but—"

Nate, rubbing his hip, said, "It definitely wasn't—"

"Sorry," Jenny said, taking her cup of tea. "Could you all talk a little quieter?"

"Right, sorry," Linds said. "Okay, Charles, I know where you're coming from, but all of us have been in mortal danger before, and in situations that were a hell of a lot scarier than last night."

"I haven't," Maddy said.

"I have," Syd chimed in as lightly as if she had just said she wanted pancakes for breakfast. She plopped down next to Jenny. Jenny regarded Sydney and frowned. The red-haired woman just smiled.

"Yeah," Gina said.

Nate said nothing, but he nodded while he studied the floor.

"I … what does that mean?" Charles asked.

"Look," Gina said. "I'm not sure if now's the time to go into our weird, shared history."

"Well, it might be if you don't want me to pack this young lady in a car and take her to the hospital right now. And even so," he said, throwing his hands up, "I can't imagine what you could say that would change my mind."

Linds took a deep breath, closed their eyes, and then said, "All right. Have you ever heard of Weeping Cedars?"

"The podcast," Charles said.

"The town that the podcast was about," Linds said.

"Okay, yes," Charles said.

"The town from Glen Moat's books?" Jenny asked.

"Yes," Linds and Nate said at the same time. Linds continued, "I'm from there. And Nate … has visited."

"Yeah, a real vacation," Nate said in his driest sarcasm.

"That town is real?" Jenny said.

"Yes, that town is real. Or it was real, now it's a ghost town. I was there when the historical society was making its podcast. I was there when everything turned inside out and upside down. I was there when a guy I knew named Jacob was murdered by his mother, and when my four friends disappeared through a doorway into another world."

"I'm sorry, what?" Charles said.

"Linds is telling the truth," Gina said. "I was there too. I was there for a lot of it. We fought the people who were behind everything—"

"At the risk of repeating myself … What?"

"Look," Linds said, sitting down next to Sydney. "I'm not sure that going into all the details will be incredibly helpful right now, but suffice it to say some very strange things started happening involving a group known as 'the Circle'—I know, that sounds crazy, and it is kind of crazy. But they tried to do a thing, a ritual, and it almost worked. And I saw terrible things, totally unnatural things, things I didn't think were possible. And I think what's happening with Jenny has something to do with those things."

Jenny leaned forward as Linds's words became fuzzy and hollow. She squeezed her eyes shut and shook her head. When she opened her eyes, the room was blurry and slow, as if smeared with syrup.

"Are you okay?" Sydney asked, leaning in close.

"No, I need some air," Jenny said. Sydney helped her to her feet and led her to the back patio. The cool air did wonders for Jenny's head. The world lost its blur, and Sydney came into focus. She sat in a plastic patio chair and peered out into the large, empty backyard.

"I don't want to be nosey," Jenny said, taking a chair opposite her friend.

Sydney raised her eyebrows and pursed her lips. She didn't look at Jenny. "You can ask me anything," she said. Her voice was devoid of its usual enthusiasm.

"You don't have to tell me, but when were you in danger? Like, what did you see that was worse than the cabin?"

For a long moment, Sydney sat and stared before she smiled. "I was taken when I was a kid."

"Fucking what?" Jenny said, leaning forward in her chair. "Like, kidnapped?"

"I guess."

"But Carson Booth … Have you talked to the police? Maybe it was the same person or—"

Sydney shook her head. "The person who took me is dead. It was my uncle."

"Oh God," Jenny said, covering her mouth with her hand.

"Yeah, I was ten. He tried to—"

"You don't have to say it—"

"—beat me to death with a rock."

Jenny felt her head snap back as if someone had punched her. She stared at Sydney, her arms and legs tingling with gooseflesh. The idea of someone wanting to hurt the young woman made no sense to Jenny at all.

People crush flowers all the time.

"I … I have no idea what to say," Jenny said.

"I remember all of it. You know how some people say they block stuff like that out? I can't. I remember everything, and I remember my dad coming in and them fighting. And he almost killed my dad."

Hands pressed Jenny down into the water. Joseph's eyes, warping in the bathroom light, stared at her with an expression that wavered between sorrow and pleasure as the waves contorted his face.

"Dad saved me, but he got really messed up. Like, it messed his brain up."

"God, how do you handle that?"

"How do you?" Sydney asked.

"Right," Jenny said. "Is your dad—I mean, how—"

"My mom takes care of him, but she really doesn't want me to see him. So, like, I almost never do. They aren't even here anymore. They moved to the coast. I was thinking about leaving, but then Maddy happened."

"I don't understand," Jenny said. "You're so … positive."

Sydney shook her head. "It's not the only thing that's ever happened to me. I've had amazing things happen, too. And, I don't know, I don't think about it much. I mean, I think about my dad, and I miss him. But it's not like the most important thing that's ever happened. I guess it is in some ways, if it didn't happen, my life would be totally different, or if my dad hadn't come in, I'd be dead. So, I don't know. I think about other stuff that's happened to me a lot more. I just want to find the happy things, you know?"

"I didn't realize we had so much in common," Jenny said.

"I'm sorry I didn't tell you when you told me, but it felt like I'd be, I don't know, stepping all over your past to tell you about mine. Like, ooh, I have one of those stories too!"

Jenny took a deep breath and surveyed the yard. It was long and wide, almost empty except for a single pine tree tucked into the back corner. It seemed wrong to her, and she couldn't think of where in Lightning Falls it might be.

"I appreciate that. But, like, now I have a new mission."

"What's that?" Sydney asked.

"I need to help you see your dad more."

Sydney smiled. "Good luck, my mom is like a wall of positivity that no one can break through."

"Weird," Jenny said, turning to stare pointedly at Sydney. The red-haired woman returned the look with a cheerful smile.

63
Danger

Wednesday, October 1, 2025 – Early Afternoon

"THAT ALL SOUNDS INSANE," Charles said, puffing his pipe and blinking through the sweet-smelling smoke.

"I feel like I say that to myself all the time now," Jenny chimed in as she and Sydney strolled hand-in-hand back into the living room. "But what are we talking about now?"

"At the cabin, you started to say that your name was Tabitha," Nate said.

"You heard that?" Jenny said.

"Yeah," Nate said. "After you've seen what I have, you start noticing the crazy details, and you don't dismiss them."

"What have you seen?" Maddy asked. "Linds told us they saw a werewolf—"

"Not a werewolf, something worse than a werewolf. Something called 'the Shepherd,'" Linds said. "But I guess you could call it that if you wanted."

"I didn't see the Shepherd, but I did read a note about him," Nate said. "No, I mostly just saw a lurching, shell-covered thing that also sometimes showed up as a drowned boy."

Jenny felt pulled in two different directions and chose not to ask about the drowned boy. "What the hell is the Shepherd?"

"The Shepherd was like a kind of herald of the Librarian. I know, sorry, a lot of strange names. Charles, I appreciate you not having an aneurysm in front of us right now. The Shepherd came from the Dark City to prepare Weeping Cedars for the Librarian. He did a lot of things, including co-opting our local news at night person, a woman named Emma Barnes. He killed her producer in front of her and then put her in the hospital."

Gina shook her head.

"That's kind of selling it short. He tore Emory in half and banished Emma to this place called 'the Shadow.'"

Charles's face was in his hands now, his pipe awkwardly held between two fingers.

"Again, I know, it's insane," Gina said. "But he banished her and several other people to this halfway point between our world and his. He was powerful. Really powerful. Much worse than your garden-variety werewolf."

"What happened to him, by the way?" Nate asked.

"We killed him. Or, well, the Green Hills Society did."

"I can't take it anymore," Charles said, though he didn't move to go.

"I hear you, man," Nate said. "But honestly, I'm begging you not to dismiss it. I lost two friends, and I won't even try to tell you how."

"What's with the shell monster?" Maddy said.

"Let's see," Nate said. "It was ... rust colored? And it had this carapace on its back, and a stalk that grew out of it, which, you know, it moved around by stabbing this bone-thing into the floor and dragging itself. We killed it—"

"'We?'" Sydney asked.

"Me and two other guys, Joe and Allen. They were ... Yeah, we went through some shit together. Anyway, we killed it, and it just turned into a kid who looked like he'd been drowned. He was some kind of demon because he kept coming back. You know, like a monster in a movie. I also teleported a few times, definitely went to another dimension, and I lost Joe and Allen somewhere I won't say because I don't want Charles to stab me. That's like the ten-thousand-foot overview."

"I just don't understand how you—" Charles said, spreading his hands. "Do you expect me to believe these things?"

"Jenny," Linds said, "why were you going to say your name was Tabitha Kusel?"

"I ... I'm not totally sure," Jenny said.

"That's not normal," Maddy said.

"I agree," Charles said, "which is why I think a neurologist is the most reasonable answer."

"But we're giving you reasons why we think there's another explanation," Gina said.

"Okay," Charles said, "let me grant that everything, and I mean everything, you've said is true. People traveling to other dimensions, werewolves, a town with a fire that won't stop burning, secret societies, all of that."

"Drowned demon shell boy," Nate said.

"Drowned demon shell boy," Charles said. "Let's say absolutely all of that is true. What does that have to do with Jennifer? Why do you think it has anything to do with her?"

Nate shrugged at Linds. "This is your thing."

Linds walked across the living room to the window and stared out. "I keep having dreams of you in a radio station."

"Wow," Charles said, standing up.

"No," Gina said, "listen. Linds is a dreamer."

"Like Jacob from Genesis," Maddy said.

"Please," Charles said. "Please, I'm asking you to listen to yourselves."

"But it's not one of the towers. It's somewhere else, like an old radio station, something from the '30s or '40s. I don't know, maybe the '60s, I don't know what radio stations looked like back then. But ... but I get the impression that it's from the '30s or '40s."

"And what is that supposed to mean?" Charles asked.

"I don't know. But I haven't dreamed like this for a few years. I only really started to when everything was happening—when the city was close to us. And I think the city is close to us now."

Charles let out a long, slow, exasperated breath. "I'm shocked," he said. "I'm shocked that you ascribe to this, Nate."

"Hey, look, I don't want to ascribe to it!" Nate said, laughing. "But I was there. I saw, shit, I don't know, something. I got a strange postcard, met a nice old man on a train, and then all hell broke loose, and then that old man was killed in a train accident, which shouldn't have been possible—"

"You met Old Bob?" Linds said, eyes wide. "I didn't know that!"

"Oh, um, yeah. I wasn't actually sure if he was real."

"There," Charles said, pointing with his pipe in his hand. "See? You can't even be sure what's real. You're dealing with a woman who has known brain trauma. I'm sorry, Jennifer, but you know it's true, and you're ascribing things she's doing to supernatural monsters. I—"

"No, sorry," Gina said, "we can't do this. We can't do the thing where the skeptic tries to pull everything apart. We," she gestured to Linds and Nate, "have experienced impossible things. Jenny is blacking out and waking up thinking she's a dead woman. And then there's the part where people came to kill you all because of what Jenny said on the radio."

"Jennifer, do you remember what you said on the radio? No. Was anyone else listening?"

"We were listening and then we turned it off," Maddy said.

"Why?" Jenny asked.

"We got distracted," Sydney said, frowning down at her hands.

"We were arguing," Maddy said.

"I see. So does anyone know what Jennifer was saying on the radio at all last night?"

Everyone shook their heads.

"Charles, I'm sorry, but I agree with Gina. The skeptic's logic isn't helping us here. Two men with shotguns came to the cabin last night to kill us. If Linds hadn't told us to get down when they did," Nate said. "at least one or two of us would be hurt or dead. And with how we were crowding the door, maybe all of us."

"I admit the men with guns are very strange, but it doesn't follow that there are other dimensions and a dark city and whatever else you think is going on here," Charles said.

"Very strange? They killed Delia," Linds said. "They hung Delia up with fishing wire. You don't think that goes beyond strange?"

"Yes, I do, but I think you're forgetting where we are. Some piece of human waste hanging a black woman from the ceiling doesn't mean that werewolves—"

"Like I said, not a werewolf," Linds said.

Charles put up his hands. "I see that I am not going to win this argument. So, I will make one final plea. Jennifer, please, I will happily drive you to the hospital, and I will stay with you while you get settled. I will go to your apartment and get your things. I will do whatever you need me to do because no one else here will do it. Please."

Jenny shook her head. "I think if nothing else were happening, if someone hadn't murdered Delia and if people hadn't come by to kill us all, I would agree with you, Charles. But something else is going on. I've seen things, too. Men in my basement, another woman's eyes staring back at me in the mirror. I have these thoughts that aren't mine. I think ... I think Tabitha Kusel is in my head somehow, and I want to get her out. And I really don't want to get shot or have any of the people I care about get shot. So, I'm not sure how to do either of those things, but I don't think being in a hospital is going to help."

Linds dropped into an easy chair and started to rub their temples.

"You all right?" Nate asked.

"Nope. Delia. They killed Delia. Why?" Linds said.

Jenny took a place on the couch next to Maddy. The image of her friend hanging from wires forced its way into her mind. She pulled Maddy close, but her presence did nothing to lessen the burning loss in Jenny's chest.

"Oh God, what about Barry?" Jenny said suddenly. "Is he okay? If they are trying to hurt the people around me, what about Barry? And Patty?"

"We don't know that that's what they're trying to do," Charles said. "They could be targeting people around Delia. Or, as insane as it sounds, the two things might not be related. I know, that sounds crazy to me too."

"Patty is fine," Linds said.

"How do you know?" Sydney asked.

"Because she keeps calling me and leaving messages demanding to know what's happening to Jenny."

"She's calling you?" Jenny asked.

"I'm sure she's calling you too, but I gave her my number last night."

"Me too, she's been messaging all morning," Nate said.

"Okay, what about Barry?" Jenny asked.

Everyone in the room traded looks. Jenny stood and started for the living room door.

"Here," Gina said, "I'll go with you … I feel like you shouldn't be alone."

As they went upstairs toward the guest room, Jenny said, "Um, thanks, by the way, for letting us crash here."

"I mean, of course. It's been a couple of years, but I'm used to this kind of thing." She shrugged. "Plus, it's really our parents' house."

"Oh," Jenny said. "Right, Linds said something about you squatting in one of your parents' places. But I didn't think they had one in Lightning Falls."

"Oh, no one told you? You're not in Lightning Falls anymore, Toto," Gina said, pointing to the guest room door.

"What?"

"We're in Enterprise."

"Oh," Jenny said, suddenly putting together why the backyard had seemed wrong.

"Empty rentals make good safehouses, I guess," Gina said. Jenny ducked into the room, rummaged through the blankets, and found her phone. The battery was nearly dead, and every app she used to talk to people showed dozens of unread messages. "Shit. Do you have a charging cable?"

"I've got a ton," Gina said. "What is that, a 'C?' Great, come on."

Jenny followed her back downstairs and texted Barry along the way. Jenny's phone buzzed as Gina handed her a cable. Jenny read the message and let out a slow sigh of relief.

Barry
Thank you for messaging me! I'm devastated. Barely holding it together, but I'm safe. I don't think anyone's coming after me. Are you safe? Please tell me you have people around you.

Jenny
Yeah, I'm safe. With Linds's sister Gina.

Barry
Keep your head down. They'll find whoever did this. Love you, man.

Jenny
Love you back, man.

"Barry is fine," Jenny said. "I'm letting him know that we're all safe."

"Jennifer, this is my last plea," Charles said. "I don't know what happened to you, but I know that you were hurt and that you're suffering some kind of brain damage. You can't remember Lightning Falls, you—"

"No one can," Linds said.

"What?" Charles said.

"No one can remember Lightning Falls. If you leave, really leave, the town is almost impossible to remember. Not here, not close by, but if you go out there, it gets fuzzy, and then it just slips away. People forget that it exists, or they say that it's somewhere it shouldn't be. I've seen people say it's in Washington."

"Yeah, I saw someone claim that it's in Idaho," Nate said.

"That's nonsense," Charles said.

"Is it? When you were in the Navy, could you remember home well?" Nate asked.

"What?" Charles said.

"When you were in the Navy, was it easy to picture home? Did you have clear memories of home?"

Charles stood, his mouth open, staring at Nate.

"Or," Linds said, "try finding the town on a map. It's not there. There are all kinds of reasons people give for why Lightning Falls is impossible to find online."

"It is on maps," Charles said. "I have a map in my car right now that has the town on it."

"Local maps, printed maps," Gina said. "Anything digital, it just goes away. Really. Look online, and it's just a forest in front of the Butte. There's the historical rest-stop, there's the trail, but there's no town."

"Tourists—" Charles began.

"Tourists come up from Enterprise or down from Clarkston. They're mostly locals to the area who can see us on the map. You know what everyone in town hears when people show up?"

"'I didn't even know this place was here,'" Maddy said, as if she were mimicking a hundred remembered voices. Gina pointed at Maddy and nodded.

"Are you saying we live in some kind of make-believe—"

"No," Gina said, exasperated and throwing her hands up. "For someone so logical, you seem to be intentionally obtuse. We're saying that something is messing with people's memories of Lightning Falls. Aren't people always missing the town when they drive up Route 3?"

"The invisible sign," Maddy said.

"Yeah," Sydney said. "But I thought that was just … I don't know, just like …."

"I'm sorry," Charles said. "But none of this means that there's a dark spirit or power or ghost or vampire lurking in the shadows. I know you all have convinced yourselves that it does—"

"Not me," Sydney said. "But I'll do whatever Jenny wants."

The room was silent. Charles finally shook his head.

"Fine. I would stay and plead my case more, but I have another person who needs me. Jennifer, please … please!" He stared at her, and then he moved his gaze from her to each person in the room. "All right then." Charles started to leave the room, but Nate stood in his way. "Nathan, don't—"

"I'm not," Nate said, laughing. He extended his hand to Charles, and they shook. Nate pulled him into a hug. "Be safe, my friend. If you need anything or if you're in danger, you call. All right?"

Charles pulled back and nodded. "You do the same," he said. Then Linds took Charles's arm and hugged him, too. Soon, everyone was saying goodbye to Charles.

Then he was gone.

"All right," Maddy said, wiping her eyes with the heels of her hands. "Now what?"

64
Now What

Wednesday, October 1, 2025 – Afternoon

NO ONE KNEW WHAT they should do next until Jenny remembered that she needed to go to the police station in Lightning Falls. Everyone agreed that that was a sensible next step. Nate offered to drive Jenny, and Linds volunteered to tag along. Sydney wanted to go too, but Maddy convinced her that they should go back to their apartments and get some things for themselves and Jenny if they were going to be out of town for a few days. Gina offered to drive the couple.

An hour later, Jenny, Linds, and Nate left together.

"How did you two … I'm not sure how to ask this. How did you know you both had similar experiences?"

"I wouldn't call our experiences similar," Linds said.

"Yeah, mine was brief, but, you know, memorable," Nate said.

"Mine lasted years. I mean, I was born there, and it wasn't all strange. But when things got crazy—yeah, that lasted a few years. But as far as how we knew? Nightmares," Linds said.

"I apparently scream in my sleep," Nate said.

"Daseth," Linds said, almost to themself. Nate shivered.

"So, wait, you two have—okay, not similar experiences—but super weird experiences in the same place on the other side of the country. Then you start the same random job in a tiny town three thousand miles away and only find out about the connection after you start living next to each other?"

"Yeah," Nate said.

"One of the many reasons I think there's something strange about Lightning Falls," Linds said. "That, the memory thing, the map thing, all of it screams 'there's something else happening here' to me. But until Cassandra's husband got killed in July, nothing had ever actually, you know, happened-happened."

"Now everything is happening," Nate said. No one had anything more to say to that.

Jenny's time at the police station was anticlimactic. They had nothing to tell her about who might have attacked her, and she remembered nothing new that she could tell them. Still, it took two hours to review her statement and answer their questions. They wanted to know why Jenny had texted all her friends to come to her, each individually. She told them that she had no memory of texting her friends and that in her delirium, she must have reached out to them each, one by one. They questioned Nate and Linds as well, though less extensively. By the time they got out, it was late afternoon.

"I need to eat," Nate said.

"Same," Jenny said.

"Me too, but I need to talk to Link about our jobs," Linds said. "Where are you guys going?"

"The Tim?" Nate asked.

"How about Cinder?" Linds suggested.

"That works," Nate said. "What do you want?"

Linds told him, and twenty minutes later, Jenny had a cheeseburger in front of her. Twenty minutes after that, Linds came in, trailed by Leddy.

"I found someone who wants to see you," Linds said, dropped into their chair, and hungrily chomped a handful of fries. Jenny stood and hugged Leddy, who squeezed her in strong arms. They sat, and Leddy told them about the search party for the people who had tried to hurt them.

"Everyone got together this morning. Town police and the sheriff didn't want us to, but we got a big group to go out and see if we could find anything." She stole a fry from Jenny's plate. "Phil and Earl think they found a casing that the police missed; Emmet thinks he found some muddy footprints on the bridge that might have boot treads from the attackers. But they could belong to anyone. Plus, how would you ever be able to prove that they were from last night instead of yesterday afternoon? Hell, they could be from this morning. The casing is kind of promising, though."

"Can they get, like, ballistics or whatever from it?" Jenny asked.

"Most of that ballistics stuff is bullshit," Leddy said. "They still allow it in court almost everywhere, but I think that's going to change soon."

"So … kind of nothing?" Jenny asked.

"For now. But the reality is that we've got your back … if you want us," Leddy said.

"How do you mean?" Linds asked around a mouthful of burger.

"We can make sure that you're not in the same situation you were in last night. You know, like, without protection." She patted the holstered pistol on her hip.

"Oh," Jenny said. "I'm not sure if—"

"It's not the worst idea," Nate said. "As long as Gina's okay with it."

Linds chewed and held up a finger. Then, after a comically large swallow, they said, "I'll ask her, but I also think it's not a terrible idea."

"Really?" Jenny asked.

"Yeah. We kept armed people around when everything happened in Weeping Cedars. Do you know how easy it would have been for people to just have walked in and shot everyone? We'd have been done in a hurry if we didn't have some kind of basic protection."

Jenny frowned. "I feel weird about that," Jenny said.

"Well," Leddy said, "it's your call, but it would make us feel better. Also, you should call Isabella; she's freaking out."

"Right," Jenny said. "Could you maybe tell her that I'm okay?"

Leddy shook her head. "You need to talk to her. In person, if you can. Maybe just stop by her office, you know?"

"Right," Jenny said. "Okay."

"We need to grab some stuff from our apartments," Nate said. "So …"

"I'll walk her down," Leddy said.

"I don't need—"

"Yes, you do," Linds, Nate, and Leddy all said in unison.

"Okay, jeez," Jenny said, forcing a half-hearted laugh. "You can escort me."

"Thank you," Leddy said, studying Jenny's face. "I will do anything to keep you safe, do you understand that?"

Jenny put her hand to her stomach and felt like she was about to start crying. She swallowed down the emotion and nodded.

"All right, there's no way you're paying for this meal, not after last night. Give me a minute and then when everyone's ready, we can get out of here."

Leddy disappeared and reappeared three minutes later, nodding. "The check is taken care of. The manager is just glad you're all alive. Ready to go?"

Leddy took Jenny's hand as they crossed the street and squeezed when they got to Isabella's office.

"You want me to stay out here?" she asked.

"Fuck no," Jenny said, before pulling her into the office building. When Jenny knocked on the door and leaned in, Isabella screamed and jumped up from her chair. She ran to Jenny and threw herself at her.

"You're okay! Are you okay? Oh my God, you're okay!" she said, squeezing Jenny, almost too tightly.

"I'm okay," Jenny said. "Just, you know, a little messed up in the head, but okay."

"Thank God you're safe!" Isabella said. She pulled back and appraised Jenny with glassy eyes before leaning in and kissing Jenny. Shocked, confused, and unsure of what to do, Jenny let it happen. A second later, Isabella broke the kiss.

"Um—" Jenny started, but Isabella interrupted her.

"Oh my God, I'm so sorry, I got carried away. I am just so overwhelmed. I've been terrified the last, like, twelve hours."

"Yeah, I—It's okay. Leddy said you wanted to see me in person, so—"

"Yes!" Isabella said, "I needed to see you were alive with my own eyes. I needed to be able to tell Chloe that you're safe; she's been worried sick. I never see her like that."

"Oh," Jenny said, glancing at Leddy, who had a 'don't ask me' look on her face. "Well, yeah, I'm okay."

"Where are you staying? Do you need anything?"

"We're taking care of them," Leddy said. "Everything is going to be fine."

"You're staying with Phil and Leddy, that's—"

"No," Leddy said. "They're keeping things pretty close to the chest, and for good reason."

The hurt look that formed on Isabella's face infuriated Jenny. How could she make this about her feelings and not about Jenny's safety?

"We're not telling anyone who doesn't absolutely need to know," Jenny said, forcing her voice to be steady and calm.

"But I want to help—"

Jenny gritted her teeth. She wanted to tell Isabella to mind her own fucking business, but she didn't need an extra layer of conflict.

"And I'm sure you will soon, but right now we already have six people piled together in a house that Linds's parents own, and we might have four more coming in and out. Please, when we get on the other side of the next day or two, or if they find the people who attacked us, everything will go back to normal, I promise."

This didn't precisely placate Isabella, but her hurt expression relaxed a little.

"All right," Isabella said. She hugged Jenny again and once more tried to kiss her. Jenny turned to try to kiss Isabella on the cheek, and they ended up like two old movie starlets, their lips smacking the air next to each other.

Leddy pried Jenny away and led her back out onto Main Street.

"That woman is insane," Leddy said. "Sorry."

"Why do you hang out with her?" Jenny asked.

"Why do you?" Leddy asked, and they both laughed when Jenny shrugged. "Come on, I'll walk you over to the others. And if you want us to come out to wherever you are—"

"We'll call after we all confer. I don't want to make the decision all by myself."

"Makes sense. Just text me and let me know, we'll have someone there right away. It'll be me or Phil first. Though Phil has been a little busy with your mom, trying to calm her down."

"God, Patty. I guess I should call her."

"Good idea, at least for Phil's sake."

After Leddy dropped Jenny off, hugged her, and comically kissed the air next to her cheek, Jenny called Patty as Nate drove them back out of town.

"Jennifer!" Patty screamed. Jenny held the phone away from her ear.

"Patty, I'm calling to let you know that I'm okay, I—"

"Are you in the hospital?"

"No, I'm with my friends. They're taking care of me."

"You have to go to the doctor! What is wrong with you? Why was someone trying to kill you? What are you hiding? What is going on? Are you on drugs? God, do you owe a pimp money?"

Jenny wasn't sure if she should laugh or cry. Linds, who was sitting in the front passenger seat, turned around and mouthed the words 'what the fuck?' Jenny only shook her head and shrugged.

"No, I don't have a pimp, and I'm not on drugs."

"Jennifer, you have to go get help! Those people have no idea what's good for you! Do you have syphilis? I was watching a documentary about—"

"I have to go. I'm okay. I'll text you later."

Jenny hung up.

"Holy shit," Nate said. Jenny's phone buzzed; the name 'Patty' appeared on the screen.

"God, I thought my parents were crazy," Linds said.

"Oh no, Patty is the champ," Jenny said. She leaned back and closed her eyes.

"So ... do you have syphilis?" Nate asked.

"Yep, I made sure to get every kind," Jenny said.

"Well, at least you're not a quitter," Linds said.

65
Uncertainty

Wednesday, October 1, 2025 – Early Evening

"LINK IS PISSED," LINDS said, pulling a slice of pizza from the box on the kitchen table. "But Charles is taking up the slack tonight. Tomorrow night too, but I'm not sure if he's going to just power through Camping Days all by himself."

"I could go back," Nate said. "Actually, no, because that would leave you all—"

"Without a man?" Gina said, raising an eyebrow.

Nate spread his hands, making a 'help me' face at Jenny. "Have any of you ever fired a gun before?" Nate asked.

Maddy held up her hand.

"Nate's right, we should have at least one person we can throw on top of someone who breaks in to murder us. Someone they can't just toss through a window," Jenny said.

"Um, thanks?" Nate said, looking down at himself.

"What about Leddy and Phil?" Linds said. "They offered to come by."

"I'm all for that," Gina said. "But I do think you should also stick around, Nate. I don't think Charles should be putting himself in danger for that stupid radio station, but if he wants to—"

"He does have to be at home for his mom," Sydney said, picking an onion off her slice.

"There's some without onions," Nate said.

"I like the taste, I just don't like the crunch," Sydney said, pulling another off.

"True—about the mother, not the onions," Linds said, taking Sydney's cast-off veggies and dropping them onto their slice.

"Okay, so let's say we have Phil come by for six hours or maybe two months," Gina said.

Linds shook their head. "I showed Gina a picture of Phil," Linds said.

"He's okay," Maddy said.

"*Okay*," Nate said, drawing the word out. "So, Phil comes over and you two get married or whatever, then what?"

"That's my question," Gina said. "Then what? We're all here, hiding out. But for how long? I don't mind the company. I actually kind of like having you all here, I'm digging the whole sorority house vibe of this place—sorry, Nate—and I'm in no rush for you all to leave. But really, what then? Do we all just shack up together until they find the assholes who tried to kill you? What are you all going to do for work in the meantime?"

No one had an answer.

"I don't think we should have Phil and Leddy here," Linds said after a long pause.

"Really?" Jenny asked. "You said it was a good idea at dinner."

"I said guns weren't a bad idea. But there's something about it that feels off to me."

"Do you think Leddy was one of the people who tried to kill us?" Sydney said around a mouthful of pizza.

"No," Linds said. "The people who tried to kill us last night were men, and they were big and heavy."

"Yeah," Jenny said, "I was thinking about that. I keep wondering if it was someone I know or not."

"Right," Linds said. "And until we know something about that, the fewer people who know about this place, the better."

"So, should we get guns then?" Maddy said.

"You raised your hands for shooting. Are you any good?" Nate asked.

"Yeah," Maddy said. "My mom fucking loves the shooting rage."

"The one south of town?" Nate asked.

"Yeah," Maddy said.

"Well, shit. I wish I'd known that. We could have gone shooting together."

"We still can," Maddy said, smiling. "I'm pretty good."

"Do you have a gun, Nate?" Gina asked.

"I have a rifle," Nate said

"Can you get it?"

"It's in the trunk of my car," Nate said. "I picked it up from my apartment today."

"Well," Linds said, "that's something, at least."

"What else did you bring?" Sydney asked.

"My rocket stuff," Nate said.

"Wait, you weren't joking about liking rockets?" asked Sydney.

"Why would I joke about that?"

"Well, I want to see a rocket fly!"

Jenny
Hey, thanks for being awesome today.
Right now, we're going to keep the house to
just the six of us who are here now.

Leddy
That makes sense. Be safe, okay? If you need
us, just tell us.

Jenny
Thank you, I really appreciate that.

Leddy
Stay safe, girl.

Volume 10, Issue 82, Wednesday, October 1, 2025

Build Ye Shelters While Ye May

By Keith Lowry, Ed. In Chief.

I HAVE THOUGHT LONG and hard about this special edition of this little paper, and I have flopped and flipped back and forth on my position. I think it's important to try to see things from both sides. And the truth is, I'm not sure there is a right or a wrong side. I think every parent and family needs to decide for themselves what is best. That said, I'm encouraging my grandchildren to go through with Camping Days this year.

Am I a monster? We have had two murders and one kidnapping over the last two-and-a-half months. That isn't much for a city, but it's a hell of a lot for us. Our county averages about one homicide a year: one for the approximately ten thousand people who live in this county. If you look at our murder rate, which is calculated per one hundred thousand people, which is the standard for this kind of thing, you find that our rate goes from 6% one year to just under 8% the next. Do you know what that means? It means our population grows and shrinks, but still, we average about one person a year.

We've had two in Lightning Falls this year. That's insane.

I knew both of the people who were killed, and I'm devastated. I don't have eloquent words for Delia the way I did for Jack. Delia was a nice woman whom I interacted with weekly, but she wasn't my close friend the way Jack was. Almost no one was as close a friend to me as Jack was. But, still, the monstrous way in which Delia Baker died is unfathomable.

And now, we've had an attack at the cabin. Men with guns. A shootout with police. What is happening to us? What is happening to our town?

I have my suspicions that the same monster that has infected so many small towns is now coming for us. The same monster that makes people break into strangers' houses to steal money, that drives people mad and makes them do insane things, that brings violence to the streets of so many towns. We have been fairly lucky up to this point that our youth has not been overwhelmed by the new, especially addictive and destructive drugs that have flooded our country recently. But I think that grace period may be over.

Now, as far as we know, there are no signs of foul play with regard to Carson Booth. So, to my mind, we may put that tragic loss aside when considering whether or not we will continue with Camping Days. Except, of course, that we learn the lesson to always enforce the buddy system. So, when it comes to the recent string of violence, I believe that none of it should affect Camping Days, since none of it has been targeted at children and teenagers.

Of course, the other reason I think that we should continue with Camping Days is that I know the people of this town, and there will not be a single campsite along the creek that isn't well-armed and protected. Anyone who intends any harm toward the children of Lightning Falls will be in for a rude, loud, and lead-heavy awakening.

So much of the point of Camping Days is to teach children self-reliance, tradition, and bravery. I trust that we will see our town exemplify exactly those virtues this week. And if my grandchildren do decide to go through with building their shelters this year, I'll be there, in my folding chair, with a lamp, a thermos of coffee, a good book, my Winchester by my side, and my dander up.

I recommend we all do the same and not, if you'll excuse my language, let the bastards win.

And give me a little time to come back to Ms. Delia Baker. She deserves a better tribute than I can muster today.

66
The Talker House

Friday, October 3, 2025 – Late Afternoon

"EVERYTHING IS OFF," MADDY said.

"I know what you mean," Linds said, yawning. "My sleep schedule is completely screwed."

"Yours?" Gina said, handing Linds and Maddy cups of coffee. "I have no idea what day it even is."

"I think that's a sign that we should start thinking about getting back to normal," Maddy said.

"I was thinking that too," Nate said.

"How do we do that?" Jenny asked. "I mean, nothing has changed, right?"

"No, but we do need to do our jobs, and we can't hang everything on Charles. And we do still need homes and incomes," Nate said.

"I mean, you could all stay here," Gina said. "Of course, I can't employ you all."

"You want us to live here?" Maddy asked.

"Yeah. I know it's currently a little crowded, but we can get another couple of beds. There's the office that we can convert into another bedroom. The attic is finished, and there's nothing up there."

"Dibs on not living in the attic," Nate said.

"Fair," Gina said.

"Aren't your parents trying to rent this place?" Maddy asked.

"Sure, but I mean, here we are, renters. They'd be happy that I'm not living alone, too. Split between all of us, it would be pretty cheap. What, like two hundred a month each?"

"If that," said Nate.

"This is nice, but we all have apartments and furniture and jobs that are connected to them," Maddy said. "I'm also enjoying the whole Talker House thing, but I feel like it's going to get crowded fast."

"Well," Gina said, "maybe there's a middle ground. You know, you guys have your places, and you can always come and hang out here."

"Sure, but that doesn't solve what we do now," Linds said.

"I have an idea," Nate said. "What if we start doing some test runs? Like, Maddy can do her show tonight at the Kusel House, and I can hang out in the lounge with my boom-stick."

"And the rest of us are down here?" Linds asked.

"Yeah, and if all goes well, maybe you'll go up tomorrow night,"

Nate said.

"Okay, I can broadcast on Saturday night," Linds said.

"No," Maddy said. "Not you, Linds, you should go tomorrow night if everything goes well. I mean, no, Nate, I want you to stay here and protect Jenny. If I'm in the Kusel House and someone tries to get in, I can hold out until the cops get there. I'll even call them beforehand to let them know where I'll be. I mean, Charles hasn't had any problems the last couple of nights."

"I want to be there," Sydney said. "I don't want you there alone."

"Syd," Maddy said, but Sydney shook her head and crossed her arms. "Fine, but you're staying close to me, and we keep everything locked. If there's even a knock on the front door, you're inside with me and we're calling the cops."

Sydney nodded enthusiastically.

"Okay," Linds said. "If things go well with you tonight, I can broadcast from the Kusel House tomorrow night. Maybe we start like that, and build up until—"

"Until what?" Jenny said. "When will any of us be confident that people aren't going to come and try to kill me again?"

"Were they trying to kill you?" Gina asked.

"Um, yeah," Nate said.

"I mean, were they trying to kill Jenny, or one of you, or all of you?"

"How would they even have known we were there?" Maddy said. "The only person they would have known would be at the cabin was Jenny."

"We have been over all of this a dozen times," Linds said. "As much as I'd love to hunker down and do a research montage, I have no idea what we're supposed to research, and we have the pressing matters of phone bills, food, and all the other mundane realities that we have to face."

"Jenny could just support us all with her other job," Sydney said. "We'll never have to go back to the towers again!"

Jenny remembered a similar conversation with Joseph and how he had convinced her to start her JustBuffs page. She thought about how he had talked about how much the community needed her and what she could do for them. She couldn't remember how she felt when he asked her to do it. She only knew that she had said 'yes.' Now, facing a similar prospect, she was torn. She already loved these people, and if doing her other job more frequently allowed them to live safe, happy lives, why wouldn't she do it? She could picture Sydney and Maddy joining her, and that also tore her in two. Still, she felt like she was made to live in a community, not hidden alone in an apartment by herself.

"I guess I could try," Jenny said.

"That seems like a complicated idea that I'm not sure I'm comfortable with," Nate said. "For a lot of reasons. So, let's try to keep our jobs and our apartments. I think Maddy's plan is a good one. Let the cops know you're there, make sure everything is super locked up, and—"

"And I can get one of my mom's guns," Maddy said, shrugging. "She's got five."

Jenny pictured Maddy shooting it out with the two men with shotguns. It made her stomach tumble.

"I don't love this," Jenny said.

"Me either, but the world isn't going to stop for us," Nate said.

67
Night

Saturday, October 4, 2025 - Night

JENNY'S EYES SNAPPED OPEN. She was shivering. Where was she? A nearly full moon shone directly overhead, and she checked her watch. 10:08.

Where the hell am I? What am I doing here?

She turned around. She was in the backyard, perhaps twenty feet from the back door. Lights peeked through the cracks in drawn curtains. She reached into the back pocket of her jeans and pulled out her phone.

A text alert bubbled up.

Headlights flashed across the backyard as someone turned onto the street. Jenny unlocked the phone. A message from her JustBuffs page popped up, and she clicked on it. Someone was offering her $50 for pictures of her feet. Jenny thought how strangely disjointed the message was with her current situation. She swiped the message away and clicked on the text message application.

A message from an unknown number appeared in her list of text messages. It read 'here.' Jenny clicked on it.

> **_Jenny_**
> Do you know where I am?

> **_Unknown Number_**
> Yes, found it in the system.

> **_Jenny_**
> Then come now, it's time.

> **_Unknown Number_**
> Half hour away.

> **_Unknown Number_**
> Here.

Jenny felt the beginning of a word form in the back of her throat, but she never learned what she was going to say. A scream erupted from the house and was immediately cut off by one thunderclap, and then another. More screams. Shouting. Nate, Maddy, Sydney. Thunderclap. Thunderclap. Screaming. Thunder. Screaming. Jenny stared in horror as the back door opened, someone stumbling out, framed by light. Three steps later, Jenny recognized Sydney sprinting away from the door.

"Run!" she screamed. "Run!"

Jenny didn't run; she froze. Her mind was slow, trying to catch up.

A short, wide figure stepped into the doorway behind Sydney. Jenny's mouth opened, and again the thunder rolled. Jenny watched Sydney sprawl and slide face down across the grass, coming to a halt several feet from her. Jenny screamed. She ran to the still shape of her friend. Glass broke somewhere a million miles away. Silence. Glass, thunder, glass. A man shouted, not Nate.

"Back here! Hurry!"

Two broad figures, one much taller than the other, stalked toward her, long shadows cradled in their arms. Jenny thought about running, but she couldn't move. She screamed and cradled Sydney's head as they came into view.

"Oh God," Phil said.

"Shut up and hurry, she spent herself contacting us," Emmet said, handing his shotgun off to Phil. He knelt down next to Jenny and held something up in front of her. "Put this on or I'll break your fucking jaw." Jenny blinked at him. He let the item unfurl from his clenched hand, and somewhere in Jenny's mind it registered as the sweater Barry had given her. He forced each of her limp hands through the sleeves. The world swam as Emmet reached down and took a huge clump of Jenny's hair in his hand.

"That should do it. Come on," he said. "Move." He waved a clenched fist in front of her.

"Stop it," Phil said. "God, what are you doing? What happened to just—"

"Shut the fuck up," Emmet said. "Help me get her into the fucking car. Hey, are you in there?" Emmet said, pulling Jenny's face close to his. "Are you in there, Shepherd? Get the fuck out here. Get the fuck out here now and help us."

"What are you doing?" a weak voice said. Jenny's eyes flicked to find Leddy standing, shaking beside Phil. She was crying, and blood covered her hands and face. "You killed them," she said.

"What is wrong with you two?" Emmet said. "Get her the fuck up now, or we'll all be dead too."

Emmet dragged her to their waiting car and threw her in the back. Phil got in next to Jenny as she curled up on the seat. Her mind rolled, and her head throbbed. Emmet slammed on the gas, and they sped away, weaving out of town with the headlights off.

"Shepherd, we need you," he shouted from the front seat. "Help us or we're fucked!"

The world slipped away as Jenny heard her mouth form the words, "I'm here."

68
In and Out

Saturday, October 4, 2025 - Night

"I DON'T THINK ANYONE'S behind us," Phil said, looking back over the seat. "Just park over there."

Jenny rubbed her eyes and her mouth. The image of Sydney's body on the grass flared in her mind, and she hugged her knees to her chest and sobbed.

"She's awake again," Leddy said from the front passenger seat.

"Good, I want to spend as little fucking time around that thing as I have to," Emmet said. "Help me get her up."

The car stopped, and Emmet turned the ignition off. Out the front door and in the back he went. Once more, he grabbed Jenny by the hair. He yanked and dragged her kicking out of the car.

"What are you fucking doing?" Phil said, hurrying around the side of the car. "Stop it, she's not doing anything."

"Do you not understand what's in there?" Emmet said, jamming his finger into Jenny's face. "None of this is right. Do you know how fucking dangerous that thing inside her is? We have to go now. Now. I mean now!"

He started dragging Jenny away from the car as she stumbled to try to keep up. She could hear roaring ahead of her, and her feet scrabbled on a stone path. An arm, strong and gentle, wrapped around her middle.

"Stop, I have her," Phil said.

"Fine, but don't fucking dawdle," Emmet said. "Come on, we need to get her up the path."

Jenny gaped up at Phil, whose face was a mask of horror.

"I'm sorry, I'm so fucking sorry," he whispered. "No one was supposed to get hurt; we made sure of that. I'm sorry, Jenny. Oh God, oh God, oh God."

"Shut the fuck up, and hurry," Emmet said.

"Why?" Leddy demanded, coming up to Jenny's other side. She put Jenny's arm around her shoulder. "Why Emmet?"

"Because your weak ass Blue Flame way of doing things has gotten us fucking nowhere for two hundred years," Emmet said.

"What the fuck are you talking about?" Leddy demanded.

"Come on, over the rocks," Emmette snarled.

Jenny was handed from one person to the next over slick stones as the waterfall thundered down next to her.

"This isn't right," Phil said as Emmet took hold of her arm and helped her over a mossy rock. "We didn't … this isn't what we believe in."

Emmet propped Jenny against a wall and held her there, his big hand against her chest. "Fine, then when we get to the top, you can tell them all how you feel. I'm sure they'll just let you walk away, right? Right?"

Jenny's head felt like something was clawing at it from the inside. "Good—" Jenny said.

"Fucking what?" Emmet said, turning to her.

She was nodding. She had no idea what she had said; the thing in her head was clawing and scratching and snuffling and snarling.

"Come on," Emmet said, dragging her up the path.

Some detached part of her confused mind told her that they were walking up next to the waterfall, but Jenny thought that was impossible. There was no path next to the waterfall. And yet, up they went in the fog of mist as the moon lingered overhead. The town started to peek above the treetops and the low rock wall that ran along the outside of the path.

"Where are we?" Phil asked.

"The gold path," Leddy said. "Didn't you know about this?"

"No," Phil said. "How did I not know this was here?"

Sharp claws cut across the inside of Jenny's eyes, and she slumped, screaming.

"God, put her down for a second," Emmet said. "Phil, throw her over your shoulder—"

Darkness took Jenny. Red shadow swirled through her mind as black lightning cut the sky of her consciousness. Three times it struck, and the world was burning. Then roaring silence swallowed everything.

She blinked. Jenny sat on the ground, cold rock pressing into the back of her neck. She wasn't sure what she was seeing. It looked like Emmet, but his head was wrong. He was peering at her sideways, his face perpendicular to his neck. And something else … what was it? His ears. They were gone.

"Fuck, fuck, fuck," Leddy was whispering as she crawled across Jenny's vision toward a handgun that lay on the dirt. "Fuck, please, just stop. Stop, we're trying to help." Jenny watched as Leddy picked up the gun and pointed it at her. "Please, don't make me do this."

"Please don't," Jenny choked.

Leddy stared at her for a long moment, and Jenny was certain that she would fire. She would fire, and the world would blink out of existence. But then, lip quivering, Leddy lowered the gun. Jenny sobbed, and a look of relief washed over Leddy's face as she tumbled onto her back and lay staring up at the sky.

"Thank God you're still in there," Leddy said.

"Where am I?" Jenny asked, frantically looking around and putting her hands to her face. Her fingers were wet and black. Her mind wanted to ask what was happening, but the words had lost all meaning to her.

"The path up to the cave," Leddy said. "Fuck. Oh, fuck me."

"Please, whatever this is, you don't have to do this. Please, Leddy, I—"

"Leddy?" Phil's voice came from Jenny's right, it was weak and pained.

"Phil," Leddy said, rolling slowly over onto her side. "You alive?"

"Yeah, holy shit, my leg though."

"Please," Jenny said. "Please, just let me go."

"I want to," Leddy said. "Give me a minute." Leddy pushed herself to her feet, groaning as she went. A gash was open in her pants from her right hip to her knee, and another across her coat from her left shoulder to her right hip. Black leggings showed through the hole in her pants, and Jenny wondered if the dark color was hiding blood, or if Leddy had gotten off easily compared to Emmet, whatever had happened to him.

"Shit, that doesn't look good," Leddy said.

Jenny turned to find Phil sitting, like her, with his back against the cliff face. His left leg was twisted and bent in three places, as if something had taken hold of his ankle and curled it up in front of him like the Wicked Witch of the East. Now it lay limp on the ground, wrong and horrific.

"You think?" Phil said, shaking with pain, cold, shock, and terror. "You've got to get her up there."

"I don't know about that," Leddy said. "You really want whatever that is to be here?"

"We've got to," Phil said.

"I'm not sure about that," Leddy said. "Emmet, what do you think? Oh, right, that fucking thing ripped his skull from his spine and turned it inside his fucking skin, Phil. And it did that to your leg. This was not what I pictured when they told me that 'the Shepherd would lead us.'"

"They'll kill you if you don't get her up there," Phil said.

"Better that they kill me than that thing does this to anyone else. I didn't agree to let a fucking werewolf loose, and I didn't sign up to kill the Talkers either. Honestly, bro, I don't think I can live with what we just did, so if we have to die right now to stop anything worse from happening, I'm happy to. Aren't you?"

Phil leveled Jenny with a steady, searching look. He nodded. Leddy gripped her gun and crawled back over to Jenny. She put the muzzle of the pistol against Jenny's temple.

"You were my friend," Leddy said, tears streaming down her face. "I love you. I'm sorry for all of this. I didn't know. I didn't, please believe me. We were just supposed to take you. But whatever's in you, I can't let it—"

The heavy thing lurched behind her eyes, and the world began to sink back.

Jenny wanted to tell her to run, but the only word that would come from her mouth was "Good—"

She didn't have a name for the kind of fear that bloomed in Leddy's eyes as the world receded and the dark thing stepped forward. But she knew, even as the darkness and the gun in Leddy's hand roared, that it would be the last time she would see Leddy alive.

69
Speaking Openly

Saturday, October 4, 2025 - Night

THE WORLD CAME STUMBLING back to Jenny in a staccato jumble of sensations. The hands under her arms, then she felt nothing. Then the dragging of her feet, followed by void. Voices murmured, silence took them, then they reasserted themselves. All was tangled, all was blurred together. The old man's voice was the first thing that made any sense.

"Why is this happening?"

"I don't know, it shouldn't be," said another voice. They were both familiar, but she couldn't place them, though they lingered just beyond her memory.

Her aching body told her that she was being carried, and then that she was being put down. Hands propped her until she was sitting upright, her legs crossed, her shoulders hunched, and her long hair hanging in front of her face. She opened her eyes, and they felt like someone had pulled them out, roughed their edges, and shoved them back in without any concern for their placement. Light flared, shadows swam, and anything beyond a few feet was a blur. She blinked, squeezed her eyes, and blinked again. She could see her hands, slick black-red in blue-tinged electric light, resting on her knees, palms up, as if she were meditating.

"She's been tampered with," a woman said. This voice was immediately familiar: Isabella. "I don't know how, but she's been tampered with."

"Why would that matter? She wore it; shouldn't that be enough?" The familiar, but unidentified, voice again.

"No," yet another voice. Barry? Was that Barry's voice? "This isn't the normal process. Honestly, no one has ever succeeded at this before."

Jenny blinked again, trying to focus. Slowly, the disparate blurs in her vision coalesced into a small crowd of people standing before her in … what was this? A cave? Was she in a cave?

Flood lights stood on tripods, filling the room with an electric glow.

"She's awake," Isabella said.

Jenny struggled to process what she was seeing. A half-dozen people crowded around, watching her. They were divided into two equal groups by a small trench cut into the floor that ran just to Jenny's right. She glanced down into it and saw clear water running along smooth stone.

She traced its path up toward a wooden door which stood open behind the crowd in the cave's stone wall.

A sound behind her turned her head. Jenny wasn't sure which ethereal substance surprise was made out of, but she figured she would have run out of the stuff by now. She was wrong. Her eyes grew wide as she took in a figure that sat cross-legged, eyes closed, head down behind her.

She tried to say Carson's name. Instead, she just said, "Good."

The boy sat next to the little canal before an open iron door. Through the door, she could see a small, brightly lit room. Between Jenny and Carson sat a low stone bench upon which she saw three items: a small tube of metal that seemed to have figures or letters etched into the side, a longer, smooth rod of reddish metal, and a dark wooden box. Jenny turned back to the crowd. Her vision was clearer now, and she recognized almost everyone. She was too broken and too confused to be surprised to see any of them. Mr. Grossman stood in the middle next to Barry and Link. Isabella stood at Barry's side with Chloe at her elbow. One man she didn't know. He had sandy blonde hair and a Van Dyke beard, and he wore khakis and a checked button-up shirt. Madly, she wondered if anyone else was there. She searched for Earl. Phil, Leddy, and Emmet had been in on whatever this was; perhaps Earl was there. She thought Earl liked her. Maybe he would help her.

You thought the rest of them liked you too, didn't you?

He had cried when the girls died in Enterprise. He had a kind heart. She wondered where he was. As her vision improved, she noticed a seventh person standing behind the rest. He was short, broad-shouldered, and bearded. He reminded her of Emmet, but older. She pictured Emmet's broken body and wanted to throw up.

Mr. Grossman stepped forward and crouched in front of her. His ancient knees cracked as he held his cane beside him and lifted her chin with his free hand.

"Shepherd, are you in there?" He asked. "Can you hear me? Shepherd, your people await your power. Lead us. Begin the ceremony. Lead your people to the knowledge of the great Librarian. Lead us into his wisdom and accept this shelter as your new home. Call your master and let him accept this offering of this bound one."

Images rushed through Jenny's mind. She wanted to vomit and tear her eyes out. She wanted to rip her flesh in half. Her mind was thrown back as the lurching thing moved forward again, wheezing and struggling, it seemed, under some great burden. It slumped forward, but instead of pushing her aside, it gripped her, pressing its milky eyes to hers.

It spoke once more.

"Good. Good. Good."

55
Waking

Tuesday, September 30, 2025 – Early Evening

THE SHEPHERD WOKE TO find two women spooning next to it. One of them, a pixie-like creature with red hair, had her hand on its new arm. The Shepherd slid out as gently as it could and watched the girl's lips work as if she were tasting something sour.

The Shepherd snuck to the door and raised its hand in the imitation of a benediction. It willed sleep over them and found little resistance. Fatigue and shock weighed them down, and the Shepherd knew they would sleep until it wanted them to wake. It could move freely. It consulted the woman's watch. It was 7:56. Technically, there was no limit to its time, but a familiar desire ached within, too powerful to ignore. Besides, questions needed answering. Did this woman have the answers it sought? It searched her mind and, yes, there was something that hadn't been there before. Some new space with new memories. It didn't know what this new region in the woman's mind was, but it was soft and permeable. The Shepherd dug the long nails of its will in and pulled the soft region of the woman's mind open. Oh yes, here was knowledge—so much knowledge! It sifted the pain and memory until it found what it was searching for.

Of course.

They had been here the whole time.

The Shepherd left the apartment and hurried silently down the hall to the basement door. It took the steps two at a time, pulling the light on as it passed. It grabbed a hammer and a long screwdriver from a toolbox on the shelves and went to a place in the basement wall. Its fingers traced the mortar around a stone. It had been perfectly done. Nothing stood out to mark it out against the rest of the wall. But the pocket of sorrow and memory knew better.

The Shepherd hammered the flat point of the screwdriver into the old masonry five, ten, twenty times. It chiseled away until the stone was free. Then it dug its fingers into the cool wall and pulled, leaving a hole which held a parcel wrapped in dark brown paper. It drew the package forth and felt the waxy surface slide under its fingers. They had been here the whole time. The Shepherd hugged its prize to its chest and breathed deeply the scents of mildew, earth, and laundry soap. Then it returned to the apartment and put the brown paper parcel on the coffee table.

It snuck back into the bedroom and gathered clothes from the dresser. Then back into the hall and into the bathroom it slipped. It turned the water on to shower what felt like a week's worth of sweat from its body. It took time to shave, exfoliate, wash, and condition, and, afterward, to blow-dry its hair. It put on its clothes slowly, savoring each step. It had been too long since it had enjoyed any of these pleasures, or any pleasures, for that matter.

Sorrow throbbed in the back of its mind, but it was secondary to its need to deliver the package and then go to the cabin. Something unexpected had delayed the process, but that was all right. Things were back on track. It wiped at the fog on the mirror, and the woman's eyes stared back at it. It liked this body, unfamiliar as it was, and wanted to stay here. It just had to stick around long enough to settle in. It also needed to snip a few more of the woman's links to the world. Many had been shorn, some by the Shepherd's people, some by others. But the woman had made new connections, and that would make things more difficult.

The Shepherd would have to unmake those tethers. And then … then they had to complete whatever the last step of the ritual was. It didn't know. No one seemed to know. But that was all right. When the door was opened and the master claimed his prize, they would all learn. Then the Shepherd's master would complete the ritual, and this body would no longer belong to the woman.

Confident in its eventual success, the Shepherd left the apartment quietly, locking up behind itself. It could feel the world; the trees, the birds, the small animals that ran and swam, and the bugs that burrowed, crawled, and flitted from place to place in the late afternoon sky. The world hummed with life and change. Change. Actual change. Eons had passed since the Shepherd had known real change; eons since the calamity that had befallen them in Weeping Cedars.

It paused. Above, a branch hung from a tree, ready to fall. It willed it to break and leave its home forever, never to hang there again. It remained in place even as the breeze tugged at its needles.

Fall, the Shepherd thought. It remained. *Fall*, it thought again, but this time its spirit went into the word and shaped it into a command. The branch swung as if struck by a stone. It twisted and snapped free, tumbling to the earth. The Shepherd knelt, picked it up, and stared at the broken wood. It gazed up at the place where it had been. The broken stub remained; the branch in its hand had not disappeared to reaffix itself to the tree. *Wonderful*, it thought. It drew the needles to its nose and breathed in vanilla and smiled.

The woman's hand dropped the branch. Hungry. It was hungry. It pulled out the woman's phone and searched her mind for the unlock code. Then it searched her mind for somewhere to get food. The Shepherd placed an order from the sandwich shop. The idea of walking in and ordering in person was appealing, but the Shepherd didn't trust the body's voice yet. Soon, however. Soon, it would speak. It longed to speak.

Order placed, it sent a text to the number under the name 'Barry' and started back toward Main Street with the wax-paper parcel under its arm. When the reply text came, it read the words, memorized them, and then deleted both messages. It didn't know how long it would stay in the body this time. It hoped to remain permanently, but the woman had unexpectedly forced it out the last time, or at least mostly out. The Shepherd had been able to cling to a little shred of her mind. But it suspected that this was because the woman wasn't aware of its presence. So, it was better to be safe.

It took a right onto the street by the apartments where the servant lived. It could sense the woman there, hoping, longing, praying that all would go as planned. She stank of desperation. It could sense the other one with her less distinctly. The Shepherd could feel the strange strands of hunger and desire that moved among the three of them—its shelter and the two women in the apartment. Nothing appealed to it less than the coupling of bodies now. Once, it had had some interest, but now there were so many greater pleasures.

The woman's body walked to the address in its mind and put the package on the doorstep. It pushed the doorbell, hearing it ring and remembering what doorbells sounded like. Then it walked across the street and hid itself in the shadow of a tall hedge. The door opened, and the old man appeared. It watched him crouch down and pick the parcel up. Even from across the street, it could see the nervous trembling in his hands. It was happy for him. A fellow servant, especially one as devoted as he, deserved some satisfaction for his work.

Then, once the door was closed, the Shepherd returned to Main Street to get its food. In the back of its mind, the pain throbbed. Fists beat against the mental cage. The girl was waking up. Jennifer. That was her name. No, not Jennifer. Jenny. Jenny. A simple name. Jenny and the Shepherd would have to come to an understanding. Either the person-shaped pain called Jenny would submit, or the Shepherd would snap her like a dry twig.

It could snap her now; the Shepherd had that power. Its master had given that. It could snuff out this woman inside, but this early, and with so many links to the world remaining, the damage would be extensive. The body might become unusable, and where would that leave the Shepherd? Back in darkness again, and unable to complete its task.

But the longer it remained, and the more of those threads they cut, the easier it would be for it to snuff the tiny light. So, it let Jenny batter the bars of her cage. The clanging didn't bother the Shepherd much.

It got to the sandwich shop, Sharko's (a ridiculous name), bought its food, and started for the cabin. A drop of rain struck the Shepherd on the head, and it smiled. The rain grew steadier as the woman's body started up the forest path to the cabin. It fumbled with the keys for a moment, unlocked the door, and stepped out of the growing storm. The Shepherd took a deep breath and could smell the electronics. Its desire grew. It locked the door, dropped the food on the couch, and walked into the broadcast room.

Ecstasy rolled over the woman's body, tingling up her legs, arms, and neck. The Shepherd let the layout of the room sink in before it stepped in and started flipping switches and pushing buttons. Moments later, the board glowed and blinked wonderfully. It checked the woman's watch. It was 8:46. Perfect. It could begin at any time.

The Shepherd decided to sit and eat first. It wouldn't be right to eat while it was talking into the microphone, and the Shepherd hadn't eaten food in countless ages. It sat at the desk and slowly devoured the Cuban sandwich, chips, and soda. The food was delicious, and the Shepherd took its time, savoring every bite. Soon, this would be the norm again, and it would invariably forget the dull monotony of perpetual, changeless fasting. Until that normality came, however, the Shepherd would savor the novelty of food that remained eaten after a person bit into it.

The Shepherd finished its meal and crumpled the trash together, enjoying the feeling of paper under its fingers. Here, too, was a chance to take one's time. To truly anticipate a moment that would come and then pass away. Here was a chance to linger in a place where time did not.

Time.

    Time like …

        Time like water.

            Time like a river flowed around the Shepherd.

                This moment came and would not come again.

                    Time did not linger there.

The Shepherd saw the unchanging towers of the city and thought of the mighty ones there who wrested from that cursed place the power that eluded so many. The Shepherd thought of how its master had granted to it some of his might, so that his servant might not be as endlessly frozen as the many threadbare souls that wandered clockwork in their madness. The Shepherd, lingering on the brink of a different breed of madness, breathed in a breath that could never be breathed again.

The Librarian's servant tasted the flow of time and lingered. Here was one of the many pleasures that only time afforded. One could stand on the precipice of the moment. One could look forward to that which was not yet and savor the anticipation. But indeed, the culmination was in the action, and to linger too long was to lose the pleasure. Letting out that one, unrepeatable breath, it reached out with its mind to the town and felt it throbbing with life. It felt the 2,000 souls within it, and a plan formed. It could, with one simple action, cut every last thread the woman had. There would even be a bonus. The hated thief was among them. If the Shepherd could sever the woman's connections and deliver the hated thief … Yes, that would please its Master immensely.

Its mind extended back to the house, and the Shepherd bid the two women wake. It felt for the thief, the wounded man, and the intelligent man. It saw them, felt them, and knew them. The Shepherd smiled. Yes, this plan would work. It drew in another singular breath, opened its mouth, and pushed the button.

For a moment, the Shepherd forgot its name. It had been so long since it had used it. But then it all flowed back.

Like riding a bike, it thought.

It … No.

Not it.

She.

She spoke.

"Good evening, Night Owls. This is Lightning Falls Radio. I'm your host, Emma Barnes, and have I got a show for you tonight."

56
News

Tuesday, September 30, 2025 — Evening

"I'VE GOT SOME NEWS, some gossip, and maybe even a trivia question if you're up for it. But first, let's make sure that just the loyal fans are listening. So, if you're not a loyal fan, if you're not part of the old guard, turn those radios off. Why? Well, maybe the baby is crying, or you forgot your laundry. Oh, do you remember what they did? You know, the person you live with, that thing they did that got under your skin? How about you bring that up now?"

The Shepherd felt the power go out of her through her voice. She could feel the radios clicking off, the idle, innocent comments slipping from the lips of lovers, friends, and relatives. She felt the town vibrating under her command.

"Okay, as Tommy James said, 'I think we're alone now.' And folks, I have to say how good it is to be back. I've been … away … it's safe to say, and I have missed so many shows. So, tonight, and maybe every night after, I'm going to go long. I don't have Tyson's Aural Theater here to follow me like in the old days, so maybe we can get something like that going soon. I'm sure there has to be an aspiring author out there who would love to try their hand at writing a radio show, right? I mean, aren't podcasts all the rage?

"Or are they? Maybe that's changed. It's been a while. I'll be honest, it's been a long time for me, and old Emma has been through a lot. Now, I realize that some of you might not know me. Some of you might be confused. That's okay. We're going to get to know each other. I'm not a very public person, but I guess it's okay for me to tell you a little about my journey.

"I used to work at a radio station in a small town in New York. Then, things happened in my town. A lot of things. Terrible things. Impossible things. Or at least so I thought. Someone I cared for was killed in front of me, which, I admit, was horrific at the time, but it's actually come in handy recently. Nothing helps you bond with someone better than a little common trauma, right?

"So, anyway, my friend was literally torn in half in front of me, and I was … hurt. Badly. I was taken to the hospital, but I didn't stay there. Well, not my … I don't know, essence? Spirit? I don't want to get controversial or take a stand on religion, or whatever, so what I'll say is that I was both there, in the hospital, and not. I was somewhere else. A new radio station, which I enjoyed as far as that went.

"Those were strange days. Strange days when I worked for my new boss. And then, well, he was also killed. That was bad. A lot of people died. I was left directionless, and, yeah, well, suffice it to say, folks, those were some pretty rough days for poor Emma. I had to deal with this worm of a producer. That was a toxic relationship if ever there was one. Oh, and the constant darkness! Wow. I was there for … Well, time doesn't work quite the same way there, so let me just say that it was a long, long, extraordinarily long time. Heck, I bet if you went there now, you might even hear me on the radio today if you tune in to the right channel. Wait! Am I bicoastal? All by myself? I … I don't know. You might be wondering right now if your faithful radio host lost her mind a little. I mean, sure, I did. How could you not, you know? No food, no sleep, no water, no anything but a twisting, churning, nightmare town.

"But I've always tried to look on the bright side of things. I met some interesting people; some stayed, some moved on. I dealt with the worm-man and went solo for a while. And that was when I caught the attention of … let's call him 'upper management.' He took a liking to me. And he had an opening. So, I left my small town and went to the big city. A tale as old as time. But folks, boy oh boy, let me tell you, this country mouse was not ready for that metropolis.

"I can't explain what it's like there. I can't explain what it's like to be turned into something … more. But I am able to tell you that it's good to be back. Good to be in a body again, to be breathing, eating, drinking, walking, and talking! Oh, I think this is a good chance to plug my new favorite eatery in town."

She shook a piece of paper and held it out in front of her.

"Hey, are you always on the move? Do you feel like you're always swimming and can't slow down? I bet that really churns up a hunger inside you! I know it does me! So, when you're feeling like you could just chomp down a whole footlong, head on over to Sharko's Sandwiches next to Red's Grocery Store on Central and Main. They've got everything from turkey to tuna, roast beef to BLTs, and Reubens to Cubans, everything you could want for your ocean-sized hunger. So, swim on down to Sharko's and get yourself a bite. It's sea-licious!

"Ugh, dear listener, this makes me long for the old days, when I could throw to Clarence and ask him to tell everyone about the town gossip. You know, I never appreciated his approach back then. But gossip is important, you know? It not only tells you about the things that aren't exactly newsworthy, but also about the people doing the gossiping.

What do they care about? What do they judge? Who do they think is good and bad?

"I didn't get that back then. I wish I had. It would have let me connect the dots a little better. And you know what, connection is such an important thing. It binds us to our community. So, you know, if you're not connected, you can slip away all the easier! And for most of us, that would be a bad thing. But, and I don't mean to be heartless, for some people, slipping away would be easier, wouldn't it? I mean, when someone carries so much pain with them, helping them move along would be a mercy. So, with that in mind, why don't we try something new? Let's play a game I like to call 'Cut the Strings!' I'm just going to send a few text messages. And ... there we go. Let's see how fast everyone can get here.

"Until then, let's play one of my favorites. How about some Bessie Smith, folks? Have you heard her yet? They call her the 'Empress of Jazz.' I just can't get enough."

57
A Dark Room

Tuesday, September 30, 2025 — Night

JENNY'S EYES FELT LIKE they were glued shut. Her body felt like nothing more than meat, weighed down by fatigue like she had never known. A wheezing beside her made her think of a ventilator. Every few seconds, something soft and distant beeped. Someone was lying behind her, their arm draped over her hip.

I'm in a hospital bed. And I'm not alone, she thought.

Gently, fingertips touched her cheek. They weren't from whoever was behind her; the direction was wrong. Someone else was there, standing beside her bed.

"Get up, darling," a woman said.

"I can't," Jenny croaked. "I can't open my eyes."

"You need to get up, or things are going to go pear-shaped for us both."

Jenny tried, but her eyes remained stubbornly closed. The picture of Delia suspended from fishing wire flashed in her mind, and she rolled in pain, bumping against the soft body next to her. The fingers on her cheek slid to her chin and cupped it lovingly.

Jenny fell back into a restless slumber until she was woken once more by a voice speaking over a tinny speaker-box. Her eyes gummed open slowly, crust cracking and falling away. The dim blue light of Hollywood nighttime painted the blurry shapes of curtains, chairs, a closet, and a woman standing before her in a sequin-threaded dress. At the woman's neck was a necklace. Her necklace. The one Delia had given Jenny. She tried to lift a hand to wipe her eyes, but her body wouldn't move.

"What's happening?" Jenny asked. "Am I dying?"

"Not yet," the woman said. "But soon, if you don't do something."

"Help me," Jenny said.

"I want to," the other woman said, pulling up a chair and sitting down in it. "But right now, someone's sitting in my chair." She glanced down at the seat she had just taken and smiled. "Not this one. Though, I guess she'll be sitting here too soon enough if you don't rally."

Jenny found breathing difficult. Her back ached, her legs and arms throbbed, and her chest felt like someone was sitting on it.

"Help me, please," Jenny said.

"Like I said," the woman said, taking a cigarette from a silver case, "I want to. But you're in the pilot's seat, for now, at least. Now, if I have it my way, you'll stay at the wheel, and I'll sit in the back most of the time. But her ..." Here she pointed to the form that lay next to Jenny. "She wants it all, and she'll get it too if you don't stop her."

"I don't understand." Jenny's hand twitched as she tried to pull it up to her face. She pictured it rising and moving with its normal ease to clear her vision. It shifted, but only an inch. She closed and opened her eyelids, trying to press away some of the gunk.

"I know," the woman said. "So, let's start with who you are. You're the dead girl who came back."

"What?"

"That's right. They killed you and brought you back, right?" the woman said.

"Joseph did," Jenny said. Her arm moved another inch. The woman, who was coming slightly more into focus, curved her bright red lips into a smile. "Joseph killed me. He killed Aurora, too, and Nolan."

"It's a shame about Nolan; I would have liked to have gotten to know him. Still, if—" she paused for a moment, "Joseph hadn't done that, I wouldn't be here. I wondered if I'd be having this conversation with a man or a woman. I'm glad he picked you instead of your beau. I don't think I could cross swords with another man, and I don't have much of your taste for the fairer sex. Don't misunderstand me, I've dabbled, but there's nothing like a man."

"Who are you?" Jenny asked, her fingers bumping against her lip.

"Your new best friend, provided we get out of here alive."

Jenny's fingers finally brushed her eyelid. Had she been sick? The skin was crusted over as if she had had some kind of infection. She rubbed lightly at first, but as her fingers found their strength and dexterity again, she rubbed more vigorously. Soon she was blinking freely, both hands working at her face, brushing away sleep, and digging out its last remnants. Her vision took a moment to focus. Then the woman in the chair finally came into full view.

"I know you," Jenny said, trying to push herself up.

"And I know you," the woman said.

"You're ... Tabitha," Jenny said.

"Aren't we all?" the woman said. "And it's Tabby."

Jenny tried to prop herself up, failed, and then tried again. She succeeded the second time and pushed herself back into her pillows. She stared down at the person next to her. A young woman lay with her bloodshot eyes wide open, her pale skin in a sheen of fever sweat. Her hair, a dirty blonde streaked with gray, lay splayed on her pillow. Gauze wrapped her body up to her neck, and over it in places, something heavier—like burlap—lay. She looked like the beginning of a mummy. That troubled Jenny, but not as much as the device inserted into the woman's mouth: a microphone lodged between her teeth. The back of it connected to a cable that hung drooping from a hook in the ceiling. The cord sagged away and then rose again to another hook and continued in slack arcs that disappeared out the door. The cable dripped with a black oil that pattered every few seconds down onto the bed and the strips of cloth that wrapped the woman.

"Who is she?"

"A slave," Tabby said. "She isn't important. Well, she is—but only until we get rid of her. And we have to, otherwise, we're both goners."

"Why is this happening? How is this happening?" Jenny asked.

"That is a very long story," the woman said. "Right now, I need you to make a choice. I need you to decide between us."

"Between you and her?" Jenny asked, glancing back and forth between them. "What does that even mean? I'm so confused."

"I know," the woman said. "And I wish I had time to give you the ins and outs right now, but I don't."

"I don't want to choose anything. I want whatever this is to be over," Jenny said.

"I know that too," she said. "But that's not an option. If you don't pick, she picks for you, and it really will be all over, just not the way you want."

Jenny shook her head. Could she believe this person? Could she believe anything? None of this could be real.

"What kind of choice is that? Who would choose her?" Jenny said, turning so that her legs hung over the side.

"Someone who wanted to disappear. Someone who wanted the pain to go away. She can make that happen. I can't. I'm here for the long haul, emphasis on 'long.' You pick her, you don't have to carry the weight of Aurora, and Nolan, and Delia. You can let it all go. You can blink out into whatever it is that comes after all this. But if you pick me, well, I can't promise you happiness, but I can promise that you'll see and do things you never dreamed were possible. And"—here the woman leaned forward and winked,—"you'll have the family you've been searching for so badly. A mama and a papa, and sisters and brothers, and you and me, we can trade off who we take to bed at night. I don't mind a little sapphic sojourn, even if it isn't my style. And I know you won't object to my tastes." She sat back and drew on her cigarette.

Jenny tried to process everything and failed. She tried to process even just one thing, but she failed at that, too. None of what the woman said made any sense to her. But when she considered the half-wrapped figure in the bed, her choice seemed clear. The lying woman's blank stare, the metal jammed between her broken teeth, and the stillness of her body were all monstrous. But if Tabby was right, Jenny could choose the mummy-woman, whatever that meant, and could finally be at peace and die. No more insanity, no more broken mind, no more reminders of the horrors she had seen and suffered. She could forget the darkness under the water and simply slip away.

She could do that. Maybe she even wanted to do that. She reached over and touched the woman's cold arm. She was dead. Jenny leaned down toward her and listened. The breathing sound was coming from the microphone, as if it somehow breathed into her, and she back into it. Or … no. No, the woman wasn't breathing back into the microphone. It was just playing the sound. Wheezing in, gasping out. Just the sounds. But that didn't make sense. That's not what microphones were supposed to do.

"They'll die too," Tabby said.

"Who?" Jenny asked, her finger tracing the line of the woman's arm up to her shoulder, where the black oil soaked the cloth strips.

"Your friends. Sydney, Maddy, Charles, Nate, and the other one."

"What?" She snapped around.

"Yes, they will die. She is calling your friends to her. And she's calling her friends too. Everyone you have left is going to die at the cabin door. They don't have weapons; they won't be able to fight. They'll just fall in a pile with their brains on the ground or their guts in the pine trees. If you die, so do they."

Jenny pictured Sydney lying on the ground and wanted to throw up. What was she supposed to do with that?

"You can save them?" Jenny asked.

"We can save them. It's as simple as unlocking a door and waiting for the police. But she won't do that. He won't let her."

"Who won't let her?" Jenny asked, exasperated. She felt stupid, like a child who was put in a class too advanced for them with no preparation.

"The Man in the Robe. The Rebellious Pupil. The Eater of Knowledge. She serves him, and he won't let her open the door," the woman said.

"I don't understand any of that," Jenny said.

"I know. But you will. If you choose me, you will. You'll understand it all. And you'll understand why Joseph did what he had to do. And we'll understand why Peter did what he had to do."

"Who is Peter?"

Tabby smiled. "You'll understand that too."

"Okay, okay, it doesn't matter, I choose you. If it will save them, I choose you."

Tabby's smile grew. "Really?"

"Yes, I choose you. I choose you so I can save them. I choose you so they don't die. So, Sydney and Maddy and Charles and Nate and … and …"

"The other one," the woman said.

"Why can't I remember their name?"

"Because they are hidden from us. They have walked where we hope to walk. They have touched fire immortal. Now, stand up and choose me."

Jenny pushed herself to her feet, her legs gave way, and she fell back down. The world shook. A scream, long and high, peeled out from the body on the bed. In its horror, Jenny recognized her own voice. It looped into itself, and the whine of feedback tore through the room. It felt like a promise of things to come.

Jenny clamped her mouth shut, pushed herself back up on wavering legs, and spoke.

"I choose you."

"Say it louder," the woman said.

"I choose you. I choose you. I don't want her. I want you."

The shade of one of the windows flew up. Green, scorching light blazed in and lit the figure on the bed aflame. Like a vampire before the sun, she burned and writhed.

"Now take that from her mouth," Tabby said, pointing at the microphone. "Take it, and, at least for the moment, we'll be free. Do it now, and then be ready. Time lingers not in this place."

58
Withdrawal

Tuesday, September 30, 2025 — Evening

EMMA FELT THE VOICES in her head and tried to ignore them. That was easy enough at first. They were faint, and she could focus on the music. Under the sway of the rhythm, she contemplated her mission. Her position was tenuous. The woman still had too many connections to the world, and Emma had too few. But in a few minutes, one of those barriers would be removed. Her predecessor hadn't had this difficulty. He arrived in power, and the body he took hadn't been meant for his permanent residence. He had also been ancient and mighty. Though in the end, she mused, he had his own, different vulnerabilities. Emma was not yet as mighty as her predecessor, but she would get stronger. There were two true things that she had learned from her new master: the first was that one must accumulate power to have it; the second was that there are far more kinds of power than she had ever dreamed.

Right now, Emma was using her most natural power, her voice. She turned off the music.

"Everyone, I know that up until now, things haven't quite gone according to plan. I was supposed to be here sooner, but … well, there's no blueprint for this exact thing. So, we're playing it by ear. Still, here I am with a little time to spare. Now, even though we're not getting me in under the wire, there isn't really enough time for me to get situated the way we wanted, so I've got to improvise and speed things along." A text popped up on the woman's phone. Emma answered it. Then another appeared, and she answered that. "Hopefully, we can get ourselves back on track in a few minutes. And let's try to make sure we don't find any more puppets in the cupboard, all right?"

She could feel that no one but the faithful were listening. But the voices in her mind kept growing louder, and she could almost make out what they were saying. She was confused. Why was there more than one voice? She thought she recognized the woman, but who was the other? She searched for the meaning of that second voice, but a knock at the cabin door interrupted her.

"Oh, well, sounds like our first guests have arrived."

Text bubbles popped up on the phone. More knocks. People called Jenny's name.

"Let's see if I timed this right—"

She sent a text message to the faithful ones who would deal with the woman's friends, deleted it, and then immediately dropped the phone. A cacophony of pain stormed through Emma's head, pounding, thrumming, drumming, bashing. She yanked her headphones off, and the ringing in her ears was suddenly deafening. What was happening in her head? Was the body having some kind of seizure or stroke? She'd never experienced anything like it. The worst she'd ever felt was the cold, slithering grip of her predecessor lifting her from her chair and reaching down into her mouth, his twisted, sharp, knobby fingers cracking down into the muscle, cartilage, and soft tissue of her throat and turning. His fingers had made soft, low, wet sounds as Emma heard herself grunt little 'o's' and 'u's' around the intrusion.

That had been a nightmare, but at least she had been in shock. The pain had been distant as she had listened to the things that happened to her. Now the pain was gargantuan, like a giant storming through her brain, smashing every nerve, yanking on every possible tendril of pain. She writhed in her seat, screaming. She pulled at her hair, clawed her face, and tried to grab her tongue to rip it out. Her hands slid down to her stomach, searching for her belly button to slip her fingers inside so she could rip herself open and let the pain unravel with her guts on the floor. She rolled from the chair. There must be a solution, there must be a way to stop the torture that opened a pit before her, promising to drop her into it without end.

Then she felt heat radiating from up on the mountain that loomed over the town. She knew immediately what it was. She had felt this kind of power before in the depths below her master's house in pits unvisited by daylight. There she had met one of the chained spirits and felt the radiating heat of its affronted pride. This was like that, only a million times hotter.

She fought it back, pushing against the heat with the force of her will. She didn't need to defeat it; she only needed a space, a little space to consider her options. She pulled the microphone close and jammed the headphones back over her ears. This is where she could be safe. She turned on the last record and let the music rise, and she thought back to a time before the darkness and constant horror.

As her mind slipped back to the leaf-blown downtown, she pictured herself: a cup of coffee in her hand, her backpack over her shoulders, and the cool of the first real sweater day of the year pleasantly caressing her cheeks. She saw herself waving to people, her eyes meeting faces she knew, and the feeling of responsibility rising in her chest.

I'm doing this for them. I'm doing this for Tom.

Emma felt safe, and the fire of the chained spirit diminished for a moment. In that momentary refuge of memory, she assessed her situation and realized that, for the present, it was hopeless. Angered, but reassured that she now understood, Emma knew what she had to do. Perhaps the men with guns would do their job, but perhaps they would not. In either case, she would return, aware of what she was up against. She would be ready when next she emerged. With one last thrust of her power, she made a space, small and hidden, in the woman's mind. She left it empty and put nothing of herself there, nothing they might detect. But it was a window through which she might slip. Of course, the moment they detected her, they might drive her out again. But if she were ready, a moment might be all she needed.

A gunshot sounded somewhere in the distance. *Too late. Too late, but I will return,* she thought. Her space prepared, the Shepherd flew from the burning fire and withdrew back into the darkness of the high tower atop the vast library of Gradludi.

70
Struggle

Saturday, October 4, 2025 - Night

JENNY DREW IN A ragged breath, her body and mind on fire. Memory, like burning metal, sliced through her. Unable to hold herself upright, she fell back, and her head hit the cave's stone floor.

"What's happening now?" Isabella demanded.

"I don't know," Grossman said. "We must trust the Shepherd."

Jenny wanted to scream, but her mouth wouldn't work. She wanted to claw at her face, but her arms wouldn't move except to twitch and jerk. Her legs kicked wildly as if she were trying to get out from under a heavy, clinging blanket. The thing in her mind slid its fingers into her ears, nails long and sharp pricked her eardrums, and the world became a shrill, piercing keening. It placed its thumbs over her eyes, rubbing and pressing until she could feel them ready to pop. The beast's fingers slid behind her jaw and worked her mouth open and closed again.

"Loutka," it whispered. "Obey me, Loutka. Where are your strings?"

Jenny could feel herself breaking. The thing leaned in and breathed into her mouth. The sound of its breath was loud and mechanical, as if broadcast over a bad speaker.

"My words, Loutka. Speak my words."

What words?

The world was a jumble.

Breath.

Voice.

Life.

Memory.

Power.

Power.

Power.

71
Dust

JENNY FELT HER MIND snap. It was a strangely tactile, physical feeling, though she knew her dissolution was psychic. She felt herself crumble, her mind and soul brittle like old leaves and ancient paper. A hot breeze rose through the lurching beast's consciousness, and she floated like dust across an empty space. She couldn't feel her body.

It isn't your body anymore.

The beast's voice no longer came from within, but echoed from the vast desolation about her. The void was vast and without form. Was it land? Sea? Neither of those words suited what appeared to her to be an endless undulation of smoke and ash. The thought came, if thoughts could come, that this must be her end, to drift here in screaming silence amid a formless, burning remnant. Snippets of her life flashed like lightning across the swirling ember clouds: Aurora playing the guitar, Nolan's laughter and innocent eyes, Sydney smiling up at the ceiling like a Peanuts character. Matina, Joseph, Patty, Maddy, her father—images strobed against cumulus soot and cinder.

She floated with the dust; she was dust. She could not breathe, but she released something within her like a breath, vital and sustaining. She let go, sensing the titanic terror that now possessed the body once hers. There was nothing left for her, and so she released herself and hoped, if she could hope, that she might simply fade utterly into the darkness.

But she did not fade. She drifted, lifted on eddies of burning air, longing for dissolution. As she tumbled and spun, a thin realization came to her. She would not dissolve. She would not fade away. She would linger among the desolation for eons, wandering shapeless through a shapeless darkness.

Too little of her remained to scream, but what was left turned itself toward the act of screaming until that was all she was.

A scream without a screamer knows nothing of time. Thus, she went, a howl through the flame without sense of time or change, scoured by the shadow to a mote that did not recognize the faces that flashed across the darkness. One sang. One smiled. One laughed. She spun and turned until she did not understand singing, or smiling, or laughing, and the faces were no longer faces.

She knew no words; she knew no meaning.

The dust was no longer dust, the heat no longer heat, and the darkness no longer darkness.

But though she did not understand it, the light remained light.

The darkness could not take that from her.

And there, somewhere far off, light shone. Golden and strange, like an unnatural sunrise waiting to break into a cursed day, it lingered below a line of black. Perhaps a billion, billion miles away, it brooded, something magnificent threatening to come forth. She had neither the will nor the power to move toward the light, yet the wind carried her thence, as if the dim embers were drawn to a more perfect illumination.

A ray of light touched her, reflected off the speck that remained, and in its brilliance, she grew. The brightness infused itself into her, like fire into iron, and she stretched and expanded. The ash about her swirled in sparkles of golden dawn, and she gathered them to herself. They joined and formed. Dust from the earth melded with incomprehensible fire. The storm spun about her and into her, gathering and gathering like a whirlwind collapsing in on itself until she stood upon a wide plain, her skin new and vital in the cresting dawn.

She turned to bask in the rising light.

Instead, she beheld the cave and the crowd of people. And, whole again, she felt herself moved once more into her own flesh. As she entered, the beast's mind opened to her, and Jenny understood her completely.

72
Distance

SHE BLINKED, AND THE monstrous thing blinked. She moved, and the terrible thing moved with her. She knew it now, what and who it had been. She saw with terrible clarity the woman who lurched under the hulking shape of tatters and echoes. She understood the woman's need to escape, to obey, to see light, to speak, and to leave the place of unchanging decay. Jenny could see the dark city full of ageless age, vistas of immutable disintegration, and tableaus of changeless mortification. She felt Emma's need, her longing, and her madness. But the thing wasn't just Emma Barnes. It was more.

Jenny knew that the thing, slumped and bloated in its layers of rough-spun tatters, should have consumed her by now. It was the Shepherd, herald of the Great Librarian of the Dark City. It was powerful beyond anything Jenny had ever conceived of. It should have destroyed Jenny utterly. And Jenny realized it thought it had.

As Jenny searched the Shepherd's mind, she found that the beast was unaware of her. It had dismissed her, and now, somehow, Jenny remained unseen and strong. The Shepherd raised Jenny's arm and spoke strange, contorted sounds into the cave. The hissing peaks and guttural valleys burned the air, and the lights flared.

As the words rose in pitch, speed, and power, Jenny felt another presence coalesce behind her, as if summoned by the Shepherd's words. Her mind, already unsteady, reeled at the weight of its immanence. Whatever this new thing was, it wasn't human. The Shepherd wasn't human, but it had once been. Jenny had the overwhelming impression that this new being had not. It was something other. Something intelligent, uncanny, and burning.

And it was waking.

She heard the clank of chains. She watched the people in front of her step back in almost comical unison. Almost. One stood still. Jenny felt the strange presence that the Shepherd had summoned vibrating behind her, shaking the world, blurring it so that she couldn't tell who the one remaining person was. All others fell to their knees at the thing's coming, but one who had stood their ground also kept their feet. Before Jenny's mind could catch up, the thing behind her spoke.

"Hello?" it said. The world vibrated around her with the strange, musical sound. The Shepherd within her trembled. Here was a power greater even than the Shepherd's. Here was might ancient and titanic.

One to free, one to bind, one to command.

The words came to her like thunder on the winds of the maelstrom in her mind.

One to free, one to bind, one to command.

She saw in her mind the items that lay on the stone bench behind her.

This is the ritual, a voice said. *This is the ritual.*

She knew that voice. She could picture the woman with the sun pendant. Tabby. Tabby was with her. Jenny struggled to keep up, to place the figures around her. The beast in her body, the great burning one behind her, and the woman in her mind. What were these things? What was she doing among them? She was so small, so fragile, so lost, and so broken. She wanted to run. She needed to escape, to get air, to breathe. She needed to run.

"Then run, little one." The voice was music, and it shook the cave so violently that Jenny was afraid the ceiling would collapse and crush them all. Yet none of the lights wavered, and no stands tipped. Though the word shuddered, it remained still. "Run," the voice said again.

Pained, sluggish, and disoriented, Jenny put her hands against the ground and pushed herself to her knees. The Shepherd, confused, tried to stop her, but the flame of the burning spirit drove it back. Jenny could see it, like a rising sun, forcing the Shepherd to retreat like a vampire.

"What is she doing?" Grossman shouted.

"I have no idea," Isabella said. "She's supposed to stay there!"

Jenny put one foot down, both hands on her knee, and pushed herself up. She turned toward the boy.

"Leave him," the great voice said. "Run, little one."

"That's the girl! She should be dead!" Link shouted.

"No, it has to be the Shepherd. Trust the Shepherd," Barry said.

Jenny put one foot down, then the next.

On the vast field of her mind where a star hung low in the eastern sky, the beast faced her, snarling and lunging. But white fire lit within its flesh, and it howled. Jenny walked and stumbled. The person who had not retreated from the spirit's presence caught her. They held her for a moment and then pushed her along toward the open wooden door behind the kneeling people.

"Stop her," Link said.

"Trust her," the thin man Jenny didn't recognize said. "The ritual has begun; the Shepherd is in control. We don't know every step, but we must perform our tasks or we will fail! Time lingers not in this place!"

Jenny took another step and reached the wooden door. Then she was through. She slumped against a wall just beyond the door. The beast snapped its burning, slathering jaws. Tabby stood next to her, radiant with light. Jenny reached for Tabby's hand. The woman took it and led Jenny along the wall until she came to its end. Tabby pulled her forward, and too late Jenny saw that there was nothing under Tabby's feet. Jenny stumbled forward, and the world fell out from under her.

73
The Pit

DAZED, JENNY PATTED THE floor around her, and her fingers met something rough. Because her body was already a bundle of aches, she wasn't sure if she had suffered any more injuries in her fall. It took her a moment to recognize a new pain in her temple. She felt a strange distance from herself, as if she had stepped outside of her surreal situation and stood with her arms crossed and shaking her head.

Well, this is exciting, she thought.

The thought felt incongruous, and to her horror, she realized that she felt like laughing. Had she finally gone mad? Did she find this funny? No … no, it wasn't humor, it was something else. Was it ease? Lightheartedness? Joy? Yes, joy. Relief. Like waking healthy after a long sickness. It was sunlight after endless drear. Sweet, lovely, magnificent life filled her as she held her temple and sat up, the floor crunching and scattering under her weight. Dust filled the air, and she coughed. Her lungs worked, tight though they were, and she almost used them to laugh.

It worked! It worked! It worked! It worked!

The thought spun in her head like a song sung by a child who set up a long and complex game of Mouse Trap and watched the final mechanism trigger perfectly.

Not quite the final mechanism, my love. One more step, Tabby's voice intoned in glee. *He sees so far!*

Joyful as she might be, Jenny was still overwhelmingly confused. She patted around for something, anything.

In your pocket. She slipped you something.

Jenny reached into her coat pockets and found a short, cold cylinder. The end was rubbery, and Jenny clicked it. Light bloomed from a small metal flashlight and illuminated what looked like the floor of some ancient medieval cell, littered with the bones of prisoners. Jenny shook her head, thinking that this must be one of the last stages of madness. Here she was, clearly out of her mind, badly hurt, surrounded by a skeleton, and in terrible danger, and she was singing songs in her head and wanting to skip up and down Main Street.

I want a phosphate!

What the living fuck was her brain doing?

I want—No … oh no … Paul.

Paul? Who the hell was Paul? Jenny felt a terrible need to reach out and touch the skull that lay near her. She gave in to the strange desire and traced the curve of its cheekbone.

"Alas," she said, and felt the desire to both laugh and cry.

I knew him well, the voice in her head said.

"Here hung those lips," Jenny said.

My son. My beautiful son. Thank you.

"I don't understand," Jenny cried, feeling her stomach heaving and her gorge rising.

I know. But I'm with you now. But the other one is still here, too. Look.

Jenny shook her head.

"No, it's too much. It's too much. Please make it all stop. I don't understand anything that's happening. Please. Please. Please."

Look, honey. You've got to look.

Jenny peered into her mind. Bound by searing light, the thing that had been Emma Barnes, wrapped in tatters, half beast, half mummy, burned and gibbered. Her clawed fingers groped helplessly toward Jenny and Tabby beside her. Young and beautiful, a feather in her headband, a small triumphant smile on her lips, Tabby reached down and took Jenny's hand.

Jenny looked from one to the other and back again.

"How do we … I mean, is she …?"

"No, she's not staying. She's got other places to be, don't you doggie?" Tabby said to the light-bound beast. "She's got to slink off to her master and heel."

"But how do we—"

"Look around, you'll find it. And when you do, she'll be on the next train to Nighttown, USA."

"Look around?" Jenny said, her mind contemplating the room.

"No, darling, not here, in the real world," Tabby said. "Hop to it, time does not linger in this place."

Jenny blinked the vision away and focused on the material world around her. The dust, though still thick, had started to clear. She crawled forward, her fingers scattering bones and rustling old canvas, leather, and metal. The more she moved, the cloudier the pit became as the air again darkened with the desiccated remains of a man.

Paul. He was my son. Oh God, he's just bones now.

Her fingers brushed the remains aside, feeling for anything that stood out from the gray decay of decades. Then, for a moment, she glimpsed it. As she pushed a femur, long and straight, aside, a flap of old cloth flipped and revealed a glimmer of silver. Jenny pulled at the scrap and revealed a bright disk. She reached out for it. Heat seared her fingers as they wrapped it round.

Then it tore her apart.

74
Before The Doors

EMMA'S MIND CLEARED. THE light had confused, hurt, and—she was ashamed to admit it—awed her. She had never seen light like that before. The chained spirit she had met had been nothing in comparison. Though the strange new light burned her, she longed for it. It promised knowledge and wisdom, power, and glory. It spoke to her like a father to a prodigal child. She wanted to hide from it; she wanted to run into it. It enveloped and consumed her.

When the light faded, she found herself in her studio, her hands on the back of her old chair. She peered into the booth, hoping to see Emory, but it was dark. Something moved to her left, and she turned.

The man sat in the corner, one leg crossed over the other, dressed in a suit like Mr. ... What had his name been? She couldn't remember. That was a shame. The day she interviewed for her job, he had been wearing a suit just like that one. This unfamiliar man smoked a cigarette, his shiny gray hair slicked back against his skull. He reminded her so much of her manager, and he might even have been him, except for his eyes. He had hundreds of them, all turning, moving, searching, and roving. She could feel two of them gazing directly at her, even if she couldn't pick out which ones they were. She knew who he was, and she wanted to threaten him, to promise that her master would overcome him. She wanted to fall at his feet and pledge her undying loyalty to him. She wanted to tear her own eyes out and hand them to him.

"I see far enough," he said in a voice low and long.

Somewhere, a door opened, and wind blew into the studio.

"Help me," Emma said.

"I must look to my own children," he said. "But perhaps the day will come when my light dawns anew, and even your traitorous master will come to me. I hope he does. Then, perhaps, my light will shine on you as well."

Perhaps. Emma's heart swelled at the idea. But until then, there would be horror. She had failed. The wind grew stronger.

"Please, he will destroy me."

"It would be better for you if he did," the Man with Many Eyes said. The air whipped past her, kicking up papers and flipping open folders and binders. Ads and news flapped past her face, notes of gossip in Clarence's looping cursive caught on the microphone.

"But I know him. He will not."

She knew he was right and despaired. Her master didn't destroy. She doubted that it was within even his vast power to destroy her in that place of ancient, immutable death. He would hurt her. He would take from her. Perhaps she would no longer shepherd the people. Perhaps she'd never be able to use her voice again. Perhaps she'd end up on a leather thong, led from place to place.

"But perhaps my dawn will come," the man said. "Or," he mused, his voice distant, "an even greater dawn than my own will come for us all."

For a moment, Emma saw what was in his mind. A light, tiny, and faint, hidden deep beyond the foundations of reality, surrounded by darkness on all sides. She wondered how it could last, for it was so small, and the darkness was so great. And yet …

As she contemplated the tiny light, she felt the first pieces of herself stripped away by the wind. She reached out for the man, but he only watched and smoked his cigarette as she came apart before him.

Unbroken night swallowed her. She floated like scattered sand across shadow and time, over valleys and plains, and among twilight-shrouded dunes. After time and no time, the familiar ghost-green glow of the unrisen moon tinged the sky. From the earth rose a broken skyline of blighted walls and bitter towers from which untattered pendants of immeasurable age stood outstretched and still. She approached the parapets and soared above them, peering down into the cobblestone streets of the walking embalmed. Down among them she dipped, twisting, pulled forward by the unrelenting call of Shadum, where her master dwelt. She flitted past the high Hill of Glory and its house of glass, skimming above the grasping, groping forest and the slack mouths and sightless eyes of its denizens.

She felt herself knit together in agony, as shadow, bone, cloth, and flesh gathered from the world and coalesced in protest about her cursed spirit. And when her eyes, newly formed, began to adjust, the pinnacles upon ancient flèche-adorned buttresses, high peaked roofs, and glowing stained-glass windows of the Great Library appeared atop a long stair. The great tower that stood at one end loomed over her, and the flapping of unseen winged things buffeted the air above her. The doors of the tower opened and radiated a dull red glow onto the long stair. From that portal emerged a wide figure, dark and cloaked, his robe stitched with symbols arcane and obscene. He regarded her from the shadow of his ancient hood.

For a moment, the wrapped, tattered, hulking Shepherd was gone. In its place, a shivering girl whose only dream had been to be on the radio like her hero, Tom Cole, knelt bewildered and afraid.

Then, under the eye of her dark master, Emma Barnes began to scream.

75
The New Settlement

THE EASE AND JOY in Jenny's heart swelled. The beast was gone, cast back into whatever darkness it had come from. The silver disk, which had burned, was now cool, and Jenny slid it into her pocket. Some part of Jenny felt sorry for the woman she had seen in the hospital bed. But her sympathy was a plucked string in a symphony of relief. She could also feel Tabby's overwhelming excitement beside her, pushing her forward. It reminded her of Sydney—if Sydney had been more jaded and cynical.

And alive.

She stood and shone her light around the pit. It wasn't too deep, perhaps six feet. She could reach the ledge easily. She wondered how the man whose skeleton lay at her feet had died. Had someone killed him and dumped him here? Had he broken his leg and died of thirst? She thought if she had time to examine the bones, she might make a guess, but right now, she had something to do. Tabby pushed her forward again. It was a strange sensation among a cacophony of strange sensations. She wanted to go forward, but the desire wasn't her own. She feared staying in the pit, but the fear didn't belong to her. She felt relieved, but at least some of the relief was alien.

Still, the feelings ached in her, and she obeyed them. She put her flashlight into her mouth and lifted her arms. Her hands slid along the pit's edge, feeling for somewhere she could grab hold of. She almost screamed when fingers touched hers. She pulled back. A split-second later, a face appeared above her. Jenny shook her head and pulled the flashlight from her mouth.

"Chloe?" she whispered. "What the fuck is going on?"

"Shhh," Chloe said, smiling. "Come on, you've got a job to do. Time does not linger—"

"—in this place, yeah," Jenny finished. "That's in my head for some reason. What the hell am I supposed to do?"

"I'll pull you up. Act hurt," Chloe whispered. "You're supposed to be the Shepherd."

"I am hurt," Jenny said. Her words felt wrong, inappropriately glib. But Tabby's giddy spirit kept the tumult of terror and pain back and away from her.

"Good, then you don't have to act that much," Chloe said, giving her a wink. Winking? She was winking right now? What on God's green earth was happening? Jenny felt absurd. "Turn off your light and I'll help you up."

Jenny obeyed and stuffed the flashlight into her coat pocket. She reached up for Chloe's hands in the dark, and the two of them worked together to help Jenny climb out of the pit. She collapsed on the woman, who promptly kissed her on the forehead.

"Glad you're safe," Chloe said.

"Safe?" Jenny whispered. "I'm safe?"

"Of course you are. He sees far," she almost giggled. "Come on." Chloe helped her to her feet and put her arm around her. "Now remember, you're beat up and hurt."

"Yeah, I can't forget it," Jenny said.

Please, why can't this be over? Just let me be sad. Let me hurt. My friends, oh God, my friends are dead!

Jenny thought of Gina, Nate, Maddy, and Delia. She wondered if Linds was safe in the Kusel House, or if someone had gotten to them, too. Was the broadcast room painted in Linds's blood? Jenny pictured Sydney on the grass and wanted to lie down and mourn for them. But the lightness and desire in her wouldn't leave her alone.

Mourn later, darling, right now is the time for victory.

Tabby's words purred in her ear. Her black-gloved hand rested on Jenny's shoulder, next to Chloe's. Jenny stumbled along, letting her new—Ally? Friend? Possessor?—carry her along.

"The Shepherd returns!" Chloe called. "Though she's a little bit worse for wear."

"Bring her here," Grossman said. "Let her use the last artifact."

"No," Isabella said, "that is my privilege! I've done everything I was asked! It's my right to control him!"

"We will all control him," the stocky, unfamiliar man said. "But the spell will be stronger if it comes from her. She wears his mantle; she stands for Shadum and its master. Her magic is greater than ours."

"When you get close," Chloe whispered, "you'll know what to do."

Jenny felt oddly confident that that was true. The people parted before her, and she separated herself from Chloe's guiding hand. She passed among them, her eyes forward. On the low stone table, two of the items—the box and the long rod—were pushed to the side. Only the small metal cylinder with carvings remained in its original place. Past the table, Carson Booth sat staring at her. She saw him with double vision. Here was the boy who had gone missing, his clothes clean, his face ruddy, his hair combed. Here too, dwelling within and around him was the great spirit that had shaken the world when it spoke. Behind Carson, in the brightly lit room, Jenny saw metal rings sunk into the floor.

They are empty now, Tabby said in her mind.

Jenny's eyes flitted to a spot in front of the rings, an indentation that looked darker than the rest of the stone floor. For a moment, she saw a pillar of flame burning there before a man bound to the iron rings. She blinked, and the vision was gone. Jenny swallowed and turned her gaze back to the low table and the small metal cylinder.

"Use the seal," Grossman said. "Use the seal and control him so that we can deliver him to your master! This is his prize!"

Tabby whispered in Jenny's ear and slid her long fingers along Jenny's arm, guiding her hand into her pocket to the cool silver disk.

Use it, Tabby breathed. Jenny didn't understand. *Let me then,* Tabby said. Jenny let Tabby guide her. She knelt before the table and brushed the cylinder aside to join the other objects. She withdrew the silver disk and held it out in front of her.

"Dwell here in this house of flesh, brother spirit!" Tabby cried with her voice. "Dwell here and put to flight all curses, all wards, and all boundaries against you. Come, herald He Who Sees Far!"

The boy's eyes burned a ghastly golden-green. Link cursed, Grossman cried out, and Isabella screamed, "Stop her!" But the boy turned his gaze upon them, and they were thrown down.

The green flame moved across his flesh and roared up around him, though it did not consume him. The electric lights sparked and shattered. He spoke words incomprehensible into the golden cave and rose to his feet. Jenny turned and watched in horror as terror twisted the faces of all but Chloe, whose countenance reflected back the light as she knelt with her hands raised.

The boy spoke for almost a minute in tones and scattered notes that hurt Jenny's ears. When he finished, he stepped forward and put his hand on Chole's head.

"Call him," he said in English.

Chloe gazed up at him, her eyes bright with tears. "Me?"

"Yes, faithful one. It is given to you to call him for your family's devotion across the years. Call him and rejoice."

He offered his hand, and Chloe stood. Within Jenny's mind, Tabby screamed in excitement, clawing at herself in ecstatic expectation. Jenny could see her rending her clothing and tearing at her hair. Her voice bestial, her movements primordial. Uncanny fear gripped Jenny, and her limbs began to quake.

Chloe raised her hands and tilted her head back. "Come, Father," she cried. "Come and see. Come to me now in this far place."

"More," the boy-thing said. "You know how. The words are in your mind."

Chloe wept, spread her arms wide, and called into the light. "Now comes the great Amber Dawn, unfettered and enthroned."

The people on the ground wailed and writhed before her.

"Come now, Unbound One! Come now, Unfettered One! Come now, Unchained Lord!"

Jenny watched in distant horror as Isabella dug her fingers into her face, drawing blood, and Link reached inside of his mouth to try to pull out his tongue.

"Oh, come to us, Prince of the Morning, Prince of the Air, Giver of Wisdom, Seer of Days, come, oh Lord of Harhain! Seeker of Lost Sons, Great Master of the Dawn, Unrisen Star, come to us that we might behold you!"

Morning light bloomed and transformed the cave.

Then Jenny beheld him.

Ancient and young, the Man Who is Full of Eyes sat before them on a huge stone throne. Many were his retainers, who knelt around the great seat of ancient mossy rock. They were strangely formed, semi-formed, and with forms ever changing. Faces of silver, faces of gold, and faces of amber stared at her from the dark around the enthroned one, and they twitched and jerked like puppets on strings.

Flanking the throne was one who froze Jenny's heart. Robed, his skin was pale, and the upper half of his face was smooth and eyeless. In his hand, he held a metal cage from which green flame rolled and wavered. About his feet, a great black serpent twisted in a writhing mass of worms that tumbled from his black lips.

Real, Jenny thought. *He's real.*

The fire that surrounded the boy who had been Carson Booth suddenly flared and caught his flesh and hair. Jenny tried to look away, but Tabby gripped her in firm hands, forcing her to stare as the flames consumed the youth, charring and melting him until only a pillar of fire remained. Then it stretched and towered, growing ever hotter and more violent. The flame moved forward, charring the floor, which was no longer the solid rock of the cave, but instead a mosaic of worn, hewn, moss-strewn stones. The pillar of heat and light bent before the enthroned figure.

"Receive now your kingdom, brother," the Unfettered Prince said, raising his hands. Between his outstretched fingers, a circlet of gold appeared. This he lowered onto the flame. When the circlet touched the fire, it changed and took on the form of a naked man. A crown upon his head, he straightened and stood before the throne.

"Take your seat," the One Who is Full of Eyes said. "Sit among those who will rule when true dawn comes."

Jenny stared as the man-thing rose into the darkness. No, not darkness. Jenny's eyes grew wider as she followed the figure and beheld hundreds of people seated in balconies above them. Each was naked and crowned, each was enthroned and regarded the rising figure with terrible, beautiful, dire, divine faces that stung her eyes and twisted her heart with dread. The balconies, which looked down on the throne, receded back and up into darkness. The number of crowned beings was great, but so were the vacant places among them. Indeed, far more numerous were the empty thrones. She thought that if all the seats were filled, they would perhaps hold thousands upon thousands. Jenny tilted her head back and saw a somber sky above the roofless gallery, and her mind flitted back to the dream of the mountain and the city built about the great pit.

Her attention was drawn back down, again, however, when the many-eyed one spoke, his voice like a great wind over a nightmare void, "You who have served my traitorous pupil, behold my mastery and despair."

Jenny watched as Levi Grossman threw up on himself and burst into flames. The broad-shouldered man with the beard dug his fingers into his eyes and reduced them to a horrid, bloody mess before his skin ignited. One by one, the people who lay on the ground erupted into candles of horror that writhed on the floor. All but Isabella. The woman who had bound Jenny's hands skittered backwards like a bug, screaming until her back met a wall and she could flee no further. Chloe walked to her and took her by the hands.

"It's okay," she said. "If he was going to burn you, you'd be like them." She nodded toward the writhing figures on the floor. "It's okay, get up." Trembling, Isabella blinked at her, and Jenny wondered what fate waited for her. "It's okay, get up," Chloe said again. Slowly, with twitching limbs, Isabella rose. "This is she," Chloe said, leading her to where the Unfettered Prince sat. He regarded the two women with his many eyes. "This is the one who was to be saved."

Isabella looked confused, and then, for a moment, relieved.

"Then, she shall be added," the one upon the throne said. Isabella looked from Chloe to the enthroned one and back again. Then realization dawned on her face, and she turned to run. She got four steps away before she froze. Twitching, she stood up straight, and her arms went out to her sides. The next moment, she dropped her forearms and let them dangle. Her legs went limp, and her mouth sagged open. A keening rose from Isabella as one of the masked retainers broke away from the crowd around the stone throne. The figure moved in jerking, pulling motions, as if it were mechanical. Jenny saw that it was a girl. A human girl. But upon her face was a mask of solid amber, and in her hands she held something of the same color. She lifted it to Isabella's face, and it stuck there. The horrid sound that came from her was suddenly silenced. Jenny knew, though she didn't know how she knew, that Isabella's cry went on, but that no one could hear it, and that no one would ever hear it again.

Not no one, whispered a voice like a silver trumpet behind her. Jenny turned but found no one. She searched the faces of all about her, but no one else seemed to notice the voice. They were all attending to Isabella.

There is one who hears all cries, the silver voice said.

Jenny turned all the way around. Her eyes were drawn to the dark indentation on the ground in front of the metal rings.

He hears, and He will comfort.

The words were like cool, calming water to her confused and parched mind, and she wanted to hear more. But the cheering of the enthroned ones drowned it as with marionette motions, Isabella followed the girl into the darkness of the crowd.

Chloe fell to her knees, her hands up in worship.

Finally, the one upon the throne turned to Jenny.

"You," he said, and Jenny understood that he was speaking to Tabby and her, "have served well, as I have seen. Now you come to your reward. Collect that which is yours and come to me and my faithful ones. Come home and be comforted. Come home and be restored. Come home."

As the word 'home' echoed in the cave, the light disappeared.

76
Closure

JENNY TRIED HER FLASHLIGHT, but it wouldn't turn on. "Chloe?" she said.

"Here," Chloe answered in the dark.

"Shit, where? Do you have a light?"

"Yeah ... but it's not working."

"What are we supposed to do?" asked Jenny.

"Hello?" A man's voice echoed from far away. Jenny thought she recognized it.

"Hello?" she called back.

"Jenny!" the man shouted. "Where are you?"

"I have no idea," Jenny said. "In a big cave. With pits! Be careful! Me and Chloe are here."

"Is anyone else there with you?" He sounded a little nearer.

"I—Actually, I'm not sure."

"Stay where you are!"

"Hey, come to my voice," Chloe said, more softly. Fingers trembling, hands searching before her, and terrified of what she might bump into, Jenny crawled until she touched something soft. She jerked back, her mind bursting with the bodies that had filled the cave only moments earlier. "It's okay, it's me," Chloe said. Then she put her arms around Jenny and whispered into her ear, comforting her. "You did so well, so well." Jenny, raw and certain that she was in shock, just let the woman hold her until, a few long minutes later, light flitted into view. Half a minute after that, a man stood before them, and Jenny shook her head in wonder as Chloe let go and ran to hug him.

"Dylan?" Jenny choked, disbelieving.

"Are either of you hurt?" Dylan asked.

"Jenny is beat to shit," Chloe said. "Come on, help me with her."

"How did you find us?" Jenny asked. Tabby mumbled something in the back of her head about Dylan, but the woman sounded sleepy, and her words were indistinct. That suited Jenny fine for the moment.

"I was always supposed to find you," Dylan said.

"She has no idea what's going on," Chloe said. "Delia died before she could tell her."

Dylan's mouth hung open, and Jenny saw the nervous young man she had known at the bookstore.

"I'm sorry, this must have been—Holy shit, this must have been the wildest thing if you didn't know—"

"Honestly," Chloe said, "it was the wildest fucking thing, and I had a pretty good idea of what was going to happen. Oh, here, hold her and give me a light." Dylan pulled an extra flashlight from his coat and handed it to Chloe, who hurried back to the stone table and scooped up the four items that lay there. She put the silver disk into Jenny's pocket.

"We don't want to leave the eye behind," Chloe said. Then she led them back to the pit where Jenny had fallen. She took the small metal cylinder and dropped it gently into the hole. "That's for Paul to keep." She turned to the others. "Okay, only one more thing to do."

Dylan and Chloe helped Jenny through the cave and into a narrow stone tunnel. They turned right at a split in the passage and soon came out onto a rocky ledge under the night sky. Warm night air hit Jenny, and she wanted to cry, but she was profoundly empty. Then a new wave of disorientation overtook her as memories flooded her mind as if released from some hidden vault.

She could see Leddy running down the street to Limler Park, her red hair streaming out behind her. She remembered kissing a boy on the swings and then reading *The Hobbit* on the same swing a few days later. She remembered sitting in Marlene's class and thinking Phil was gross whenever she'd go to Leddy's house. She remembered Isabella and her brothers. She could feel the anxiety and fear as she knelt, praying, when her mother brought strange men home. She remembered dances, working at the record store, and graduating from high school. The memories came, but they were thin and distant—faded versions of what had once been hers.

She felt her life pouring into her like the waters of the falls into the pool below. She breathed deeply the scent of the stone, the moss, and the pines.

"Are you alright?" Dylan asked her.

"Not really," Jenny said.

"Well," Dylan said, "let's get you to the hospital. Um, and there's a really messed-up scene on the way down. Just don't look, okay?"

They helped her down past Emmet, Phil, and Leddy, who lay in heaps. Jenny remembered what the Shepherd, that twisted remnant of the woman Emma Barnes, had done to them. She remembered how it had felt, how they had broken, and how they had tasted. It took all of her remaining strength not to vomit.

When they reached the path's bottom, they directed Jenny to the side of the waterfall's pool. Chloe stripped, and Dylan helped Jenny take her clothes off. He did his best to avert his eyes. She didn't know why she was going along with it, but she had nothing left with which to resist. Quaking and holding on to Chloe, she waded down into the freezing shallows as Dylan focused on her face and the falling water. Jenny barely felt the cold or heard Chloe's words as she dipped down into the water and rose, letting the spray wash her clean. She lingered in the mist where the warm night air met the freezing water. Breathing, washing blood from her, and sensing Tabby in the back of her head, Jenny didn't know how to feel. Chloe ran her hands over Jenny's shoulders and through her hair as if she were untangling knots. Jenny felt both strangely close to and distant from the woman.

"Come with me," Chloe said. She led Jenny into the falling water. It pelted her, stinging her shoulders and breasts. Three times, Chloe cupped her hands above Jenny's head and shouted into the night. "*Buď zavřena!*"

Then Chloe pulled her from the water and hugged her close. She was weeping. She kissed Jenny's forehead, cheeks, lips, eyes, and nose.

"You've done it," she said. Jenny, worn beyond words, fell into her and kissed her.

When they came out, their goosebump-covered bodies steaming, they dressed. Dylan and Chloe led Jenny to a small black sedan parked behind Emmet's car.

"Ride in the back with her," Dylan said. Chloe helped Jenny into the back seat, where Jenny leaned her head against the window, tired and bewildered. Dylan took off quickly, but carefully.

"Cops," Chloe said, as they turned onto Main Street.

Jenny looked through the glass as they pulled up next to a police car while they waited for pedestrians to cross the street. Officer Gadke sat in the front seat of his cruiser, talking to a blonde woman who Jenny guessed was in her fifties. The woman glanced up, over the car, and at Jenny. Officer Gadke followed her gaze and saw Jenny. He waved.

Wave back at him and smile.

Jenny considered the thought and almost dismissed it. But, finding no reserves left in her to resist anything, she smiled at the red-haired police officer and raised her hand. Then Dylan pulled away, up the road, and out of town.

Considering the passing trees through her half-resolved reflection, Jenny said, "I don't understand anything."

"I know. But there's plenty of time to go back over it all," Chloe said. "Come on, let's get you to the emergency room."

77
Memories

Sunday, October 5, 2025 – Early Morning

A BLUE SUV ROLLED slowly up Route 3 as its driver and passenger scanned the pines, searching for the turn.

"Do you think it'll still be hard to find?" the dark-haired passenger asked. She wore a gray tank top, tight jeans, and a complication of bracelets on both arms.

"Couldn't say," the man said. He had a southern accent, which she always found funny. She imagined it had been decades since he had lived anywhere anyone would consider 'the south.'

"There," she said, pointing. The sign stood in a little clearing beside the left-hand turn. The driver turned left and then, a hundred yards up, turned right onto the main road.

"It's going to be on the right here pretty quick," she said.

"I know," he said, amused. She wondered if the man ever got really annoyed. She had tried to push his buttons a hundred times, but he had never risen to her taunting. He turned again, and the SUV crunched up the stone driveway. They passed the old, rusted legs of some bygone structure before he pulled the car around to sit parallel to the front porch. He put the vehicle in park and turned the key.

"Ready?" he asked.

"Nope, but here we are," she said.

She threw her door open and dragged her coat out behind her. She hated riding with it on, but she also hated the cold. Shrugging into the heavy overcoat, she kicked the door behind her and heard it slam. The man took the stairs in two steps, pulled the screen door open, and put his hand to the latch.

"Open," he said. It clicked. He did the same trick to the apartment door on the right.

"Empty?" she said.

"She's at the hospital. She'll be out tomorrow. The other one won't be out until next week, so we'll get a hotel room."

"You don't want to stay at the house in Enterprise?" she asked.

"Don't be morbid," he said. "Or flippant. Those people were brave. We should be so lucky to die as honorably as they did. That's not usually in the cards for people like us."

"I know. It's also an active triple murder crime scene," she said. "I doubt we'd be able to slip in and out undetected."

"You want to get her clothes?" he asked.

"Why, don't you want to rummage through her panties?"

"I thought I'd leave that to you," he said, smiling.

"What are you going to do?" she asked.

"Breathe it in," he said. He sat on the sofa and did precisely that, taking a long, slow breath in through his nose. She left him to it. Before going to Jenny's bedroom, however, she ducked into the bathroom, grateful for the relief and a few minutes alone. It had been a long drive.

Hands washed and dried, she rummaged under the sink and in the medicine cabinet. She was shocked that there weren't prescriptions by the dozen. Then, into the bedroom she went and found no duffel bag. She returned to the living room and told the man.

"She probably brought it with her to the rental house. Grab the spare from the SUV," he said.

Grumbling, she did so and returned to fill it with as many clothes as she could cram. She had always appreciated Jenny's style, and she didn't want to deny her the retro look she'd been cultivating since she returned home. Once she jammed the bag full of T-shirts, skirts, jeans, underwear, and a few pairs of socks, she lugged it back out and dropped it on the floor.

"It's not here," she said. "Maybe at the rental?"

"More likely with her at the hospital," he said. "They would have put it on her at the end." He touched his forehead and scowled.

"You okay?"

He grimaced and nodded. "He's eager. So am I. But we have to be patient. Can you be patient?"

"Yes, daddy," she said in her most annoying voice. He smirked. "I know," she said. "If you were my daddy, I would have turned out differently."

"Well, I'm glad I'm not, for a score of reasons," he said, pushing himself back up. "You get her toiletries and such?"

"Nope, probably at the rental."

"Right," he said. He considered the Glen Moat book on the table. "Looks like she's finished with this one. Let's get her another one before we see her."

"Yep, I'm sure that will smooth everything over," she said. She scanned the apartment and shrugged. "I think we're good here."

He agreed. He locked the doors behind them with a word, and she stripped her coat off again before jumping into the SUV.

"So, down to Enterprise?"

He nodded. "If it's in the rental, we'll have to wait until night," he said.

"Okay. What about the hospital?"

He shook his head. "Too soon. She'll get out tomorrow, and Chloe will take care of her. We'll bide our time. Have you ever seen Lake Wallowa?"

She shook her head.

"Well, you're in for a treat."

He pulled the SUV out of the driveway and back onto the main road. He took them down along Main Street and past the library, which seemed to have suffered major structural damage. Caution tape, scaffolding, and huge blue tarps surrounded one side of the building. He turned right, drove to the end of the road, and parked in front of a small, but pretty, ranch-style house.

"What's this?"

"This is where my best friend lived," he said. "You can stay here."

She watched him walk up to the front door and put his hand on it. The door opened, and he walked inside. She scanned the street and found no one about. She wondered what it would be like to live in a small town where the streets were empty and nothing ever happened. She decided it would be far too boring for her.

She breathed against the window and poked at the condensation as he closed the front door and came walking back up the cement path to the sidewalk. He circled the car, got in, and put a small brown paper bag into the center console's storage compartment.

"What's that?"

"Memories," he said, patting the paper. "Little rectangular pieces of the past. All right, let's get to roving."

He took them away from the house and then away from the town. South they went through the pines until the forest gave way to rolling grassy fields. She breathed on the window again and poked at the circle of breath, leaving little holes with wet centers that jiggled like a dozen eyes.

The Quiet Rumble

Volume 10, Issue 83, Sunday, October 5, 2025

Foundations

By Keith Lowry, Ed. In Chief.

I'll ask your indulgence for my timing. I am writing this before bed on Saturday and setting it to post on Sunday. That is, of course, what I normally do, but given the potentially active nature of the situation downtown, this little post may be out of date by the time it goes up.

As I'm writing this, three things of note are happening. The first is that Kira Cerny is appropriately enjoying her win as First Camper. Most people in town already knew Kira as the enthusiastic daughter of Pastor Cerny, a young lady who has been active for years in local charities. This week, we got to see more of her astonishing character when she saved a younger camper from being swept away by the swollen waters of Kusel Creek. I can't think of anyone more deserving than Kira to receive the honor. Her family has done this town proud for almost 125 years, and Kira looks like she might outdo them all.

The second thing is that dozens of families are concluding a well-deserved and dry Movie Night after two soaking wet days along the Kusel's banks. When I was a boy, Movie Night involved a lot of blanket-wrapped kids piling into the new Mist Theater (it had been the Silver Ring Theater through the '40s) and watching cartoons, Buck Rogers, and Dracula or The Invisible Man. My kids also went to the Mist, but by the '90s, Movie Night had started to shift. Instead of gathering at the theater, kids had sleepovers with friends. VHS tapes and DVDs replaced the theater, and though I appreciate the convenience of it all, I think we lost something wonderful in the process. We traded the extremely minor inconvenience of walking down to the Mist for the comforts of home, and in the bargain, we lost a real common experience, something the kids could take with them as they grew up.

But, of course, that's just me, an old man lamenting the loss of what was good and, I suppose, missing the good of what replaced it.

The third thing of note is that right now, engineers, police, and firefighters are crowding Main and Library to try to assess the extent of the damage to the southeast corner of the library. This is, of course, the topic on which this little article might be out of date before it posts. As of now, the empty building to the south of the library is still standing, though I've been told that its foundations have been significantly undermined. In fact, it seems that the empty building shows signs of progressive deterioration that might have been caught if it had been in regular use.

Fortunately, from all reports, no one was hurt in the collapse, which took place just after 11:00 PM. It is, however, quite a blow to our town, since, as most of you know, the library was just reopened this afternoon to rather significant fanfare. I've reached out to Mr. Grossman to ask him about the books he donated today and whether he knows if they were damaged in the collapse. I'm still waiting to hear back.

In situations like this, you just have to wait and see before you can really make an educated guess about the final state of things. However, I'm hopeful. As of now, there is no fire, which is a miracle. And books are resilient, in both the metaphorical and literal senses of the word. I think we'll be able to recover most of what went tumbling down.

Now, it's late, and I've had a scotch, so forgive me if I conclude with a bit of philosophical whimsy. But it seems to me that after these thankfully mostly uneventful Camping Days, we should look to our foundations. We should walk around them, give them a good going over, and decide where we need to shore things up. And while our literal foundations may need some work after more than a month of unusually copious precipitation, I think this year's Camping Days and the character of our First Camper suggest that our community's foundations are pretty darned solid.

And that makes me hopeful for the future.

I just hope that I don't wake up and find out that this whole post is already out of date.

78
Object Permanence

Monday, October 13, 2025 – Early Afternoon

JENNY THREW THE OVERNIGHT bag over her shoulder. It clacked dully with the sound of pill bottles. She turned to the hospital bed and smiled.

"You ready?"

The woman who sat on top of the covers was barely recognizable. Her bald head sported two bandages that hid bright red, stapled incisions and a halo of light-blonde peach fuzz. Bruises smeared her face, head, and neck with deep purple, lilac, and sickly yellow. Jenny knew they continued down the woman's back, arms, rear end, and thighs under bandages that crossed the woman's body from her knees up. She appeared paler than normal, the black tattoos on her arms standing out like ink on a newspaper page. The white T-shirt and baggy gray sweatpants contrasted starkly with her usual, bold style.

Sydney nodded, not meeting Jenny's eyes.

"Can you turn, or do you need me to do it?"

"No, yeah, I can," Sydney said weakly, pushing down on the mattress and slowly moving one leg to bend over the edge of the bed and then the other.

"Amazing," Jenny said, walking up to her injured friend.

"Yeah," Sydney said, her voice hollow and flat.

"You can move them, that's a hell of a start," Jenny said.

Tell her not to worry, they'll fix her right up, Tabby said.

"The people we're going to meet, they can help," Jenny said.

Sydney nodded, but Jenny could tell she didn't believe her, or maybe she didn't care. She was missing Maddy's, Nate's, and Gina's funerals. She was losing her ability to say 'goodbye' to almost the only people she loved in the world. Her job, health, and home had all disappeared in the blink of an eye. Life had shed its color, and Jenny imagined there didn't seem like much reason to believe in anything anymore.

Jenny understood entirely.

She put her arms under Sydney's armpits and helped her into the waiting wheelchair.

"Pull the curtain," Chloe whispered from the hall. Jenny pulled the privacy curtain around them as footsteps approached the room.

"Um, she's helping her with a personal matter," Jenny heard Chloe say. "Can you come back in like ten minutes?"

The nurse said something that Jenny couldn't hear, but Jenny wasn't concerned. This was the time they were supposed to collect Sydney, and it would work out fine.

The Man could see far. He was full of eyes.

The nurse's footsteps padded away.

"All good," Chloe said.

"You ready?" Jenny asked, running her hand under Sydney's chin. The wounded woman nodded once, staring blankly down at her knees. Jenny smiled and stepped behind the chair, grabbing its handles. "Don't worry, Syd, everything's going to get better." She leaned down and kissed her on the cheek. Sydney's hand came up and held Jenny's face against hers. Jenny felt her start to shake. She tasted the first tear that rolled down. She kissed her again, stood, and pushed her out through the privacy curtain.

"Left," Chloe said. And left they went.

When they exited through the side door, a blue SUV was waiting for them. Jenny froze. She had known he would be here and had tried to prepare for it. She'd talked it through with Chloe and with Tabby. But none of that made this moment any easier. There he was, leaning against the vehicle, his hands in his pockets. Tall, sun-tanned, with white hair as short as Sydney's, wearing old jeans and a white button-up shirt, Joseph smiled at her from under aviator sunglasses. Her stomach was a block of ice.

She glanced at the hood of the car, and the ice shattered into a thousand splinters. Jenny had known he was going to be there, but she hadn't known *she* would.

Matina sat on the hood in short shorts under the unseasonably hot October sun. Her dark hair fell around her bare shoulders, and light glinted off sunglasses that were the twins of the ones Joseph wore.

"I wonder if we all get a pair," Chloe said.

"Syd," Jenny said, leaning down close to her ear. "You're going to meet two people I—" She didn't know how to finish that sentence.

The back door of the SUV opened, and Dylan stepped out. He was wearing a green Baker's Books T-shirt. Jenny wheeled Sydney up and stopped ten feet from Joseph. Chloe did not; she ran up and threw her arms around the tall man whom she called 'Uncle Joe' as he picked her up from the ground.

Please go to him, Tabby said. *I haven't seen him in so long. Please, Jenny.*

Jenny felt the ache in her stomach and couldn't say no to Tabby.

Her longing was too powerful, her need for reunion too great.

You want to take over? Jenny asked her.

No, no, this is for both of us.

Joseph put Chloe down and, keeping her at his side, he turned to Jenny.

"Hello, darling," Joseph said.

No, not just Joseph.

"Hello, dear one," Jenny's words slid out in a strange confluence of will and submission that she had not become accustomed to. She stepped forward tentatively, and then again. Then Joseph lifted Jenny into the air.

And Peter lifted Tabby.

"I've missed you so much," the man said to the woman. "I wish I could have told you everything. I wish you could have known. But I wasn't allowed."

"All that death," the woman said, her body shaking, the tears running. "I loved them."

"So did I. I still do. I still do. But we are here. We are together again. And we have family again. Forgive me if you can. But if you can't, then let me try to make amends."

The woman said nothing more as she held him, suspended in his embrace. Jenny wept; Joseph wept. Tabby sobbed; Peter sobbed.

When the man let the woman down again, Jenny felt herself come forward, or perhaps Tabby withdrew.

"How long have you been like this?" Jenny asked, searching for the right words to describe their situation.

"Since I was a child," Joseph said. "Since before they sent me to that camp, before I met her great uncle." He looked down at Chloe. "He was my best friend. He was family. But now that's all of you. And, I have to say it, you're a fine-looking group. Matina, come down and say 'hello.'"

Matina slid from the hood and leveled a long, sullen stare in Jenny's direction. Jenny approached her and reached down to take her hand, holding Matina's fingers in hers. They didn't speak as their palms slid together and their fingers entwined. Matina leaned forward and touched her forehead to Jenny's. They breathed into each other, mouths open, eyes closed. Then Matina kissed her, and Jenny felt Tabby recede further into the back of her mind. This, at least, she could have to herself. They kissed for a long, silent moment until Jenny finally pulled back.

"Does everyone get one of those?" Chloe asked.

"I had the same question," Dylan said.

Jenny felt herself doing something new. Or, if not new, something that she felt like she hadn't done in ages. She laughed. Matina laughed too. Then their arms were around each other, and their laughter turned once more to tears.

Aurora, Jenny thought. *You should be here. Oh God, why aren't you here?*

They held each other until Jenny heard Joseph's voice. "Hello, Sydney, I'm Joseph." Jenny turned to see her confused friend.

"Jenny," Sydney said.

"It's okay, Syd." She had no idea why she said it. It shouldn't be okay. But she left Matina and returned to Sydney's side. "It's okay. You're going to be okay. We all are."

"Looks like you're in a bad way, my dear. How about we take you somewhere where you can get fixed up, good as new?"

Sydney looked like she wanted to protest, but was too tired to muster the energy. Dylan and Joseph lifted her into the back seat. Jenny slid in next to her.

"Are we taking this?" Dylan asked, his hands on the back of the wheelchair.

"Nope, I've got one in the back. Leave it for them to find. All right, folks, let's skedaddle before they come looking for the girl with the best taste in haircuts," Joseph said, running his large hand over his crewcut.

Matina climbed into the front passenger seat. Chloe slid in next to Jenny, and Dylan sat in the back. As they drove off, Jenny turned and regarded the red-haired young man.

"I don't understand," Jenny said. "Tabby's been trying to explain the whole thing to me, but I think my brain is kind of boiled."

"That will pass," Joseph said from the front seat. "I'll help you with that."

"What do you want to know?" Dylan said.

"I guess—was it all an act? Were you just pretending the whole time?"

"Pretending to what? Be nervous around you? To work for Delia? I mean, I really worked for her. And you definitely make me nervous," he said, smiling bashfully.

"I guess I'm just trying to untangle what parts were real and what parts were just like … some kind of mechanism."

"Everything was real, everything is mechanism," Joseph said. "The whole show is one big clockwork, you'll see. But that word, 'real,' it only goes so deep."

Jenny felt Tabby rousing herself. She was curious and came forward again. Joseph started patting his side as if feeling for something.

"What do you mean?" Chloe asked.

"Well, real is only as real as reality gets. If this whole thing, this world, other worlds, if they are all just a big, mindless mechanism, then big, mindless mechanism is what 'real' means. If that's the case, then everything is just as real as everything else."

Jenny responded, but it was Tabby who made the words. "But if there's something deeper …"

"If there's something deeper," Joseph replied, "then that's what 'real' means, and then some things can be more real, and others less. And then your question has meaning."

Jenny recognized the mode Joseph was slipping into, and so did Tabby. For the first time, she got a hint of which parts of him were Peter. She wondered what aspects of her would become Tabby. Tabby immediately answered her question, at least a little.

"So, it's the foundation that determines the reality? What is at the core, the root of all things, that is the measure of everything else?"

"Precisely," Joseph said.

I feel like I'm endlessly repeating myself, but I don't understand, Jenny said to Tabby.

My darling, we're going to have to talk about our reading habits, Tabby said, laughing as if she were made of bells.

They drove for an hour, until they were sufficiently far away that Joseph felt comfortable pulling over next to a small lake.

"What are we doing?" Jenny asked.

"Saying 'goodbye' to someone," Matina said. She held up a brown paper bag before opening her door. Everyone got out except Sydney and Dylan. He stayed with her in the car and held her hand as she stared blankly down at her knees.

"She's going to be okay," Joseph said, studying the bald woman.

"Are you sure?" Jenny asked.

"Oh yes. We're going to get her as good as new, and then she'll have all of you. Can't think of a better group to heal with."

"Are you going to tell me why you did what you did? I don't … I can't pretend like you didn't destroy me."

"Yes, but that won't fix it. Knowing *why* almost never fixes anything. But maybe if you see how it destroyed me too … Well, I guess I don't know. But do know that I love you, and I'm going to be by your side until my last day. And if you can't see your way to forgiving me, and my last day comes at your hands … Well, that seems fair to me."

Jenny crossed her arms and felt Tabby standing behind her. "Okay," they said together. "I can live with that."

The group walked together to the lakeside, and Joseph pulled out a book of matches and held them up to Jenny.

"So, wait, what are we doing?" Jenny asked.

"You have to burn it," Joseph said.

"Why? What is it?"

"Take a look." He nodded, and Matina opened the bag.

Jenny looked in and frowned.

"Figured you'd want to do the honors," Matina said.

"More than that, it won't work if you don't do it," Joseph said. "That's not normal, by the way, usually anyone could do the honors. But this is a special circumstance."

"I'm a broken record, I know," Jenny said. "But … what?"

"We don't make the rules," Joseph said. "Your ghost, your fire. Besides, their people did the same thing after they thought they'd won."

They burned all my clothes, Tabby said. *They thought that would keep me away.*

Jenny reached inside the bag and felt the past two months run softly under her fingertips. Everything had happened so quickly. She didn't understand anything, and a deep, screaming part of her told her to run away and do anything other than what Joseph told her to do. But that part of her was muffled and distant, as if sunk below fathoms of dark waters.

She took the matches and, after Matina put the bag on the ground, lit the whole book before dropping it into the bag. The bag and its contents caught and burned. The last two months rose before her, first in a thin wavering tongue, and then in a widening, growing billow. Patty driving her home from Sunrise, Delia welcoming her back, Isabella tying her hands, Barry, Phil, Leddy, Earl, and even Emmet. She saw Maddy, Nate, Gina, Charles, and … the other one. Why … why couldn't she remember their name?

They rose together in the smoke, and Jenny wondered if that was all any of it had ever been, just smoke. It had come and gone so quickly, and what was left? Sydney. Sydney remained.

The group stood in a semi-circle around the little pyre, and both Chloe and Matina put their arms around Jenny as they watched. When all that remained was a pile of smoldering ash, Chloe spit onto it.

"Good riddance," she said.

Then Joseph kicked the remains into the water.

"We are beset on every side," he said as some of the remnant sank, and the rest spread across the water's surface.

"Yes," Matina said. "But thankfully, He sees far."

Joseph put his hand on her cheek, leaned down, and kissed the top of her head. She hugged the big man tightly. Jenny watched and wondered. She had never seen the two of them affectionate with each other, and she wondered what had transpired between them in the past year. The group waited until the ashes were no longer visible on the water's surface and then piled back into the car.

"I'm starving," Chloe said.

"Me too," said Dylan.

"All right then," Joseph said. "Let's get something to eat. Any ideas? Actually," he chuckled, peering at Jenny in the rear-view mirror, "let's let the lady of the house pick. What do you want to eat, Venena?"

LINDS POURED SUGAR INTO their coffee and stirred. The diner was so quiet that they could hear Charles breathing.

"Are you taking over Link's job?" Linds asked. They tasted their coffee, put it back down, and stirred more sugar in.

"Yeah, what's left of it anyway. I think they have some idea that they're doing something good by replacing one black man with another."

Linds smirked. "Can't take black jobs away," Linds said.

Charles wheezed a half-hearted laugh.

"At least you get to keep regular hours now."

"I don't want to keep regular hours," Charles said. "I liked that job. Hell, I loved that job."

"Yeah," Linds said. "Me too."

They sat in silence. Linds, finally happy with the sweetness of their coffee, drank slowly but steadily until the cup was empty. When the waitress returned, they repeated the ritual.

"You really need to leave today?" Charles finally asked.

"Yeah, I mean, I don't work for the town anymore, and the apartment belongs to the town."

"Well, I hear the man they are putting in charge is a real softy. I'm sure a foxy young thing like yourself could convince him to let you stay."

Linds laughed and reached across the table, taking Charles's hand. "Believe me, if I thought either of us wanted that ..."

Charles laughed and cried. He took his glasses off and put them on the table. He held Linds's hand while he wiped his eyes with his napkin and shook his head.

"Where will you go?"

"I feel like I answer that question every few years now," Linds said. "I'm dreaming again, so I'm going to let that point me in the right direction."

Charles frowned, his skepticism evident in his furrowed brow. "Where do you think they are leading you?"

"Right now? South. There's something ... maybe someone ... south."

"Someone?" Charles asked.

"Yeah ... I think so, anyway. I see, this is silly, but I see red hair."

"Like Sydney's."

"No. Natural, long, and—" Linds took a long, deep breath.

"And what?"

"Dead kids. Lots of dead kids," Linds said.

"Well, that's … a lot," Charles said. "Have you thought about maybe talking to someone? You know, a therapist? There's no way any of this has been good for you. I don't want to upset you, but I think you probably need real help. I'm not trying to offend you, but you've been through more than—"

Linds squeezed his hand and smiled. "I'm not sure any therapist would be able to hear what I have to say and not try to commit me."

"Then maybe—" Charles began.

"But I'm not alone, Charles. I'm not the only one who has seen what I've seen. Do you really think animals tore Leddy and Phil and Emmet apart on the mountainside?"

"No."

"Where do you think everyone else went?"

"I don't know."

"Then what do you think happened?" Linds asked.

"I don't know, but I think almost anything is more likely than some kind of wolf creature tearing people apart and eating them whole."

Linds thought back to a bike ride they had once taken. They felt once more the fear that had paralyzed them as they watched the beast searching for them in the dark streets of Weeping Cedars.

"And that is where we disagree," Linds said. They held up a hand. "I know, the fact that we disagree is something that you think is insane in and of itself. I get it. So, I'll promise you this. If I ever stop finding other people who tell me that they've seen the kinds of things I've seen, I'll immediately check myself into the nearest mental health center. I give you my word."

"Just because other people reinforce—"

Linds shook their head.

"All right," Charles said. "I'm not your father. You're going to run your pasty ass off to Mexico, and there's nothing I can do about it."

"I don't think I'm going that far. California, I think. Maybe … maybe San Francisco. I'm not sure."

He squeezed their hand again and then let go.

"Well, just know that you always have a home here. Though I can't imagine you'll ever want to come back again."

"I don't know. After Gina, I can't imagine my parents will want to stay up here now," Linds said, pushing their plate back and surveying the diner, half-full of quiet people staring down at half-eaten meals. "But I honestly don't know."

Charles stared at the table. "I still can't—"

"I know," Linds said.

"Do you ever dream about them?"

"Who?"

"Nate. Maddy."

Linds nodded and let the world blur as they remembered. "I see Earl coming in the front door and Emmet behind him. I see Nate …" Linds shuddered. "I see Nate. He sees Earl's gun and lifts his rifle. He yells, 'Get behind me, God damn it,' and then he fires. And Earl just crumples. Then Emmet comes in behind Earl—"

"You think you're seeing it like it really happened?"

Linds shrugged. "I see my sister dying, kneeling over Nate's body. I see Maddy shielding Sydney. I see her shouting for Sydney to run. If my mind is making that up, then maybe you're right about me being crazy."

Charles swallowed. "If your dreams tell you that they all died bravely, then I'm not going to argue this time."

Linds nodded. They left the diner and walked down Main Street.

"You think that's a coincidence?" Linds asked, pointing to the half-collapsed mess that had been the town library.

"I have no idea what to think about that," he said.

"That's fair," Linds said.

Buzzing hummed out of Charles's pocket. He pulled his phone out and shook his head. "Patty again," he said.

"Didn't know you two were close."

"I barely know the woman," Charles said. "But you'd think we were best friends with how much she's been calling me. But then, I don't blame her. I'm sure she feels like she lost more than most. Her daughter, her friends, her pastor."

"I think we lost more than she did. At least Jenny's still alive."

Charles nodded. "Have you talked to her?" he asked.

"No, she won't answer my calls," Linds said. "I think … I don't know, but I think she's with dangerous people now."

"What kind of dangerous people?" Charles asked.

"The kind that scare me," Linds said. They turned off Main and continued to Linds's apartment, where a U-Haul van sat rumbling with its back doors open.

"Your parents taking you?"

"No, an old friend," Linds said. "He made the trip out when I told him what was happening."

The apartment door opened, and a tall, white man with short brown hair and beard shuffled his way out with two suitcases and a backpack.

He was wearing a checked, short-sleeved button-up shirt and faded jeans.

"Hey," he said.

"Hey," Linds said, taking one of the suitcases. "Charles, this is Tom, Tom, Charles."

"Tom? You're Linds's dad?" Charles said, shaking the man's hand.

"No, he's my father," Linds said, smirking.

"That's a priest joke," Tom said. "And no, I'm neither. Just an old friend from the trenches."

"The trenches," Charles laughed. "Of where?"

"Upstate New York," Tom said, smiling.

"I keep hearing how dangerous it is up there," Charles said.

"Yeah," Tom said, "you have no idea."

"I've tried to tell him," Linds said, pushing bags into the back of the van. "But he is ever the skeptic."

"Well, every good horror story needs one of those," Tom said.

"Is that what you think this is, a horror story?" Charles asked.

"Yeah, of course," Tom said, staring down at his scuffed boots. "Unless it's not."

Linds hugged Charles and got into the passenger seat. The two men shook hands again, and the van was off, driving south through town. It turned right at the edge of town onto Founder's Road, passed the gravel driveway, and then left. When they came to Route 3, they bore right toward Enterprise.

Behind them, the forest rose and spread, climbing up the side of the butte where rocks scattered and clung to the mountain. The stones, ancient and sharp, littered and split, cast their long, dark shadows upon the earth. Down, through the twisting ways, the darkness wove in crack and crevice, through tunnel and channel. In that darkness, beyond a chamber where six pits lay, one an open tomb, a second room spread sentinel before a final, doored chamber. Within, ancient iron looped across the stone where chains invisible no longer fettered an unseen prisoner. And before those metal rings, curved an indentation, like a shallow bowl in the timeless rock, darkened as if it once held a pillar of fire.

Thank You for Reading Lightning Falls!

To learn more about Emma Barnes and Linds, listen to the *Weeping Cedars* podcast.

To learn more about what Nate endured, look for *Welcome To Weeping Cedars*, a novelization of his first encounter with the nightmare.

To see other glimpses of other characters and locations from this book, listen to *Wrought of Amber* and read the short story collection *Shards of Amber* while you listen.

For all of this and more, visit:

www.WeepingCedars.com

About the Editor

Dawn E. Dagger is an author and editor who hails from rural Ohio. She is obsessed with anything literary, caffeinated, or in need of research. She has been a fan of Weeping Cedars since 2020 and can confidently say that the world of Weeping Cedars has changed her life. When she's not writing, reading, researching, or deep in any other creative endeavors, she can be found at home, snuggling her cats and wonderful husband, safe from the horrors of the world.

About the Author

J.W.G. Wise writes twisting horror stories from one side of a hundred-year-old duplex in Pennsylvania, where he abides in a love/terror relationship with small-town America. He lives with his loving and lovely wife, the only force that keeps him from wandering into the streets of the Dark City alone one idle Thursday afternoon.